Isolde Martyn was born in Warwickshire and grew up in London with a burning desire to become a historical novelist. It took a while. In the meantime, she gained a history honours degree from Exeter University, specialising in Yorkist England, and worked variously as a university tutor, book editor, archivist and parent. A founding member of the Plantagenet Society of Australia and former chair of the Sydney Branch of the Richard III Society, she now lives in Sydney.

Her first two novels *The Lady and the Unicorn* and *The Knight and the Rose* both won the 'Romantic Book of the Year' Award in Australia and have been published in Australia, America, Germany and audio. Isolde's debut novel also won the prestigious Rita for 'Best First Novel 2000' awarded by Romance Writers of America, and was nominated for 'Best Historical Novel 2000' by *Romantic Times*.

www.isoldemartyn.com

Also by Isolde Martyn

THE SILVER BRIDE

FLEUR-DE-LIS

ISOLDE MARTYN

PAN
Pan Macmillan Australia

First published 2004 in Macmillan by Pan Macmillan Australia Pty Ltd
This Pan edition published in 2004 by Pan Macmillan Australia Pty Limited
St Martins Tower, 31 Market Street, Sydney

National Library of Australia
cataloguing-in-publication data:

Isolde Martyn.
Fleur-de-lis.

ISBN 0 330 42134 4.

1. France – History – Revolution, 1789–1799 – Fiction. I. Title.

A823.3

Cover image kindly reproduced with the permission of
The Art of Elisabeth Louise Vigee le Brun
http://www.batguano.com/vigee.html
An international effort by her admirers

Typeset in Bembo by Post Pre-press Group
Printed in Australia by McPherson's Printing Group

Papers used by Pan Macmillan Australia Pty Ltd are natural, recyclable products
made from wood grown in sustainable forests. The manufacturing processes
conform to the environmental regulations of the country of origin.

For my daughter Claire and son Leo
– the freedom to speak our thoughts
without fear is precious – keep it safe.

In the Spring of 1793, the unity of revolutionary France was crumbling. Ringed by enemy monarchies and ravaged by dissent within, the inexperienced government, brimful with idealism, was struggling to equip its armies and feed its people.

But the theatres were still playing, the former chefs to the grand seigneurs were opening cafés and restaurants, and it was still possible to fall in love.

THE MEMOIRS OF FRANÇOISE-ANTOINETTE DE

MONTBULLIOU, 1816

List of Characters

PHILIPPE DE MONTBUILLOU★	Fleur's brother, an émigré (fugitive) in Coblenz
MARGUERITE ⎱ ★ HENRIETTE ⎰ CÉCILE	daughters of the Duc de Montbulliou by his first marriage, half-sisters to Fleur
MATTHIEU BOSANQUET★	a gentleman of Paris
MARIE-ANNE CORDAY	an old schoolfriend of Fleur's living in Caen
MME DE BRETTEVILLE	Marie-Anne's aunt
DEPUTY RAOUL DE VILLARET★	a deputy of the Convention and member of the Committee for General Security
ROBINET★	a *sans-culotte* (working-class) friend of Raoul's
LAURENT ESNAULT	a lawyer in Caen
ABBÉ GOMBAULT	fugitive priest from Caen, under deportation order for refusing to swear loyalty to the revolutionary government

In Paris

ANDRÉ BEUGNEUX★	close friend and lodger of Matthieu Bosanquet
MACHIAVELLI★	a snaky boarder of Matthieu Bosanquet
PIERRE MANSART★	Fleur's business agent

MARIE-JEAN HÉRAULT DE SÉCHELLES	formerly king's advocate and advocate-general of the Parlement of Paris. Member of the Convention for Seine et Oise
FELIX QUETTEHOU★	nephew to Matthieu Bosanquet and printer with extremist views. Influential member of the Paris Commune (city authority)
COLUMBINE (FEATHERS)★ JUANITA (WATERSPOUT)★ ALBERT (WHISKERS)★ RAYMOND (BEANPOLE)★	actors at the Chat Rouge
EMILIE LEMOINE★	a grisette (working-class Parisienne)
ARMAND GENSONNÉ	friend of Raoul de Villaret and member of the Girondin faction in the Convention
FRANÇOIS BOISSY D'ANGLAS	son of Raoul de Villaret's godfather. Former comte and major domo to the King of France's brother, the Comte d'Artois. Member of the Convention
JEAN-PAUL MARAT	Sardinian. Formerly a doctor and scientist, now a journalist and popular radical. Member of the Convention

JACQUES-LOUIS DAVID	Raoul's early mentor, official artist of the Revolution and a member of the Jacobin faction in the Convention
GEORGES DANTON	lawyer and famous orator. Minister of Justice during the September 'disturbances'. Member of the Convention
MAXIMILIEN ROBESPIERRE	leader of the Jacobin deputies in the Convention
JEAN-BAPTISTE CARRIER	friend of Quettehou and procurator from the Auvergne. Member of the Convention
GEORGES-AUGUSTE COUTHON	supporter of Robespierre. Member of the Convention
LOUIS-ANTOINE DE SAINT-JUST	supporter of Robespierre. Member of the Convention
HENRI DE CRAON★	emigré (fugitive) in London, friend of Fleur's brother, Philippe
MME MANON ROLAND	wife to M. Roland, a former minister of the Girondin government
FRANÇOIS-NICHOLAS BUZOT	Mme Roland's clandestine lover and member of the Girondin faction in the Convention

Prologue

*What country before ever existed a century and a half
without a rebellion? And what country can preserve its
liberties if their rulers are not warned from time to time
that their people preserve the spirit of resistance?*

THOMAS JEFFERSON, AMERICAN AMBASSADOR TO FRANCE

JANUARY 1789

Since the stable behind the Clef d'Or was
where he had been initiated into making love
some seven years earlier, Raoul de Villaret
rode into the town of Clerville in the January
twilight wondering whether he should just pass
through or halt and revisit the generous 'magda-
lene' who had provided such a delightful tutorial.

Not for an anniversary encore, of course – Bibi must be prodding forty by now, and at twenty-two, he had become choosy – but perhaps to say thank you for the only decent memory he had of the place.

His stomach complained of hunger and he frowned against the knife-edged wind as he rode towards the town square, knowing he would be unlikely to find a decent supper before he reached Rennes. The rivers were frozen over, the grindstones of the watermills were locked in ice and there was little flour. He had seen desperate hunger in the haggard faces of the migrating workers he had passed on the road. He doubted they would find labour in Clerville or anywhere else in the region; he doubted also that the King's call for every parish to submit a written list of grievances would make much difference. The incidents of unrest were growing and it looked as though he was encountering one now.

The Place Saint-Denis was still crammed with the poorer people who had come in for market day and there was a great deal of angry shouting going on. They had snared a grain transport. The carters, pulled from the running board, were struggling within the crowd, and the four-dragoon escort had foolishly let themselves be isolated in front of the market cross. Astride on top of the grain sacks, defying the soldiers' muskets, a gaunt workman was addressing the crowd.

'The King does not wish our children to starve, patriots!' he exclaimed, his dialect proclaiming him a local man. 'It is his evil counsellors and that Austrian bitch who are trying to squeeze every last sou from us. Take the grain to feed your children, *mes braves*, and you,' he snarled at the dragoons, 'shoot us if you dare!'

Another man sprang up onto the cart and jabbed a finger in the air. 'Go and observe the fine English lawns, *mes amis*, the strutting peacocks, the mulberry trees. Why should we labour while the Duc de Montbuillou leads a life of idleness? We're not even allowed to shoot his doves for eating our peas. Has he done anything to keep us from starvation? No! Break open his barns, I say! *Allons!* Let us seize the grain and feed our children!'

'To the chateau!' a woman bawled. 'Burn it down!'

'And be broken on the wheel?' scoffed someone.

'Starve then!' the second orator exclaimed. 'The only difference between us and the *noblesse* is in the ledgers! I say burn the records which make slaves of us! To arms!'

One of the dragoons fired above the head of the speaker, merely to frighten him, but the crowd erupted in bitter fury.

Raoul reined his horse Nostradamus round. The *chateau*? For years, he had tried to forget the Chateau de Clerville, vowing never to set foot within its detestable proximity, but the painting was there. Jacques-Louis David's painting! He could not let a work of David's be destroyed, even though he loathed every oiled pore of this particular canvas; even though to see its brilliance again would make him remember that humiliating month at Clerville when he had been David's apprentice.

With hatred burning anew, he circumnavigated the square through the back streets and spurred out of the town ahead of the mob. As he rode, it was not just David's impatient snarl Raoul recalled, but the sting of the Duc de Montbulliou's horsewhip across his shoulders and the sniggers of the duke's daughters. Their hateful laughter whirled around his temples, so infecting his senses that he grew hot with shame beneath his greatcoat, remembering the ripe, pointing breasts flaunted to torment him.

He drew rein at the gates of the chateau, smiting his riding crop against the ironwork, gratified that the old gatekeeper hobbled forward in his sabots with a respectful touch of his forelock. Thank God for that! So no ghost of a thin, gauche sixteen-year-old was recognisable any more.

'There is a mob on the way,' Raoul exclaimed, but the ancient cupped his ear and grinned. 'Open the gate, damn you! *Holà*, you!' Raoul snatched off his tricorne hat and gestured frantically to a boy loitering in the doorway of the gatekeeper's cottage. 'Run to the servants' quarters as quick as you can and warn them. There's a rabble coming to burn the chateau. And you, man, for Christ's sake, let me through!'

He glanced back impatiently. The torches flaring behind him on the road were distant enough. The old fellow, fumbling now with sudden fear, unlocked the gates to let him in. Instead of following the carriage drive, Raoul turned into the *basse-cour*. His memory served him well; beyond the clipped hedges that hemmed in the lawns and flowerbeds was a copse sheltering an English grotto. Little had changed in six years. The old artificial cave was as he remembered it, large enough to tether Nostradamus out of sight. He listened again but the winter dusk was quiet. Even on foot the rioters would not take long to reach the chateau, for it lay but one mile from the outskirts of the dirty, impoverished town like a pendant jewel around a beggar's neck.

Jamming his hat firmly down and with his neckerchief back to front so he might draw it up to hide his face, Raoul made stealthily for the rear terrace and tested the second window of the billiard room. The frame slid up easily as it always had. He adroitly climbed over the sill into the cold gloom of the unlit room and, skirting the billiard table, he softly opened the door to the *salon*. Despite the heavy odour of lavender polish, a faint hint of mustiness spoiled the elegant room like the whiff of sweat from beneath a nobleman's expensive waistcoat.

Only the candelabra on the harpsichord had been lit. Raoul's gaze slid round the walls and halted at the painting which hung beside the opposite door. Not David's, but a more recent portrait of Montbulliou and his son. Both faces mocked Raoul with their supercilious expressions just as they had done in real life. The duke's eyes bore smugly into his, forcing him to remember the shame and the violence, the raised whip beating him painfully to his knees. *Merde*, it was tempting to drive his knife into that smirking, canvas mouth. Raoul dragged his stare away and, pulling his neckerchief up over his mouth and nose, let himself into the vestibule. David's painting did not hang there either. Time was running out. The tick-tock of the grandfather clock echoed up the great staircase and he could hear raised voices in the common room.

Could the painting be in one of the bedchambers? The sound of breaking glass drove him to take the quickest way – up the backstairs – to Montbulliou's dressing-room. A startled footman collided with him in the hall, but he thrust the man roughly aside with a warning to save himself, then hurtled up the stairs to the duke's apartments. Glad of the scant lighting, he edged cautiously forward. The upper floor was chill and silent. There was no evidence of the family. Just as well. It would have been a unique pleasure to scar the duke's face; an unwise pleasure that might send him to the galleys or the Bastille.

Orange-flower water and pomade! The dressing-room stank of the duke, but there above the shining, polished side table hung his quarry – David's masterpiece, a greater work than any of the artist's more heroic paintings. Or so Raoul thought. He stared at it for a moment, reabsorbing its magnificent sensual power. Gauzy, lascivious and heartless, the duke's three oldest daughters – the goddesses Venus, Minerva and Juno – watched from their frame as he came closer.

The fourth daughter in the painting was not looking at him. She had been nine years old and too fat to play a beauteous goddess. Instead, she had been coerced to model as the chubby Cupid offering a golden apple as a prize. A fruit so real and luscious that Raoul could have snatched it from the canvas; the apple that the youth Paris was to award to the goddess he judged to be the loveliest. But Paris was not in the painting; David had made the beholder of the painting Paris. *No, you judge*, he had said to the world.

The sound of splintering wood and shouting jolted Raoul back to reality. Swiftly, he dragged a Louis Quinze chair across to the wall, grinning as he stepped with mudded soles onto its fine brocade. Then he drew his knife from its sheath.

'*Get down!*'

A young girl stood in the inner doorway, pointing a pair of duelling pistols at him. The weapons wobbled but there was determination in the plump young face. Cupid! He had no trouble recognising her. Long brown hair, loose save for a band that held it free of her forehead, tumbled down to an indiscernible waist clad in tawny velvet. About fifteen now, but still round as an English pudding!

'Shoot me then,' he challenged, and turned his back to her.

'I mean it, *thief*!' said the girl.

Raoul ignored her. He was halfway through hacking the top edge of the canvas free when a bullet exploded into the frame, missing his fingers by a skin's breadth.

'*Diable!*'

In the second she had to toss the spent weapon away and change the loaded one to her right hand, he was off the chair and grabbing her wrist. The child held on, her breath short, her mouth in a grim line. She had courage. Only with a sharp twist did he manage to prise the weapon from her, and then she began to kick and pummel him. Raoul tried to wrench himself free. He had to get back to his task before the mob broke in, but, like a little terrier, the girl had his shoe off and now she had hold of his stockinged foot.

It was the bitter scream of a woman in the courtyard below that made her let go. Cursing, Raoul stooped, tugging his stocking back into his knee breeches. Then, not taking his gaze from the girl's eyes, he backed away, quickly disarming the loaded pistol. He tucked it in his belt and grabbed up his shoe. Perhaps the chit thought he was going to beat her with it, for she blinked up at him from her hands and knees in consternation. But he was wrong; she was listening intently.

'What is going on?' she asked, frowning.

'Don't you know?' Safe behind his neckerchief disguise, he looked down at her confused face with the greatest of pleasure. 'They are ransacking your chateau, Cupid.'

'Cupid? Why are you calling me that? Who are you talking about?'

'Your people, your poor overtaxed peasants. They are going to –' Good God, what was he doing wasting time? '*Lock the door!*'

With another oath he sprang back on the chair and started working at the painting again.

The girl showed some sense. She calmly turned the key and returned to his side, looking at him like a puzzled puppy.

'You should save yourself, mademoiselle,' he exclaimed, then cursed himself for his weakness.

'I –' She glanced round her helplessly. 'Yes – yes, thank you. I'll hide.' She stared at the locked door, clearly wondering whether she could reach her hiding hole.

'At the back of the linen cupboard?' he scoffed. 'The smoke will reach you there.' He could hear feet on the stairs, boots tramping the precious carpet.

'How do you know about th– ?'

'Get out before they kill you!' He jabbed a finger towards her father's bedchamber. 'Out by the passage!' She stared at him appalled as he wrenched the last corner of the painting free. 'Oh, come on!' he cried. Thrusting the canvas under his arm, he propelled the foolish child by the elbow towards the inner door. 'Wait, take this.' He seized a Sèvres figurine from the mantelshelf and thrust it into her arms. 'Hold up your skirt.'

'What!' But she obeyed as he seized whatever else he could from the shelf and desk: a small timepiece, a porcelain dish – all dropped into her keeping. 'Come on! Quickly!'

He knew the passageway or thought he could find it; her older sisters had locked him into it seven years ago, but it was Cupid who ran her hands over the carved panelling and twisted the bottom grape. A tiny wooden door clicked open at waist height disclosing a lever.

The mob was kicking at the door of the outer chamber.

'Get it open, damn you!'

'I've never worked it by myself,' she protested, wriggling the lever.

'You won't be alive to try again. Yes, that way!' Raoul sighed in relief as a hidden door in the wall slid open. A dank, earthy smell filled the chamber. He shoved the girl into the opening, seized a candlestick and awkwardly pushed in after her. There was scarcely time to yank the lever panel to before the room's outer door splintered.

'Don't move!' He laid his fingers warningly across her lips. She froze beneath his hand and they waited while, beyond the wall, the mob began to destroy her father's beautiful room. He could feel her seething panic against his fingertips.

'What, none of 'em?' yelled someone. 'A piddling lie. Put a torch up the backside of one of the lackeys and they'll soon blab.'

'That stink, what is it?' Could they smell the fetid damp?

'Your bloody boots, I daresay.'

The canvas was heavy beneath Raoul's arm. He longed to let it drop but he dared not move. It seemed an eternity before the violence outside ceased and the duke's rooms were silent. The girl tried to shake free. At least she was not hysterical. Raoul slowly lifted his hand from her mouth.

'Stay still. I need to find my flint.' Her breath was irregular as he knelt and lit the candle, keeping it well away from her petticoats. 'That's better, eh? You're a brave girl.' It was a grudging admission but not well received. After all, she could not study his relieved face behind the neckcloth. Although she was intelligent enough to hold her tongue, the knuckles clutching her laden skirt to her waist glimmered white.

'Come on!' he said, gruffer now, and swallowed his own misgivings. 'We'll go the hard way.'

It was not easy to see without a lantern. The candle dazzled them and the chit struggled to clutch her trophies one-handed, freeing her right hand to shield her eyes so she might manage the stone steps. Raoul had less visibility than her and moved forward cautiously. But he remembered these stairs in the darkness – how her half-sisters had locked him in; how, smouldering with anger, he had been compelled to edge his way down them, his courage lit only by the thought of revenge. Back then he had fought off the irrational fear that had threatened to choke him; the terror of being enclosed. Even now the sweat of fear was prickling on his skin.

'How did you know of this?' the girl whispered.

'Be quiet!'

'Are you the same thief who stole my father's snuffbox from his escritoire last week? Did you –?'

'*Be quiet!*'

It would take merely one push to send this girl tumbling down the narrow stairwell. Only the fact that she had had no part in her half-sisters' escapade kept her alive.

She was silent but not for long. 'Do you have to wear that stupid scarf?' She halted and twisted round to speak, her cheeks shiny and pimpled in the flickering light. He ignored her and with a huffy little shrug she continued the descent. The dankness had a disturbing trace of smoke in it as they reached ground level. Merciful God, he hoped that the rest of the passage was clear and he would be able to get the trapdoor open.

'Not far now,' he muttered, marvelling at how well the girl was bearing up. How brave would she be if she had to feel her way alone, in total darkness, with rats running across her bare feet?

'I'm freezing.'

Gallantry battled with common sense. His greatcoat would have drowned her and impeded her progress. 'Like the rest of France,' he answered.

His boots squelched in the water puddled in the passageway. They must be clear of the house now. Another twenty paces should take them beyond the stable to the glasshouse.

The passageway ended in a wall of earth. The crude ladder, left for the convenience of escaping dukes or – more likely – visiting whores, looked too rotten and ancient to bear Raoul's weight while he dislodged the trapdoor. 'Hold these!' He loaded the girl's overburdened arms and she waited stoically while he pushed upwards. The trapdoor did not move. Cursing, he tried again, straining as he had that time before when some fool gardener had left a barrow over it. Heaving with all his strength, he felt it give, and slowly he pushed it upwards. The sweeter air, even though it was scented with potting earth and horse manure, smelled more blessed to him than a mistress's perfume or a roasting duck.

Worth trying the ladder now, he decided, but the second rung snapped under his foot. He sprang onto the third rung and up so swiftly that it took his weight and he was able to scramble out. 'Hand me up the painting.'

'Only if you promise not to shut me in.'

'Would I have damn well bothered with you if that were my plan?' He took the booty she passed up piece by piece. 'Now put that candle out!' He passed down a tub for her to stand on, and helped her hoist herself up. Brushing her skirts and palms, she joined him like a comrade-in-arms as he stood staring out through the glass.

'Oh, good God!' she whispered. The panes beyond the potting trays were dirty but there was no mistaking the fire lighting the windows of the chateau. He heard the draw of breath and slapped his palm against her mouth before her involuntary scream burst forth.

'There is nothing you can do,' he muttered, frowning down at her. 'Stay calm.' Her shoulders trembled and he kept hold until her shaking gradually ceased. She shook him off and glared through the window.

'They're taking out the horses,' she muttered, cursing beneath her breath.

'So now is a good time to run.'

'I'm not going anywhere,' she exclaimed. 'This

is my home, give me back my father's pistol. I'll kill myself if I have to.'

'Oh no, you'll live,' he promised, his voice a hiss of menace. Despite her courage, let her know what it was like to feel helpless and hungry for a while. 'Where are the rest of your accursed family?'

'At court. Maman died a few months ago.' The pain in her voice was still raw. He did not answer. 'Oh, *bon Dieu*, someone's coming.'

'Keep your nerve.'

The latch of the door that led out to the stables rattled. Raoul pressed her down under the potting shelf and crouched beside her.

'Who's in there?' A lantern waved. 'I know you're hiding. Who's there, I say?'

'A friend.'

'Growing cabbages, are you? Come out and show yourself.'

'I'm enjoying a woman,' Raoul called out. 'You have a quarrel with that?'

'I said *show yourself*!'

To Raoul's astonishment, the duke's daughter let out a rich gurgle of feminine laughter worthy of any nubile chambermaid.

'Sounds like you are already doing that.' A chuckle filled the silence. 'Well, don't be long. We're going to torch everything before we leave.'

She giggled again, a small self-satisfied laugh, as the latch was dropped, then in a less courageous voice, she demanded: 'What did you mean, "enjoying a woman"?' Was she taunting him?

'Where did you learn to laugh like that?' he

countered, wondering if she was already corrupted by her despicable half-sisters.

'From Celeste, one of the maids. She giggles like that whenever my brother tries to kiss her.'

Well, thank heaven for Celeste, he thought grimly, mentally adding 'seduction of maid-servants' to his list of grudges. A great pity King Louis had not asked for *cahiers de dolerances* against individual lords. His most Christian Majesty could sell them afterwards as scandal sheets.

'Come on.' Raoul prodded her down towards the glass door furthest from the chateau. 'My horse is hidden at the grotto. Can you lead the way?'

'Of course!' The reply was haughty.

Then what would he do with her? Deal with that later, he willed himself. Now he needed to concentrate on getting the pair of them out of the grounds.

He followed her along the kitchen garden wall behind the *basse-cour* and then they skirted a small hedge, keeping their heads ducked in case the flames shooting up from the glowing windows lit their presence. Once the girl looked back across the lawn, her face white and horrified at the screaming and the demoniac figures running to and forth.

'Go on!'

She halted, out of breath with her exertion, against an oak. 'How did you kn–? Jesu!' A mighty, inhuman trampling came towards them. Raoul cocked the pistol, taking aim but then an ugly braying erupted from the bushes and a dark shape lurched towards them.

'Blanchette,' Cupid exclaimed in relief, floundering in the darkness to find the creature's head. 'The chaplain's donkey.'

'Wonderful!' Raoul took her arm to drag her away.

'But we can't leave her here.'

'Yes, we can,' he snarled. This was the last thing he needed crashing along with them, but the donkey did not share his opinion. It followed. All he needed now was a celestial choir and a couple of shepherds and they could volunteer for next Noel in the cathedral. No, forget the shepherds. They were probably splintering the Louis Quinze chairs.

He heard the sound of Nostradamus's hoofs and the rattle of his bridle before they reached the grotto. Someone was trying to make off with him. A huge fellow! Fierce and not just desperate but armed with a cleaver. Oh God, he would have to jump the wretch and –

'Thomas!' admonished Cupid primly, recklessly shoving in front of him. 'That is not your horse.'

'Stand back, man, or I'll shoot,' growled Raoul, pushing her aside. He raised the pistol.

'But you haven't got it lo–' Oh God, a far too clever child!

'Yes, I have,' lied Raoul. 'Did you hear me, scoundrel, stand back from that horse.'

'Mademoiselle,' exclaimed the huge man, his face softening. '*Nom de ciel*, is that you?'

'This is Thomas, our underchef,' said Cupid cheerfully, obviously feeling correct etiquette was necessary. 'And this man is a thief but he has been generous enough to help me escape even though I annoyed him.'

And now it was the unsuspecting Thomas's turn to play knight errant, decided Raoul. Yes, he remembered the man vaguely. Cupid was a burden to foist upon a serving man's shoulders; it might be a risk to put the girl in the fellow's hands, but he certainly sounded gentler than he looked.

'Attend to mademoiselle's safety, *mon brave*. Take her and the damned donkey and get out of here!'

A gasp came from the darkness, followed by a silence as though the huge man was weighing the matter. 'Very well,' he answered finally.

'But where shall I go?' Cupid's hands tugged beseechingly at the front of Raoul's greatcoat as though he had become her nurse.

'Now don't be foolish, little one,' he exclaimed. 'You have family.'

'But they have all gone to Versailles. Shall I –?'

'No! Not Versailles,' he advised swiftly. The court was no safe place for a young girl. 'Somewhere else, eh?' He shook her elbows. 'Some other relative?'

'An uncle in Normandy but I hardly –'

'Then go to him. Thomas will take you. Get going, man. I will see you on your way!'

The lodge gates had been ripped down and the cottage was on fire but astonishingly there was no one about. 'Come on!' Raoul wrapped his coat round the girl and, drawing his horse behind them, hurried her past, hoping she had not seen the old gatekeeper lying in a puddle of his own blood.

Unfit, Cupid halted, bent over with the pain in her side from running. Raoul urged her into the cover of the bushes edging the Clerville road. 'I'm leaving,' he told her as the large man came lumbering up with the donkey. 'Go with Thomas now and do as he says.'

The girl straightened. 'Who are you? How shall I know you again? Why won't you let me see your face?'

'Because, being a Montbulliou, you might have me hanged,' he answered coldly, retrieving his coat.

'You *are* a thief!' she retorted matter-of-factly.

'Yes, mademoiselle, not worthy to lick your shoes.' The bitterness in him rose like bile as if he tasted the words. Marguerite, the girl's oldest half-sister, had lashed him with that taunt. He tied the canvas across his saddle pommel. He would secure it better later. 'Adieu, Cupid. Be content that I have not shot you through the heart.'

'If I'm Cupid, Monsieur Thief, maybe I've shot you through yours.' A witty retort and no thanks to follow.

Hardly a surprise, he thought as he swung up onto his horse, and was glad to be free of her.

He looked back once. She still stood there watching. The firelight adding a flickering outline: her stroking the donkey's neck and the cook with his hand upon her shoulder.

Raoul turned his face away from the town, galloping up the road until he came to the first track and then he rode across country, skirting Clerville. The burning chateau lit the night sky behind him, blinding the stars. What a shame, he jibed at the duke's absent son and haughty daughters, there goes part of your inheritance!

1

We have often in the past learned that the temperament of the French is such that it requires extreme danger to draw out its entire strength.

GEORGES DANTON

MARCH 1793

'I am glad you do not know about equality, mademoiselle,' Fleur told her donkey as they took the shorter way over the hill, 'else I should be carrying your load.' She reached out a fond hand to Blanchette's nose and received a friendly huff in return.

They threaded their way warily among the oaks, alert for the startle of birds' wings that might warn them of wild boar or two-legged danger. Fleur was humming softly under her breath. Her weekly sortie to Caen had been satisfactory; no one had challenged her and her disguise as a boy had worked yet again. Even if any of the citizens of Caen remembered a plump schoolgirl who had once attended Trinité School, they would hardly see the resemblance in a thin lad, peaky from a winter of hunger. Now she and Blanchette had only to descend and cross the main track that traversed the forest and then they would be almost home.

It was amazing what contented Fleur these days. Once she would have been heartbroken to leave the excitement of the town; these days she found reassurance in the forest, for oaks and elms did not change the laws from one day to the next. This was her refuge. To think that as a child she had daydreamed of living in a woodland cottage like a hidden princess. She had never guessed it would become a necessity, that her kind would be hunted like foxes. *Ciel!* She had even conformed to wearing a revolutionary rosette of white, red and blue on her cap; a wonder that Blanchette was not expected to wear one too!

There had been several times since 1791 when starvation had nearly taken her, when thieving or else bringing down a pigeon with her catapult had enabled her and Tante Estelle to survive. And it was worse now. Because the grand seigneurs had fled and foresters were no longer employed to scare away poachers, the peasants were slaughtering the deer and other game as if the forest could be easily replenished. Soon there would be nothing. Many a time Fleur had wished the man who had forced her to leave her father's chateau had shot her through the heart, for the future was as bleak and desperate as her past.

She and Tante Estelle endured a meagre existence. Cécile, her half-sister, was somewhere in England, and her uncle and brother had fled Paris in '91 to join the King's brothers in Coblenz. If they returned, it meant the guillotine; the Paris mob had already slaughtered Papa and Marguerite, God rest their souls! And even in the depths of Grimbosq Fleur lived in uncertainty, for any relatives of émigrés were suspect and if the authorities discovered she was the daughter of the infamous Duc de Montbulliou, there would be no acquittal. This cursed Revolution! Even innocent Thomas, who had brought her safely to her uncle's house, was barely eking out a living selling sausages in Bayeux.

'*Diable!* What now?' She froze as sounds of a scuffle reached her from the road. Her friend in Caen, Marie-Anne Corday, had warned her that she took too many risks, especially journeying on her own so much. She tiptoed forward and quietly edged aside the budding hawthorn fronds so she might glimpse the road below.

Two masked horsemen were attacking a third rider, a large, older man who thrust his stick this way and that, trying to keep a seat on his terrified horse. His assailants were far too nimble for him and one of their blades drove into his belly. He gave a fierce yelp of agony. Bicorne hat and wig went flying as he tumbled off onto the slaty track and lay there convulsing. From her hiding place above the thicket of hazel, holly and brambles that coated the lower slope, Fleur watched appalled as the man's violent spasms gradually ceased. Was he dead? Perhaps not, for one of the brigands dismounted and kicked him over onto his back. Just as the villain drew back his arm to slash the man's windpipe, Fleur did the only thing she could think of to save him.

'*Holà!*' she bawled as if she had comrades lagging behind in the forest, and reached for her catapult. 'Pierre, Jacques, *vite*! Stop slacking!'

The startled assassin tensed. He might have finished the bloody task but Fleur shot a stone into the flank of the other brigand's horse. It reared, terrifying the traveller's steed into flight, and bolted, leaving the second murderer to fling himself into the saddle and spur off after them. Since the track disappeared round a bend within some fifty paces, Fleur could not be sure they were truly gone. Her one extravagance, the pistol hidden beneath her jacket, might bring down one of the brigands. The other? It would have to be the knife in her belt.

With a huge shove, she drove Blanchette forward and hastened to where the man lay sprawled. Blood was staining the lower part of his waistcoat.

'Oh, monsieur!' Heedless of whether the assassins would return, Fleur threw herself to her knees. After such throes, she was positive the traveller

4

must be dead, but she still reached beneath the expensive lace frill that cuffed his wrist, hoping there might be a faint pulse. Blanchette stepped back with a whinny, suspicious of the prone human.

The man's eyes opened a crack. 'Cross yourself, boy!' he hissed through clenched teeth. 'Respect the dead! Remove your cap!'

Amazed at his quick-wittedness, she instantly obeyed, snatched off her bonnet, bent her head as if in prayer and then rose to her feet, waving to the hillside. '*Holà!* Jacques, there is a dead man here.'

'Well done, lad!' muttered the traveller through the corner of his mouth. 'Have they gone?'

'I cannot be certain.' Fleur sprang up, whistled with all the vigour of a peasant stripling and waved to her imaginary companions. 'Down here, Pierre!'

How badly wounded was the traveller? Was he going to die? With dusk coming on, she could not leave him here to be run over by a carriage or some courier riding like the Devil. The bubbling blood persuaded her. He could bleed to death while she fetched help from the charcoal-burners or sabot-makers who worked in the forest. The nearest cottage was hers. Dared she take him there? The man did not look like a revolutionary, even though his tumbled hat paid lip service to Equality with a *tricolore* cockade, but it was hard to know these days. Human birds sang different songs depending who was listening.

'Give it another moment,' the injured man rasped, his face contorting as if every word hurt.

5

'Kneel and search my pockets as if you are looking for clues of identity. Pull things out. Examine them.'

Fleur obeyed, her movements exaggerated, and finally the drum of retreating hooves told her the brigands had gone. With a loud breath of relief, she straightened up.

'Cl-clever lad.' The whisper of praise took strength. He winced as she pressed the handkerchief from his pocket against the wound. 'You would make a fine actor.'

'Who are you, monsieur?' He was old. In his fifties, she guessed. That face had seen a lot of living. The florid skin, now ominously pale, was slack over his cheekbones; deep lines traversed the high, clammy forehead; and the cropped, coarse hair, flattened from the wig, held scant proof that it had once been mousy.

'Bosanquet, Matthieu Bosanquet.' He tried to sit up but the pain was great.

Fleur undid the leather flask at her belt and, nursing his shoulders, let him take a swig of water. 'I live close by. If I could assist you onto Blanchette . . .'

'Blanch— ah, yes. Quickly, eh?'

Glancing over her shoulder all the time lest the assassins return, she swiftly unbuckled the panniers from the donkey, and refastened the girth belt about Blanchette's shaggy pelt so that Monsieur Bosanquet could grip the leather while she put her arms beneath his shoulders and heaved him forwards onto his knees. He was so close to fainting that only his powerful willpower finally got him onto Blanchette.

'There is only one thing you can depend on in this life,' he gasped, grabbing hold of the wooden yoke and wincing as she urged his leg across the Passion cross of dark hair on the donkey's back. 'Yourself. But you come a fair second, *mon fils*.' It was an effort not to stare at the spreading stain or the scarlet beading upon the fobwatch chain; Fleur busied herself hoicking the bristly panniers across her back.

'Not far.' The smile on her face was forced. The man's broad shoulders were slumping precariously and his panting breath was loud in her ears as she tugged Blanchette's leading rein coaxingly: '*Proot!*' But the velvety ears shook rebelliously. *Do not misbehave*, she pleaded silently. The little hooves at first refused to move but then, as though sensing her panic, Blanchette reluctantly began to follow her.

Mercifully, M. Bosanquet was still conscious by the time they reached the cottage but trudging up the narrow path between the grasping gorse seemed to have taken forever.

Her aunt, Estelle de Thury, once a grand lady of Bayeux, was waiting for her, anxiety creasing the brow that expensive creams had once protected; the apron she would have scorned to wear before her husband's exile crushed by roughened fingers.

'Never tell me,' she exclaimed, relief replaced by asperity as she noted Fleur's companion and rescued the baskets from her niece's burdened shoulders. 'He was sold at half-price?'

'No, madame,' ground out the stranger's voice with momentous effort. 'I was . . . *given* . . . away.'

Fleur and her aunt made M. Bosanquet comfortable on their only bed and examined his injuries beneath a succession of tallow lights. Cleansed, the wound beneath his striped satin waistcoat did not look spectacular. It was rather the tiny froths of air in the seepage that bothered all three of them.

'What madness possessed you, Fleur? We could have a dead man on our hands,' whispered her aunt, drawing her out of the room and shutting the door behind them. 'He needs a physician, child. Oh, if only we lived closer to Caen, I am sure Marie-Anne's aunt would have taken him in.'

'What choice, *hein*?' Fleur muttered, tugging off her cap and running an exasperated hand through her curls. 'I will leave for Caen before first light. There's a new doctor from Cherbourg who's set up in the Rue Saint-Pierre. Maybe he will not ask any questions. It will be a risk but . . .' She shrugged; for nearly two years she had been living in fear of arrest. 'And I am sure our guest will not want much to eat,' she added wryly as her aunt darted a look at the meagre supplies that had to last them the week. 'Besides, there is coin. Enough to pay the doctor's fee. Have a look!'

Her aunt looked through the buff-skin wallet and gave a weary nod, tucking back a lock of dark, lank hair that had been too long denied the curling tong. As she replaced the *porte-monnaie* beside the fobwatch and pocket book on the scoured table, she let her chilblained hand linger on its soft leather. 'Like one your uncle had,' she murmured, and then in silence scraped a knuckle across her damp cheekbone. 'No use crying, I suppose.' It was bravely spoken with a sniff and lift of the Thury shoulders. '*Tiens*, child, you took a risk bringing the stranger here. Shouldn't we ask old Guillaume or one of the other forest people to take him in?'

'Tomorrow, perhaps.' Too exhausted to argue, Fleur let her sabots thud to the earth floor and leaned her forehead on the heel of her hand.

'No news from your uncle, I suppose?'

'No.' Poor Tante Estelle. A penniless fugitive, Uncle Charles's letters came by circuitous routes and they never had correspondence from Fleur's brother, Philippe. Deprived of the rank of duke, two splendid chateaux, a luxurious Paris mansion, not to mention access to the smelly glories of Versailles and all the sinecures that would have been his under the *ci-devant* King Louis XVI, Philippe was bitter and morose, according to Uncle Charles.

Fleur heaved the wicker pannier of supplies onto the table. 'Marie-Anne and Mme de Bretteville gave me some dinner. I kept some for you. And I met the gypsies again. Paco asked after you. Would you unpack all this while I see to Blanchette?'

Her aunt tore into the wrapping and was already gobbling the cheese before Fleur reached the door. 'You will get indigestion, Tante,' she chided fondly, but once outside in the frosty twilight her smile vanished. Wrapping her arms batlike around her thin shoulders to keep away the shivers, she headed for Blanchette's stall.

'I cannot bear much more of this,' she confided wearily into the long ears as she hugged the donkey. The journey to Caen had worn her out and she must tread the same path tomorrow. Then, despising herself for weakness, Fleur whispered a prayer for M. Bosanquet. If anyone needed God's help, he did.

'You consider I should put my affairs in order, eh, doctor?' M. Bosanquet demanded, wincing as the physician set aside the wadge of linen and gently felt the telltale rigidity of the abdomen.

'I did not say that, monsieur.' The doctor stooped, his ear to the patient's belly, but as he straightened, the swift exchange of glances with Tante Estelle on the other side of the bed confirmed his suspicions.

'You did not need to, man. I have studied men's faces long enough to know when they dissemble. How long? Days? *Hours?*'

'The injury is indeed severe.'

'*Ma foi!* Then I need a lawyer more than a doctor,' groaned the patient, clutching at Tante Estelle's sleeve as she mopped his brow. 'Is there one in Caen or have they all gone to Paris to make mischief? What about that old devil Esnault? He and I were pupils at the Abbaye aux Hommes.'

The doctor felt Bosanquet's pulse. 'I will acquaint Citizen Esnault with your predicament and give him directions. It will save the boy here making another trip to town. I am also prepared to forward a message to your family on your behalf.'

Diable! Fleur sent her aunt a troubled look behind the doctor's back. M. Esnault's tongue was said to be as long as the road to Paris! Why not invite the whole of Caen?

'Your fees are in my wallet, doctor. Ask the lad.'

Outside the bedchamber, the physician was far more forthright.

'Since you are not his relatives, I will not mince words. If the blade has damaged the gentleman's intestine, waste will seep out and infect the rest of his belly within a few days. Just make him as comfortable as you can.'

'Ah well, the Devil will be sharpening his toasting fork, I daresay,' M. Bosanquet remarked cheerfully to Fleur as she set the wallet and other contents of his pockets back next to the pillow, but his skin was ashen. 'It seems I need to make my last confession.' He gave a derogatory sniff and, chewing his lip, added, 'I wish I didn't give a fig as to whether a priest is a republican or a kisser of royal shoe buckles, but I am an old-fashioned soul at heart. There . . . there is no chance of fetching a nonjuring fellow, is there?'

'We-we might be able to manage it,' muttered Fleur. 'The priest of Saint-Gilles has been visiting the forest.' Hiding might be a more apt description, since he had refused to take an oath to the Republic and was under a deportation order. 'I shall see if any of the forest people know of his whereabouts.'

'Gombault, eh?' His fingers scrabbled at her sleeve.

'Abbé Gombault, yes.' She frowned. 'You are well informed, monsieur.'

'My mother knew them all. Ah, don't scowl so, boy. I am no danger to him. Thinking of slitting my throat if I blabbed?' His ability to run ahead of her thoughts was quite unsettling.

'If I had to, monsieur.'

'I do not know your circumstances, *mon brave*, and I'll ask no questions – gentility gone sour, perhaps.' The eyes flicking over her clearly suspected more, for these days anyone could move a stone and find an *aristo* hiding beneath it, but he cleared his throat. '*Bien*, I've plenty of money with me to pay a score of lawyers and my board.'

She had noticed. 'I am glad of that, monsieur.'

'Yes, so am I.' Fleur's aunt was back, studying him from the doorway.

Their guest bestowed his wistful expression upon her as if inviting her absolution. 'I know I am an infernal nuisance, madame.' His voice was heavy with emotion. 'But could you or the lad spare the time to read to me? I'd rather not be on my own until I get used to the notion of . . . going.'

'Well, you will have the late King Louis to keep you company in hell, I daresay, sir,' Fleur's aunt exclaimed tartly, fiddling with the cotton fichu around her bodice, 'and . . . and a score of philosophers who should have known better.' With a sob, she fled.

'*Tante*.' Fleur hastened after her and found her cradling her head against the wall.

12

'Ignore me, *mignonne*. You know how it is.'

Did she? Had Tante Estelle glimpsed her own mortality in M. Bosanquet's face? She turned the older woman and drew her into her arms.

'Oh, Fleur.' For a few minutes her aunt wept against her shoulder and then she roused herself. 'Whatever happens to you, do not waste a moment of life. I wish your uncle were here. I wish I had not squandered . . . I wish I had known he and I would be parted. Promise me, child.'

'I promise,' Fleur hushed her, not understanding clearly what she meant. With the prospect of starvation facing them, squandering anything was as likely as jumping over the moon. 'Come back and be kind to poor Monsieur Bosanquet,' she coaxed, straightening her aunt's cap and using an apron corner to soak up the tears.

'No, you shall read to him. Oh but, Fleur, there is only the prayer book left. We burnt the rest, remember.'

'Then prayers it is, since I cannot remember the jest Marie-Anne told me yesterday,' Fleur answered dryly. How did one comfort a dying man when everyone now believed that the Supreme Being was some sort of celestial clockmaker?

'Can you remember any Molière, the scenes we used to read together?' Fleur remembered every precious line, the laughter, the shawls, the pilfered waistcoats from her uncle's *garde-robe*. That had been in '89 when Thomas had delivered her to her uncle's doorstep in Caen like an unfranked letter. She thought of the abandoned library with sadness.

Molière's plays were among the few books her aunt had brought to the cottage, books they had burnt last winter, scene by scene.

She might have been giving M. Bosanquet news that he would live, judging by the delight which flooded his face as she stood at the end of the bed declaring: ' "Follow me! I'm going out to show off my clothes in the town . . ." '

'Bravo, *Le Bourgeois Gentilhomme*! But I think something less humorous, *mon petit*; it hurts to laugh and I think you could make me laugh a great deal, yes? How about: "Aristotle and the philosophers can say what they like, but there's nothing to equal tobacco: it's . . . it's . . ." '

' ". . . an honest man's habit . . ." ' she finished, grinning. 'How did you guess I could read, monsieur?'

'I heard you humming as you made ready for bed last night. An unlettered peasant would not know a melody by the youngest of the Bachs – or has the Revolution enlightened all of us?'

It was necessary to meet his gaze evenly. 'As you say, monsieur, gentility gone sour.'

'But not expiring, eh, like some? Now read to me.'

By the time the last fingers of daylight struggled in between the blinds, Fleur was exhausted and exhilarated. For a few hours she had lost herself in a saner, happier world, but now Tante Estelle stood silently waiting for her to finish declaiming and sent her out into the shadows to gather firewood.

Had she managed to distract M. Bosanquet from the omnipresent pain in his belly and the darkness of death that awaited him, she wondered. It had to be darkness. Surely it was not Divine Will that had killed the King, tossed down the nobility and placed France at war with half of Europe? She almost envied M. Bosanquet's approaching night.

Tante Estelle kept vigil beside M. Bosanquet's bed throughout the small hours while Fleur curled up next to the kitchen hearth. As the sun rose, the girl took her turn again. The sick man hardly dared move now and the thin mouth of the wound was yellowing.

'Tell me about yourself, monsieur,' Fleur asked, not willing to reopen the book. They had both had a surfeit of prayers. As the gentleman had admitted, heaven would not be holding its breath to welcome him, and Fleur was reluctant to disclose secrets, for the fever was mounting and soon he would succumb to delirium.

'I live in Paris, 47 Rue des Bonnes Soeurs,' he told her, adding like a pompous bourgeois, 'A man of property.'

'Then what are you doing coming to Caen, monsieur?'

'Each year on my mother's birthday, I come to visit her grave.' Sadness clouded the air between them. 'You know, I'll wager all I own that the attack on me was planned.'

'Have you so many enemies?' Fleur asked, trying to dispel his sorrow with a teasing smile.

'Only one,' and he added with feeling, 'God willing. My nephew, Felix Quettehou. He loathes me, covets my wealth to build up his business.'

'But it is up to you how you bequeath it. Have you no children?'

'Never married, not–not the marrying kind, and yet –' He blinked at the window where a rosy dawn suffused the sky. 'Child, I have been doing some hard thinking about this matter. Call your aunt in, will you, please.'

Puzzled, Fleur coaxed her aunt to leave off chopping the shrivelled wild garlic that would enhance a thin pottage.

M. Bosanquet cleared his throat, tightened his face at the agony this caused, and then waited for their full attention as though he were a lawyer addressing a *parlement*. 'I have a proposition.' He paused. 'You live a meagre existence here. What are you, aristocrats in hiding?' Tante Estelle's mouth tightened. Neither woman answered. 'And this pretty creature.' He reached out a hand to take Fleur's fingers.

Tante Estelle's shoulder stiffened. 'Go outside, child!' she snapped.

'*Tante!*' Fleur had lost her childhood the day the chateau had burned down.

Had it not been painful, M. Bosanquet might have laughed; he had to be content with a grimace instead of a smile. 'I may be an old fool but I can tell a lovely boy from a girl. Why this masquerade, *ma petite*?' he asked, his fingers closing tight on hers.

16

'It is safer for her, monsieur. Two women living on their own,' her aunt replied. 'The forest people respect us. Others will not. Now, come to the point, old fool. I have not all day.'

'The point, eh.' He clenched his teeth and sank back against the pillow. 'I thought to leave my properties in Paris to a friend but . . .' The Adam's apple moved painfully. 'Fill this pipe again for me, child.'

'You think your nephew may have hired the assassins, monsieur?' Fleur packed the clay barrel with tobacco from his pouch.

'Ha, clever child, now there is a theatre piece for you! I made no secret of my annual pilgrimage to Caen.' He watched her poor efforts at lighting the pipe. 'I will not leave my nephew a sou!' The draw of tobacco flavour gave him fresh heart. 'There must be no question, you understand,' he told her aunt through the wispy smoke. 'No challenge! My *point* is, what if I bequeath my property to you?' His effort to give Tante Estelle a charming smile failed tragically. 'What are you, in your fifties? Still some life left, eh?'

'Man's already delirious,' muttered her aunt, but it was more than rouge pinkened her cheeks. 'Foolish old roué.'

'I was never more serious in my life, woman. I behold here a young lady who is quick-witted, resourceful, hungry and poor. Will you condemn her to starvation and loneliness? Marry me, Estelle-whoever-you-are, become Madame Bosanquet, and I will make my will in your favour. You shall never starve again and this sweet young flower will soon find a beau in Paris.'

Fleur laughed, not impolitely but out of aston-ishment, and glanced for her aunt's reaction. Tante Estelle humphed.

'No, listen to me, woman,' he retorted. 'You both need a new identity, else why does this child dress as a youth? Why do you hide her away in a forest when she is the age to seek a husband? What have you to lose? I shall be dead within the week.'

Fleur's aunt bristled. 'Paris, indeed! Would you send us to be massacred, to live among murderers where the cobblestones are clogged with blood? At least here we are safe.'

'Safe, here?' M. Bosanquet's eyes had grown shrewd. 'What about those innocent women dragged to Caen bound to the guns just because they were related to the priest at Saint-Jacques? Oh, I heard all about that last time I came here. Do not delude yourselves, mesdames, the Revolution is like a hungry sea creature. It will slowly reach out its tentacles and devour all of France. You should have seen the deputy who overtook me on the road – the light of revolu-tion in his eyes, a true believer. There will be a guillotine in the Place Saint-Sauveur before the year is over. Why do you not accept my offer, you old goose?'

'Be quiet, sir!' Her aunt clasped her hands against her ears.

Fleur patted his arm. 'Dear monsieur, your offer to us is very generous but, well – your nephew, if he is so greedy for your money that he tried to kill you, he will contest your will and –'

'– and murder us!' finished her aunt.

'I have friends in Paris, madame.'

'They did not do much for your safety!'

'No, to tell you the truth, but this journey for Maman I always do alone. I did not think my – my nephew would be so desperate. If I could make the journey back to Paris, I would destroy – *aïe!*' A stab of pain twisted in his belly. 'For the love of God, when the priest comes, let him marry us.'

'No!' snapped Tante Estelle, and flounced out; the vigorous chop of the cleaver recommenced.

'Oh, monsieur.' Fleur rescued the pipe. 'She prays my uncle is still alive.'

His expression was genuinely rueful. 'But she wore no wedding band.'

'She sold it to feed us through the first winter here.'

M. Bosanquet swallowed and turned his face to the wall. 'Oh, Christ!'

'*Tiens!*' Fleur rose from the stool, paced to the shutters and stood for a moment considering, before she swung round decisively. 'My aunt may not be able to wed you, monsieur, but I certainly can!'

2

Let us be wary of confusing savage man with the man we have before our eyes.

JEAN JACQUES ROUSSEAU, *A DISCOURSE UPON THE ORIGIN AND THE FOUNDATION OF THE INEQUALITY AMONG MANKIND*

'Wife to widow in one day!' Marie-Anne exclaimed, pulling hard at the laces of the quilted linen stays she had lent to Fleur. 'You do experience life to its full.'

Fleur clenched her teeth and held on to the chest of drawers, wondering whether, if she lost her grip, she and the respectable Marie-Anne Corday would tumble backwards through the second-storey window in full view of Caen's Rue Saint-Jean.

'Life to its full!' she gasped. 'Oh yes, like the time I was set upon by those young ruffians behind the butter market and arrived on your doorstep black and blue.'

'Fortunate they were not older,' clucked Marie-Anne with the weight of her superior years. 'Take this.' She generously scooped out one of the last two *eau de millefleurs* sachets from the box on the chest of drawers. 'Down your chemise, Madame Bosanquet.'

Fleur tucked the tiny perfumed pillow down between her breasts with a smile. *Madame Bosanquet!* She tasted the name on her tongue as though it were some exotic sweetmeat. And now she was in Caen at Marie-Anne's aunt's house with a new identity, and the man who had given it to her was in a coffin.

Her wedding had hardly been the matter of dreams – vows to a dying stranger old enough to be her grandfather! Not for her a carriage pulled by four greys or a gown of ivory Brussels pointlace over silken petticoats. No seigneur of the family gave her away; instead old Guillaume, a sabot-maker who lived on the edge of the forest, had played her absent brother's part. Philippe would be livid that his permission had not been sought, but M. Bosanquet's condition had left no time for niceties. The will had been drawn up beforehand with M. Esnault's help. Oh, it was almost like a theatre piece – the lawyer not suspecting that the boy in work-stained trousers chopping wood behind the cottage had not yet been made 'the wife' who was to receive all M. Bosanquet's worldly goods.

The rest of the dying man's affairs had been managed by a conspiracy of priests. Abbé Gombault officiated at the marriage and heard the dying man's confession, staying until the last, and then he and Guillaume carted the body to monsieur's mother's grave at the Chapel of Our Lady at la Délivrande where the local curé had buried him according to Church rites. The hastiness of it worried Fleur but she had not dared risk a public funeral or a coroner's investigation. Better to leave the cottage, the abbé suggested, and set out for Paris as soon as possible. The trouble was she and Tante Estelle needed official passes to leave the district of Calvados.

'Fleur, are you listening to me? How does it feel?' If Marie-Anne was wondering whether she could still breathe, the answer was no.

'Damnably *inconfortable!*' groaned Fleur, staring down at her thrust-up bosom as though her breasts were something alien. She had been used to flattening them beneath a towel.

'*Language!*' her older friend scolded amiably. 'Well, I am relieved you are back to dressing as a young lady, even if you do not sound like one. At least the mayor will be impressed. He will be so occupied admiring your curves, you will have the pass for Paris in an instant.'

Fleur's dry answer was lost in black bombazine as Marie-Anne flung the mourning gown over her friend's head.

'Only a few tucks necessary.' Deft fingers twitched the bodice straight. 'I cannot believe how much weight you have shed since leaving school.'

'About the only compensation.' Fleur drew Marie-Anne's black hat over her short curls and strode to the mirror above the mantelpiece. '*Ciel!*' The girl in the looking glass was unrecognisable. The high cheekbones were new to her and the crescent smudges of fatigue beneath her eyes suggested she was older than her nineteen years. The scratch where a flying chip of firewood had grazed her chin did not help either. 'At least I look like a widow,' she declared, arranging the veil over her hair. 'Yes?'

Marie-Anne nodded behind her, fingertips rising surreptitiously to brush the moisture from the hint of crow's feet; perhaps she was remembering mourning for her *maman* in this very gown. Fleur hoped it was that and not pity.

'I appreciate you letting me borrow this. You have been a good friend to me during the troubles, Marie-Anne.' For a moment the two young women clung to each other.

'You had better go and get those passes if you want to take the Paris diligence at two o'clock this afternoon.'

'One last touch.' Fleur reached out to the pewter tray on Marie-Anne's bureau and withdrew a pinch of sand.

'What on earth . . .' In amazement Marie-Anne stared as Fleur lifted her veil and threw back her head to drop the fine particles into her eyes.

23

'It's the small details that are important. My late and brief husband's advice. The first glimpse can be the most convincing. There, do I look as though I have been weeping?'

'Absolutely, Fleur.'

'I do not want to be arrested, do I?' This time she did not mistake the pity. 'It is my last chance to live a normal life. Now, wish me well, dear Marie-Anne.'

'Indeed, I do. Wait, do not forget the gloves, and no striding.'

'Or whistling, spitting or swearing. To arms, *hein*?' And with a back of ramrod rigidity that their teachers at the Abbaye aux Dames would have beamed upon, Fleur descended the winding stairs to the courtyard with a courage that was barely skin-deep.

By the time she reached the bridge at the end of the Rue Saint-Jean, she was as jumpy as a deer hearing the hunter. Why was it wearing a gown made her more ill at ease than her workman's clothes? Why did people stare so? She was trying to walk with a feminine gait. Or was it merely curiosity, because they thought her a stranger and wondered whom among the townsfolk she grieved for?

The broad façade of the two-hundred-year-old Hôtel d'Escoville which now served as the *hôtel de ville* (or, if you spoke in revolutionary jargon, the 'common hall') glared down at her like some grand courtier of Louis XIV's Versailles, daring her to enter its courtyard. She would have darted across to the Église Saint-Pierre and sent a beseeching prayer to Our Lady save that a pair of national guardsmen were lolling in its doorway watching her and it was now the Temple of Reason. *Ciel!*

With somewhat undue haste, she turned out of the cold wind into the shelter of the cobbled courtyard and halted. Another time she might have studied the ornate splendour of the dormer windows and Italianate turrets; instead she stared open-mouthed at the biblical statue of Judith holding the bloody head of Holofernes. An omen? It could be her head if the mayor grew too curious and began to ask questions with sticky tendrils and barbs. *Nom de Diable!* And there was another severed head! This time Goliath's, dangling from the shepherd boy David's hand.

'Looks gormless, *hein*? Wouldn't employ him to guard my flocks!' cackled an elderly woman, emerging, balanced by empty buckets from the arched porch on Fleur's left. Well, yes, David's face did look vacuous. 'Lost, are you?'

'Good morning, I was seeking the mayor.'

'Probably taking a nap,' chuckled the crone, and spat ambiguously. 'Well, go on up, dearie,' she chided, noting Fleur's hesitation. 'We are all equal now, ain't we?'

No, probably not, if you were male and called yourself an official, thought Fleur testily as she climbed the curving stone stairs and found herself upon a small, open balcony. With a choice of doors, she knocked upon the grander. Someone inside grunted and, with a deep breath, she let herself in. The chamber, which took up the entire wing, was pleasantly warm after the chill of the street and smelled of polished wood – a while since she had savoured that aroma of power.

At the far end of the room a man in a high-collared dark blue coat stood outlined against the window, his back turned. A dress sword hung from the *tricolore* sash that crossed his right shoulder, and a fulsome band of revolutionary colours encircled his waist. He gave her an uninterested glance over his shoulder as she closed the door behind her, but then as she straightened and waited for him to address her, he looked round again. Fleur lowered her gaze swiftly. The boy of two days ago would have stared back but a virtuous widow anxious for a pass needed to show some deference.

'*Monsieur le Maire?*' Her voice, so husky she barely recognised it, bruised the silence of the room and she knew instantly she was wrong. Someone else coughed and peered round from the high-backed chair that headed the long table; a scrawny man wearing the scarlet woollen bonnet which had become à la mode among supporters of the Revolution. One glance and the fellow ignored her, rustling his papers with an air of self-importance.

To whom should she address her request for a pass? A caped greatcoat was flung across one of the chairs. Fawn gauntlets, riding crop and a beaver hat profusely ornamented with scarlet, blue and white plumes lay together upon the table. Did these belong to the man at the window? Was he merely a visitor passing through?

She stepped forward, observing with misgivings the fellow dwarfed by the high chair-back. One really should not make swift judgments about people from their appearances, but with his unkempt hanks straggling across a greasy collar, he looked more like a slop-seller than a clerk.

'Good morning, monsieur,' she began serenely. 'I came to see the mayor but . . .' She faltered, conscious that the room had stilled, that the gentleman at the window was suddenly listening intently. The person at the table cleared his throat, picked up a quill from the ink pot then jabbed it back in again. 'Citizen Fournay. I am the acting municipal officer,' he growled. 'Citizen Enguerrand is not in Caen at present and Mayor Legoupil-Duclos is indisposed until further notice.'

An ill beginning. 'Ah, I see, well then, Citizen Fournay, perhaps you can assist me. I need a pass to return to Paris.'

'Paris?' He was at last bothering to look at her. A leer, definitely a leer, surfaced between the long sideburns, and Fleur's flesh crawled. This was even worse than the other man's interest. Here she was veiled and gowned in black – clearly grieving – and this wretch had the audacity to . . . Her spine stiffened, her gloved nails pressed into her palms but she bit back a retort. At least she was not alone with the creature, for the man at the window stretched purposefully, the subtle crack of his clasped hands reminding the municipal officer of his presence.

'Why do you need a pass, Widow . . . ?' Fournay asked with a sniff, recalling his duty.

'My name is Bosanquet, Citizen Fournay. Possibly you have heard what happened?' Fournay stared at her stonily. 'We were attacked,' she added with breathless indignation. 'Monsieur, my husband was badly wounded. The forest people who helped us fetched Dr Talbert but unfortunately . . .' Wary of saying too much, she dramatically knuckled her cheek beneath her veil then drew a handkerchief from her reticule.

'Yes, yes, I heard. Bosanquet, *hein*? Originally from these parts, yes?'

'From Calvados, yes, but my husband preferred to reside in Paris. The brigands took our papers. That is why I need a new pass from you.'

'Royalists, probably.' About to spit upon the glossy floor, he seemed to remember his new status and shrugged instead. 'A pass – just for you, then?'

'And my aunt. She will be accompanying me.'

'Most people are running away from Paris. Why do you not remain here?'

Fleur ignored his amusement. 'I have property there, Monsieur Fournay. Urgent matters to be dealt with, as you can imagine.'

'Property, you say?'

She could have bitten her tongue off. Fool she was, this creature would now want a bribe. Property? M. Bosanquet might own a hovel near a sewer for all she knew.

'I assume you would like the passes issued to

you now.' Fournay rubbed his thumb and fingertips together meaningfully. 'Or perhaps you would like to collect the documents from my house tonight.'

'Now will do.' Unwillingly she drew off her gloves, careful to keep the hard skin of her hands hidden. Apart from Marie-Anne's late mother's wedding ring, borrowed to give her story credence, Fleur's only adornment was an aquamarine in a simple setting that Maman had given her on her fifteenth birthday. *Nom de Ciel*, she could not give away the wedding ring. With a bitter heart, she forced herself to drop the aquamarine into his cupped hand.

'Not enough!' he mouthed at her.

'*Let me see that!*'

They both started and sprang apart like disturbed lovers. The other man had left the casement, his spurred boots sounding ominously on the wooden boards; his fist unfurled slowly, menacingly, between them, waiting. Fleur gave a hiss of breath; must she pay this upstart too?

Muttering, Fournay relinquished the ring into the outstretched, uncalloused palm. Fleur's gaze followed the midnight blue sleeve of the stranger's coat and blinked in astonishment at the gold braid epaulette embellishing his unsashed shoulder. If a different man had been wearing such an over-adorned uniform, she would have been amused at the absurdity, but he wore the republican colours like a victor who knew his own worth. *Grand Dieu!* Both these men were dangerous.

Fournay swallowed loudly but it was Fleur who was being weighed along with her ring. The cool stare was examining her. No nervousness, no trembling like a mouse, she told herself, just show a reasonable respect. Play the innocent widow, not the frightened aristocrat.

'Gentlemen, I should like to be on my way this afternoon,' she admonished gently, and with a finely measured confidence she managed to lift her gaze from the man's uppermost gold button. She was aware of dark-brown hair restrained in a queue, of freckles faintly scattered across strong cheekbones, of fine teeth; but it was his eyes, bronze-hued, cold and intelligent, scrutinising her from beneath arched brows, that mesmerised her. A chill humour glinted in those dark depths.

'Perhaps you would like to unveil.'

Something inside Fleur's body unfurled, awakened, as if it recognised a call to arms from the voice of a general. Her mind protested, uncomprehending such alien, sudden stirring.

'Citizeness?' The hard, golden eyes searched ruthlessly for rebellion. Slowly, reluctantly, she set back the black gauze. Search all you like, her gaze told him. Thank God she had rubbed the sand into her eyes.

Was he pretending suspicion, playing with her like a tomcat amused with a little widow mouse? She was armed for such battles. Her sisters might have served apprenticeships in flirting; Fleur's had been in survival and she knew when the hunter sensed a killing might be at hand.

Feel the character! Beneath the stranger's inspection, she deftly glanced away, letting her eyes water with unshed tears. Yes, she could do that. Not only had she played the tragic heroine in family theatricals, the last four years had taught her how to weep. *Timing, oh yes, that too.*

Slowly, she raised her eyes once more to the stranger, letting her misery turn to blandness, as if, just like the statue in the courtyard, she possessed a hollowness not worth further acquaintance. The ploy worked.

'Let her have a pass.' Losing interest in her, her inquisitor examined the ring, holding it up between his thumb and forefinger before tossing it back to the municipal officer without any comment. With a snort, Fournay swiftly pocketed it in his waistcoat. '*Mais non*, Citizen Fournay,' the visitor scolded, 'you will donate it towards the local fund for the national guard. This nation does not run on venality any more.' The clipped observation matched the young man's cold smile as he watched the older man tug the gem back out with an ill grace, then he said softly: 'Now make out the widow's papers, Fournay. I have not all day.'

With a grimace, the municipal officer resumed his seat and, riffling through the pile of papers, selected a clean sheet. 'I'm not much at the shape of things, citizen,' he muttered.

For an instant the stranger did not comprehend and then a slow smile crooked his mouth. 'My pleasure. Are you ready?'

'Yes,' growled the other, plucking a quill from the inkwell. '"Pass, given to Citizeness Bosanquet, widow."' The scratching halted. 'Age?'

'Twenty-three,' she lied.

'Height? How tall are you, citizeness?'

'I-I don't know, Monsieur Fournay.' Her glance flew unthinking to the young official's face. More than her height was being estimated by his trawling gaze but Fleur dared not rebuke him.

'Set down five foot four inches.'

'Hair brown, then?'

'With a tint of chestnut, Fournay.'

'Eyes?'

'Do not glance away, citizeness. *Blue as an Italian lake.*'

The quill spluttered: 'Blue.'

'Nose?'

'Turn your head if you please, citizeness.' A command not a request. His lower lip curled consideringly, and hidden in the folds of her skirts, so did Fleur's fists. 'Neither long nor yet retroussé,' murmured the maddeningly amiable voice, but Fournay was not enjoying the game.

'*Merde*, it's a cursed pass not a poem, citizen. Get on with it!'

'Please, messieurs, I do not wish to delay you,' protested Fleur, but she was pinioned beneath the young man's scrutiny like a butterfly about to be labelled.

'Small, straight,' growled Fournay. 'Chin?'

'Gently rounded, I should say.'

'*Round* will do. Face?'

'Enchantingly tragic and . . .' The soft laugh was measured. The full nib waited angrily. 'Set down "*oval*", citizen.' He watched critically as Fournay

32

scattered sand across the painful writing and unfortunate blots, then he slid the calculated charm back into cold officiousness: 'You have forgotten to date it. Year II of the French Republic, remember.' With that verbal slap, he bestowed a brisk, dismissive nod on Fleur, then strode back to resume his vigilance at the casement. 'And do not forget the other woman's,' he called out over his shoulder.

'I need to see her, don't I?' muttered Fournay, unsure of procedure, but at a shrug of the visitor's shoulders he tugged out another sheet and took Fleur through her aunt's description.

She should have been grateful for the young official's playful interference, but he terrified her. No doubt some former schoolteacher or impoverished merchant's son! A self-satisfied nobody wallowing in his shiny new superiority, anxious to put notches on his belt! If he could spring to advancement by having her declared an enemy of the Revolution, he would do just that. And Paris would be teeming with men like him. It was all she could do to hide her nervousness as she watched Fournay fill in the last details for her aunt.

'Thank you,' she said politely, relieved that the papers were finally in her hands, and darted a glance at the figure by the window. Head flung back arrogantly, he stood legs astride, hands clasped behind him. No doubt as smug as Narcissus. Could he see his reflection in the diamond panes?

'For heaven's sake, go, citizeness,' he drawled without turning. 'You have what you came for.'

Feeling as though she had just survived an

audience with the Devil, Fleur sped down the stairs. The icy intelligence of that face haunted her. What had he discovered about her from the ring? She glanced up swiftly. He was gone from the window but the prickle between her shoulder blades intensified as she crossed the courtyard. As foolish as Orpheus, she could not resist looking round and discovered him standing on the balcony, framed by the high arch of golden limestone, watching her like a brooding god wondering whether to make mischief.

Fleur jerked her head forwards again, drawing down her veil over her flaming cheeks, and walked – *don't stride!* – as calmly as she could towards the street. Someone else in the courtyard was staring too: a workman sitting legs apart on a step with his crib beside him, swigging from a leather flask. Workman? No, the correct term now was *sans-culotte* if you did not wear breeches like your betters.

'Bonjour, madame.' A different *sans-culotte*, cheerful and gnarled, paused in barrowing firewood off a cart and waited for her to pass.

'Pardon me,' she exclaimed, 'can you tell me the name of that man up there on the balcony behind us?'

A grey moustache waggled as the old fellow looked her over and then peered round. 'What, the whippersnapper you can't see for the golden gee-gaws and furbelows? Probably snooping to see if we are doing our job.' Fleur let a smile light her eyes and his grin broadened. 'A representative *en mission* from the Committee for General Security in Paris, that

34

one. Been setting up committees of surveillance all over Calvados. Fancy him for a beau, eh, citizeness?'

Quel malheur! A creature from the bubbling vent of the volcano! 'I suspect France is his only bedfellow, monsieur,' she replied brightly. *Zut, zut, zut!* Why of all the people in Caen did she have to cross that one's path?

Something was not consistent. Raoul leaned forward to meet the questioning stare from his agent, gave an almost imperceptible nod and raised his left hand to heart height. Anyone noticing might have thought the curl of his second and third fingers were but idle flexing.

Follow her!

The young widow's shapely curves inspired his admiration until she disappeared into the shadow of the archway. It was a damnable while since he had seen a woman so desirable and intriguing, and the male half of Caen must be thinking so too, judging by the ancient workman who set down his barrow to speak with her and the soldiers who strode in whistling at her.

Did the Widow Bosanquet realise how tragically beautiful she was? His own appreciation, Raoul rationalised, was as much professional as instinctive, for his hand ached to draw her. Persephone mourning for the sunlight. Yes, naked upon a bed in Tartarus after her abduction, awaiting the mighty god of the underworld. Virginal, afraid but excited, unclothed save for a wisp of black veiling across her thighs. Oh yes.

Fournay inconveniently interrupted his fantasy, lolling against the doorframe, chewing his grimy nails. Smug eyes blatantly assumed that he had been watching the girl.

'The intendant is late arriving. Think he might be trying to snub you, citizen?'

Raoul drew a deep breath and followed the municipal officer back into the chamber. 'Plenty of time,' he growled. 'Have you finished your lists?' He watched the fellow slide back resentfully into the chair, and then, slipping a hand into his coat pocket, drew out a fistful of coins, bestowed one in the fund box and withdrew the widow's ring.

'Ha, knew you would do that,' sneered the local man.

'I have given more than it's worth.' Raoul thrust the bauble under the official's nose. 'There is no jeweller's mark, see.'

Fournay would not have known a turquoise from a ruby. He grunted: 'Think she was an *aristo*? Do you want to have her brought back for questioning?' The narrow eyes sparked.

Raoul shook his head indifferently but his fingers fondled the ring. 'Have *you* ever seen her before?'

'Can't say I have. I suppose she is from Paris. Hard to tell, eh, she spoke so soft.'

'But her dialect is not Parisian and it is not from Calvados. Further west, maybe.'

'Pretty piece of tail, eh, and she's returning up your way. Nice coincidence, that. You could follow matters up.'

'Just a little widow,' Raoul said with a tight smile that told Fournay to damn well mind his own business.

Fleur did not go directly back to Marie-Anne's. She headed nostalgically for the Rue Basse, her feet drawn with the obedience of a student up the hill towards the squat grey spire of the Abbaye aux Dames. She drew breath at the top of the rise, frowning at the mass of horse dung fouling the approach to the Trinité School's gatehouse and the revolutionary posters slapped upon the limestone walls. '*Egallite*' was badly spelt in whitewash across the great oak door, and a fresh stain of urine was drying on the wall behind the national guardsmen on duty. Did nothing decent endure any more? she thought angrily, longing for the peace and order those walls had given her.

Oh, such dreams! Marie-Anne, secretary to the abbess, with a head full of snippings from the works of Voltaire or Rousseau, so naively jubilant at news of the fall of the Bastille in distant Paris. And cheerful little Fleur, five years younger, always listening and questioning. Golden days, the brief calm before the Revolution smashed through her life again like a stone through glass.

Mercifully Fleur and her aunt had already fled Caen when the rabble dragged the nuns from their classrooms for a beating and the authorities had closed the school. Now most of her teachers were in hiding, still defiantly living according to the rules of St Benedict, and Queen Matilda's proud abbey had become a storeroom and uniform factory. 'It would break your heart to see it,' Marie-Anne had told her sadly. The queen's tomb desecrated by soldiers' graffiti. No plainsong, no constant murmur of prayers, no –

Turning away, Fleur froze inwardly. The *sans-culotte* from the courtyard was leaning against a wall. Holding it up? That was too much of a coincidence.

Pretending she had not even noticed him, Fleur crossed the muddy road and descended the hill along the Rue Haute. She had intended to make a farewell call on the former abbess-headmistress, Mme de Pontécoulant, in the Place Saint-Sauveur, but that was now out of the question. Too dangerous for both of them. Instead she cut down the stairs of the narrow Venelle Maillard and turned right. Was he still following her? Dropping her handkerchief, she stooped to retrieve it, glancing back. Oh, he was, curse him! Well, she must convince him she was a stranger. Fumbling in her pocket, pretending that her pass paper was an address, she stared up searchingly at the shutters of the houses and then retraced her way up the steps, as if lost, passing the man without a glance. With a deep breath, she knocked on one of the doors.

'Bonjour, my name is Bosanquet,' she explained. 'I am seeking friends of my late husband's, Monsieur and Madame Aunay.' She repeated the futile request at a second house further along and then, with her shoulders bent as if utterly dispirited, made her way to the busy thoroughfare of the Rue Saint-Pierre.

Oh, he was good at dogging her, but she managed to lose him between the market stalls and a courtyard. Then she hobbled back towards the Rue Saint-Jean.

'Oh, Fleur, thank goodness, you are back,' exclaimed Tante Estelle, collapsing into an armchair and fanning herself vigorously. 'Did you get the passes?'

'Yes, but I was followed,' muttered Fleur, stripping off her gloves and stooping to hush Azar, Marie-Anne's little dog. 'A workman from the Hôtel d'Escoville.'

'You think the man fancied you, dear heart?' Marie-Anne appeared from the kitchen, wiping her hands on her waistcloth.

'I doubt it.' Fleur pulled off the pinching shoes. 'Some upstart from the Committee for General Security is making everyone jump. It is all right, Tante, no one asked where I was staying.'

'Oh, but we have nothing to hide,' Marie-Anne's elderly aunt, Mme de Bretteville, declared, scooping up the dog and cuddling him to her pockmarked cheek. 'Hush, Azar! And, besides, Marie-Anne has some very influential admirers.'

Marie-Anne made a face. 'And I am not marrying Hyppolyte or Gustave, even if they ask me, which they won't. Men may enjoy the rarity of arguing politics with a woman but they do not want intelligent conversation at breakfast. Come and talk to me while I finish making dinner.' She tugged Fleur into the kitchen. 'Who was he? This fellow from Paris,' she demanded, closing the kitchen door.

'Down! Get off there, Ninette! There is hardly enough for us.' The dislodged cat landed stolidly on all fours and, affronted, retreated to wash her paws.

Fleur dipped her finger in the sauce on the hob. 'Some upstart anxious to clamber to glory over the rubble by setting up surveillance committees.'

Marie-Anne raised her eyebrows in disgust. 'A Jacobin?'

'I don't know. Do Jacobins flirt?' Fleur explored the pile of journals lying beside the chopping board. *Le Journal de la République*, Brissot's *Le Patriot* and Husson's *Courier*, all a week old.

'My friend Hyppolyte passed them on to me,' explained Marie-Anne, jabbing a finger at *Le Journal*. 'See, they are not giving the government a chance.' Picking up the cleaver, she began to take out her fury on a waiting onion. 'Imagine how hard it must be for inexperienced ministers. France torn by civil war and ringed by enemies. Armies, let alone the poor to feed and clothe. I mean, it's not going to happen overnight, getting everything right. Organisation takes time. And this constant vile criticism by Marat and Robespierre. Promise me you will go along to the Convention and write to me exactly what is being said.'

'If it is safe.' Fleur set down the gazette and lifted up Ninette, tickling the soft fur behind the cat's ears. She watched the cleaver descend. 'I may be sticking my head in "the little window" by going to Paris.'

'Paris!' Marie-Anne fumed. More bits of onion scattered, startling the cat out of Fleur's arms. 'Why is everyone so scared of Paris? There is no king, no court any more. Why must we let Paris dictate to the rest of France?' The chopper stilled as her friend's face softened. 'Oh, Fleur, I envy you and yet . . . You will be careful, won't you?'

'I have done with starving like a dog and I think I had rather risk the guillotine than suffer another winter in the cottage.' Fleur wriggled her toes, glaring at the chilblains showing beneath her darned stockings.

'Oh, *ma pauvre*.' Marie-Anne came round the table to hug her. 'Why did you not say so, you goose? We could have helped you.'

'You had hardly sufficient either.' She took her friend's hand gratefully. 'No, Marie-Anne, I am like the miller's youngest son – it is time I set out into the world to seek my fortune. Another door is opening and I have to go through it. We need to tell ourselves that things will get better. Stories for infants, hmm?'

'They will, they must! We knew it was never going to be easy. Victims and martyrs, yes, there have been, of course, but what war is bloodless? And it has been a war – against greed and self-interest. A few wallowing in luxury and vanity while the masses went hungry. You always shared my dreams, Fleur. Do not despair. It will be all right, you'll see. We have almost won.'

Fleur's eyes glistened. 'I wish I had your faith.' She stood up and paced to the window. 'But,' she said, slapping her fist against her thigh, 'I cannot cower in a forest for the rest of my life. If Paris offers me opportunities, I am resolved I shall seize them with both hands, whatever the cost.' And there would be a price. There always was.

Turning, she put on her brightest smile. 'You must come and visit me when I am settled in – if it is not too dangerous. Promise?'

'Oh, try and stop me. I shall afford it somehow.' Marie-Anne held out her hands to take Fleur's. 'I know I've seen little of you these last two years but I shall miss you and pray for you.'

Fleur would need her prayers. Idealistic Marie-Anne thought her merely the niece of a lesser noble but she only knew a fraction of the truth. Fleur had not spoken of her grief. Marie-Anne did not know that Fleur's papa, le Duc de Montbulliou, and Marguerite, her eldest half-sister, had each had a knife drawn across their throats as though they were common beasts. That was in Paris! And it was going to take every ounce of Fleur's courage to go there. *But to stay would be even worse.*

3

Dearest Marie-Anne,
How I wish to share with you both the thrill and
misgivings that Paris affords me. I shall survive! I am
resolved on it. I just pray that the haughty deputy will
not pry too deeply into poor M. Bosanquet's demise . . .

EXTRACT FROM THE LETTERS OF FRANÇOISE-ANTOINETTE DE

MONTBULLIOU, 1793

La Veuve Bosanquet. Just a little widow? Raoul's disciplined mind filed the matter away and he thought no more upon the girl until nine o'clock that evening when the inn servant brought supper to his bedchamber. Time to set his report for the Committee for General Security aside. Closing his portable escritoire, he sat down at the cross-barred table and began to scan the local broadsheet while he dined. There was no mention of Bosanquet's attack. Nor had the young woman behaved in a particularly suspicious manner after she had left the common hall. Seeking out friends of her husband apparently, though it did not explain why she had been lurking around the old Trinité School. An old pupil, perhaps.

Raoul tossed the newspaper aside. He was halfway through the *echaudés* and *vin mousseux* when a stranger knocked and made free to let himself in.

'Citizen Deputy?' Before Raoul could manage an answer, the man removed his bicorne hat, set it upon the cloth and sat himself down uninvited in the chair opposite. He was in his fifties, clean-shaven, hair powdered and curled, and reputable-looking if one ignored the faint spatter of gravy that had never fully washed out of his muslin cravat.

Raoul cleansed his lips with a napkin and eyed the older man with asperity. 'I believe I am not acquainted with you, citizen.'

'Name's Esnault, I'm a lawyer. I apologise for disturbing you, Citizen de Villaret, but I understand you are returning to Paris tomorrow.'

'I am not a courier, citizen. I do not interest myself with other people's packages.'

'No, of course you do not,' the other man leaned forward, veined hands clasped, 'but do you interest yourself in murder?'

Even though he followed Esnault's directions, Raoul wasted an hour of the next morning before he found the track in the forest of Grimbosq which led to what he supposed was the dwelling where Matthieu Bosanquet had died. It looked inhabited, except there was no smoke rising from the single chimney even though firewood was neatly stacked along the front wall. A poor attempt had been made to garden, and behind the dwelling he could see a small byre with a manger still wispy with hay. Some of the manure was recent.

'*Holà?*' He rapped on the door with his riding crop and, hearing no answer, undid the latch and let himself into the dark interior. Drying herbs brushed against his hat like thick cobwebs. He cast the hat upon the cleared table and, thrusting open the shutters, permitted the frosty air to dilute yesterday's smells of cooked onions and swept-up hearth ash. The room was too tidy. He lifted the inverted cooking pot left behind on the bare hearth. It had been used recently. Not needed any more. Curious. Peasants never discarded anything.

Not a leaf or shaking of boot soil disfigured the rammed-earth floor and when he ran a finger along the shelf which still held a pitcher of dried peas, it dislodged no mouse turds nor came away dusty. If Matthieu Bosanquet had been rescued by the inhabitants of the *bassot*, why were they not here any more?

And someone had lived here – until yesterday afternoon, he guessed, when the young woman and her supposed aunt had taken the diligence to Paris. Gone – before Esnault or the physician had second thoughts.

People in a hurry were often careless. He eyed the inner door hopefully but the bedchamber also was devoid of character, save for an old square of leather hanging batlike from a wall nail, which peasants wore to keep the rain off. A faint smell of incense hung in the room. Someone had given the dying man the last rites. Who?

The simple bed had been stripped of its linen and the only other item of furnishing was a chest. Raoul knelt and thumbed the contents: two covers – one twill, one green wool; an ancient sheepskin pelisse; worn sheets, old but quality – looted, perhaps; and darned work clothes – boy's trousers. And, forgotten in the trouser pocket, he found a gypsy comb with a pair of wagtails painted on it curiously tangled with a catapult. He dropped the lid shut. If the dying Bosanquet had occupied the bed, where had the pretty widow slept during her vigil? Not beside the kitchen fire? He leaned against the doorway, observing that not only was there a well-scrubbed table, but on either side of it two crudely made chairs. Only the father in a peasant dwelling such as this sat at a table – if he was lucky. The rest of the family stood to eat.

Citizen Esnault was right. There was a mystery here, else why would the inhabitants have fled? Did they fear interrogation? Witnesses calling themselves Estelle and Guillaume had signed the will and where were they now? Raoul frowned as he latched the door behind him. He did not have time to seek them out and it was not really his responsibility to investigate further, but he would. Oh yes, he certainly would.

The Cherbourg diligence rumbled to a halt at noon outside the two-storeyed offices of the Messageries Nationale in the Rue Notre Dame des Victoires. It was Thursday, three days since the coach had left Caen, and its stiff passengers, eight adults and three children, had had a surfeit of each other. Forced proximity for hour after hour enticed intimacies from people you would not meet otherwise: people like the lascivious card-player from Lisieux, or the bad-tempered crone from Carentan, who stared at you for hours on end and wondered at your secrets. Tante Estelle, unused to public coaches, had nearly betrayed her noble origins on several occasions and was probably suffering from bruised toes where Fleur had needed to deliver discreet, swift warnings. Then there had been the passport checks by officious local upstarts almost every two leagues.

As they had reached the environs of Paris, the stink of the city had intensified like a miasma in the interior of the coach. Fleur had noticed her aunt clutching her small portmanteau as if she had Queen Marie Antoinette's famous necklace inside it, and realised Tante Estelle was striving to hide a very genuine fear. They were risking their lives daring to come to the lair of the very dragon that had devastated France, murdered innocents, but Fleur felt excitement and danger seeping through her veins like Papa's brandy. It was infuriating not to be able to see out, to begin to assess the enemy

– seven years since she had last visited Paris – but the passenger from Cherbourg had drawn the shutters down so he might nap, and the window on the other side was monopolised by two fidgeting children who squeaked worse than fledglings.

'Your passes, citizens!'

Fleur's blue blood ran cold at the formidable tone. Two national guards were waiting for the passengers to disembark, examining everyone's papers with calculated menace – and these were Parisians; she could not gull them so easily. Well, if she could face a deputy of the Convention, Fleur could manage these two. But would she have to get used to this unpleasant ogling? Being a woman was definitely not easy.

Her confidence teetered precariously like a novice tightroper when the Cherbourg importer was marched off for further interrogation. Welcome to Paris!

'I never expected to set foot in this pit of vipers ever again,' muttered Tante Estelle, swishing her skirts from the nose of a stray dog. 'Do not stride so.' She bustled across behind Fleur to a choice of three fiacres for hire. 'Can we afford this?'

'Yes, if I haggle,' Fleur muttered grimly, deciding which of the drivers wore the most honest expression.

'Surely . . .'

'Unless you would prefer we hire a barrowman and walk?'

Her aunt's snort of disapproval justified the intense bargaining that followed.

'I am beginning to think you have plenty of your father in you,' muttered Tante Estelle, as the ill-sprung fiacre jolted forwards. Fleur slid her thinner purse back into her bag, aware that M. Bosanquet's money was running out like water through a leaking bucket, but she still gave her aunt a comforting smile.

'Nearly there. A few days and Paris will not seem so foreign to us.'

Regrettably, the older lady was not in the least enthused. 'There's no convincing you, is there, child? What do donkeys do but go out into the middle of the field when there's a storm coming and –'

'– and any horses in the meadow always follow it,' finished Fleur, hoping that Blanchette was happy with Guillaume. 'So I'm the donkey, am I?'

'And I'm the foolish nag. Now do stop bouncing and sit like a lady.'

But Fleur was exuberant, staring at everything like a short-sighted child with her first pair of spectacles. Chickens scattered and hawkers bawled at their conveyance as it trundled along, flourishing their wares: tricolore ribbons, handkerchiefs commemorating the fall of the Bastille, and cockades in button to saucer sizes. The long street they turned up was much like those in Caen, lined with shops. Above them rose several-storey stone dwellings with plain casements embellished by painted shutters and tasteful little balconies. There was no pavement; the street was pockmarked with puddles and the passers-by nimbly sprang back as the coach bowled past. No wonder most of the men wore black stockings with their breeches. But suddenly there was something wrong. People started running in the same direction, some with barrows, others with panniers. Women snatched up babies in one hand, their skirts in the other, and further down the street a press of people were almost fighting their way inside a shop.

'What's happening?' Fleur unlatched the window and called out to the driver who had slowed his horses.

'A new supply of soap, citizeness. Better if it was bread, eh?'

'I never observed the Parisians were *that* bothered about washing,' muttered her aunt as the coach gathered pace again, but Fleur did not answer; her spirits were sinking. Beggars were everywhere, hardly able to cover their shoulders against the cold March wind, holding out their hands piteously. It did not auger well. Had she and Tante Estelle survived a cruel winter to face a summer of starvation? Paris did seem to have less food than Caen. Turning a corner, the fiacre rattled past closed shops. Outside a baker's stretched a queue of women, half the street long, their faces pinched. Cold, sullen eyes watched their vehicle pass. Fleur leaned her head back against the seat. A creature of the street sisterhood thumped on the side of the fiacre hoping that it carried potential customers and, seeing only two ladies inside, spat. Was the woman a desperate mother forced to sell her body for food for her children? Oh God, thought Fleur, would she be reduced to that if M. Bosanquet proved a liar?

Tante Estelle's contemptuous mutterings continued. Paris had indeed been taken over by the masses, but at what cost? Proud walls that had glimpsed the Sun King, Louis XIV, ride past were daubed with charcoal slogans; posters gushed patriotism and worse. '*Vive Marat!*' and '*I love Danton!*' were mild sentiments compared to the broadsheet that been discarded on the coach seat beside Fleur. It informed her that Brissot, the leader of the ruling deputies, had been intimate with his maman, and a crude cartoon implied that the minister of the interior, Roland, was a contortionist. Was that physically possible? Her cheeks heating, Fleur began to acquire a new vocabulary.

'Give me that!' Tante Estelle snatched the paper. 'I have never seen so much scurrilous –'

'Sshh.' Fleur darted her a warning look.

'I was going to say the streets look filthier than ever.' The aristocrat lowered her voice with dignity. 'Look at that creature relieving himself.'

'I am trying not to. Have you noticed how few horses there are?'

'Requisitioned to pull gun carriages instead of curricles,' said her aunt. 'Is there nothing that has not been ruined.' They were passing a low wall studded with ugly iron stumps. No doubt the railings had been wrenched off to melt down for guns or else to use as – Fleur shivered – crude bayonets.

Her aunt must have been thinking the same.

'Oh, child, when I think of your poor father and sister being slaughtered like beasts.'

'Please, Tante,' snapped Fleur, terrified lest the driver could hear. 'I thought we agreed never to mention that.' *Nom de Ciel*, did her aunt think she had forgotten? 'This . . . this looks a quieter neighbourhood.' She pretended to admire a medieval, half-timbered dwelling, determined to keep her fear safely lidded.

Tante Estelle shrugged, unimpressed. 'Do not raise your hopes. Bosanquet had more hot air than a furnace. Mark my words, you have inherited nothing more than an attic room in some stinking tenement. Look at that! Worse than jackdaws. No privacy! And what if these boarders he told us about refuse to let us in?'

Fleur sat back, disdaining to stare at the laundry hanging from every window. Inside, she tried to disengage from the rising panic. I will manage, she vowed and grabbed at the strap as the fiacre swung round a corner.

'Forty-seven Rue des Bonnes Soeurs, *hein*?'

The hired vehicle reined in outside a smallish seventeenth-century building flanking a courtyard on three sides. Their arrival was observed by a man lounging against the outside wall, seemingly doing nothing but watching the world pass. Fleur sighed; there seemed to be a lot of idlers in the streets. Probably an out-of-work servant. Equality was all very well but the great houses of the noblesse had at least provided employment. The sluggard stopped picking his teeth and slouched off, whistling a summons to someone. No doubt their arrival would fuel neighbourhood gossip.

Fleur carried her meagre bag into the court-yard, her stomach growling. The smell of ground coffee hung in the air above her, competing with the clean aroma of freshly sawn wood. This old house, like most along the street, had three storeys – apartments, judging by the irregularity of the window fittings. The upper casements were neatly curtained with long drapes, while on the ground floor, cloths tucked over strings sufficed and half the shutters were missing. A dog with a torn ear bounded out to yap at Fleur's skirts, and from an upper iron balcony festooned with foliage a violin rasped haltingly. Several barefooted children left their play among the muddy potholes and came to gape at the newcomers. One whistled away the dog. A woman sitting on a doorstep suckling her baby in the sunlight gaped at Fleur as though she had eight legs and a sinister pair of spinnerets, and then, becoming aware of the newcomer's bereave-ment, crossed herself and turned the infant to her other breast. In the shade a joiner humming Mozart set down his hammer.

'Bosanquet?' Fleur called out. The artisan wiped his hands on the seat of his trousers and pointed to the door at the back of the courtyard.

The wing edging the rear of the yard presented a more uniform appearance. The lion doorknocker gleamed, the step was unsullied, the boot-scraper clean. A thin gentleman in breeches and silk stock-ings opened the door, but before Fleur could speak, he burst into tears at the sight of her mourning clothes. He introduced himself between sobs as M. Bosanquet's friend and boarder. 'André B-B-Beugneux' showed them into what passed for a modest dining room, and withdrew with a wail of anguish, promising that they would be brought coffee.

'Well, better than I expected,' admitted Tante Estelle grudgingly, inspecting the silver candelabra and the other ornaments upon the mahogany sideboard as though she was walking down a line of soldiers, 'if one can stomach the neighbourhood – and the boarders! Beugneux! He pretends to refinement but . . .' she shrugged. 'I cannot wait to meet the foreigner, Signor Machiavelli. I wonder if he is dripping with emotion as well.'

Fleur ignored the sarcasm. What was the role of a widow? Should she be taking charge? Wearily she sat down at the table and hoped that the bewigged, wailing creature who had greeted them would be solicitous enough to hurry the refreshments.

'I am the one supposed to be doing the weeping,' she observed. 'Isn't his reaction rather excessive?'

'Yes, indeed,' answered her aunt. 'I begin to suspect that the late Monsieur Bosanquet had – shall we say – *hidden* depths.'

It was not kind to mimic the poor man's stammer but Fleur could not resist. 'Well, my l-late husband has a w-w-watering p-pot of a l-l-lodger.'

'Fleur! Desist! You are a grown woman and a widow.'

Just as well, for a rather more composed M. Beugneux shortly reappeared, bearing a tray set with a coffee service. Clearly grateful when Fleur indicated that he should join them, he set his coat-tails aside and sat down upon the dining chair opposite her. 'I am sorry that I welcomed you so poorly, mesdames, b-but . . .' His voice choked and a lace-cuffed hand gestured apologetically.

'Be at ease, monsieur,' Fleur reassured him, then annoyed her aunt by reaching out a gloved hand to touch his sleeve. 'I am glad my husband has good friends who mourn his passing.' She waited while he blew his nose with genteel grace. The whiff of lavender filled the air.

Clearly in the autumn of his life, thought Fleur, discreetly studying the crannies of M. Beugneux's face, and was not in the least surprised that he still preferred the dress of the ancien regime: heeled morocco shoes, satin breeches, embroidered coat and waistcoat, silk jabot and powdered wig. But the added colouring and beauty spot were unattractive. Strange to think that until three years ago most of the nobility, including her papa, had rouged their cheeks and looked so. And this gentleman's eyes reminded her of a lizard in one of Mama's picture books – sleepy-wise, watching her from beneath the layers of crinkled skin. It was she who felt under the glass now, but there was no lechery in his study: no hostility, either, only a wariness, for she could order him from what was now her house.

'I apologise for my distress, m-madame. Monsieur B–B–Bosanquet and I have been together for a long time. He was in such good spirits, so well when he left here. B–but –' He moistened his lips as if that would erase the difficulty of what he felt compelled to say. 'I–I am devastated to find that Matthieu never told me of your existence, madame.'

Swampy ground, this. Fleur was tempted to explain the circumstances of her marriage but it was too early for trust. He might have already allied himself with Monsieur's obnoxious nephew.

'I am happy to acquaint you in due course with how Monsieur Bosanquet and I came to know one another, monsieur.' She drew breath – a lie, for she still had to iron the wrinkles out of her story – and added truthfully, 'but I am sure you understand that it is painful to talk of these things at the moment. Monsieur . . . my husband spoke of you at the last. "Tell André that I bear him the deepest affection." He wished you to have this, monsieur.' She drew out the silver watch and chain from her purse and set it before him upon the cloth.

For an instant M. Beugneux could not bear to touch it, and then he gathered it up with reverence as though it were a holy relic. Fingering the dial glass lovingly, he swallowed and asked, 'W–was it very painful, his dying?'

'He was brave but gradually he slipped in and out of unconsciousness until finally his spirit was overwhelmed.' She saw that genuine tears filled the crevices of the man's face and she reached out a sympathetic hand. 'Monsieur Beugneux, you and I have a great deal to talk about, but these things can wait.'

'Your p-pardon.' The silence between the three of them was embarrassing and then M. Beugneux shook his head as if trying to reassemble his thoughts. 'I-I have taken the liberty of arranging a gathering the day after tomorrow at . . . at one of the temples of reason to bid poor Matthieu adieu. If you do not feel up to attending . . .'

It was something she must endure. And M. Bosanquet did deserve a memorial service. Aloud she said, 'Of course. I rely on you to be my support, monsieur.'

'I am your servant in that, madame.' He leaned forward across the cloth and carried her hand to his lips. A sad gesture, like the last line of a tragedy. 'You are very gracious, Madame B-Bosanquet. I had b-braced myself to find you neither charming nor so generous. I-I would like to feel we are almost family.'

Tante Estelle gave one of her disapproving coughs, but he appeared not to notice as he rose and went to the sideboard. 'I should give you these.' He took out a bunch of keys. 'M-Matthieu usually carried them with him. They are yours now.' A gesture of confidence, thought Fleur. He could have bided his time to hand them over. 'Now what else? Ah yes, Monsieur Mansart, your husband's business agent, will be at the church – p-pardon, t-temple of reason – and he will arrange to call and acquaint you with how your finances stand.'

'My husband, God rest his soul, spoke little business with me. Is there anything I should know straightaway?'

M. Beugneux shook his head. 'I think you should save any questions for M. Mansart, madame. I expect you wish to sell 2 Venelle Sorel.'

Fleur swallowed. Another property! 'Is it far?'

'Off the Rue de Sévigné, madame.'

A censorious intake of breath from Tante Estelle prompted Fleur to say swiftly, 'Well, I shall save all my questions for Monsieur Mansart.' She ignored her aunt's fingers tugging like a small child's at the back of her skirt. Two Venelle Sorel! Was that where the *filles de nuit* roamed looking for customers?

'Would you care to show us over the house, Monsieur Beugneux?'

His mortification showed on his face. 'P-pardon, I am at fault here. You will wish to rest and bestow your things. Come.'

'Venelle Sorel! A gaming house, you may be sure!' Tante Estelle exclaimed behind her hand, delaying Fleur from leaving the room. '*Mon Dieu*, or else a house of ill repute! You had better let me deal with this Monsieur Mansart. A young woman like you must not concern herself with these matters.'

Fleur's curiosity was piqued. Had M. Bosanquet owned a brothel?

'Is something amiss?' M. Beugneux stood anxiously at the door.

'No, it is – it is just that Monsieur Bosanquet requested me to permit Signor Machiavelli to remain as part of the household. An Italian, I suppose. His chef?' A blunder!

Jaw slack, M. Bosanquet's friend was staring at Fleur as though she had suggested they invite his Holiness the Pope to stay the night. He recovered his astonishment and sucked in his rouged cheeks. 'I will introduce you presently, madame. This way, if you p-please. Most of the rooms are Spartan, I'm afraid.' The stammer was less obvious now. Or maybe she was becoming used to it.

What had she said that was so astounding? she wondered, as she followed him up the stairs, but enlightenment did not follow. He began with the attic. Nothing remarkable. The discarded bric-a-brac that inhabited such places, and a dusty travelling trunk. One day she would explore the contents. The two rooms on the uppermost landing were furnished with narrow beds and washstands but unoccupied. The first room on the next floor boasted paintings and mirrors but the bed and dressing chair were draped with dustcovers. M. Beugneux did not open the second door at the end of the landing. 'This is my *chambre*. You wish to see it?'

'Thank you. Not just now,' murmured Fleur, anxious to see if the rest of the house displayed any enlightenment about the man she had married.

'In here is M-Matthieu's *chambre*.' The room was in darkness, necessitating M. Beugneux draw back the faded purply-red brocade which curtained the high west-facing window.

Lit by daylight, the room revealed a bed against

the far wall with a canopy of mulberry taffeta falling gracefully either side of the bolster and a surfeit of squab cushions. A *feather* bed, Fleur guessed and said a little prayer of thanks as she stared about her. A Persian carpet lay in front of the hearth. She could imagine the luxury of taking a bath before a glowing fire but those days were probably gone. Two ornately framed mirrors hinted that '*cher* Matthieu' had set store on his appearance, or perhaps it was to increase the light. What moved Fleur most was a copy of Molière's *Le Bourgeois Gentilhomme* on the small table beside the bed. She stroked appreciative fingers across the leather cover.

She began to ask, 'Did monsieur have a libr–?'

'Uugh! W-what is –?' Tante Estelle had run out of words. She could only point a shaking finger. Glittering eyes were watching them from beneath the slowly moving cushions on the bed.

'Ohhh!' exclaimed Fleur.

'Oh, the naughty creature! That,' explained M. Beugneux, with a mixture of apology and mischief as he turned from securing the curtains with tasselled cords, 'is Machiavelli! The wicked fellow has escaped from his box again. Not Italian at all, and no culinary skills except in catching larder pests.'

'A snake!' shrieked Tante Estelle.

'A p-p-python and as good a p-protector as any watchdog, madame. M-Machiavelli frightened the Commune guard when they searched the house. Nothing was taken from this chamber, nothing!'

Fleur came cautiously forward and peered at the creature's fat coils. Its skin was a multitude of coffee-coloured islands floating against dark waterways. Sinister but beautiful.

'Why should the Commune guard search here?' she asked, frowning. The last thing she needed was to have married a man under suspicion.

'A random inspection – "d-domiciliary visit" – to make c-cowards of us all.' M. Beugneux flicked at a nonexistent speck of dust on the back of his friend's dressing chair without meeting her eyes. So it was not the whole truth.

'How tame is this creature?' Her aunt stared at the reptile from across the carpet. It stared back.

'Not in the least venomous, I assure you, nor dangerous unless you are a mouse or rat. Fortunately we have a good supply of those. Matthieu let him have a rabbit once a year on his b-birthday.' His shudder was delicate. 'He does not need to be fed often. Warmth is of the essence. Now you have been introduced, I shall put him back in his b-box.'

Fleur had the feeling she had just passed some sort of test. 'Will he let me touch him?'

'Of course, madame,' monsieur beamed. 'He is yours now. Spread your arms out so.' He arranged her arms like a scarecrow's and then, with both hands, lifted Machiavelli off the coverlet and draped him about her shoulders. She let the python slither slowly along her arms. He was heavy but his skin was smooth and not unpleasant against hers. The originality thrilled her. It was love at first sight.

'You shall have to instruct me how to look after him, monsieur.'

'Fleur, no!' protested Tante Estelle. 'Mice! We are talking about things with . . . with whiskers that can run up under your petticoats.'

'I fear there are a great many creatures with whiskers in Paris that may do that.' M. Beugneux's face beyond her aunt's back belied the gravity of his tone. He rolled his gaze heavenwards and gave Fleur such a kind, funny, conspiratorial smile that she turned away, unable, snake-laden, to put a hand to her mouth to stifle her laughter. 'I shall naturally take responsibility for stocking Machiavelli's larder, Madame Bosanquet.'

There was a yearning in the softly spoken promise that made Fleur glance back swiftly over her shoulder and read the question in his sad eyes. It had been there ever since he introduced himself; he was willing to do anything not to be turned out.

'Excellent.' She unloaded Machiavelli back onto the bed. 'Monsieur Bosanquet particularly requested me to ensure you and Citizen Python here remain as boarders.'

The gentleman dropped to his knees and lifted the hem of her black gown to his lips. 'Your servant, madame, your most obedient servant.'

This sort of fulsome adoration from such an elderly creature was a new experience and Fleur found it necessary to examine the room again. She blinked in astonishment at the superb painting of David and Jonathan gazing in fraternal admiration at each other. Could it be a Greuze? As for the bronze Cupid on the mantelshelf, pah, she disliked it on sight. It reminded her of standing for hours as a child holding out an apple so a bad-tempered maestro and his pimply apprentice could make sketches.

'What exactly did my husband do for an income, monsieur?'

M. Beugneux draped Machiavelli across his own shoulders, stroking the python's skin. 'Dear Matthieu had all manner of enterprises, madame, but I would have thought . . . I fear none of them have fared well since the Revolution, what with the nobility losing much of their income and so forth.'

'What enterprises?' Better to be honest.

'You mean you do not know about the lace manufactory or the property in the Marais?' He was clearly amazed at Fleur's ignorance. 'Did Matthieu not explain anything?'

'We did not see much of each other.' She hastened to allay any suspicion. 'You could say he was almost like a father to me rather than a husband.'

'Ah.' M. Beugneux smiled as if the thought pleased him greatly. Shifting the python's head, he took out his new acquisition, his face saddening as he ran a thumb across the timepiece. 'Mansart, Matthieu's man of affairs will acquaint you with how matters stand.'

'I shall need to purchase some . . . necessities, monsieur.' Fleur ignored her aunt's sharp glance. 'There is no maidservant I may send out, is there?'

'"P-partner in work", they are called now. No,

63

I am afraid not. One of the neighbours comes in to clean. You could hire a fiacre to take you to the linen market tomorrow, perhaps.' Fleur inclined her head. 'Then I shall leave you to settle in.' He indicated that the room was at her disposal.

'At least there is plenty of storage,' observed her aunt. 'I shall unpack later.' She grandly bestowed her portmanteau in the bottom of the cleared wardrobe. It was all she had left of her once luxurious life.

'One moment, mons- Monsieur Beugneux, is there a bedchamber for my aunt?' It was more a command than a question, but Fleur added tactfully, 'I am sure that you do not wish to share with Citizen Machiavelli, Tante.'

Her new acquaintance smiled. They began to understand one another.

4

Dearest Marie-Anne,
There has been an incident. Perhaps I was wrong to
force this change upon my aunt but there is no going
back for me. Fortune is one instant liberal and then
most perverse . . .

EXTRACT FROM THE LETTERS OF FRANÇOISE-ANTOINETTE DE
MONTBULLIOU, 1793

For the ostentatious, the arcades of the Palais Royal, maggot-like with hungry orators, ubiquitous jugglers and feather-fingered pickpockets, was a mecca. Which was exactly why, on his return to Paris, Raoul preferred to meet his old friend and fellow deputy, Marie-Jean Hérault de Séchelles, next afternoon in the Café Bancelin on the corner of the Rue Charlot. Even that establishment was crowded and Raoul was forced to circumnavigate twin girl dancers from Marseilles whose carmagnole jackets revealed more than they covered, a squat vendor selling wart cures, and a bony prostitute who trailed Raoul to Hérault's table and drew her skirt high above a taffeta garter.

'Very attractive, citizeness, but we're busy.' Hérault, ex-President of the Legislative Assembly and Raoul's senior by several years, cast aside the news sheet he was reading and rose to embrace Raoul. Their friendship went back a sentimental distance that took in a coincidence of ideals and, beyond that, a pair of noble military papas.

Raoul slung his greatcoat on the back of the chair. Sitting down, he idly picked up the broadsheet, scanned its headline, and pushed it back across the table. 'Dr Marat?' he asked with a curl of lip.

'That hack gets more profane. He uses vitriol instead of ink.'

Raoul laughed. 'In '89 you said he was speaking the language of the people. What more can he do to shock us except grow crude and yap louder?'

'Oh, *you* are patted on the head, *mon brave*.' Hérault poured him a glass of *vin ordinaire* from the carafe. 'You have been zealously occupied. *I*, on the other hand, am accused of spending my time déshabillé in the foothills of Mont Blanc, horizontally amusing a certain former marquise.'

'Marat wrote that? Show me.'

'No, he said it to Catherine Evrard who repeated it to Elénore Duplay who told Max

Robespierre. Your health!' They clinked glasses. 'Not bad,' murmured Hérault, testing a mouthful before he leaned languidly back. 'So, did you have a satisfactory sojourn *en mission* in Normandy?'

Raoul grinned. 'Not half so good as you in Haute Savoie.' His friend's tanned, aristocratic cheekbones told their own account. 'And was *la belle* Adèle amused?'

'Actually, I believe she was. We lived on love and *fonduta*.' His gaze rambled appreciatively over the bosom of a girl on the next table. 'Where did you go, de Villaret? Just Calvados?'

'As far as Cherbourg. I set up committees of surveillance, and spoke in all the Jacobin clubs. Our associates in the provinces required a great deal of encouragement. *Diable!* In some places I might have been an Englishman for all the welcome I received. They are frightened of us, Hérault.' He tapped his fingers on the broadsheet. 'These poisonous tirades of Marat's are part of the trouble, but most of it goes back to last September.'

' "Our country in danger", eh?' That was Hérault's euphemism for the disturbances which had occurred after the Austrian and Prussian bayonets had pricked the French armies back into their heartland and seized Verdun. The disastrous news had panicked Paris. Hérault had made a fiery speech of patriotism in the National Assembly, but it was Georges Danton, roaring with angry passion, and placard writers like Marat and Fabre d'Eglantine, who had incited the Paris mob to drag the priests and aristocratic inmates out of the prisons and execute them before they could become traitors and saboteurs: *'Let the blood of traitors be the first holocaust to Liberty!'* Ordinary citizens still winced with the shame of it. So did Raoul. Only extremists like Marat gloated about the blood-letting.

'Go away!' growled Raoul, thrusting the cheap whore back as she tried to slide her arms round his neck. 'I found a few passionate Jacobins in Caen but most people in Normandy do not want any more changes. They haven't come to terms with the King's execution either. The unrest in Brittany and further south is unsettling them.'

'I suppose your rural ignoramuses think the present government is doing a fine job. *Merde!*' Hérault crumpled the broadsheet and launched it at the cleavage of the persistent prostitute. 'This Girondin government could not even organise a game of boules. We have generals deserting daily.'

Certainly, the new Republic seemed to be blundering riderless all over the place, but Raoul did not envy the inexperienced ministers. Given time, they might achieve much, except Marat was not giving them a chance and the people, still hungry, were growing impatient. The Revolution was falling to its knees like someone being stoned from all sides.

'We certainly do not need any more Septembers,' he stated emphatically.

'You think I want that!' His friend leaned forward, cuffs clinking upon the oilskin tablecloth. 'I am glad you are back in Paris,' the well-bred voice lowered to a safer volume, 'because we are going to have to jettison the present government. Brittany, as you say, is tottering; the counter-revolution in La Vendée is infecting the rest of the country. The English refused us flour last year. That devil of a minister, William Pitt! His gold will soon turn the whole seaboard against us. I need you to recruit your friends from the Plain to side with us. We have to clean out the ministries before the house we have built with hard work and sacrifice topples in on itself.'

Raoul listened, running a finger pensively along the edge of the table. Many of the Plain – the deputies who sat on the floor of the Assembly – had always voted on their individual principles and tried to avoid being part of a faction. Now it looked as though they were going to be forced to choose between supporting the Girondins who were running the government or joining the growing opposition, 'the Mountain' deputies like himself. He, Hérault and his old master, the artist Jacques-Louis David, were all members of the Jacobin Club, an institution on the Rue Saint-Honore where the issues of the day were vehemently discussed. Raoul had cut his political teeth there. Now there were Jacobin Clubs in most of France's major towns. The participants ranged from moderate ex-noblemen to rabid *enragés* like Deputy Marat. Well, it would be an interesting year and Raoul wondered if he would be alive at the end of it. *Not if France's enemies prevailed*. Hérault was right. Something had to be done soon.

'*Bof!*' his friend exclaimed. 'These fools running the country may be able to burble Cicero and hold intellectual dinner parties, but when it comes to putting bread in the people's stomachs or getting supplies to the army, they are out of touch with reality. They talk but they make no decisions.' Hérault in full flow was like a hot-air balloon; it was no use interrupting until his flight of oratory was over. 'Here we are at war with most of Europe and who is giving the orders? Manon Roland, the ex-minister of war's wife, a convent-bred bitch who wouldn't know one end of a musket from the other, for God's sake! Has old Roland nothing in his breeches? Pathetic, *hein!*'

'Quite true, you cannot fight a war with fans and rattles,' Raoul agreed. The damnable problem was that every republican had his own agenda and the wondrous ideals of '89 that had united everyone in hope and fraternity seemed to have dissipated. 'What are you proposing, Hérault?' he asked quietly, downing the last of his wine.

'That we find competent, experienced administrators to run the war and nominate them to this new committee on public safety.'

'I'll certainly support you on that.' It might mean the Committee of General Security Raoul was on would lose its pre-eminence, but saving France was more important than any personal glory.

'And I was wondering if you could give me a hand with drafting a constitution?'

'What's wrong with the one that old Condorcet's drawn up?' Raoul asked.

'It has three hundred and sixty-eight articles. Imagine the *pique-nique* the Girondins will enjoy, discussing each clause for hours on end.'

'Ah. Of course, I'll help you. I'm honoured you asked me.'

Hérault sat back satisfied. '*Bien!*' He summoned a waiter and ordered coffee.

'This is part of the trouble,' Raoul said cynically as the cups were set before them. 'Everyone wants coffee.'

His companion ignored the irony and changed the subject. 'So, did you find any remnants of the Montbulliou family reduced to growing cabbages in Normandy? No fat derrières you recognised?'

Raoul shook his head. 'Too busy.' He had given more thought to the pretty curves of Madame Bosanquet than to finding the youngest Montbulliou girl. 'I'd still like to know if the chit survived.'

'Guilt?' probed Hérault.

'No,' replied Raoul honestly, 'just curiosity. Closing the file, if you like. I did discover that one of the Montbulliou girls boarded at the Trinité School in Caen until the convent was closed down. Oh yes, and that an uncle on the mother's side, one of the Thury-Estry family, was arrested in Bayeux for counter-revolutionary activities.'

'Have you questioned him? Or has he paid the price?'

'No, this was a couple of years ago. He ran away to Coblenz and all his property was confiscated. The rest of his family fled before they could be arrested. Nothing has been heard of them since.'

'In your girl's shoes, I would have bribed my way onto a boat out of Cherbourg.'

'Well, I'm waiting to hear further but there is talk that one of Montbulliou's four daughters died of inflammation of the lungs in London. That could have been her. A third sister died in a riding accident. Which leaves one daughter and the son unaccounted for. He would be about twenty now. It is assumed he is in Coblenz as well.'

'And you are positive the *ci-devant* Duc de Montbulliou is dead?'

'Oh, yes,' Raoul answered with certainty. 'Montbulliou and his eldest daughter, Marguerite, the Vicomtesse de Nogent, died in the disturbances in September.' He swirled the last drop of wine before he emptied the glass. His shrug suggested lack of further interest in the matter but Hérault looked up with a slow grin.

'I think you have found another quarry, you sly rogue, de Villaret.' A finger briefly jabbed his shoulder.

'Maybe.'

'So did you seduce some lovely Norman innocent, or have you abandoned her among the apple trees utterly ignorant of your lusty thoughts?'

'I had little time for an *affaire*.' Raoul pushed his coffee cup aside. And certainly not with a suspect who might have planned her elderly husband's death. 'Drink up, Hérault, if you are going to walk back to the Rue Saint-Honoré with me. I have a report to finish for tomorrow. Are you likely to be presiding at the Convention?'

'Tomorrow, no, and just as well, I have to get on with drafting the new constitution and then attend a memorial service at a temple of reason.'

'Anyone I know?'

'No,' smiled Hérault. 'Someone who tried to put a few investments my way. I may have a few debts to collect.'

Raoul's chair scraped the flagstones. 'May the Supreme Being smile upon your enterprise.'

His friend responded sweetly with a finger and led the way out.

'Oh my!' Fleur paid off the hired fiacre and turned to join her aunt on the corner of a road off the Rue de Sévigné. The Marais, with its narrow streets and antiquated mansions hidden behind high walls, had lost the glory it had enjoyed in the days of Henri of Navarre and Louis XIV. The rich had rebuilt elsewhere. Now the section wore a confused air. Artisans had invaded the streets closest to the river; the revolutionaries had set up the two prisons of La Force. The boulevard to the east with its Chinese baths, cafés, a choice of theatres and Dr Curtius's Waxworks (oh yes, the fiacre had brought them the long way round) was slowly scratching into the Marais's genteel polish.

Tante Estelle was gazing open-mouthed at the façade above the doorway fronting the alley. Large letters of faded black proclaimed '*Le Chat Rouge*' and alongside them was a weathered painting – a saucy, peeling feline licking a paw and glancing provocatively down at likely customers.

'A café!' Fleur nearly whooped. Oh, she would write to Bayeux to her friend Thomas, her father's *sous-chef*, without delay.

Her aunt glanced round nervously. 'We are conspicuous enough as it is. Try the keys that dreadful creature gave you.'

'He is not a dreadful creature,' argued Fleur, withdrawing the house keys from her pocket.

'B–B–Beugneux,' sneered her aunt. 'I have strong suspicions about him.'

'I do not know why you should think him improper. He behaved impeccably towards us and it is evident he cared deeply for "*mon cher* Matthieu".'

'Exactly,' muttered the older woman as the lock obligingly withdrew its tongue.

Fleur let herself in and wrinkled her nose. The interior smelled like an old kitchen cloth. The table linens covering the five long trestles were clean but marred by old stains and wax dribbles from the candlesticks. To the right of the entrance was a serving area and a shelf ornamented with vases and dusty, long-stemmed glasses. Beyond, a large fireplace dominated the wall with a variety of coffee pots standing stoically along its generous hearth waiting for someone to light the fire to keep them warm. It really required a stove rather than a wasteful hearth to warm a chamber this size. Afternoon light poured in through the small panes of a long window to her left, illuminating pairs of painted laurel garlands interweaving up the sepia walls. Glancing around at the cracks in the plaster and the powdery paint, Fleur was reminded of the tired, blemished old courtesan she had glimpsed earlier from the fiacre.

But in kindly candlelight with the firelight dancing? Oh, this could be a haven of warmth and laughter. A laughing, joyous mistress to the men of Paris. Fleur blushed. Whatever was she thinking!

'Dreadful! Bosanquet must have been running this on air,' sniffed her aunt as if she smelled the immorality too. 'No lighting to speak of, either. I will wager no one respectable ever came near this place.' Only a few sconces decorated the walls, and most of the candleholders in the central wooden candelabra were empty. 'You would be lucky to see the faces of your neighbours if you supped here.' She swished up a corner of the tablecloth and rattled a bench. It wobbled. 'Poor quality. All of it. Besides, the risk of fire is gargantuan. There can be no question of you keeping this.'

'But we have not investigated it thoroughly, Tante Estelle.'

The groan was middle-aged. 'Must we?'

Fleur's attention had been snared: a row of candle stubs sentried the edge of a meagre platform centred in front of the far wall with a proscenium painted with garlands of flowers built out around it. A small stage with no curtain, merely a screen of sporting wood nymphs separating it from a door behind. A stage. A tiny stage!

With a scream of delight, she sprang up onto the blocks and whirled, arms outflung.

' "How can I ever forget the dreadful danger which first brought us together, your noble courage in risking your life to snatch me from the fury of the wave, your tender solicitude when you brought me to the shore, and the unremitting ardour of your love which neither time nor adversity has diminished, a love for which . . ."' She broke off laughing. 'Act one, *The Miser*. Where have you gone, Tante?'

'Actresses rank but a fraction above whores in polite society. Kindly stop behaving like one.'

'You never said that when we put on plays during your visit to Clerville or when Marie-Anne and I read *Tartuffe* to you in Caen.'

'Totally different circumstances.' Tante Estelle's powdered head reappeared from below the serving bar. 'Well, there are plenty of napkins and glasses,' she called out, but her niece did not answer. Fleur had unlocked the door behind the screen and was gazing with utter rapture at a rack of costumes. The pre-1780 ones were rather worn, but the more recent were of surprisingly fine quality, as good as she and her sisters had worn – such a bevy of silk and brocade as she had not seen in years.

Some costumes were disgustingly scandalous: wicked flesh-coloured stockings pinned to gauzy, gold-spangled Greek draperies sewn with glass beading, and metallic breast cones that would have been Sunday clothing for an Amazon. Indeed, some of the men's clothing was just as scanty. Not the two creamy togas edged with purple but the Roman kilt made of gold-painted leather straps and an Egyptian loincloth gathered beneath a central flap of stiff brocade. And there were all the accessories an actor might dream of – sandals, boots, spurs, helmets, pikes, musketeers' plumed hats, torques and breastplates fit for heroes. Fleur slid a medieval cross-hilted sword from its scabbard and thrust the tip at her image in the looking glass.

On the other side of the room long periwigs and neat curled queues hung from a row of pegs, while towering monstrosities à la Marie Antoinette, perched on faceless wooden stands, stared at her from a deep shelf. Fans – lace and plumes – hung on hooks from a wooden batten above a dressing table. Laughing before the mirror, Fleur discarded her hat and reached up for a wig.

'No, leave it,' exclaimed her aunt, catching her arm. 'Think of the lice. It is bound to be infested.'

Fleur shrugged and instead gleefully unscrewed one of the multitude of jars crowding the table surface. 'Greasepaint.' She breathed in the aroma with as much delight as if it was a perfumed rose.

'Your mama always reckoned that Great-Grandmother had a dissolute past. Now I am certain of it!' Tante Estelle glowered at Fleur's ecstatic reflection. 'Put that down. We shall have no more actresses in the family! Come along, I daresay we should see the rest of this dubious establishment. I have no doubt there are gaming boards stashed away somewhere.'

Fleur reluctantly followed her aunt back into the dining area and through into a kitchen that would have thrown her father's head cook into an apoplexy. Clearly the café had served few meals, for although space existed for storage and preparation, there was no *potager* to heat food and a dearth of any utensils, pans or chopping boards. If only Thomas were here. She had written to him before she left Caen, advising him of her address in Paris, but she would write again tonight. Oh, if she were not so short of time; Thomas's advice would have been worth a king's banquet, but she must use her own judgment.

'What is through here? Try the keys, child!'

Armed with a candlestick, her aunt stalwartly led the way down wooden stairs into the surprisingly modest cellar. Onions were birthing long thin shoots on a pile of sacking, and judging from the scattering of neat oval turds, a family of rats and their smaller cousins had feasted royally on a forgotten pumpkin. Wooden racks covered two walls but the wine stocks they held were not plentiful. Fleur opened the furthermost door.

'Just coal. Oh!' A rash mouse shot out across the floor and disappeared beneath the lowest shelf of bottles.

'Disgusting.' Tante Estelle seized a discarded broom handle and swung it vigorously beneath the rack.

How long had this place been neglected? Only a few weeks, perhaps.

'I really need to come here by night,' Fleur mused aloud, locking the cellar door behind her, and turning to stare up speculatively at the fruit and laurel wreath motifs decorating the dark green ceiling.

'At night! Over my dead body!'

'Do not say so,' whispered Fleur with a shudder. She was suddenly aware of the chill of the place and the lengthening shadows. 'We had better lock up. I must fetch my hat from the costume chamber.'

Now that the light was fading in the outer room, the wigs on the stands had taken on a sinister mien, like severed heads. For an instant, Fleur wondered where they had come from, for some were of the most expensive quality. Then she heard a ghostly whisper and a woman's soft laugh.

Snatching up her hat, she rushed out, locking the door swiftly.

'What is the matter, Fleur?'

'N-nothing, Tante. It is later than I thought. We should go.' Yes, she thought, darting a glance about her as they walked down the street back the way the coach had brought them, this might be an *avenue des souers* after nightfall. She began to feel vulnerable. Was it her imagination that the passers-by seemed more furtive than when they had arrived? It was hard to progress swiftly for the street was badly furrowed and, like everywhere else, there was no pavement and the gutters were soupy with dirt and refuse. It had started to drizzle, a light, feathery rain which was little more than an inconvenience. Fleur glanced about her and froze as she caught sight of a man who looked very like the fellow who had been lurking in the Rue des Bonnes Soeurs. Could he have followed them? Surely not. But he wore the same surliness and brown jacket. No, her imagination was playing tricks just as it had in the theatre-café. She would not remark on it but she was uneasy as they looked up the street in either direction to summon another fiacre. Only a large private coach lumbered into view, but to their astonishment the driver drew rein beside them. The badly scratched insignia on the door should have alerted them to danger.

'You wish to be taken somewhere, citizeness?' If this was democracy at work, then perhaps there were advantages in a republic.

'Oh yes,' said her aunt with relief. 'Rue des Bonnes Soeurs.'

'You pay before you get in these days.' The driver named a figure that seemed even more outrageous than the fare they had paid earlier, but Fleur, still shaken from her imagining in the costume room, did not haggle and helped her aunt aboard.

'I shall be glad when we reach the house, Fleur. This district will be dangerous once night falls, and to think it was so respectable. I remember when —'

Fleur's hand tightened warningly over the older woman's arm. 'It seems dangerous now, Tante,' she said grimly, 'and I am sure there was a cutpurse following us as we left the café.' She changed seats, lowered the window and glanced back. 'Heavens! He is chasing after the coach. *We are in a hurry, if you please, citizen,*' she called out, rapping to the driver. 'Well, at least the thief will be exhausted before we get anywhere near Rue des Bonnes Soeurs.'

'Mercy!' Jolted, Tante Estelle grabbed at the leather handle as the carriage bowled down the narrow street at a neck-breaking pace.

The press of carts, fiacres and one-horse cabriolets across the Place des Victoires slowed the vehicle.

'Have we lost him?'

Fleur lowered the window again. 'I think he's been left behind but there are too many people around to be sure. You know, this is extremely luxurious for a hire vehicle.' She wriggled against the cushions, which reminded her of Papa's best sprung coach. It was excellent to feel such softness again. They proceeded in fits and starts through the traffic but as they reached the Rue de Grenelle something hit the side of the coach.

'Loose stone,' muttered Tante Estelle. 'The roads were bad enough when we had a monarchy. I doubt this so-called Convention will do any better. Instead of one useless king, we have hundreds.'

A loose stone when they were going no faster than a walking pace? Then another stone bombarded the framework, and another. The two women stared at one another in growing consternation, jerking away from the doors as a scatter of pebbles hit the window glass, followed by the softer plop of mud. The coachman swore loudly.

'Make haste!' Fleur rapped upon the front of the coach with the flat of her hand.

The vehicle speeded up. Fleur caught the leather hand strap as the vehicle lurched but the shouting was all around them, and it was as if a giant had seized the coach and was tossing it from hand to hand. Fleur was thrown headfirst against the facing seat. Tante Estelle fared worse and Fleur dragged her ashen aunt up from the floor, her heart fearful.

'I do not want to die, not like this. Not like –' Panicked fingers scrabbled at her, trying to grip hold, a breath away from screaming.

'No, you don't!' growled Fleur, shaking her. 'Be quiet!' Tante Estelle shuddered, her eyes bulging with fear. 'Listen to me! They cannot hurt us. We have done nothing.' Even as Fleur rationalised, her courage was fraying fast, but one of them had to keep a cool head. There was no mysterious masked thief to save her this time.

A man was shouting: 'Stop the coach, I say! Over here, patriots! I need your help.' The bawling came from above them and the scrabble of heavy boots thudded upon the roof.

'Sweet Mary protect us, Fleur!' Tante Estelle crossed herself as the vehicle came to a halt; her fingers fumbled for her rosary.

'What is death but a few minutes of pain and then oblivion?' Fleur whispered. 'Courage.'

As the door was wrenched open, the older woman shrank back in terror from the fierce faces peering in.

'Haul 'em out!' bawled a harridan from the crowd. 'See what we've snared.'

'What in hell do you want?' snarled Fleur. The dialect of a Caen peasant was the safest she could manage as she squeezed Tante Estelle's trembling hand, but it was like facing a Medusa's head of hissing snakes. A burly fellow in the *pantalons* of the working class reached out to grab her right wrist and jerked her from the refuge of the coach.

'*Salaud!*' she hissed, jabbing two fingers into his

eyes – it had worked with the young ruffians in Caen. The man swore, jerking back, but other vicious hands hauled Fleur down onto the street. The crowd about her was deep and growing, its mood rumbling and volatile.

'Take your hands off me!' exclaimed her aunt, slapping at her assailants as she too was dragged out onto the filthy, puddled ground.

'Why pick on us?' exclaimed Fleur, gasping and squirming to free herself as the beast holding her groped at her breast. 'This-is-not-our-carriage!'

'Citizens, don't be deceived by this little tart!' exclaimed a scathing voice from above and the cutpurse who had been stalking them sprang down from beside the driver. His grin was malevolent. With one leering look at the terrified women, he directed a glob of spit onto the stony road. 'Oh, how I like to see 'em cowering. *Voilà*, what did I tell you! *Aristo* scum! Afraid to face us, see!' He planted himself in front of them, scrawny, bare arms akimbo, his gaze running over them like a whetting knife.

Words came unbidden to her mind; the dreadful words of a letter sent to Marie-Anne last autumn by an acquaintance in Paris: 'They hanged a nobleman from a lamppost and then they hacked off his head and set it on a pike so they might parade it through the streets.'

Fleur's jaw trembled but she forced herself to mock him. '*Holà*, you need spectacles, you fool, or else a brain bigger than a walnut. I'm an actress not an *aristo*.' Pulling herself away from the slackening hold upon her, she rearranged her bodice with an aggrieved air and tried to maintain the provincial accent. 'The coach was for hire, ask him!' She directed a plea towards the coachman but the utter coward, refusing to meet her eyes, suddenly took his chance and whipped his horses into a violent plunge forward. The crowd sprang aside, not bothering to give chase.

'Still the lady, isn't she?' The burly man allied himself with the thief. 'You know how you tell an actress from an *aristo*, citizens? You string her up and see if she gives a better performance.' The laughter gurgled around the two women like quicksand.

'Ha! That's a good one. Never seen her act before, have we, citizens?'

Fleur rolled her eyes as if exasperated by his stupidity and someone guffawed, but her larger enemy exchanged an evil glance with the man who had stalked them.

'An actress, eh, so why is she in black then, and what about this old crow?' He jabbed a savage finger into Tante Estelle's shoulder. 'Scared of us, isn't she! Why's that?' He seized her aunt's fichu and jerked her up onto her toes. 'Why isn't she wearing a cockade?'

Oh God! It must have fallen off unnoticed at the café.

'Pick on someone else, you dolts,' Fleur snarled through clenched teeth. 'You'd be in b–b–black if your s–sister had just died of scarlet fever! I'm . . .

I'm an actress playing at the Chat Rouge.' She had never felt so afraid in all her life, not even when the mob had invaded the chateau. Had Papa and Marguerite been as terrified as this when they were hauled out onto the street? 'The Chat Rouge,' she repeated, trying to distract their attention from her aunt, 'in the Marais.' Tante Estelle gazed at Fleur in absolute horror.

'It's closed down,' jeered the thief. His hand swooped up from behind her, grabbing the high neck of her gown, half choking her.

'Not any more, *bête*!' spluttered Fleur, trying to kick backwards at him. Words were now an effort but they were her only weapons. 'They ha . . . ve a new entertainment starting on Friday. Now . . . let-me-go! You followed me from there, you bastard!' She squirmed, trying to turn round to confront her accuser.

'Such a pretty liar.' The foul stench of her captor's breath filled her nostrils. 'Well, citizens, maybe this little *putain* should entertain us in a private room at the Lion d'Argent before we string her up.' His hand slid meaningfully down the front of her skirt and fumbled inwards. Fleur shrieked her fury, struggling with all her might. Better to inflame them further and die a swift cruel death than be raped and tormented shamefully.

'Citizens!' A voice of authority sliced through the uproar. Two newcomers were forcing their way through the rabble.

The cutpurse wrenched his victim's arm behind her back. 'Another word, whore, and you're already dead,' he snarled and a knife blade pricked between her shoulderblades. He took her answering shudder for acquiescence and loosened his hold only to cruelly enmesh his fingers in her hair and compel her to her knees. Fleur's head was forced viciously down like a victim's awaiting the blade of the guillotine. She heard him curse crudely beneath his breath as black knee boots strode briskly into the range of her vision. A pair of buckled green leather shoes followed and portly calves stockinged in sable silk stopped a puddle away from where she knelt. There was a snag in one. *Help me*, she prayed to the strangers, wincing as her captor's grip grew even tighter.

'Come now, citizens,' drawled a second, more languid voice, 'if you have captured enemies of the state, they must be dealt with under the law.' The green toecaps turned slightly as if their owner must be exchanging glances with his companion. Tense silence. Fleur dared not breathe and then an old man voice's exclaimed from the back of the crowd: 'You are right, Citizen Hérault.'

'Yes,' said another in a deferential tone. 'We'll take 'em to the Commune and denounce 'em there.' The rabble muttered agreement.

'On what charge, my friends?' The voice of the man who had spoilt their entertainment was disturbingly familiar. The boots of glossy, expensive leatherwork halted less than a pace in front of Fleur and swivelled slowly as if their owner was scrutinising the crowd. The hush deepened to fearful respect. No longer a mob, there was a shuffling back of feet, as if the newcomer was slowly committing the individual faces to memory. In front of Fleur, the greatcoat swung to stillness at the man's shining heels. 'Who does the woman say she is?' rapped out that voice above her head.

'An actress,' someone called out helpfully.

'No, I know her. She's a traitor's widow,' shouted the man holding Fleur. 'Can't any of you fools tell the difference?' With a cruel twist of his hand he yanked at her hair, jerking her head up so hard that tears started. 'Tell them you are a liar.'

'I have done nothing wrong,' she gasped out to the man looming over her. She was aware of loosened dark hair curling wildly over the white stock, but the face beneath the high-crowned hat was behind her blur of tears.

'Oh, she can act,' sneered the stranger. 'I have seen her do so. Release her, citizen, if you please. I shall report this matter to the Committee for General Security. We shall be keeping her and her companion under surveillance. Not all actors are patriots.'

A violent hand thrust Fleur forward. She ended up sprawled ignominiously, her gloved hands splayed in the mud at the bootcaps of her rescuer. With a careful hand, he tilted his high-crowned hat, and Fleur stared up with astonishment into the sardonic eyes of the arrogant deputy she had encountered in Caen. He made no move to help her to her feet; instead he gazed down upon her like some eastern king assessing a newly purchased slave. If he was silently waiting for her to embrace his leathered calves in loving gratitude, he could whistle for that. Fleur was grateful but not *that* grateful.

The green shoes moved in. '*Attention!*' murmured the one called Hérault in warning.

Fleur swiftly lowered her head, afraid the second man would order her to be taken for questioning.

'Not all deputies are patriots either!' snarled her former captor. He drove a savage boot into Fleur, slamming her forward. Her arms bore the brunt and she crouched, bruised and shaken, cradling her breast like a terrified child, lest his fist come at her as well. She heard the spittle leave his mouth but she jerked sideways. It landed upon her rescuer's boot. Tension seethed in the air above her head as though two male beasts were eyeing each other off, and then the thief gave way, shouldering his way angrily through the crowd.

Was it over? She let her breath out slowly in case anyone else in the crowd accused her, but the entertainment was finished and the outer edge began to fray; barrows wove back into the traffic and the passers-by continued on their way. Neither the deputy nor his more debonair companion made any effort to assist her. In fact, her rescuer deliberately folded his arms. What wondrous manners the Revolution bred. Trying not to cry, muddy, bedraggled and dishonoured, Fleur clambered to her feet unaided.

Tante Estelle must have read her mind for she narrowed her brow admonishingly and Fleur bit back an angry comment. Although the people

closest were dispersing, it was not without back-
ward glances, and the burly man and the old
harridan hung around, a distance off but watching
still. By the saints, it would not take much to have
those wretches crying for their blood again. No
wonder their two rescuers did not wish to be contaminated by so much as touching her. They had
taken a risk in helping her, she realised, feeling a
little guilty now. Perhaps they were even genuinely
suspicious of her. Except that the heavier-built
man with the powdered blond hair had turned his
expensively coated back on the spectators and was
blatantly admiring her through his quizzing glass.

And this Committee for General Security!
What in God's name was that? The last thing she
and Tante Estelle needed was to be dragged before
some half-literate investigation committee! Under
surveillance? Her hostile acquaintance from Caen
was calmly studying her as though she had become
an infernal nuisance to him. Fleur's chin rose
defiantly.

'You are missing your sash and epaulette,
monsieur.'

Cynical amusement flared briefly at her spirit.
'Thank you for your help, Hérault,' he said pointedly over his shoulder, his cold golden gaze holding
hers, and she knew his tone chided her for her lack
of gratitude.

'Oh, monsieur, your pardon. Indeed, you have
saved our lives.' Tante Estelle put a shaky arm round
her niece.

'Not monsieur but *citizen*,' their rescuer corrected

indifferently. 'You would be well to remember that.' He deliberately used the informal, disrespectful term of address usually reserved for intimates or children, and Fleur felt the anger ripple through her aunt.

'You really know these women?' the man's companion asked.

'A little widow from Caen.' Contempt laced his tone.

'Yes, a little widow from Caen,' retorted Fleur, with a toss of her head. She glared up at the deputy, bitterly resenting the fact that she was once more in his debt.

'Fortunate we intervened,' the handsome blond man commented. 'By the look of you, my lovely, you need to improve your acting if you want to keep body and soul together these days. You need a bit more patronage, eh?' It was spoken with friendly lasciviousness and a flash of teeth. A fine hand squeezed her sore forearm, testing her bones through her sleeve. Fleur flinched but he laughed. 'Which theatre are you playing at? I'll come along and put you under *my* surveillance.'

Irritation curled her other rescuer's mouth. 'How in the name of reason did you manage to cause so much trouble?' He addressed this question to her aunt, making Fleur feel as though she still had plaits and milk teeth.

'All we did was hire a fiacre,' protested Tante Estelle in an aggrieved tone. 'Is that so wrong?'

'Of course,' retorted the deputy, his hostility towards them scarcely concealed. 'Good citizens, *honest* citizens, walk.'

'Yes,' agreed the man called Hérault. 'Unless you are a government official or a member of the Convention. For you, it is safer to walk.'

'Walk, with a rabble like that loose?' The lady's voice quavered.

'We have had a revolution, or hadn't you noticed, citizeness?'

Sensibly, Tante Estelle made no answer to that jibe.

'I suggest you seek advice on the new manners required in Paris before you venture out again,' he continued smoothly, the disdain in his voice unmistakable. Well, he certainly would not be the one to ask if his manners were anything to go by.

'Yes, indeed,' muttered Tante Estelle with teeth-clenched humility. Her hand felt backwards for Fleur's and pressed it cautiously. Thank heaven this creature thrown up by the Revolution did not know who they really were; he might smell more fragrant than the bastard who had just stalked them but his manners and politics made him as great an enemy.

'If the coach that hurtled past us was the one you hired, no wonder it drew attention.' He waited, testing her. Fleur drew a breath and then stared at him with feigned blankness, while the icy finger of horror poked his meaning home. She should have recognised the coat of arms! God have mercy, the carriage had belonged to the Princess de Lamballe, the Queen's dearest friend, who had been massacred by the people. But to know the insignia was to condemn herself.

She swallowed. 'You . . .' The word erupted hoarsely. 'You mean . . .' It was an effort to gather the strength back into her voice. 'Are you saying it belonged to someone famous? S-some former aristocrat?'

De Villaret did not answer but regarded her with scarcely disguised suspicion.

'I-I never thought. Oh God!' Fleur felt faint in truth. Tante Estelle was staring at her, concerned.

'Do you know your way home?' Citizen Hérault asked not unkindly. At least he had given up ogling her.

Home? She gulped back the tears of humiliation and shock. Home? A hovel? Return to the forest and live worse than peasants? She blinked, and looked up to be surprised at the pity in the deputy's expression, as if he had knowledge of her dilemma.

'Ah, yes,' he drawled, 'home.' He expected her to retreat. But Fleur had never turned down a challenge and the man's attitude goaded her into defiance. She was not going to slink back to her kennel like a beaten dog. A few days' respite to find her feet without toppling into further danger was all she required; a few days to learn how to cope with this anarchic city. She shook her head as if to brush away these distrait thoughts and discovered the two men were still staring at her, her rescuer academically, as though she was some chemical solution he had tipped acid into and was waiting to see the result.

'*Holà*, citizeness? Did you hear me?' Citizen Hérault repeated his question.

Fleur pulled her wits together. She darted a glance at one of the dark alleyways; the burly workman was still watching her intently.

'No,' she whispered, hating herself for her cowardice and fearful where the honesty might lead her. 'No, I do not know my way home. Not yet.'

'Where are you staying?' It was the deputy who asked.

What could she answer him? She did not want him to know, she did not want any more to do with him. He was too suspicious, too clever. If he started investigating –

'Forty-seven Rue des Bonnes Soeurs,' her aunt informed them.

'Then we shall see you home,' the flirtatious Hérault answered. He did not offer either woman his arm but glanced at his disagreeable companion, who merely shrugged and waved his hand towards the corner.

'We shall follow at a distance.' So they were to be treated as lepers, as suspects. The odious deputy must have read the fear in Tante Estelle's face for he added in a casual manner, 'Do not fear any harm shall come to you – unless you have something to hide.'

Harm? Oh it was so tempting to scorn their condescending help but she was genuinely frightened, for her aunt more than herself.

'That would be most generous of – you.' Her aunt humbly used the informal address, though it must have tasted like bile to do so, and tucked her arm through Fleur's. 'Come, my child.' *Before these men change their minds!*

Proudly, their fear concealed, the two women began the walk back. They were forced to glance behind for instructions whenever they came to a corner, for the men kept a discreet, uncontaminated distance behind them.

'Our pigs at Thury-Estry had better manners,' muttered her aunt. 'If this is the new France . . .' A curse sufficiently vile eluded her. 'Once our emigrés get themselves organised . . .'

'Hush, Tante. We must not talk so.'

'But you think it, do you not?'

Fleur nodded gravely, though, to be honest, she could remember noblemen as rude and crass as these so-called patriots.

'I suppose we have to be grateful,' her aunt muttered. 'Those *sans-culottes* animals could have murdered us in cold blood like they did your poor father.'

It was appallingly true. 'We were stupid. From now on we shall have to be very careful. The rules are different now and we must learn them if we want to survive.'

'Let us return to Caen, Fleur. It was safer there. I beg you, sell these properties.'

'I promised to look after Monsieur Beugneux and Machiavelli.'

Tante Estelle scowled with disapproval but replied, 'Then let them leave with us. Anything, Fleur, but let us quit this foul place.'

'No! No, we must give it a little longer. Supposing the Republic is never overthrown? What then? We have to survive somehow.'

'*Tiens*, if that's the case, then we must leave France. Join your uncle in Coblenz or your sister in London.' Shakily, she added, trying to be brave, 'I daresay I can put up with the ghastly food.'

'Better than starving,' agreed Fleur, 'but how? With this mania for passes, I daresay that soon we shall be needing a passport to go to the end of the street, let alone get out of Paris. Trying to leave France is like running the gauntlet, with some officious shark at every town wanting to inspect our papers and know our business. We are hedged by enemies, Tante.'

'And coming here has made it worse. We should have gone to England when the troubles began. It is my fault, Fleur, I thought you would be safe to continue your schooling, I thought –'

'No one could have imagined what was going to happen, Tante Estelle. We must make the best of things. Oh, I do believe we have reached the Rue Saint-Honoré, thank heaven.'

During the entire fifteen-minute walk, Fleur was acutely aware of their protectors' scrutiny; the gooseflesh along her spine tingled, as if her walk and the sway of her hips were being evaluated. The men were conversing but more than once she heard their soft laughter like a mockery. It was hard not to suppose that they were laughing at her! Ignore them, she told herself, but the possibility chafed her. Twice she had stumbled on the uneven rubble and blushed in embarrassment, then as they stood on the corner of the Rue Saint-Honoré, her already muddied dress was spattered further by filth from the wheels of a passing cart.

'It is fortunate you are in black, little widow,' whispered the deputy as the men drew level with the women to cross the street.

Fleur shrugged, trying to be worldly. The deputy was smiling but still with that hint of a sneer; the amber eyes were amused as she scowled at him and looked away.

'Almost there,' exclaimed Citizen Hérault in the slightly slurred way Fleur was beginning to recognise. The gentlemen of Paris really rolled their *rrs*.

The man was right, thank God! Fleur's breath came more easily as she began to recognise the shops they were passing. The clientele were better dressed now, more respectable – no rough workmen in sight, nor, thank heaven, the horrid creature who had almost caused their deaths. Fleur had no illusions about her escorts; if that knife-pulling troublemaker had returned to waylay them with an angry mob, there would have been no more knight-errantry on the part of their rescuers. They would have put their own skins first.

There was the church where M. Bosanquet's passing was to be remembered tomorrow. Yes, they were almost home. She halted her aunt on the next corner and waited as the men caught up with them. 'We need trouble you no further, citizens. Our lodgings are but a little further, only in the next street.'

'What a shame,' murmured Citizen Hérault with charming insolence. 'I was enjoying the view.

Marie-Jean Hérault de Séchelles at your service, deputy for Seine-et-Oise.' With an ancien régime flourish, he doffed his broad-brimmed plumed hat. 'Unfortunately, it is no longer de rigeur to kiss a lady's hand. In the name of France, citizeness, au revoir.' Taking hold of her shoulders, he gave her a vigorous kiss on each cheek.

Fleur arched a rebellious eyebrow at his indifferent companion, who made no such move. 'Oh, I do not always follow the fashion,' he remarked, sensing her reluctance to have him touch her. 'Raoul de Villaret,' he inclined his head curtly, 'and I am at nobody's service any more, thank God!' But his hand reached out and caught her chin; his thumb, uninvited, rubbed across her indignant lips. 'Go back to the country, little widow. The men in Paris eat morsels like you for breakfast.'

5

*In republics . . . the extreme difference in wealth
leaves the mass of people subservient to a handful of
individuals . . .*

JEAN-PAUL MARAT, *THE CHAINS OF SLAVERY*

Why had he bothered warning her? Raoul wondered. It was not as if he cared what happened to the provincial little Delilah, but even on her hands and knees with the mob salivating for her blood, there had been pride and defiance in her. *Tiens*, if he received any more unsavoury information from Caen, he would certainly investigate her further and it would be easier now that he knew where she lived. Perhaps the great watchmaker in the sky intended him to be her nemesis, and if she were responsible for her husband's death, he would make sure she paid.

'Taking little piece, apart from her dialect,' murmured Hérault. '"You are missing your sash and epaulette,"' he mimicked. 'What else were you missing when you saw her last, my dear fellow? Your shirt and breeches?'

'Have you ever heard of female spiders that devour their mates?'

'"Devour" meaning "eat", or "devour" meaning "consume in passion"?'

'Precisely, Hérault,' and wearing his most enigmatic expression, Raoul left the former *avocat-général* of the Parlement of Paris standing on the corner looking baffled.

Next morning's rain faltered respectfully for the commemorative service at the local temple of reason. Fleur sat numbly in her hastily cleaned black gown as small groups of mourners slid onto the chairs behind her. Her thoughts were not on the Supreme Being finding room in his mansion for her late and brief husband, but, as they had been all night, on the image of the dark-haired deputy. *Under surveillance.* It was not just that Fate had flung him into her life twice within a week, but there was something else: not exactly a familiarity but a faint sense of déjà vu. She shook her head as if that would exorcise her unease and tried to be dutiful; poor M. Bosanquet lay in a grave at la Délivrande and she should be praying earnestly for his soul's journey through the darkness.

'Citizeness.' A hand shook her shoulder from behind. Half rising, Fleur took in the expensive caped greatcoat and silken breeches, and barely concealed her panic. Hérault! *Nom d'un chien!* How had he known about the service? Was she indeed under the Republic's surveillance?

'Christ have mercy!' muttered Tante Estelle beside her.

Fleur sent a prayer to the empty altar behind her as Hérault saluted her with his right hand on his heart. 'Citizeness Bosanquet, I believe? Your humble servant. My condolences.'

Humble was he, and pretending not to know her? Fleur inclined her head politely, reluctantly grateful that he expected her to behave as though yesterday's shameful meeting had never taken place.

'Marie-Jean Hérault de Séchelles.' He rippled his name forth rapidly; then, as though leaving her to digest this impressive information, he half knelt and shielded his face reverently with his hand, his lips moving in prayer.

'To think the Queen once sent him a specially embroidered scarf,' whispered M. Beugneux, pale behind his lacy cuff. '*Avocat-général* he was, and not only a d-deputy b-but P-President of the –' Further information was prevented as they realised that M. Hérault had resumed his seat and was showing a curiosity in who was attending. Another man joined him, shaking his hand discreetly, and glanced coldly at Fleur without a word of greeting. She barely noticed, though, because a revelation hit her like a catapult pebble.

Hérault de Séchelles. Oh what a fool she was! She had seen the name in several of Marie-Anne's newspapers. He was *the* Hérault de Séchelles, one of the leading revolutionaries; a loathsome creature who had betrayed his own kind and, by the expensive look of him, used the Revolution to advance his own selfish interest. She resisted the urge to storm out of the temple as if the traitor had infected the air, for he was surely one of the foul orators to be blamed for the massacre of her father and sister. And was she to be his next victim, to be hauled before a tribunal because she refused to take her clothes off for him?

She stared bleakly at an altar bereft of candles. If the Revolution had dared to rename God, what chance had Fleur, a Montbuillou, to survive among such ruthless wolves? Beside her, her aunt crossed herself with a trembling hand. Real tears prickled behind Fleur's lashes, and an intense longing for a shoulder to weep on, for someone to take care of her for once, overcame her.

'M-madame?' M. Beugneux's crinkled face was displaying concern.

Fleur blinked at him, droplets running down her cheeks, knowing she might contaminate all she touched. Sister to a rebel, niece to an emigré, a duke's daughter and now involved with a murdered stranger, she had already reserved her place on a tumbril. And she had selfishly dragged Tante

Estelle to this dangerous city where there was no one to trust.

'Madame Bosanquet?' M. Beugneux repeated, his faded blue eyes full of pity.

Then the words of Matthieu Bosanquet came back to her: *'There is only one thing you can depend on in your life – yourself.'* She must pretend for all she was worth. Pretend that she was not afraid.

'I will survive,' she replied with feeling and managed a watery smile.

The old man drew breath to answer but the celebrant, flaunting an opulent *tricolore* rosette in support of the new Republic, coughed loudly, demanding attention. 'In the name of the *sans-culotte* Jesus Christ, I welcome you here to our temple of reason.'

The priest seemed like a gull perched on the edge of the pulpit, his eye sharp and head thrown back aggressively as he performed his duty. Disapproval of the deceased's morals spewed out of the morass of revolutionary phrases and religious clichés that followed.

What had poor Matthieu Bosanquet done to earn so little respect? It was hard not to notice M. Beugneux's knuckles whitening. Fleur reached for his hand consolingly and ignored Tante Estelle's shoulder-wriggle of censure. On the other side of him, Bosanquet's business agent, Pierre Mansart, still a stranger to her, surreptitiously eased his watch out of his waistcoat pocket, and behind her the former aristocrat, Hérault, twisted a loose button on his coat cuffs.

It was deplorable. Fleur had seen young children conduct garden burials for departed rabbits with far more respect. But anger would be indelicate, so she sat through the remainder of the service ignoring the priest, her gaze fixed upon her lap.

'Citizeness?' M. Mansart stood back to let Fleur and her aunt lead the congregation down the nave. Then he and M. Beugneux flanked her with fatherly solicitude as she took her place in the drizzle on the steps outside and waited for the variety of mourners to trickle by, gaping as if she were a pickled monster in a museum. No doubt gossip had condemned her as a money-grabbing baggage already.

Aware of the closer, curious glances of M. Mansart, she played the grieving widow, employing a muffled sob and a handkerchief clutched to her lips as a defence against any unwelcome questions. She had only to recall her beloved maman's last moments dying from an infection of the lungs, and tears, sparse but bitter, came forth to glint upon her cheekbones and further dampen the delicate gauze.

She felt a hypocrite. It was poor M. Beugneux who, truly mourning Matthieu Bosanquet, delivered the necessary phrases and pressed the dark gloved hands, while she whispered polite thanks like a modest provincial.

It was indeed an ordeal; hard-miened faces, as impatient as the priest's, seemed to be assessing the quality of her clothing, but behind them, hemming the crowd, female gulps punctuated the silences and several times a male nose was ostentatiously blown. The emotion emanated only from a cluster of four, two men and two women – one blonde, one tall and olive-skinned – who had sat together at the back of the temple. Unwilling to approach, they humbly eyed Fleur from across the churchyard. Former servants, perhaps? Two long, thin feathers rising from the short blonde's bonnet quivered noticeably as if their owner trembled now and again. The other sobbing woman might be Italian or Spanish, her black hair piled beneath a scarlet bonnet à la Révolution. Maybe they had both bestowed their favours on M. Bosanquet for there was definitely a skittish lack of gentility about them.

'They look like a pair of *putains* to me,' muttered Tante Estelle from behind her. Fleur inclined her head to them and the women bobbed, spreading their skirts. One of the men, the owner of some stunning whiskers, clasped his hat to his chest in reverence and bowed, but the little group still made no move to bestow their condolences.

'Citizen? Ouch!' A gloved hand fastened itself about Fleur's wrist as she proffered it, and squeezed painfully.

'Why, Tante Fleur, I have heard that the wives of Indian rajahs throw themselves on the funeral pyre. It's an admirable custom, don't you think?' There was no mistaking the venom in that whisper. Fleur tried to free herself but the man who had sat in the chair next to Hérault held her fast. 'Think you can cheat me, do you?'

As M. Mansart started to intervene at her cry of alarm, her assailant released her and stepped back.

'Introduce us,' requested Fleur coolly.

'Save your breath, Mansart. I can introduce myself to this little cheat. Felix Quettehou, Matthieu Bosanquet's heir.' He removed his tricorne hat mockingly and, turning, bestowed an ugly smile on M. Beugneux. 'Lost your share as well, have you, you old *pédé*?'

Even disregarding his disgusting behaviour, Fleur instantly disliked the ferret eyes glinting behind the knobbly bridge of a thin nose. He looked to be scarcely thirty, but while some balding men might retain a debonair handsomeness, the skull and forehead emerging from the sparseness of Quettehou's sandy hair looked to be unpleasantly bony. Added to which, his complexion lacked any colour to redeem it.

'This is hardly the t-ti—' M. Beugneux protested, the large hands aflutter.

'No, indeed,' snapped Fleur, reassured that M. Mansart was still beside her. 'Have you no respect, citizen?'

'Adventuress!' Quettehou snarled, jutting his neck forward. 'Imposter! I will see you damned, you lying trollop.' He adjusted his grip meaningfully on his walking cane and looked as though he would have liked to have laid it about her shoulders.

Fleur recoiled but M. Mansart stepped between them. 'Your manners, sir, are wanting!'

'The will is a fake, you fool. The whole world knows it.'

Too old to fight a duel for such an insult, M. Mansart stood his ground, pushing his spectacles firmly up his nose. 'Are you calling the worthy citizens who witnessed the will liars as well, Citizen Quettehou?'

'A sabot-maker and some rapscallion priest! It's no more a will than this creature here is a real man.' A bony forefinger stabbed into M. Beugneux's waistcoat before he swung back to Fleur. 'As for you, Widow Bosanquet,' his lips curled back to show his predatory, yellowing teeth, 'you will wish you had never been born by the time I finish with you. I will ruin you and anyone else who takes your side!' The entire graveyard hushed. Only the birds were not embarrassed.

'I rejoice to see I have acquired such delightful relations,' she declared sarcastically. 'You really must come and see if there is any bric-a-brac you want.'

'Why, you –'

Years of breeding compelled Tante Estelle to intervene. 'A word, if you please, citizen.' Quettehou, scowling like a schoolmaster thwarted in midthwack, permitted her to draw him away through the shocked crowd.

'La Veuve Bosanquet?' A familiar voice, redolent with charm and bonhomie, issued from the porch, deliberately patching the uncomfortable atmosphere quite as if he had anticipated it, and everyone respectfully hushed to watch the most distinguished mourner take Fleur's hand. Why had Hérault lingered in the church? To make inquiries or merely to execute a dramatic emergence on the steps?

'Forgive me, citizeness,' he was saying, 'but I did not know until today that Monsieur Bosanquet was married.' He bestowed a nod of recognition on Mansart, who replied on Fleur's behalf: 'Monsieur Bosanquet preferred that madame should remain in the country.'

'Ah.'

'Were you a friend of my husband's, Citizen Hérault?' Fleur asked, unsmiling.

'A fellow investor, and a patron of one of his establishments,' the deputy added with a lowering of voice. Aware that his flamboyant presence seemed to be arousing further comment and that the feathered blonde was cocking her head provocatively, he gave the woman a fast, furtive glance before returning his attention to Fleur. 'Your husband was a versatile man, Citizeness Bosanquet,' he continued. 'He dabbled in all sorts of enterprises, but I understand he was not doing so well of late. The property near the Rue de Sévigné – you know about that? A drain, of course. There are too many similar establishments now. And it is a pity his lace-making investment in the city proved disastrous, but one sees so much competition elsewhere, Brussels, eh? And of course, as with many luxury manufactories in France in recent years, the market has dried up.'

'Decapitated,' murmured Fleur into her handkerchief. At her elbow, M. Beugneux broke into a fit of coughing.

Unable to see her face, Hérault was evidently not sure how to take the remark, for he busied himself genially nodding to the other mourners. 'Forgive my impertinence, citizeness, but have you considered what you are going to do about the café? You have informed her of her circumstances, I take it, Citizen Mansart?'

'No, Citizen Deputy, we have hardly had time to go into details. I have yet to show her the ledgers.'

'Then I assume you will be selling it, citizeness, as soon as possible.'

'No, Citizen Hérault,' Fleur answered calmly, resolving to be rebellious. 'I am considering the appointment of a new manager.' Amazement altered both men's expressions. She glanced away modestly. How pleasant to see one of the haughty heroes of the Revolution speechless.

'A risky enterprise for a young widow,' Hérault exclaimed at last, exchanging glances with Mansart. 'You are a woman of hidden parts.'

'An extremely courageous lady, if I may say so, citizen,' declared Mansart, adapting quick-wittedly to his client's viewpoint.

Hidden parts! Behind her veil Fleur frowned, for Hérault's gaze had grown once more overfriendly. Could he have concluded she was a provincial actress and therefore fair game? Embarrassed, it was her turn now to glance about, her fingers tucking back a loose curl.

The worldly Jacobin set a hand on her arm. 'Pardon me, but may I have a private word with you, citizeness?'

She was reluctant to permit this traitor to draw her to one side among the graves, but it would have been impolite to refuse and, to be charitable, he had rescued her yesterday.

'You will have to forgive my candour, but, well, if you are intending to make a go of things in Paris, citizeness, may I offer you some counsel?' Fleur inclined her head with deliberate awkwardness, relieved he had not recognised the signs of a fellow aristocrat. 'I suggest, citizeness, that you find a way to reduce your late husband's debts as soon as possible. Most of these people are creditors come to assess your means of repayment. To be honest, I daresay I am come here for that purpose too.' Fleur swallowed. This was the last truth she had expected. 'Indeed,' he added, 'indelicate as it is to raise the matter here, I think you should know that your husband borrowed more from me than anyone else.'

'I see,' she said uncertainly. 'Forgive me, but I have not been apprised of the extent of money owing to you or indeed anyone. If you would give me a little time to look into matters and decide how I should best proceed, I shall do my best to pay you back.'

'I am prepared,' he was looking down, rubbing a thumb over the shiny knob of his cane, 'to waive the debt for certain considerations.'

All the alarm bells were sounding in Fleur's mind. 'Considerations?' she echoed.

'Yes.' The man's warm glance rolled upwards, lingering appreciatively on the curves of her breast. 'Favours.'

'Of course, favours,' she repeated with feigned puzzlement. It was a small satisfaction to see him redden at the virginal noncomprehension in her face. 'Well, I shall discuss your proposal with Monsieur Mansart and see what he thinks.'

'No! I mean, no, do not raise the issue with Mansart. You and I can perhaps discuss this again.'

'When I am less ignorant, you mean?'

He did not know she was playing with him. 'Yes,' he said, letting out a breath and observing his shoe buckles. Her silence embarrassed him further before he added: 'May I give you some friendly advice?'

'From so illustrious a person as yourself, of course.' *And I would very much like to slap your face either now or some time in the future.*

'As you . . . as you are obviously a young woman of respectable breeding . . .' She waited, but no irony gleamed down at her. 'I-I urge you to distance yourself from any matters of business, citizeness, especially the café.' Sure of his superiority again, he continued: 'People respect virtue and patriotism these days. You may have already observed how volatile this city is. It is easy to make enemies and it is easy for your enemies to find new friends.' He glanced meaningfully towards Felix Quettehou, who stood apart, glowering at them. 'I think you need to choose your company and choose it well.'

'Yes,' said Fleur, wondering how he classified himself. 'I understand what you are saying, Citizen Deputy, and I thank you – both for your assistance yesterday and your good counsel today. I intend to become a model of propriety.'

'Oh.' The gentleman's face coloured slightly. 'Excellent, a woman of good sense. Now, perhaps I should go and trickle a little oil onto troubled waters for you, *hein*? I am about to be appointed to the Committee of Public Safety, and Quettehou will not want to fall foul of any member of that, I assure you, even if he is a friend of Deputy Marat.'

'Marat? *The* Marat?'

'Yes, Quettehou used to print some of Marat's works. Indeed, I marvel your husband did not inform you.'

Ignoring the remark, she set a hand upon his lace cuff, displaying the manners of a bourgeois rather than an aristocrat. 'Pardon my ignorance, but this committee you mentioned, Citizen Hérault, what exactly is it?'

He did not seem to mind the gesture or the question. 'A new committee, citizeness. It is being urged upon the government. It will be elected mostly from the Montagnards – the deputies that sit on the sloping seats in the hall of the Convention.'

'The Mountain. I have heard of it.' Yes, mentioned in a pamphlet Marie-Anne had shown her with disgust. The Montagnards certainly seemed to be louder and far more extreme than the Girondins, who were in control of the government.

'Then you may know that while we are not exactly a disciplined group, we do have a club at the old order of St James's monastery in Rue Saint-Honoré, not far from the Église Saint-Roch. That's why we call ourselves the Jacobins.

'And actually, if you have the time, Citizeness Bosanquet, why not come along to the Convention when it is in session? We are a democracy now. The gallery is open to the people.'

'And this Jacobin Club, is it exclusive?'

'No, visitors are welcome, but if anyone wants to join, he needs to be nominated by another member and the club has to take a vote.' *He!* So it was exclusive. 'There are some women who support us. I daresay you could call in at one of their meetings. Oh, here is Citizen Beugneux.' The latter was bearing down upon them frowning – an odd knight in armour but perhaps she looked as though she needed rescuing.

'Your . . . your companion yesterday, Citizen Hérault,' she asked quickly. 'Is he also owed money by Monsieur Bosanquet?' This former noble might consider it bad manners to refer to yesterday's incident but it was necessary for her peace of mind.

At least the man looked puzzled rather than affronted. 'Oh, you mean Raoul de Villaret, citizeness. *Diable*, no, I have no recollection of them being acquainted and I have never encountered him at the Chat Rouge, but your husband had fingers in many pies.

'Citizen Beugneux, I believe.' He nodded to the older gentleman, the courtesy rather tepid, and then turned once more to Fleur with an expression of greater interest than was acceptable. 'Perhaps I may call upon you in a day or so.' She inclined her head so sternly that he had to accept the gentle reproof. 'Thank you, then,' he murmured politely. 'I wish your enterprise well, citizeness,' and he sauntered off after her new nephew, who was striding away, angrily lashing his walking stick at the nettles adjoining the puddled path.

M. Beugneux sniffed. 'The fellow is impressive and useful b-but I really think you should avoid his type, my dear,' he sniffed. 'The man's a roué even if his p-papa was noblesse *de l'epée*, and he's a Jacobin. Detestable creatures! Still, I daresay p-poor Matthieu would have laughed to see him here. A P-President of the Convention! Oh dear me,' Grief overcame him somewhat excessively again, necessitating the vigorous use of a silken handkerchief.

Ciel! She had just been propositioned by the President of the Convention! At least her companion's nose-blowing gave her a chance to recover her wits and refrain from laughing. 'President!' she exclaimed, taking his arm.

'Oh, not all the time. A few of them rotate the office just as they do the committees.'

'Citizen Hérault says he is to become a member of the Committee of Public Safety.'

'Oh là, not another group with a fancy name! They're cropping up like w-weeds, dear madame. The C-Committee for General Security, the Commune committees. Why bother with ministers of state? There will be a c-committee for stray dogs and a committee for investigating committees before the week is out.'

Fleur smothered a giggle. 'He suggested I should go along to the Convention and hear some of the debates.'

'By all means, my dear, if you are truly interested in such matters, but I cannot understand why you should be, and there are some very d–dubious p–persons who have begun to frequent the p–public gallery. The Furies, I believe, is the current name bestowed upon them.' He patted her hand. 'No, no, a young woman like you should be seen in far better company.' And that would not be easy, thought Fleur.

'However, now to contradict myself,' M. Beugneux continued, 'there are some p–people I think you should meet – our company of actors at the Chat Rouge.' He discreetly raised his forefinger, obviously a prearranged signal, and the disreputable little troop of four approached. So the café stage *had* been used. How wonderful, Fleur thought wickedly, her own group of actors! And she could not resist bestowing her own nicknames upon them immediately.

Whiskers's bow was flamboyant and fulsome. 'Madame, we extend to you our deepest sympathies, the passing of a great spirit.'

The little blonde nodded, the black feathers stuck in the back of her bonnet bouncing distractingly. '*Chère madame*, we shall remember dear Matthieu with the profoundest gratitude.'

The exotic waterpot gulped and a burst of sobs gurgled forth. 'Oh, what is to become of us now that our beloved Bosanquet is gone.'

The beanpole struck a tragic pose, his wrist pressed passionately against his brow. 'One would have thought the gates of the citadel would have been flung open.' Then seeing Fleur's blank stare, he added, 'Shakespeare, English writer.'

'Oh.' All four were staring at her like fledglings waiting for her to open her beak. Fleur cleared her throat. 'I expect you wish to hear my decision on the future of the café.' Four heads nodded frantically. 'I need to give the matter some thought but at present it is my intent to reopen it as soon as possible.'

'You mean you still wish to employ us?' The stocky actor, Whiskers, stepped forward, studying her afresh with an expression of worldliness tinged with pity – clearly this convent-bred girl from the country did not understand what she was taking on.

'If I can, yes, and I expect you to honour your contracts. Come to the café this time next week and I shall answer all your questions. Now, I see that my husband's agent is waiting to speak to me. Au revoir.'

'*Eh bien*,' she heard one of the actresses remark as she walked away on M. Beugneux's arm, 'there still is a god.'

'A goddess!' corrected the beanpole, kissing his fingers loudly. 'We are saved, *mes amis*. Who would have believed in such a miracle?'

Fleur wondered what in heaven she had got herself into. The other cluster of mourners were still eyeing her but there was not a handkerchief among them. Distant relatives, perhaps?

'Who are those people?' she asked, summoning Mansart to join her.

M. Bosanquet's man of affairs sucked in his cheeks and ran a hand across his chin. 'Those?' he echoed ominously. 'Those, I am afraid, are your husband's creditors.'

'All of them?'

'Yes, citizeness; all of them.'

6

Monsieur Esnault!
As you say, it sounds as though the trail has gone cold
in Caen. No matter, I shall continue to pursue my
investigations in Paris. Justice must be done and seen to
be done!

AN EXTRACT FROM A LETTER OF RAOUL DE VILLARET,

MEMBER OF THE COMMITTEE FOR GENERAL SECURITY, 1793

'Oh, but this is terrible, Monsieur Mansart!'
exclaimed Fleur next morning, her chin
nesting in her hands as she stared at the
sheaf of billets fanned out in front of her. 'I can
understand about the lace manufactory but these
other ventures. All failed!'

'I fear so, madame.' They were sitting side by side

in front of the let-down shelf of M. Bosanquet's secretaire like harpsichordists playing a duet and, as if the performance was over, M. Mansart closed the ledger before him. 'I thought it best to terminate the leases since all the premises were rented, that is, except for the café. The workers have been paid off but the suppliers are another matter.'

The doorknocker resounded for the umpteenth time that morning, echoing throughout the apartment. Fleur pushed her chair back and walked across to the window to peer discreetly out. Another bill being delivered! Worse and worse. She hesitated before she swung round, wondering how much she could rely on Mansart.

'Straight as a governess's backbone,' her husband had told her, and certainly he seemed a gentleman, neat in clothing and manners and, to judge by his frown lines and eyebrows not yet grown bushy, still in his forties and past the fire-in-the-belly ambition of young men like de Villaret. Mind, she wondered if the head beneath the brown wig had ever enthused about anything save accounting. What was black in her ledger was the fact that Mansart had accepted her husband's final will unquestioningly, and not pressed her for any payment in cash or 'favours'.

'This is just the beginning, I am sorry to say, madame.' He stood up to face her. 'Your creditors will probably allow you a week's indulgence since you are newly widowed, but then they will be all out in the courtyard clamouring with a vengeance.

I should hide away any valuables if I were you. The bailiff will be round in no time.'

A week, only a week, and she had promised the actors work and now –

'What choices do I have?'

'Sell up the café immediately, though you will not get a good price for it. Or you must sell this house, or . . .'

'Or become a member of Hérault de Séchelles's seraglio.' Mansart blushed like a nun at her straight-forwardness, and she added bitterly, 'It is how things are done in Paris, *n'est-ce pas,* monsieur?'

'Your good looks, madame, give you that extra choice.'

'Is that your advice?'

'You have a serious enemy in Quettehou, madame, and I would wager my livelihood that he will challenge the will, so it would definitely be an advantage to have a powerful protector in these uncertain times.' He swallowed, adding with reluc-tance, 'And certainly if such an *affaire* could be handled with discretion, you might find yourself wealthier in the short term.'

'I see.' Her fingers tapped angrily on the polished chair-back. A whore or a beggar. In the country she might find firewood; here in the city she must thieve or buy it before she could cook a meal, and in winter it would be worse. And to think she imagined her fortunes had improved.

'Or . . .' Mansart was regarding her specula-tively, 'you could take a gamble, madame, throw good money after bad.'

'What exactly do you mean, monsieur?'

'You could reopen the café, hire the most expensive acts in Paris and maybe fool a buyer into thinking a profit could be made.' He laid the ledger on top of its two companions. 'I have another client to see, madame, and must take my leave. You still have a few days to think it over.'

Think it over? She was nineteen, taught by a governess and then convent educated. She could trap a rabbit or bring down a pigeon, but what did she know about running a theatre-café? And there was so much competition.

Paris had a plethora of theatres: the National, the Molière, Citizeness Montansier's, the Palace, the Vaudeville, the Cavern and the plentiful boulevard entertainments. Then there was music: grand opera by Lesueur, or *opéra-comique* such as Grétry's, and feasts of Gluck and Haydn at the academy. The box of broadsheets and reviews she had found in M. Bosanquet's bedchamber told of a multitude of patriotic dramas over the past years. The mother who lost all her sons in the war against Austria. The wife who divorced her aristocratic husband to marry her republican lover. Last year's most popular play, run by the Théatre-Français, had been about some peasant who ballooned heroically to the moon (clearly not a cheese one), where the king was badgered by an overbearing queen. The playwright then shifted the last act to France, whose king had accepted the restraints of a constitutional monarchy and now presided over a felicitous people. Well, with King Louis guillotined, they would not be playing that one to a packed theatre any more, nor quoting the fulsome reviews. One theatre had even had a re-enactment of the storming of the Bastille, rather ambitious for a boulevard theatre, but perhaps the sentiment, if not the spectacle, was there. And at the moment there was *The Widow of Malabar, The Devil's Castle* and *A Daughter for Marrying*.

'Ah, Fleur.' Her aunt swept into the room and stared at the closed accounting books. 'You are finished already?' she asked sharply. 'But I understood you were to apprise us both of Bosanquet's estate, Monsieur Mansart.'

'It is perfectly all right, Tante,' intervened Fleur. 'I have managed to get my mind around the figures. You had better go, monsieur, or you shall be late.'

'Au revoir, madame.' M. Mansart gave Fleur a half-bow. At the door, he paused. 'I am not sure why Monsieur Bosanquet suddenly decided to marry after all those years as a bachelor, but permit me to say he made the right decision.'

Well, at least someone in Paris had confidence in her.

Her aunt peered over the papers. 'You have decided to rid yourself of that disgusting café, I take it.'

'No, Tante Estelle, I have not,' muttered Fleur, sweeping the bills into a pile and stuffing them into the secretaire drawer.

'But it is out of the question to keep it, you foolish creature. An unmarried girl –'

'But I am *not* an unmarried girl, Tante,' Fleur

interrupted dangerously. 'Not any more, and I'm not going to starve either.' And I *shall* find an entertainer who will bring the customers flocking to the Chat Rouge, she added silently.

But she needed to understand Paris; she needed time.

'What are you doing with this toy, Raoul?' The Girondin deputy, Armand Gensonné, idly flicked the catapult that was hanging on the side of the easel in the rented room above Raoul's apartment.

Perhaps the sunlit studio with its exposed medieval beams was not exactly the appropriate stage for a morning argument on patriotism, but Raoul, with Hérault's warning in mind, was trying to talk some sense into Armand. He had whetted his argument with freshly brewed coffee and a *coup* of cognac, but so far his opinions had made no impact.

'That is certainly not a toy,' he retorted. 'Watch!' He shifted Boniface, the neighbour's cat, from the casement sill, prodded the window open further and then selected a small pebble from a dish beside his palette and inserted it into the sling. The missile missed the nearest chimneypot and hit the tiles instead, scattering some dozy pigeons into a panicky ascent before it dropped into the water butt in the tiny courtyard below.

'And which Goliath are you trying to miss?'

'You, of course.' Raoul stuffed the catapult into his coat pocket. 'Now stop trying to change the subject!' Of all the Girondins, Armand was the one he knew the best and respected the most, but his friend could be as stubborn as hell and, what's more, when he chose to be, vaguer than someone who had ridden headfirst into a tree. Raoul glared across at him in exasperation. 'You aren't going to heed a word I say, are you? Trying to make you recognise the danger is as cussed hard as convincing the Pope to turn heathen.'

Armand shrugged. He was prowling now among the propped-up canvases. 'The only way to prove this government is right is for our ministers to stay in the saddle. Fancy you even suggesting we should let go the reins in midgallop. Resign, *non!*' He emphasised his point by jabbing a tapering paintbrush into the air.

Raoul gave a growl. 'For the good of France, Armand,' he exclaimed. 'Look, it's why we toppled the Bastille. So that we could get rid of an incompetent government, not replace it with another one. The whole of Europe is against France, the supply lines cannot meet our soldiers' needs, the price of food is rising daily, the *assignat* is barely worth the paper it's printed on, and the counter-revolutionaries are stirring up the rest of the country. Paris does not believe your government can deliver what is needed and, I am sorry, nor do I. If the ministers cannot do the work properly, they should have the courage to admit it *for the good of France* and resign.'

That was the trouble, he decided: if one gave a political man a whiff of power, he became snared like an opium-eater, unable to see his own blemishes in the mirror of public opinion. Armand, with his eloquence and breadth of vision, was one of the few Girondin deputies who might be able to persuade the ministers to surrender their posts; the other Girondins were either too much philosophers to be pragmatic or else too naive to see that the support of the Plain was swiftly disappearing. Basically they were intellectual snobs who thought the ordinary people too ignorant to have any involvement in law-making.

Armand's smile was tired. 'Much as I respect you, Raoul my poor friend, you are becoming such a pesty Jacobin that you begin to believe your own rhetoric. It is not our ministers' fault that half the generals are deserting to the Austrians. Do you really believe that the Mountain can handle the situation any better? We are trying to achieve what a thousand years of history failed to do, and the people, of course, expect instant happiness. It is totally impractical.' He picked up a painting of a girl with her shoulder bare and the folds of her ribboned shepherdess costume falling tantalisingly away from the curve of her left breast. 'I would not mind this one over my bedroom mantelshelf,' he remarked appreciatively, setting it on the easel.

'The generals are deserting because they believe we will lose.' Raoul grabbed the canvas and thrust it back in its place on the floor against the wall. 'We need unity, Armand, leadership not just orators. Danton says —'

'Danton! We're not climbing into bed with that

bastard. Besides, we can't afford him. The holes in his pockets are as big as the Place de la Révolution.'

'He's only trying to warn you, for God's sake. France needs strong government, otherwise the Republic will tumble like a house of cards. The people are hungry, Armand, desperately hungry. Have any of your government ministers ever known how that feels? Do you?'

'No.' Armand's voice had lost its amiability. He gathered up Boniface from a patch of sunlight and stood at the window, his gaze more distant than the haphazard roofs cluttering the view. The purr of the fondled cat filled the brooding silence. 'Marat's friends have wrecked our printing presses,' he said grimly over his shoulder. 'You think that speaks of unity?'

Intolerant now, the ginger cat sprang down, its moulting hairs catching the light.

'No, of course not, but issuing an order for Marat's arrest is not going to solve anything. It will just make the *sans-culottes* more irate.'

'It is so easy to criticise, so hard to govern.' Armand turned from the casement and flicked at the tawny hairs adhering to his earth green coat. 'Maybe we shall have to do without Paris, *mon brave*. Maybe we need to move the Convention to a city where we haven't got hacks, washerwomen and beggars telling us our business.'

'You cannot be serious. *Nom d'un chien!* The Mountain will accuse you of seeking to divide France further and conspiring with the monarchists.'

'Then let them. We will stand on our laurels. We

killed the King.' His blue eyes rose to fix Raoul's gaze. 'We *all* killed the King.'

For a long moment Raoul stared back and then he acknowledged, 'Yes, for the good of the people and for the best of reasons. Armand, I am warning you, if we can throw an incompetent king overboard because he put his religion and antiquated principles before the people's good, then we can certainly jettison the Rolands and their cronies.'

But his friend merely tugged his watch from his waistcoat pocket. 'Boissy's coach will be here at any moment. Time to go. I would still like to buy that shepherdess painting, by the way.'

'No, you would not,' growled Raoul. 'It is too passé. One of my old efforts.' He scooped up the cat and strode to the door. 'Believe me, hanging that on your wall would not do your reputation or mine much good.'

Armand picked up his hat from the table and followed him out. 'Ah, but I'm not inviting the Convention into my bedchamber to view it. How much do you want?'

Raoul locked the door behind them and tried one last time: 'Think about what I said. The people want bread, Armand. And if they can't have bread, they'll want circuses. And whatever happens, I do not want you to be the clown.'

The Convention met on the first floor of the old Tuilleries Palace in the former theatre which lay between the two wings now called the Pavilions of Unity and Liberty. An apt meeting place, decided

Fleur, for M. Beugneux had warned her that the deputies performed for a gallery that mercilessly booed any boring bleaters and drummed their heels in delight at the handsome and profane. This then was the popular daily entertainment and it was free if you didn't mind the waft of armpits and stale clothing.

Fleur, crammed in a corner against the wall because she had been advised to arrive early, had ample time to study her fellow spectators. They were mostly working-class women. A few men of bourgeois appearance stood behind the back row and several ordered the younger females to give up their places. Broadsheet writers insinuated themselves, scruffy fellows most of them, making ready to bend like question marks over their notes. Stained fingers drew out paper from writing cases; penknives flashed busily, sharpening quills or cleansing fingernails. Inkwell lids flipped up like predatory crustaceans waiting to catch the morning's morsels.

Fleur began to wonder whether she wanted to remain in such a crowd but her way out was blocked by a whole bench of noisy market creatures, talented at bawling in public. It seemed she must resign herself to remaining there for an hour or so or earn their abuse. This might be her means of understanding what was going on in Paris. At least the experience would be something she could write about to Marie-Anne, and it was a heady feeling to find herself at the heart of the Revolution and catch a glimpse of the leaders mentioned in the Parisian pamphlets. She became so absorbed in watching the representatives of the people's Republic seep into the hall that she totally forgot her discomfort, and when the man occupying the president's seat rang a bell to hush the hall to business, Fleur felt the tingling anticipation of seeing laws that would affect all France flower into life beneath her gaze – history, living and breathing.

The speeches in the hour that followed were as exciting as watching a puddle evaporate. For the most part, the deputies looked very ordinary and certainly not as she had imagined the villains who had scythed through the knees of the aristocracy and voted to guillotine King Louis. Many of these men must have been the stalwarts who had proclaimed the Declaration of the Rights of Man and vowed never to disband until they had made a better France, but she heard nothing remarkable from them. Instead these so-called revolutionaries yawned, scratched, ahemmed and generally looked bored. The only thing one revolutionary spent the first half-hour trying to liberate was the food from the gaps between his teeth; another spat towards the aisle whenever he disagreed with a speaker. Marie-Anne would not have been impressed; if these were the men intent on slapping the dough of France into a different shape, it was hardly likely that life would be better for the whole nation or that France would set an example to the world.

The deputies perched on the benches in the sloping rear of the hall, mostly men in their thirties, must be the Mountain – the Jacobins; and those sitting in the level area in front of the rostrum had to be the Plain – the unaffiliated deputies. If any member wished to address the assembly, he had to queue up in front of the platform where the President of the Convention sat, register his name and seat himself on the bench reserved for the morning's speakers. Then when it was his turn, he would be invited to step up to the lectern, which was draped in the scarlet, blue and white of the Revolution.

Making a speech here required considerable confidence, for not only did the women in the gallery hiss and mutter at the speaker like snakes on Medusa's head, but the general conduct of the representatives of the people seemed very informal and often insulting. Half the time the listeners either paid no attention or else they kept interrupting as if it was a game to unnerve the speaker. They wandered in and out at will; they conversed loudly among themselves; they passed messages; and some of them lay sprawled asleep, snoring loudly. Democracy at work?

But what a galaxy of creatures these representatives were! From men who had been powdered by their hairdressers and wore their waistcoats and breeches with fastidious elegance, to those with greasy, matted hair who obviously put liberty and equality before soap and water. And not a woman deputy among them. No wonder the women sitting in the gallery felt it important to be noisy and outspoken.

Towards midmorning the atmosphere changed, the floor of the Convention filled up and the calibre of the speakers improved.

'Rob-es-pierre, Rob-es-pierre,' chanted the gallery girls as a dapper, youngish man in a swallow-tailed coat stepped up to speak. The whole place hushed as he shuffled his papers. His oratory did not exactly move Fleur as it did the other women, but his attack on the government and the way the war against Austria was being run was certainly well prepared. There was no humour in this Robespierre as he studied them over the top of his pince-nez, but the carefully timed phrases sounded as though they came from the heart.

Fleur could not hear the government's defence because all the women sharing her bench started hollering at two late arrivals. The large-bosomed *sans-culotte* beside her squeaked loudly, bouncing her assets excitedly at a brown-haired deputy in his early thirties.

'*Holà*, Gensonné!' she screamed, springing to her feet, all thighs and elbows. Delirious, palpitating womanhood, she subsided by Fleur as ecstatic as if she had seen the Angel Gabriel. 'He smiled at me,' she whispered dreamily. 'I adore his eyes.'

Well, conceded Fleur, Gensonné's eyes were certainly his best feature if you discounted his lustrous, curling hair, but the man's mouth was definitely too effeminate for her taste and the smile had been merely the genial serenity of a man with more important matters on his mind.

'Pah, I'd rather have his friend,' a voice behind

them said scathingly and bawled out in a voice that almost deafened Fleur, 'Give us a smile!'

The other women yelled and drummed their heels in support. Fleur leaned forward only to jerk back immediately. Gensonné's companion was Raoul de Villaret! When he nodded indifferently at the gallery, the women shrieked even louder. Fleur shrank back against the wall. Thank God, he was too intent on stooping to speak to a seated deputy to bother with ogling his admirers, for she would have been mortified if he had recognised her.

'*Beau, hein?*' the voice behind Fleur exclaimed. 'Only twenty-seven too.'

'He can climb on my rostrum any day,' giggled someone else.

Fleur edged in rashly, 'He looks too self-centred to me.'

Her immediate neighbour had recovered from her rapture. 'Well, I have a friend who says de Villaret gave her the best night in years,' she declared authoritatively, wriggling with superiority. 'Fingers like a pianist. Painted her in the –'

'Woo-hohhh,' chorused the women.

So he painted naked women, did he? Fleur studied de Villaret's well-proportioned back with a mixture of spinsterish contempt and fascination.

Gensonné's ample admirer tweaked Fleur's black veil mischievously. 'I haven't seen you here before, citizeness. Didn't your old man like you taking an interest?'

'I am new to Paris,' Fleur answered cautiously.

'*Non*, really! Have you not been to the Jacobin

Club in the Rue Saint-Honoré yet? What, you haven't?' Blue eyes widened in disbelief. 'Oh, you must! That's where the decisions are really made.'

Oh, yes, that was if you ignored the ministers of state, the Cordelier Club and its notorious Danton, the Paris Commune dominated by the odious writer Marat, not to mention all the city sections and whoever made the most noise in the national guard! Fleur had not spent the last year in utter ignorance.

'If you are anxious to have your say, citizeness,' prattled her neighbour cheerfully, thumping her knee, 'you should come along there later today. Much more interesting than here.' De Villaret had finished his conversation and as he straightened and turned round, the woman behind Fleur sprang to her feet. '*Holà*, Raouly darling.'

Before Fleur could duck out of sight, Raouly darling glanced up. What man wouldn't at such a hollering? He touched a gloved hand to the brim of his beaver, acknowledging his agitated admirer, and then his gaze fell upon Fleur, conspicuous in her black. He stared openly and then with a flash of teeth bestowed a smile upon her and the glowing woman behind her.

Zut, she swore inwardly, her face warm behind the veil, but surely there were plenty of widows in Paris. He might not have recognised her.

'Ah, there's my other sweetheart.' Her new companion annoyingly bounced with excitement as a beefy, pockmarked fellow set his ploughman's hands upon the lectern. The man's voice carried excellently and his well-delivered cadences would have not disgraced the senate of ancient Greece or Rome.

'Isn't he wonderful? A real volcano, our Danton. Are you all right, *ma chère*? You look a trifle queasy to me.'

'The h-heat. I feel queasy.' Fleur thrust a handkerchief to her mouth in an effort to hide her loathing. Georges Danton! The infamous, venal, bloody degenerate who had instigated the September massacres! Fleur shuddered. Had the woman beside her cheered on the butchers that murdered Papa just as she was cheering now? 'Pardon me, citizeness, I need some air.'

'Baby on the way, *hein*?'

No, she was not with child. Against a barrage of protests, Fleur squeezed her way between the rail and the row of feet; one pair kicked her viciously for ruining the view and she almost tumbled across several impatient knees with the pain. The air of the corridor – deserted, thank heaven – was at least less contaminated. She leaned against the marble balustrade of the staircase with a deep sigh, her eyes closed.

'I hope you are not going to be sick, citizeness.'

Fleur snapped to attention. Of all people, it was Raoul de Villaret who stood below, left arm across his chest supporting his right elbow. He was stroking his jaw thoughtfully. What might have passed for a grin curled his mouth.

'Stay there and I just might be,' muttered Fleur beneath her breath, annoyed that she was not even

133

permitted to feel faint without his interference. Why was he suddenly running up a friendly flag? Did the arrogant bastard think she had left in embarrassment because he had caught her watching him? Damnation, she thought in panic, maybe she had better let him think just that. With a deep breath, she straightened up and slowly descended the staircase with as much grace as she could. What mischief was brewing for her now? Out of the cauldron to a waiting fire? With a mind full of misgivings, she reached the last few stairs.

'Citizeness Bosanquet? Are you grown so coy of a sudden? I presume it is you hiding behind the black lace.' Insolent devil!

'Citizen,' she greeted him with a pretence of shyness, resisting the strong temptation to sweep past him dismissively like a former duchess.

Raoul de Villaret deliberately stepped in front of her and Fleur found herself halted, disconcertingly, at eye level with him. The man was arresting – in more ways than the obvious! If he had been an aristocrat in a pre-revolutionary salon, she might have teased him, she conceded; but with or without the artillery of handsome looks, he was a revolutionary and dangerous.

'You are exceedingly active for a lady so recently bereaved, citizeness,' he accused amiably, his dark eyes full of amusement. Did he think her a courtesan selecting her next lover from the power-hungry and the influential? Then, without permission, he outrageously set back her veil.

'You need sunshine, patriot.' But then he

frowned. 'Has something made you unwell, citizeness?' His gaze flicked from her waist to her hips. *Nom d'un chien!* He too was trying to discover whether she might be breeding.

Reddening, she held her temper. The thought of any man's child ripening inside her was scandalous to her maidenly mind, but if he supposed her a widow, it was not an unreasonable assumption. Really, if the man were more civil, she would have thanked him for rescuing her yesterday. Now it required an effort not to slap him for his impertinence.

'It was hot and crowded in the gallery, citizen. Nothing more, I assure you.' Why had she said that – as if her condition was any of his business! 'As to being here, I find it best to occupy my mind.' Her irritation was close to boiling over. 'Do not let me keep you, Citizen de Villaret. Should you not be inside the hall listening to the great Danton?' It was an effort to keep the distaste from her voice.

She put up her hand to tug her veil back into place but he presumptuously set a hand upon her tight sleeve.

'A moment, please. It is fortunate to see you here, citizeness, since I desire to return something of yours.' With a smile that was annoyingly enigmatic, he slid a hand into his coat pocket.

'I am sure you have nothing there that is of the slightest concern to me, citizen.' A slight purr of flirtation sweetened Fleur's reproof but then memory jolted her. Her ring! *Ciel!* Had he retrieved it?

Never say this interfering upstart had tried to trace the ring's provenance.

'Oh, but I have,' he corrected roguishly, and possessing himself of her gloved hand, he pressed something far larger than jewellery into her palm and closed her fingers over it. 'I am sure we shall meet again, citizeness.'

Beyond words, she stood still as a bronze statue until the doors of the assembly hall closed behind his insufferable back.

Raoul de Villaret had found her catapult.

7

*I certainly would not wish to live in a new republic,
however good its laws are.*

JEAN JACQUES ROUSSEAU, *A DISCOURSE UPON THE ORIGIN
AND THE FOUNDATION OF THE INEQUALITY AMONG MANKIND*

Nom d'un chien! De Villaret had her on a
leash and wanted her to know it, and
Fleur, her emotions jumping grasshopper-
like from fear to bravado, finally opted for anger.
She arrived back at her inheritance in a scarcely
controlled fury to find her aunt in an almost equal
lather, waving a letter in one hand and smelling
salts, lent her by M. Beugneux, in the other.

Since the gentleman tactfully disappeared up
the stairs with surprising agility, Fleur was left

alone to deal with her aunt's distress. It seemed the letter had imparted information guaranteed to threaten one's sanity, or so Tante Estelle informed her with fulsome agitation. Marie-Anne's aunt, Mme de Bretteville, had written to say that the Abbé Gombault had been arrested for refusing to take the oath of loyalty to the Republic and accept the edict of deportation, and was to receive the death penalty. To add to that horror, Guillaume had left Grimbosq and gone to Bayeux to evade the soldiers who had been seeking him for questioning over M. Bosanquet's demise.

Fleur sank down upon the sofa in the parlour, Mme de Bretteville's neat writing dancing before her eyes. She seemed to bring disaster to all who knew her. And where was Blanchette? Had Guillaume taken her with him?

'And note the postscript from Marie-Anne,' exclaimed her aunt. 'After we left, that meddling lawyer, Esnault, went nosing through the Trinité School library for lists of pupils over the last five years.'

'What's left of it. That would have taken him no more than a few minutes. He would have found nothing.' Fleur read the postscript again. 'I will hazard the republicans are looking for the estate records Marie-Anne and the abbess have hidden. They would not be bothering with the likes of me. Everyone knows they have been trying to find out the extent of the abbey's holdings for the last year so they can seize everything.' Her aunt looked unconvinced. 'Maybe they think an old pupil has them hidden. Oh, but this news of Abbé Gombault is heartbreaking.'

'I have had enough!' fumed Tante Estelle, dashing her fists against her black skirts. 'Last night you told me you intend to become a tradeswoman and reopen that revolting café, and now this morning you have been to the Convention. How can you have the gall to set foot among those regicides? And to think that rascal Hérault and his odious companion know where we live. They will be soon sniffing round asking questions, mark my words. That,' she pointed to the letter, 'is just too much of a coincidence.'

She was probably right, but Fleur kept her own panic strapped down.

'Tante.' She reached out a soothing hand but the older woman flinched, jowls and lace lappets quivering.

'I will not be pacified. And . . . and, furthermore, I have no intention of sharing a house with . . . with snakes, or mixing with actors and sodomites any longer.' Fleur's eyes widened. 'You and I are returning to Caen, niece, and there's an end to it. I have booked us two seats on tomorrow's diligence.'

It was necessary to take a deep breath and be firm. 'No, Tante.'

'No! How dare you answer me so! You will do as I say, mademoiselle.'

Fleur's spine stiffened at being addressed like some common serving girl. 'No, madame,' she retorted, risking the fact that her aunt looked angry enough to hit her.

'You foolish girl! I will not tolerate your disobedience!'

Her aunt's rare outbursts of fury never lasted long. Fleur glared back at her and made no answer. Eventually the older woman sat down, her mouth a cat's behind of sulky umbrage.

'Please understand, Tante Estelle.' Fleur judged it timely to rise and cross to kneel beside her aunt's armchair. 'Yes, you are right, you should return to Calvados, for you are not a Montbulliou, but I must stay in Paris. There are people here who are depending on me for a living, and if I can manage to reopen the café, I will be able to send you enough to live on. You must not mistake my disobedience for ingratitude. You have been so kind taking me in and seeing to my schooling.'

'Oh, Fleur.' Calmer now, the older woman's fingers sought her hand. 'No, it is you who have done the looking after me since your uncle fled. I am afraid, Fleur. Paris is making a coward of me.'

'Then you must leave Paris.' Fleur pulled out her handkerchief from an inner pocket and her catapult tumbled free. 'Oh,' she whispered.

Tante Estelle glanced at it. 'Thank you, you keep it. I could never even throw a cushion at your uncle to hit him properly.'

Now was not the time to feel hysterical with laughter. 'Oh, Tante Estelle, I am not expecting you to use it. It was given back to me this morning by de Villaret.' Her aunt looked blank. 'The odious companion, remember. It seems someone has been to Grimbosq.'

'Oh.' Trembling fingers flew to the older woman's lips. 'Jesu, Fleur, wh-what are you going to do? You must leave Paris, darling. Now we have a little money, we could try to reach the border. Your uncle –'

'I intend to face de Villaret. You must see that to run away would surely inflame his suspicions further. Françoise-Antoinette de Montbuillou should be keeping her head out of sight, whereas the parvenu opportunist Citizeness Fleur Bosanquet is made of different mettle. He cannot prove I had a hand in Monsieur Bosanquet's death.'

The tick-tock of the clock punctuated the silence.

'Oh,' sighed her aunt finally, 'I do not know what your uncle would say to such harebrained bravery. No, I will not have it. We must leave, both of us. Stay in this terrible city and you might as well invite the executioner to put your name on his list.' Fingertips smoothed a curl back from her niece's cheek. 'Poor, foolish child. You always were stubborn.'

'You have not been listening, Tante.' Fleur scrambled up from her knees. 'Not only may it be impossible for us to get passes to leave Paris now, but the world has changed, forever perhaps, and I have to make my way as best I can. And it is more than that. You see, I-I think I have stopped being frightened.'

Her aunt, matriarchal sentiments back in place, tossed an exasperated gaze to the plaster garlands embellishing the ceiling. 'More's the pity then. Fear might jiggle some sense into you. Oh, how can you talk so stupidly? The bloodthirsty rogues out there can arrest us merely for being related to counter-revolutionaries.'

'Perhaps, but I am not going to sit in here like a milksop wringing my hands. I was meant to come to Paris. Go if you wish, but I am staying.'

'But, Lord, child, we cannot remain here with that hateful nephew and now de Villaret scenting blood. Heavens!' A new thought had struck her. 'Besides, there is no question of a young girl staying here without a chaperone. Your honour, your virtue, Fleur. You will never find a husband.'

'I have found one, remember.'

'But a proper one, Fleur, a *living* one.'

'Dead ones are much easier to deal with.' Any intimacy was inconceivable. Lovers and husbands asked too many questions. 'I do not need a chaperone now I am a widow.'

'In name only.'

'Tante, please understand I am not a child any more. If I can survive by my wits in the forest, then I can survive here. If de Villaret orders my arrest, so be it. I must do as much as I can while I can.' She gathered up her hat and veil. 'Now you will have to forgive me, I wish to be seen as a good revolutionary.'

'But w-where are you going now?'

'To the Jacobin Club.'

Tante Estelle crossed herself. 'How can you flaunt yourself among those criminals,' she spluttered. 'You young people – Oh, I vow I no longer

142

understand you. You used to be such a biddable child.'

'It is like this, Tante. Remember Cécile was terrified of dogs after one of Papa's hounds bit her at Clerville when she was little?'

'And what is that to the point, pray?'

'Maman decided the only way to cure her was to give her a dog of her own.' Oh dear, her aunt was still looking at her with pity. 'Well, Tante,' she announced grandly as though it was a declaration of war, 'I am going to show the dogs I am not afraid. I might even buy collars for some of them.'

'And this de Villaret?'

No, she thought, one had to draw the line between common sense and folly.

'Oh yes, Tante, especially de Villaret!'

The Jacobin Club met in the old monastery of St James, which consisted mainly of a huge hall that lay at right angles to the Rue de Saint-Honoré. A placard directed Fleur round the side to the main entrance, which opened onto a large courtyard containing a tall, healthy Tree of Liberty, encircled by a picket fence. Only a rose window in the end wall and the square turret straddling the steep roof hinted at the building's former use. An immense flag now hung at an angle from a broad wooden placard which proclaimed not only the Society of Jacobins but also its principles in painted capitals. Fleur rattled the great doors but they were locked, then a small door alongside it opened and she was beckoned out of the cold. Two artisans wearing red liberty bonnets stood waiting before a table where their papers were being officiously scrutinised; a brawny *sans-culotte*, legs astride, appeared to be guarding the doorway to the hall and the stairs to the gallery.

'Where do you think you are going?' he asked Fleur.

'I am just looking while I wait,' she retorted, standing on tiptoes to see past his shoulder. The club was obviously in full session, for the hall was packed and warm with people. Oblique columns of April sunlight poured through the high dormer windows into a great chamber smoky with pipe tobacco. Draped down the west wall, between two huge, high windows made up of small square panes, was a painted cloth banner depicting a lifesize virile ploughman standing in the simplicity of a Rousseauist field of impeccably turned furrows. His muscled arm was blissfully flung round his pregnant, adoring wife, and a chubby infant clutched at his brown *pantalons*, staring towards some idealistic future.

Or was it the painted ploughman admiring the wall-hanging of the half-naked young woman opposite (in a Phrygian hat surmounted by a chicken) which showed where revolutionary aspirations were skittling? Despite the criss-crossing tricolore braid, the mademoiselle's Grecian draperies had been neatly peeled back by the artist's hand to reveal round, perfect breasts. Clearly, this nubile 'new France' was not to encourage a state of relaxed *déshabillé* among the women who seemed to make up a quarter of the audience, but it certainly might distract the male listeners from the speeches.

The *sans-culotte* doorkeeper, who seemed to be meditating upon the painting's naked bosom, dragged his gaze away and stepped back to let the other visitors through.

'You there, sister, where's your membership card and ticket?' rasped the whiskered man behind the table.

Fleur turned, wondering how she might gain a temporary pass. Would she need to lie about her age? But then a chubby brown arm swept round her shoulders; her buxom acquaintance of this morning evidently had been watching for several friends to arrive and had sprung up like a friendly bitch to vouch for her. Within seconds she was inside the hall and the most recent arrivals were shuffling along the hindmost bench to make room for the pair of them.

'Feeling better, darlin'?'

'Much.'

A workaday palm was proffered: 'Emilie Lemoine.'

'Hush!' A man in front of them swung round testily.

'I'm Fleur Bosanquet.' They shook hands. 'What are they debating, Emilie?'

'Well, we're doing *assignats*, but shortly we'll be onto education for girls. Have you read Olympe de Gouges's *Declaration of the Rights of Woman*?'

'No, but I certainly shall if you recommend it. Are we allowed down here?' Fleur could see that all the other females were up in the gallery, but

Emilie tapped her own nose and giggled. 'Not going to guillotine us, are they? Where's your pluck, Fleur Bosanquet?'

Her pluck was melting fast, but she supposed if she was going to face up to these people she might as well do it with trumpets blaring. The speaker on the rostrum was reaching the height of his argument. Fleur vigorously huzzahed him as he finished, for he proclaimed himself a disciple of the *ci-devant* encyclopaedist Marquis de Condorçet, who supported the view that women should be able to vote and hold office.

'Who's that?' whispered Fleur. A blotchy-faced fellow, wearing an ermine collar that clashed absurdly with the bandanna which tethered unruly hair darkly against his brow, had taken the stand.

'You don't know Marat! He's club president this week.'

'You mean he's a member?'

'Of course, everyone worth knowing is a card-holder here.'

Jean-Paul Marat! Fleur gazed wide-eyed at the hateful bête noire of Marie-Anne's circle. The man made a great show, repeatedly thumping fist against palm, as he spoke against the Girondin government. His language, punctuated by vulgarities, was fast and passionate and the mournful dark eyes were lit with fury. Fleur, not informed like her neighbours on *assignats*, public works programmes on government corruption, listened intently but Emilie drummed her heels and shrieked her approval along with the women upstairs.

The man who spoke after Marat, however, had a voice as flat as Holland and Fleur's mind began to drift back to her own problems. She was not even aware of Marat ringing the time bell or a new speaker mounting the platform until Raoul de Villaret's voice crashed through her reverie like a fist slamming down upon a table.

'Of course women have a right to education,' he exclaimed, 'but expanding our schools and colleges to accommodate them is an expensive process that may take decades It is the boys who are our future. They must be educated first if we are to ensure we have men of vision who will lead us into the next century.'

'Pooh!' bawled Emilie.

'What about women of vision?' shouted a woman in the gallery.

'There's no such thing,' guffawed one of the men.

'Give us votes!' shouted another female voice.

'Yes, give us a chance to vote against male idiots.'

'Not if you're not educated,' a man yelled at the gallery, and was applauded by his male companions.

'Patriots!' De Villaret held up his hand to quieten the furore. 'Patriots, it has taken over seventeen centuries since the birth of the *sans-culotte* Jesus for many of our brothers gathered here this afternoon to be given the right to vote. Change is necessary, certainly, but it must be gradual. Our republican sisters cannot expect either equality or education at the scratch of a quill.'

It was reckless of Fleur to draw attention to herself but she could not stand such masculine dogma. Besides, it was not being anti-revolutionary. Her heart was palpitating and she would probably tumble headlong in the first sentence but . . .

'Citizen,' she cried, springing vehemently to her feet. 'Are you blind?' The sudden hush of interest around her was disconcerting. Had her voice carried so clearly? 'Are you deaf too? Half of France is composed of women and yet you seek to muzzle us, to make obedient lap-dogs of us.'

'Woof, woof,' bawled a youth and Fleur felt her cheeks heating at the male chuckles.

'Go on.' De Villaret's unemotional tone carried authority that quietened the chamber. He leaned his forearm along the lectern, his unreadable gaze settling disconcertingly on her. *Fingers like a pianist.* For an instant her mind froze, but the female cogs and wheels inside her seemed to tighten her breathing and create mayhem in all sorts of surprising places. Imagine posing for him in gauzy draperies. She forgot the rows of people separating them.

'Go on! He won't eat you.' A female hand was tugging insistently at the lower edge of her bodice jacket. 'Keep going!'

'We – women – are not spaniels!'

'No but you can lick my toes any day, cherie,' sniggered a male voice.

Other crude comments bombarded her but she could be dogged too. 'Why are we women not allowed to vote?'

'Because, sweetheart,' bellowed one of the men,

waving his pipe, 'when we get home after a day's work we want supper, not yapping about politics! And what's more, Rousseau's Sophie would agree with me.'

'Yes, that's your place there!' A male forefinger pointed towards the painted ploughman's wife.

'No, there!' guffawed a man on their bench, casting lascivious eyes at France's nakedness on the other wall. Emilie clouted him.

Was it worth trying to make herself heard when the fathers and husbands in the audience were resolved not to take her seriously? Still Fleur kept on her feet. 'I despise Rousseau's "Sophie" and I completely endorse Citizen Condorçet's suffrage proposals and so should all of you! Is any man here denying that women have souls or feelings or minds?' she demanded, but it was to her enemy on the rostrum that she flung the question.

With a disturbingly sensual grace, Raoul de Villaret pushed back the lock of hair that had loosened from his queue and smiled across at her with what she took for despicable condescension. Or was it pity?

'Citizeness, I am not denying any of that. You must admit, however, that very few of you women have been educated to have any real grasp of the difficulties of government and yet you would vote, despite that ignorance.' He let that sink in and added: 'On what grounds will you elect a deputy, citizeness? Because you like his swagger, because he smiled up at you in the gallery. You are blushing, citizeness.' Compassionately, he swung his gaze

149

from her and looked up to include all the other women. 'Oh, I will concur that girls need to be educated, but I totally abhor giving women voting rights in the present situation.' The drumming of heavy masculine heels supported him.

'When will you give us equality?' snapped Fleur. 'It took only a quick scratch of a quill to overthrow a thousand years of monarchy.'

'A lot of scratches of the quill, my pretty trouble-maker.' De Villaret's smile was unmistakably patronising. 'You are not wrong . . .' He paused for the laughter to hush. 'You are not wrong to demand equality but let us educate you first, citizeness.' His voice descended to a sensual purr of masculine conceit, and then he straightened, waiting for the applause, his expression of triumph withheld as laughter and shouts of 'Bravo!' echoed around the hall, rocking Fleur as if the very air vibrated.

Fleur subsided onto the bench beside Emilie, who was bouncing up and down, applauding her.

'I'll volunteer to educate you, darling!' exclaimed a bawdy voice; a neighbouring male paw slapped the only available part of her backside. 'What about tonight?'

Shame scorched her face, but the agent provocateur of her humiliation, de Villaret, bestowed a smile gleaming with white teeth in her direction. 'You wish to add anything, citizeness?'

'Yes,' she shouted, rising to her feet again. 'You are old-fashioned despite your youth, citizen, and you are a coward. I do not know what few experiences with women have given you this blinkered attitude towards my sex but I suggest that you are carrying ancient values like the ass you are.' She sat down heavily, her heart thumping as though it was trying to escape her rib cage. The laughter around her was suffocating. It was tempting to flee the hall but that would be a female thing to do. Dear God, why was she thinking so treacherously? *Female?* This female would sit it out.

Deputy de Villaret was laughing as he stepped down but the other men were not finished with Fleur. One of the Jacobins sitting near the front stood up, swung round to face the audience, and waggled his fingers behind his head like donkey's ears.

'Hee-haw,' yelled someone and then most of the men were doing it either at the women upstairs or at the back bench.

It was Emilie who jumped to her feet now. 'You *salauds*! Asses the lot of you! Come on, citizenesses of France! Will you listen further to such imbeciles?' The women in the gallery rose from the benches like a flock of squawking rooks and clattered down the stairs in their wooden sabots as heavily as they could. Emilie grabbed Fleur's arm and they marched out together. It was wrong. They should have stayed.

'Nice speech,' said one of the *sans-culotte* women, tapping her pipe out on the fence protecting the Tree of Liberty. 'Will you come and enjoy a beer with us, citizeness?'

Fleur was amazed; they were actually asking *her*. Two days ago some of these furies might have been willing to hang her from a lamppost. 'W-what time is it, please?' she answered hesitantly.

'Quarter to four, *ange*.' Someone pulled out a gentleman's watch. Who had owned that – a tumbril victim?

'Oh, that late. Forgive me, I have to meet someone.' The sudden scowls showed they did not like her refusing. 'Truly, a business matter.' And just as well; they seemed a touchy lot, and with *her* past she was bound inadvertently to say something to offend them. Emilie's disappointment seemed genuine, and on impulse Fleur gave her a hug. 'Thank you for supporting me.'

The round face beneath the gathered cotton cap shone with pleasure. 'I always come here when I can get away from the stall. I sell used clothing – not doing badly either, if you need something. You coming tomorrow?'

'I'll try to.'

Fleur arrived back at the Rue des Bonnes Soeurs somewhat grazed from having run the masculine gauntlet, but with a delicious idea unfurling.

'I have decided,' she announced to M. Beugneux, who blinked up sleepily from his armchair like a noonday owl, 'I am going ahead with reopening the Chat Rouge and we are going to put on a performance that all Paris will talk about.'

'Just as well,' replied M. Beugneux dryly, straightening his velvet sleeves over his frothy cuffs, 'for a fellow called Thomas has arrived to manage it and the man's too large to argue with. And what shall we do with the donkey?'

'Donkey!' shrieked Fleur with immense delight. 'Thomas *and Blanchette*!'

'Your friend has gone across the street to negotiate some temporary accommodation for the long-eared madame. I take it she is a friend of yours as well?' He held up a finger and listened. '*Voilà!* They are back, I believe.'

Fleur hurtled down the stairs and threw open the front door.

Weathered, bald as a pebble but no less rotund, the large, kindly man who had escorted her to Caen stood there grinning, with Blanchette drawn up beside him.

'Oh, Thomas! *Thomas!*' Fleur flung herself into his arms. He gave her a smacking Gallic embrace and whirled her up into the air.

'Bonjour, *ma petite!*' he laughed, scuffing the tears of joy from her cheek as he set her down.

'Oh, Thomas, and you brought Blanchette!' She could hardly breathe for happiness as she turned to fling her arms about the little donkey.

'All it needs is the thief of Clerville,' chuckled the underch'ef dryly, 'and we have quite a reunion. Guillaume sends his regards. He says the gypsies also send their good wishes. Ah, bonjour, madame,' he called up to Tante Estelle, who had leaned out of the upstairs window to investigate the hubbub. 'Hasn't she grown into a beauty?'

'Are you talking about my niece or the donkey?' her aunt retorted. 'Because I tell you this, Thomas, they both lack brains coming to Paris and so, I fear, do you.'

The underchef gave her a cheeky bow and turned back to Fleur. He stared at her across the donkey's pelt, his levity vanished. Perhaps he could read the struggle and hunger of the recent years in her face as she could in his.

'I am glad to be here, Fleur,' he said, close to tears. 'Bayeux was . . .' his large, capable hands flexed, 'a struggle.'

'It won't be easy here, either,' Fleur warned him gravely. 'It could be far worse.'

'*Ça ira*,' he reassured her, quoting the Marseillaise. *It will be all right.* 'Besides, *petite*,' he added immodestly, his cheerfulness bursting irresistibly forth, 'who else makes food as delicious as I do! Something the Parisians are about to find out, *hein*?'

Fleur's aunt, dressed for hours of tedious travel in a diligence, confronted her niece at breakfast a few days later. A different aunt, a shoulders-back aunt, a most unusually up-early aunt. Fleur braced herself for a scolding.

'I have been doing some common-sense thinking about our conversation the other day, child, especially what you said about not being afraid any more, which was quite an admirable sentiment, given the circumstances, and I have decided that I must stop behaving like a coward.' She then spoilt her speech by adding disgustedly, 'Heavens, Fleur, you have straw in your hair.'

'Oh, have I?' Fleur bit her lower lip apologetically. 'That is from feeding Blanchette. Thomas and the carpenter, Jacques Caillou, have been making a byre for her, and Caillou's children think she is wonderful. They are going to lead her through the streets with a placard showing the Chat –' The avalanche of words rolled to a halt. 'But you are still leaving?' she asked solemnly.

'Yes, I thought you understood I had made that decision. But I am not going back to Calvados, not yet. I am going to do something for myself. I am going east to Coblenz to find your uncle. There is a diligence leaving for Rheims in two hours. I daresay I shall find some way to cross the frontier.'

'But that is wonderful.' Fleur threw her arms round her. But what of a pass? Would the authorities grant her one?

'Wonderful!' scoffed her aunt after a dutiful embrace. 'Utter madness, like walking in front of a firing squad. But it is missing Charles that is destroying me. If I haven't much time left and he is still alive, I want to spend every moment with him.'

'You will have years and years together.' In genteel poverty! Her uncle's few letters lamented a lack of money. Everyone said the emigrés lived on nostalgia, revenge and air. Her aunt shrugged but Fleur assured her, 'No, no, I am sure he will rejoice to see you.'

'Well, we shall see. You were right to remind me that my duty to you is done. It has set me free.' It was bravely said, although one could see her aunt's resolve was like a custard but newly set.

'You *will* find Oncle Charles,' exclaimed Fleur encouragingly. 'Oh, I know you will.'

Her aunt made use of a handkerchief. 'I shall see

Philippe, of course, and seek news of your sister too. I vow I'll find some means to send you word.' Then she held Fleur back from her. 'Only nineteen. Dear me, if times were not amiss you would scarcely be launched into society. A schoolroom chit.' *Or married off.*

'I will manage. And I have friends to advise me now.'

'Mansart and Thomas, yes, but I would give Beugneux notice, him and the snake. There is a definite similarity between them.' She shuddered. 'Ugh. He has that same narrow-eyed glint as though he is laughing at me. Oh, you may giggle, child. "There are none so deaf as those that will not hear." But he has his uses. Look! Here is my pass.'

'Let me see.' Fleur examined the paper in amazement. It looked quite genuine.

'He acquired it for me. See, it says I am needed to oversee the birth of my first grandchild.' M. Beugneux clearly had hidden talents. Perhaps he was anxious to be rid of Tante Estelle.

'Oh dear,' sniffed her aunt. 'I do not know what your brother will say to my abandoning you. He will not be pleased with either of us.'

'It is none of Philippe's business any more.'

'It will be if you find yourself in trouble. No, do not interrupt me. You are older than your years, Fleur, but be very careful. People can be malicious. I mean those who use the power of gossip like a surgeon's knife and can make fast work of your reputation. Versailles was like that. You may scoff. Maybe the butterflies that fluttered prettily among the rosebushes are all gone now, but it is not just the dung beetles who marched on the palace that want to fly, it is the scorpions and the spiders you must be careful of.'

'*Tante!*' spluttered Fleur, hugging her again. 'That was quite a speech. I will watch where I tread, I promise.'

'There is a reckless streak in most of the Mont-bullious.' Her aunt sucked in her cheeks with the knowing observance of an in-law and set her niece aside. 'Now, if you will kindly fetch my bag down . . . and,' her expression became somewhat sheep-ish, 'I was wondering if there is something from the house that we could pawn to pay for my fare.'

'However did you manage to reserve a seat on the diligence without any money?'

A gloved hand waved airily. 'Oh, Monsieur Beugneux arranged all that. Now what about the money, dear?'

There was just the picture in M. Bosanquet's bedchamber – an old-fashioned, frothy painting of a simpering girl and her beau flirting on a garden seesaw by an artist called Fragonard.

'I'll go straightaway.'

The shopkeeper where Fleur took the picture made an immediate offer. He said that it might be one of a set.

By the time she handed a tense aunt up into the diligence, Fleur was tempted to persuade her to stay. It was not easy saying farewell to the woman who had given her so much. For not only had Tante Estelle and Oncle Charles taken her in when she had arrived on their doorstep with Thomas back in '89, they had placed her in the Trinité School. Their house in Caen, the wonderful library, the musical evenings, the play readings, had brought Fleur such happiness after the lonely months at Clerville. But in '91 when Oncle Charles had decided to leave France to join the King's brothers in Coblenz, her world disintegrated for a second time. As punishment for her uncle's desertion, the revolutionaries demanded everything he owned be surrendered to the state. She and Tante Estelle had been forced into the streets with muskets. Next day an order had been issued for their arrest and, forewarned by friends, they had left Caen for the hardship of Grimbosq.

'God keep you safe, *chère Tante*.' Fleur stepped back from the diligence moist-eyed, fearful she might never see her again. Although the travelling pass had been scrutinised without a comment, it would be inspected at least twenty times before the coach reached the disputed border district and Tante Estelle still had to contrive to pass across the enemy lines. 'Au revoir,' Fleur called out, wiping away her tears. It was not easy; like casting off in a longboat from the mother ship and watching her sail away, and yet Fleur also felt a wondrous sense of liberation.

Fleur drove herself like a galley slave for the rest of the morning, mostly because she felt guilty that she had impelled Tante Estelle to depart, and partly because the trickle of creditors dirtying the doorstep was increasing to a flood. Leaving an obliging M. Beugneux to fob them off in his distrait fashion, Fleur escaped with Thomas to inspect the Chat Rouge.

Even seeing the café in the déshabillé of daylight, Thomas began to stride around the cutting block in the kitchen, his mind cooking up the future, while Fleur scuffed the mouse droppings under the cupboard with the back of her heel and watched him in delighted relief. His enthusiasm was no surprise. After helping run an all-weather, sausage stall at Bayeux, management of a Paris café was definitely a carrot worth munching.

Fleur spent the rest of the rainy afternoon trotting after him through puddles at the Parisian produce markets until they finally surrendered to complaints from sore feet and decadently indulged in hot chocolate and crêpes on the Pont-Neuf. A good place to debate whether the Chat Rouge could afford to serve more substantial fare such as *tourte de saumon frais* or *rognons de mouton au vin de Champagne*, for the plethora of cafés along the boulevards and the Palais Royal arcades provoked daunting comparisons. It would mean increasing her debts by a hundredfold. Dare she risk it? Unlike his holy namesake, however, Thomas had no doubts. Parisians were going to taste the cuisine of la belle Normandie as they never had before, and what was more, they were going to adore it. *Vachement!*

Nor was the next day spent idling. Thomas, almost as round as he was high, made a formidable bodyguard for Fleur and the slight M. Mansart when they visited the tenements occupied by M. Bosanquet's lace-makers. Fleur's exuberance might have been a trifle optimistic but she promised her employees that if she could make the Chat Rouge a prosperous concern, she would give them not only work but bonuses. Meantime, if they would be prepared to leave the bobbined blonde silk at home, they might come and help Thomas prepare the café in exchange for a hearty meal and provisions to take back to their families. Paris, it seemed, was one great rumbling stomach. One day, if she had the means, Fleur vowed, she would ladle out broth to the hungry mothers of the Marais. She knew what it was like always to be ravenous.

After these negotiations she hastened to attend the late afternoon session of the Jacobin Club. This time she sat in the gallery, close to the rostrum, and paid meticulous attention to the speakers, who included the popular deputy from Arras, Robespierre. He was as neat as he had been at the Convention. The revers of his slate-blue summer coat leafed a white organdie stock, and his hair was scrolled and powdered. The heavy lidded eyes behind the spectacles noticed everything. Such thick lenses did not compliment him (without them, some would have accounted him handsome) but were in service as his weapon and his shield. He hid behind his spectacles yet punctuated statements by removing them, staring intently at his listeners and then putting the glasses back on to continue. Interesting. Maybe, thought Fleur, she should seek out a *lunetier* and order some spectacles to make her new persona seem older and more bourgeois.

Deputy de Villaret was missing from the throng, thank goodness, for she was too tired to engage in any fire across his bows. At least, not yet – but her idea was growing like warm yeast.

M. Beugneux was still up on her return and together they sat with Thomas drinking the last of the chocolate at the kitchen table. Her gentleman boarder was brimful with gossipy anecdotes about many of the deputies and encouraged Fleur when she mimicked Robespierre. Tante Estelle would have been quite horrified but Fleur was growing more elated by the moment. This was indeed freedom.

'*Tiens*,' Thomas exclaimed eventually, mopping tears of laughter from the fans of creases around his eyes, and departed for his bedchamber.

Fleur lit her candle for the stairs and then remembered her manners. 'I have not had a chance to thank you properly for my aunt's pass, Monsieur Beugneux.' Tiptoes were required to reach his altitude and bestow a kiss on his cheek.

'Self-interest, madame.' The face, crinkled like an ageing mushroom, smiled wickedly. 'Either she w-went or I did. Besides, I think it was t-time you slid free of your nursery reins, little one. The Chat Rouge will miaow again, hmm?'

It would have been respectable to digest such sentiments with disapproval, shock even, but Fleur was too honest for that. 'I shall not ask you how you acquired the pass then,' she said sensibly and took up the candlestick.

'A moment, if you p-please. You have been kinder than I could deserve or expect. I-I would b-be highly honoured if you were to consider me family, Madame Bosanquet. I feel sure poor Matthieu would have approved.'

Why not? She was free to do so without Tante Estelle to huff and complain. Having lost so many relatives, it was refreshing to acquire one. 'Of course,' she beamed.

'And I may call you Fleur?'

She held out her free hand. 'Consider it agreed.' He raised her fingers to his lips.

'Madame, I shall do all in my power to be your liegeman.' How quaint. She was smiling as she climbed the stairs. 'Fleur . . .' She turned. 'Now I understand why Matthieu did what he did. Pardon my frankness, but permit me to say that although you may look like a mademoiselle from the provinces, you think like a true Parisian.'

The muse is a temperamental caller. Sometimes she leaves a visiting card and does not return for days. Searching for the elusive creature, Fleur spent all next day at the Convention and blunted several quills that evening at the secretaire with Machiavelli curled about her chair-back.

'Monsieur Beugneux?' She rearranged the python and sighed with the weariness of self-doubt. 'The café needs to offer an entertainment that will set tongues wagging. What do you think of this?'

The day's broadsheets were set aside as he leaned over and accepted her notes. He read swiftly and then, setting his pince-nez aside, ran a finger inside the neck of his needle-point jabot as if it were choking him. An unusual gesture for a man of his sensibility.

'My dear,' he said gently, 'if you are intent on pulling these tails – which I suspect you are – have a care. Is not excellent food enough?'

'Omelettes and eggs,' replied Fleur, receiving back her fistful of notes.

'Breaking eggs, yes, I understand, but people are touchy, little one. They may prefer to break us instead.'

Next day, the actors were in turn amazed, enthused and incapable. Fleur was not sure whether it was keeping their liberty that concerned them or whether they all found her inspiration for the opening night beyond their collective abilities.

'No, no, I really meant like this,' exclaimed Fleur, joining Juanita – Waterspout – on the little stage. It was easier to show than explain all over again since most of what she was suggesting lay in silent mimicry. The audience of M. Beugneux and the other thespians made no effort to interrupt. They applauded with old-fashioned handclapping when she was done and glanced from one to the other.

'Well?' pleaded the new proprietress, searching their expressions for the real verdict.

'Dear madame,' began Whiskers and then he

looked to where M. Beugneux sat, one hand resting elegantly upon his walking cane. In fact, they were all looking at him.

The white face crumpled in surrender and he cleared his throat. Curiously, in this company M. Beugneux's stammer was almost gone. 'W-what you have just done, my dear Madame Bosanquet, was remarkable, quite remarkable. You demonstrate a keen and, dare I say, somewhat cruel eye for the foibles of those who seek to rule our destinies. The performance you are suggesting will bring Paris flocking. It may also bring about the café's closure and your incarceration. If, however, you can avoid this for several performances and then return your patrons to entertainment somewhat blander by comparison, you will have made sufficient money to keep the café going for a further week and –'

'And by then everyone will know of the excellence of my terrines and lobsters.' Thomas joined them, wiping his hands on the cloth aproning his huge stomach.

'A star danced when you were born, madame.' Beanpole kissed his fingers to Fleur.

'Was that consent then?' She rather thought it was but restrained herself; employers were not supposed to bounce with excitement. 'Bien! Which of you will play the part?'

Why were they all staring at her with that mixture of compassion and indulgence?

'Oh, my dear,' M. Beugneux told her with pity, 'nobody can – except you!'

❦

'But it is Saturday night, de Villaret.'

Raoul moved the Palais de Justice ink pot, that was still rebelliously flaunting a royal fleur-de-lis, out of the way of Hérault's breeches. His visitor had annoyingly made himself comfortable on the edge of the desk, which having belonged previously to a *ci-devant* economist, creaked in despair.

'Saturday night,' repeated Hérault, fiddling with the writing quills, 'but I daresay that fact has escaped you. Leave this. Have some amusement Paris is full of music and laughter tonight. You need a woman and I have found just the one for you.'

Shifting his attention from the dispatch from M. Esnault, Raoul raised a disbelieving eyebrow. 'My dear Hérault, I can find my own women.' Like the intriguing widow, if only she would let him close enough to snare her tailfeathers instead of scurrying away whenever he so much as glanced in her direction.

His attention returned to Esnault's letter; the abbé who had officiated at Bosanquet's funeral was a nonjuring priest who had been on the run for the last few months. Not only was this exceedingly curious, but Esnault stated that there been no other reports of robbery along the stretch of road where Bosanquet had been attacked – at least not in recent months. Nor, it seemed, had M. Bosanquet made any mention to his acquaintances in Caen of an approaching marriage the previous year when he had visited his mother's grave.

'De Villaret!'

'All right, Hérault, what's this one's name?'

'La Coquette. *Incroyable! Piquante!*' He blew on his fingers meaningfully. 'No, do not make a face. I saw her perform at the Chat Rouge last night. It is under new management, and they are really most innovative.'

'Don't tell me – the Dance of the Seven Tricolores?' Raoul drawled, pelting a loose rosette at Hérault, who held it against his chest and wriggled like a full-breasted Salome.

'Ha, very patriotic, de Villaret.' He cast it back against Raoul's unshaven chin. 'You should suggest it to Madame Roland. She can wear them for Buzot. I admit . . .' He stretched his noble frame and yawned. 'I admit there is the usual pink tights and spangles fare provided afterwards – as tepid as bathing at Nice in July – but it is the main performance that had me riveted. This new actress, La Coquette, is an amazing mimic. One of the best acts I have ever seen, and I insist you come along tonight. I doubt they will run the show for more than a few evenings, it is so damnably risqué. Tell you what, if La Coquette does not astound you, we will both get disgustingly drunk at my expense. I've reserved a table.' He picked up a copying trellis and stretched it into a straight line.

'I don't like that playful expression of yours, Hérault. You remind me of a Frans Hals portrait.' The smirky cavalier came to mind. 'And there is more to interest me here, believe me.' He slapped a hand upon Esnault's report. 'No, I leave La Coquette to you, my dear fellow.'

Hérault lifted his hands in questionable generosity. 'Oh, I have another little chicken to pursue. La Coquette is unquestionably *yours*.'

8

Dearest Marie-Anne,
I find myself provoking an enemy whom I should
avoid at all costs. I can only surmise there must be an
unfortunate recklessness in my character . . .

EXTRACT FROM THE LETTERS OF FRANÇOISE-ANTOINETTE DE

MONTBULLIOU, 1793

'Is anyone going to tell her?' Columbine asked Juanita, who was wreaking havoc on Fleur's rib cage as she drew tight the laces that secured the whalebones. Wearing a panniered dress on stage required fortitude.

'Tell me what?' gasped Fleur, losing hold of the dressing table and nearly sending all three of them toppling against the rack of the dressing-room.

The candles around the greasepots danced with the breeze of the girls' muffled shrieks. 'Tell me,' echoed the image in the mirror.

Columbine, unfeathered for once, looked far too secretive. 'Just that Citizen Hérault declared to half the Convention yesterday that Thomas was a *chef extraordinaire*.'

'And we have run out of seats and sauce à la Calvados, I suppose,' finished Fleur. 'That was not what you were going to say at all, Columbine.'

'No,' giggled Columbine, 'but I will tell you . . . *later*.'

Across from Raoul, Hérault freed the multiple flounces of his cravat from the protection of the napkin and wiped his fingers. 'Were those not the best *coquilles Saint-Jacques* you have ever tasted?'

It was necessary to shout the reply above the noise of the other patrons of the Chat Rouge since every bench and stool was occupied. Even the fleas would soon be reduced to standing room.

'Indeed, Hérault, I am sure they would taste even better if you had *la belle* Adéle lined up as a dessert.'

'Ah but I have a change of menu in mind.' Hérault stared about the restaurant as if seeking someone, and with a shrug of resignation returned his attention to Raoul with a laconic smile. 'It is your just *dessert* I was considering when I brought you here, *mon ami*. This is where the night becomes truly interesting.'

'Really?' Raoul had found the entertainment so

far pleasant but unremarkable, yet he had to admit that the mood of the evening was already beginning to change. Perhaps there was some truth to *électricité*, the substance the farmer-general Lavoisier claimed lurked invisibly in the air, for he could sense the growing excitement emanating around him. The well-fed, excellently wined audience – and Hérault seemed to be acquainted with half of them, judging by the nods and grins – was thrumming with anticipation. Around them, the waiters were snuffing out most of the table candelabra. Along the little stage, Argentan lamps flickered into obedience for the second act of the evening.

A drum roll hushed the entire café and then a woman swept out from behind the screen.

'La Coquette,' whispered Hérault. '*Diable*, I wish the lighting were less grotesque.' Then he, like everyone else, forgot to breathe.

Creamy breasts rose from the actress's tight corsage in beauteous sufficiency to provoke every male into lip-moisturing silence. A black velvet ribbon enhanced the beauty of her throat, but the rest of her appearance was little to Raoul's taste. He disliked the fussiness of the former Versailles fashions: the gross panniers upholding creamy skirts of some sort of silky fabric threaded with gold, the lead-white complexion, the rouged cheeks, the unnecessary beauty spots and the powdered, ridiculously towering hairstyle made famous by Marie Antoinette.

What followed was a satire on the ancien régime. The girl aped the mannerisms of the defunct aristocracy like one born to it. Although Raoul grinned like everyone else, the performance was predictable pap for an audience that would be wise to snigger.

Warming to her spectators, La Coquette grew more personal. Her victim was not the imprisoned Marie Antoinette but the new uncrowned queen, Manon Roland. Raoul drew a breath. The audience tensed at her antics and then guffawed heartily.

'By God,' muttered Raoul, laughing. He himself had visited the Rolands' house and seen the dame des Girondins sewing or writing letters, not saying a word but eavesdropping intently on what was being said. 'Manon will not be amused when she hears of this. This creature has her pilloried.'

'I told you the girl was remarkable. I hope she repeats last night's performance.'

The actress disappeared behind a screen painted with pretty nymphs. 'Encore!' roared her audience, thumping the tables, splattering the dripping wax. The whiskered drummer stood beside the proscenium, drawing emotions from the taut skin of his drum. Surprise, shock, laughter beat out from his sticks and shone on his greasy, lugubrious cheeks as out towards him fluttered a silken stocking. Its partner followed. Ribbons slunk and garters crawled like pretty insects over the top of the screen. The powdered headdress, reanimated, fought with the quarrelsome fan above the heads of the naked nymphs. Petticoats, tossed over the top, were gathered up by a stooping, rebellious, blonde maid-servant who found herself attacked in the rear by naked panniers that had suddenly taken on an aggressive masculinity.

The drumming subsided to a waiting beat as the harassed maid carried in a hat stand laden with garments, and then the rhythm gathered new momentum. From behind the screen to a crescendo of sound came La Coquette – or at least Raoul assumed it must be her – this time in breeches, shirt and jacket. White paint still disguised her face in garish fashion and her short hair was so sleeked and dark with pomade that it was impossible to guess at her true colouring. Despite her slight form, she moved so like a man that Raoul began to suppose her of ambiguous gender and wondered if he had imagined the pretty cleavage and that was why Hérault had dragged him here – to play a jest. A Le Coquet, perhaps? Or were there two of them? A brother and sister?

First of all, the young actress exchanged the jacket for a striped waistcoat, queued wig and spectacles, peering at the audience warily from behind heavy round frames and thick lenses. Max Robespierre, the fastidious luminary of the Jacobins and champion of the people! First Manon, now Max! Raoul's interest quickened. This was dangerous entertainment.

On stage, the false Max yawned and closed an imaginary door behind him, turned the invisible key and then slid a top bolt in, turned, hesitated, turned back and slid the bottom bolt too. Then he stepped away, paused, and swung back, testing the latch. Next he began miming the practising of a speech, using the spectacles in perfect mimicry. The audience loved it. La Coquette was good, very good.

Then it was Danton's turn. This time the actress tied on a wax mask – a wonderful replica of Danton's pockmarked cheeks and bullish expression – Mlle Grosholz's handiwork from the waxworks on the Boulevard du Temple, perhaps? Oh, very resourceful! And the tousled wig looked just like Danton's tangled, unruly hair. Pretending she was at the lectern of the Convention, La Coquette thundered out in mime a rousing speech, pausing occasionally to ogle the gallery.

Then this character, too, was discarded with the mask. Who next? Raoul waited in anticipation, enjoying himself hugely. This was better than the milk-and-water melodrama the other theatres put on. The performer slid her arms into a dark blue coat and exchanged her unkempt hairpiece for a dark, unpowdered wig and turned to sternly peruse the audience. Another deputy, but who? Her arm slid along the edge of the invisible lectern and a silent speech began. Now and then she raised her other hand to thrust back the lock of hair that had been deliberately loosened from the velvet bow. This deputy paused in his speech to take formidable note of his listeners' faces. The patrons around the café were awed, too, by the power of the actress's gaze and then suddenly they began to chuckle. At the laughter La Coquette gave a broad, open-mouthed smile at the imaginary gallery and a lift of eyebrows. Why was everyone finding it so

amusing? Raoul had not worked out who . . .
Hérault was doubled with laughter. And then the
performer raised two hands behind her head and
flapped them. Some sort of rabbit?

'Who is she supposed to –?'

'You, you ass.' Hérault clouted him in the chest.

In disbelief, Raoul glanced about him and saw
the spluttering audience at the nearest tables were
watching for his reaction. Nonplussed, he looked
back to the tiny stage. The laughter was no longer
directed there. As if she suddenly realised one of
her victims was present, a brief expression of panic
furrowed La Coquette's white forehead. For an
instant, she seemed to lose control.

Serve her right, thought Raoul, but now she
was looking to where he sat and suddenly, brilliantly, she was back in the saddle and reining the
audience in. Is he there? her expression asked them
and they roared out: '*Oui!*'

She bit her lip, then the red slash of a mouth
became sickle-shaped with exaggerated embarrassment and she made a cravat of her hands against
her throat, glancing from side to side. You can take
a joke, her eyes told him, sparkling with mischief,
then she appeared agitated again, as if by his reaction. For an instant she began to walk away, then
came back to centre stage. White-gloved hands
gestured to her bosom. Who, me? No, it wasn't me.
The red mouth squashed into a rosette, pouting
once more in his direction, the eyes sheepish and
then provocative.

Then she forgot him, disappeared round the

screen, and re-emerged with a thunderous expression and a red band around her forehead and a copy of the gutter *L'Ami du Peuple* in her hand – Marat. Christ! Was she crazy!

Raoul missed the subtleties of the performance that followed. He was still reeling. Was that how he looked when he spoke in public? So formidable?

His friend leaned close. 'What do you think of her? Brilliant, eh? Has you in a pickle jar, *hein*?'

'It's seditious.'

'Absolutely!'

'Who owns this place?' The sharp whisper had made rich men tremble.

'Why, none other than the little widow we rescued from the mob.' Hérault's glass lingered near his lips as though he was savouring more than the wine. Raoul set his down swiftly before he spilt it. 'Don't trespass there, *mon ami*,' his companion was saying. 'La Veuve Bosanquet is in debt to me up to her pretty neck and I intend to enjoy each delicious reimbursement.'

'Dangerous pickings.' Raoul's voice was cruel. 'Marat could mince her and her actress to bloody pieces for this.' But Hérault could not hear him; La Coquette had finished her act. It was no longer acceptable for Parisians to clap. Instead, shouts of 'Bravo!' filled the restaurant. Her admirers slapped the tables. They emptied the juddering vases. Dripping flowers hurtled at her feet. Who was she/he?

Raoul suddenly felt used, sullied, as though some hidden voyeur had been watching him all week. Aware he was still observed by those around him, he leaned back nonchalantly, resting his chin on clasped fingers. 'I could have the woman in prison for this,' he repeated, his smile barely skin-deep.

'Or you could have her in your bed,' chuckled Hérault, leaning closer. 'A most exquisite and highly preferable revenge.'

'I suppose now you will tell me that La Coquette is a boy?'

'Seduce her and find out!' The flat of Hérault's hand shook the glasses. 'Encore! Encore!'

Behind the screen, Fleur was shaking as Columbine put an arm round her and ushered her quickly out to where Juanita was waiting with her mourning clothes. She was glad of their busy fingers tugging off her shirt and unwinding the bands, for she was incapable of managing for herself.

'Encore!' The shouts had not subsided and she darted a panicked look towards the outer door.

'Always leave 'em wanting more,' giggled Columbine.

'Is she decent?' Whiskers – Albert – made his entrance, his face in rapture. '*Incroyable!*'

'*Fabuloso* yet again!' Raymond, the taller of her two actors, plastered Fleur's hand with a kiss, while Juanita hastily wiped the white disguise away and Columbine slid a curled brown wig clothed with a black bonnet and mantilla over La Coquette's oiled-smooth hair.

'Citizen de Villaret is out there!' Fleur blurted to M. Beugneux, who had just come in. Fear was smashing about inside her like a panicked bird, but he seemed quite unruffled by the announcement; in fact, the deep lines around his mouth twitched into a thin smile.

'Yes, I am afraid Citizen Hérault is responsible, my dear. I fear we neglected to tell you he admired your performance last night.'

Fleur suppressed an unladylike expletive. Admired her performance? And brought his friend along so he might gloat and whisper: '*There goes the widow mouse. I only have to reach out my paw for her.*' De Villaret, of all people! Did he have a sense of humour? She doubted it. *Nom d'un chien!* What would he do to her and the café?

'May I say you were unquestionably *magnifique*, madame.' M. Beugneux bowed over her hand with all the charm of a Versailles courtier. 'Do not show fear, *petite*,' he muttered beneath his breath. The blue eyes flicked sideways to Juanita and Columbine. He was right. It would not do for patrons to hear hysterics from behind the stage.

'I had a good teacher, monsieur,' Fleur said cheerfully with a deep curtsy, keeping her wits. '*Merci*, a thousandfold.'

Beneath the veneer of stammers and almost melodramatic emotion, M. Beugneux was proving a man of surprises. It was to his tutoring she owed the polish of her mimicry of Mme Roland, Max Robespierre and Jean-Paul Marat.

The sudden rattle of the outside doorhandle startled her. For an instant she was terrified that an angry Raoul de Villaret would force his way in, but the booming voice belonged to Thomas.

'You have done it, *ma belle*!' her chef exclaimed, manoeuvring his bulk through the door, his fist encircling a bottle of the sparkling *vin de Champagne*. 'We have had to turn people away. The place is as crammed as a miser's cellar.'

'Ah, you should have seen de Villaret's expression, *patronne*,' threw in Albert. 'That gorgeously fierce jaw nearly hit the floor.' He mimicked de Villaret's astonished expression and had Fleur close to hysteria.

'Oh, was that de Villaret?' exclaimed Thomas, his expression sobering and he regarded his *patronne* with a brief, sudden sobriety before the dimpled smile resurfaced. Then he kissed her on both cheeks and lifted her into the air.

The rented room, stifled all day, took a breath as Raoul flung open the windows. The impertinent night breeze, pleasured by the warble of a nightingale from a neighbouring courtyard, shouldered the curtains apart and riffled thoughtlessly through the letters on his bureau. For a moment Raoul stood on the tiny iron balcony above the Rue Saint-Antoine, staring unseeing at the veiled moon, and then he closed out the noises of the world. There was enough light from the street oil lamps to assist his undressing but Raoul struck a flint to the entire candelabra that presided over his quills and ink pots. Too lazy to climb the stairs to his studio, he tipped out his pen tray and found the stick of charcoal. Humming, he drew out the sketch of the Widow Bosanquet from his writing desk drawer and, selecting a fresh page in his sketchbook, made a drawing of La Coquette. Then, with a soft laugh, he ripped it out and placed the two side by side.

Had M. Bosanquet engaged in receiving goods that had, well, shall one say, avoided the tolls and fees of the farmers-general under the monarchy, or the taxes of the new regime? Goods that had conveniently fallen off the back of carts? Such thoughts had briefly flittered through Fleur's mind as she had been hastened, euphoric with champagne and cheap triumph, through the cellar of the café to surface magically among some derelict looms in the basement of a tenement in the next street.

The purpose of the journey, which she scarcely remembered, was to circumnavigate the attentions of a certain pair of deputies, one drunk, the other broodingly sober. This was explained to her calmly by M. Beugneux over breakfast next morning as he poured her a third cup of coffee before M. Mansart arrived. She was on no account to reveal the cellar's concealed exit to anyone. Fleur, her temples throbbing, concurred.

A half-hour later a jubilant M. Mansart was despatched to the Convention to pay off an instalment of the debt owed to Hérault de Séchelles, and the new proprietress of the Chat Rouge, her colour less pasty now, set out with M. Beugneux for her new El Dorado.

The news that one of the small panes of the café window had been broken and a crumpled newspaper thrust through accompanied by a firebrand, cleared any remaining haziness from Fleur's mind. It was fortunate one of the kitchenhands who was now sleeping on the premises had still been awake and had swiftly tugged down the flaming curtain and beaten out the fire. Well, if they now had patrons, they certainly had enemies. She brazened out the news before her kitchen staff of former lace-makers with an optimism that was becoming more fragile by the minute. Finally, Thomas made her a small, steel-strength coffee and urged M. Beugneux to escort her home.

Was Felix Quettehou behind the fire? she wondered silently as they began their walk back. A rival proprietor, perhaps? De Villaret? Surely not. She doubted spitefulness was one of his vices.

'*Mon Dieu!*' hissed M. Beugneux, and Fleur started in panic as a coach braked beside them and two national guard sprang down from the running board.

'Inside, if you please, citizeness. Not you, old man! Just the woman!'

Oh, dear God! Well, it had been a calculated risk and now she must pay for her sedition. But it was too soon, just when she had begun to taste some sweetness again in life. Which of the deputies lacked a sense of humour? Or was it Mme Roland, the bourgeois *eminence grise* behind the current government? What penalty would be exacted? The carriage ride today and the scaffold within a week? Or would she be thrust into some prison cell to languish for her audacity?

Poker-backed, she closed her eyes and tried to think clearly how she must defend herself. However, the vehicle halted just before the end of the Rue de Sévigné. Fleur's eyes flashed wide as the door opened and a man stepped lightly in and rapped for the driver to proceed.

'I thought you might prefer this to being questioned at my office adjoining the tribunal,' Raoul de Villaret murmured coolly as he removed his high-crowned hat, tossed it onto the seat beside him and leaned back against the leather cushions opposite her. It was easier to stare at the long fingers clasped around the metal top of his swordstick than to dare read his face.

Inwardly Fleur loaded the powder and readied the guns. Outwardly, she regarded him with dislike. 'I have no idea what this is about, citizen,' she answered serenely, and took an unreasonable interest in a passing cart.

'I trust your affairs in Caen are well in hand?'

That startled her into looking across at her inquisitor. 'Citizen?'

'I understood inquiries were being made in order to apprehend the brigands who attacked your husband. I received a report yesterday afternoon.' So it was not about last night. Oh my God, but yes, it was – he had sent the carriage to collect her at the Chat Rouge. He had known she would be there. So he now had a two-pronged fork to jab her with! Pray heaven, he did not know she was La Coquette!

'There was certainly no need for Citizen Fournay

to bother himself with the matter, Citizen de Villaret. My husband was quite coherent before he died and guessed who was responsible, and I assure you he did not blame anyone in Caen.'

'Oh, it is not Fournay who is concerning himself. It is Citizen Esnault.'

Damn Esnault! And damn this man! He had noticed her hands tighten in her lap. 'I have only met the gentleman once,' she said calmly, forcing herself to appear at ease. 'He was an old schoolfriend of my husband.'

'I understand he witnessed Matthieu Bosanquet's will?'

'I am not sure of the purpose of this conversation, Citizen de Villaret, but if Citizen Esnault – or you, for that matter – are implying that I somehow *compelled* Matthieu into leaving me his worldly goods, the answer is no. I find myself in debt to here.' She tapped her high black collar. 'My late husband enjoyed a gamble, not at the gaming tables but in business. Of late, because times are so changeable, he did not do well. Ask Citizen Hérault. He is my husband's major debtor.'

The clever eyes regarding her conceded nothing. Indeed his jaw hardened. Did he believe her?

'Were you and Monsieur Bosanquet acquainted for long before your marriage?'

'That is none of your business, citizen.'

'I could make it so.' Oh, he was playing with her, the sudden velvet of his voice contrary to his words. Did a doe in the forest recognise the intent gleam of a different hunt in a stag's eyes? Fleur did now, looking into the face of the man opposite her. The sudden smile as he leaned forward held infinitely more danger than an unbuttoned rapier. 'You provoke interest, citizeness.'

'Maybe, but I certainly do not seek it.' Not from you, her glance told him but something deep inside her was opening. 'And let me return this.' Her fingers fumbled through her skirt to her pocket and drew out the catapult. 'I have no idea what you meant by presenting it to me. Perhaps I am missing out on some peculiar form of Parisian humour.'

He took it from her and sat back, testing the leather thongs that tethered the sling, but his gaze did not leave her face. 'Not a pocket mirror nor needle case for you, madame, but a lethal toy.'

In other circumstances, she might have found the implication amusing, even flattering. 'Why should you imagine it is mine?' He was silent, watching her. 'I am not a murderess.'

'Money can commission villainy.' He allowed that to sink in, and, unnerved by his silence, she abruptly turned her head to the half-open window and leaned her chin upon her glove.

'How old are you? Not twenty-three, I suspect.'

'What difference does it make?' she retorted. 'You want some sort of confession. Very well, I shoot cats like the guillotined king once did and I strangled the rest of the nursery when I was three.'

'You must have had phenomenal strength.' His eyes examined her with appreciation. 'Wouldn't it have been easier to nudge them out of the cribs like cuckoos do?' The humour was brief. He was back to playing Torquemada. 'I asked, how old are you?'

'A hundred and four! Will that acquit me?'

'Citizeness!' His tone turned staccato. '*How old are you?*'

Fleur glared at him. 'Nearly twenty. *Why?*'

'Nineteen, then,' the cool voice corrected, replete. 'Thank you.'

Refusing to turn her head, she paid his tardy politeness with an icy nod.

'I understand you are the new owner of the Chat Rouge.'

In the street, the buildings ran by swiftly like sand through a minute glass.

'You are going to close me down.'

'Oh yes, I could do that.' There was a serrated tone beneath the refusal to commit. So he intended to make her pay for last night's mockery.

'Is it *livres* you require, Monsieur de Villaret, like your friend Hérault? Or is it to be something less obvious to placate your Jacobin morality.' With a lift of chin, she pretended to note the upper windows of the passing tenements.

'What do you take me for, widow?'

Well, that certainly hit, but the silence which followed maddened her. 'Then what is it you want – oh!'

The window shutter slammed down beside her.

'I want your full attention, citizeness.' De Villaret withdrew his hand slowly and sat back with languid ease, clearly gratified he had sent her pulses racing. 'What do you suppose would please me?' The white teeth were almost clenched.

'A-a sense of humour?' she suggested courageously.

'Very good, but not the right answer.'

Fleur's breath refused to grow even.

He leaned forward. 'La Coquette.' Oh, *nom d'un chien*! So he was only after the actress. Relief should have flooded through her aristocratic veins but instead she felt thrown aside. How could he prefer a painted houri to the *ci-devant* Mlle de Montbulliou? Astonished at her own feelings, she could only blink at him.

'L-La Coquette?' she echoed bleakly.

'A meeting with La Coquette – tonight. Those are my terms.'

'W-what if she refuses?' *Show the dogs you are not afraid.* 'As-as her employer, I have the duty to protect her.'

He burst out laughing. 'Nineteen and an abbess already! No, do not bridle so. I do not mean to insult you.' The brown eyes sparkled roguishly. 'Of course, I merely wish to impress upon your actress that she is playing with fire. So are you!' Steel rasped through his voice again. 'As I say, arrange a rendezvous for me, or,' he lifted the top of his cane and poised it to knock the driver's panel, 'it will be so easy to incarcerate you in the nearest prison and send your theatre troupe to join you.' He smiled at her panic. 'No? Not yet?' The cane was lowered. 'In that case, I should be very careful which deputies you permit La Coquette to mock in future. Word spreads like fire in this hayloft of a city. Danton will be amused, I'm sure – I know him well enough to make that forecast – but Marat could destroy you in a paragraph, even send the rabble to find you . . . or perhaps he has already? I believe you had a fire.'

The fire! Yes, she had recklessly challenged half of Paris. Later she would deal with that. Now she was alone in a coach with Raoul de Villaret and out of her depth. So La Coquette had embarrassed him. Well, that was something. Out loud she asked: 'And you? Were you *amused*, Citizen de Villaret?'

The well-clad shoulders shrugged. 'I thought La Coq–' He broke off and gave her a sharp look. 'You were there, were you?'

Damnation! 'N-no, but I'm told that –'

'You were there, citizeness,' he declared emphatically, 'counting the takings, I expect.'

She sprang to her feet and rapped against the coach with her palm. But he caught her wrist and thrust her down.

'Since this is an unofficial meeting, I have no need to listen to any more of your insults,' she seethed.

'Who said it was unofficial?' She struggled but his grip was strong. 'I seem to remember rescuing you several times, you ungrateful girl. Perhaps you would like to face the mob again. Crowds are very easily arranged and lampposts are plentiful. Ouuch!'

Having kicked him hard, Fleur collapsed fuming on the seat, curling her toes with the pain. Raoul de Villaret was gazing at her with what

186

looked suspiciously like a desire to put her across his knee.

'V-very well,' she exclaimed, before he could acquire a fondness for the notion. 'I will speak with La Coquette. I shall tell him to expect you at the café before tonight's performance.'

'*Him!* A nice try, citizeness.' Smiling, he pulled open the flap and ordered the coachman to let him down. 'Until this evening, then,' he murmured, lifting his hat mockingly. 'Take her back to Rue de Sévigné. The exercise will do her good.'

'Adieu, you *salaud*,' she muttered angrily, subsiding against the seat-back, forgetting the driver's flap was still open.

'Congratulations, citizeness.' A lone eye peered in at her and a rumble of a chuckle reached her. 'Most passengers only go one way.'

In a towering, pomaded wig dusted with powder of orris and crushed cuttlebone and decorated with a three-masted ship, make-up that made her look as though she had sneezed in a flour sack, sufficient eau de Cologne to drench a four-storey brothel and side panniers beneath her skirts that would not let a licentious man come broadside, Fleur paced up and down the theatre dressing-room. Columbine and Juanita had enthusiastically offered to stand in for her with de Villaret, but as Thomas pointed out, Juanita was too tall and even a stupid man would notice that. As for Columbine, she would reel him in and Fleur wanted to get rid of the man, not have him hanging around the premises penning lovesick poems to bits of Columbine's anatomy. Not that the Jacobin was capable of writing anything except arrest warrants.

Monseigneur-High-and-Mighty-Deputy de Villaret was late, probably deliberately so, curse him. Well, if they started slapping the tables out there for her, it would be his loss. Why was her heart thumping so? *Ciel*, her nerves were jangling worse than when she had made her stage debut, and, oh, she must keep her voice low and flirtatious.

As she heard de Villaret's voice outside the door, she instinctively stepped back. Rain spangled the greatcoat and beaver of the deputy, who let himself in without knocking. If for an instant he seemed assaulted by the hurricane of scent that must have hit him full-face, he did not let it show and closed the door behind him.

The cluttered room seemed diminished by his being there and she sensed the very air grow taut with anticipation. Realising her hand was clenched tightly about her hairbrush, Fleur willed herself to set it down with nonchalance. Picking up her plumed fan instead – the feminine weapon and buckler of the ancien régime – she unfurled it and fanned irritably as if his presence was heating the room to an intolerable degree. He seemed not to mind; the golden eyes studied her as though she was an insect encased in amber, then he remembered his manners.

'*Mademoiselle, je suis enchanté.*' He stepped forward and carried her reluctant hand to his lips. A libertine flourish. Who was she dealing with? A profligate who professed sober republican virtues, or was she witnessing an abrupt uncloaking of a puritan chrysalis into a dissolute moth?

'*Mais non*,' she trilled, fan aflutter. 'I am the one who is flattered. You liked my performance last night, then, citizen?'

His mouth curled, giving a glimpse of fine white teeth, but the man's eyes burned with a cold fire. 'My dear mademoiselle, I am sure you could perform brilliantly *anywhere*.'

Rake! Her palm itched to slap that challenging smile.

'It depends on how *appreciative* my audience is,' she found herself saying recklessly and brought her lashes down like a veil against him. 'I understand from Madame Bosanquet that you are here out of regard for my safety. How very brave of you.'

'I wish merely to point out that there are less dangerous ways to earn a living, citizeness.'

Was there an offer hidden in those simple words? Fleur had enjoyed no apprenticeship in flirting like her sisters had, but feminine instinct, and that suspicious tautening between her thighs, recognised the hunter circling closer now. Trying to keep her hand steady, she picked up the dish of sweetmeats an admirer had sent her, and held it out to de Villaret, but he shook his head. She placed an almond between her lips, an excuse not to answer.

He took the dish from her impatiently and nestled it back among the cosmetic pots. 'I congratulate you on your obvious talents, mademoiselle, but it only requires one of your victims, such as myself, to denounce you to the authorities for sedition and you will end up in La Pélagie.'

The prison for prostitutes. Fleur blanched inwardly and then her anger grew.

'Oh, citizen,' she purred, reaching out a lace-gloved finger to tease at his stock, 'I am positive you would make sure that no harm comes to La Coquette.'

Lazily his fingers fastened round hers and stroked upwards. 'That depends.'

She pulled away with a soft laugh and turned to her mirror, fastening the paste diamonds into her ears.

'How sweet that you can still blush beneath that appalling make-up, mademoiselle,' he commented dryly. 'Surely I cannot have embarrassed you.'

In the mirror she watched him move up behind her. Skilful hands closed in, parenthesising her small waist. She held her breath; a few inches more and he might touch her breasts, or at least the bared curves that thrust up above the stiff bodice. She desperately wanted to experience such a sensation. Her sisters had told her it was enjoyable, but the alert eyes of the man in the reflection were calculating, like a demon about to snatch a soul.

Instinctive modesty compelled her to set her hands restrainingly upon his cuffs, but with a swift flick of the wrist it was he who now had her arms gently imprisoned against her waist. 'It is so easy to make a prisoner of someone,' he murmured, drawing her shoulders to lean against him, 'in so many ways.' Again the ambiguity.

Something beyond the control of her mind made the rebel inside her quiver pleasurably at such subtle custody.

His lips brushed her shoulder. 'I should need some reward for my protection from now on, and this reckless sedition will have to cease.'

'Reward, citizen?' Her answer was a beguiling, sensual sigh.

'Tonight.' The man's words were a soft breath upon her cheek. La Coquette was hard put not to giggle; seducers were so deploringly predictable. 'After your performance, come to my table.' It was an imperious statement, which was easily translated into sheets or a chaise longue; undo a button here, a lace there. It reminded her of the necessity to flex her feminine strength in modest protest against the man who held her.

His hands released her. The sudden freedom left her desolate but Raoul de Villaret was not done. He adventured his palms upwards over the figured brocade to stroke his fingertips across her skin under the silk edge of her gown. It was unbelievably tantalising. For a breathless instant Fleur wished herself exposed to his touch, to his gaze, like a concubine to her master. He had hardly touched her and she wanted more, much more. But it was the actress La Coquette she was playing who was aflutter at such temptation; the hidden aristocrat must never lose control with the likes of this man. As de Villaret himself had warned: the rakes of Paris devoured innocents.

'Tonight? That depends,' La Coquette replied

huskily as she shrugged free. 'You must go, citizen. I have work to do.' She appraised her appalling reflection in the mirror and turned, flirtatiously tugging his watch from his waistcoat pocket to glance at its iridescent hands.

'So have I.' Another threat. He sternly withdrew the watch from her fingers and slid it into his pocket. 'I shall return later.'

'*Tiens.*' She made dimples of her cheeks, her voice a sultry murmur: 'I can fit you in between Doctor Marat and Citizen Danton but,' her lower lip quivered, 'I do ask how much protection one poor actress can need.'

Clearly he did not believe her. Admiration, dislike even, flickered in the depths of his golden eyes.

'Oh-hoo, madame, are you ready?' Columbine cooed through the keyhole. The latch rattled. 'Shall I signal your entrance, chérie?'

The spell was broken. The sorcerer released her. It was he who opened the door and with a questioning lift of brow demanded her signature to his unwritten treaty. La Coquette gave him a sultry look and an indifferent wriggle of her shoulder. Hidden behind the cosmetics, the duke's daughter thought herself safely immune. She set her sights beyond the open door, cleared her mind and nodded to Columbine. The drumming began.

It was dressed as the sombre, virtuous Widow Bosanquet that Fleur finally appeared beside the small table reserved for Citizen de Villaret in the shadows against the side wall. Unfortunately for him, he had been kept waiting a considerable time. On the other hand, only a few drowsy patrons remained to witness the imminent drama. He did not show courtesy by standing so she seated herself without his licence. Behind de Villaret's back, she glimpsed her acting troupe clustering at the serving bar to covertly watch her latest performance; the men in disbelief, the actresses in glee.

'You wish to say something, citoyenne? *Un coup de rouge?*' Male words. The empty, waiting wine-glass was pushed towards her; the carafe lifted with chill amusement.

'It seems you have been kept waiting to no avail.' Her fingers upturned the glass symbolically upon its bowl. 'I regret, sir, that this establishment is under new management and does not permit its performers to mingle with the customers.'

Surprisingly, he was not unpleasant. Instead, he drew a line in the tablecloth with his fingernail. 'I was led to believe the arrangement was agreeable to La Coquette.'

'My actresses are not *filles de nuit.*' Fleur rearranged her skirts like an annoyed dowager. 'You would need to inquire at her lodgings. What she does in her private life is her business, but in regard to her public life, as I told you this morning, she deserves my protection.' Dear God, he was right, she did sound like some indignant mother superior. 'In fact, how dare you assume that because she is an actress, she is beneath your respect? No doubt you intend to threaten her with imprisonment in La Pélagie if she refuses to sleep with you.'

She watched the man's eyebrows rise at her vehemence. 'How very noble of you, citizen. Has the Revolution not yet rid our society of such condescension and male bigotry? Oh, you make me so furious! Why do you not abolish the law that degrades these people?' She waved her hand towards the troupe. They were contriving to hold Thomas, now free from his kitchen, in lively conversation but they were still, out of both loyalty and self-preservation, keeping a wary eye on her. Their livelihood, after all, depended on her liberty. 'Are you listening to me, citizen?'

He seemed to be completely distracted by her chef's immense person.

'I beg your pardon,' he answered, and propped his chin upon his fist in deceptive obedience.

'No,' she continued, 'you would rather sneer at them and blackmail a talented actress into behaving like a harlot for your pleasure. Well, negotiate the needs of your pathetic life somewhere else. I will not have my theatre turned into a bordello. Close me down out of spite, if you desire. Now leave! My staff have to clean up the mess.'

It was as if she was implying the spilt wine and the stained tablecloths were his fault. Raoul de Villaret stared at her in fascination.

'Feeling better?' he asked, reaching for his hat.

'Didn't you listen to a word I said, citizen?' Fleur asked, miffed beyond endurance. His attention kept streaking sideways to her chef, or was it

Columbine who might serve as second best? Goodness, here she had been nerving herself to confront him and now the horrid man was not even bothered at having his arrangements aborted. 'Are you not . . . not displeased?' she demanded, tense hands clasped upon the cloth.

A foolish grin smudged the intelligent lines of cheek and brow. Was he too inebriated to rattle threats? 'No, citizeness.'

'Then kindly remove yourself, citizen.'

He skittered a handful of coins across the table and, humming, sauntered off into the cold April air.

Fleur shrugged at her employees and sank back on her chair with a sense of utter failure. It wasn't the end, but it wasn't a beginning either.

Raoul paused at the door to look back to where the girl still sat at the table. The actors had moved across and were leaning over her like children around a widowed parent but she was not answering them. Weariness spoke in the slender back drooping like a flower that needed sunlight and water.

'Goodnight, citizen. We must all get some sleep, *hein*?' Raoul swung round. The cook was holding open the door for him.

His voice surfaced coldly. 'The owner has certainly turned around the fortunes of this place, or is it down to you?'

The large jowls quivered. 'I'll tell you a secret, Deputy. You get some chopped garlic and butter and you heat it in a pan, eh? And then just before opening time you waft the pan around outside. La Coquette's the same. Gets the customers in. As for *la petite citoyenne* there, she is the heartbeat of us all.' The cheerful expression reassembled into sadder folds. 'Do not close us down, citizen; it was in good humour. We mean you and the Republic no harm.'

Raoul did not answer.

Outside the wind still blew like winter. He did not like being made a fool of, but the boy once belted by an angry duke had grown into a man who enjoyed being in control – of his own emotions and other people's.

Only nineteen!

His hands, achingly, remembered the slender, delightful feel of La Coquette, the delicate bones too easily discernible, the height of her against him. Treated it like a game, had she? Well, the game was only just beginning.

9

Your worst foes are amongst yourselves . . .

JEAN-PAUL MARAT, ADDRESS TO THE FRIENDS OF LIBERTY

Arriving early for a session of the Committee for General Security, Raoul made himself comfortable in an armchair next to the stove in the vestibule outside the committee room with a cup of coffee and a newspaper. Within seconds a confident hand batted the paper, and his old master, Jacques-Louis David, now an influential Jacobin deputy and the cultural spine of the Republic, tossed back his coat-tails and flung himself down in the chair opposite. Raoul nodded casually. David's scowls no longer daunted him.

'Bonjour, young Raoul. What a kerfuffle yesterday,

eh? A government warrant out for Marat's arrest! Serious stuff – inciting the people to murder and pillage, eh? You should have heard Robespierre huffing about it. Says they might as well indict the entire Mountain.'

It was respectful for Raoul to look attentive although he had been at the Convention when the motion had been carried. Serious business indeed! Like the vote on the King's fate, it was one of the few times each deputy had been required to stand up and announce to the gallery how he was voting, and now everyone knew who sided with the Girondin government and who supported Marat and Robespierre. His friend Armand had voted for the indictment, which now put him within the sights of the Mountain's verbal cannons.

'Separates the sheep from the goats.' Raoul shook his paper back into its folds and tossed it on the small table next to him.

'It's an all-out attack on us Jacobins, of course.' David brushed a finger to and fro across the indent of his chin as he always did when agitated. 'But, by God, it will force both sides of the Mountain into bed together.'

Raoul agreed; it would certainly unite any deputies – extreme as well as moderate – who felt the ministers had been half-hearted in consolidating the gains of the Revolution. 'Do you think they can make the charge stick?' he asked with a soupçon of deference. It was as well to keep his famous mentor sweet.

'First they have to catch Marat, don't they?' The

great master leaned forward confidentially, hands clapped upon the meeting of breeches and stockings. 'But, by the same token, there's a lot of people who're hoping the government nails him this time. Not me, I might add, but let's be honest, the fellow's a bloody Jeremiah, always bellyaching. There isn't one of us he hasn't hurled some filth at and it sticks, curse the bastard. *Eh bien.*' He sat back and, perceiving a loose thread issuing from a waistcoat buttonhole, investigated it. 'Did your mission in Calvados go well?'

'Yes, I think so, sir. Ah, good morning, Danton.'

Danton slapped a friendly hand on Raoul's shoulder on his way into the committee room but his jibe was for David. 'Finished the *Tennis Court Oath* painting yet?'

'More cheek and I'll paint you behind a pillar, Georges,' David called out after him and rose to his feet. 'Doing any portraits, are you, Raoul?'

'Some sketches now and again, sir.' No longer a pupil, Raoul smiled lazily, noting the wiry grey hairs proliferating among the artist's dark curls. The cyst beneath the skin of David's left cheek had grown a little since they had last met.

'Some pretty model, eh?'

The days were long gone when the great master had painted two-dimensional frothy women in silken panniers or taken commissions to depict the heirs of the noblesse in Grecian costume. Neoclassicism, with its sharp defining lines, had taken its nod from him. He painted men creating history or, to be precise, taking oaths – whether it was *The*

Oath of the Horatii, now in an Italian gallery, or the not-yet-finished *Tennis Court Oath* with its idealism oozing like perspiration from the bistre wash. And heroes! David liked patriotic heroes. *The Death of Socrates* had been so à la mode before the Revolution that every aristocrat in France had bought a copy.

'Yes, there is a girl,' Raoul drawled.

'Ha, sly dog!' A fist slammed his shoulder. 'One way to get her clothes off, eh?'

'I suspect it may require more ingenuity than that.'

'Oh, a clever hussy, is she? Women don't know their place any more. Well, busy morning, *mon gars*. If you ever want to give me a hand with any of the public festivals, let me know.'

'Thank you, sir, I'll bear that in mind.'

And that was all he would do. Raoul had endured enough of David as an employer to last him to the grave. David was a genius, no question, and he had changed public thinking: painters and sculptors were no longer seen as tradesmen but as cultured men worthy of being invited to the salons of the beau monde. But Raoul could not forgive the great master for spitefully destroying the entire Academy of Arts because they had once refused him membership. A few arteries of aristocratic blood still ran deep in Raoul despite his politics.

'Deputies! Are you coming in?' the *suisse* manning the doors called out tactfully.

Not all the fourteen members of the Committee for General Security were present but the green baize covering the large oval table was already untidy with coffee cups and dispatches, and Danton's pipe smoke drifted beneath the ceiling mouldings, as Raoul sat down in his usual seat opposite David's.

Danton leaned forward so the morning sunlight would not dazzle him as it crawled across the room, his fleshy fingers splaying the morning's agenda.

'Now we've all read your report, it's time we discussed your visit to Normandy, de Villaret. Looks like Caen is a hotbed of Girondin sympathisers.'

'It would seem that way,' he informed them. 'Of course, that is not to say we have no support there.'

'Well, you did a good job,' Danton conceded after they had discussed Raoul's conclusions at some length. The others bleated obligingly. 'I had a quick look through today's business,' he continued, sitting back, his thumbs circling each other like busy bobbins, 'and there's something confidential come in this morning that you might not have seen yet. Prisoners – all aristocrats – have been escaping from the women's section of La Force prison.'

Raoul raised an inquiring eyebrow, his interest sincere. La Force was in the Marais district, close to the Chat Rouge. There had been no mention of these escapes in the official reports; no tidbits dropped to the broadsheet hacks.

'We are not even certain how they are getting out. Since you live in Le Marais, de Villaret, this is just up your street, so to speak. How about you take a week to look into it?'

'But of course.' It gave him an official opportunity to investigate La Veuve Bosanquet.

'De Villaret.' Danton delayed him after the morning session ended. 'Warn your friends in the Plain – I was thinking of Boissy in particular – that they can no longer look after goats as well as cabbages. It's one or the other. We shall *expect* their votes in future.'

'I understand.'

'Just make sure *they* do.'

There were two reasons, not three, for the abrupt disappearance of the brazen, mysterious La Coquette. Firstly, the Chat Rouge's *carte du jour* had successfully seduced clientele from rival establishments. Secondly, the acting troupe, happily high on an appreciative audience, were now producing an excellent balance of entertainment themselves, without Fleur's involvement. Thirdly, the fire had been a warning from someone. Oh and there was a fourth reason. Not that Fleur was a coward precisely, but with republican foxes like de Villaret and Hérault sniffing around her chicken coop, she felt safer in her widow's bombazine than behind the lascivious silks of La Coquette.

Safe up to a point. Immersing herself in the daily activities of the Chat Rouge was a better antidote to worry than snuff or opium in marshmallow, and Fleur was deeply worried not only that she had heard nothing from Tante Estelle but also that Raoul de Villaret might still be investigating Matthieu's death.

But at least she was no longer hungry and, despite living in a city at war and occupied by her family's enemies, Fleur was revelling in her busy, bourgeois existence. She and Blanchette accompanied Thomas's cheerful bulk as he pushed a barrow around Les Halles in the early morning, and she enjoyed listening to him haggle over everything from beef flanks to glacé chestnuts.

Whenever she could afford the time, the Widow Bosanquet was careful to keep up attendance at the Jacobin Club or the Convention to give the appearance of a loyal patriot – suitably cockaded. (Perhaps there was a streak of Protestant blood in her, misbegotten generations back by some ancestor who had had the sense to save himself from being massacred on St Bartholomew's Day.) Attending the club had its blessings. Not only did she discover Emilie's giggly, golden-hearted company to be exhilarating (even if her coarse wit was sometimes shocking), but the young used-clothing seller was also Fleur's exuberant source of all the tittle-tattle that chirruped in the undergrowth of alleys and laneways – everything from the price of bread to the more sobering accounts of how some aristocrat had died that morning. Fleur dared not hush her on the latter but sometimes she recognised a name or remembered a face and it was necessary to stopper her outrage and let the actress in her take over. While the Widow Bosanquet sat nodding over the *verre du chocolate*, the *ci-devant* Françoise-Antoinette de Montbulliou inwardly wiped away tears.

She also learned more about her unwanted nephew-in-law, Felix Quettehou. The swallow-tailed, well-dressed deputy at the funeral was not his week-day persona. Lord no, Emilie declared, Quettehou normally wore the bandanna and trousers of the *sans-culottes*. Well, he had to, didn't he, seeing as he was a printer who took commissions from the *enragés*, cranking out incendiary prose that accused the imprisoned Queen Marie Antoinette of every-thing from bestiality to incest with her children.

'Look, this is another one of his,' Emilie giggled, spluttering biscuit as she perched on a stool at the Chat Rouge. 'See, I told you, it's far worse than Marat's paper.'

Fleur picked up the broadsheet and read it with growing horror. It provided an education in crudity – not only a foul cartoon but gutter lies beyond her modest imagination – with Quettehou's name rib-boning the printer's line at its base.

She swallowed, feeling even more out of her depth. 'I wonder if he was behind the fire,' she said suddenly. 'Except that we haven't had any trouble since we've started doing well.'

'Well, you wouldn't, would you, Fleur love,' gurgled Emilie. 'If it was him, he wouldn't want to destroy a goldmine. Reckon it must have been. If it had been some other café owner, they'd have had another go at you by now. No, I reckon he'll try and do it legal-like.' She slid to the floor and shook her striped skirts into order. 'Well, are we going to the club today or not?'

It was queuing to enter the gallery of the Jacobin Club that Fleur nearly encountered the artist David, slicing his way self-importantly through the waiting women. Her start of recognition made him glance back at her. It was hardly likely he would recognise her but she wasn't taking chances. The moment he bustled on, she surreptitiously moved to the other side of Emilie. Another deputy to avoid; another painful memory stirred up.

She must have been about nine years old when her father had summoned David to Clerville to paint her half-sisters. God knows what commission the great man had extracted, for he was famous even then. It was an episode she had pushed into the attic of her memory to grow cobwebs. She wanted to forget forever David's expression of distaste when her father had insisted that *all* his daughters be in the painting. The artist's gaze had crawled over her chubby torso with blatant distaste. In the end he had depicted her as a hideous Cupid with her plump thighs swathed in some sort of Grecian loin cloth and a gauzy scarf, which looked as though it had blown conveniently out of the ether, across her podgy chest.

Hours of posing for sketches by the foul-tempered David or worse, the pimply, boastful apprentices he had brought to mix his paints and do the boring tasks. Well, one of them got his comeuppance. Her sisters had amused themselves by pretending they admired the upstart, encouraging his swaggering, tormenting him with moistened lips and easing up their draperies. Oh, they had been cruel, but it had all ended when they shut him in the hidden passageway behind her father's *chambre à coucher* and –

Cheers crashed in upon her memories. Fleur landed back in the present with a thud. Around her, the *sans-culotte* women were craning like a disturbed bird colony.

'*Merde!* That's Marat!' Emilie's mouth was grape-shaped with astonishment. 'He's sticking his neck out coming here. The government have ordered his arrest.' She tugged Fleur vigorously towards the doorway as huzzahs broke out around them and suddenly there was a great commotion as the Jacobins rushed out of the hall to welcome their hero.

Although Fleur had mimicked this most famous of revolutionaries, she had only seen him from a distance. Now she looked at him with different eyes, realising just how important he was. The darling of the *sans-culottes*. Close up, he definitely wasn't a demigod. In fact, the man who posed between the double doors, kissing his fingers to his worshippers . . . well, he still looked ordinary to her.

And he was coming past them. Like beggars from the Gospels, women reached out to touch this new, rather short messiah. The men, paying more than lip service to equality, thumped his back. Close up, the famous bandanna was not just an eccentricity, an attention-drawing device that proclaimed Jean-Paul Marat the people's beloved bandit, it also strove to conceal an inflammation spreading from his scalp. No one should have stared but everyone did. Leprosy, was it? No, some other sort of skin disease.

Around his shoulders he wore the same grubby, narrow pelt of ermine. A two-fingered gesture to the monarchy of Europe, Fleur supposed. The rest of his apparel was unremarkable: cotton shirt, leather waistcoat and mouse-coloured trousers that ended at bare calves held up by a belt softened by years of service. Inconspicuous. No wonder the soldiers sent by the Girondin ministry had failed to find him.

He strode up to the rostrum, gleeful as a monkey, and verbally jingled his freedom at his enemies. He had decided to face the indictment, he announced. There was a moment's silence while his audience digested this and then they cheered, no, roared! If their hero felt confident enough to confront the government, well, *formidable*! Encouraged, approved of, Marat's oratory grew more vehement, condemning the Girondins and their ministers in language not fit for delicate ears. Beneath the shocking colour of his words, Fleur discerned the phrases of an educated man. Marie-Anne had been correct to say that this man was dangerous, and for other reasons too, it struck Fleur; not just conviction caused his stridency, but the constant, smarting whip of his disease. Was it killing him? Did he sense his tide was ebbing, or did the river of hate gushing out of his mouth somehow give him a brief oblivion?

He did not stay at the rostrum long but made his way back down the hall, shaking the hands thrust out to him, as though he were a victorious general. No one had ushered the women up to the gallery so they were still clustered around the neck of the hall. As Marat reached them they surged forward to pay homage as though he was another Christ, Emilie among them, and Fleur was left, noticeable in her reticence. To her absolute horror, Marat freed himself from the pats and fawning and pushed through to confront her.

'So you are the cheeky bitch who owns the Chat Rouge.' Legs astride, he stopped before her, blatantly exploring the curve of her breasts. 'You are fucking lucky I saw the funny side of things. *Merde*, I could have the people rip the place apart any time I bloody well choose.'

His vulgar language did not shock Fleur; she had heard coarse language in the marketplace in Caen.

'Yes, I realise that, Citizen Marat. I am grateful for your tolerance and I do apologise for La Coquette teasing you as part of her performance, but we needed to draw in customers.' She beamed up at him and received a grin in absolution. 'At least you would have found yourself in good company on stage,' she teased.

'Yes, old Max and Georges, I hear,' he chortled, rising onto his toes to see where Max Robespierre was; then the workman eyes flickered back to her. 'Though why your actress was lampooning that young dog, de Villaret, had me really vexed until I discovered that he's *screwing* the little bitch. No wonder we haven't seen hide nor hair of him for the last week.'

Well, that was a punch between the eyes. This

time she felt her face go red. She must be blushing like a smoky Paris sunset. What made it all the more insufferable was that before she could splutter an answer that was neither furious nor foolish, Marat leaned close and whispered: 'And tell La Coquette if she wants to mimic me in future, I'll give her lessons – for a price!' and he slid an impertinent hand to Fleur's derriere and goosed her.

'There is nothing about goosing in the New Testament,' Fleur muttered later to a jubilant Emilie, trying to impress upon her new friend that for her part, she considered all revolutionaries, and Marat in particular, far from holy, before the two women parted at the Place des Innocents.

Screwing La Coquette! They were rabid dogs, the lot of them. Ideals! Pah, give these deputies the chance of extra money for looking the other way, or offer them a tumble on a mattress, and their morals went out the window quicker than a sneeze.

'Where are Columbine and Juanita?' she demanded, marching into her café and stopping short at the uproar. Chairs were sprawled at ugly angles, benches lay on their sides, half-a-dozen voices were exclaiming from the cellars and Juanita was sitting on the stage cradling a squashed *bergère* hat, her feet adangle, and wailing loudly.

'*Nom de Diable!* What is going on?'

'We've had a visitation, *patronne*.' Thomas, wiping his hands on his apron, emerged from the kitchen as if he had been listening for her. 'The section gendarmes *and* the national guard. They've been searching the entire neighbourhood. Orders of your friend, de Villaret.'

'Friend!' At least the café had not been singled out, she thought, suppressing the reflex of panic. 'Did they damage anything?'

'Best see for yourself, *petite*.' He jerked his head towards the dressing-room. 'There's the worst of it.'

Fleur halted in the doorway, wrinkling her nose at the fulsome reek of stale orange-water. Tights, tabards, bodices and skirts lay in a melee on the floor, the cosmetics pots had been swiped from the dressing table and that too had been tugged away from the wall, but it was the grotesque tangle of wigs that turned her stomach. It reminded her too much of the foul executions in the Place de la Revolution.

'Apart from the cosmetics, is there any actual damage?'

'Look at this!' Columbine held out the costume Fleur had worn for the first half of her performance. Ugly rents disfigured the exquisite *poult de soie* skirt.

'And you should see the cellar, *patronne*. Bloody imbeciles should be killing foreigners, not bayonetting onions,' muttered Thomas. 'But the bastards didn't start drinking and they didn't steal so I suppose we must be grateful for small mercies.'

'Get Juanita to help you, Columbine, and sort out how much is damaged,' Fleur ordered, and swept off towards the cellar stairs with Thomas behind her. 'You say de Villaret was with them.'

'Yes, *petite*, with the gendarmes, it was about

two hours ago. Poor Gaspard was here on his own. He had no choice but to let them search. And then the soldiers came.'

Below stairs, the staff, with much grunting and effort, were heaving the wine racks and the barrels back against the walls. One of the former lace-makers was stitching up the rip in a sack of flour; another was shooing onions back into a box.

'The main thing is to not let this disrupt today's menu,' Fleur declared to Thomas. 'We can deal with most of this tomorrow morning.' She commiserated with Gaspard and then clapped her hands, 'Back to your normal jobs, please, and thank you for clearing up the mess.'

Once everyone had dispersed, she took a candle and made her own swift exploration, more out of curiosity than to check for damage. Where was the door that M. Beugneux had taken her through to avoid de Villaret? It had to be here somewhere, or had she been so soused in champagne that she had imagined it? The cellar walls seemed solid and disappointingly dull. No sign of concealed doors anywhere. Puzzled, she returned to her upstairs realm.

Within half an hour the chaos of the dressing-room had been shelved, hung or wiped. The soldiers, with *sans-culotte* relish, had only bayonetted the two gowns that might have passed muster at old Versailles.

'This is so unnecessary,' fumed Fleur. 'Indeed, we should be recompensed.'

'You are not going to confront de Villaret, surely?' squeaked Juanita.

'I do not mind seeing him on your behalf, *patronne*,' Columbine offered somewhat too eagerly.

'No, I have no wish to foist such an unpleasant task onto you,' replied Fleur firmly. She flung the two costumes over her shoulder and headed off to the Palais de Justice with an expression St Joan might have worn to fight the English; but she had not counted on April turning so clement. The brocade gowns were heavy to carry and by the time she reached the bridge to the Île de la Cité, she was hot, weary and regretting her hasty temper, especially as the medieval walls of the Conciergerie prison, which now specialised in prisoners who had been condemned to death, stretched up before her, high and menacing. She crossed the Pont au Change, halted in front of the clock on the corner tower of the Palais de Justice and drew a deep breath. It was not too late to reconsider. The doors of the huge guardroom that lay beneath the palace were propped open. The interior was like a huge whitewashed crypt and noisy with soldiers. Was she a fool to come here? She was no longer an aristocrat, she reminded herself, but a bourgeois businesswoman. Having an affair with La Coquette, was he?

Refuelled with anger, she marched up to the iron railings enclosing the busy forecourt of the Palais de Justice. It might be easiest to edge in behind the cartload of potatoes that was trundling in, but one of the whiskered guards manning the gilded gates thrust his pike across her way.

'*Holà*, you there! Just where do you think you are going? Let's see those!'

Stupid of her. Clutching expensive, old-fashioned gowns made her look thoroughly suspicious. The guard strode up so close she could smell the tobacco on his breath. Studying her face for guilt, he began to search through the folds of the gowns. 'I am here to see Deputy de Villaret,' she muttered unwillingly.

'Oooh, likes ballgowns, does he?' smirked the other guard. 'I would have said he was a breeches and waistcoat fellow myself, but it's surprising what weapons are hidden in a woman's skirts these days. Hold the deputy's finery, friend, while I check the rest of the citizeness.'

Fleur was convinced that the only reason the sentries let her in – after they had finished fumbling her for knives or pistols – was to annoy de Villaret. Scarlet-faced, furious and excessively manhandled, she hastened into the middle of the courtyard then faltered. A huge, decaying maypole wearing a weathered *tricolore* ribbon stood incongruously to her right. To her left rose the steep roof of Sainte-Chapelle, the chapel of the Valois kings, its precious windows blessedly intact. At least they had not used the jewel-like glass for artillery practice but, judging by the large cabinets that were being barrowed in up the steps, it no longer echoed with plainsong or organ music. Ahead of her a trio of old gossips sat knitting at the base of broad stone steps leading up to the law courts. Three men, lawyers to judge by their robes, were clustered halfway up, deep in discussion.

'*Oi!* Dressmaker, that way! *Là!*' The first guard

was pointing at a wicket gate beneath a low archway to the right of the stairs where more guards were checking a visitor's papers. *Zut!*

This time she was more poised. Time for a dazzling smile and a dash of La Coquette.

'I am here to see Citizen de Villaret,' she requested, and strove to disguise her horror as she realised the tall gentleman in front of her was no visitor but a new prisoner having his name taken. The gentleman glanced back at her as if seeking a fellow sufferer and then, judging her to be merely a seamstress and a *sans-culotte*, coldly jerked his chin up.

'Take no notice of his haughtiness, chicken,' joked the sergeant. 'He won't have that head much longer.' Showing off to her, he violently drove the butt of his musket into the prisoner's side.

'Thank you.' Hard to smile instead of run.

'Take her along, Morel, and no lingering!'

Sick to her stomach, Fleur forced herself to follow the whistling young soldier up a small flight of stairs whose masonry was charred from a recent fire.

'Ever been here before, citizeness?' The straw the soldier was chewing waggled.

'No.' *And I never want to come here again.* Her voice sounded overloud in the corridor. He nodded acquaintance as they passed a soldier escorting a woman with hands tied behind her back.

'Going to the tribunal,' explained Fleur's escort cheerfully. 'See down there, that's the women's court.' The small square courtyard seemed pathetic, dwarfed on all sides by louring walls. Only a smidgin of grass had endured the winter and a lonely tree struggled to lend some gentleness. Several ladies were crammed into a tiny patch of sunlight and a small child played in the dirt at their feet; on the other side of the yard, watched by more guards, a young man and a girl were holding each other's hands. 'Saying au revoir,' quipped Fleur's young escort, pulling the straw from his mouth and flicking it out the casement. 'Entertaining, *hein*?'

Fleur stared, unable to answer as the young man was dragged back by the arms, a soldier either side of him. The girl's loud scream of protest battered the walls of the courtyard. 'Better than the theatre any day, don't you agree, citizeness?'

Words were impossible. She no longer noticed now which way they went. Behind her, through the open window, the girl's sobs were turning to despair. Another corridor, another guard barring her way with a pike, her papers examined, another corridor, more questions, and then an antechamber.

'What's her business?' demanded a *sans-culotte* with a pistol stuck in his belt.

'She's here to see Deputy de Villaret!' A pinch through her skirts punctuated the declaration.

'Company, citizen,' the man announced to someone inside as he opened the door a crack. 'Another seamstress touting for night work.' A moustached face grinned down at her. 'What's your price, darling?'

'You can dream!' muttered Fleur, squeezing past before he could grab her. Her derrière must be as blue as the royal flag with so much pinching. Behind her the door closed.

De Villaret did not look up at his visitor. His jacket and stock were hung on the back of his chair, and he was engrossed at his writing table. A leather-clad volume, heavy with authority, lay at his elbow. He appeared to be making notes, not signing warrants and other fearsome documents as she expected, but her imagination was racing as she absorbed the bare walls and floor devoid of welcome. Had wretched prisoners stood here trembling, jabbed forward at the short point of a pike? What madness was this, to force a confrontation with a man she should avoid? She had gone too far in her anger, trading on his attraction to La Coquette. Besides, it was the imaginary woman he admired, not her.

'Yes, citizeness?' He slowly looked up from his notes, wearing the officious expression he had worn in Caen. 'Yes, what is the matter?'

The matter, the *immediate* matter was that . . . *Nom de Diable!* She blinked at de Villaret, uncertain how to proceed, for the controlled interest in his golden eyes was somehow depriving the room of air. His study of her missed nothing: the clutched gowns, her heated complexion and the hair escaping so disorderly from her small hat.

'What did you want to say to me?' The question offered no emotional guide.

'I make no apology for disturbing you, citizen. I am exceedingly angry. Your men . . .' The words tumbled out tepid when they should be scalding.

'Yes, citizeness? What about my men?'

'They – well, they damaged these costumes when they – I mean you – searched my premises.' The injustice of it rallied her. 'I insist on reparation.'

'Show me.' The chair scraped back. The man's shirtsleeves fell gracefully into place as he came round the desk to her. Damn him, did he have to come so close? It was he who eased the gowns from her grasp, laid them across his desk and examined the rents. 'Yes, I agree with you.' Striding to the door, he jammed it open with his heel. 'Mauger!' The surly *sans-culotte* looked astonished at the burden suddenly thrust into his arms. 'Take these to the former duchess. Tell her the mending must be done straightaway.' He closed the door, the mocking lift of his brow questioning whether his visitor was satisfied.

Fleur recoiled. 'You-you are making a *duchess* mend them.'

'Equality, citizeness.' His expression was devoid of sympathy. 'Besides, she is good at sewing and has nothing better to do. I will send the soldiers who were responsible for the damage to your restaurant to return the dresses tomorrow morning. They will apologise. Why are you still looking so angry? Did you expect me to be unreasonable?'

'Of course,' snapped Fleur, 'and . . . and I have been disgracefully fumbled by half the revolutionary army of France trying to reach you and achieve . . .'

'Recompense? Poor citizeness, I should have thought you were used to that.' With this ambiguous remark he stood back, freeing her path to the door as if he assumed she wished to leave immediately and then when she made no move, regarded her with curiosity: 'Is there something else you wish to discuss with me?'

'Indeed, yes,' she spluttered. 'Yes, there is! Marat . . . *Marat!* has informed me that you are conducting a liaison with my employee.'

For an infinitesimal moment his face froze, but perhaps it was her imagination. 'Which one?' The edges of the man's mouth lifted slowly, teasingly. He returned to his desk and leaned back against it, surveying her with lazy amusement.

'Which one?' she retorted, trying not to sound sour, but this was beyond endurance 'Good God, citizen, you can't mean –?'

He had pity on her. 'Ah, you mean La Coquette.' The long fingers stroked across his chin as if the matter required perusal. 'Yes, I believe I am.'

'But that is not possible,' she exclaimed.

A dark eyebrow arched insolently and he spread his hands, glancing down over his shirt and breeches before he raised his head. 'I find no problem, citizeness.'

'Well . . . well, I do!' She retreated as he took a step towards her 'And you may close me down if my sentiments annoy you. I expressly forbade such a liaison.'

'Did you? Oh yes, I recall. Well, these things happen. But I doubt you would be pleased to see your café close unless you wish to pay your debts to Hérault de Séchelles in a different coin. Now, delightful as this interruption is, I have a great deal of work to do. Permit me to see you to the gate.'

The door was being held open. She had no choice but to brush past him, her skirts snatched in as though his libertine habits might infect her clothing. Except the wind was not quite blown out of her sails.

'You may mock me, citizen, but I absolutely forbid you to carry on this . . . this *affaire*, otherwise I shall be forced to dismiss the woman!' Oh, this was ridiculous, she thought, briskly walking ahead of him through the gallery. How could she possibly be envious of a creature made of nothing but greasepaint? Columbine, it had to be Columbine or — She glared round at the man behind her with fresh suspicion. Had this damnable scoundrel been boasting?

'Ah, be fair. You know as well as I, citizeness,' he remarked cheerfully as he followed her down the stairs, 'that La Coquette is a law unto herself, and I clearly remember it was you who advised me to approach her privately.' That brought her up short as she reached the lower floor.

'Yes, I did, citizen,' she admitted, glaring up at him, wishing she did not like the way his dark hair curled with a republican liberty of its own. 'But are you sure you have the right actress, citizen? After all, she was in costume when you met her at the café, and I employ several.'

His forehead creased in surprise but she could sense the suppressed laughter. 'Of course, not the

blonde girl nor the southerner but the brunette.'
He gestured to her to precede him and she felt his
gaze licking like flames at her back. 'Your height,
actually,' he murmured, 'same colouring too.' Then
he was level with her, covering the distance with
an easy stride. Fleur, unable to think of a cutting
answer, was fuming. A strong hand caught her
gloved wrist and compelled her to stop. 'Be honest,
my dear Citizeness Bosanquet, as a woman of the
world, you surely cannot object to my liaison with
La Coquette unless the late nights are affecting her
performances on stage. Are they?'

Fleur gazed at him open-mouthed. Goodness,
she must look like a waterspout on the roof of
Notre Dame. Wiping the entertained look off de
Villaret's damnable face would have assuaged her
temper. 'But La Coquette has not been perform-
ing,' she replied through clenched teeth.

'Hasn't she?' Polite surprise was laced with cha-
grin. 'Indeed? Maybe I am wearing her out. I try to
organise interesting diversions to entertain her.' His
appraising gaze rose lazily up her skirts, over her
bosom and waited, alert now, testing. 'Indeed, I am
planning to escort her to a balloon ascent in the
Bois de Boulogne on Saturday if the weather is
sympathetic.' He saw Fleur through the wicket
gate.

'A *b-balloon*!' Curse it, she was beginning to
sound like M. Beugneux at his most agitated.

'Have you never seen a balloon?' he asked
charitably.

Oh, he was playing games with her. Holding

out a rattle for her unworldly hands to snatch at. Fleur swept ahead of him across the courtyard, buckling her temper down, then turned, trying to behave with sophistication. 'A balloon? No, I have not.' Outwardly she stayed serene; inwardly she felt like a little girl who was missing out on presents. 'A republican balloon, I assume?' she added provocatively. 'I am sure the Convention has sufficient hot air to send one as far as London.'

The deputy's eyes gleamed with the love of battle. Sympathy with the exact blend of sarcasm was weighed out to a nicety. 'No balloons, and a widow too!' he purred with fake pity. '*Incroyable!* But why do you not come on Saturday if the weather is fine? I am going to arrange a breakfast hamper. Do you drink champagne, citizeness, or is it yet another vice you do not permit yourself?'

'Oh, I permit myself all manner of vices,' Fleur murmured silkily, aiming for nonchalance, and then recognising that the hook was dangling, handsomely baited, added swiftly, 'It is the company I am fastidious about. I daresay it could be very amusing. However . . .' Oh God, she must not sound so enticed. It was necessary to frown down meaningfully at her widow's skirts.

'I am sure your late husband would not disapprove of your participation as a spectator, citizeness.'

'He . . . Matthieu was a great believer in public entertainment, sir. Yes, why not, I shall attend.' Oh, she should have turned on her heel by now. To be seduced so easily and by a balloon!

'*Bien!* Permit me to send the details to your house tomorrow.' She inclined her head and then saw the official in him take over. 'A warning, citizeness. *Aristos* have been escaping from La Force, which is why we have been searching all the premises in your section. I assume you and your employees – as good patriots – will inform me at once if you see or hear anything unusual. And, citizeness, *be careful*. It is no game these traitors are playing.'

With a stern inclination of her head, Fleur withdrew, feeling like a duelling opponent who had just been pinked – twice. The Devil! The lowdown, unspeakable, insufferable – It was a mistake to glance back over her shoulder. The rogue was watching her with the smiling complacence of a fisherman who had just hauled in his supper.

At least he had not been searching the Chat Rouge because of her, she reasoned, remembering his warning. As for knowing about her debts, his friend, Hérault, must have divulged that morsel. But the matter of La Coquette . . . She was going to wring the truth out of Columbine. It had to be Columbine, she decided. Juanita was too tall and none of the other women would have the gall. By the time she arrived back at the café, she was ravenous for food and an explanation from the jaunty blonde, but the actors had not yet returned for the evening's performance. She collapsed onto a chair at her special table beside the wall and toed off her shoes. Half-concealed by a wicker screen, the table afforded her some privacy as well as an opportunity to observe the interplay of staff and customers.

'Did you receive justice, *patronne*?' asked Thomas, setting a bowl of divinely smelling pottage in front of her.

'The trouble with that man,' declared Fleur, waving her spoon fiercely in a nonaristocratic fashion, 'is that he is a rake first and a revolutionary second. This is delicious. Why are you making faces?' She wriggled round in her chair. 'Oh!'

Behind her in the gap between the painted flowers on the wall and the screen stood Felix Quettehou wearing his workman's breeches and Madras bandanna.

'Bonsoir, Tante Bosanquet,' he exclaimed. 'May I?' and slid into the chair opposite. 'I have come to apologise.'

'It must be the weather affecting everyone,' she murmured, exchanging glances with Thomas, and gestured to the soup. 'Will you have some?'

Quettehou nodded. 'That is exceedingly generous considering my rudeness at my uncle's funeral.' He half turned in his chair. 'This is quite incredible. I never believed that anyone could turn this hole into a success. *Félicitations!*' He accepted a glass of sauterne from one of the waiters and raised it to Fleur. 'You are quite a businesswoman.'

'And you are a printer and section representative at the Commune, citizen?'

'I move with the times and I am prospering. Paris devours broadsheets like a desperate fledgling and, like you, I have acquired powerful friends.

Hérault is quite a feather in your hat.' The probing came again. 'Is that how you met my uncle – through him?'

'No. Ah, here is your soup,' she said, hiding her relief. 'Tell me what you think of it.'

He grinned at Thomas and tried some. 'A little too rich for me, *mon brave*, but yes, still good, not that I am an expert.'

Thomas waggled an insulting finger behind Quettehou's head and disappeared.

'How do you distribute your broadsheets?' asked Fleur, dabbing her lips with a napkin.

'I have regulars but I listen out for large gatherings, opportunities when my men can distribute the pages easily to a large number. I ask around. Do *you* know of anything this coming week?'

'There is some sort of balloon ascent on Saturday if the weather is clement.'

'Ah, that's it exactly. Thank you, Tante. Are you interested in balloons?'

'This will be the first time I have seen one. Yes, I am tempted to attend.' She took a sip of her Bourbonne water. 'So, Monsieur Quettehou, is it easy combining your work and your duty as a patriot? Your work with the section must take much of your time.'

He nodded. 'There is a great deal to be done if we are to consolidate the changes since the Bastille fell. The Church's filthy grip on so much land and wealth has to be broken, and I want to see Marie Antoinette and all the other aristocratic houris who lived off the rest of us guillotined.'

'But you believe in owning property and making a profit?'

'Of course, how else can progress be effected? It's not drunken peasants who are going to lead France into the next century but people like us, people who can harness money with hard work, ingenuity with opportunity.' He glanced about him meaningfully before returning his attention to her. 'People who can make others work efficiently.'

'You flatter me.'

'And I am mortified that last week I insulted you.' His fingers stretched towards her apologetically before withdrawing to the edge of the table. 'Some time I should like to hear the circumstances of how you met my uncle.' Like this very instant, his expression suggested.

Fleur stood up, shaking out her skirts. 'Another time. You must forgive me if I attend to my duties. No, please, finish your soup. We have just installed a billiard table if you wish to play and there will be some entertainment in an hour.'

Already standing, he shook his head. 'I, too, have business that needs attending. Am I forgiven for my previous insults, Tante Bosanquet? You must understand that the shock of my uncle's death . . .' Had deprived him of manners, when most likely he had arranged his uncle's murder?

Compelled to shake his hand, she shuddered inwardly at the damp slide of his flesh beneath her palm and watched with relief as he left the café.

'It must be our day for unwelcome visitors,' she declared to Thomas, as she cleared the table.

'There's more, I'm afraid, *patronne*. Columbine is indisposed and cannot play tonight. Juanita will do her solos instead and said not to worry you.'

'Indisposed?' The word rose to a surprising crescendo.

Thomas's brow creased in puzzlement. 'You think it is a lie, *patronne*?'

'I-I heard a rumour that she was having an *affaire de coeur.*'

'Ah!' It was a Gallic 'ah' redolent with understanding.

Fleur bit her lip, half in mind to charge round to Columbine's lodgings and see for herself. No, that was foolish. 'Thomas, I know this will sound frivolous but I think you and I have earned ourselves a free morning. The café can manage without us for a few hours. Would you be my escort on Saturday to a balloon ascent?'

'*Patronne!*' His eyes were spherical. 'My pleasure!'

'*Bon.* Now, is there anything I can help with?'

'If you can see what else needs putting to rights in the cellar, *petite*, that would be excellent. I haven't had time to scratch myself.'

Anxious to be busy, Fleur lit a candle and went downstairs. No one had swept up the flutter of onion and garlic skins displaced by the search.

Where was it the prisoners were escaping from? La Force? The old Hôtel de Caumont de La Force, scarce a street away. These old mansions must all have warrens of cellars and passages beneath them. She set down the broom and took up the candlestick. The walls seemed solid. No concealed doors, no trapdoors either.

For an instant she remembered the day her world at Clerville had ended, recalled the little she knew of the thief who had helped her. To her fifteen-year-old self, he had been old, but now it did not seem so. Slender shouldered, he must have been only in his early twenties which would make him, why, not even thirty. That was if he was not rotting in some gibbet by now or lying headless in an unmarked grave. The Revolution had at least been efficient in emptying the world of cutpurses. It was no longer acceptable to thieve from one's equals, and thieving from anyone with a title was a privilege reserved for the government.

'Citizeness, Chef said to tell you that there are two soldiers here with the gowns.' Already? De Villaret must have commandeered a battalion of duchesses.

'Tell Thomas to offer them a free meal if they are decent men just doing their duty.'

She returned upstairs but there was no sign of any military save for a pair of officers happy at the billiard table. The returned gowns were draped over the screen by her table.

'I hope you do not mind that I did not delay the soldiers,' muttered Thomas as she inspected the wonderful mending. 'Louts like them do not like apologising. They might have noted your face for the future. Better to be careful, *hein*?'

'*D'accord*,' she agreed amiably, grateful for his thoughtfulness, and carried the dresses back to their racks. She lit the candles in the dressing-room and sat down before the mirror. One of La Coquette's several wigs sat blankly on its stand but the others were not in evidence. That was no surprise. There was still a pile of crumpled garments waiting to be pressed before they were hung back up. Or perhaps Columbine had treacherously sequestered one of them.

Saturday, she thought wearily; should she resurrect La Coquette and sail into the Bois de Boulogne with all flags aloft? Or should the Widow Bosanquet make a subdued, stately appearance? Perhaps she should call at Columbine's lodging off the Vielle Rue de Temple and ascertain the truth, but tonight she did not want any answers. What should I do? she asked her reflection. The tired Fleur in the mirror, nineteen and unwed, stared back, wide-eyed. The candles flamed like altar lights either side of a painting.

She could remember one girl in the convent confiding naughtily that if you took off all your clothes and sat naked before a mirror at midnight on New Year's Eve, the face of your true love would be revealed. Well, New Year was months away and she was not about to sit naked for any-one, and especially not de Villaret.

The eyes in the mirror grew wistful. There was only one man she yearned to meet again, the masked thief who had led her to safety down the secret passageway he should not have known of. *Her mysterious thief!* A hero in her daydreams but no doubt some boring artisan or a dismissed footman of Papa's – there had been plenty of those; except there had been a curious authority about the man. Not a servant's sneering hauteur or the swaggering tyranny of the newly moneyed but the calm ease of a man who knew himself and liked the fellow he saw in his shaving glass.

Yes, *her fantasy*. So many moments wasted in wondering; webs spun by night to catch a fantasy and in the morning broken by reality. Fleur buried her face in the shelter of her trembling fingers. Take each day as it comes! Just as she had in the forest. After all, the future might be brutish and short.

10

Dearest Marie-Anne,
They tell me that one of the reasons for Dr Marat's
violent bitterness is that his experiments and discourses
on the nature of Light have been disregarded by the
academies. I am about to embark on an experiment of my
own – to observe whether the hot air needed to make a
balloon rise exceeds the energy exerted by a certain citizen
in pursuit of the female sex. The most infuriating man
in all the world! I find myself forever out of temper with
him but I rejoice to believe that he thinks the same of me.

EXTRACT FROM THE LETTERS OF FRANÇOISE-ANTOINETTE DE
MONTBULLIOU, 1793

The Bois de Boulogne might have too many trees – after all, it had been the hunting park of the kings since the days of Henri of Navarre – but there were a few broad swards where a balloon might be launched on a calm morning, and it was far enough from the heart of Paris not to attract a huge crowd. In any case, it was not as if the balloon was going to be cast off. No, it would be safely anchored by ropes. They were just going to experiment with how long it would stay in the air with three men on board. A process completely and utterly manageable. Or so Raoul thought as Deputy Boissy d'Anglas's coach, carrying Boissy, Armand and himself, traversed the cobbles of Saint-Honoré and headed towards the Porte Maillot.

'Oh, you haven't brought a book with you, Armand,' he exclaimed in disgust. '*Nom d'un chien*, it's a balloon ascent.'

His friend shrugged. 'It could get boring.'

'You are sure this Robinet fellow is trustworthy, Raoul?' Boissy, the son of Raoul's godfather, asked again, searching his pockets for his snuffbox. As it was mostly his money paying for the balloon, he had some justification for concern.

'Yes, Boissy, there were eight there last night to guard the apparatus – I made sure they had cudgels with them – and I've arranged for some national guard to be there this morning just in case.'

Armand whistled. 'Friends in high places, *hein*, Raoul.' He offered his snuff to Boissy.

'Low, by the sound of it,' snapped Boissy. He

tapped a sprinkling of powder onto the back of his hand and took a snort.

'Well, none of them will be as high as you in a few hours' time, *mon brave*, believe me. You will be able to write a new treatise on transportation *en ballon*,' chuckled Raoul. Unless, of course, the weather changed, but the great watchmaker in the sky could not have given them a sweeter morning after last night's showers. Today would be a respite from the endless bickering in the Convention, and since there had been no escapes from La Force prison during the week, Raoul intended to enjoy himself; besides, he had seduction on his mind if the day went well.

A quarter of an hour later he eased down the window shutter and checked his watch dial in the light of the lantern that swung on the outside of the vehicle. Perhaps they should have left earlier; the early morning traffic in the city had been heavier than he had anticipated. 'Are you sure you will not join the ascent, Armand? You can take my place.'

'*Diable*, no! I will stick to criticising Marat. It is just as dangerous but I can still keep my feet on terra firma.'

'To each his own!' Raoul shrugged. The horses were slowing. '*Merde*,' he exclaimed in astonishment. 'Damn it, I thought we understood this was to be a private business.'

The common ground around the ascent site looked as though a horde of gypsies, without their caravans, had moved in. Dark rolls and crescents on the ground beside dead fires stirred, stretching out pale limbs as the carriage wheels bowled past.

'By the look of them, it's the rabble from the homeless camp on the other side of the park,' muttered Boissy. '*Mon Dieu*, Raoul, I never intended this.'

'Nor I,' growled Raoul.

Even with his liberal principles pinned on his chest, Boissy, *ci-devant* major domo to Artois, the dead King's brother, was an aristocratic bird ripe for plucking. *Merde!* Every hack writer in Paris would be loading their verbal pistols to shoot him down. But with Artois baring his teeth at the Revolution from his safe kennel in Coblenz, who could blame anyone for being suspicious? Even Raoul wondered whether a healthy bribe from across the border might have tempted a continuation of his friend's discreet services. After all, if the Revolution failed, Boissy's old master might one day become a king.

Boissy's hand tightened on his walking cane, tense, but he did not voice his fear. 'Let us get on with it, then, but if anything has been pilfered . . .'

Raoul did not answer. He sprang from the coach and marched towards the huddle of carts and bricks in the centre of the field.

'Drink, citizen?' A lemonade-seller, bent under the weight of her pack, hobbled towards him. A gaggle of others materialised beside her, honking:

'Rosettes, citizen?'

'Beer, Deputy?'

'Broadsheets? Latest news?'

'Show me that!' Raoul could just about make

out the glimmer of capitals announcing a balloon ascent. Damn!

''Ere, citizen!' Half-a-dozen urchins plucked at his coat-tails. 'When is this balloon thing gonna go up then?'

Checking that his watch and wallet were still in his possession, Raoul swung round and shook his head helplessly at his travelling companions before he caught sight of Robinet lounging beside the brick wall they had built the day before. He headed over to him with a merciless expression.

Lifted an inch from the ground by his coat revers and pressed up against the wooden frame holding the balloon membrane, the *sans-culotte* vigorously shook his head, protesting he had not organised the circus that surrounded them. The moment he was lowered he grabbed a shovel and dashed across to fuel the glowing brazier with an alacrity that was rarely glimpsed.

'Well?' Dewlaps quivering, Boissy stomped up wearing an expression like a keg of gunpowder with its lit fuse at kissing point. 'Well?'

'I do not know who damn well spread the information – I'll geld the bastard later – but it will be worse before it gets better.'

'Worse?' echoed Armand.

'Much worse. Someone's printed a broadsheet. It looks like we'll be getting half of Paris.'

Fleur, and no doubt her neighbours, was woken at a most ungodly hour by an urgent rapping on the front door. A cheerful member of the national guard saluted her, presented two passes, informed her the weather had cleared and she was to expect a fiacre at five o'clock. Fleur blinked blearily at the cloudless sky, closed the front door and swore loudly about revolutionaries and one in particular. Later she was grateful for de Villaret's planning; the narrow artery into the Bois de Boulogne was already clogged with carts and coaches by the time the fiacre reached the park gates.

'The only consolation,' she told Thomas, sleepily stifling a yawn, 'is that Columbine will detest having to get up so early. I wonder if he sent a hired vehicle for her too.'

Thomas chuckled. 'Well, if he is planning to seduce the pair of you at a champagne *pique-nique*, he's going to have not just me but an audience of thousands. Don't frown, *mignonne*, at the rate we're progressing, you'll be lucky if you get there in time to enjoy the crumbs.'

Finally, it was easier to walk, and with her burly, devoted chef for protection, it had seemed a good idea to Fleur at first. However, as they explored the frayed edges of the crowd cramming into the balloon site, she was far too aware of hungry eyes calculating what valuables she might carry. Pushing through to the front seemed impolitic.

'Not at all what I expected,' chortled Thomas, craning his neck to see their goal. 'You are looking pale, *patronne*.' He pinched her cheek. 'You need some breakfast. Let's hope they have saved you some.'

Fleur had never seen so many people in one place. Even the branches of the nearby oaks were laden with human rooks. 'I think we should leave, Thomas. I-I do not care for this at all.'

'Ha, it won't take long to find him. Let's make for the balloon, *hein*?' Her chef flipped up his brown coat-tails. 'Just hold onto my belt.' With a sigh, she shuffled on obediently in his giant wake.

She had not told Thomas of her experience with the mob that first week in Paris. That must be what was making her edgy, she rationalised, but deep down she sensed danger. In the woods she would have noticed a sudden stillness or been warned by a startled bird, but here . . . No, she must stay calm. After all, there were plenty of bourgeois spectators like her tangled in the crowd. How stupid to be anxious; this was no restless rabble but a mixture of people in Sunday humour on a calm and sunny morning. There was a balloon ascent to watch and even if she did not discover Citizen de Villaret and Columbine in this press, at least Thomas would enjoy some well-earned leisure.

'Ouuuch!' A hand sliced down painfully on her arm. She instantly lost her grip on Thomas's belt. A rough youth had elbowed his way in front of her, cutting her off, and another man was pushing into her from the back. Something hard and curved hooked around her right ankle. She jabbed her parasol down to free herself.

'Thomas!' she screamed as her assailant yanked hard; some cutpurse was bent on pitching her headfirst beneath the crowd's feet. 'Thomas!' Then the youth swivelled swiftly, a small knife ready in his fist. '*Thomas!*'

The chef's muscular arm swiped the youth aside as though he were some flimsy cranefly and curled round Fleur's waist. Protecting her with his body, Thomas almost carried her the rest of the way.

Righted like a toppled black chesspiece safely behind the cordon of national guard protecting the ascent site, Fleur repinned her hat with a shaking hand. She had never thought she would be so glad to see a blue and white uniform.

'C-can you observe Columbine anywhere, Thomas?' she asked, trying to sound sensible and ignore the fact that she desperately wanted to run away. But where? Behind her was a sea of faces concealing her attackers in secure anonymity; ahead was de Villaret.

'No, no sign of Columbine in any guise,' Thomas chuckled, scanning the figures moving around in the smoke, 'but there's the deputy, *patronne*, and he certainly hasn't an actress on his arm.' He put his fingers in his mouth and whistled. 'He's waving us through.'

'A moment.' She fumbled for a handkerchief. The acrid smell was strong enough to bring tears to her eyes, and God knows what they were burning, but it was the after-shock that rendered her fragile.

Thomas waited patiently, clearly enjoying himself. 'Cheer up, little one. At least the stink will keep the hordes at bay.' He was right. Like wolves lurking around a traveller's night campfire, the spectators were being cautious. 'Feeling better now?'

Better? Walking the plank off a pirate ship into a shark-filled ocean might be more appealing. Her shoes were sodden from the dew on the ankle-high grass, and she wished herself at the café with a heartening mug of coffee to warm her hands on, not standing in some foggy clearing with the lousy and the murderous. Mind, she had to admit the risen sun was splashing dabs of colour into this grey world and insinuating its gentle warmth between her shoulderblades. Tucking her arm into Thomas's, she let him draw her around the covered carts.

The ingenuity of the enterprise astonished her. A low iron brazier was burning within a circle of bricks. At least four feet high and two feet thick, the wall looked to be a hasty, unmortared construction. It was broken in three places: to allow access to the brazier, to keep the large wicker basket that would ride beneath the balloon clear of the heat, and to accommodate the huge bulk of the green and red striped balloon skin which flowed out across the grass like an immense semiflaccid tent enclosed in mesh. Four men stood outside the wall holding long beams of wood. They were lifting the vast wooden hoop, which equatored the balloon skin, above the brazier. The fire must have been wafting heat into the membrane for some hours, for the lower half of the balloon was already billowing.

'The worst is over, *patronne*,' remarked Thomas. 'I suppose they'll unhook the hoop once it is full enough to stand on its own.'

Fleur mopped her eyes with her knuckle. The stink was hard to escape. All manner of rubbish – rags, worn-out shoes, logs and slivered furniture – was piled high outside the first break in the wall, and two workmen with neckerchiefs protecting their mouths and nostrils were leaning on their shovels watching the brazier. The procedure still looked hazardous. If the brazier burned too fiercely, it might well set fire to the balloon skin and a lot of republican money would go up in smoke. Who was paying for this frivolity? The government? Out of confiscated Church property, no doubt!

The balloon's keepers moved about the grass twitching the balloon fabric like fussy tailors. One of them was Raoul de Villaret in summer breeches of white nankeen. No plumes today – a true revolutionary now with his wide shirtsleeves unleashed from the discipline of his coat. He raised his hand gracefully in greeting and stepped over the cat's cradle of ropes to join them.

'I commend you for punctuality, citizeness.' The unblemished teeth gleamed in a holiday smile. 'You want some?' He indicated a brunette lemonade-seller rattling her cups at them hopefully on the edge of the crowd.

'No, thank you.' It was necessary for Fleur to drag her gaze away diffidently from his speculative grin and stare coolly about her.

'I thought you might have brought Hérault with you, citizeness.'

'Why should I do that?' she asked with genuine

surprise, wondering why his grin instantly broadened. 'And . . .' She cleared her throat, '. . . and is La Coquette here?'

'I suspect she would not miss this for all the world.' The man's dark lashes fell and rose on a gaze practised at conceding nothing. Instead, he took her elbow with the ease of a beau. 'Come, permit me to introduce you to the man behind this enterprise.'

Fleur had little choice, but she faltered as she recognised the shorter of the two gentlemen who rose from checking the rope knots. His name escaped her but she had met him before the Revolution, when King Louis's younger brother, the Comte d'Artois, had visited Clerville. He came from a Protestant noble family and, yes, she would swear he had been one of the Comte's close circle, but what was he now? It would be a euphemism to call him a survivor; traitor might be more apt. He might have given away a title, but not his wealth. The cut of his coat, pristine stock and expensive shoe leather pronounced his hypocrisy.

'May I present Deputy Boissy d'Anglas, the reckless instigator of all this.'

Reckless? Indifferent, certainly. The former courtier was too preoccupied with the balloon to waste his breath on any conversation with the likes of her, but Fleur was taking no chance that he might recognise a fellow aristocrat. Behaving like a milkmaid invited into a ballroom, she rubbed her palm nervously on her skirt before she held it out, and declared in an overloud Calvados dialect, 'An honour to meet you.'

But she had overplayed. Beside her de Villaret froze; his recovery, however, was exemplary.

'And this is Deputy Armand Gensonné, known for flights of eloquence. I have no doubt he will shortly be adding balloon hyperbole to his speeches. Citizens, La Veuve Bosanquet and Thomas, chef of Le Chat Rouge.'

She had supposed him in his late twenties, but face to face Armand Gensonné looked older than he had at the Convention, although there were no grey strands in his ebullient light brown hair. Emilie was right. He did have rather beautiful eyes, translucent with marvellously long lashes, but his prissy mouth and dimpled chin lacked the male strength of de Villaret's jawline. Ha! Emilie would go green as emerald when she heard that her new friend had been in kissing distance of this idol.

'Is something amusing you, madame?' Gensonné's smile was thinning.

Fleur shook her head, demurer now. 'No, citizen, I daresay I am feeling rather bemused by the occasion.' An understatement! Aware that the conversation was stumbling miserably, she raised a gloved hand to her eyes in search of inspiration and peered through the smoke at the brazier. 'Cow pats?' she exclaimed, astonished to see open barrels of dry dung being lugged off a cart and carried across to the stokers.

'It's a form of greeting in Normandy, Armand,' de Villaret said dryly. 'We shall get her used to Parisian ways eventually.' He placed his hand in the small of her back and steered her away from the others. Thomas did not follow. The lemonade-seller had found a customer.

The custodian touch sent a flurry of panic through Fleur's insides. What on earth did he expect from her? Heavens! It had been idiocy to come this morning. He was too dangerous, too suspicious, and the sideways glance he was giving her this instant was not appreciative. Well, if her excessive display of peasant manners had made him lose interest in her company, so much the better. Maybe now he would swallow the lie that her mother had been lady's maid to the nobility.

'They are heating the air inside the envelope to make it lift,' he informed her as they walked past a huge basket roped to the balloon membrane outside a second gap in the brick edifice.

'Thank you,' Fleur replied sweetly. 'We are so dense in Normandy, I doubt I could have worked that out for myself.'

'Then I am glad I enlightened you, citeziness,' he countered, his imperious hand urging her forwards again. The golden-brown eyes were speculative. 'The more obnoxious the smell, the greater the lift . . . apparently.'

'If that is the theory, Citizen de Villaret, this stench should lift your friend's balloon over the rainbow. Are we sending citizen mice up too?' One attendant was releasing small balloons over the heads of the fidgeting populace.

Her guide ignored her sarcasm, kicking at a guy rope with his buckled shoe. 'To check the wind direction with their tails?' The maddening gaze rose up her skirts. 'It's been done already. Mice and dogs.' This prompted him to turn his head in Thomas's direction. '*Tiens, tiens*, your guard mastiff seems to have found an attractive bone. Shall you whistle him to heel or can you trust a deputy of the people to look after your virtue for a little longer?'

Fleur followed his stare; her chef's sudden animation over a second cup of cordial was rather touching. 'As you wish, Citizen Deputy,' she murmured with appropriate meekness, and, aware that her escort was watching her every move, she endeavoured to open her new parasol, hoping it might deflect his scrutiny. 'Please, I should hate to detain you from more enticing pursuits, citizen.'

'You mean seducing La Coquette? Permit me, citizeness.' He removed the sunshade from her clasp; a scarlet pagoda swiftly flowered across the spines.

'Oh, how disappointing,' she purred, twirling it before she settled it against her shoulder. 'The seller swore it was inscribed with the wit of the Convention.' And before de Villaret could manage a reply, she tugged off her glove and sank gracefully, her ebony skirts billowing, to test the texture of the balloon skin. Seduce *La Coquette*! Her heart was resounding so much like a regimental drum that it was necessary – and safer – to inspect the fabric with a display of deep interest.

'Fascinating.' She held out her hand for him to assist her to her feet.

'I think so.' The answer hid layers of meaning.

His touch even through her glove shook her equilibrium. 'Do you want me to explain how all this works?'

'You fear my woman's brain might be strained in the attempt, citizen?'

'Is that a possibility?' he retorted so straightfaced that he made her laugh. 'That is better. Stop peppering me with grapeshot, Citizeness Bosanquet. I have a thick skin. Besides, I would have hardly invited you as well as La Coquette if I found your company tedious. Shall I show you the ropes?' he asked dryly, but the brief twist of his lips implied there was more to be explored between them.

'Yes, if you please, citizen.' Fleur beamed with sufficient innocence to confuse him. Just you try! Safely chaperoned by Thomas and the crowd, she could momentarily afford the game, although she was wondering what the ground rules were. Neither Columbine or Juanita had materialised in a froth of perfumed expertise to lure him from her side.

At least it was flattering to be thought worthy of a lecture salted with measurements, formulas and proportions as they walked round the swelling membrane and inspected the large willow basket, which was to carry the aviators. Fleur listened, sincerely interested, while Citizen de Villaret, with masculine delight in detail, persisted in explaining the dynamics of shifting three men. It was a conversation safe from sedition or seduction, and as the fabric before her began to take on a force of its own like a troubled ocean, Fleur mistakenly forgot to be on guard. With all the happy excitement of a nineteen year old, she waved her parasol across to where Thomas lingered with the lemonade-seller.

'Pray, excuse me, citizeness. I will find out how much time is left.' De Villaret left her. She waited, feeling at ease, glad that the weather had not turned fickle. To be sure there were a few drowsy clouds moving very slowly, but the morning was warm now and the air tranquil.

A roar of approval broke from the crowd as the huge balloon slowly heaved itself free of the ground and rose majestically above the basket. Fleur caught her breath, impressed at how immense it looked. De Villaret, shielding his eyes with a broadsheet, was staring upwards, as rapt as Deputy Boissy, who signalled imperiously to one of the stokers. The workman cast aside his shovel and climbed into the basket. Fleur wondered who else would join him and whether they would be coerced, for she doubted someone like Boissy would risk his own skin. Mind, there were precedents: her papa had once told her that when M. Rosier had made his first ascent in a free balloon back in '83, he had planned to use two convicted criminals, but he had changed his mind at the last minute and made the ascent himself.

Or did they have a more spectacular passenger in mind? The smile slid from Fleur's face as a new thought hit her. De Villaret had mentioned an actress named Mme Thible, a daring creature who had ascended to a height of nine thousand feet with no less a witness to admire her valour than the King of Sweden. Surely de Villaret had not cajoled Columbine into making a spectacular arrival as La Coquette. Could that be why he had invited her as well, to witness her protegée's magnificent ascent?

The deputy returned, eyes alight with challenge. 'Boissy says you may step inside the gondola if you wish.' Her ignorance amused him. 'The basket, citizeness!' he enlightened her. 'It is quite secure. I have just checked the anchoring to be sure.'

'How kind of your friend.' Fleur was genuinely touched by the thought. 'And I am not afraid, citizen,' she declared, countering the teasing challenge in his eyes. No, she could have skipped in delight as they circumnavigated the ascent area back to the gondola. To be sure, standing beneath such a globe of air was somewhat daunting but it was still safely tethered and presumably there would be a little wicker gate that you could –

'Oh!' she squeaked in shock as the deputy's strong arms swung her high, well clear of the side, and planted her, feet first, into the basket. Blushing, she virtuously straightened her bodice, ignoring de Villaret's amusement.

'I am told this gondola is far smaller than the one Montgolfier used.' He folded her escaped sunshade and handed it across the leather-clad edge that separated them like a country stile. 'How does it feel?'

'*Formidable!*' Fleur beamed across to where Thomas and Deputy Gensonné stood talking to the people beyond the cordon of guards, and gestured in marvel at the huge bubble of hot air above her. Then she remembered her manners.

'Thank you for permitting me aboard,' she called out to the balloon's owner.

Boissy, testing the ties on the canvas bags attached to the outside of the gondola, straightened, blew the hair out of his eyes, and jerked his head meaningfully towards a half-dozen yelling boys who had broken through the cordon and were chasing each other among the ropes. 'Deal with them, Raoul, before someone gets hurt!'

The basket was divided into two compartments and Fleur turned to greet the occupant on the other side, a broad fellow with pepper-and-salt hair cropped short. This was the pilot, she supposed, but he had his back to her.

'Bonjour, citizen.'

He grunted, too busy fiddling with the ropes. Just another surly *sans-culotte* in leather waistcoat and greasy cap. Oh well, thought Fleur, determined not to feel uncomfortable; best to observe what she could before the men removed her like unwanted ballast. Then the fellow turned. It was the workman who had stalked her in Caen!

Panic shot though her. It was an effort to resist crossing herself. Instead her hands coiled into fists. So Raoul de Villaret had suspected her from the start. The catapult, the threats in the carriage and now this? What cruel game was he playing?

'Scared, Citizeness Bosanquet?' asked the *sans-culotte* insolently. His hedgehog eyes were the sort that didn't open wide.

Fleur shook her head and tried to behave with nonchalance. 'The compartment is roomier than I expected,' she remarked, turning slowly. It was sufficient for three thin people to stand with elbow room. Hessian tableclothed a board that shifted under her soles like a boat as hot air surges buffeted the balloon, and a cold object rolled against her ankle. 'Oh,' she exclaimed in astonishment, stepping back. 'It's champagne!'

'Pass it to me!' The pilot seized the bottle, wrapped it in his jacket and stashed it down beside him.

The massive bladder of air was straining to lift further. The activity around the balloon intensified.

'W-wherever will you land?' she asked.

'Wherever the bloody thing decides to come down, citizeness. I could be meeting the Supreme Being in a matter of minutes. Nice thought, *hein*?' So it was that dangerous. No wonder the fellow looked so resentful. Then the heavy moustache wriggled and he laughed. 'It's not going anywhere, citizeness. Didn't they tell you it's not a free flight? We could be tethered halfway to heaven for bloody hours.'

A tethered ascent? How disappointing! She wondered uneasily whether the fickle crowd was aware that the performance would be tediously static, unless the balloon casing ripped or caught fire. The people were growling already. No, they weren't; the noise from the crowd was laughter, for the wicked urchins were running hither and thither, screaming in glee. All the attendants were after them now. Fleur bit her lip, trying to hide her amusement. Boissy and Gensonné had given chase as well, but the boys ducked through the ropes and dodged like rabbits. As fast as one was caught and thrust back into the crowd, he wriggled free and sprinted back into the melee. It was good-natured. Several of the soldiers broke rank to help and the spectators, opportunistic like all crowds, pushed closer.

The basket shifted. Fleur, alarmed by the increasing determination of the balloon to heave free, began to wonder if she should try to scramble out, but there were no toeholds in the wicker wall for a lady to manage the breast-high barrier on her own with dignity. She glanced around for de Villaret and saw him and a workman fall sprawling across the anchor rope in a tangle of boots and fists.

'Perhaps you could help me to disembark,' she called to the pilot as the basket lurched more violently, but he was frantically grabbing at the ropes. She heard Thomas's voice, glimpsed him trying to break past the national guard who were using their muskets now to force back the crowd. De Villaret was shouting too, running back towards them. She grabbed the side in panic, determined to scramble out at any cost, but the gondola jerked up into the air, tossing her backwards into the bottom of the basket. The crowd screamed.

Fleur struggled onto her hands and knees. With a gasp, she grabbed the leather edge and hauled herself up, only to utter a peasant exclamation at the carpet of upturned faces with mouths like nesting holes beneath her. The basket was head-height and rising fast.

Good God! No wonder people were shouting. It was not just the spectacle; de Villaret had seized the loosened anchor rope and was being carried along beneath the gondola like a human pendant. Already they were too far above the ground for him to jump to safety.

'Take it down this instant!' she yelled at the pilot but he seemed mesmerised by de Villaret's plight. 'He will be killed. Do something!'

'How can I, woman? This arse of a thing won't take orders.'

The balloon was sweeping sideways. Boissy and Gensonné were running after it across the grass, trying to grab the other trailing ropes but already these were well beyond their reach. It was heading for the woods! Merciful God! De Villaret would be smashed into the upper branches and there was nothing she could do.

But the deputy had a strong grip and the will to live. Hand over hand, heels clinching the rope like a sailor's, he managed to haul himself up until he was parallel with the basket. Kicking his legs up sideways, he struggled to pull himself up over the wicker barrier but the balloon was lifting at a more alarming rate. Fleur grabbed the deputy's arms. The loose folds of his shirt slithered from her grasp. With a grimace, he heaved himself up and she seized his elbow and pulled. No use. Dear God! The balloon, out of control, was at the air's mercy. They were above the canopy of the trees now. She

might be glad of de Villaret out of her life, but not
this way!

'Please, don't let go! You mustn't let go,' she
cried, looking round frantically for help. The *sans-
culotte* was leaning out perilously over the opposite
edge in a vain effort to tilt the gondola. With a
supreme effort, de Villaret shifted his hands along
the rail to the corner where a sandbag dangled. It
briefly gave him the hold he needed. With Fleur
tugging at him in a massive effort, his arrival in the
gondola was swift and sudden and the pair of them
went tumbling down in a tangle of skirts and
folded parasol. The air slapped out of Fleur's lungs
as his weight fell across her and the loud bravos
somewhere below turned to bawdy whistles. It was
worse than being jammed in a laundry basket.

'Thank you, citizeness.' De Villaret's voice
sounded cool as he eased himself slowly onto his
elbows, but pearls of sweat glittered on his forehead.

'You are crushing me, citizen,' Fleur pointed out
huskily. It was not amusing to be his mattress; one
of his thighs was heavy across her hip, his right
knee was lying between hers, and something hard
and parasol-like seemed to be pressing uncomfortably between her shoulderblades.

'My apologies.' The arrogant deputy made no
attempt to shift himself. His gaze was bemused. Or
maybe it was shock, she decided forgivingly, wriggling to extricate herself from such compromising
proximity. The strong wrists that had saved his life
seemed to be accidentally braceletting hers. Being
straddled twenty foot above the ground by a dazed

republican, with a balloonist sniggering at her, was not to be endured.

'I have had enough of these games. Take us down this instant!' she exclaimed to the balloon's incompetent pilot.

'Oh, to be sure, citizeness!' muttered the *sans-culotte*. 'Has she a mouse's turd for a brain? I told her already there's no driving the bloody thing.'

'Altitude sickness.' The humour was an effort; de Villaret's expression was strained. 'Citizeness?' His elegant fingers repositioned themselves, offering assistance. Chivalry from a revolutionary who had helped to demolish a monarchy? Fleur, with little choice, placed her hands in his and was drawn to her feet. The pilot muttered crudely.

'Go to the devil!' de Villaret snarled. The mischievous responding shrug argued the fellow's amusement; colour was seeping back beneath the workman's stubble.

Fleur ranged herself supportively beside her escort to glare at the offender. 'I thought you said this was not a free flight,' she accused. 'Did you organise this?' Then the unpleasant thought struck her that de Villaret was quite capable of planning such a clever spectacle. 'Did *you*?'

'No!' Her escort's voice was pure ice. 'Do I strike you as suicidal? Did *you*? The scandal will bring your patrons flocking, though you may not live to enjoy – *Oh, mon Dieu!*' His indignant scowl was vanquished by an expression of absolute wonder. About to slap him, Fleur dragged her disconcerted glare from his face and looked down.

'Oh, *oh!*' she whispered in utter awe.

In unexpected unison, all three of them gazed in enchantment at the passing canopy of the oak trees far below their feet.

'Wave to your chef, reassure him,' de Villaret advised, finally breaking the silence, his withering tone undeterred by the adventure. 'Or are you in danger of losing your breakfast?'

'I-I cannot see him.' The field of the ascent was already hidden.

'He will see you, though. It may inspire him. Eggs *à la ballon*, perhaps.' He was smiling broadly now. St Michael, returning with angelic sweat after driving Lucifer from heaven, might have smirked with equal exhilaration.

She laughed at the absurdity, patting the rim of the gondola with excited palms, and because the progress of the balloon was so stately, forgot for a few moments to be afraid. 'Oh, this is wonderful, wonderful. It is so incredibly gentle.'

The world as she had never seen it lay spread out for her delight. To the right she glimpsed a small, pretty mansion, like a doll's house, with a walled garden and lily ponds. To her left a looking-glass glimmer betrayed a lake, and a flutter of ducks rose towards them. Roads, narrow as ribbons, stretched like lacing across the forest.

'*Quelle merveille!*' The man beside her seemed as entranced as she was. Below them a small herd of deer fled daintily into the trees.

'This must be how birds see the world,' she cried excitedly.

'I wonder. Their eyes are positioned at the side compared to ours. Look there! No, there, see the rabbit? Now if I were a hawk.' He pressed fingers over his right eye in experiment. Oh yes, he would swoop.

'I am thankful you are not!' Fleur exclaimed, and watched the creature streak safely across the grass.

They were moving serenely but at a remarkable speed considering it was so calm. While the basket had been tethered upon the ground there had been no movement in the air at all, but now the balloon seemed like a dandelion seed blown by some gigantic invisible breath. And it was still soaring. In an instant the oaks would be as small as models in a child's toy farmyard.

De Villaret might be awed with pleasure but he frequently stared up inside the balloon as if to check the integrity of the fabric. There was some unspoken communication between him and the pilot. It was clearly he, not the *sans-culotte*, who had a better understanding of how the thing must be managed.

Realisation struck Fleur. Already her ears were hurting and she wondered if a human head might explode at a certain height. She swallowed in fear and then realised doing so eased the pain but not her growing terror. The great bladder would rise and rise until the air within the thin membrane started cooling and then it would plummet. At least one nobleman had died already in a ballooning experiment. She gulped again to clear her hearing and wondered how fast they would fall. The best would be to be killed instantly, the worst to be crippled.

De Villaret set his hand over her whitening knuckles. 'I see you realise how dangerous this is.'

Fleur met his gaze. 'Yes, but it will be a magnificent way to die.'

The deputy made no answer, his mouth tightening as he looked once more below. No doubt wishing to comfort her, he pointed. 'That is where half our audience came from. The last refuge of the homeless and destitute.' Fleur smelled the smoke before she saw the higgledy-piggledy, unpleasant tumble of boxes and canvas untidying the edge of the woods. Catching sight of the balloon, several women rose shrieking from beside their cooking fire. De Villaret waved to them in friendly fashion but one terrified pregnant woman fell to her knees and crossed herself.

'Try a blessing instead, citizen,' chortled the pilot. 'Pitiful cow! Probably thinks you are the Second Coming.' A crippled beggar crawled out and brandished his crutch skywards as though they carried a godlike responsibility for his impediment. Then a few barefooted children futilely gave chase; the balloon's shadow was moving faster.

'I hope that poor creature does not give birth before her time,' whispered Fleur, her own spirits seesawing between euphoria and terror. If God existed, they would soon find out. 'Was . . . was Citizen Boissy expecting to make the ascent?' She was trying not to scan the green and red seams above her for weakness. Better to force herself to admire the scatter of clouds and identify the snowy owner of each shadow dappling the fields. The balloon was floating far, far too high.

'Poor Boissy,' said the man beside her. 'He was hoping to impress the Academy of Science.'

A whistle from the pilot made them turn to stare to where his grimy fingernail pointed. Beneath a purple-brown haze, the city of Paris stretched across the western horizon from the northern grassy hill Fleur guessed to be Montmartre, south across the clutter of roofs to the neat rectangular baroque palaces of the north bank. The Cathedral of Notre Dame and the silver-grey pepper-pot turrets of the ancient palace of the Valois kings rose from the island heart of the city. To the south of the river she identified the glinting domes of Les Invalides, the veteran soldiers' home, and the Panthéon, where the famous philosophers Voltaire and Rousseau were interred.

'The *gloire de France*!' de Villaret murmured, his face alight. 'I swear I will die rather than see Austrian and Prussian flags over our city, eh, Robinet?'

The *sans-culotte* rubbed a hand across his rough cheeks. 'Well, I do not give a toss if I do not see tomorrow's sunrise, citizen. I would not have missed this for anything.'

'Nor I,' echoed Fleur.

'I am very glad, Citizeness Bosanquet,' murmured the revolutionary beside her, 'for I think it is time for confession, don't you?'

11

Feeling like Faustus with a few last moments to fathom Helen of Troy, Raoul stood before the unsuspecting La Coquette, his white sleeves flaring, his hair pirate wild. His hand itched for his sketchbook, and the bit of his brain that had any sense left was praying that they would not end the day tangled in a tree or spiked like paper billets on the desk of God.

The young widow was not praying. Her cheeks were flushed with excitement; the morning burnished her hair, and her eyes were wild and bright. *A magnificent way to die?*

'Confession?' she flung back courageously. 'Have we the time? It could take hours.'

He could have pressed her on Bosanquet's murder, instead he dragged the crumpled paper from the pocket of his breeches. This meddling actress did not realise what her mischief had cost. The broadsheet hacks would label this enterprise a frivolity and accuse Boissy of wasting money that could have been donated to the state coffers.

'This was to be a quiet launch,' he informed her coldly.

Citizeness Bosanquet tugged the wrinkled paper balloon into visibility. 'While you seduced La Coquette? *Sacré bleu!* Citizen, we are thousands of feet up and you still want to play the inquisitor!' She looked as fierce as an Amazon; a pity she was not dressed for the part as well.

'We are going to be flying across the Seine if either of you could be bothered looking,' threw in Robinet.

'Was this done with malice, citizeness, or just for notoriety?' Raoul hit the paper with the back of his hand. 'Come now, admit it. The boys were paid to cause a diversion while some hireling released the balloon.'

She swallowed and found a scathing answer: 'Eggs

à la ballon for the masses? We only have a small kitchen at the Chat Rouge, citizen. One has to be practical.'

He was close to shaking her. 'Citizeness, I have no doubt we shall all be omelettes shortly. Will it hurt to tell the truth?' Somehow honesty between them mattered, but she turned from him, cradling her shoulders and glancing up uneasily at the coloured globe above her.

'Is the truth important any longer, Deputy de Villaret? It seems to be getting colder by the instant. Are we going to freeze, do you think?'

Had she been merely a widow, he would have observed the proprieties, but she was also an actress, and Raoul was an opportunist – a swiftly cooling opportunist. Wrapping his arms about her from behind to warm himself was infinitely tempting but the back of the girl's skirt was fashionably padded with a bustle.

'You are right.' He drew her from her corner. 'Stand behind me,' he insisted and, finding her wrists, dragged them about his waist. The citeness shivered, but she lay her cheek against his shoulder, and he gradually felt her resistance give way and her soft breasts press against his ribs. Had they been alone, he would have eased her into his arms and tasted her; making love to her in a balloon might indeed be a magnificent way to die.

'You *must* be cold, citizen,' she taunted him through gritted teeth, her warm breath moistening his shirt. 'And during an interrogation too!' The broadsheet fidgeted angrily in her fingers, annoying the tiered ruffles of his shirt.

Devil take her! 'If demanding a reasonable explanation –' he began.

'Reasonable!' Before he could stop her, the annoying chit began to rip the paper and would have flung it over the side had he not seized it. 'I wish I had brought my late husband's encyclopaedia along this morning,' she exclaimed, struggling delightfully to free her wrists, 'so I might find sufficient words to describe your unspeakable behaviour. Let me go! I am not a human warming pan!'

'Take his republican arse before a tribunal, citizeness,' jeered Robinet. 'Besides, he's only belly-aching because he owns half this bloody thing.'

'Unfortunately for you, citizeness,' declared Raoul, releasing her with punctilious politeness as though it were an act of mercy, 'I make it my business to recognise the peculiarities of our printing presses. It's a useful pastime.' He was facing her now, brandishing the broadsheet. 'Your nephew Quettehou printed this.' His gaze did not leave her face, as his fingers crushed the paper theatrically and dismissed it to the floor of the gondola. 'Pass the knife, Robinet!'

His antagonist gasped as though he had already drawn blood. 'W-what are you going to do?' she demanded, recoiling, her eyes wide.

Raoul revelled in her discomfort. She might be an excellent actress, possibly a murderess and a pretty liar, but the wicker was against her back now. Cornered, well and truly!

'Do? Lighten the load, of course,' he retorted witheringly, then turned away to lean over the leathered rail and saw loose the sandbags on their side.

The first hurtled to the river with a frightening celerity. Fishermen boating in the shallows grabbed their oars, two ducks went airborne and a gaggle of washerwomen took to their heels squawking. Frowning, Raoul cut the second bag free. Significantly, the balloon did not rise further. Words were unnecessary as he grimly passed back the blade to its owner.

Robinet severed the bags on his side of their small wicker republic and then, with his back turned, relieved himself over the side. 'Lightening the load,' he explained, rebuttoning his trousers flap.

Raoul folded his arms, trying not to shiver. Was this what it felt like to stand in shirtsleeves on a tumbril in the frosty air waiting for death? Did the girl realise how close they were to it? Aloud, he said, 'Well, citizeness, I believe it's your cue.'

'I told Quettehou about the balloon launch, yes.' The girl's aqua eyes were angry slashes of fury. 'But two rogues in the crowd tried to kill me this morning and . . . and . . . I do not know what it all means.' The sigh was excellent, the sudden change of mood impressive. Her despairing gaze slid over the innards of the balloon as though she expected to see the outside air thrust through it like a fist. Then she looked once more at Raoul and rallied – a peroration delivered through clenched teeth. '*Diable!* I do not care whether you think me a gold-raking murderess or not. I will see you in hell, de Villaret!'

'Bravo!' muttered Robinet out of the actress's hearing as she bestowed a furious back on them.

'Is this the interval? If I had known I was to have entertainment as well, I'd have done this for free. Better tell her you know she is La Coquette and we'll be into act two.'

The actress's eyes became gems of aquamarine. Only the blush of rose stealing back into her pale countenance betrayed her.

'Are you?' Raoul asked.

'In mourning?' She drew a mocking hand down between her breasts. It seemed unintentionally seductive.

'But *out of mourning*?' he drawled and watched her moist lips part. Oh, there should have been champagne and wine, a slow, lazy luncheon. 'You may not realise that balloons,' he continued, choosing new weapons, and glancing down at the earth before he satiated his appetite on the gorgeous-lashed eyes warily watching him, 'balloons such as this were invented for a brief assault on the enemy defences,' and he straightened, allowing his gaze to saunter slowly up over the closely buttoned black jacket to linger on her lips, 'sufficient only to get a man over the battlements.'

'The wind's changing,' muttered Robinet, launching spit over the side for emphasis and watching how the air moved it.

'I do not want a liaison with you.' The insistence was gently done; like Raoul, she was conscious of the *sans-culotte* listening beyond his shoulder. 'It would be supping with the Devil and I do not have a long spoon.'

'That is a pity. You may live to regret it.' Raoul's

smile was bittersweet. She might think the rapiers were set back on the wall but . . . He checked upwards and caught his breath. The green and red stripes were rippling dangerously. Time for a peace treaty if there was a heaven. He swallowed and told her, 'You have my apology, for what it is worth, citizeness.' Behind her, Robinet, pale as ashes, crossed himself. Towards the west across the sling of the Seine, the forest flanking the Chateau of Saint-Germain waited like a stack of bayonets.

'Thank you at least for the experience. I do think that this,' the citizeness gestured nobly to a field of sheep below them, 'is wonderful.'

'The sheep?' Raoul asked dryly. The fields were getting larger by the second. Oh God! There might be squashed mutton for dinner.

'No,' the citizeness spluttered, tears and rash laughter battling within her as she realised what was happening, '. . . d-don't think me ungrateful, to be c-courted in a balloon. Oh Christ.' She crossed herself, gripping the rail with her free hand.

'Ungrateful!' He could outdo the entire Convention in volatility. 'Get down!' he shouted, shoving her to her knees. 'Brace yourself! And you, man, get down!'

'*Merde!*' Robinet grabbed the slackening ropes.

Raoul's stomach was trying to change places with his heart. He quickly crouched, jamming his soles against the outside frame, cradling the girl's head against his chest. The feel of her hair soft beneath his fingers might be the last sensa–

263

The gondola hit the field with a violent jolt and spewed out the humans like used flowers shaken from a brisk housewife's vase.

De Villaret took the impact against his shoulder with the other two stacked pancake-like upon him. For an instant Fleur thought she had squashed the life out of one revolutionary at least for he lay so still beneath her, and then when Robinet rolled off her back and the load upon the deputy's chest lessened, the maddeningly golden-brown eyes opened. The exuberant grin told her nothing was broken; his concern was for her.

'Are you unharmed, citizeness?' he asked as she unpeeled herself rapidly from his arms.

Yes, she was. A silly black hat tipped over one eye, the Duc de Montbulliou's surviving daughter was on her hands and knees in the mire, and close to mirthful hysterics.

A mosaic pressed into soft mud, de Villaret became aware of moist large brown eyes, generously lashed, and a lugubrious muzzle from which a bunch of half-chewed grass suspended motionless. The large physiognomy was swiftly joined by other astonished faces, slightly whiskered, as a herd of milk cows gathered to see the greatest event since the arrival of the summer bull. It was not so different from the Bois de Boulogne.

Raoul swivelled his head with difficulty and groaned at what filled his narrow view. 'Cow pats!'

'Oh Lord!' exclaimed Fleur, weeping with

laughter at the steaming dung inches from her muddy hands. 'Some things don't change.'

Raoul took charge. It was natural to him, an old habit not easily broken despite the infant democracy enveloping him. The bespattered little widow accepted his hand. Tugged upright, she swore beneath her breath and then permitted him to assist her out of the mud. At least she was not screaming at him. Furrows of cocoa-coloured mud sucked at Raoul's bootsoles as he, enjoying the curl of smaller fingers in his, conducted her across to the grass. He could have accused the girl of being gleeful but she now had her lips tightly pleated. It seemed they had landed near a gate, which flanked a water trough. It explained the milking shed on the horizon; it also explained the excessive mire. A fly caught in a doughball would have been sympathetic. The soft mud had saved their lives.

'Well, Citizen Gensonné won't find us.' Robinet squelched ashore, hiding something behind his back. The lady untangled her fingers.

'I'll hire a cart from the farm,' Raoul announced, though he did not feel too certain.

'Your poor balloon.' The chit's amusement was scarcely masked as they gazed upon the mess of rigging. The cows were still standing around it in fascination.

'*Your poor balloon*,' echoed Robinet, sniggering at the mud neatly caking Raoul's back from hair to heel. '*Mon Dieu*, citizen, you look like a half-dipped chocolate bonbon. A marvel this survived.' He held out the champagne as a peace offering.

Raoul crouched and rubbed the bottle clean on the grass. 'It is de rigeur,' he explained exuberantly to the mud-splashed citizeness. 'Standard equipment. You offer it to irate farmers, and if they are not appeased, you use it to fight your way out of a difficult situation.'

'But it wasn't a free flight,' she pointed out.

'Ah.' His smile might have charmed Marie Antoinette into feeling secure.

'Nothing is free these days, citizeness,' snickered Robinet. 'You'll be paying later.'

And what did that mean? Fleur's good humour at being alive plummeted. The deputy gave her a slow, roguish stare as he dragged the edge of his boot along the long grass. It was as if she had been bargained for and the paperwork finalised. But if her mind rapped out a frantic call to arms, the rest of her was trying not to listen. He was so deliciously debonair about the whole business. At least the front half of him was.

'So shall I stay with madame here, or don't you trust me?' Robinet was asking.

De Villaret's wicked gaze released her. 'No, damn your eyes,' the deputy answered, 'but I'll go nevertheless. See if your parasol has survived, citizeness, and hit him if he tries anything.'

Fleur managed to breathe again. 'Will you?' she asked Robinet mischievously.

'Yes, given encouragement, *ma fille.*'

'Try packing this up first,' drawled de Villaret,

and then, with a mocking salute, he climbed the gate and set off whistling up a milking track towards the sprawl of buildings untidying the fields. Halfway across the meadow, she saw him check his step for an instant and lift a hand to favour his shoulder.

'He's hurting. Why did he not just unlatch the gate?'

'Likes to do things differently. Don't you?'

Like playing tribunals in balloons, thought Fleur, licking her fingers clean of honey an hour later. The airborne champagne, couriered by a deputy of the Convention, had certainly opened helpful doors and cupboards. The local peasant farmer and his vast *tricoteuse* of a wife would be able to boast about this for the next twelve months, and in return for providing such an extraordinary spectacle, the aviators had been rewarded with a patriotic meal washed down by frequent cidery toasts to increasingly blurred republican ideals.

When the men finally staggered off singing across the fields to salvage the remnants of the balloon, Fleur leaned against the outside wall of the farmhouse and tried to tilt her lurching mind in a sensible direction. Misguided or otherwise, she reached the conclusion that she should return to Paris unobtrusively without de Villaret, so she set off east down a cart track that had looked drier, shorter and less meandering from several hundred feet up. Had she been less inebriated, she might have remembered she was not in breeches and jacket, nor armed with a knife and pistol, or that acquiring conveyance into the city once she reached the road from Dreux might cost more than her pocket or virtue could permit. The air was still and warm enough to make her wintery skirts a confounded nuisance, and the puddled, furrowed ground moved unsteadily beneath her feet, due to the balloon, the cider or perhaps both. All in all, she found the trudge exhausting and was neither surprised nor disappointed when a peasant cart drawn by two oxen eventually overtook her.

'What the Devil are you doing?' yelled de Villaret, springing from the driver's board.

'Exercising . . .' Fleur beamed in happy rebellion, squaring up to him. 'Ex-exercising my rights as a citizen of the R-republic, D-deputy,' and she saluted.

The man was utterly sober. 'Well, I regret to inform you that women, particularly foxed ones, have not yet been granted any rights.' His scowling, taunting face deserved at least a verbal swipe but before Fleur could think of a perfect retort, he swooped. She landed unceremoniously on the plank seat like a sack of flour dropped from a derrick. 'Drive on!' he ordered imperiously. 'And you, citizeness,' he added, climbing back on board with a grimace, 'are worse than all the plagues of Egypt. We were scouring the fields for you.'

'Some of us were,' yawned Robinet from behind. He was sprawled upon the sad remains of the balloon ropes, eyes shut.

'I am not foxed.' Fleur primly straightened her shoulders, swishing her skirts free of contamination from male thighs. 'Deluded, p-possibly, but not f-foxed. I have never been f-foxed in my entire life.'

De Villaret muttered something not for her hearing and lapsed into a grim silence.

'That's women for you,' muttered their obese host.

'Yes,' Fleur agreed, irrationally content. Bumping along was hardly a happier state than walking but she could now see over the hedgerows. In fact she was one of the few women in France – in the world, actually – who had seen higher than over the hedgerows. She had flown! This morning's heady, wonderful adventure had been worth every moment and even if she was sharing it with an infuriating revolutionary, at least he was an attractive, if muddy, one.

'How is your shoulder?' she asked to appease him, for every rut was jarring.

The dark eyebrows rose. 'Such solicitude,' he drawled. 'Well, it would be devilishly easier if you could move over a fraction. I fear I am in danger of bruising the other one as well if I fall off this damned thing. Our friend there is taking up half the board. If you will permit, citizeness?' And he shifted his arm so that it lay along the rail behind her back.

With two male thighs like grindstones either side of her, it was hardly romantic or comfortable but Fleur was aware of de Villaret's every breath. He must be aware of hers; for the Jacobin was not just watching the passing, undulating fields. The curl of his fingers rested only a few inches from her breast. Was this what it felt like to have a lover? This reckless, sudden ache to be touched? It must be the carafe of cider still playing backgammon with her brain, Fleur decided. She stared down modestly at her clasped hands, and then sideways at the nankeen of de Villaret's breeches against her black skirt, imagining the muscles toned from riding and from rapierplay edging her naked skin. Within her lap, her hands made mirrored question marks; ah, now she understood that other hunger. Her befuddled mind had known that to ride back into the city in his company would be foolhardy. Civil war raged within her and common sense endorsed her earlier decision. His approval was not desirable. It never could be.

The driver nudged his huge leg closer to her with a chuckle, and a rumble of some rude ditty composed for longboats came from behind them.

'Find a cork for it, Robinet!' de Villaret growled as the wheels battled a deep rut. Pain sharpened the apex of lines stretching out from the edges of his eyelids.

Fleur wriggled round. 'Pass me an empty sack, citizen.'

'Boards too hard for your derrière, madame?' The sans-culotte shoved the cleanest looking over to her.

'Lean forward,' she ordered de Villaret. Folding the sacking into a pad, she slid the hessian against the wooden backboard behind his shoulder.

'Thank you.' He leaned back gingerly, his stony profile softening. She noticed his arm was again behind her, his hand almost an epaulette.

'Oohh, thank you, *maman*,' chortled Robinet.

'You should see a physician when we get back, citizen,' Fleur advised. 'You might have dislocated something.'

'My brain, I suspect.'

'It's the kiss to make him better that he really wants, darling,' chortled Robinet.

'Citizen Robinet,' said Fleur gravely, 'if there is another sack to hand, I suggest you climb into it headfirst.' She ignored the mocking rise of a *sans-culotte* finger and attempted to put her more enigmatic companion in his place as well, especially while the deputy still had his eyes closed. Without that intelligent stare to scythe her, she might discover some answers to questions she had almost forgotten.

'So, citizen,' she purred with deceptive amiability, 'why was Columbine not there this morning?'

The dark lashes flicked open. 'Which one *is* Columbine?' he asked lazily.

He was convincing; the pace of Fleur's breathing faltered. The long fingers by her shoulder flexed.

'L-La Coquette.' It was necessary to clear her throat but her voice sounded husky, alien, as she added disapprovingly, 'the actress you have been having an *affaire* with, citizen.'

'I haven't been *having* an *affaire*. *We* are having an *affaire*.' And he shut his eyes again, his fingertips making faint indents on the pouched gathers of her sleeve. 'Nothing is free.'

More words like these voiced in a dangerous

male purr and something would overflow from her – emotional phrases that would be regretted later. Perplexed, she could only stare at the rusty swaying rumps of the labouring oxen as they travelled on in silence. The revolutionary shifted drowsily and idly gazed out across the ploughed furrows, showing no awareness that a nearby heart was thundering in haphazard confusion. Jealousy was not an emotion she had been aware of until now. Unless he meant . . .

'I had a mistress once.' The massive carter's unexpected comment startled his companions and not just the sunshine warmed Fleur's complexion. 'But then my wife found out,' he added morosely. 'Easier for you dwelling in a city.'

'Why are *you* complaining?' rumbled Robinet. 'You have haystacks and meadows.'

'Meadows! That there meadow, see.' A plump, speckled arm waved a whip towards a lush pasture. 'Looks soft, eh? But women complain. Eh, how they complain. Damp, thistles, ants, flies.' He slapped a hairy hand down on Fleur's leg and squeezed. 'Grass stains.'

'Pardon me,' ground out Fleur, hoisting the farmer's wandering hand back across his gross knee, and instinctively edged back against de Villaret.

'Petition the Convention, *mon brave*,' sniggered Robinet. 'Get 'em to pass a law against women complaining.' No one applauded.

'Must have cost a lot, your balloon,' the peasant remarked, jerking an ear towards the ropes and basket. They had left behind the waterproofed membrane.

The deputy did not answer. He batted a fly with his free hand, and the others took the hint.

Fleur's fermented-apple euphoria had finally vaporised. By 'we', this two-faced Jacobin had meant Columbine, *definitely Columbine.* He was a rake, a hypocritical bloody republican rake! She stiffened forwards, away from the dissolute shirtsleeve, resolving that from now on she would keep her distance from Deputy de Villaret no matter how enticing the invitation. All for a balloon! *Ciel,* how could she be so irresponsible, fanciful, reckless? Poor Thomas must be frantic with worry. She brushed a hand across her knees; the worst of the dirt had flaked away but some of it was ingrained into the fabric as it was into her reputation.

Nothing is free.

Good grief, this foolish scrape might be in one of those revolting broadsheets tomorrow. Christ forbid that word of this ever reached her brother in Coblenz. And her attempt to appear respectable had been a disaster. Even Hérault had warned her. Oh, if only these oxen would go faster. She hazarded another sideways glance at de Villaret and sighed. The Jacobin was indifferently observing a hovering goshawk. Probably deciding which premises to search tomorrow, she thought testily.

Raoul was actually relishing the passing play of light across the shadow growth of young wheat while he tried to forget politics and the sacrifices that might be needed on his part to protect Boissy, not to mention the escapes from La Force prison that were still his responsibility to solve. At least he and his fellow aviators were alive, and this was ridiculously idyllic. Idyllic? Aside, that was, from his aching shoulder, the fermenting, buzzing puddles, the clinging stink of byre, the plebeian chaperones – at least the oxen were sober – and the fact that the intriguing adventuress whom he was longing to seduce was possibly a murderess.

Had he been Fragonard, he would have loved this scene. A peasant hay cart – the hay an artistic amendment – in a sunlit lane! They should be wearing straw hats. No, perhaps not; the girl's incongruous black clothes and bowed head would draw the viewer's eye. Call the painting *After the Funeral*. The plain afternoon sky needed a wash of clouds to add interest, but the fresh green of the hawthorn and the rutted track with its tangled trimming of dead-nettles, cow–parsley and brambles would do well enough. Such charming depictions were now considered frivolous. Not his style, ever.

The hero in such a *frivolous* painting would have stolen an arm about his companion's waist and kissed her all the way back to the Porte Saint-Cloud, but then an artist's hero did not have an unmannerly representative of the Commune behind him listening to every rustle. Listening? *Merde*, the bastard was snoring! Raoul twisted round painfully and jabbed him. 'Turn over!' The grizzled moustache vibrated and Robinet rolled onto his side with a mutter. Wincing, Raoul lifted his arm away from the backrest and rubbed his wrist.

'You miss the countryside, citizeness?' he asked her as a white admiral butterfly performed in front of them. His companion hesitated too long, then shook her head, unwilling to be drawn.

What was she at now, this damnable spinning coin of a creature? Raoul still had not got her measure and he was curious to discover why had she deliberately broadened her country vowels in front of his friends this morning. He could think of no reason unless she knew that Boissy had been high in Artois's service, but why should that disconcert her? Here or there he could hear a phrase perfectly delivered, as if she was cleverly borrowing her tones from the noblesse. Part of her acting talent, but he would swear she had served in an exalted household before the Revolution. A lady's maid perhaps, for she kept her own person proper. Maybe the noble family had been arrested. It would explain her reticence.

'Did you grow up in a town, citizeness?'

Her neat breasts rose maddeningly beneath the figured damask. 'The last few years I have come close to starvation. Will that suffice?' Her chin jutted higher, challenging him. 'I dislike my past, citizen. I am sure you would too.'

'Things will improve,' he murmured. Oh, he would paint her, soon, yes, and then he would make love to her.

The lane halted at the Dreux road. Curving ruts dictated the cart should turn east to Paris and the oxen knew it too, falling in resignedly behind a wain packed precariously high with spiky movables and iced with insolent children.

'Improve?' The widow lifted a disdainful eyebrow at the children's protruding tongues and waggling fingers as if these epitomised the future. 'So long as you are not talking about some form of mother-hood on behalf of the Revolution,' she said dryly. 'Citizen Hérault tells me I should turn respectable.'

The remark found some tiny unpatrolled square of sensitivity. Raoul took a deep breath. 'Not with him, I trust. You'll have to deal with *la belle* Suzanne, not to mention *chère* Adèle, a former marquise in Haut Savoie who is waiting for his return.'

'*Quel dommage,*' she teased. 'He has already sent me an invitation to Le Nid.'

'Do not go. It's a cottage seraglio, thigh deep in satin cushions. He's caused a shortage. Bread, soap and cushions. No wonder there have been riots.'

She laughed and Raoul felt foolishly gratified.

'So what will improve?' she asked him shyly. He let his expression tell her something else. *Our rapport*, he answered silently, and wondered if Hérault had already kissed her and whether she had liked it.

'I mean France,' he said aloud, enjoying the way the sunlight discovered bronze glints in her nut-brown hair.

'Do you think so?' She bit her lip thoughtfully, her aqua gaze perusing his face. Tiny touches of bronze flecked the irises of her eyes. He must remember that when he painted her.

'Imagine France as a woman, citeness,' Raoul suggested, his gaze admiring the curves of her breasts beneath the vertical bands of black satin. 'She has run away from her family and has to decide whether to be happy with her new lover and not care what Europe thinks of her.'

The widow's lashes lowered, moved like a courtesan's fan, to tease. 'And what if she is dismayed that her lover has slain her father and his servants in order to seize her? France may need convincing that she will not end in hell paying for her sins.'

He grinned. 'Ah, like any sensible woman she should accept her lover's protection and the decisions he makes on her behalf. He has risked all for love of her.'

'But he offers her such an uncertain future, Citizen de Villaret.' Her voice was low, velvety. 'Society sees their union as unlawful and whispers she is a whore. And, alas, who is this true lover? It seems to me that poor France is being abused and knows not where to trust.' The kissable lips pouted. Flirtatious La Coquette was showing in the widow's eyes like a mischievous ghost at a window. 'I wager you the fickle jade may go for a soldier at the end of the day, lured by a fine uniform. Perhaps only a general's martial laurels can redeem her reputation.'

Diable, the chit somehow knew how to prick him. Raoul did not answer. Past anger resurged; his father had wanted to send him to the military academy, to follow the family tradition. '*Put away the palette, boy! Behave like a man! There is nothing finer than to be a soldier on behalf of your country.*' The final quarrel had been bitterest of all, the accusations on both sides ejected in ugly passion. Cut off penniless at fifteen, rebellious, surly and sure that he was right and the old man was wrong.

Raoul stared across the fields and with an

aching heart remembered home – Berri – a child-hood pastiche of golden summer. Behind the placid beauty had been the lowing misery of cows robbed of their calves; in their exquisite salon, his weeping mother had rocked in unhappiness, plead-ing with him to make his peace.

'So, Deputy, should France fall for a soldier?' the girl prompted, reminding him that he had not answered.

'Soldiers need continual glory,' he answered curtly, 'and the price of glory is continual war.'

It was Fleur's turn not to answer. De Villaret had taken her light words personally. Darkness glim-mered in his eyes; his mouth was a downward arc of displeasure. And there she had been merely teas-ing him about the hero, General Lafayette, who had regrettably fled across the border and was now a prisoner of the Austrians.

'Are *you* France's true lover, citizen?' she jibed mischievously.

He had recovered his composure, and amuse-ment once more crinkled the corners of his eyes. 'I would be so, citizeness.' The words were like silk drawn caressingly across her skin as the golden gaze lowered and rose again appreciatively. 'If France would have the courage to submit herself to me.'

If she had been standing up, she might have melted, thought Fleur. He was good at this.

'Ah, that's what I call a decent bit of flirting,' applauded the driver. 'Wish I could do it like that. What's France going to do, eh?' Fleur's stays did not protect her ribs from the meaningful elbow jab by the leering farmer, but she still had some ammunition left against the man on her left.

'I believe France is still undecided,' she announced, and added, 'I noticed this morning, Citizen Deputy, that you didn't open the gate in case the cows misunderstood. I rather think that you learned that the hard way. People misunderstand easily, don't they?'

How very perceptive of her! 'Maybe.' Raoul refused to be drawn. The girl was rattling him to see what pawls and ratchets still worked, but it was the farmer who took a turn at cranking up his distinguished passenger's principles as they trundled past the last of the hawthorn to plod down the strung-out line of houses that would accompany them now until they reached the city.

'What do you think about the Paris Commune, Deputy? Getting too big for their boots?'

The dishevelled deputy regarded his own muddied boots, while Fleur, the object of his seduction campaign, put her fingers to her lips to smother her laughter. Raoul smiled at her; yes, this conversation would sail again when they had jettisoned the unwelcome ballast.

'The reason I'm asking, Deputy,' pursued the farmer, rubbing a grubby finger along an itch in his moustache, 'is that one of my neighbours was selling his vegetables at Les Halles market yesterday and heard the stall-keepers sayin' Mama Roland is agitating to shift the Convention from Paris to some other city where the Commune is weaker and the people will not interfere. Any truth in it?'

'She will not succeed.'

'Ha, but look at Brittany, and further south – La Vendée. Seems like the rest of France is turning against Paris. What do you say to that? A worry, huh?'

'Yes, it is,' de Villaret agreed, glancing at Fleur to see if he had her interest, 'and it's easy to see why federalism is so attractive. Calvados, for instance, is governed by men like Lévêque and Doulcet who want no interference from a central government in Paris. Don't you agree, citizeness?' It was a stab in the dark. He was testing her. Who she knew, what she knew, who she was; but he had left it too late. The shadow of the Porte Saint-Cloud fell across the cart.

Behind them, the *sans-culotte*, stirring on his bedding like a dog instinctively scenting when home is near, struggled to a sitting position, scratched his chest and blinked blearily. 'Christ! The city already?

'No, Robinet, this is a facsimile,' muttered de Villaret. 'If you look carefully, you will see that everyone has cloven hooves. We did nominate you for the Heavenly Convention but Citizen Peter had to draw the line somewhere.'

'Passes! Step down!' Officialdom emerged briskly out of the sentry box beneath the high arch and slid suspicious eyes over the dry mud appliquéd to the lower half of Fleur's skirts as she followed the farmer down. Incredibly, Robinet was the cleanest of the four of them. De Villaret, respectable only from the front, instinctively reached for his coat before he sprang down and grimaced, empty-handed. 'Ah.'

'He is actually a Jacobin deputy.' Fleur tried hard to keep a grave face as she spoke.

Large apple-red cheeks were sucked into concaves: 'Oh yes,' said portly officialdom, 'and what's he been speaking at, citizeness, a farmyard assembly?'

De Villaret tried his most austere expression. 'Friend, if I were an aristocrat, I'd be escaping from Paris, not entering it covered in cow dung.'

Robinet leaned forward and poked the deputy. 'Ah, but you could be an aristocrat rescuing another aristocrat, Raoul. Want to know how he got covered in shit, *mon brave*? He fell out of a balloon.'

'Go to the Devil!' growled de Villaret.

Fleur turned her face to the cart and surrendered to laughter.

'Well, what *do* you want, then?' growled the deputy, glaring at the disbelieving officer. 'My pocket watch left as surety?'

'Bribery, eh? That's an offence.' The fellow sauntered round to the back of the cart. 'You can give me a ride as far as the Place de Vendôme. It's the end of my duty for today.' He settled himself on the back of the cart, legs dangling. 'Heard you at the Jacobin Club, Deputy. Heard about the balloon too. It's all over Paris.'

Glaring at the giggling widow, Raoul swore and, setting assertive hands around her waist, swung her back up onto the driver's board before she could squeak out an argument.

'Well, Citizen Quettehou will be happy,' she exclaimed cheerfully to nettle him further. 'And you can set me down near the Place de Vendôme as well.'

'It is no hardship to take you straight to your lodging.' Raoul's hands stayed long enough on her waist to feel the quick intake of breath. So she was far from immune to his pursuit! Or was she fearful of his suspicion rather than his desire?

'You mistake my meaning, Citizen de Villaret,' the widow in her lied primly. 'Thank you for the experience this morning. It was quite . . . unforgettable and I would not have missed it for the world, but I have no wish for our names to be linked further.' He was pleased to see her face and throat had turned to rose. 'I'm sorry about your balloon. And I appreciate your . . . your offer, but I am afraid deepening our acquaintance is out of the question.'

'I think you are in error, citizeness.' He seated himself beside her again and the farmer flicked the whip. The oxen started stoically.

'Error? That is a very sinister word, Deputy de Villaret, but I am not afraid of you.'

'I am delighted to hear it,' returned Raoul. They progressed in silence.

She tugged the veil of her hat down but people were staring, putting two and two together and making a dozen. The cart's load and passengers had become an entertainment. Oh, there would be hell to pay for this. Raoul's mind slid into ways and means of diluting the damage, and then with a pang of guilt he remembered the citizeness's tale of some attempt on her life. He must look into this, question her and the chef further. It would give him better reason to annoy her at the café.

'I am sorry about this,' he said, wondering why he was apologising, and reached out a hand to her tense fists.

'Don't be,' she said cryptically. 'But it wasn't my fault either.'

Confident that only she could hear him above the rattle of carts and bawl of stall-keepers, Raoul warned her, 'I don't give up easily. Don't run from me unless . . . unless Hérault has already cozened his way into your affections with perfume and gewgaws?'

'Do you imagine I am so easily bought?' No anger but a sigh. 'To be plain with you, Citizen de Villaret, I . . . I met someone once that I would like to meet again.' Each word was weighed out for him with an apothecary's care.

'A *ci-devant* lord with a pretty face.' Raoul could not resist the sneer.

'A thief, actually.' She lifted her chin – Joan of Arc, smug after conquering Orléans, might have looked just so – and she was clearly relishing his astonished expression. 'He-he helped me once. I-I could have been killed.'

'A thief elevated to hero?' he laughed, with a cynical memory of his own. 'And if this criminal comes knocking at the door?'

'I would not let him in,' she murmured coyly, her gaze sliding away as the cart halted in the jam of vehicles. Mysterious behind her veil, she added breathily: 'Besides, he won't. He will enter by the window unasked, I'm sure.' Before he could stop her, she sprang up, stepped past him and swung herself down onto the cobbles. 'Au revoir,' she beamed with a mocking twirl of skirts, and kissed her hand to Robinet and the officer.

'No!' Raoul stayed the farmer's whip hand, in two minds whether to pursue her. Liked thieves, did she? Well, he wasn't without experience.

'*Holà*, Citizen Deputy!' An insolent hand buffeted his head. 'Are we going to hold up the traffic all day while you daydream?' Robinet stepped over the backboard and landed beside him in an aroma of garlic, sweat and cow dung.

Raoul shook his mind from a reverie that had him slowly freeing La Coquette from a gauzy peignoir and surfaced to the torrent of invective from the cooper's cart queued behind them. 'Oh, *d'accord*, we're going!' he shouted back, giving a Parisian gesture.

'Well, now you've no choice, Deputy.' Robinet clapped Raoul's bruised shoulder with deliberate glee. 'Looks like *you'll* have to go in by the window as well.'

12

Patriots,
There are many uses for a balloon. It is the return to
earth that creates the problems.

EXTRACT FROM A SPEECH OF RAOUL DE VILLARET,

MINUTES OF THE CONVENTION, 1793

Concealed behind a Passy water stall, Fleur watched as the cart, snared between a fiacre and a cartful of lashed barrels, was herded down the Rue Saint-Honoré. If that was an end to her association with de Villaret she should have been glad, but by the time she reached her house, she was feeling as abandoned and deflated as the unroped balloon.

'*Mon Dieu*,' exclaimed M. Beugneux, relief

flooding his face as he flung open the door with Thomas in his wake, 'I thought p-pastoral activities went out of fashion when the *ci-devant* Queen left Versailles.'

Fleur stared down wryly at her spattered skirt as she drew each of her soles across the boot-scraper. 'Haven't you heard of mode *à la crotte*?'

The gentleman's thin mouth twisted in impious pity as he plucked a hatpin of impertinent straw from her hair. 'My dear child, I really think you should come inside before the trend sets P-Paris ablaze. Thomas here has almost been reduced to a nothingness.'

'*Patronne.*' The large man was in tears as he embraced her. 'What happened to you? The deputy's friends and I tried to follow but –'

'It is all right, Thomas, we all survived, but I am sorry I caused you such concern.' Ushered into the small salon, she sank down on a chair and gratefully accepted a *café noir.* 'I am back to earth as you can see but, believe me, there were moments –' The two men listened without interruption as she told of her adventure.

'*Formidable,*' applauded M. Beugneux afterwards, 'but, as you will have observed, the trouble with dirt is that it adheres to all manner of things. I really think you should see this.' He unfolded a pamphlet from his coat pocket. 'As you see, the ink is hardly dry. Your acquaintance Emilie Lemoine brought it round shortly before your return.'

It was Marat's broadsheet *L'Ami du Peuple.*

*My brothers, my friends, it should be drawn to your
notice that two of our deputies are wasting money
on hot air to impress their charms upon a femme
galante. The people want to know, nay, demand
to be told, the source of their funds for such an
expensive enterprise. Have these citizens another,
more lucrative sideline – like dipping into the public
coffers or diverting army supplies? What says La
Minette Rouge or, judging by her modiste, should
we say, Noire? 'Alors, people of Paris, it will take
more than getting a balloon up to impress me!'*

Black pussycat! Fleur gasped. Marat meant her.
'But this is lies,' she exclaimed in outrage. 'I have never
. . . Why I . . . I only met Citizen Boissy . . . today.'

M. Beugneux refilled her coffee cup. 'Hmm,
you understand the phrase *femme galante*, of course,
my dear?'

Oh, she did: actresses, mistresses, the 'other'
women who made men's relationships triangular.
Fleur felt her face growing hot. 'This is absolutely
vile,' she exclaimed, rising from her chair in fury.

'I daresay Marat has been longing to bring the
aristocrat Boissy d'Anglas down and this is his
moment. Where are you going, *petite*?'

Fleur paused at the door. 'Why, I am going
round to the Jacobin Club to tell Marat what he
can do with his broadsheet.'

M. Beugneux frowned and set aside his cup and
saucer. 'I suppose there is no hope of dissuading
you, my child? There has been enough hot air
about today and M–Marat doesn't need any more

to inflate him to the heights of Mount Olympus. Besides, while your appearance is charmingly rural, it lacks . . .' he raised his quizzing glass at her dishevelled appearance, 'shall we say, authority.'

The exertion of the hasty walk creamed off some of her fury but on reaching the Jacobin Club just as the session was conveniently breaking up, Fleur, now cleanly gloved and gowned, cranked herself up to take on the *enragé* of *enragés*. The broadsheet in her hand like a bayonet, she charged in, scanning the chamber for Marat with as much ferocity as a well-paid dragoon ordered to search the undergrowth for royalists.

'Fleur!' With a gleaming shake of her hoop earrings, Emilie caught her arm. 'It is you. Bonjour! I heard about the balloon. What sport, *hein*?'

'That's why I'm here. Where is Marat?' It was a wonder she couldn't smell him – except that she'd heard he bathed daily to relieve his skin condition – but there he was, scruffy as ever, debating some point with the tall – unusual for a native of the Auvergne! – Deputy Jean-Baptiste Carrier and two other men below the rostrum. Fleur marched on past the benches and straight into the cluster. Carrier, shocked at her audacity, paused in midsentence.

'Miaow!' said someone.

Cheeks burning, Fleur tried to shake off Emilie's restraining hand. 'I wish to speak with you, citizen, in private.'

'Want to levitate with him as well, *ma belle*?' Carrier asked snidely.

'Here will do, citizeness,' replied Marat, his gnome's eyes wicked.

The amused male audience was disconcerting but Fleur took a deep breath and brandished *L'Ami du Peuple*. 'If you call yourself a writer, you should be better informed . . . *and accurate!*'

The beloved of the people sucked in his cheeks. 'Moi, chérie?'

'Yes! You made up most of this.' She rattled the paper. 'Where is your integrity? This is just gossip to titillate the ignorant.'

'Wooohoo.' The cluster of listeners about her was multiplying.

'You imply I am an adulteress. You slander me without any thought for the truth or how this may put me out of business.'

'I should imagine it will bring customers racing in, sweetheart.' The impudent hack was smiling.

'But you quote me, Citizen Marat. I *never* said these things! How can you justify such vilification? Oh, I was prepared to have respect for you, citizen, but such utter rubbish convinces me you are prepared to prostitute truth just to sell more of this.' She crumpled it and shook the contents of her fist. 'You owe me an apology, Citizen Marat.'

'*Ma petite fille*, this is, shall we say, a little revenge for La Coquette's impertinence.'

Ignoring Emilie's warning tug, Fleur held her ground. 'I do not mind apologising for that, Citizen Marat. At least my actress didn't misquote or cheapen you. And as for you saying that the Republic does not need balloons, well, let me –'

'Oh, hold your tongue, you trollop,' Felix Quettehou drawled, materialising at Marat's side like a pantaloned guardian angel. 'Shall we ban her from the club, citizens? Give her a spanking and send her home?' He smirked at her astonished face.

'I'm a good hand with a slipper,' threw in Deputy Carrier, but the great man flung up a hand to silence them both.

'Young woman, are you telling me that this morning's expensive little enterprise served *any* purpose?'

'Yes, it did, Citizen Marat, if you want France to win this war against Austria. Don't you know balloons can be steered over the enemy's line or into citadels and forts and . . . well, someone has to pay the money and take the risks and –'

'– impress whores?' Quettehou sneered, making full use of their audience to add, 'If you are so virtuous, Citizeness Bosanquet, go home and sew for the army!'

Trying to ignore the humiliation, Fleur straightened her shoulders, unable to think of any words acid enough to hurl in his face. 'This is none of your business, Citizen Quettehou.'

'Isn't it?' Receiving an encouraging nod from Carrier, her horrid nephew continued: 'You seduce an old, dying man into signing my inheritance over to you and now you are dragging his good name through the gutter.'

Fleur stepped back as though he had slapped her; the expressions around her were no longer indulgent.

'I did not seduce your uncle, Citizen Quette-hou. I tried to save his life and my involvement in the whole business this morning was an accident.'

'*Grieving* widows do not go to balloon ascents.'

The despicable cur! Fleur stared bleakly at her own defeat. It was time to retreat with tattered banners and a huff of virtue – or she could try fainting. But before she could even employ the first strategy, Marat said quietly: 'I hear someone set fire to your café premises, citizeness.'

'Yes, citizen.'

'It wasn't me, Citizeness Bosanquet. I appreciate good food too much.' With a hand on the small of her back, the great man steered her out of the group and walked her towards the door. 'I have some terrible faults, sweetheart, but arson isn't one of them.'

'I never accused –'

'No, you didn't, child. I am glad you didn't think I was responsible.'

It was necessary to ask one more question. She swallowed, her gaze modest, and asked: 'They won't march anyone into a tumbril, will they, because of this? I should not want that to happen. If the people believe –'

'Sentimental about de Villaret, are you?' An ink-stained finger flicked her cheek. 'Oh, I know he's pursuing you. I should cut a wide berth round that young blade if I were you. Take my advice. Go home and forget about him. He's like the rest of us. The Revolution is our wife; our mistresses are just . . . mistresses.' Then, with a chuckle, he tugged the pistol from his belt and playfully aimed it at one of the neighbouring windows. 'It's not de Villaret but Boissy d'Anglas I have my sight trained on. Money to burn and friends across the Rhine.' He fired. The window pane cracked and a whole platoon of outraged pigeons took to the skies. 'You have good nerves, *ma fille*. Have I made my point?'

Fleur, white as a flag of surrender, recovered her deafened wits. 'Someone could have been behind that glass,' she accused.

'What is one life to save many,' Marat's gaze was piercing now, 'so long as France is served? By the way, de Villaret needs to arm himself. The Girondins are after me, but for now they'll be pleased with whatever Jacobin bird they can shoot at, and he'll do nicely.'

'Why are you putting yourself through the mangle, Raoul, pretending that it was only you who financed the balloon enterprise? Boissy's a big lad. He should look after himself.' Armand, for once laden with a tennis racquet rather than a work of philosophy, encountered Raoul next morning in the forecourt outside the wing of the Tuilleries Palace where the Convention was in Sunday session.

Raoul smiled. The fastidious Boissy would shudder at being likened to a stable hand. 'It's all right, Armand. I can defend myself.' And I have a debt to repay, he added silently. When Raoul's father had cut off his defiant son's allowance, it had been his godfather, Boissy's papa, who had persuaded the famous David to take Raoul on as an apprentice. 'I imagine your Girondin friends have their knives already whetted,' he added.

'I am sorry, Raoul. You know they've been waiting for an opportunity like this. Even Manon Roland is in the gallery.'

'Then I had best get this over with. Are you coming in?'

'No, this is one debate I will not be part of. Good luck, my friend.' He embraced him in Gallic fashion. 'Ah, wait, I forgot. Did you know your rural Venus accosted Marat at the Jacobin Club last night?'

'She did *what*?'

'Accused him of vilifying her. You'd better go. Hérault's over there waiting for you. At least your friends are rallying.'

But Hérault, with Marat's broadsheet poking out of his redingote pocket, did not look in the least sympathetic. 'Have you read *L'Ami du Peuple*?' he growled, unfolding his arms and falling in beside Raoul as they entered the vestibule.

'Oh, I saw it.'

'Insufferable! You must deny everything they throw at you and let Marat have Boissy's head if that's what he wants. It'll keep the Girondins off our backs.'

Raoul stopped and swung round on him. 'For God's sake, Hérault, I am not going to let Marat crucify Boissy just because he worked for royalty. I am playing this my way!' and he strode through the great doors alone.

It was an hour later when he finally left his seat among the Mountain deputies to take the rostrum. If the word 'balloon' was mentioned any more today, he wouldn't be keeping his fists in his pockets, he vowed silently as he climbed the steps to answer the volley fired at him by the Girondin deputies.

The latter were jubilant. They had been bombarded with so many accusations of filching government funds, collaborating with the Austrians and selling army supplies to fill their own pockets in the last weeks that they were now squawking like exuberant carrion crows at having a Jacobin to pick at. *Salauds!*

'You may proceed, citizen.'

Raoul calmly inclined his head to the president and began to present his answers. Lucidly, he hoped. For every government jeer, he hurled back chapter and verse on the use of balloons in war and commerce. He bared his breast for the Girondins to shoot at, claiming that it was he who had financed the entire ascent.

'You're a liar, de Villaret,' roared Marat.

'Audit my papers then!'

It was honest. This morning, despite Boissy's protests, Raoul had paid the bills for yesterday's bricks and cables; but now, facing the tough men who had weathered the Revolution, he wondered if that had been enough. The squabbling Convention was out of control. Nothing less than an exorbitant donation to the public coffers would dampen this fire – unless they demanded his head as well.

When he finally stepped back down onto the floor of the assembly, he knew what it felt like to be crossed off the morning's tumbril list. He was going to be a lot poorer by sunset but at least the Girondin government needed money more than it needed executions.

Georges Danton took the rostrum after him and in tones that a Pericles or Marcus Antonius would have been proud of, grandly began to defend the cause of love. Raoul, roused by pokes from his companions, listened in growing horror. It would have been rather amusing had he not been the 'damsel in distress' this particular Saint-Georges was rescuing.

'*Diable!* Hérault, is this your doing?' he muttered behind his hand. It was tempting but ill-advised to march his companion outside behind a hedge and punch him on that well-bred nose.

'Saved you a fortune, haven't I?' chortled Hérault. 'Isn't Danton a marvel? Look up there, *mon brave*, have you ever seen so many women snivelling?' It was a wonder Hérault had not solicited Citizeness Bosanquet to go into a dramatic swoon in the gallery while she tossed out broadsheets advertising breakfast. At least she wasn't here, thank God.

'Would you like your face rearranged now or later, Hérault?'

'Such ingratitude! At least you cannot rearrange Danton's. It's already been done.'

Moved by Danton's stentorian magnificence, the session broke up moist-eyed and forgiving, and Raoul, with a coterie of sentimental Jacobins protecting him as though he were a prize stud at a horse fair, ended up in a tub-thumping, drunken haze in Danton's wine cellar singing 'Ça Ira'.

At 47 Rue des Bonnes Soeurs, Fleur set down Matthieu Bosanquet's coffeepot before she spilt its contents on the tray cloth, and listened to Emilie in utter astonishment.

'Oh, Citizen Danton spoke so prettily, love, you could have heard a flea jump, an' it was as if . . . as if he was speaking directly to the heart of each and every one of us patriots.' Emilie clasped her hands at her breast like a nun in ecstasy.

'Sentimental rubbish,' protested Fleur, 'and not a word of truth in it.'

'So you may say, my duck, but you and de Villaret are the talk of Paris. There'll be a cram at your café tonight.'

'I wish I had not been indisposed,' growled Fleur. Yesterday's excitement had brought on her monthly flux and she had missed attending the Convention. 'Truly, I'd like to wring their necks, de Villaret's and Danton's. True love, pfft!'

Her friend looked as disappointed as a child told not to believe in fairies. '*Merde*, I wish someone would link my name with Armand Gensonné's like that.' Emilie's infatuation was remarkable, considering her politics and that she knew very little about Gensonné other than he looked good in his breeches and had once smiled at her. 'And to be kissed in a balloon.' Emilie's sigh was volcanic.

'I don't care how many thousand fools swear

they saw us kissing,' repeated Fleur through clenched teeth. 'De Villaret did *not* kiss me.'

'Still, maybe he will paint your picture now. With nothing on.' Emilie giggled.

'Pfft, that's about as likely as Citizen Robespierre being a monarchist,' muttered Fleur. If de Villaret suggested that, she would smash his canvas down on his head with the greatest of pleasure.

Raoul woke up groggily. He remembered drinking some spectacular wine that had been acquired by Danton in dubious circumstances, but the rest of his recall was cloudy to say the least. When reality struggled to the surface of his drowsy, aching brain, he discovered he was lying on someone's flagstone floor with his mouth as dry as blotting paper, and that the nearby bubbling sounds were not coming from fermenting grapes but a snoring Hérault.

He relieved himself in a bucket and, stumbling upstairs from the cellar, discovered that someone had inconveniently snuffed out the sun. Navigating the dark, lurching courtyard, he halted to clumsily sluice his face at the rainwater butt, and since that did as much good as a wart on a princess's nose, submerged his head to the tip of his ears and then stood, ostrich-like, waiting for his reason to return.

It did. With a vengeance – or certainly part of it did! His conscience dictated that he should offer some sort of apology to a particular young widow without delay and this required strong coffee, a fiacre and some grovelling. The first matter was easily settled, courtesy of the pretty nursemaid in charge of Danton's children. The second took somewhat longer, but a coach eventually unloaded him in the Rue des Bonnes Soeurs. The grovelling?

Sober enough to wish to avoid an audience, and observing that an aproned carpenter and his apprentice were sitting untidily on a doorstep in the courtyard of number forty-seven passing a bottle back and forth, Raoul retreated towards the nearest alleyway. It led him to a narrow lane that conveniently spined the back walls. He counted the buildings, miscalculated and repeated the effort, hoping he had found the right gate. It was locked, nor did any candles flicker behind any of the upper windows. Perhaps he should leave matters until tomorrow, but he was here now and maybe she might even . . . No, in his less than exuberant state, he knew some fantasies were improbable. He lingered, concealed in the shadows, eyeing the high wall, and then he heard someone hurrying along the alley. A woman, shoulders bent as though she huddled into her shawl, moved with furtive haste along the lane towards him. For an instant he assumed it could not possibly be Citizeness Bosanquet, but the creature darted a swift glance to left and right and then, before Raoul could gather the right bouquet of words to thrust at her, she deftly inserted a key into the gate and let herself through into the Bosanquet garden, hurriedly locking it behind her. He heard another door whine open, and close.

'Oh, *sacré Christus*, child! Don't scream!' The woman intruder spun round on the landing at the challenge, holding a finger to her scarlet lips, and Fleur gazed, round-eyed, at M. Beugneux. Not only was her gentleman boarder wearing one of the dressing-room's wigs, more modest than the one Fleur had used for La Coquette, but from neck to waist he was snugly buttoned into a woman's brown bodice jacket. Her astonished stare took in his ample female bosom – stuffed with what? – and slid down over the voluminous bustled skirt. He raised the hem with a rebellious pucker to show flat-heeled shoes – women's, nevertheless.

'It is not what you think.'

'I'm not thinking anything,' retorted Fleur. 'But if it's not what you expect I'm supposed to think, what should I think?'

M. Beugneux's face crinkled further. 'I can –' He stopped and his gloved hand darted up, silencing any further response from her. They froze and listened but the house was silent save for the distant snores of Thomas from the floor above. Beneath the cascade of ringlets, the gentleman's shoulders slumped in relief. 'Oh dear, my nerves are all over the place. Go back to bed, dear child. I owe you an explanation, but will it keep till morning?'

'I suppose so,' Fleur whispered back. 'But I want the truth. You will have plenty of time to think up an explanation but it had better be exceedingly good.'

'Oh, you shall have the truth, child, but you might prefer lies. Go to bed now.'

'Wait, monsieur, Machiavelli wasn't in his box when I got back.'

'Then it was probably just him we heard.' M. Beugneux crossed himself in relief. 'He will turn up. Sleep well.'

Sleep well! With a python on the loose, an elderly man posing as a woman on the other side of the hall and her reputation ruined by de Villaret and his despicable cronies! Fleur's nerves were hopping like dislodged fleas. All she needed was Felix Quettehou to break in and her day would be complete.

Raoul slid over the windowsill and allowed his eyes to become accustomed to the darkness. Someone was moving about on the floor above and he heard a woman exclaim. Less befuddled now, he moved like a cat, soft-pawed, through the downstairs rooms and paused beside a secretaire in the parlour. His eye might not be so alert to assess, nor his mind to remember, but his curiosity as to what lay behind the marquetry foliage was too great to resist. Besides, it would give the girl time to remove her outer garments. Far easier to negotiate with a woman in a peignoir, without the ramparts of stays and petticoats.

Pulling the heavy curtains tight across the salon window, he drew a tinderbox out of his coat pocket and lit its small companion candle, orientating it so that its special shield reflected all the light across the table. The secretaire was locked. He searched in his pockets for the wire he always carried in case he forgot his door keys. The drop front yielded within minutes like an easy woman but held no female secrets within its drawers. All the papers belonged to Matthieu Bosanquet. Letters, old leases and invitations, addresses, receipts – archives of a busy life – but no dutiful letters from a young wife in the provinces, which was odd. Several, though, from Felix Quettehou the printer, all about money: requests for loans, but the most recent had been short and vindictive:

If you don't pay up, I'll print the truth.

This house was brimming with secrets. He retied the tape about the bundle. Then, fingers sensitive as a physician's, he ran a hand over the interior of each of the small compartments. Nothing. Disappointed, he set each pile of papers carefully back. What else beside her alleged marriage vows had linked the young actress to Matthieu Bosanquet? The girl in the balloon gondola had displayed nerves of steel. But surely not a murderess? Surely she was not working in the printer Quettehou's interests? Every feeling in Raoul hallooed that argument down because he wanted her. Infinitely desirable, courageous and a wonderful blend of mischief and something else – an innocence with men. Well, she wanted a romantic thief. He smiled stupidly at the ceiling and then remembered the duke's chit of a daughter pointing her papa's pistols at him. There was a thought! God forbid the alluring widow kept pistols in her boudoir. Apologise, he told himself, but with style! And with luck, she might cook him breakfast afterwards.

But with the cautious testing of each tread as he climbed the stairs, Raoul began wondering at his madness. Twice the creaking nearly betrayed him. Three doors. Were all the rooms occupied? Grinning, he stooped and felt the carpet before each. One piece was hardly worn. He ignored that door and listened against the door on the left. The quiet was almost too intense. He tried the handle. Locked. Which left the room at the back. He waited and then slid a delicate touch around the handle. It turned.

Inside the darkened room, a movement to his right froze him. Damn it! He was jumping like a spinster aunt at his own reflection. He ventured further, thankful this was not the frothy boudoir of a whore de luxe, but it hardly seemed a woman's taste either. *Was* this her bedchamber? Yes, he recognised the familiar, light perfume in the air before he heard the rustle of the bedclothes. The curtains were securely drawn but he managed to distinguish the drapes of the dark canopy framing the head and foot of the bed against the far wall.

If he were wise, he should slide a hand over her mouth lest she alarm the whole street with a scream, but there were more delicate ways of waking a sleeping woman, particularly this one. Sitting down upon the counterpane towards the foot of the bed, Raoul let his imagination charge ahead, but he was not out of control. Not yet. A peace treaty needed to be set on the table before he . . . well . . . raised the matter of a nocturnal alliance.

'Citizeness?' he whispered softly but as he reached out to rock her ankle through the coverlet, the point of a rapier pricked through the stock beneath his jaw.

'Do not move!' She had emerged from the darkness to stand behind him.

With steel pricking his skin, he could hardly swallow. 'I . . . would not dream of it.'

'De Villaret!' Her astonishment dissipated in seconds before he could disarm her. 'I thought it was . . . Why, *you bastard*!' Her voice was a soft hiss of venom in the darkness. 'How dare you come here!'

'You told me that your thief would come by the window, so I . . .' *Diable!*

Across the pace of shadowy air, he sensed her struggling for words.

'But he's *my* thief, damn you!' The rapier shook with indignation, tickling his neck in deadly fashion. '*Mon Dieu*, are all the men in Paris demented tonight?'

He must be. And who else did she . . . ? On the edge of his vision, someone shifted. *Diable!* Raoul realised with a jolt that if she was holding the weapon, who the blazes was lying in her bed?

'Put the blade away, citizeness,' he said firmly, wishing he could read her face, and skewed his gaze sideways trying to distinguish the shape beneath the bedclothes – the man's dark hair upon the pillow. Not someone's mighty bulk, thank God! Which excluded Hérault or Danton, and anyway both of them were sleeping off the drink. Who the hell was it? Some *inconnu*? The thought that she was already taken winded him. He had been too confident.

'I cannot believe your utter insolence, Deputy.' With renewed control, the girl let the steel point stroke down his cheekbone. Then she jabbed him beneath the chin again. 'Do you not understand a plain "no", citizen, or must I daub the word above my front door with a row of lamps beneath it?'

'I did not come to ravish you.' Mere inches from Raoul's thigh, her lover stirred beneath the bedclothes. It would only take a scream from her to wake the sluggard. Or was the man feigning sleep and biding his time to settle the quarrel? Raoul braced himself in readiness.

'No?' He winced at the contempt in her voice. 'Ah, you just happened to be strolling past my windows and decided to leave your card in my bedchamber.'

'I came to apologise and . . . I had not realised you already have a lover in your bed, citizeness,' he drawled finally with what he hoped passed for dignity. But the huffy offence he felt must have been evident, for the girl began to laugh and her control of the sword became so precarious that she stepped back, trying to stifle her spluttering in the sleeve of her peignoir.

'What is so amusing?' Raoul demanded in a fierce whisper and tried to stand.

'*Stay where you are!*' She thrust the thin blade back towards his chest, forcing him back down.

'Why don't you defend her?' he sneered at the supine occupant of the bed. The coward did not stir.

'He cannot answer you, citizen.' Hysteria flickered on the edge of her soft, mocking laugh. The rapier was beyond her control, wavering danger-ously. He cautiously pushed it aside with the back of his hand and swallowed, his flesh prickling. 'Cannot?' He snatched another look at the cover-let and edged to his feet. 'In God's name, madame, who is in your bed?'

The rapier fell to the floor and she doubled over, her hands crossed over her ribs with laughter. 'You really want to know?'

He must have fainted. By the time he struggled to his senses, his hands were bound and a huge, brawny fellow whose hands smelled of onions was hoisting him across the back of a hairy beast. If this was a nightmare, why could he not wake up? The drinking bout at Danton's. He must be still in the wine cellar. Yes, that was it. But the smell of hay and newly emitted horse dung filled his nostrils and the memory of lying on the floor with a monstrous snake slithering across him seemed terrifyingly vivid. Recall hit him with the impact of icy water and with it the knowledge that he, one of the proud conquerors of the Bastille, had ignominiously lost consciousness on a woman's boudoir floor.

The ground, a mess of hay, looked damnably close. Oh God, they had him over the back of an ass! Him, Deputy Raoul de Villaret! They were in some sort of stall. He struggled, swearing loudly. The donkey backed in panic.

'Hush, Deputy,' scolded a female voice, 'or you will become utterly notorious.' Mme Bosanquet materialised at the head of the beast and clicked her tongue to calm the creature. How was she managing to grab one of Raoul's feet when both her arms were embracing the donkey's neck?

'Stay still,' rumbled a menacing voice from beneath the belly of the creature. Strong hands were lashing Raoul's ankles to his wrists. A face, sweaty and familiar, loomed up in the candlelight. 'You may be a deputy, my friend,' muttered the Chat Rouge's massive chef, 'but it doesn't give you the right to abduct defenceless young widows and invade their boudoirs. Have you no self-respect?'

'Defenceless!' spluttered Raoul, trying again to wrench himself free. '*Her*, defenceless! She sleeps with a bloody python. Get me off this damned animal at once!'

'Hush now, stop blustering.' The girl, bundled bearlike against the cold in some sort of thick wrap, crouched beside Raoul and stroked his forehead. Her fingers smelled of honeysuckle and donkey. 'Thomas will take you home. Where do you live?'

'I am not telling you,' snarled Raoul, jerking his head away from her touch. He did not want to seduce this vixen any longer; he wanted to put her across his knee.

'Then you had better lead Blanchette round the streets until the deputy sees sense, Thomas. But I do warn you, Citizen de Villaret, it will provide marvellous copy for *L'Ami du Peuple*. Of course, if you bribe Marat, he might forego the pleasure of publishing. Ah, but he's not venal, is he? What a pity.'

'Oh, my God!' Strangling her was fast becoming a pleasurable thought.

'Don't rely on the Almighty to be sympathetic,' lobbed in her chef. 'He rode donkeys too, remember.'

Too angry to answer the blasphemy, Raoul lapsed into furious silence as they led him out, only comforted by the fact that most of Paris was still snoring. The donkey's hooves clicked loudly on the haphazard cobbling as they crossed the silent courtyard and Raoul buried his face in the thick pelt, praying no curtains twitched to witness his humiliation.

'Wait, madame!' whispered Thomas as they reached the street. He held the lantern aloft and checked the knots. 'As good as a trussed chicken.'

'I'll give you trussed chicken!' fumed Raoul, glaring at two pairs of feet. 'Now, let me off this creature, you little harpy! You've had your jest.'

'Feel free to shout for help, Deputy,' retorted the outrageous chit, 'but the scandal will be all over the city faster than the news of a fall in bread prices. Now, *where* would you like to go?'

'I – oh, Rue Saint-Antoine, damn you!'

'A tedious ride, then.' She crouched once more. Hands, used to work, petalled his face, and then she laughed and kissed his hair playfully. 'Bon voyage.'

'She's not receiving!'

Raoul jammed his foot in Fleur's hallway before the gaunt woman could shut the door in his face a second time. The baby she was holding blew a kiss at him.

'What, not even a deputy of the Convention?'

he drawled with a raise of eyebrows. 'Go to Citizeness Bosanquet again. Advise her I shall wait until she is ready to see me but pray tell her not to be long. I am not a patient man.' The decadent custom of ladies entertaining gentlemen callers while their servants took hours to dress them had disappeared from Paris – regrettably. He could have strangled her slowly in her chemise.

He waited. The woman could have shown him into the salon, not left him on the step like a muddy sabot. He could sense the eyes at the windows. Across the courtyard a joiner stopped singing the role of Figaro and was staring at him with a mechanic's curiosity.

The creak of stair within the house made Raoul swing round hopefully only to encounter a tall, thin elderly man who looked as astonished as he. The gentleman paused and then continued down the stairs, the skirts of a dull *surtout* coat slithering behind him.

'If you are here for payment, I will give you the address of Citizen Mansart. He is dealing with all madame's affairs.'

'He isn't dealing with this one.'

'Oh, forgive me.' The distrait look vanished; the lines cobwebbing the man's whitened face deepened, and the thin red mouth puckered into a vague hint of welcome. 'Citizen de Villaret, of course, of course. Come in. Madame Bosanquet is already at the café. Perhaps there is something I can help you with.' Had this ancient fop witnessed his humiliation last night?

'You have the advantage of me, sir.' Raoul removed his hat since the woman had not reappeared to take it, and pulling off his gloves, laid them upon the small hall table.

'Oh, B-Beugneux. André Beugneux.' The clasp of fingers was tepid. Raoul was offered a chair in the salon and sat down opposite his host, wondering – and not only about last night's donkey. Who was this leftover from the ancien régime?

'I g-gather you have demonstrated some interest in Madame Bosanquet's past,' the older man remarked. 'You left the secretaire open.'

'Careless of me.' Very careless.

'Utterly,' the man concurred. 'So what are you h-here for? To apologise . . . *again*? Or is this an official call?'

'I know that those responsible for Matthieu Bosanquet's unfortunate death have not yet been found, Citizen Beugneux, and I dislike mysteries. If I can help clear Citizeness Bosanquet of any suspicion, I shall count myself useful to her.'

'H-how thoughtful of you, Deputy.' Beugneux withdrew a porcelain snuff box from his pocket, flicked it open and offered Raoul a share. Refused, the older man took a pinch, loosened it upon his wrist and inhaled. 'Widows, particularly those recently bereaved,' he observed languidly, 'are beset with a whole rainbow of emotions and, as you may have observed, our little provincial citizeness is scarcely out of the schoolroom. Do you not think it wise to let her come to terms with her loss? You place temptation in her way at a time when

Fleur is exceedingly . . .' the thin white fingers spread, 'vulnerable.'

Fleur. Her name rested in Raoul's mind like a blossom on his palm. Yes, *Fleur*.

'Warning me off, citizen?' he retorted with asperity. 'Are you some relative to her?' What right had this scented nobody to interfere? And Fleur Bosanquet had shown no sign of grieving – except when she remembered!

The old gentleman raised his quizzing glass. 'My d-dear young man, your p-persistent attention has become rather a nuisance, a p-public nuisance! Since M-Matthieu Bosanquet was a friend of mine, I really do feel he w-would want me to safeguard his widow.'

'I am sure he would, citizen. No doubt you too might have had reasons to rejoice in his demise.'

'Tsk, tsk!' The quizzing glass was permitted to fall. 'As you will have observed when you examined his will last night, D-deputy, it left nothing to me.'

'Except his young, charitable widow. What happened to the aunt from Caen? Was she some hired actress?'

The answer was withheld. Beugneux moistened his lips like some ancient reptile before he replied, 'I hear you m-met Citizen Machiavelli and had an interesting journey home.' The old eyes, pouched with frail skin, narrowed at him. 'Stay away, Deputy, find amusement elsewhere or your adventures this morning may become an amusing anecdote for P-Paris. As I believe you are aware, madame's nephew owns a p-p-printing press.'

With a shrug at the threat, Raoul rose to leave, his expression no less stern. 'Murder is not something that is acceptable to the Republic of France, citizen,' he warned as M. Beugneux saw him out.

'You surprise me.' The man's eyes glittered as he pulled open the door. 'Then I am mistaken in what I observed last September. Adieu, monsieur.'

If bread had been more abundant in Paris, Fleur would have fed the chestnut-headed *pochards* that had swum up waggling their tail feathers at her, but it might have started a riot. Instead she joined M. Beugneux on the path and linked her arm through his. Thankfully he wore a commonplace *surtout*, the colour of squashed olives, over his usual plumage and they made an innocuous pair unlikely to draw attention.

Strolling through the gardens of the old Palais de Luxembourg did not restore her spirits like the forest trees of Grimbosq. Fresh green leaves had struggled out into the city's smoky air; a red squirrel streaked like a flame up one of the tree trunks, but the hubbub of hooves, wheels, dogs and touters could still be heard from the Rue d'Enfer. The swept paths and clumps of jonquils were more joyous than the mired streets with their broken cobbles, and at least their conversation could not be overheard.

M. Beugneux had not yet come to the point of revelation. He had been skating around that particular crack in the ice ever since they left the house and had only this minute informed her that

311

de Villaret had called while she had still been asleep.

'My dear, this admirer of yours is becoming a trifle *de trop* and he really has the manners of the times – none at all.'

'Only when he's trying to frighten. Perhaps I should have spoken with him this morning, monsieur. Maybe I could have found out why he really broke into the house.'

'I suspect he was following me, my dear, which does present a rather large problem – for both of us.'

'Then you had better tell me what this is about.' Perhaps de Villaret was not really interested in her at all – a relief and a disappointment – but what in God's name had M. Beugneux been playing at?

'The aristocrats that escaped from La Force, *petite*. I was hoping not to involve you, but I regret to say they are hiding on your property, little one.'

She halted, withdrawing her arm from his. A crack in the ice? A cursed great, gargantuan hole! My God, this was the last thing she expected. 'What, at the house?'

'Not at the moment.' The gentleman seemed relieved that she did not faint or turn hysterical. 'No, my dear, at the Chat Rouge.'

She did not know whether to be relieved or furious but she must give nothing away. 'The voices I heard on my first visit! Not ghosts at all.'

He shook his head. 'A few days more in prison and they would be.' His frown grew deeper. 'I congratulate you on your sangfroid . . . and admirable discretion.' He was studying her with renewed curiosity. 'So you heard them, when was that?'

'The first afternoon I was there with my aunt. Not since, I promise you.' Her gloved hand curled round his arm. 'You!' she said in wonderment. 'All the while it has been you rescuing them?'

He pinkened and glanced away modestly, the flutter of eyelash judged perfectly. 'With a little assistance.'

'Oh, M. Beugneux, how very brave.' Inside, she was wondering how many more malevolent tricks God had up his sleeve for her. No one was what they seemed any more. What else could cursed well happen? Emilie admitting she was an English spy? The python the Emperor of Austria in disguise?

'But now I have endangered you, dear child, and we have de Villaret lurking on our doorstep as if, forgive the vulgarity, you are a bitch in heat.'

'*Ciel!* I have my own reasons for not encouraging him but . . .' God protect them! She and M. Beugneux might not be standing in the Jardins de Luxembourg in a week's time; they could be in a tumbril with their hands tied behind their back and – 'Oh, God!'

'I will spare you the details of my adventures, my dear child. The less you know, the better, and there are others involved whose names I should prefer not to divulge. You do understand?'

'Of course.' Such ludicrously genteel conversation! They might be discussing the weather.

'You probably wish us to find another hiding

place. They only stay a night or so until the hub-bub dies down and then we move them on.'

'No,' replied Fleur resolutely. 'You must continue to use the Chat Rouge. I presume my late husband turned a blind eye to such activities, or was he part of this as well?'

The puckered cheeks were drawn into concaves; the answer was careful: 'I did not involve him.' Nothing more was added.

'And your stammer, monsieur?'

'It comes,' he shrugged, 'and goes.' The silence between them was no longer companionable; the gusty April wind irritatingly tried to make away with her hat and veil. '*Oh là là*, if you wish me to move my lodgings . . .'

Fleur halted. 'No! No, my husband wished you to remain.' Perhaps it was absurd to invoke M. Bosanquet's last hours as though his every word was gospel, yet it seemed the only star to steer by. 'But only,' she added, 'so long as you do not endanger Thomas or any of the staff.'

'*D'accord.*' Her hand was raised gallantly to his lips. 'I salute your courage. Meantime, I perceive you find yourself unhappily between the hammer and the anvil.' He offered his arm again, and they strolled on like father and daughter. 'On the one hand, this Jacobin deputy should be avoided like *la peste*, on the other hand, I hear that he faced a public drubbing in the Convention and only emerged a free man because that odious creature, Georges Danton, stood up for him and convinced the house he was a man in love. With you, madame. I can see that you might be tempted to return his ardour. That young man has a fine physique and a quick mind. Too quick.'

Fleur nodded, biting back a short Caen oath; today was getting worse by the minute.

'I fear this morning's little rap over the knuckles is hardly likely to put him off. Drat this wind!' M. Beugneux clapped the tricorne hat to his wig's horizontal curls.

'And the more he hangs around, the more dangerous it is for you and your poor fugitives, monsieur.' Let alone her, she added as a postscript. M. Beugneux might find himself rescuing her from La Force.

'Hmm, it seems best that my friends and I cease our activities for a while.'

People might go to the scaffold and all because of de Villaret's suspicions. They walked on in silence. 'I just cannot understand why he is so interested in me,' she muttered, more to herself than her companion. 'Do I honestly look like a murderess?'

'You look . . .' The old man stopped and stared down at her. 'Do you never gaze in your mirror, child?'

'Not really, only to use tweezers, that sort of thing. I couldn't afford a mirror until I came to Paris. Ah,' she patted his hand, 'yes, I understand what you are saying, monsieur, and that is very gentlemanly of you, but you're wrong. He suspects that I'm a fraud, that I murdered Matthieu.'

'And,' said Matthieu's friend, 'did you?'

❧

Armand frowned at the fountain where one of the coppery nymphs was sporting a scarlet cap of Liberty. 'I have the greatest respect for the fair sex,' he murmured, 'but they can be a confounded nuisance. Everywhere I go that wretched grisette turns up looking like a lovesick loon. No, behind us, the chit below the statue.'

Raoul glanced down the main walk of the Tuilleries gardens, and then idly to the side, where he noticed an apron straining across a generous bosom, a mass of lustreless hair escaping from a mobbed cap, a sunburned snub nose and a mouth temporarily shaped like an unlucky horseshoe.

'And I thought you were talking about Madame Roland, Armand.'

'That is not amusing.' His friend waved a fly away. 'I just wish women would stay where they are meant to be, wearing a kitchen apron or nothing at all. Women like her reduce our debates to vaudeville.'

'That is democracy, Armand.'

'Don't you sound so devilish superior, Raoul. I noticed you started playing to the gallery once you realised that Widow Pussycat was up there. We're here to make laws, not indulge in ogling. Uuugh, and look at that chit watching my every move.'

'Since you rarely move at all, with your nose constantly in a book, it can't be very exciting for her.' Laughing, Raoul punched his lapel. 'It's all right, Armand,' he said soothingly, 'when we've ousted you from government, we intend to ban all women's clubs – *especially knitting ones*,' he added with feeling, noting the pair of grim *tricoteuses* who were handing out broadsheets to passers-by. 'Anyway, Armand, the puss in question doesn't like being stroked, not by me at any rate.'

'Do I detect a challenge taken? *Mon Dieu*, that atrocious accent. Who'd want to wake up to that?'

'My interest is mainly professional. Listen, she appears out of nowhere in Caen, claiming to be married to an elderly Parisian who has just been attacked and killed; the witnesses to her marriage have disappeared. Then she comes to Paris, magics up a chef who makes a foie gras to die for, mimics Marat *and me*, and has half the city flocking to watch her performance. One instant, she's La Coquette; the next, she's a bourgeois widow, all vestal virgin and it's "keep your hands on the table". *Diable*, Armand, I'm fascinated. What is she going to do next?'

'So you suspect her of murder?'

'Yes . . . no. I'm utterly confused. Damn it, every time I meet her, the air is electric. You have to admit the girl's a little Venus – beautiful breasts, a killing smile and those lovely eyes. And she's not stupid. She wouldn't be running that damn café of hers so well if she were. She's intriguing. In fact, yes, I wouldn't mind waking up to all that every so often.' He waited for a reply.

'Ah, well.' Armand, some inches taller, merely blinked down at him and shrugged.

The subject seemed to be closed and Raoul, conscious of having displayed a far from professional attitude, swallowed and asked soberly: 'So what did you want to talk about with me?' If there was any mention of a donkey, he was not sure how he would handle matters, especially as he had just this minute made an utter ass of himself yet again.

'I wanted to warn you about this morning's session.'

Raoul looked down and ran a thumb distractedly across his fingernails. 'So your faction is *still* baying for blood? I have never diverted public money.'

'They want a scapegoat to throw to the people, Raoul, and you'll do a treat.'

'I was protecting Boissy.'

'I know that. Look, if the paperwork is in order, neither of you have anything to worry about. What I don't understand, and nor do my colleagues, is why Danton felt it was necessary to defend you.'

'I daresay he was feeling sentimental.'

'Or that he suspected you were guilty.'

Raoul's anger exploded. 'Armand, how long have we known each other? You know I would die for the good of France. So would Boissy. *Mon Dieu*, we should be rowing in one direction, man, not squabbling like a pack of curs. Tell your colleagues they can examine the bills and the receipts. They can even read the correspondence between Boissy and myself on the potential use of balloons in transportation.'

'Oh, you don't need to convince me. Convince them.' Armand nodded to a crowd of *sans-culotte*s sauntering past. 'Do something public and patriotic. Like finding out who is syphoning the traitors out of La Force.'

'Very well.' Raoul was seething. 'And you can do something public and patriotic too. Right there!' and before he stormed away, he shoved his Girondin friend towards the girl beneath the statue.

'Have you seen who is gracing us with his company, *patronne?*' Columbine rearranged her scarf so it exposed even more cleavage; on stage Juanita suddenly seemed to be singing louder.

'Want me to tell Thomas to add extra salt to the potage, madame?' whispered Albert. 'Ah, too late.'

Fleur watched with annoyance; her chef had decided not only to serve Raoul de Villaret personally as though their customer was a Bourbon monarch, but now he was standing back, smoothing his hands on his large rear, while the deputy considered the first mouthful. Then, having concurred over its worth, Thomas actually sat down and gossipped with the cursed devil as though they were friends met over a game of boules. M. Beugneux was right; it would take more than a ride on an ass to shame de Villaret. She just could not afford to let him frequent the café. It would be too dangerous.

As if he sensed her interest, the man in question let his gaze languidly scan the restaurant and found her watching him. No, he was not shamed. Instead, he placidly tore the *pain de campagne* and returned his attention to Thomas. It was tempting to ignore him, but the trouble with fire was that the brilliant dancing flames offered not just light and heat but entertainment. Perhaps she could stand the heat for an instant without being scorched.

Sweeping up to the seated deputy, her smile was like a flag of truce. 'I did not think I would see you here again, citizen.' Hands clasped serenely, she absorbed the warmth of his stare with too dangerous a delight.

'I do not believe in bearing grudges, citizeness,' de Villaret answered, cleansing his lips with a napkin. 'Where else in the city can I find food so superlative?' At that compliment, Thomas rose, smirking, and left her carpeted.

'Please.' Raoul gestured to the empty seat. 'Won't you join me?' He let it sound like a threat but, to his delight, his pretty tormentor not only sat down opposite but, setting his high crowned hat to one side, propped her elbows on the tablecloth in true *sans-culotte* fashion.

'I am glad you are not feeling surly, citizen,' Fleur Bosanquet murmured huskily. 'I wanted to apologise for what I did.' *She* was apologising? He watched her fingers playing lovingly over the metal buckle decorating his hat.

'The donkey ride? Oh, surely not.' Summoning up a sense of humour afterwards had not been easy. 'And the python?'

'Perhaps not the python,' she admitted. 'I never asked him to leave his box.'

'*You* are enjoying this,' Raoul accused, demolishing the meagre breadroll further.

Fleur made her grin mischievous and stroked an impetuous finger teasingly round the hat brim. 'Don't look so fierce, Deputy. According to Danton, you are supposed to be aflame with passion.'

'Don't flatter yourself. The only thing I am feeling passionate about this morning is finding the traitor who is aiding those aristocrats from La Force,' Raoul answered and watched her fingers freeze. 'However, you do well to remind me, citizeness. What do you suggest?' He stared at her with a look that Marcus Antonius might have used on Cleopatra.

'Oh,' Fleur exclaimed. The Jacobin knew his power. She was glad the rest of the café could not see her face. What would it be like to untie the ribbon band that held his hair and tangle her fingers in such dark luxury, dragging his face towards her, feeling his kisses on her face and throat? She had never kissed a man on the mouth, and this man had a gorgeous mouth and a smile that could have commanded her soul. But he wasn't smiling.

'I thought, mistakenly, citizeness, that you might sense the *électricité* that Volta speaks of.' Raoul found the ensuing silence hurtful. The widow was staring at him as though he had just read her name for the tumbrils. He fingered the spoon again, and wondered if the quiet was just an omission. Perhaps patience was necessary. Perhaps it was she who needed the stroking. 'Look, I, too, apologise for last night.'

His left hand set down the spoon and reached out with a will of its own. He possessed himself of her wrist, thumbing over the satin skin above her pulse, and felt his own blood quicken.

Fleur tried to slow her telltale heartbeat. What did it matter if the Girondins gored this Jacobin, she reminded herself. M. Beugneux's work was far more important. He must not be arrested.

What the hell was she playing at? Raoul wondered. Her racing pulse meant she wanted him or else . . . or else she was afraid.

'Sometimes,' he said gently, his thumb meaningfully scuffing the calluses on her fingers, 'sometimes you look so frail, as though you have not just this café but the whole world dragging at your skirts. Will you not let me help you?'

And let him help her to the scaffold? Fleur tore her gaze away. He might not intend to endanger her but his touch was unlocking doors that led to the Place de la Revolution.

'There is nothing wrong, Citizen de Villaret,' she answered sensibly, trying to withdraw her hand. 'Truly. Things are a thousand times better than they were.'

'*Than they were.* What is it that frightens you? Is it *my* fault?' He raised her fingers to his lips and she felt his breath against her skin. 'If you think me an ogre, then know me better. Let me prove to you that I can take care of you.'

'You are mistaken.' She jerked her hand away.

So she was rejecting him. Raoul could not speak further. The shame of Clerville rose again like bile – those haughty Sirens luring him to believe that they admired him then bringing him tumbling down into the dirt and rubbing his face in it. The hideous blundering out of the hidden passageway into the duke's bedchamber to see him tupping a chambermaid, and then being horsewhipped. And accused of voyeurism. Did she not realise he was a man who hated to look a fool? He might have deserved her derision last night but now his forgiveness was wearing as thin as a beggar's shirt.

Fleur cursed inwardly. Clearly she had damaged the man's honour. Why was he so touchy? She sensed his anger seething. 'Your pardon, citizen.' Her glance took in the busy waiters. 'Things are busy – I had better –' But she needed to dampen down the heat of his fury. 'Citizen de Villaret . . .' Heavens, what could she say to this complex being so she might hold him. She needed a thread as delicate as a spider's weaving. 'Give me . . . time.'

The harsh lines that had drawn tight around his mouth eased but his eyes were like streaked tigereye, soft-hued yet stone. 'I can't.'

She looked away, chasing the tail of words that would not come to her. 'Believe me, citizen, it is easier not to become embroiled.'

'And let the lamp be your only companion in the mausoleum. That, too, will burn low.' Fleur gazed at him perplexed. The web was being spun on either side.

' "*The grave's a fine and private place,*
But none, I think, do there embrace." '

'Is that English?' she chided. 'You quote what I cannot understand.' A translation was not offered. She rose to her feet, shaking her skirts.

'Listen to me.' De Villaret's strong fingers tightened once more about her wrist, and he scraped back his chair and stood too. 'I promise not to ask of you anything you are not prepared to give.' The silence grew again, unanswered. He tugged her closer. 'Other women have a kinsman or husband to rule and protect them. You are only nineteen and you're resourceful, yes, all of this,' he gestured to their surroundings, 'but let me –'

'Oh I understand the protection.' There was *protection* and . . . well . . . protection. She gave him the benefit of altruism. 'But *rule* me?' She almost hurled the phrase back and then leashed her temper. Men were reared to assume sovereignty in the same way they expected every meal to be put in front of them. 'No! I manage. I have always managed.'

'Not this, you know I do not mean with this.'

The restaurant buzzed around them and the circle of phrases was back to the beginning. Desire and resolve tightened his face. Her answer was not acceptable. The marking out was public. He would not accept a rebuff as Hérault had. No, the sensual glint in the golden-brown eyes declared his determination to accept nothing but her surrender, and Fleur was unsettled, tempted, immeasurably flattered and determined to refuse. If she had possessed the freedom to choose a lover for his physique, she would have set a laurel wreath upon de Villaret's brow, but she would not take a man just because she liked the way his dark lustrous hair was drawn back or the nice way his mouth lifted when he smiled. Not so intelligent and suspicious a man as this.

Was this a genuine rope to tug her from the quicksand? Hardly. She could not believe that a

Jacobin like him could want the Widow Bosanquet without a cartload of self-interest thrown in: a payback for her mockery on stage, because he had to make Danton's assertion true to save his reputation, or even the macabre challenge of dangerous intimacy with a possible murderess. *What do you mean?* her expression challenged.

'I mean the attempts on your life,' he was saying. 'You should not be out alone so late at night. Last night, for instance.'

'But I was n–' She bit off the word. *Mon Dieu*, he must have seen M. Beugneux! 'Your shoulder comes with a price, citizen,' she said quickly.

'You still don't trust me?' he asked.

'Of course not, Deputy. You admitted you are only loitering round here because you are still trying to sniff out what is happening at La Force.'

'That's very hurtful.' His hand released her.

'But so very true.' Pain disturbed her voice, lending it sincerity. 'I think you had better leave.'

Raoul took up his hat with a sigh. 'Very well, I cannot ask you to promise me anything, but my advice is free. You may not permit me to protect you but I will – as much as I may.'

Why of all men did this Jacobin have all the grace and splendour that plucked at her senses? How hard to be cold, to force him away, when she longed for him to draw her close. But everyone she loved had been taken from her. To love him could be to destroy him. 'Thank you, citizen, but I cannot in all honesty encourage your attention any further. I don't deserve it. Now, may I see you out?' The customers were watching now and the public face she turned to the world was serene and controlled.

At the door, de Villaret permitted her to help him on with his greatcoat in wifely fashion.

'I forgot to give these back to you.' He fetched something out of his coat pocket and held out her missing comb and the ring she had surrendered in Caen. *He forgot!* And now it looked to the customers as though they had an understanding. To take back her ring, her mother's ring, was beyond her refusal but her simple comb . . .

Raoul dropped them into her cupped palm. 'Smile at me, Fleur,' he murmured, savouring her beautiful face. 'The Convention thinks we're in love.'

'The Convention can –' Beyond him she saw the soldiers had halted their billiards. 'Deputy, this will not –' But he caught her chin, tilting her face so that she was forced to look at him.

'I want you, Fleur,' he said simply. 'I want to make love to you. And if you will not welcome my attentions, then for your own safety,' his fingers stroked her throat, 'do not bestow your *favours* on anyone else.'

Her lower lip curled, defiance flaring. 'Is that a threat?'

'No,' he lied, hurt and ruthlessness unsheathed in his voice. 'It's a warning.'

13

. . . the rendezvous of style and the place where the graces link pleasure and love . . .

MAYEUR DE SAINT-PAUL WRITING OF THE PALAIS-ROYAL

Fleur cleared de Villaret's table, wishing she had used a fire bucket on him rather than her feeble wits. Instead of catapulting the deputy from her life, she'd almost let the man kiss her. Well, actually she'd almost kissed him . . . oh, *nom d'un chien*! Fetching quills and ink, she tried to write out the new placard. The soups especially mocked her. Twice she spelt bouillabaisse with an excess of s's and wasted good cardboard. Finally, she let the pen drop from her fingers and buried her face in her hands. Not only had she yearned for de

Villaret to touch her, but she had felt the physical animal magnetism that Mesmer spoke on, and more besides. The longing to share thoughts and hopes, to demand loyalty and . . .

Oh this was bad and, worse, useless. A Jacobin! Her father and sister would haunt her from their graves if she betrayed them, and as for her brother . . .

'Thomas,' she exclaimed, pushing away the menus and with them temptation. 'It's time I did the books.'

The desire to seek out de Villaret's forbidden company was almost irresistible, and traipsing through Les Halles markets, supervising the installation of a faïence stove that would keep the customers cosy and amiable, overseeing renovations to provide permanent accommodation for Blanchette, setting up a daily trestle outside the café to ladle out potage to the poor or, well . . . just shelling peas . . . were time-consuming but hardly thrilling substitutes. For two weeks Fleur steeled herself not to visit the Convention or the Jacobin Club, but then she discovered during one of Hérault's weekly visits to the café to collect his payments that she need not have been so cautious. Not only had the annoying Deputy de Villaret been out of Paris – on business as an elected member in his home district of Berri – but on his return he and Hérault had been industriously working on a new constitution for France. So he had lost interest in her, thought Fleur sadly; if only they had been on the same side. But it was for the best; the deputy might have been licking his wounds but he certainly had not called off the intense police presence in the neighbourhood of La Force and the Chat Rouge.

Towards the end of the second week, however, the streets of the Marais returned to normal. Marat had surrendered himself for trial, calling the Girondin government's bluff, and extra gendarmes were needed to ensure public order around the Conciergerie where 'the man of the people' was being held.

Free from surveillance, the staff at the Chat Rouge relaxed and M. Beugneux began returning to the Rue des Bonnes Soeurs at odd hours and in different guises once more. Only Fleur still felt she was being watched. Since the attempt on her life in the Bois de Boulogne, Thomas had insisted that she must not venture into the streets without one of their staff, but Fleur had never lacked courage. It was time she showed her enemies that she was not afraid; besides, hearing the notorious Olympe de Gouges speaking to the women's group at the Jacobin Club was an occasion Fleur would not miss. Not only was Olympe a dramatist, but she had written *The Declaration of the Rights of Women and Citizens* and offered to defend King Louis at his trial, a reckless gesture that had frightened off most of her admirers. To Fleur it made her a double heroine.

The evening, like last year's military campaign, proved a disaster. A rainstorm, worse than any they had suffered during the winter, had the women huddling together as hail lashed the club roof with the violence of a Bible stoning, and the infamous speaker failed to turn up. It was mid-evening before the heavy rain finally abated, leaving puddles glinting like giant moonstones in the yard of the club and a chill breeze shaking the dripping leaves of the Tree of Liberty.

The women dispersed quickly. Fleur was humming as she walked along the Rue Saint-Honoré until her forest instinct made her neck prickle. Her gloved hand rose involuntarily to her throat. She was displaying no jewellery under her shawl; just a modest cross lay beneath her bodice, and her pocket hung lightly between her skirt and petticoats. Remembering the sinister man who had incited the mob against her, she began to hurry. The footsteps, some thirty paces behind her, increased pace, only slackening when she slowed, and crossing the street after she did. Fleur stopped strategically in front of a milliner's window, judging the rascal following her would be forced to halt just where a lamp hung pendant across the street. She darted a sideways glance. It wasn't the lean fellow skulking after her but a large man in a heavy black coachman's cape with his tricorne hat pulled down and his collar turned up. He did not have the furtive edginess of a pickpocket but she was sure she had encountered him before. Fear streaked up her spine. She tried to wave down a fiacre but all the coachmen were whipping their horses towards the Palais Royal, so instead of continuing west along the Rue Saint-Honoré, Fleur scuttled the other way towards the palace's lights like a panicked rabbit, hoping to throw off this predator among the crowded arcades.

Glittering with lamps and shimmering pavements, the civilised façade and graceful galleries seemed welcoming, but Fleur realised quickly that at night this was not the safest refuge for an unaccompanied woman and she braved herself for bawdy solicitations.

The myriad stalls that had seemed respectable by day blazed with coloured lanterns, and the clientele was now loud and brazen. Cheap scent and chocolate, pineapple and peppermint, crêpes and vomit, coffee and spilt wine, lavender and urine pervaded the night air. A roar of male carousing came from one of the striped pavilions. Hand-organs, fiddles, hurdy-gurdies – and somewhere a German baritone – battered air already vibrating; conversation was shouted. Cigar smoke crawled up from gambling cellars and billiard halls; and below the upper balustrades, in windows that had seemed innocent by day, sat candlelit whores. Surrounded by people, Fleur felt desperately alone.

Still, it should be easy to find a fiacre, she decided, scolding herself for her fears – except it had begun to rain again and the Théâtre Français must have just emptied, for a chattering tide of people was surging across the gardens, and Fleur could hear the wheels of coaches and the shouts of hirelings in the street beyond. She plunged in against the current of the throng, making slow progress to reach the closest arcade but, to her dismay, the man was still following. The shops along the gallery were closing as she passed; if she could just lose him by playing hide and seek among the columns . . . But the shadows were already possessed by creatures of the night: shifting pickpockets and prostitutes; slumbering beggars like ragged clumps in doorways; creatures of indeterminate sex with lead-white faces and huge mouths, their hair dyed, voluminous and tangled; and thin, bony children whose faces told too much. Maybe she should turn and confront her hunter, but her body stumbled on through the nightmare. Soldiers, sloshing with ale, halloed her at the portal of a gambling hall, trying to coax her down the dark stairs. She pushed through their jeering midst, looking neither left nor right like some prim virgin. It was unlike her. The *patronne* of the Chat Rouge usually shook off raucous suggestions with an amiable retort. But Fleur was out of control. She felt the same panic she had in the crowd at the balloon ascent. Someone in Paris wanted her dead and he was still following. Oh God! She hurried on. Cafés like her own mocked her panic, their scarlet curtains and painted ceilings suddenly alien, exclusive. At the end of the arcade she paused in the shadows, her heart running fast. No, this wasn't irrational. The other times had not been imagination.

'Move on!' A knife tip pressed between her ribs. Fleur's breathing nearly stopped. 'You're on my ground.' A *fille de nuit* whirled her round and slammed a hand across her face. 'I said *get out of here*!'

'She looks more wholesome than you, Lisette,' boomed a male voice; a callused, grimy palm thrust Fleur back against the stone pillar. 'Let's have a look at you, eh. Nice cloth.' While its owner groped, a mouth with half its teeth missing grinned down at her. Fleur sagged deliberately, eyes downcast, and then she whammed her fist into the fellow's nose and took to her heels. Skirting the trees, she fled across the garden out into the pattering rain that was scattering the revellers.

A strong hand grasped her shoulder and she gave a shrill squeal of shock.

'C-citizen!'

De Villaret stood at her side, real and substantial, the raindrops sparkling on his hair and shoulders as he lifted his hat to her. The askew earth righted itself.

'I beg your pardon. I did not mean to startle you so.' If he was surprised at seeing her there alone, he hid it well, asking courteously, 'Are you here with friends, or will you join us? We're going inside out of the rain.' He gestured to a party of gentlemen deliberating beside one of the tables outside the Café de Foy. Danton's laughter rumbled across to her as he slapped a waiter on the back and she saw the glint of Hérault's fair hair among them.

'No, at least, thank you but . . .' She swallowed, catching sight of the dark Nemesis lurking among the trees like some foul spider. 'Citizen, I am being followed. I-I don't know what to do. I don't want to lead him home.'

De Villaret's expression did not change but the glint of adventure flickered in his eyes. 'I see,' he said calmly, taking care not to stare beyond her. 'Let us move towards the tables. Is he watching you now?'

'Yes,' Fleur gasped. 'Yes, he's gone across to the portal of the jeweller's.' De Villaret sensibly did not look round. 'It's . . . it's not my imagination. I swear it.'

'Of course not, citizeness. I will see you home.' The kindness in his voice nearly overwhelmed her. She needed a friend at this moment. It was ridiculous to feel so fragile, close to tears. And de Villaret was an opportunist; she knew that, but his eyes were looking at her with gentleness.

'But your friends . . . I do not want to spoil your evening.'

'It would spoil my evening to know you were in danger and I had not helped you,' de Villaret asserted. 'Come!' He took her hand and led her into the well-lit foyer of the café. 'Wait here a moment, then I'll join you.' Fleur nodded gratefully, and waited while he gathered up his hat and swordstick. His companions had seen her now.

'Well, well.' Hérault strode up to her. 'Spying on the enemy?' He raised her hand to his lips. For an instant, the aristocrat in Fleur sprang up defensively, but it was the café behind her that he meant.

Her smile was cosmetic. 'Something like that.'

'There's another payment due. You know that?'

'You'll be paid, citizen. Haven't you said the Chat Rouge serves the best food in Paris?'

'Perhaps I should raise my interest then. Tsk, tsk, and you still haven't come to Le Nid, *ma belle*. Why not? We have the most marvellous parties.'

'It's the cushions.'

'*What?*' Hérault was startled even further when his fellow deputy rearranged him to the side.

'Pleasant dreams, *mon brave*,' de Villaret fare-welled with relish and, setting a possessive hand beneath Fleur's elbow, steered her out across the courtyard. 'Why aren't you presiding at your café?' he demanded in a husbandly tone.

'There was a women's meeting at the Jacobin Club,' explained Fleur, glancing over her shoulder. 'He's still following me.'

'Ignore him. You were saying . . .'

'I wanted to hear Olympe de Gouges.'

The deputy gave a disapproving snort. 'Not very wise of you.' And what was that supposed to mean? But he had slowed to a stroll and was offering her his arm. Fleur slid her hand through, realising the world was becoming manageable again.

Then he stopped, confronting her. 'Are you hungry, Fleur Bosanquet?'

'Yes,' she admitted softly, realising, yes, she was. Tantalising aromas of coffee and port rose around her where before she had only scented danger. The restaurants and halls glowed like brilliant embers. And de Villaret at his most charming was lethal.

'What is your desire then?' The words were a caress and she felt deliciously tempted.

'I do not know the Palais Royal, citizen. I came here once with Thom—'

'Not know it?' He laughed. 'How can you live in Paris and claim such ignorance? Shall it be Italian *glaces* – though I warn you they are better value and more genuine in the Rue des Italiennes.'

'Oh, here will do,' Fleur answered. 'But not ices.'

'Hmm.' He scanned the arcades on either side. 'Then not the Grotte Flamande – it's mostly billiards and the entertainment's not fare for women – nor La Barrière, the new chef's untried, though they say he makes *pâté fou*. If you are swooning with hunger, they do a decent supper at Café Liberté,' he jabbed his cane towards the lights at the end of the gallery, 'or pasta in the Rue de Beaujolais, but as it's after nine, it may be a crush with the après theatre crowd, though you might see the ex-Duc d'Orléans there. Citizen Égalité himself—'

'No, there, please,' Fleur cut in swiftly, nodding towards the Liberté.

'Citizeness, it shall be my pleasure.'

It was not quite what she expected. The powdered maitre of the Liberté, wearing his obligatory *tricolore*, fulsomely welcomed de Villaret by name. Having passed the lady's shawl and the customer's hat and cane to an underling, he requested an entwined couple in one of the more private stalls to disconnect and resume their tangling elsewhere, then he fussily *mouchoired* the cushioned, crescent-shaped bench before he permitted the new arrivals to be seated. Fleur was caught between dismay at the enforced intimacy and the urge to laugh.

'Perhaps I should tell my waiters to dust the benches,' she giggled, and sobered as de Villaret slid in after her. With a painted screen beside her, she was snared in a luxuriant velvet cul-de-sac. Around them, the warm shadows, concealing other clients, whispered of confidences. It was definitely a rendezvous.

'Hmm,' she commented, trailing a silken cushion with the back of her hand. 'I thought there was a shortage.'

'Feeling safer?' He eased the loose satin bolster behind his back with the nonchalance of a pasha settling on a divan with his latest concubine. Safer! Sitting thigh by thigh with a Jacobin, and no oxen or gall-tongued *sans-culotte* to chaperone them! 'Wine or champagne *mousseux*? We missed out last week.' *We?*

'Oh, wine,' Fleur declared. 'Did you not know there is a war?'

'You *are* feeling better. How about *vin de l'Hermitage* then?' His nod instantly summoned the hovering waiter.

'The staff know you,' she observed, but she was looking around at the other customers – what she could glimpse of them. Most of them were in an embrace.

'The Liberté caters for rakes and roués,' de Villaret countered witheringly as though he could read her thoughts. 'You pay extra for the degree of shadow; I bring all my mistresses and even the women I find wandering in the Palais Royal here. That's better. Now take the poker from your spine,

337

citezeness! A lot of restaurants are lit as dimly as this, but the food is excellent and I did offer you a choice. Here's the wine. This will put heart into you.'

Well, her knuckles had been well and truly rapped.

'The Chinese have a saying,' he told her, touching his glass to hers. '*May you live in interesting times.*'

'It sounds like a curse. Especially now.' She glanced round at the brass-ringed crimson curtains, knowing who lurked beyond the windowpanes. Would her pursuer stay in wait?

'Be at ease. He cannot harm you.' At ease? When the concern in de Villaret's eyes was exploding the fortifications she had been building all last week?

'It's becoming too frequent,' she said softly.

'Attempts on your life?' His expression hardened. 'Or that you perpetually need rescuing. Am I missing something?'

'Oh, I do it deliberately to earn your attention, I promise you. Maybe I should start extricating aristocrats from La Force.'

His fingers tightened around the stem of his glass, then he raised it and drank, watching her. 'It would certainly bring me running, but I don't find that remark particularly amusing.'

'I'm sorry.' She gazed down at her napkin.

He changed the subject. 'Was the de Gouges woman worth listening to?'

'She did not turn up.'

That made him smile. 'All promises and no

delivery – just like Manon Roland.' He let that
settle and, to tease conversation out of her, added,
'Don't you think one of the reasons the Revolution
happened was because our culture was becoming
effeminate?'

'Oh, that is nonsense.' Fleur forgot about the
man lurking outside and contemplated the pleasure of aiming a damp sole at her rescuer's ankle.

'Is it nonsense, citizeness? Old France was like
that crone Madame du Barry, powdered and
puffed up with other people's hair, hair that poor
women had to sell to feed their wretched children. Where was France's manhood? Wafting
around Versailles with painted faces, beauty spots,
wigs and lace. Pah, every inch of life was berib-
boned, full of whirls and flourishes.' Goodness,
thought Fleur, had meeting M. Beugneux inspired
this lecture? 'Look, I believe Rousseau was right,'
continued her companion. 'We're missing virtue.
There's an honesty we have to get back to. I'm
sorry.' He broke off, and met the devilry in Fleur's
face.

'Women staying at home with their sewing
instead of attending meetings, you mean?'

'Well . . .' Fortunately for him, the waiter arrived.

'If I were La Coquette,' Fleur informed him after
she had ordered, 'you would be trying to seduce me
and I would be accusing you of hypocrisy.'

For an instant de Villaret looked affronted and
then he launched a counter-offensive. 'And what
am I doing now? Charity work for widows?' He
leaned forward, watching her. 'But you are La

Coquette, aren't you? Fleur . . . La Coquette . . . Which of you is real?'

'La Coquette doesn't exist,' said Fleur quietly. 'Please don't imagine she could. I only did it to bring the customers in.' She watched him lean back like a lawyer who had extracted an admission. 'There, you have your confession at last, but it took you a while, citizen. Maybe you should take all suspects out to dine. Interrogation *au coq* . . . or *truffé*,' she added lamely, her cheeks growing warm. *Au coq! Mon Dieu*, sometimes she didn't behave as though she was nineteen but nine. 'I–I didn't mean *that*.'

'I know, but I like it when you make mistakes.' He leaned an elbow on the tablecloth, his chin cupped in his hand. 'Let me confess too. My name is Raoul, Fleur Bosanquet, and I don't think you murdered anyone.'

'You don't?' She felt like an insect being slowly bound with silken threads. 'Raoul?'

'Raoul.' The name growled provocatively. *Ciel!* The Jacobin was going to kiss her and she was going to let him.

The waiter coughed.

'Not in cold blood at any rate,' added de Villaret, forced to shift back as a dessert descended between them, its rosy sides wobbling.

Fleur drew a deep breath and somehow found her spoon. 'I should tell Thomas to try something like this.' She licked the fluffy mixture of cream and rosewater from her lips. 'Maybe with chocolate. We do not have enough chocolate on our menu.' De

340

Villaret made no comment, seeming content to savour her enjoyment. 'Your charity to widows,' she added huskily, refusing more wine, 'does it come at a price?'

A slow roguish smile curled about his mouth. 'You mercenary baggage!' he murmured, permitting the waiter to refill his glass. 'Of course it does, especially after midnight.'

Would he cage her here till midnight? She finished her dessert in silence, her thoughts as confused as a ransacked house. 'Why are you looking at me like that?'

'What, like Newton brained by an apple?'

'Something like that.'

'Well,' he sighed, 'I am wondering if we can begin again, Fleur-de-Lis. Whether we can try and imagine there is only now.'

'Now?'

'Definitely now.' He was dangerously close. She longed to feel his fingers steal beneath her curls; she wanted him to draw her face to his. 'No future, no past, just now.'

The deputy was wearing the grin of a general who knows the second campaign has been a success. But there was something else as he lifted his glass towards her: not just a speculative desire that made something deep inside her ripple with longing but a tenderness in his smile that made her feel treasured.

'Oh,' she whispered. 'Now is all we can wish for.' With all her senses seduced, Fleur wanted to hold this moment between her palms as though it were a fragile dove that might take flight at any moment and leave her lonely and lost. But this wasn't real. Tomorrow he would return to his investigations and she would be forever watching the street corners, waiting for the knock on the door and the national guard with warrants.

Glass met glass. Fleur took a sip and grimaced. The wine tasted sour after the sweetness.

'I lied just then,' she recanted. 'I want to know about your past.'

There was a long pause. His gaze moved pensively and slowly, very slowly, up her black brocade buttons as though he was slowly undoing each. 'What do you need to know?'

Need? Her whole body was burning. Fanning herself, she tried to keep her voice steady. 'W-what was your profession before you became caught up in the Revolution?'

'I was trained as an artist.' He seemed glad to be distracted by the cheese platter that was being placed between them. His knife sliced into the ripe softness.

Fleur drew a breath and checked herself. No, she could never tell him that she had sat for the great David as a child.

A silence settled between them before he added, 'I painted portraits. I should like to paint you.' And not just your face, his gaze told her.

'Do you –' She swallowed; words were hard to disentangle in her growing confusion. 'Do you always tell the truth as an artist?'

'The truth.' The word sounded like a sigh. One

of his dark eyebrows lifted fractionally – she did like his eyebrows – in the cynical way that was becoming familiar. 'No, people do not want the truth. Some would say portrait painters are as much the sediment of society as prostitutes. We take money to massage another's vanity. Have you seen any of David's work? Some say he is the lackey of the Revolution. What do you think?' Fleur was not sure whether his clever mind was still setting traps for her.

'Well, I suppose if he is painting history being made, it makes him a sort of visual chronicler. Just that alone should make him valuable to posterity, shouldn't it?' But she could imagine King Louis's brothers burning David's *Tennis Court Oath* in the palace yard at Versailles if ever things returned to normal. 'I do not know what *you* think of David's techniques, citizen, but as an ignorant observer I think them excellent except . . .'

'Except?'

'Except the women in his early paintings are so useless. *The Oath of the Horatii*, for instance. It is all military glory, men together, and the women are just a wailing heap in the background with nothing to say for themselves at all.' *Mon Dieu!* That was a mistake. Where was the provincial nobody from Calvados supposed to have seen such a masterpiece? 'But you have distracted me, citizen,' she chided. 'You do not need my opinion. We were talking about you. How did your family feel about you taking up a paintbrush?'

'Instead of a musket or a lawyer's quill?' His eyes

lost their soft gleam as though she had stumbled on a hidden lode of pain. 'Diable, it would be an understatement to say my father was displeased. In his opinion, soldiering was the only worthwhile career. We parted on bitter terms. I left home without his blessing.'

'It bothered you?' Too light a word. Too late, she saw the sharp lines slashed from flare of nostril to a mouth curled down in strong displeasure.

'Not at the time,' he answered with a dismissive shrug. So he was wary she might dig deeper.

Trying to be more subtle, she asked: 'I've often wondered, as an artist, do you . . . you must look at the world with a different eye? Are we not blocks and triangles of light to you?'

'The beautiful Fleur Bosanquet reduced to geometry!' De Villaret tilted his head and smiled his slow, lazy smile as if she had given him given carte blanche to stare his fill. 'That is a fascinating suggestion. Has some other artist told you that is how he thinks of you?' His hand rose in worship to the column of her throat.

Fired by his touch, Fleur needed to restore the conversation to a more prosaic level before she melted to a cinder.

'Oh, a boy who had aspirations as a painter once told me I looked like a toad with indigestion. Oh, Ciel! You've spilt your wine. Hold still.' She uploaded the salt cellar generously over his shirt cuff.

De Villaret, recovering from almost choking, exclaimed hoarsely, 'Then the young clod was either blind or stupid.'

Frowning sweetly, Fleur even gave the matter some thought. 'Stupid, I'm afraid, and rather a braggart. What's the matter?'

He dragged his other hand across his forehead. 'I'm sorry,' he exclaimed, clearly making a courteous effort to continue the conversation. 'How old were you then?'

I *must* be boring him, decided Fleur. He probably expected us to be intertwined by now. Even the couple who had just come into the restaurant were already embracing. And she must look so dowdy, buttoned to the chin in this tedious black when all the other women here were wearing evening necklines. But he repeated his question.

'Oh.' She stared at the cloth. 'About nine. I was rather fat as a child but he had no right to be so rude.'

That was a mistake. The Jacobin was frowning as if he feared she might suddenly balloon out of shape that very instant, but he did not tease her. Instead he refilled their glasses with painstaking care. 'Did you retaliate?' he asked.

Encouraged, Fleur nodded impishly. 'I brib– no matter.' She bit her lip. Oh, she had nearly tripped then.

'Oh no, don't hold back now, Fleur.' Imperious fingers tilted her chin up. 'I want to know exactly what you did.'

'I-I hid a toad in his satchel,' she lied, editing out the bribe she had given the footman to do the task. 'T-tell me, did you make a decent living from your art?'

'A toad?' The edge of his thumb skimmed her lower lip. Oh *bon Dieu*, she wanted to open her lips and taste . . .

'A-a very little toad. At least so I . . .' Oh God, the intense gleam in those beautiful eyes. If only he weren't her enemy.

'A toad with indigestion,' he repeated. '*Nom d'un chien!*' Released, Fleur regarded him with huffy confusion as the man's long fingers rose to hide his laughter and his shoulders visibly shook. 'Oh, Fleur, Fleur.'

She glared at him. Not that he noticed. If she could ever, *ever* say that de Villaret had come close to hysteria, no, not hysteria, losing control might be more apt, this moment was it.

'Yes, well, need we dwell on that?' she retorted tersely.

He swallowed, trying to rearrange his features into at least a semblance of sobriety, and offered her the cheese platter. As if Roquefort or Chester would placate her! Unappeased, Fleur served herself. 'I asked if you'd made a decent living from your art,' she growled. 'Commissions and things like that.' She pushed the plate back and he served himself the new Norman cheese that was à la mode, taking care not to look at her.

'I . . . yes . . .' The damn man was sucking in his cheeks as though he was close to bursting into laughter again. 'Yes, I had plenty of commissions before the Bastille fell but suddenly life pointed me in a different direction.' He dabbed his lips with his napkin before he gazed back at her. 'Somehow

I ended up a deputy.' There was a different warmth in his expression now. Something had changed, softened further, but the desire was still there crackling invisibly in the air between them.

'That cannot have been as easy as it sounds,' she said softly.

'I had help,' he answered, letting his eyes wander lazily over her with an artist's freedom. 'My mentor was ambitious. He climbed high, changing his coat to suit the fashion. I suppose I seized hold of his coat-tails and held on.'

'No.' She leaned back, shaking her head. 'You believed.'

His expression grew distant. 'Yes, and I still believe. I know what it is like to be at someone's beck and call. I believe in equality and freedom of opportunity.'

But not for women. Aloud, Fleur said, 'So do I. But there are always ruthless men who use the dreams of others to make money, aren't there? Wherever there is a niche, they exploit it. The Revolution took place, don't you think, because people were hungry and desperate, and yet nothing has changed. I sometimes wonder whether the Revolution occurred because a lot of people were bored. They sneered at the King and Queen so much that even the ordinary people started to sneer as well. I suppose you think that a foolish observation.'

'No, a most acute one, and you are right about greed too. That is why Robespierre and Marat have earned the people's love. They don't exploit anyone to line their pockets.'

'Do you?'

'No! *Diable*, citizeness, a few morsels of Norman cheese and you are as fierce as a *tricoteuse*.'

'An honest question, *Raoul*.'

'I draw a salary, no sinecure – I work for it – and I derive some income from my grandfather on my mother's side. Now let us talk about you, citizeness.' Somehow his hand had moved across to take hers. 'Apart from being a duplicitous, argumentative minx, no doubt engendered by being overweight as a child . . .' He paused, the golden gaze reflecting the lamps and mirroring her face. 'You were thin with hunger back in Caen. Why? Bosanquet would not have let his future wife starve. What really happened?'

Duplicitous, sadly, yes! The teasing bruised her. Her soul yearned for no lies between them, but she must play this game forever. Should she offer an explanation of the catapult? Perhaps a bone of truth was necessary for him to chew on.

'It is quite simple. I was starving and Monsieur Bosanquet was dying. He offered me marriage to keep his possessions out of his nephew's hands. I was hungry, so tired of being hungry, so I agreed.' She looked up and hoped she saw understanding in his eyes. His mouth was tight with satisfaction. Another admission for his dossier. 'I am not a Medusa, if that is what you suspect.'

'Would I be feting you if I thought that?'

'Yes,' she admitted, 'I think you might. You are a very clever man, Citizen de Villaret. Too clever for me.'

'Raoul! And you have not told me one half of it, Fleur. Why did your husband not leave the inheritance to his friend Monsieur Beugneux? Or were you already well acquainted with Bosanquet?' So he *had* been poking a stick into the tree to see what bees flew out.

'With Monsieur Bosanquet, no. No, truly, it was the sudden whim of a dying man and I'm very grateful to him. As God is my witness, Raoul, I never set eyes on Matthieu Bosanquet until I found him wounded on the road and took him back to my cottage.' She held her breath, expecting him to ask her why she had been living in Grimbosq.

'Bosanquet must have seen much merit in you.' He turned her hand over. Her mother's ring twisted beneath his touch.

The sensual scrape of his thumb across her palm set off a warning tocsin. She had already confided too much. 'Oh, I nursed him, read to him.'

'A good Samaritan. Hmm, but remember your Gospels; there were several Samaritans, the traveller *and* a woman at the well. Will you let me drink?' He kept hold of her hand so she could not withdraw it across the cloth.

'Oh,' her lower lip quivered, 'you would soon go on your way.'

'It isn't necessary to believe, you know, just trust.'

'Do you not think it is tempting?' Her heart was thumping like a soldier's drum.

'No yokes, no bridles,' he promised.

'No future,' she answered bleakly.

349

'Safer so.' Raoul leaned forwards, his face alive with idealism. Had he stood so looking up at the steep walls of the Bastille the day it fell? 'We are on the edge of a new age, Fleur. Take a breath and jump!'

'You don't know me.' *I would endanger you, and if you find out who I am, you will endanger me.* What had Marat said? *The Revolution is our wife.*

'Does it matter? I'm your destiny, Fleur, believe me. I've wanted to have you ever since we met in Caen and fate keeps tossing you to me.' His hands framed her face and his lips touched hers, caressingly at first and then he deepened the kiss, skimming his hands down to her shoulders and holding her with a fierce, beautiful possessiveness. Oh, *bon Dieu*, no wonder lovers spent so much time embracing.

'Citizen, it —' she protested when he drew his face back.

'Raoul,' he corrected. 'Listen to me, Fleur. This thief you spoke of the other day. He's an illusion. Thieves are neither kind nor loyal. They only steal hearts in fairytales. Did you see his face? I doubt you'd even know the scoundrel now.'

'That may be true.'

'Or is it . . .' The astute smile belonged to a victor. 'Could it be that you are not what you seem, sweet citizeness, and I might discover too much?'

'Ah, you have it, Monsieur Interrogator. I am undone at last. I admit everything. I am one of King George's spies sent to lure you to my pillow.'

'Excellent.' His eyes were dancing with

roguishness. 'Pillows, I like. We could come to an arrangement. I will feed you tidbits of tantalising but false information about army supplies and the strategic plans of the national guard to please William Pitt, and meanwhile you can . . .' his voice was a great beast's purr, 'tantalise me.' He carried her hand to his lips.

'Raoul, it is not possible. I am sorry.'

The silence was disturbing, cruel. Outwardly he seemed amused but she sensed the words had sunk into the bone.

'You heard about the Tennis Court Oath when you were in Calvados, citizeness?'

'All of France knows of it.' What path was he leading her on now? Yes, she knew that when King Louis had summoned the States General to sort out France's deficit, the demands of the representatives who were neither nobles nor churchmen had angered the royal temper.

'Remember, Fleur, when the King forbade the Third Estate to meet and ordered the doors of their assembly hall locked against them, what did they do?'

'Why, they went to a nearby tennis court and took an oath not to disperse until they had achieved reform.'

Raoul de Villaret took her chin in his hand. 'I want you, Fleur Bosanquet. That is my demand and you may lock your door against me but I'm a revolutionary, I do not keep to the rules.' And letting go of her, he abruptly snapped his fingers for the maitre to bring the *billet*.

Outside, they walked briskly to the Rue de Montpensier, where the horses of the hire coaches shifted miserably in their harness. The rain was heavy again. Sufficient to make any stalking rascal abscond, she hoped, but she was relieved that de Villaret mounted the fiacre steps after her.

'This is kind, but I am sure it is inconveniencing you,' she protested politely.

'I should be on your guard if I were you,' he replied cryptically, and rapped the driver's panel.

From him? It was her own perfidious passion that would betray her if he so much as touched her.

After the flow of words between them earlier, the patter of rain on the coach roof and the hooves echoing in the street were suddenly lonely sounds. Fleur wanted to reassure him that it was not his fault she dared not deepen their friendship, but to even hint at her true reasons was to open a Pandora's box.

'Raoul . . .'

The word was innocent, just his name, but a word can whirl and change with the play of breath and become an incantation. The spell of halves was broken. Her companion reached out and took a second savouring of what he truly wanted. The man's skill was magnificent, enthralling. Fleur had never imagined a kiss could be so compelling. Winding her arms shyly about his neck, she parted her lips and he instantly deepened the kiss with a soft growl of pleasure. It was too easy to forget he was an enemy. Within her a subtle alchemy was refining her anger into a nobler emotion. Insatiable, his mouth teased and tormented her, now demanding, now hardening. His hand rose to her breast and unlooped the fastenings. She was unsure, until his fingers stroked down inside the opening of her gown, touching her breast through the frail fabric of her chemise. A wonderful sensation spiralled down her body.

Was this why Eve was driven from Paradise – because she learned to feel and wanted more, rivalling the Supreme Being in her demand for worship? Fleur's skin, sensitive as it hungered for each stroke of Raoul's fingers, alerted all her senses, arousing a different hunger between her thighs.

'Rue des Bonnes Soeurs, Fleur.' She surfaced to find that suddenly the buttons were being tucked back into their silken slits, her breasts packaged back. 'Send for me if you have any more trouble, citizeness.' How formal he sounded now, she thought regretfully. 'Or would you like me to put a guard on your house?'

'You can do that?'

'I can.'

'No, that's not necessary. Perhaps he was a footpad and, seeing me on my own, he . . . Oh, please tell the driver it is the next gateway.'

The fiacre braked at the entrance to the courtyard and de Villaret sprang out and helped her down. The rain was easing and the sky was growing dappled; the moon wore a seductive veil of cloud half-drawn across her face.

Raoul stared up the street the way they had

come and then, with an expert eye, inspected the courtyard.

'Thank you for your kindness,' she began.

'I keep a ledger, Fleur, and I will call in the debt, make no mistake.' And then he added with humour, 'One of Thomas's dinners will be welcome.'

'Of course.' She kept her voice light.

'Wait here,' he told the driver, and taking her elbow, he steered her across the courtyard to her doorway.

'Did you know your patrons at the Chat Rouge call you "the Bastille" behind your back?'

'The Bastille!'

'They are taking wagers as to when you will fall.'

'But the business is doing well.'

'Not fail, *fall*.'

'I see,' she replied coolly. 'Well, they are wasting their time to be bothering with such a trifle. They might remember that when the Bastille fell, there was hardly anything inside. Thank you for warning me. I shall be on my guard in July when the anniversary comes around.'

'I was there when the Bastille surrendered,' he murmured, his face a shadow to her. 'When you do fall, *ma douce*, I will be the one to take you. Goodnight, Fleur.' He carried her hand to his lips.

It was tempting to hurl things around when she reached her boudoir a few minutes later, but restlessly she swung round and sped down to the kitchen where she lifted Machiavelli out of his crate. He regarded her soulfully. Not that she trusted a python's judgment. He was probably thinking of rabbits. Damn de Villaret! Did men have nothing in their heads but revolution and seduction?

It was then a spatter of gravel hit the windowpane.

14

Frenchmen! Free and frivolous! Will you never be aware of the evils threatening you? Will you always fall asleep on the edge of an abyss?

JEAN-PAUL MARAT, *L'AMI DU PEUPLE*

'Well, I'd never have wagered you'd whittle down to a beauty, Toinette,' the man who had been following her declared gruffly, tossing his hat and whip onto the small table beside her armchair.

'I d-didn't recognise you, Philippe. To think all evening it was you following me.'

Her brother the twenty-one-year old duke stood before her clothed like a coachman. He smelled like one too, of horses, sweat and stale clothing. Perhaps it was all part of his disguise.

'And a fine dance you led me, Toinette.' He formally took her hand and kissed her cheek, still with the boyish awkwardness she remembered. Sad that despite the mature broadening of his shoulders and the stubble upon his cheeks, there had been no learning of easy charm since they had last met, but no doubt he was very weary.

'I–I'll fetch you something to drink,' she offered nervously.

'I need more than that.' So would the conversation. Two years of silence was a dampener to any reunion.

'Of course.' Alone in the kitchen she had time to collect her wits along with the cheese and precious bread from the Chat Rouge. Was he intending to stay?

At least Philippe had the manners to open the door so she might carry the tray in. The repast was off the plate instantly. He ate like a soldier and she watched him guiltily, wondering why she did not like him better.

'A fancy place you have here, Toinette.' He took a swig of the wine; it passed muster.

The single candle lit the uncomfortable air between them. Her sibling's sprawled form in the armchair opposite seemed an illusion.

'They know me here as Fleur,' she corrected, rising to refill the wineglass on the small table at his elbow. 'My schoolfriends at Trinité called me that.'

'Fleur.' He tasted the correction on his tongue

as though it were a poisonous lozenge. 'How very childish. Safer, I suppose.' The long legs shifted, shedding a large comma of dried mud from his boot soles. 'I brought you a missive from our aunt.'

'That was my next question.' Fleur took the letter and swiftly slit it open. 'Oh, I am so thankful she reached safety.'

'I'm not. The stupid woman has done nothing but grumble since she arrived.'

'Yes, she fusses, but she's not stupid. I was glad of her company the last two years, believe me.' His morose expression deepened. 'I doubted I should ever see you again, Philippe. I should have appreciated a letter, just one.'

'We are at war, in case you haven't noticed,' he retorted coldly. What was it he wanted of her? Money, she suspected.

'Isn't it dangerous for you to be back in France?'

'My God, of course it is, but shall we say I have some business in Paris and it seems I need to carry out my family obligations. Our aunt insisted. I can see why.' His scowl implied he preferred her fat and indolent.

'What family obligations, Philippe? Surely you cannot mean me. As you see, I am hardly in need of help.'

'*Zum Henker damit!*' he swore, rising to help himself from the decanter. 'The old baggage is right. You are grown headstrong. She tells me you consort with actors and such riffraff.'

'Actors are recognised as citizens now,' she exclaimed defensively.

358

'Pshaw! Whores, bawds.' He turned haughtily. 'You were bred for better than that, a decent alliance through the marriage bed.' He was evaluating her like a merchant, and the blood rose shamefully, heating her cheeks. One didn't march out and slam the door on a duke, but it was tempting. Married! True, if the Revolution had not occurred, an alliance with another noble family would have been arranged, but she had now tasted independence.

'This is Tante Estelle's meddling.' Fleur rose. She needed the wine as well. 'You didn't care a scrap till now.'

'Time has a way of running fast,' he muttered, making himself comfortable again and crossing his boots at the ankles. 'And now you are nineteen, I believe. I forgot that you would be in need of a guardian to see to such matters.' Again, the calculating appraisal.

'Nonsense, Philippe. Besides, I am still in mourning. Indeed, surely it is you who needs a son to carry on the title.'

'With me a royalist and guillotine fodder? If I am killed, your son will have my title.'

'You are forgetting Cécile is safe in England.'

'She's dead.' He delivered it like a dish of poison and watched Fleur digest the horrid revelation. The memory of a golden-haired minx shimmered between them: Cécile, the youngest of her three half-sisters. Philippe flung himself out of the chair. 'Christ, sometimes it drives me almost mad. Our lands, our family, the respect . . .'

'When . . .' Fleur tried to swallow the pain and find her voice. 'What happened to her?'

He toed the carpet edge, avoiding her eyes. 'I don't know for certain,' he muttered, dully running a hand along the mantelshelf. 'Inflammation of the lungs, I suppose. But it's my guess she was half dead from hunger.'

'H-how did you find out?'

'My friend, the Chevalier Henri de Craon – you know, I was at school with him. Well, he was an émigré in London at the time. It seems someone found his name among Cécile's papers and wrote to him. That's how I heard.'

'Oh God!' Tears could come later. Fleur knuckled them away beneath his stare and sat down feeling like a hollow statue. There was no pity in her brother's face, no comforting arms held out to her, only a stony resolution. 'Philippe,' she whispered, but it was for what might have been that she grieved. Her brother had always been a stranger. Heels disappearing into the branches of a tree; spurred boots against a horse's flanks as he rode to hunt; trunks packed for military school; or his arm flung up in dispassionate farewell from a carriage window. This was all she knew of him.

'It is just you and me, little sister.' Philippe's callused fingers caught her chin. 'So now you understand your value and your duty.'

'I supported our aunt and myself for two years,' she pointed out, jerking her head free.

'And came precious close to starving, I hear. Let us waste no more time arguing.' Like an auctioneer, he was glancing about him at the ornaments and paintings. If he recognised the evidence of master artists, he made no comment. 'You are to sell up and return to the country where it is safer. We will win this war eventually but it may take longer than we anticipated.'

'No, Philippe, leaving Paris is quite out of the question.' For once she was almost thankful for the Revolution. 'I have responsibilities. Business is going well. Besides, people are dependent on me for work. I cannot let them down.'

'You always were slow-witted, Toinette, but I never thought you bourgeois. Can you not see, when Brunswick and the Emperor break through with their armies, the *sans-culottes* will turn on the likes of you like rabid dogs. We are not dealing with rational human beings. Christ, girl, all it needs is for the ignorant rabble to dislike the shape of your face and they'll tear you apart.' He did not need to remind her of last September; the slaughter of her father and sister was too painful.

'I must live with that possibility,' she said softly, remembering the crowd gathered round the fiacre. 'I am not afraid.'

'I do not give a damn whether you are afraid or not,' he exclaimed, pacing once more to the fireplace, then swinging round. 'You have a duty to marry while you're still in good looks. From what our aunt tells me of Bosanquet's holdings, selling them should buy you a *ci-devant* noble and some of the Church land that's come onto the market. That should suffice until I can claim back our estates.

No, save your breath! You're scarce out of school so don't argue with me!' His hand came down, slicing against the macasser on the back of her armchair. 'What could our aunt be thinking of, leaving you unchaperoned, vulnerable to some impoverished Casanova!'

'Philippe!' She twisted round, glaring. This was too much like facing her father with holes ripped in her stockings from climbing the roof of the orangery. Shear away the wild tangle of hair and put a powdered wig on him and it could have been a younger version of her autocratic Papa standing there. Even his mannerisms, the way he rubbed his thumb to and fro across his closed fist, were inherited.

'No, don't make excuses. I want you away from the republican filth who are sniffing around your skirts.' How dare he underestimate her! Fleur stiffened her shoulders, ready for battle. 'Why are you looking at me like that? You've not lost your virginity, have you? Tante Estelle – '

'I-beg-your-pardon?' she ground out, every staccato syllable frosted.

He moved closer, louring over her. 'Oh, have I offended your virtue, Toinette? Well, that's a relief. At least it proves you have some left.'

She snatched up the cup of wine and tossed the contents straight in his face. 'How dare you insult me in such a vile fashion. If I was a man, I would call you out for that.' She flung a shaking arm towards the door. 'Please leave!'

He laughed down at her, ignoring the clear

droplets dripping down his unshaven chin. 'Lord, we have been corrupted, haven't we? I didn't think to see you behaving like a gutter trollop.' He raised a hand and for an instant she thought he would hit her. 'See what comes of mixing with the creatures that murdered Papa and Marguerite! Or had you forgotten?'

'No, I have not forgotten. How could I? But I'm surviving, Philippe. I've managed to stay alive since we lost everything and I resent you storming in here telling me how to behave as though I were still a child. Go now, *now*! Before I have you thrown out. And if you wish to return in better temper tomorrow, do so, but this is *my* house, not yours, and I will not endure your insults.'

'Do as she says.' M. Beugneux made such a theatrical entrance that he nearly tipped Fleur into hysterical laughter. 'Is this vile creature bothering you?'

Philippe's sneer could have soured cream. 'Who is this fop?'

'I am a good friend of this lady's late husband. My name is André Beugneux.' The gentleman made an old-fashioned bow with such a flourish of lace kerchief that her brother's beetlebrows instantly rose in irritation. 'I will not ask who you are or why you are here, young man. These days it is not a courtesy, but do as madame says.'

Before she could stop him, Philippe's hands fastened into M. Beugneux's lace jabot, almost lifting him out of his buckled shoes. 'You never saw me,' he growled, half choking him. 'You heard nothing.' He flung the old man away from him as though his very touch defiled him. 'Worse and worse, sister,' he drawled, turning his head. 'Republicans and ageing Ganymedes. I will return tomorrow night. See that we're not disturbed. Out of my way, old man!' With a glower at them both, he took his leave.

Philippe was impatiently skulking in the shadows of the back garden when Fleur returned from the café with Thomas late next evening. Once Thomas was up in his room, Fleur let her brother in and they climbed the stairs to the salon in silence.

'You took your time.'

'I have a business to run,' she answered, tugging off her gloves. 'Unless you have something else to say to me, it has been a long day and I am tired.' She collapsed in her chair and heeled her shoes off. Was that bourgeois enough for him?

'I have, as a matter of fact,' he answered coldly. 'Maybe you could be useful before we marry you off. After all, it's a war and one must make sacrifices.'

Fleur braced herself. He sounded just like the republican government when it wanted a large donation. 'You want me to put on breeches and join the royalist army?'

'No, and there's no need to take that tone of voice with me.' The curtains were drawn but he walked across to the window and glanced down into the front courtyard, suspicious of the shadows, before he tugged the heavy curtains more closely to and turned with an expression worthy of an irate governess. 'I have been listening to the gossip about you.'

'Ah, the balloon,' she murmured carelessly and enjoyed the disapproval. 'Did you know I am probably the first French aviatrix?'

Philippe was not impressed. 'This deputy, Raoul de Villaret.'

'Oh, him. I thought you might have meant Hérault de Séchelles, he is so amusing. Oh, stop gaping at me.'

A brief astonishment crossed his face. 'I had no idea you moved in such inner circles.' Then the sneer returned. So he thought her a republican courtesan! She avoided mentioning her encounter with Marat. *That* would shock him.

'Do you think I am such a fool, Philippe? I am teasing you about Hérault and, believe me, I have been at great pains to discourage any intimacy with de Villaret. I do not need you or anyone else to point out the dangers. I am a Montbulliou.' Her head was high. 'Why are you laughing at me?'

Philippe shook his head and the furtive expression she had always disliked came into his eyes. 'We have a role for you and it's more important than being a Montbulliou.'

'We?'

'The others I met with today. Other royalists.' He took his time.

'I thought I was supposed to be the brood mare,' she prompted.

'Well, we may still achieve that. Henri de Craon's

365

interested in having a look at you some time. But for now we want you to encourage de Villaret.'

'You are too late. I've told him I am not interested.'

'Don't be foolish. It's never too late. We want you to take him as your lover.'

Fleur was lost for words. Not only did he seem too easily led but the insult was grotesque hypocrisy, especially after yesterday's fraternal dressing-down. 'What am I supposed to do?' she asked eventually. 'Talk of politics in my chemise?' The thought of Raoul seeing her undressed was most unsettling.

'Or without it.'

'How dare you!' She turned away before she hit him, but rough hands dragged her round to face him.

'You will do it for France. You are not allowed a choice, Toinette. It's your duty.'

'And the family honour?' she almost spat at him. 'What if I become pregnant? You wish a Jacobin's bastard to get your title?'

'Don't be ridiculous. Bastards can't inherit.'

'Well, perhaps I'll persuade darling Raoul to change the law.'

'You vixen,' he laughed, catching her wrists. 'Anyway, the cur is from the Protestant noblesse. He fell out with his father and turned renegade. Maybe you can talk him into turning his coat again. Didn't you know?'

A nobleman. No, she didn't. Curse men to hell! The lot of them!

'I won't do it,' she snarled, struggling to free herself.

366

'You will or I will have someone denounce the old roué upstairs.'

'But you can't. He is one of us and –'

'Expendable,' he cut in, before she could divulge that M. Beugneux was doing more for France than he was. 'Very expendable. An ageing sodomite by the stink of him.'

'By God, you mean it, don't you?'

'Oh yes, Toinette. The rules of war are dirty. I will do anything to get my lands back, *and you shall too!*'

'Bonjour, petite, I've brought you two gifts,' M. Beugneux announced, joining Fleur in the kitchen next morning. 'Firstly, this.' He tugged a set of *passe-partouts* from his coat pocket. 'You never know when you might need it and . . . *voilà!*' He dropped a drawstring bag onto the kitchen table and drew out one of her calfskin shoes.

Fleur straightened from putting Machiavelli back in his box. 'Oh, so you had my shoe, monsieur! I thought I had lost it but –'

'These are for you,' he interrupted excitedly, tipping out a pair of new boots onto the kitchen table. The aroma of new leather filled the kitchen. 'To thank you for your generosity. And there's another reason. Watch!' He twisted the heel of the right foot and extracted a blade some two inches long. 'Only one side is sharp, but drawn unexpectedly across a man's throat from behind, it could be lethal. Not easy to handle, but there, it may save your life some day.'

Fleur was not sure whether to be horrified or flattered at such forethought, but his pleasure in giving demanded an equal response in her. 'Oh, Monsieur Beugneux.' She threw her arms round his waist and nestled against his flowered waistcoat. 'That's *formidable*. I shall try out the *passe-partouts* on all our doors and thank you for the boots.'

His hands stroked her back. 'Listen, I've made promises. We shall be using the cellar at the café tonight. If anything goes wrong, you and Thomas must disclaim all knowledge. Don't do anything to defend me. Promise, *hein*?'

'Must you run the risk?' she beseeched him. 'If de Villaret starts investigating again, he –' She felt a betraying blush creep over her face and throat.

'I can't delay matters, little one. I shall have to take the risk.' Thrusting the boots into her hand, he leant down and kissed her cheek. 'Bread and circuses, Fleur, and I'll do everything in my power to thwart these butchers. They haven't the bread but, by God, we have the circuses.'

'This is a surprise,' drawled Raoul de Villaret, scabbarding his umbrella in the rack at 47 Rue des Bonnes Soeurs later that evening. He set his hat upon the brass hook and drew off his leather gloves.

Fleur dutifully helped him shed his double-breasted redingote and ushered him into the warm salon. 'I would have made the invitation earlier for supper but we were short of hands at the café. You seem in good spirits, citizen. Pray, do sit down.'

Being contrary, he stood with his back to the hearth instead, hands clasped behind his back. Oh yes, she could see the haughty blood in him now. No wonder he was at ease with Hérault de Séchelles and Boissy d'Anglas. What was it that people said about religious converts – that they could be more fanatic about their new faith than those born to it? And here before her fire stood a true believer, a debonair disciple to Saint Jean Jacques Rousseau.

This evening the man's dress was unquestionably patriotic: the cuffs on his gleaming boots echoed the dark blue of his sleeves and pantaloons, which set off the scarlet front of his tunic and the crisp white cascades of his stock. Even the misbehaviour of the hair strands escaping from his queue looked politically wonderful. Of course, it needed a crooked tooth to just mar that heart-stealing smile to a revolutionary niceness but one cannot have everything. The young slop-sellers and gallery viragoes would have been drumming their heels for him today, no question.

'Haven't you heard the news, citizeness?' Eyes the hue of filtered cider were watching her with the roguish glint that was becoming increasingly familiar. 'Marat was freed this afternoon.'

'Oh, yes, I heard,' replied Fleur, stroking a finger along the brocade arm of her chair, her gaze swiftly averted to a more decorous angle, 'but I would have thought that after his attack on your friend Boissy, you would have been pleased to see him muzzled. I can't say I'm rejoicing.'

He grinned. 'Oh, seeing the Girondins so embarrassed at his acquittal is far more satisfying. They've set themselves a very uncomfortable precedent. We deputies are supposed to have immunity to speak freely, so by ripping Marat's away, they've left themselves open to being brought to trial as well.'

'Which could leave you vulnerable too, Deputy,' Fleur pointed out. 'Weren't you one of the pigeons the Girondins were trying to bring down?'

A flash of white teeth showed he dismissed such a possibility. 'In a melee of feathers with you, my dear citizeness? They don't share your skill with the slingshot, do they?'

'I don't know what you are talking about,' demurred Fleur, her voice a purr. 'Would you care for some refreshment, Raoul?' She rose, smoothing her skirts.

'No, thank you, some of us went to the Café de Foy. Closer than the Chat Rouge, Fleur.' His gaze lingered thoughtfully upon her cap with its edging of black lace and slid down to the neckline of her simple housegown. He had never seen her throat and shoulders uncovered before. Not that her bodice was risqué; she had fluffed up the black gauze kerchief and it obscured most of her cleavage. 'Now what was it you wished to discuss?' The ironic lilt to his voice suggested, oh so very subtly, that the word 'discuss' might be coaxed to a different meaning.

'Well, to come to the point,' said Fleur briskly, sitting down again. She wasn't sure whether it was the warmth of the fire or his amused smile that was making her temperature rise. He sat down at last, stretched out his legs across the rug towards her as though it was his hearth and crossed his ankles. One hand curled into a pedestal for his chin.

'Hmm,' he said.

Fleur withdrew her toes swiftly into the shelter of her skirts. 'I want to find out who is behind these attempts on my life. I have my suspicions but I want evidence. I thought maybe you could give me the name of someone I can hire.'

'For a bodyguard?' Sprawled back, he seemed relaxed but she could see the fox in his nature was very much on the alert.

'No, to watch Felix Quettehou. I am convinced he sent the assassins to attack my husband.'

'Are you sure it is not those very assassins who seek your life in case you might recognise them?'

'I doubt it. Besides, if they were mere brigands, I imagine they would wish to remain in Calvados. I'd be no danger to them here.'

'What about Citizen Beugneux?'

Fleur looked at him sharply. 'But he was Matthieu's friend.'

'A lover's quarrel, perhaps.'

The shock that M. Beugneux could be a murderer froze her for an instant before she dismissed the ludicrous suggestion. 'He wasn't mentioned in my husband's will. There would be no point in his killing me, whereas Felix Quettehou was next of kin and would have inherited.'

'What about you?' For an infinitesimal moment, she thought he meant her, before he added, 'Who is *your* next of kin, Fleur-de-Lis? Your aunt? What's happened to her?'

'Can we omit the "de-Lis" part, citizen?' exclaimed Fleur, rising to her feet. 'The royalist connotations might be misconstrued.' He did not stand out of courtesy and seemed calmly amused by the verbal rap.

'You haven't answered the question.' He slowly turned a ring on the third finger of his right hand. The lazy stare was deceptive; he was thinking like a gendarme. 'You never do. I hazard there is something in your accent from further west than Calvados. Would you have connections in Brittany, perhaps?'

'Stop behaving like a tribunal,' she replied irritably. 'I was born there, if you must know. My mother was a lady's maid. She never married.'

'Then what were you doing in Caen?'

'I went to school there. My aunt married well. She paid for my education but we fell on hard times. Now can we return to the present?' She forced herself to sit back down, wishing that her eyes were not constantly drawn to the man opposite her.

'Maybe we should go through each incident, one by one,' he was saying. 'Tell me what happened the day the mob attacked you.'

On safer ground, Fleur suppressed a sigh of relief, but she began to narrate what had occurred. Having rejected his attention, she had needed a reasonable excuse to lure him back, and it was for patriotic reasons, she rationalised. Not only was the deputy well away from the cellar of the Chat Rouge but if Philippe's friends were watching her house, they would presume she was carrying out her brother's orders.

She was telling Raoul about Quettehou's outburst at the funeral, when something was disturbed in the kitchen below.

Every house has its noises: the shutter that rattles when the wind shinnies up beneath the tiles, the rhythm of rain from roof to the barrel in the yard, but this sound . . . Oh, *bon Dieu*, had Philippe returned?

Raoul de Villaret heard it too. The long fingers stroking the sphinx arm of his chair paused for an infinitesimal moment. She read it in his face, the intensity – as if a string had been tuned to exactitude.

'Is that Beugneux? Shall we ask him to chaperone us?' Oh, the Jacobin was testy tonight. Had he been expecting kisses?

'No, it sounds like Machiavelli has escaped again.'

'Who?'

'Your friend the python. He's nocturnal. He gets restless. I'd better go and put him back in his box.'

'He's very noisy for a reptile.'

'Well, yes, goodness, he actually broke a plate last night,' she lied.

'Did he? *Mon Dieu!*' He stood up. 'Go on, then, reprimand the rascal. I'll stay here if you don't mind.'

She grinned, hard put to disguise her relief. 'May I bring you some refreshment?'

He shook his head and opened the door for her. It was all too easy.

The bottom of the stairs and the kitchen were in darkness. Fleur took a deep breath and turned the handle. As she stepped in, a gloved hand slammed against her mouth from behind the door.

'Shh, *c'est moi!*' The hand loosened with a rustle of taffeta.

'Monsieur! *Mon Dieu!*' He was not alone. She could hear the nervous breathing of someone, several someones. 'I'm going to light the candle,' she said, fumbling with the flint. '*Zut!*' An unlady-like oath but the occasion warranted it.

'Don't move!' a strange voice rasped as the candle flame grew. Two national guardsmen stood with muskets trained on her. On close inspection, they were women.

'She's a friend,' hissed M. Beugneux.

'Not for much longer,' muttered Fleur, glaring at his female regalia. 'Are you out of your mind bringing them here?'

'Your cursed deputy has set a cordon round the café.' M. Beugneux had never sounded so weary and desperate and he looked fit to faint.

'My cursed deputy is upstairs in the salon.'

'Christ!' His complexion was grey beneath the cosmetics and in horror Fleur saw there was a different scarlet blossoming on the caped collar of his red jacket. 'Just a flesh wound,' he hissed. 'For the love of God, stay calm!'

'Calm?'

'Shall we shoot her, monsieur?'

'*Sacré bleu!* Put that damn thing away!' M. Beugneux pushed the gun muzzle downwards and, rallying his spirits, swung round on Fleur. 'Get his breeches off him!'

'What!'

'Seduce him!'

She stared at the soldiers. The landing upstairs creaked.

'Anything I can do?' shouted Raoul.

Fleur rushed to the door. 'No, I'll be back in an instant,' she called up with a serenity that would have earned her a part at the Comédie Française.

M. Beugneux held out a bottle of champagne. 'For France!'

'*Ardinghello.*' De Villaret pushed the book back between its neighbours. 'Wilhelm Heinse. It's about an artist in Florence who goes to the Greek Islands and enjoys . . . What's this?' He glanced down at the bottle she had thrust into his hands.

'Shall we go somewhere more comfortable? Monsieur Beugneux will be down for his chocolate soon and I'd rather not get embroiled,' she added with feeling.

'If you wish.' His expression was disturbingly suspicious. 'You are looking pale. What happened?'

'It's Machiavelli, he . . .'

'Yes?'

'He'd . . . he'd . . . vomited up a dead rat. You probably heard me swearing.'

'Ah.' He waved his free hand: 'Do you want me to . . .'

'No,' she said hurriedly, sweeping past him to take two glasses from the cabinet. 'I've cleared it up and put him back in his box. I gave him a good talking-to about being so greedy. He did look apologetic – for a python.'

'Come then.' Raoul waited while she lit a candlestick and blew out the candelabra, and held the door open for her with his boot cap. He was humming the Marseillaise as he followed her up the stairs.

The bedroom was still warm from the western sun. Fleur set the glasses upon the dressing table, freeing her hands to tug the lower window down and pull the curtains.

'S-sit down.' She waved a hand with a nonchalance she did not feel. 'Wherever you like.' De Villaret was leaning back against the closed door, his eyebrows raised in polite astonishment as he glanced from the bed to the only chair. Perhaps the bed held python-like memories for he stayed where he was. 'Would you like to open the champagne, please.'

'I thought we might save it for later.' He set the bottle on the floor and straightened, eyeing her like a hawk waiting for a songbird to fly into his orbit.

'L-later?' As Fleur watched the artist's fingers deftly seek beneath his coat collar and unbutton the back fastening of his stock, she discovered her body was acquiring a sensual urgency of its own. 'Please, m-make yourself comfortable,' she added foolishly.

'Are you sure about this?' His voice sounded distrait, as though his mind was running counterwise.

'S-sure? Oh, *this*?' She nodded. 'Yes. W-why, aren't you?'

'Sudden changes of mind and heart, Fleur. The weathervane could spin again.'

'Yes,' she swallowed. 'I daresay it is a turnaround but . . . You don't look very happy.'

'This is my stunned look.'

She had heard that women let down their hair when they were with their lovers. Well, she had better do that, then maybe he would look more relaxed – except that she hadn't any long hair to let down. She frowned at her reflection in the glass and saw he had moved closer and was watching her. It made her feel extremely strange. Perhaps she should let down *his* hair instead, or maybe she should make his breeches a priority. She glanced at the mirror. There were buttons either side of his waist. It should not be too difficult but she was trembling.

Raoul stared in fascination as she removed her lace-trimmed cap, watching his mirrored image as she did so. Then she turned and, coming across to him, pulled his linen stock free and tossed it behind her. The ribbon gathering his dark hair was slowly untied. He made no move to touch her, delighting in the torment of restraint.

This wasn't too difficult, thought Fleur, but she must not make him suspect that it was his breeches that were so important. Imagining she was a famous courtesan, she tugged the upper buttons of his shirt undone. Dark hair mantled his chest and she stopped instinctively to tease a finger curiously through the tangle before she skated her palms over his silk waistcoat and up beneath the taffeta lining of his coat to slide it back over his shoulders. The sleeves stuck and he waited while she solved that dilemma. The coat fell softly at his heels. Then she leaned up and brushed her lips against his, while her fingers unfastened the buttons of his waistband. At last she had his breeches down.

'Ohh!' Suddenly the man was no longer passive.

Raoul, aching for her to touch him, grabbed Fleur's hand and pressed it against his under-breeches so she might feel how aroused he was. Aquamarine eyes blinked up at him in total astonishment. What in hell was going on here? One instant she was behaving like a houri and the next minute she was red with embarrassment. If she was untried, a virgin gift to be unwrapped carefully and his to initiate . . . The quiver of sexual fear in her touch exhilarated him beyond belief. He had never wanted a woman as much as he wanted her.

Zut! She had forgotten that men's breeches were fastened at the knee and he could pull them up again in an instant. De Villaret's had small buttons and little buckles. She needed to get them over his shoes, which was extremely difficult when he seemed to want her to stay holding him. And that particular part of him seemed to have a life of its own. Her touching him there actually made him groan. It seemed to be with tormented pleasure. This really was quite fascinating, but she did need to make sure he wasn't going to be able to chase after the escaped prisoners.

'Pardon,' she murmured and, withdrawing her hand, sank in a billow of skirts to remove his shoes. Those at least came off easily. No bourgeois laces there. Kneeling, she undid the buckles at her knees and pulled the breeches down and free of his feet with a sense of triumph. He gasped, a sort of anticipatory gasp as if he expected her to do something else. His hand fondled her hair but she didn't look up. Unhurriedly she untied the garters that held his white stockings, and slid each down. He had handsome calves. Muscular but sleek. And rather nice feet too, she thought. Not bony but just, well, nice. And clean.

Then she made the mistake of looking up. He had placed a hand where he had earlier wanted hers and his expression reminded her of a man who was trying not to lose control.

She tossed his breeches to one side and stood up to face him, trying to conceal her ignorance.

'This is unexpected,' he said with effort, as though words had become elusive.

Something was wrong. He wasn't behaving like a man burning with lust. Far from it. He wasn't even trying to hold her, and his expression was a mixture of exasperation, fascination and something else. Something lethal. Did he suspect she had been trying to distract him? Well, not trying. At least she had achieved her objective.

Maybe more kissing was needed if he was in this strange mood.

'Do you not want this?' She wound her arms about his neck and stood on tiptoe so she was snug against him. Something was pushing very hard against her thighs.

'Not want this?' He was studying her face with the intensity of an inquisitor. 'On the contrary, I want it very much.' At last the man folded an arm about her, taking control with a pent-up mastery. His left hand possessively slid between her throat and cheek and held her firmly while he kissed her, a mocking kiss, powerfully controlled like its master.

'Surprise me some more,' he murmured against her mouth. But how could she when she was unlearned in love?

'I think it's your turn, Raoul.' She was breathless now. His kisses alternated between playful – teasing the side of her mouth or caressing her throat – and hungry across the bared valley where the ends of the black gauze neckerchief were tucked into her bodice. He tugged the gauze out and kissed the tops of her breasts while his fingers deftly freed the buttons of her caraco jacket and pushed it down to her elbows. It was an irritation that her stays were like armour against him, for Fleur felt the wanton longing to press her naked breasts against his chest. Instinct had conquered restraint, and passion, caution. She wanted to drown in that golden-brown gaze.

It was easy now to free the buttons of his waistcoat and find the fastenings of his shirt. He gave a growl of pleasure. His fingers were pulling the laces of her stays loose as skilfully as any servant. He was practised, very practised.

Our mistresses are just mistresses; Marat's words came back to her. She was going to lose her precious honour, her chastity, and not just to a revolutionary but a Jacobin. *For France?* No, not for France or her family, this was her own private revolution. La Bastille was definitely about to fall.

'I have been longing for this moment ever since I first set eyes on you but it's going to have to wait.' He had her by the shoulders now. 'Who's down there? A very active snake named André Beugneux?'

Oh, bon Dieu! Fleur took a deep breath. So he had guessed. This had all been a ruse. 'It's just that . . .'

'That he has the annoying habit of rescuing people who don't deserve it.'

She swallowed, struggling for a phrase to haul herself to safety, and stared miserably as he strode to the window where he flung aside a curtain and stood staring out, arms folded. Should she fall on her knees and beg for his compassion?

'Raoul.' It was a heart's breath, as she drew close to the stubborn shoulders. *Diable!* She liked this man, despite his politics, despite his prejudices. And now she was going to risk everything in her belief that beneath the single-minded veneer was a fair-minded human being. 'They're girls. My age, Raoul.'

The silence was cruel. The man seemed frozen. Fleur prayed. Was there some prearranged signal? Were his soldiers alert out there in the darkness ready to move in? It seemed an eternity as she waited, hardly daring to breathe, before he dragged the curtain back across and turned. The icy anger in his face terrified her.

'He's been using the Chat Rouge as a refuge before he moves them on, hasn't he?'

Instinct told Fleur she must not lie. 'Yes.'

'And now he's bringing them here to your house, putting your life at risk?'

'T-tonight was the first time. Because you put a cordon around the Marais again.'

'But he got them through it.' His mouth tightened.

'W-what are you going to do?' There was a pistol in the dressing-table drawer if she could get to it.

His eyes raked over her disarray. 'I'm going to make love to you. That's my price. You've bought my silence for one night.'

'Why?' The word was wrenched out. A desperate attempt to save the precious shards of something that had beauty and value.

'Oh, you want me totally abject too, do you? My values dragged in the dust of your chariot.'

'That's not it at all,' protested Fleur. 'I have been honest with you, I think, Raoul. I ask no less of you.'

'*Why*? *Mon Dieu!* Because, you infuriating hoyden, I want you.' He gestured, as if his hands might catch the meaning from the air. 'Because . . . because there is a sense of destiny in everything coming to this, to now, this moment. I cannot explain any better than that.' Then he glared at her. 'Yes, I can.

You are a thorn, a contagion – a God-given responsibility and I can't give you up.' His features desperate, as if the cockerel had crowed for him as it had for St Peter, he flung himself away from her into the centre of the room. Fleur stood, still as a mouse, knowing her life and M. Beugneux's still hung in this man's balance.

'I have a further condition,' Raoul de Villaret added huskily. 'The escapes from La Force must cease instantly or else I shall arrest the old man – and you, citizeness.' It was no bluff. 'You will tell him that your life is hostage for his obedience.' He turned, very much under control, to face her. 'I mean it.'

'Shall . . .' Her voice sounded rusty. 'Shall I summon Monsieur Beugneux? Do you wish to speak with him yourself?'

'No, I shall have nothing to do with him. I have seen nothing and heard nothing, and if you want my advice, you will ask him to leave these premises tomorrow.' Well, she would think further on that. 'Does anyone else know?' he ground out.

'No, you have only me to contend with.'

He strode to the door and for an instant she thought he was leaving, but he picked up the champagne. 'This is the only chance left to you, Fleur. Don't expect mercy a third time.'

The stopper's wire cage was twisted free. She watched his thumbs prise out the cork slowly. He came across to the dressing table and silently filled the flutes.

'I know, Raoul,' she said softly, believing that she understood. 'Thank you.'

He handed her the glass. Above the crystal rim his eyes watched her, bereft of gentleness.

'To survival,' she said, and tapped her glass to his.

The physical act, the tasting of a wine that had been nourished as grapes and prepared to give pleasure, began to thaw the frozen wilderness between them.

He picked up his coat and slung it over the back of the chair. So he was staying. The price demanded was to be paid straightaway. Fleur, her thoughts in disarray, gathered up the rest of his clothes and laid them across the seat.

'The Republic values virtue, Fleur,' he murmured, emptying his glass and refilling it. 'You want to sacrifice yours. Why?'

And how was she going to answer that? For France? Where did her loyalties lie?

'I asked you for time. It ran out this evening.'

The hungry, exultant way he was gazing at her stole her breath away. She felt beautiful, desired and owned. What had begun in Caen needed to be fulfilled; now the price had been agreed, he would accept nothing less.

Raoul de Villaret glanced towards the bed, then smiled and held out his hand to her in a regal gesture. It could have been a treaty made between nations and consummated between the son and daughter of an emperor and a king.

Fleur placed her hand in his. 'I have never lain with a man before,' she said. 'Be kind to me, please.'

Raoul carried her fingers to his lips. 'Fleur, I may be an opportunist but I would not exchange one night with you for all the gold and gems in France. *Allons, mon coeur.*'

The slow dawning woke Raoul from a deep slumber and for a confused instant he creased his brow at the purple overhanging and the unfamiliar gilt and ruby wallpaper a few inches from his shoulder before he remembered why, and his gaze fell on the girl who lay unclothed beside him. He eased the sheet from beneath her arm to uncover a firm, sweet breast. His artist's mind estimated the mix of colours to depict the perfection of her skin, while his body hardened with anticipated pleasure. He leant over her, adoring this young goddess while his hand slid down the gorgeous curve of her thigh, across the gentle swell and through the silky triangle of fur.

'I'm still asleep,' she murmured.

'But I am not.' He bestowed a kiss on her shoulder and turned her over. 'I cannot get enough of you.' She smiled dreamily and stretched out her arms to him. Persephone at ease, all her senses lulled by slumber, but he suspected she had been awake for some time. The sea-blue eyes opened, asplash with mischief. So she had no regrets. Excellent!

'Goodness! *Raoul!* Is what you are doing legal?'

'It's an ancient tradition in France. In Berri they do it nightly.'

'Oh! That is so nice.' It was still a surprise that kissing might be done below the décolleté level and that parts of her had been designed for pleasure not just motherhood. 'And what else do they do in Berri?'

'Well, let me see, when a couple marry, the bridegroom brings all these shoes –'

'Shoes!'

'Hush, lie still! Yes, shoes! He brings them to the bride and he kneels down before her and tries each one of them on her foot. Only one will fit her. It's prearranged, of course, but it's rather quaint.'

'So – oh, keep doing that – the bride tries on all these shoes belonging to other people and only her shoe fits.'

'Of course. Then the bridegroom stands up and takes her hand and everyone cheers.'

Will you ever do that for me? No, she could not ask that. This union was purely transitory.

Afterwards, she lay with her head against his breast while his fingers still played, impossibly straightening the recalcitrant curls that embellished her neck.

'I want to paint you, Fleur,' he murmured, his breath soft against her forehead. 'I've wanted to paint you ever since I watched you that morning at the Hôtel d'Escoville.'

'I remember. You stood at the balustrade like a brooding god, Raoul. Very dangerous and very tempting.' Her finger traced his lower lip. 'You still are. I'm not sure I shall agree. Modelling is hard work. I've done it before.'

'You'll be lying down.' His voice was a gravelly purr. 'And you get the pomegranates and wisps of veiling free.'

'And what do you get?'
'Artistic satisfaction.'
'Can I have that too?'
'Yes, *yes*, indeed. Would you like an advance?'

15

One last effort is needed, it must be a terrible, a decisive blow.

JEAN NICHOLAS PACHE, MAYOR OF PARIS, 1793

'So you decided to be patriotic,' sneered Philippe, falling in beside Fleur as she hurried up Rue de Sévigné to the Chat Rouge. 'Wasn't too unpleasant, was it? Be thankful the bastard is good-looking.'

She counted to ten, so did the bells of the city. It was hard to walk faster than he did, but she tried. She did not want company, least of all his. Not while she felt like the rope in a tug of war. Live for today, whispered Raoul de Villaret between caresses. Live for tomorrow, demanded her brother.

Should she feel ashamed at having lost her virtue? Part of her revelled in the heady freedom to choose where to bestow her favours. Maman and Tante Estelle would not have approved. But it was too late for regrets. She must make the best of things. And what future did she have? Certainly no marriage chest or a booking in heaven, just an uncertain lover who would abandon her if he ever found out her true identity.

'Did you go through his coat pockets?'

'*Comment?*'

'Do-you-have-anything-for-us?' he asked as though she were a simpleton.

'You can't go through someone's pockets while you're sleeping with them.' And besides, she had been next to the wall – between the wall and a very hard . . . Her glove swiftly masked a smile.

'Oh, can't you?' Philippe smirked. 'Kept you busy, did he? Well, do it next time.' Then he added with a somewhat belated brotherly concern, 'I hope you told him to use a sheath.' Fleur stared at him open-mouthed. '*Un chapeau anglais*, Toinette. I cannot believe you are so ignorant. For all you know, the man may be carrying syphilis or gleet – soldier's pox, you ninny. For God's sake! We agreed you don't want his child.'

'Go away, Philippe,' she snarled, crossing the road. Next instant, he would want chapter and verse.

'No, you listen to me!' He chased after her and, grabbing her arm like an aggressive beggar, shoved her into a shadowy archway that portalled one of the ancient mansions. 'Last night was just the beginning. We want you to get into de Villaret's rooms and go through his papers.'

Slammed against the wall, Fleur gazed up at him in horror. 'You are out of your mind! Now let go of me. I'm late as it is and I've got a business to run.'

'You bourgeois little trollop.' His nostrils flared. She thought he would shake her but then he released his painful grip on her shoulders. 'I'll say one thing for you, you've a good head on your shoulders.'

'And I intend to keep it there,' she retorted. 'And I'm not making money. I am still paying off Monsieur Bosanquet's creditors, including Hérault de Séchelles.' She ducked under his arm and, grabbing up her skirts, hastened on. Next minute he would be suggesting she pay off her debts between the sheets and pass on the savings to him.

'And don't suggest otherwise,' she snapped as he caught up with her. 'I'm not doing any more dirty work for you.'

'Where's the risk? The regicides have organised a celebration for that animal Marat's acquittal. De Villaret will be there with the rest of them. He won't disturb you.'

'No! Apart from the fact I have no idea what I'd be looking for, de Villaret is no fool. He's highly suspicious of me as it is.'

Her brother disregarded her protest. 'We know he was hunting for traitors in Calvados. We want his list of suspects.'

'I think you are wasting your time, Philippe.' She halted. 'And I wouldn't come any further if I were you, there have been a lot of soldiers around La Force.'

He scowled at the cluster of national guard ahead on the corner. 'You wouldn't be sweet on this damn regicide, would you, Toinette?'

Fleur did not like the gleam of cruelty in his eyes.

'He may be a Jacobin, Philippe, but I've met far worse.'

'You reckon so, little sister? Then you had better read these and then perhaps there will be no more nonsense about disobeying me.'

Fleur shut herself in the dressing-room at the Chat Rouge, her heart heavy with misgivings. The first document was a letter addressed to her brother in Coblenz.

Monseigneur le Duc,
So I must address you and apologise if I am the
first to bear the tragic news of your father's death.
I saw with my own eyes the despicable circumstances
in which your father was murdered. I was one of the
priests taken to the Abbaye Prison.

Fleur's eyes clouded with tears but she dashed them away.

Your father was dragged ahead of me before this
mockery that called itself a tribunal. They declared

him guilty and he was hauled out into the street
where fiends armed with sabres dispatched him. Two
or three of those ahead of me suffered the same fate
and then I was forced to take my turn before the
gutter lawyers. Mercifully one of the national guard
who knew me spoke up on my behalf and I was
given my liberty. On stepping out into the street,
I was embraced as a patriot by the same foul
butchers who had just slain my fellows. I recognised
M. de Villaret, a ci-devant *deputy of the National*
Assembly from Berri. His hands and coat were
stained with innocents' blood and there was a
crazed look on his face.

An abbot who was fortunate to survive the massacres
at La Force prison tells me this same deputy was at
the prison just before your unfortunate sister, the
Vicomtesse de Nogent, paid the price for being our
poor Queen's friend.

The immediacy of the writing, the character of
the author and the purity of his intentions in
writing to her brother argued that there was little
reason for her to doubt the veracity of his testimony.

The second letter was even more damning.
Bertrand, the turnkey at the Abbaye Prison, testified
to seeing de Villaret killing one of the prisoners in
the street on the second of September. He recognised him because the young man had visited the
prison before in company with the Minister of
Justice.

The cruel phrases etched themselves on her
mind. Fleur forced herself to read the priest's letter

a second time and then she sat staring at the wall. She had thought it possible to fall in love but now it seemed far easier to hate.

Running along the Rue Saint-Honoré an hour later, garbed like a youth, dodging the soldiers lest she be forced to show her papers, Fleur knew the risk was high. She had left her house in her widow's clothes and changed in the stable, not an easy task with Blanchette nudging her for carrots and hopeful for an outing.

Beyond her immediate neighbourhood Fleur slowed and sauntered along in her old Calvados manner, whistling, one hand stuffed in the pocket of her jacket and a sealed letter under her arm as though she was an errand boy. By the time she reached the Rue Saint-Antoine she had a heel blister from one of her new boots, but the hidden blade gave her confidence, as did the small knife she carried in a leather sheath beneath her workman's carmagnole.

The ancient gabled cornerhouse where Raoul de Villaret lodged was three storeys high and had been divided up into apartments. A list of residents' names was daubed on the wall just within the main door, which opened directly onto the street, and fortunately there was no inquisitive concierge or *suisse* to witness her visit.

De Villaret was living on the second and third floors. Fleur sprang up the polished wooden stairs with swift, light feet and came to a gasping halt on the uppermost landing outside a solid-looking door.

She knocked. When no one answered, she crouched and unknotted her handkerchief, which contained a wire and the ring of *passe-partouts*. *Ciel!* If the soldiers had caught her with those, the consequences wouldn't bear thinking about. Crossing herself, she said a swift prayer and knelt to put an eye to the keyhole. A half-finished face stared back at her. Hérault's!

It was only a painting on an easel. In fact the room was full of faces, she discovered to her astonishment as she softly closed the door behind her. The quayside waft of linseed was recognisable and she discerned oil of spike lavender and drier fragrances that took her back to childhood, to the time that David had come to Clerville and set up his temporary studio in the old nursery. Forgotten words bubbled up from memory as she gazed about her: pouncing and *impasto*, glazes and scrumbles; and the colours: sienna and ochre, green earth and rose madder, massicot and azurite. For an instant she closed her eyes and imagined Maman again, beautiful in her lace and hooped gown standing at David's shoulder smiling. 'Keep still, Cupid,' she had teased, 'or your arrow will hit the wrong heart.'

And it had. She had made a mistake and now she had just made another; this was de Villaret's studio, not his domicile. It was a spacious room, perfect for an artist, amply lit with windows on both sides, and the low ceiling with its exposed beams lent a Renaissance atmosphere. A place to concentrate on work, for there was no comfort here: no furniture to speak of, save for a simple wooden chair and a chaise longue.

Fleur turned to go then hesitated. This all belonged to de Villaret; the lover she now hated. For an instant she had the urge to overturn the cabinet with its drawers of poisonous pigments and hurl crimson lake at Hérault's half-finished grin. Instead she resolved to explore her enemy's domain. To destroy you need to understand, she told herself.

It was orderly. Families of brushes, camel hair and hog, hung on a string between the medieval beams like victims *à la lanterne*. The palette knives were precisely set, like an executioner's tools upon a scaffold of a table. She found casts of hands and faces and a human leg bone in a wooden crate. In a drawer she found chicken skin, ivory and vellum: animal sacrifices to the art of miniature painting.

Tiptoeing her fingers through the frames stacked against the old Louis Quinze wallpaper, she discovered a leather portfolio secured at the sides with red tape. It yielded sketches of marquises and courtesans, dukes and deputies, their political allegiances no longer keeping them from brushing cheeks. De Villaret's clients must have liked how he depicted them and paid, for there were few final portraits propped against the wall. Most of these people were dead now, she supposed; severed, like dead flowerheads. All dead while *you* prosper, she whispered, running a finger across one aristocratic portrait that bore the confident signature. *Did this proud marquise refuse to pay your price?*

A shabbier portfolio contained evidence of experiment and more variety of subjects. Some sketches must have been done years ago for the paper was poorer quality and foxed with age. One study moved her – a man and a woman's inter-woven hands. Both wore wedding rings and Fleur's first assumption was that they were a husband and wife, except there was such a poignancy revealed in the interweave of fingers that she was left wonder-ing whether they were lovers, each snared in a loveless marriage. Such love, it almost made her weep. Oh, how could a regicide so cunning and murderous show such sensitivity?

Biting back self-loathing at the memory of last night's surrender, she swallowed the tears and resolutely worked her way through the pile. A *modello* made her pause again – a small-scale paint-ing of a larger project: Marcus Antonius dying for love of Cleopatra, self-disgust fighting a war with adoration across his contorted face.

Fleur could see David's influence but here was a sensitivity lacking in the great master's heroic figures; a dying man whose hand reached out to the beholder as if to say: I may have failed at the last but I have *lived*!

Nor was de Villaret's Cleopatra like one of David's weepy women, but defiant and tragic. The woman's soul was in her eyes.

It was magnificent.

On the shelf a clock chimed the half-hour, reminding her she was staying too long with no result to show for it. She straightened with a sigh only to notice a sketchbook open upon the chair. His current work, perhaps? Curiosity won her over. In an instant she was on her knees with the book open before her on the floor.

And there she found pastels of the woman who had modelled for Cleopatra, close sketches of her from the waist up in a drawstring cotton bodice with a rose satin sash, and one of her asleep on the chaise longue with a sheet half drawn over her sprawled nakedness. Fleur glared at the chaise longue. Oh, he had found comfort here, all right. The bloody, treacherous son of a whore! *'Artist's fingers,'* Emilie had said. Damn him! Yes, he had artist's fingers. Every inch of her skin had experienced them, even . . . Well, he must be laughing. Having killed her father, he had now taken her honour. She turned the page in fury, and stared, wide-eyed in astonishment, at her own image.

La Coquette, cheeky and flirtatious, in stays and greasepaint, and, facing the actress on a different sheet with a grave and challenging expression, herself as a widow. De Villaret must have drawn her from memory, but what disturbed Fleur was that the two drawings were on the same scale, at the same angle and the matching jawlines were unmistakable. Each of the sketches was clearly dated: the actress sketch had been done the very day he had seen her satire. But the first sketch – *mon Dieu*, this had been done in Caen.

For the moment she could not bear to turn another page. It was as if he had been spying on her the entire time. The clever rogue must have known she was La Coquette when he had sent the coach to arrest her, before the balloon fiasco, before she had even thought of confessing.

Hate simmering, she flicked on through the sketchbook and found several more drawings. Herself at the Café Liberté, laughing, and one of her as a country girl, sitting demurely in a pony cart gazing down at her hands folded in her lap as though she were being driven home from a funeral. Avid for more, she was disappointed to find the rest of the workbook unused but there was a loose sheet tucked in at the back of the folder.

Fleur took it out and gasped. Oh, now she understood the term erotic. A man in a Greek tunic, his legs bare, was pushing open a wooden door. The man's pose was not exactly furtive but he wore soft buskins on his naked feet as though he wished to tread softly. The room he was entering, like a voyeur, contained a scrolled couch and, sitting mermaid-like with her legs curled beneath her, was a semiclad girl. A Grecian filet glinted gold against the creature's auburn curls. One of her breasts was uncovered, and the white folds of her chiton were only fastened over one shoulder, as if she had been distracted while dressing by the tiny dog that was standing with its front legs against the couch. The filmy fabric gaped enticingly to reveal the young woman's other breast as she leaned down, snapping her fingers teasingly. She was not looking at the dog but staring at the man who stood observing her. Her red lips were parted in shock at being caught *inflagrante* but her eyes were subtly assessing her visitor's intent. It was a look that Fleur had glimpsed before; the covert glance of a maid at her employer; the swift appraisal her sisters had given male callers; a look as old as Eve's.

Persephone was scrawled beneath the sketch. Persephone in the Underworld after her abduction. Fleur gazed once more on the girl's features. The face, not so easily recognisable as the other sketches, was hers. She was Persephone, torn between virtue and inevitability. And the god coming to possess her – Fleur sat back on her knees, her face scorched with shame. This too was dated. Caen, 18 March.

The whistling and heavy feet on the stair shook her to reality. She grabbed a small urn from among the model props and shrank against the wall behind the door, holding the pot up ready to strike him hard.

'Raoul, are you back?' The door was hammered again. Oh God, she'd not locked it. The oath that followed was one of Robinet's ripest.

Should she pretend she was here to model? That de Villaret had gone to buy more oils? No! Wine! Fleur held her breath; the urn waited. 'Stupid *cul*'s left it unlocked,' muttered the *sansculotte*, peering in. The door closed again. He must have possessed a set of keys, for a key turned in the outside lock and was removed.

Fleur let out her breath. A different door rattled on a lower landing, then a few moments later she heard Robinet greeting someone down in the street. De Villaret? She darted to the window, but it was just an old woman, perhaps one of the other tenants. Quickly Fleur tried to remember the right rod to free herself from the studio. Her hands ran with sweat but finally she made the lock surrender.

Two apartments shared the lower landing. She broke into the one that lay beneath the studio and found herself in de Villaret's other sanctum; his *tricolore* sash, greatcoat and deputy's plumed hat hung from a nail on the door, and a rolled-up banner was angled in a corner. It was a pleasant room with a tall window that opened onto a tiny iron balcony overlooking the street. Behind a screen in one corner was a marble wash stand with a large bowl and ewer, a small canister of tooth powder, two bottles of essence, razor, strop and shaving tray. Above it, mockingly coroneting an ornately framed mirror, was a *sans-culotte* workman's bonnet. The escritoire, predictably, was locked and might demand ingenuity to open it.

Pockets, Philippe had said. She groped the lining of the greatcoat; its inner pocket yielded up an ancient errand list, a card of speech notes and a small folded packet, which made her blush when she glimpsed the pink ribboned sheath inside. She cursed its owner and shoved it back in its wrapper. The caring man who had led her through the steps of lovemaking was nothing more than a selfish blackguard, safeguarding himself against fatherhood and soldier's pox. Well, Fleur hoped he got soldier's pox and every other malady of the bedchamber; she hoped bits of him dropped off and . . . Fleur stormed towards the *salaud*'s wardrobe and then stopped, scraping her tears away. She must be businesslike. Yes, detached and scrupulous in her exploration.

The armoire, like most gentlemen's, contained some forty shirts, quality ones with underarm gussets, all neatly stacked; a pile of detachable cuffs, both sober and frivolous; and an ample supply of ironed linen stocks, with and without crimped ruffles. It was the blue coat de Villaret had worn at the Palais Royal that almost unhorsed her. She slid a hand into one of the flapped pockets and caught her breath, hearing voices below and the ominous creak of wooden stairs.

Not again! If it were de Villaret returning . . . Without a second thought, Fleur wriggled her feet between the spare shoes inside the wardrobe and hastily pressed herself against the back, drawing the twin doors to. The tails of his coats – the man had plenty – tickled her arms, and the aroma of other men's tobacco hung in the folds, but the rich, spicier scent the deputy wore drove into her with every breath. What if he discovered her?

Fleur froze, her hands splayed against the splintery wood behind her. One of the boards curiously gave beneath her fingerpads.

The outside knocking was deferential, the voice out of breath: 'Your clean sheets, citizen! No, not there? Bloody stairs!' The panting laundress departed, cursing.

Pushing aside the thicket of clothing, Fleur stepped out onto the carpet; then, opening the wardrobe doors wide, she jerked aside the commissioner's tunic de Villaret had worn in Caen and eased forward on all fours across his satchel and shoes to explore the back of the wardrobe. It seemed quite solid but then as she ventured higher, one of the panels pivoted inwards. As she pushed the upper end of the board, the lower end seesawed out at thigh height, revealing a cavity. A false back! *Formidable!* This was like something out of a storybook.

One knee on the bottom of the wardrobe, she dipped her arm inside the hollow. Her fingers scrabbled against leather but her knuckles were touching something rough and fibrous. Familiar from her recent exploration in his studio, Fleur recognised canvas. A rolled up painting, no less. Why would he –?

It was not easy to extract but she managed and, pink from her exertion, sat back on her heels and examined her treasure. Happy in its rolled state, it fought at being unfurled and her arms were aching and stretched as the picture was revealed. Good God! She let go in shock. It bounced against her lap and speedily rescrolled itself some distance from her knees. For a moment she studied it as though it were some snake that might attack again, and then, with painful breath, she pinioned the middle lower edge and readjusted her weight so she was straddled over it, hands and knees holding each corner.

Fair, lost faces simpered from another life. Her half-sisters. *The Judgement of Paris*. On the right-hand side, thrust in at the cajolement of Maman, was Fleur herself, smirking with a nine-year-old's self-confidence, the cupid bow alert for mischief.

Fleur ran a finger over the jagged corner. Four years of wondering who the man was who stole it and why? Why of all the treasures in her father's chateau, had the thief chosen this? And how had the painting found its way into de Villaret's hands? Why would he want it? Because it was David's? She rolled it up, her emotions a tempest of anger, disbelief and sorrow as she stowed it back in its hiding place and tidied the shoes back in front.

Raw, she sat down before the writing desk in the chair de Villaret must sit in to write his letters and picked the lock. Lifting down the board, she scanned the pigeonholes and drew out a slim, leather-bound notebook. Only the first few pages were used – notes for several speeches – but on a whim she turned the notebook back to front and read, in burgeoning horror, the cold-blooded note of her father and sister's slaughter in the September massacres. Her immediate family were listed, one by one, in de Villaret's pleasant – oh, so legible – script with a control and dispassion that was absolutely terrifying. Fleur felt like a fly that had blundered into some foul and monstrous web.

Philippe de Montbuillou	*emigré. Last heard of in Coblenz, wanted for anti-revolutionary activities*
Marguerite	*Vicomtesse de Nogent, ci-devant lady-in-waiting to Marie Antoinette, perished*

	with the Princess de Lamballe in disturbances September 1792
Henriette-Josephine	*Marquise d'Aurillac, died in hunting accident, 1788*
Cécile	*Suicide, December 1792, Frith Street, Soho, London – 'enceinté en acte de décès'*

Good God! According to the death certificate, her sister had been carrying a child. Fleur crossed herself, cursing the foul beast who had made Cécile pregnant and then abandoned her to starve. How in God's name had de Villaret discovered so much *and why*? There was one last entry:

Françoise-Antoinette	*daughter by de Montbulliou's second wife, educated at Trinité School, Caen?*

Underscored beneath her name were the words:

I have found her!

Raoul reached the Rue Saint-Antoine in a devil of a hurry. His morning was in chaos. The reception for Marat had gone well but afterwards Danton had called a brief meeting of the Committee for General Security. Raoul received a congratulatory clap on the shoulder for assurances that the escapes at La Force would cease, and then in the same breath was told that his colleagues wanted him to

404

leave immediately for Caen and report back on any adverse federalist activity. It was urgent. Seeing that Marat had been acquitted, the committee was concerned that the angry Girondin government might carry out its threat to move its headquarters away from Paris, and Caen would be ideal. Who else on the committee was so well qualified to be their eyes and ears? A coach would be waiting for him at the Cour de Messagèries and an official of the Central Paris Commune who was travelling on to Cherbourg would be joining him.

Well, what was a good Jacobin to do in such a situation? Ask his colleagues for an extra day to say farewell to his new treasure? A fine lead balloon that would have proved.

So now he was rushing back to his lodgings in a sweat, wondering where Fleur might be and whether he had time to see her. He could hardly expect a sensitive new mistress to be satisfied by a few scrawled lines. For the first time he actually felt like damning the Revolution; initiating his beautiful Fleur further in the field of love had been consuming most of his thoughts all morning.

'*Mon Dieu*, man!' he swore, almost colliding with Robinet as the latter materialised on the bottom stair in the hallway. 'What in hell are you at?'

'You have a visitor, *mon ami*,' muttered the *sans-culotte*, jabbing the mouth of his pipe towards the ceiling. 'I heard someone moving around in your room and I think they are still there. No one has come past.'

'*Diable!* Not Thérèse!' Of all days! Raoul's

model and previous mistress had never returned her key but he hadn't seen her for months. *Merde!* He needed a staircase scene with Thérèse like he needed a bullet hole in the head. She had the face of Helen of Troy and the voice of a town crier.

Robinet shrugged. 'I knocked. Thérèse always used to answer the door if it was her. I reckon you've got a thief.' The gleeful look that accompanied this conclusion was not at all helpful.

'Well, I'm not in the mood for fisticuffs,' muttered Raoul. 'Damn it, I've got to leave for Normandy this afternoon. Lend me your cudgel and fetch the national guard, *hein*? There's a patrol just around the corner.'

Cursing silently, he was careful to tread on the sides of the stairs as he climbed and to avoid the especially creaky ones close to the landing. Tomfoolery! He would be lucky to have time to write to Fleur, let alone kiss her goodbye. Damn it, he wanted to feel her soft, sweet body against him and breathe in the perfume of her hair against his cheek. He could almost smell the fragrance.

Shaking such thoughts away, he tightened his hold on the cudgel, unlocked his door and pushed it back slowly. It pressed against the laundry pannier behind it. Well, that was reassuring, but the room was dark, the curtains drawn. Surely he had . . .

'*Bon Christ!*' He smelled the ashes before his mind took in the escritoire with its drawers all open and plundered. Foolishly, he took a step towards the window, irritated that he must deal with this intrusion now, and then he heard the door close behind him. Oh God, the scent of honeysuckle was not imaginary. Only a darling sylph like her could have fitted between the pannier and the doorjamb but what . . . ?

'Fleur?'

The answer was a bitter laugh.

'No, I'm not Fleur. You know that. I am the daughter of the Duc de Montbulliou whose death you ordered and witnessed. I am the sister of the Vicomtesse de Nogent whose death you ordered. I am the sister of the émigré, Philippe de Montbulliou, whom you want to send to the guillotine. I intend to go to the guillotine, too, Raoul de Villaret, just as you planned, but unfortunately you won't be alive to see me mount the scaffold because I am going to kill you.'

His back to her, Raoul slowly set down the cudgel. 'Would you like more light so you can relish my dying spasms better?' Raising his arms languidly, he slowly pushed one of the curtains back. Inside, he was shaken, ill-prepared. This ugly discovery was too precipitant. He had imagined enlightening her between caresses, easing the dream out into reality when she was languid from his lovemaking. But, now, yes, he could believe her hurt, but how . . . ?

'*Fleur.*' He made her name a soft sigh of entreaty as he turned, his leisurely calm a mask, and froze, slack-jawed in horror.

An urchin stepped out to confront him, a pistol in either hand – Raoul's delightful mistress of last night in yet another guise. But now contempt and loathing disfigured her lovely face, and the contempt was for him. Oh, God, thought Raoul, she means it! She really means it.

With his hands lifted in surrender, he struggled for words to defend himself. 'Yes, I guessed who you were, my darling, that evening at the Palais-Royal, but as for the rest, you are mis–' He broke off, his breath painful as he glimpsed the ravaged notebook and the ashes scattering his opened escritoire.

'I'm not mistaken.'

At Clerville she had been fifteen years old. She had fired at him and missed; this time she was nineteen and her hands were steady.

'I want you to leave here, my darling,' he said, trying to keep his voice even. 'The guard are on their way. Robinet has gone to alert them. I didn't – we didn't – know it was you.' She didn't respond. 'Give me the pistols, my darling.' He took a step closer.

'Stay where you are, you unspeakable monster!'

'Fleur, please.' Oh God, he could feel the sweat trickling between his shoulderblades. 'Please, my darling, I swear I will answer any questions where and when you choose but *not here*. You have to *leave here now*.'

'Don't you understand, you Antichrist, I don't *care* whether I die or not.'

'But I do,' he said, 'I care if you die.' He had seen desperation in many forms; linked to courage, it was invincible and deadly, and Fleur had courage.

He had to give her something to live for but

what could he – the revolutionary she despised – offer Françoise-Antoinette de Montbulliou?

'You can't shoot a dream, Fleur. I'm your thief.' He had to disarm her now before they came. He would not be able to protect her from the questions afterwards. 'Your thief at Clerville. You shot and missed, remember. And we went through the tunnel.' The sound of heavy boots reached him from the street, the soldiers were into the hall, mounting the stairs. 'The donkey, you must remember the donkey.' A lift of cynical eyebrow in her tense face merely sneered at his pathetic squirming. 'Oh Christ, Cupid! For God's sake, shoot me and be damned!'

Her eyes widened, like a wounded animal's, and then she sagged, arms dropping to her sides, as Robinet burst in.

The *sans-culotte* halted, gaping. Behind him, three soldiers primed for violence braked, cramming the doorway.

'Deputy!' Robinet recovered first. Behind him, uncertain now, the soldiers straightened, saluting.

'Patriots.' Raoul inclined his head in stern courtesy. 'As you see, someone has searched my papers. I thought the rascal was still here but if he is, he's hidden himself damnably well.'

'Who's that then?' The officer insinuated himself to the front, his expression like a mastiff bailing up a kill. Raoul sucked in his cheeks. How did one explain a girl dressed as a *sans-culotte* with cocked pistols in her hands?

'This . . . this is my . . . my new model. I was considering painting her as –'

'Gallant France,' Robinet cut in helpfully.

'Yes,' Raoul agreed, his suavity precarious, 'Gallant France.'

Gallant France was gripping his guns. Even if the fanatic despair had vaporised, she could still kill two of them before they overpowered her and he headed her list.

'Why's she holding them pistols at the ready?' asked the officer suspiciously.

'To shoot the thief,' she answered for herself. Her voice was poisonous honey. 'Hadn't you better find him, patriots?'

'Do put the small arms down, my dear,' drawled Raoul, 'or at least put the safety catches on. You are making these fine fellows edgy. Patriots, let me introduce you to the famous actress and aviatrix, La Coquette.' He watched displeasure tighten her face. The soldiers' stares slid downwards.

'Enough of that,' growled their officer. 'We'll search the premises right away, Deputy.'

'Citizens,' Raoul murmured, delaying them further, 'I value my neighbours' goodwill. No bay-onets in the dirty washing, *hein*. They like their clothes unslashed. If you find the rascal, bring him to me first. I'd like to set eyes on him.' He saw them to the door and leaned against the doorjamb, watching them disperse.

'I'm going downstairs,' he announced, trying to reduce the atmosphere in the room to normality. To glance back at the girl might be to destroy the brittle calm. 'Wait until the soldiers are gone, Robinet, then take the citizeness back to her house if she'll let you. My pistols can go too. They're glued to her palms. She can keep them for the time being. And don't ask her questions, Robinet. I'd prefer a quiet funeral but let's not make it a double one. Oh, and you'll need to order a coffin for me. There's been rather a high demand of late.'

As he reached the doorway, he braced himself for her shot.

16

Dearest Marie-Anne,
Oh, my spirits are so bruised, but I must count myself
fortunate to still be alive . . . Fleur

EXTRACT FROM THE LETTERS OF FRANÇOISE-ANTOINETTE DE
MONTBULLIOU, 1793

Gallant France was tense and pale as Robinet, whistling nervously beneath his
breath, escorted her back to the Rue des
Bonnes Soeurs. The pistols were in her belt, and her
sullen silence had forestalled any advice on his part,
but by the time they halted outside Blanchette's
stable, he could not resist any longer.

'I wouldn't shoot the deputy if I were you,' he
cautioned her. 'If it's a crime of passion, kiss and

make up. There are plenty of worse *culs* than him. He'll make it up to you when he gets back from Caen.'

'Caen!'

'Yes, leaving this afternoon. What have I –?' Appalled to see she had one of the pistols out and cocked in a flash, Robinet's jaw sagged.

'Go home!' Fleur's voice was a low growl of warning.

'I know he said you could hang onto 'em but they're not toys, you kn –'

'Robinet, the way I feel at this moment, I am quite capable of putting a shot through anyone and you're the easiest target. Go!'

Fleur let herself into the stable and pushed home the bolt. Wrapping her arms around her donkey's neck, she wept silently against the dark cross. Blanchette nuzzled her, hoping she would fill up the corner manger; one of them had to have some thought for the future and a full stomach. Fleur shook the donkey's feed out for her and then sank down onto the straw in a miserable knot of arms and elbows.

Now revenge had clawed its way into her mind, it squatted there filling every cranny like a malodorous evil crushing all reason.

Shame and misery flayed her, but above all, guilt. When the news of Papa and Marguerite's deaths had reached her in the forest, she had been young and resilient, preoccupied with the urgent need to keep herself and her aunt from starving. The royalist agent who had managed to flee to

Caen with the intelligence had been uncertain of his facts, and the terror in faraway Paris had seemed unreal. Fleur's family had been among hundreds of victims and it had felt almost like a natural tragedy, as though they had been caught in a flood, distant, inevitable and unavoidable. Nor, happy in the enclosed world of the Trinité School, had she ever truly mourned Henriette, a sister she had not seen for years.

But now *all* her half-sisters were dead. And she was dishonoured by her lack of feeling. Doubly so, since she had even lacked the courage to kill Papa and Marguerite's murderer. Fleur drew out de Villaret's flintlock and ran her fingers over the brass barrel. Why *had* he stalked her family like an angel of death? Was it some insult by her father in the Hall of Mirrors at Versailles? Kisses refused by a teasing Marguerite while the Queen watched? How very small of him! And to think she had believed there was an honourable man within this murderer, that she could forgive him anything for love.

Love! God forgive her, she had fallen like some easy dove brought down by the talons of this hawk. Two-faced bastard! And to be going off to Caen today without even telling her!

Thief! Never! How could de Villaret be *her* thief? Thomas must have foolishly told the story but . . . Ah, *bon Dieu*, what if he was? *Thief?* No, murderer! And her dreams were now in shards.

The bell of the Église Saint-Roch shook her back to practicalities. Quickly she changed into her black skirt and clawed her fingers through her hair, trying to think straight. She must speak with Philippe but not yet, for she was hurting so much inside. She just could not face him with her wounds so raw.

'*Patronne?*'

Thomas was back. Fleur held her breath, hugging the pistol against her heart. *Go away, Thomas!* Leave me alone! I despise humanity, I loathe myself and the only dignity I have left would be to pull this small piece of metal back and make an end to it all.

His footsteps disappeared inside the house but a few minutes later he was back and the latch rattled. 'Are you in there, *patronne*? I've just seen Emilie. She's been at the celebrations for Marat. I thought you'd have been there. Are you all r–'

'I don't give a damn about wretched Marat!' Fleur pushed back the bolt and flung open the door.

Her massive friend sucked in his cheeks as he set eyes on her and then leant forward and plucked a straw from her skirt. She must look as though she'd escaped some filthy madhouse; woodcurls and hay clung to her bustle and dusted her hem. 'Marat!' she spat out. 'Marat will end up smelling of roses whatever happens.'

'*Oh, bon Dieu!*' Realising her hasty words, she clapped a hand to her mouth.

'I doubt it. Not a good joke, *patronne*,' chuckled Thomas, glancing back over his shoulder in case anyone had heard. 'Nor a good day by the look of you.' He swept a huge arm about her shoulders. 'What's it to be? A dose of laudanum and a good lie-down or some cutlets and a *vin extraordinaire*?'

'Oh, Thomas.' The comforting aromas of the Chat Rouge that clung to him filled her breathing as they entered the house together. Her heart ached but she was still alive.

At the Messageries Nationale, Raoul eyed the hired two-wheel cabriolet with irritation. Was this mission so urgent they couldn't find him a better vehicle? And the weather had turned foul. Cursing inwardly, he slung his bag to the porter and took shelter out of the rain beneath a gateway. Unslinging his writing compendium, he leant it upon his knee and flicked open the inkwell.

'Citizen, the post-chaise is ready to leave,' insisted the driver, coming up behind him.

'*Moment*,' murmured Raoul, swinging round. The man gaped at the *tricolore* sash, which had been hidden by Raoul's coat, and snapped to attention.

'Deputy.' He touched his forehead in salute.

'Is there something else?' Raoul waited pointedly for the fellow to give him some privacy.

'No, Deputy. Of course, Deputy. My apologies.' He retreated, red-cheeked, to explain the delay to the other government passenger.

Raoul closed his eyes for an instant, trying to clear his thoughts. He not only ached to hold Fleur in his arms and make her listen but he wanted her trust more than anything in the whole world. And to have to leave Paris when . . . Oh God, how could he make matters right? Another man might have let the coach leave without him, but the Revolution was more important than his personal business. Still . . .

A haughty voice yelled out, 'Infernal nuisance! How long are you going to keep us waiting?'

'Yes, indeed,' exclaimed a woman. 'You tell him.'

Raoul jerked his head round towards the coach with an icy smile. 'Convention business, citizen,' he drawled malevolently. The heavily jowled official took one look at his uniform and instantly hushed. Several of the nearby passengers who were waiting for public conveyances watched him as though he were a beast escaped from a circus intent on mauling them, but somewhere in the yard Raoul sensed some other observer and it bothered him. There was no face he recognised and yet the feeling would not leave him.

He made two attempts at his message to Fleur – pride would not let him be abject – rejected both and stuffed the crushed papers in his pocket before he scrawled one line, folded the sheet and summoned an errand boy to take it.

Then with a last uneasy glance about him, as though he were seeing Paris for the last time, he sprang up the steps of the carriage.

The bells of Saint-Eustache, which stood at the north-west corner of the Halles market, were striking three as Fleur repeated:

'My Great-Aunt Sophie has the measles. I wish to buy some special fruit for her.'

Zut! she fumed, meeting the old stall-keeper's blank expression. She was sure she had come to the right stall . . . 'My Great-Aunt –'

'It's all right, madame.' The mouth cracked open in a gap-toothed grin. 'I think my friend up the street has just the thing, but first I need to make sure.'

In her present mood, Fleur was not amused at his teasing. 'Then tell *your friend* I need to buy some fruit urgently.' The stallholder shrugged, and waited until his apprentice had finished serving another customer before he whispered his instructions and sent the boy off. With a leer, he offered Fleur a carrot. She took it with a sigh, wondering whether it was some kind of prearranged signal, and was still munching it when her brother loomed up, a leather apron around his thighs and a lumpy sack of beans over his shoulder.

'You'd better have something important to tell me,' he muttered, swinging his burden to the ground and unstringing the opening for her inspection. '*Ciel!* Don't blurt it out here, you foolish chit!'

'I wasn't going to,' hissed Fleur, leaning down to examine the produce. 'If you don't want to know –'

His fingers bit into the soft flesh of her arm. 'Behind you is a cabbage stall, and behind that a laneway. I want you to walk down it and stop at the second cart waiting there. Don't look round!' He hoisted the sack. 'Go on!' he mouthed, and strode away.

Fleur obeyed his instructions, puzzled that Philippe did not follow her up the alley.

'Can I help you, citizeness?' The shaggy-haired carter lolling on the driver's board of the second cart took a pipe from his mouth.

'I don't suppose you'd be interested to know that my Great-Aunt Sophie has the measles?' Fleur asked wearily.

'Double doors up on the right, citizeness.'

Entering, she found herself alone in a small warehouse and surrounded by innocent crates of potatoes, a bland, exotic vegetable, still not very popular in Paris. This was not a company she or Thomas had dealt with and the café owner in her surfaced; she stooped over one of the boxes and burrowed her arm in, curious to see if the quality vegetables were merely on the surface, and froze. Her fingers had encountered metal. They were smuggling arms.

'The others won't be pleased you came here.' Her brother drew the doors to and leaned against the crossbar with his arms folded. 'What do you want, Toinette?'

'I'm here to tell you how much I despise you,' she hissed now they had privacy. 'You ordered me to prostitute myself knowing full well that de Villaret was our father's murderer.'

'And it didn't take much for you to spread yourself for him,' he sneered, striding across to face her. 'My, my, Toinette, what a milksop you are. A few minutes on your back for the sake of France and you're complaining.'

'I don't have to list –'

Instantly his hand clamped her wrist and pulled

419

her to him. 'We're fighting this war every way we know how. Anything to get our lands back, you hear me! If I tell you to sleep with Robespierre, you'll do it. Now why are you here? What did you find at de Villaret's lodgings? Any notes on Calvados that we can use?'

'I found his notebook.'

'Yes? Come on, I haven't all day.'

'It was all about us. *Us*, Philippe! H . . . he knows everything about our family. It was all there, the date each of our sisters died, our father's murder. He even has David's portrait of us, Philippe, the one that hung in Papa's dressing-room.'

There was no shock in Philippe's face, only a tightening of muscle that added cruelty.

'It must be some old vendetta between his blood and ours, don't you think? Something Papa never told –'

'Stop yapping, Toinette. What exactly did the notebook say about me?'

'Last heard of in Coblenz. Oh, don't look relieved. He knows who I am. He can denounce me any time he pleases. I think you have to get out of Paris now. He's left for Caen but –'

'Be quiet, let me think!' Her brother dragged his fingers either side of his stubbled chin. 'Caen, you say? And there was nothing else of significance in his papers?'

'I-I didn't have time. H-he found me going through his papers.' She refused to hang her head.

'Oh Christ in heaven, how could you be so –? I hope you thought of a good excuse.'

'No, I tried to shoot him.'

It would have been wonderful to see Philippe gaping at her if it wasn't so serious. Then he reached some sort of decision.

'I don't think you need to worry, Toinette.'

'But what about de Villaret?' asked Fleur faintly, wondering if her ears were functioning. The comfortable, forgiving tone in his voice contradicted the vindictive calculation in his smile.

'Oh, we'll knock him off in a dark alley the moment he gets back from Calvados.'

He was lying, but *why* she wasn't sure. Nor was she sure she wanted de Villaret cudgelled to death. Somehow he was hers to deal with.

'Toinette, you're a brave girl. You're one of us!' The chuck under the chin might be well meant but it was patronising. 'Listen.' His voice sank to a whisper. 'We're planning to do a deal with the federalists. Toulon, Marseilles, Nantes are all saying they don't want Paris dictating to them. The tide is turning, believe me. And we have a new, easier role for you. No, don't look at me like that. My friend Henri de Craon and some other émigrés in England are prepared to come back and help us.' She waited, dreading what would come next. 'Your café could be really vital. It's not just a gold mine, it's a mecca. You understand what I mean. All sorts of customers, because of the cuisine. We could organise things from there. Of course, Henri'll have to use another name, but if he ties the knot with you and we make it fully legal, that is, a civil ceremony and a nonjuring priest as well – all fair and square

– then he can use the café as a cover and it could buy more of these.' He kicked the nearest crate.

'Potatoes, Philippe?'

'No, for – Oh, you're joking.' He looked as though he wanted to end the conversation.

'There's one thing you've forgotten, Philippe.'

'And what's that?'

'I don't like Henri. I never liked him. He always completely ignored me whenever he came to Clerville.'

'Women!' Her brother's arms rose in a gesture of disbelief. 'You were nine, Toinette, and fat. Damn it, girl, none of us stays the same. Just because the fellow didn't make small talk with you about your doll's house.' He was completely misreading her stillness, ignoring her hands clenched at her side. 'It may impress you to know that Henri was planning to join the Knights of the Dagger.' She must have looked blank for he added impatiently, 'The royalists who took an oath to rescue the King.'

'*Did* he?'

Philippe ignored her sarcasm. 'No, he was winding up his affairs in London to do so but then the bastards executed the King sooner than we all expected.'

'And now you want me to give him everything I own. I cannot believe that you could come up with such a cold-hearted scheme, or is it your fellow conspirators who suggested such a thing? Anyway, it's out of the question. It's my café . . . yes, and Thomas's in a sense. I have been struggling to pay off all the debts and now you want to cream off any profit.'

'Damnation, Toinette, de Craon will let you manage it if that's all that is bothering you. Gives him a chance to get on with organising the campaign. But some of your profit will have to go to that. Stop being so female and difficult.'

'Dear me, Philippe, me difficult? Are you aware that during this conversation you haven't once considered how I feel?'

'You? Curse it all, Toinette, I'm trying to arrange a decent marriage for you. De Craon's descended from one of Louis XIV's marshals. And it's not as though you are a great prize, things being the way they are and . . .'

'And . . .' she prompted dryly.

'And . . .' he shrugged, 'and if these times were less topsy-turvy, his family, well, what's left of 'em, would demand his bride to be untouched, but you being . . .' at least he had the grace to look sheepish, 'a widow, he cannot expect that. Why are you being so obdurate?' He met her scowling expression with a curled lip. 'Listen to me, if Papa were still alive and he told you you'd be marrying de Craon, there would be no argument. Well, I'm your guardian and head of the family, and I'm telling you that is exactly what you will do and there will be no more argument. You'll like him well enough. When we've rid France of these bloody madmen, he'll get his chateau back.'

'You think so?' She enjoyed saying that.

'Their government's about to fall in a heap and they're quarrelling among themselves like a pack of hungry dogs. We'll have 'em soon, you'll see, and the heads rolling in the Place de la Revolution will be plenty, I can promise you that. Going, are you?' He sounded surprised.

It was too easy to fall into her old childhood role and let herself be bullied but she was her own mistress now.

'Yes,' answered Fleur, pausing at the door. 'The thought doesn't thrill me but when can I expect to see you again, Philippe?'

'We're going out of Paris to . . . towards Clerville. We're seeing what support we can muster to help our leader, the Comte de Puisaye, and whether we can link up with the insurrection in La Vendée. I can't say how long I'll be away.'

'I'll manage,' she replied curtly, suspicious of today's openness when before he had been so miserly in sharing his plans, and then added, 'Philippe, you are only twenty-one, with life still ahead of you. These friends of yours, do not let them rush you into anything. Think before you act.' The charm that was possible flared only briefly in his smile but then he joined her, his hand upon the latch. 'Wait, Toinette, I need any money or jewellery you have on you.'

She was carrying very little. Wearily, she emptied her purse into his palm but he caught her hand before she could snatch it away. He wanted the aquamarine. 'Ah, I can get more for this.'

'No! It was Maman's.' She tried to free herself. 'You ask too much!'

'Do you think she would have withheld it? *Do you*? Now give it me!'

'Let go, Philippe!'

With her lips a tight seam of displeasure, she drew off her ring.

Briefly a gentleman, he opened the door for her. 'Take care, Toinette. And . . . and if de Villaret should get back before I do, just keep him at a dangle. It's me he's after and I'll deal with him, I promise you.'

Raoul slept – or at least pretended to – as much as was possible in an ancient vehicle that pranced along over every rut and stone with the exuberance of a puppy. Sleeping was a way of avoiding conversation. He spread himself along the seat on his side of the coach, ignoring the glowers of the *ci-devant* tax collector and his wife, and tried desperately to focus his mind on his mission.

Caen was a warm womb waiting for the Girondin seed; idealism waiting to take to the streets with federalist fervour. When he reached Calvados he must reassure their loyalists and arrest any of the administration or military who supported a rebellion against Paris. Arrest them, yes, and terrify them into passivity before releasing them (or at least that was his intent, though a few might deserve a more drastic sentence). Paris had to retain its predominance over France, otherwise there would be no hope of withstanding the Austrian emperor and his allies. Just the thought of that meddling Marie Antoinette set at liberty to take her revenge was chilling. Women! Women were . . . Fleur!

It was useless trying to think of anything but her. Why had fate flung her to him again and again if it was not his destiny to care for her? But it was a destiny that ran counter to his common sense. Here he was, a man of reason, a devout Jacobin, lusting after a royalist who wanted to shoot him. Wanting her was a heresy, but making love to Fleur had felt so very good and he longed to do it again. His mind and body knew no peace now. Just remembering her sweet, slender body beneath his. Damn! Growing cursedly uncomfortable, he sat up and shifted his writing case discreetly across his thighs.

'What in hell . . . ?' They were thrown from their seats as the coach suddenly careered off the road. Raoul reached instinctively for one of his pistols before he remembered that Fleur had taken them. A couple of shots cracked through the air and they heard a scream, then something human thudded back into the bodywork of the coach. Hoofs thundered past the vehicle and in seconds the carriage horses had been drawn to a halt.

'Out!' The door was flung open and Raoul found himself staring down the muzzle of a blunderbuss. 'Your rapier, man! Disarm!' Scowling, Raoul obeyed and stepped down onto the forest floor with an ill grace. There were at least four horsemen. In the poor light he could only see the mask of the man closest but he did not think they were common highwaymen. Deserters, probably. One of them was unhooking the lantern from the coach. Two of the others had pistols pointing at him. The growing darkness was on his side but he doubted he could outrun them even if he headed for where the trees were thickest.

'Do something!' pleaded the tax collector, trying to calm his hysterical wife as he helped her out. Unarmed against four? raged Raoul. Oh yes, and he could walk on water.

'Credentials!' The pistol jerked a command at him. Credentials! Jaw clenched, Raoul slowly unbuttoned his tunic then raised his hands to collar height while the man thrust a hand into his breast pocket and withdrew the pass and letter of authority. The man with the torch kneed his horse close so his leader might examine the papers.

'Deputy,' crooned the leader with a maliciousness that made Raoul wonder if he would see next day's sunrise. Vindictive eyes met his as the man refolded the papers and slid them inside his riding boot. Then he signalled to Raoul to step away from the coach and nodded to his colleague, who raised his pistols and shot the other two passengers.

'Jesus!' screamed Raoul as the older man fell choking to his knees and crashed forward onto the leaves. The woman had been hurled back into the coach by the impact of the shot. Her breath came in short, desperate gasps. Raoul swung round to help her.

'Leave her!'

'But she's not –'

'I said *leave her*!'

'What kind of bastard are you?'

Two of them had dismounted. They surrounded

him now. The woman's heaving filled the silence between them.

In a few seconds they roughly stripped Raoul of his tunic, sash and shoes.

'Now, your turn.' The leader laughed. 'I want you to grovel for mercy, king-killer!'

'Go to hell!' Raoul jerked his head back defiantly.

He struggled as two of them grabbed him by the arms while the third drove a fist into his stomach. Gasping, he tumbled to his knees, doubled over in agony. A savage kick from behind sent him sprawling face down.

'Spread him.'

Spread him! Oh Christ, what were they going to do to him? He tried to resist as gloved hands savagely dragged his arms out across the ground.

'We're wasting time. What's this about?' protested one of the men.

'Bring the torch closer! Citizen animal, here, was a second-rate painter before he took to murdering.'

'*Who are you?*'

The pistol shot deafened him. Searing pain ripped up his arm. Someone was screaming an oath and he realised it was him. Where his right hand had been was a mass of blood.

'I said *who are you?*' Each word was a gasp. This was it. His revolution and his life were over but somehow it mattered that death had a name.

'Philippe, Duc de Montbulliou.'

Death did have a name.

'Finish it!' One of the others was edgy.

'Oh, I'll finish it. A piece of him at a time. A shot for every hurt this cur has inflicted on my family.'

Tense, Raoul gritted his teeth and waited for the bastard to fire again. He heard the click of metal.

But the burst of fire came from the coach. One of the attackers screamed and toppled from his saddle. Raoul scrambled to his heels.

His breath came in short bursts. If he could only . . . Shots rang out at him. Something exploded below his hip, a throbbing pain so intense that he almost passed out, but his mind kept burning like a candle flame that wouldn't die. Then he felt the crack of pain against his skull and the candle went out.

'It's just as well you didn't shoot Monsieur de Villaret, *ma petite*, else we should all be looking through the little window tomorrow morning,' M. Beugneux exclaimed, wincing with discomfort as he eased the bolster behind his back with his good hand. 'Ah, reheated br-broth, how enthralling. It's my shoulder that is w-wounded, not my appetite.'

'Hmff.' The broth was steaming and Fleur needed to navigate it past the carved teak elephant, the pedestal bearing a naked Pompeian athlete and the Viennese harpsichord. The chef followed her in with a tray of coffee, and paused, goggled-eyed.

'*Formidable*,' he exclaimed. 'This is a museum, monsieur. How did you acquire all this stuff?'

Beneath his tasselled nightcap, M. Beugneux's smirk was reminiscent of Machiavelli's expression after his latest rat, but the gentleman offered no explanations.

'Eh, *patronne*, I forgot.' Thomas fumbled in his leather waistcoat pocket. 'This arrived for you from the Messageries while I was out in the stable. I thought it best to wait until you were in a better frame of mind.'

Fleur bit back a retort as she unfolded the unsealed paper. It contained a single sentence. She read it aloud in absolute fury.

Judge not, that ye be not judged. R.

'It's the Sermon on the Mount,' M Beugneux observed unnecessarily.

'The Order from the Mountain more like!' Fleur flounced angrily from the bedside. The audacity of the scoundrel! 'How dare *he* quote the Bible at me!'

Not when the Republic guillotined good men like the Abbé Gombault and turned nuns out to starve! *Judge not, that ye be not judged.* So de Villaret was not prepared to answer for his sins and his message was a clear warning that she was in his power. Well if he thought he was going to be returning to an obedient little skirt waiting to be tumbled, he was mistaken.

'Judge, *hein*? Oh, I've judged you all right, you hypocrite!' With intense satisfaction, she crushed the paper and lobbed it into the fire, pleased to see de Villaret's handwriting brown and fracture in the flame. 'There!' Hands clasped behind her back, she stood defiantly, daring them to argue.

Cold blue eyes condemned her still for the afternoon's rashness. 'The deputy is not a stupid man.' M. Beugneux blew a long, slow breath across the bowl and mopped the rime of broth from his thin lips with a shaky right hand.

He was right. Her rashness this morning had put them all at risk.

'You think I let the horse run away with the cart, do you?' she challenged, singling out M. Beugneux, but it was Thomas who nodded.

Found guilty, Fleur folded her arms defensively and turned to glare at whatever painting hung over the fireplace. A martyred Saint Stephen gazed heavenwards with her.

'*Mon Dieu*, if that vindictive cur thinks I am going to purr around his bootcuffs when he gets back . . .' she muttered over her shoulder. 'Maybe he's already denounced me. Maybe it'll be a matter of days. Hours, even.' If she was being melodramatic, she had good reason. Like many citizens going about their everyday lives, Fleur had tried to ignore the slam of the guillotine's falling blade, but the two worlds were at last colliding.

'Truth has a strange way of bubbling out, given time,' M. Beugneux remarked. '*Maybe* things aren't what they seem.'

'Like you, *hein*?' Thomas employed the nail of his little finger as a toothpick, and then added, 'You know what, *patronne*, I'd say your father had more enemies than there are fleas on a dog's rump. De Villaret was one of many.'

Fleur found her way to the open window and

stood looking out on the moonlit backyard, her arms cradling her body. A rat skittered soundlessly along the top of the wall.

Papa had hanged the ratcatcher at Clerville for poaching. Quick to judge and slow to forgive, that had been Papa. Like the day he had horsewhipped one of David's young apprentices for a misdemeanour. She recalled crouching by the balustrade and watching the struggling youth, hurling abuse at her father, hauled down the staircase by two of the footmen. And Papa had stood wigless, clothed in his silken dressing-gown, looking on from above like some vengeful king, while her sisters had quietly closed the door of their bedchamber and then burst into shrieks of laughter.

Papa must have noticed the rustle of Fleur's dress for after the boy had been dragged off along the servants' passage, he had swung round to confront her.

'So you saw, Françoise-Antoinette. And what did you make of that?'

'I do not know, Papa,' she had replied honestly, 'I saw you beat that boy.'

'You saw impudence rewarded. Remember that, child. Give an inch and filth like him will take a mile.'

'Yes, Papa.' But at nine years old she had not understood the sudden afternoon violence nor why her father had been bare-legged. It was several years later that she had discovered her sisters had maliciously shut the apprentice in the secret passage behind her father's private apartments. The lad had fumbled his way along behind Papa's *salle à coucher* while her father had been tupping the chambermaid. Hearing the noise, Papa had discovered him behind the panelling and had been so furious, he had seized his riding crop and viciously beaten the lad, refusing to hear his explanation and accusing him of deliberately playing the voyeur. Yes, the apprentice had been a prize braggart – even Fleur had taken revenge on him for calling her names – but he had deserved a fair hearing.

'I'm sorry, *patronne*,' Thomas interrupted her thoughts. He stood behind her now, his large hands upon her shoulders. 'I disliked the duke and I never thought much of your sisters or the boy either. All the servants got heartily sick of their pranks and your father never once took them to task.'

'So you didn't like my family,' she whispered bleakly and then surprised herself. 'Well, Thomas, I suppose nor did I overmuch. Looking back now, I can see they were all utterly selfish.' She slid from his supportive hands, needing to stand alone. 'But it's all right for you to say so, but I have betrayed them by . . . by consorting with the man responsible for their murder, and I cannot forgive myself nor him.'

'But who exactly is accusing the deputy?' M. Beugneux had the look of a weary magistrate. 'Have you seen the testimony your brother mentioned?'

'Yes, he gave me the copies.' Fleur thrust her hand through the slit in her skirt and produced a folded square from her petticoat pocket. '*Voilà!*'

The patient perused the documents at arm's

length then handed them up to Thomas. 'There is no evidence that these men actually saw de Villaret kill either your father or your sister,' he argued.

'*Nom d'un chien!* Bertrand saw him kill someone and he was spattered in blood. Someone's blood, if not Papa's. Well?' She dared them to disagree. 'And don't tell me he was an innocent bystander. He's dedicated to the Revolution and utterly ruthless. All the Jacobins are.'

Thomas shrugged. 'Maybe, maybe not, *ma petite*. He saved your life at Clerville, didn't he?'

'How can we be sure it wasn't him who incited the people to march against the chateau in the first place?' she asked, accepting a cup of coffee. 'All I know is that ever since then he's been stalking my family like a hunter, picking us off one by one. It was all in his notebook. You should have seen it. Each date my sisters died. Oh, I've been so stupid, taken in by the easy charm . . . It would have taken one shot to revenge Papa's and Marguerite's deaths and I did not have the courage.'

The creased face opposite refused to judge her. 'It takes courage to live. Killing is easy.'

'I have no more heart to do either.' It was even more shameful that M. Beugneux, a quiet hero of the counter-revolution, should be absolving her so generously. 'I've lost my way. I've betrayed my family, my noble blood, my honour.'

'No, *patronne*,' protested Thomas, putting an arm about her. 'In a time when there is little to eat, you've given people work. Isn't that right, monsieur?'

'Yes, that's true, Fleur,' said M. Beugneux.

'Matthieu would have been proud of you. Not only do you have to keep going for their sakes, *ma petite*, but you have to make up your own mind about what is important. Don't be a clock for others to wind. I have drawn my own conclusions. So should –'

The furious rapping of the front-door knocker ignited panic in all their faces.

'Open in the name of the Republic!'

It was Fleur who dropped her cup. It caught the lip of the coal scuttle and shattered around her feet, splashing its contents over her skirt.

'*Zut!*' she exclaimed, trying to make light of it. But the knocking came again, louder this time. 'It's . . . well . . . why are we all looking so worried?' Her forced cheerfulness did not reassure the others. De Villaret could have left orders for Françoise-Antoinette de Montbulliou to be guillotined while he was away. A clean finale that would not tax his emotions.

Thomas rubbed a hand across his chin. 'Jeanne's out queuing for bread. I'll answer it.' He jerked his head at the back door. 'You want to leave, *patronne*?'

'If they're here to make an arrest . . .' She thought about draping Machiavelli around her or arming herself. 'No, what does it matter. I'm past caring.'

'How very brave.' M. Beugneux calmly flicked open a cavity in his ring and shook the contents into his cup. 'One should always be prepared,' he murmured. 'There is a certain quality to a knocking, don't you think, and this shrieks violence.'

435

The knocking echoed again.

'OPEN IN THE NAME OF THE REPUBLIC!'

The Republic proved to be Felix Quettehou, *enragé* in ink-stained trousers, scarlet waistcoat, a shirt open to his belt and a bandanna which, had it sported a feather, would have made him look more like an American native than a Parisian. He ordered his escort – two section guards – to wait outside.

Deliberately keeping the printer waiting while she changed her skirt, Fleur eventually entered the salon with a stately chill that would have frozen puddles, and swept a discreet glance around the furniture to make sure her guest had removed none of the ornaments. Behind her cold demeanour she was feeling as frail as a snail shell but she was not going to let this irritating in-law crush her.

'Will this take long, Citizen Quettehou? I have to be at the café shortly.' She clasped her hands at her waist, blatantly impatient.

'The café, yes.' Matthieu's obnoxious nephew moved past each of the paintings, rocking to and fro on his feet like a sergeant inspecting his men, before he grinned back at her over his shoulder. 'I am going to lay my cards on the table. You remember there was a fire at your café, a most unfortunate act of vandalism.' Fleur nodded. 'Well, I keep my ear to the ground – one does of necessity these days – and there are one or two unpleasant rumours going round.'

'You mean it's going to happen again, citizen?'

His cheeks puffed out somewhat and he nodded.

'And who is behind this vandalism?'

'Well, I am.' The man's chest, hairless and garlic in colour, inflated proudly. How did one answer such a scoundrel? 'Nothing personal, Tante Fleur,' he leered. 'You must understand that.' What other fairytale would he have her believe – that King Louis still had his head on his shoulders? 'You see, it's only a matter of time before I find the evidence to prove what a conniving little actress you are, and believe me, I will, or . . . or we could come to some arrangement. I let you continue here,' he waved a hand to include the house, 'and you make over all your deeds to me. No?' He smiled deprecatingly as she slowly shook her head. 'Alternatively, we could become partners. You're quite a resourceful little baggage. How about you marry me and safeguard your future?'

Fleur grabbed the mantelshelf for support.

'I can see I have taken the wind out of your sails, dear aunt.'

Her fingers curled slowly around the silver candelabra. Marrying Quettehou made the prospect of a seventy-year-old ploughman with bad breath seem appealing. 'And . . . and if I don't entertain this magnanimous offer of yours?'

'Pfft.'

'*Pfft?*'

'Pfft! There is so much crime in Paris these days. One could almost accuse the authorities of turning a blind eye.'

She restrained herself from propelling the

candelabra through the air. He deserved a setdown but she did not want any more attacks on her life. She must handle this carefully. 'You really are such a sweet, thoughtful fellow to warn me and I do thank you for the proposal but although I find printers ink so,' here she let her gaze absorb his full manly beauty, 'so utterly compelling, I am still in mourning for my beloved husband. But I will give your offer some serious thought.' She let go of the silverware and shook the small handbell, hoping that Thomas would assist her promptly. This was one visitor that must not linger. 'Return to me in a month, Felix.' Graciously offering her hand to him at shoulder height, she added charmingly, 'Maybe my heart will ignite and we can run the printing works and café together. With your unscrupulousness and my duplicity, just imagine what advantages our children will have.'

Quettehou had lost his smugness and was staring at her, clearly torn between cynical disbelief and vanity, vanity that she might be genuinely encouraging him.

'You shall have a fortnight to think about it. It's not long.' He possessed himself of her fingers and trickled his lips down the back of her hand. 'Not long at all.'

As Thomas showed him out, Fleur tried not to wipe her wrist on her skirt. At the salon door she paused. Surely the secretaire had been closed properly? With her temper mounting, she let down the writing table. The papers in the flanking pigeon-holes looked unrifled except . . . Except there was a single document longer than the rest beneath her letters from Marie-Anne, letters she likely would not reread.

Unfolded, it proved to be a properly witnessed will. Fleur's heart skipped a beat.

And the signature – leaving the house and café to Felix Quettehou – was not her late husband's, it was hers!

17

Si j'faisons quelque belle action,   *If I perform some*
wondrous deed,

Si j'mourrons pour la patrie,   *If I die for my*
country,

On nous place au Panthéon   *In the Panthéon, they*
will place me.

'ENFIN V'LA QU'C'EST DONC FINI', FRENCH REVOLUTION SONG

'**M**en!' snorted Columbine, hands on hips, as she admired the repainted pussycat sign. 'If the Revolution hadn't closed down all the nunneries, I'd think about taking the veil, I honestly would. That revolting Quettehou threatening the Chat Rouge and your handsome deputy gone two weeks and not a word.'

Since she had tried to shoot the 'handsome deputy' before he left, Fleur hardly expected correspondence from him, especially anything signed 'love, Raoul'. She was amazed to find herself still at liberty.

'You are welcome to de Villaret, Columbine, but I assure you, pythons are better. They don't argue, they just hiss.'

'Wait a minute, *patronne!*' exclaimed the blonde, hastening after her into the café. 'Are you talking about Machiavelli? Oh, don't tell me he was at your house all this time. And here I've been making inquiries all over the place.' She clapped her hands together. '*Quelle merveille!* Oh, please let me use him in one of my acts. I promise I'll look after him. Could you bring him here tomorrow?'

'If Monsieur Beugneux agrees.'

'Oh, please, please, and have you time to sit down and listen to my idea? It will take your mind off your wicked Raoul. Oh là là, what have we here? Another deputy!'

Fleur swung round to see Armand Gensonné blocking the doorway, staring about him aloofly. What had brought this rush of blood to his haughty head? Hardly the urge to play dominoes or watch Columbine's dexterity with gauze. Then she noticed a very dour Robinet behind him and a horrible feeling of foreboding enveloped her.

'Citizens, let me find you a table.' The blonde sashayed towards them.

Fleur froze as Gensonné removed his tricorne hat and ignored Columbine. No man ignored

Columbine unless he had something very serious on his mind.

'Madame, I regret . . .' His large hand fumbled with his hat. 'Deputy de Villaret was murdered on his journey to Caen. It-it took some time for the local officers to make an identification.'

It was Columbine who found Fleur a chair before she fell.

For the next week Fleur stoically carried out her duties but at night she sat distrait, bewildered by the world, realising that she would have given her life to hear Raoul's voice again. And while she hid her aching heart and, out of remorse, forgave the suspicions and lies that had lain between them, the Jacobins cropped hay out of her lover's death with nauseating gusto. Not just snippings from de Villaret's speeches but predictable words like 'patriot', 'martyr' and 'hero' peppered the journals for days while the hacks scrabbled around for follow-up epithets. A week later the news sheets spoke of 'daring aviator', 'a thinker ahead of his time' and 'a Frenchman worthy of Mount Olympus'. But when one writer, too lazy to check his facts, described Fleur as 'de Villaret's widow', the Chat Rouge was suddenly pestered by people frothing condolences in return for free cups of café au lait. The latter included Marat and a flotilla of his admirers, who propped their mud-crusted heels on the tables, emptied their pipes onto the floor and drank the Chat Rouge dry of crème and *chocolat*.

Hérault came to the café to offer commiseration, but since his visits coincided with Columbine's sinuous performance with Machiavelli, Fleur concluded the actress was ranking high on his shopping list. She herself was impervious to the recruiting procedures for his seraglio, but she found his teasing friendship distracting. Perhaps his interest would keep Quettehou at bay.

'Why are you complaining, citizeness?' Hérault chided as Fleur showed him the latest gazette. 'Notoriety is good for business. I daresay poor old de Villaret would have been vastly amused. And this is for you.' He pushed a black-edged card across the serving ledge. Curious, Fleur wiped her hands on a cloth and picked up the invitation.

'The Panthéon!' she exclaimed.

'Of course! Dear old Raoul is to be buried among the greatest of this century: Rousseau, Voltaire, Mirabeau and the first martyr of the Revolution, poor Lepeletier.'

'Wasn't he stabbed in a café?' Fleur suppressed a sarcastic tone.

'Yes.' Hérault was provoked into glancing round uneasily. 'But it was at the Palais-Royal and the day before the King was guillotined. Raoul will be our second martyr. The coffin is arriving tomorrow and we'll have a gun carriage convey it through the city streets with lictors and virgins leading the way.'

'Did he manage to leave any?' muttered Fleur beneath her breath.

The Jacobin eyed her with a blend of sympathy and speculation. 'So the Bastille did fall. You've kept me wondering. Rest assured I'm around to pick up the pieces.'

'So I've observed this last week. However, I don't want to be swept up and glued back like a broken ornament.' She held out the invitation. 'Please give this to someone who will enjoy *la gloire*. As I told you before, the deputy and I parted on bad terms. If I have wounds to lick, I'll do it privately.'

'Don't be naive, citizeness,' he retorted, refusing to take it back. 'As a good patriot, you *will* attend the funeral. The procession's going to start at the Jacobin Club by the Tree of Liberty. It should be an excellent spectacle. David has designed some special costumes. Mind, it won't be as good as Lepeletier's. Did you see that? No? A pity. David had him displayed for four days in the Place de Piques on top of the pedestal where the statue of Louis XIV stood and, of course, it was January, which helped – you can't do that with a body in high summer. But I tell you, it made a big impression, bloodstained shirt draped on a pike. Paris talked about it for weeks. Only thing that ruined it was his daughter wasn't very cooperative even though we made her a "Daughter of the Nation". Didn't deserve it, wealthy little cow.

'Anyway, David's doing his best, especially since Raoul was once his apprentice.' That jarred Fleur. Jarred her so much that she did not protest as he added, 'I'm off south on another commission myself very soon, one less lethal, I hope. A swift trip to Mont Blanc. I'd be pleased if you'd attend a soirée at Le Nid before I go.' He leaned across and kissed her on either cheek. 'Tomorrow, I will see you at the Panthéon.' It was an order.

Apprentice to David? The empty two-handled pan she had just picked up somehow crashed to the floor. She stood dazed as the startled customers glanced up from their chess and newspapers. A gentle arm – Juanita's – came round her shoulders.

'I am such a fool,' Fleur exclaimed, smacking her forehead with the heel of her palm. De Villaret had known about the secret passage at Clerville because her sisters had shut him in it. He was the apprentice her furious father had horsewhipped all those years ago. *The apprentice, the thief and the deputy.* Had he been picking them off ever since?

'You are not with child, are you?' whispered Juanita anxiously.

Diable, she innocently hoped not. That would be the greatest irony of all.

It was not every day that one's only lover and greatest enemy was interred among the mighty. Lacking a tragic wife for de Villaret, the Jacobins intended Citizeness Bosanquet to play the grief-stricken fiancée. David had even sent her a message suggesting she hurl herself upon the coffin, and please could she weep copiously – the people would love that. But Fleur had no intention of being paraded like some black-draped war trophy, nor would she sit near the coffin alongside the butchers of the Revolution.

Fleur did, however, close the Chat Rouge on

the morning of de Villaret's funeral and, insisting
Thomas and Emilie leave ahead of her to attend
the service, she crossed the old bridge to the Île de
la Cité and paused in shock opposite the cathedral,
where carters were offloading sacks of stockfeed
and bales of straw. That was expected – nothing
was sacred any more – but it was the damage to the
beautiful façade that bruised her soul. Was there no
end to ignorance, stupidity and such appalling
vanity? Above the main portal of Notre Dame,
every one of the Biblical kings had been smashed
out of their niches. What gave these vandals the
right to destroy these priceless sculptures?

She lingered on the Pont-au-Double and stared
unseeing at the lantern spires rising beyond the
quays of the Left Bank. She was loath to continue,
loath to turn back. No past worth remembering,
no future either. God was binding chains around
her ankles to weigh her down, and the grey river,
reflecting the gathering rain clouds, ran beneath
the bridge uncaring, its mindlessness beckoning
her to a desperate oblivion. Survival was not everything. Existing in a city at war was a challenge she
had met, but now . . . Now life no longer held any
savour for her, for the fire that lit her soul was flickering out. Why should the memory of feeling
safe in de Villaret's arms flood her mind suddenly?
Instinctively safe in the embrace of a murderer!

As Fleur hesitated, the bell of the Palais de Justice began to toll. A lone booming bell from Notre
Dame gave answer, and across the city, on either
side of the Seine, the towers and spires replied in

slow, doleful chorus so that the sound became one vast heartbeat for the whole of Paris. This was for Raoul de Villaret? Downriver Fleur heard the drums, the hooves and the marching feet crossing the Pont Neuf. Tears trickling down her face, she began to run.

She reached the Rue Soufflot before the cortege and stood with her back to the wall of Montaigu College, her blood churning, her breath uncertain and her reeling mind still a mosaic of cobbles and corners. But she was here in time, opposite the modern, domed Panthéon, watching as the carriages spewed out the new noblesse, led by the Adam and Eve of the Girondin government – the drab M. and Mme Roland.

The republican unity was transitory. The Girondins might object to trailing behind a Jacobin coffin but they were here because public tribute was expected even if it meant rubbing shoulders with the coarser, vulgar orators. Mme Roland swept into the temple without a glance at the pinch-faced poor who were seeping in from the Court of Miracles and the sewers of nearby Saint-Séverin to eddy restlessly before the temple. The ravenous students from the abolished colleges jolting their scrawled banners for a dead hero did not warrant acknowledgment.

Silent, sad and detached, Fleur waited.

Led by youths and maidens in Grecian robes and laurel leaves, the procession of Jacobin deputies, Commune dignitaries and national guard marched stony-faced to a muffled drumbeat as they accompanied the gun carriage bearing the coffin through the hushed crowd. Seeing de Villaret's sash, the one he had worn at Caen, looped on a pike like a Roman legion banner in front of the bier was no surprise after what they had done for the stabbed Lepeletier. It was Raoul's plumed hat on top of his coffin that was almost her undoing – this at last was reality, the living breathing man who had made love to her and planned her death lay lifeless in that wooden box.

Instinctively, Fleur pushed forward into the crowd as it surged at the stark mausoleum. She had almost left it too late but, yes, she would go in, hide at the back like Christ's humble penitent, well away from the deputies brandishing their patriotism. The national guards let her through just in time to avoid the six bearers as they emerged from the central doorway of the Panthéon to shoulder the casket. There was a dull thud of the body sliding as bull-shouldered Danton grabbed the handle on his side and heaved. Taller than the others, he and Hérault took the main weight at the front, with Boissy and Gensonné uncomfortable in the middle, and at the rear, hardly bearing the weight at all, David and, surprisingly, Marat, looking like a stained leftover on a second-hand clothing stall. Sweaty in the heat, he still wore the signature strip of ermine, and blotches of livid, irritable skin made islands on his nose and chin. As they went past, he was the only one to notice Fleur's shadowy presence.

'You want to take my place, Chat Rouge?' he

called back outrageously, making the others lose stride and the *haute bourgeoisie* sneer over their shoulders.

Standing at the packed rear of the temple, Fleur could see nothing of the funeral bier beneath the dome, nor in her tangle of guilt did she want to. The opening hymn to the Republic required compliance but she felt incapable of paying more than lip service. Those around her sung fervently. Then the speeches began, Jacobin eulogies oozing with patriotism. Eulogies for a martyred murderer!

Well, she hoped de Villaret's soul was being tumbriled down the road to hell, with her father and his other victims lining the route and hissing him in. Knowing the damnable rogue, he'd come back and haunt her just to annoy. She should not weep but . . . dead. Oh, *bon Dieu*, it was as if she were treading some precarious plank flung down across an abyss from which she might tumble down into hysteria on one side and, on the other, grief.

The temple rustled as the congregation jostled for kneeling space. Peeping through her fingers, Fleur could at last see the coffin resting beneath the gloomy dome and the deputies sitting in rows in the east and west aisles. Envy was not one of her vices but she was becoming squashed and uncomfortable. The guards were misguidedly letting some of the *bas peuple* in, and the air, what there was of it, was fetid with unsponged skin and stale clothing.

Someone's knees were poking into her soles and she wriggled forward. Then a man's shabbily

449

trousered thighs annoyingly edged in close beside her. She shuffled discreetly leftwards but a bare hand fastened round her sleeve.

'I have been looking for you everywhere,' whispered an impatient male voice. 'Outside, now!'

She was never sure afterwards how her feet carried her out of the Panthéon or indeed what kept her upright; only that within seconds she found herself shaky and momentarily speechless in a corridor of air between the soldiers and the outside stonework.

'Well, that was easy,' said her abductor smoothly. 'We can talk here or perhaps a cell at La Force might be appropriate.' He seemed unperturbed by the crowd.

'With no distractions,' she agreed blithely, gesturing at their surroundings, and, wondering if she was out of her mind, added, 'But I really think you should go back in there.'

'With no distractions?' her escort reiterated, his smile only skin-deep. 'Round there, perhaps?' He gestured for her to precede him towards the corner of the building. 'Anyway, who's being buried?'

'You are.'

It was the theatrical exit line of the century, worthy of an audience of thousands, except the singing hordes were not listening, and there was no door for her to leave by.

Raoul, unquestionably alive, if somewhat battered, recovered first. His bruised jaw clenched. 'This is for me?' The words were not exactly ground out. When a vastly amused M. Beugneux had redirected him to find *la patronne* at the Panthéon, there had been no explanation.

'Surely you deserve it?' Fleur Bosanquet asked with the enchanting innocence she seemed to keep for playing him. Any astonishment at her victim's shirtsleeve appearance in workman's waistcoat was now abandoned and the cunning little cat was recklessly appraising the unaccustomed sight of his shortened hair curling about his forehead in ancient Roman fashion. She looked like Delilah thinking about sharpening the scissors further. Had they not been standing outside a Panthéon packed with diamond patriots gathered to remember his short, rebellious life, Raoul might have been tempted to squeeze the life out of her pretty throat. Either that or find somewhere nearby in the old abbey grounds where he might exact his revenge more pleasurably. The black, gauzy fichu begged to be ripped away, the tempting creamy cleavage plundered except – *His funeral?* Questioning his own sanity and whether being alive was a sudden inconvenience, Raoul took another look at the monstrous flowerbed of people.

'Christ!' he muttered, and grabbed his would-be murderess's right hand and hauled her back towards the tomblike entrance. 'You are right, citizeness, it would be impolite not to attend.'

At the threshold, he halted. The revolutionary te deum was in crescendo. 'Well now, my little actress,' he murmured, 'we can walk up the nave demurely like a bourgeois married couple or you can wait here. But if you leave, I will hunt you to the ends of the earth.' Only a fool with a sense of drama would have proceeded and he knew Fleur could not resist.

'I haven't a posy,' she retorted coquettishly.

'Don't worry, I'll be buying you a wreath shortly. Let us get this over, shall we?' He elbowed his way through the crowd near the door. Further in, the guards were keeping the naves clear. Pikes suddenly barred his path.

'You can't go through, citizen.'

'But it's my –'

'Invitation,' purred Fleur, brandishing a crumpled card, and proceeded sweetly on. Raoul thrust the pike aside and hastened after her.

'Why is it I have this uncontrollable urge to throw you off the Pont Neuf?'

'Lack of imagination, I daresay.'

People suddenly forgot the words to the anthem as they passed. Graciously smiling, La Veuve Bosanquet glided along beside Raoul with infuriating competence. Given encouragement, the wretched girl would start waving like a princess.

'Marie Antoinette's in prison. They don't need a substitute,' he warned and increased his stride. It could have been a romantic melodrama if the chit had not been a royalist Medusa.

His coffin – well, someone's – swathed in the republican flag, had not been placed before the dismantled altar but in the centre of the temple beneath the dome with the festooned pike propped up at one end like a macabre gravestone.

Several lines of shiny-faced choirboys faced it from the far side.

As he reached the revolutionary elite, privileged on rows of chairs in front of the steps that descended from the north and south naves, Raoul bestowed a lift of eyebrow on the Girondins' solemn faces. No one recognised him at first in his *sans-culotte* clothing, then Armand, usually away with the fairies, dropped his prayer book in astonishment and received a schoolmistress's silent rebuke from Mme Roland. Slowly, the rest of the row turned, goggle-eyed like children at a puppet show. Observing the Jacobins on the opposite side, Raoul saw Hérault direct an outraged look at Fleur Bosanquet as though she had engineered this unexpected resurrection – the scoundrel had probably spent the last two weeks trying to lure her to his cushions. This was priceless. Best of all, David's beatific expression, which he always wore when ceremonies were going well, had metamorphosed into open-beaked astonishment.

With theatrical timing, Raoul paused by his coffin but his frown as he became aware of the blood spatters on the tricolore sash wreathing the pike was honest.

'*Bon Dieu*, what the hell are you doing here?' Armand broke rank and, tackling the barricade of knees with rare exuberance, emerged free to embrace Raoul in true French fashion.

'Isn't it customary for the dead to attend?'

Across Armand's shoulder, Raoul watched the distracted choirmaster fall off his box. The boys' voices faltered to giggles and a wave of exclamations rippled backwards from the closest rows. But when the deceased sprang up onto the coffin, the entire Panthéon erupted in disgusted yells.

'Brothers!' Raoul shouted and held up his hand for the hubbub to cease. As the *sans-culottes* at the front recognised him, the protestation hushed to awe and slowly the whole temple fell silent.

'Patriots!' Oh God, this was pleasurable. His voice carried with ease among the columns. 'I do not know what stranger you honour in this coffin but it isn't Raoul de Villaret. I am Raoul de Villaret and lucky to be alive, gloriously alive.' Oh, he had them in the palm of his hand now. And, like Marcus Antonius, he had a corpse to stand over. 'My friends, I was attacked on the way to Caen by royalists. They stole my papers and left me for dead. *See!*' He pushed back the hair that lapped his forehead. Even Fleur, who had planned his murder, forgot to act and gaped up at him like the rest, her lips divinely parted. Raoul resisted that invitation and concentrated on his audience. 'Friends,' he cried, his fists to his chest, 'only the courage of a loyal *sans-culotte* saved me. I wish he stood here now so we might honour him. Two of my fellow patriots were shot down beside me.'

'What happened to your hand, de Villaret?' Marat came capering out to shout the question but it was David who had cued him. The great master's gaze met Raoul's, artist to artist, his expression white with grey stirred in.

Raoul grimly tugged off his glove; above the

bandaged knuckles, his fourth and fifth fingers were missing.

'The royalists tried to destroy my hand, the hand that signed the death warrant of a king.' Pivoting on his feet, de Villaret held his right arm up so the people packed into all four sections of the Panthéon could see, and then his gaze selected Fleur. Oh God, yes, he blamed her. 'But I shall sign their death warrants.'

The girl trembled, for an instant she looked as though her legs might dissolve beneath her, and he relished the flash of terror before she suppressed it, gazing up at him artlessly like a lamb about to be slaughtered. *I have you now*, his eyes told her. With one gesture, he could turn this crowd upon her. They would eat her heart out.

He swung back to face the people. 'Do the vermin that attacked me think to cripple the Revolution?' The spectators held their breath. 'See,' he roared, 'I can still fight against tyranny!' It hurt his damaged palm but he rasped out the rapier that hung on his belt and thrust it heavenwards. Light danced upon the blade – well, what light there was. The congregation cheered and beyond the open doors the curious crowd rushed forward shouting.

Ah, this was almost worth being shot at. 'Patriots, brothers and sisters of the Revolution, we have fought to free France from its servile yoke. We are no more beasts of burden to those men who let our children starve, men who judged us, men who did not question us because they did not want to hear our answers. But those carrion are still out there, waiting for us to die beneath the invaders' boots. They are still out there. Their agent provocateurs are in our great cities, turning our people against Paris, against you, against the Convention – the Convention that was democratically elected. Only in unity can we preserve our liberty! Only in unity can we defeat the enemy!' Raoul tossed his sword to his other hand and drove his wounded fist up through the air. The crowd roared.

Fleur panicked. The man was inciting another massacre. He was cranking up the hatred, almost whetting their blades for them.

'Out there –' he began.

She had to stop this before the streets ran with blood.

'Citizens,' she shouted, springing up onto the coffin in front of him. 'Rejoice!'

De Villaret, thank God, was too astonished to push her down but the people's indignation reached her like a breath so foul it nearly toppled her. With a deep gasp, she flung her hands towards the great dome. 'People of Paris, we have already triumphed over death. The citizen lives. Kiss your children, embrace your wives! Let this be a day of celebration. Of love! *Vive la France!*' She swivelled round with difficulty and, stooping, carried his bandaged hand to her lips in an act of homage.

'Love!' heckled someone who sounded like Quettehou. 'We need BREAD.'

'*Get down!*' De Villaret's smile was angelic; his words a fierce hiss of fury.

'*No!*' she exclaimed, rising and swirling round to kiss her hands to the congregation. 'HAPPINESS! HOPE!' And Paris roared back. Beaming, Fleur drew breath and launched into one of the songs beloved by the *sans-culottes*: ' "Ah! ça ira, ça ira, ça!" ' Ooof!

De Villaret sprang down, hauling her with him. Behind the coffin, the voices soared and the feet of the Revolution stamped the chorus of 'Ça ira'.

> '*Ah! Just you wait! Just you wait! Just you wait!*
> *The people are shouting this again and again.*
> *Just you wait! Just you wait! Just you wait!*
> *Despite your treachery, we'll prevail.*'

'The patriot here,' de Villaret kept his good arm like an iron band about her waist as the deputies closed about them, 'can never leave the stage. Thank you, *ma mie*.' The venom in his voice would have poisoned a village.

'I can't breathe,' she hissed, trying to free herself without anyone noticing.

'Good,' his voice replied in her ear. 'So long as you can't talk.' His boot nudged the flag-draped bier. Who in hell was standing in for him?

'This is in very bad taste in my opinion.' The muse of the Girondins, Mme Manon Roland, pushed through, snatching her brown skirts aside from brushing Fleur's black bombazine. Both her younger admirer, Buzot, and her ageing husband followed in the wake of her bustle. 'Did *you* orchestrate this travesty?' she snapped, brandishing her parasol menacingly at David's kneecaps.

The master of ceremonies inclined his head. 'My dear Manon, we could have done this for Buzot if you needed a second coming, but let's find out, shall we?' He started to peel back the flag petticoating the bier and then laughed at the woman's delicate shudder. 'No? I thought not.' Already the wheels of David's artistic mind were in full revolution. He stepped forward to clasp Raoul's shoulder but he was looking speculatively at Fleur. 'A day of love. Very good! Lead the girl out like a bride.'

'*Comment?*' Raoul was fit to strangle her. 'She's a widow,' he protested.

'We've just done the marri– no, I-I can't.' Fleur was in agreement with de Villaret for once, but David took no notice.

'Widowed France! The symbolism. Think of the symbolism. Move, Raoul! Now! Before they reach the last line! Repeat the final chorus,' he ordered the choirmaster. 'The rest of you follow in pairs. Stop sulking, Manon! Quickly! And you,' he snapped his fingers at one of the military officers, 'set a guard around the coffin!' Swiftly rearranging the cloak that proclaimed him a deputy, the great man turned on his heel. 'Behind me, now! *Now!*' And the great master of French art started down the nave with the solemnity of an archbishop.

Suppressing a curse, Raoul rearranged himself so that his hale hand might secure Fleur's. 'Till death us do part,' he muttered malevolently.

'Amen to that,' Fleur retorted, her chin raised haughtily.

'We'll conquer the enemies that still remain,
Sing alleluia as our refrain.
Oh, just you wait, just you wait, just you wait.

Those who are down, we'll elevate
Those who are high, we'll bring 'em down.
Ah, just you wait, just you wait, just you wait!
This true catechism we'll impart
And like fanatics, spread the word
To obey this with all your heart
Until it's done by all of France
Oh, just you wait, just you wait, just you wait
Despite your treachery, we'll advance.'

Two by two, like animals on Noah's ark, the deputies fell in behind as though they had been rehearsing all week. The congregation beamed on approvingly. Only Quettehou's face, dark against a flanking pillar, was a mask of fury. The people cramming the doorway parted to let them through and closed in behind the procession.

Fleur's euphoria was beginning to vaporise, leaving a residue of horror at the price she might pay for her audacity. She seesawed between reckless elation and wild despair; one instant exhilarated that de Villaret was alive, the next afraid because he was leading her out towards the mob. Was this how the Queen had felt, made to parade before the pikes and smile and smile?

They waited a few paces back while David tested the crowd. The rain had come.

'And where would you like to spend the night, you harpy?' de Villaret growled through his teeth while he beamed at the rabble. What answer did he expect? La Force?

'Not in your bed, you bastard.' She tried to tug her fingers free. If only she could tunnel into the living mass, away from him, away so she could rally her courage. 'Your master's whistling us. You'll earn some brisket if you behave.'

The double doors framed them as they posed like royalty – constitutional newlyweds – while David wound up his speech to the crowd. When he finally stepped aside with a flourish, Fleur blew kisses from her fingers to the shouts of 'Bravo!' and simpered at de Villaret like a besotted bride.

'When I have finished with you, chérie,' her companion threatened softly, pulling her close as if to kiss her cheek, 'you will be praying for the little window.'

'You think *I* planned your death?' she protested as he held up her hand to the crowd like a victorious wrestler.

'Since you tried to shoot me the morning I left Paris, yes!' He kissed her hand, still keeping firm hold of it. Then, with an unkind laugh, he drew her breast to breast. His mouth came down on hers and the crowd roared. Fleur emerged knowing she was dealing with one very furious man.

'It will only take a word from me,' he whispered, smiling into her eyes. 'They will tear you apart.'

'Try it,' she ground out, her smile gracious. 'Two can play this game.' And kissed him back. 'What's it to be, Raouly darling? Your head or mine?'

He laughed at the challenge but as he drew breath to enlighten her, an enterprising student grabbed his ankles and he collapsed backwards with a yell onto a chair of arms and was hoisted shoulder high. Before Fleur could resist, she too found herself jolted, her buttocks bounced between two unequal shoulders. It was electrifying, uncomfortable and horrific. At least her boots, tightly laced, stayed on her feet. Her shoes would have gone long ago. She slapped at a hand groping to souvenir a garter.

'*Wait!*' she cried.

The edge of fear in her voice reached Raoul. He looked back over his shoulder and for an instant let an exultant, cruel smile curl his mouth, but then he relented and bade the fellows carrying him slow down while those carrying the actress caught up. 'Don't put your hands up her petticoats, *mes amis,*' he warned, his voice dark. 'She's mine, all mine.'

One young woman dragged free the laurel wreath that necklaced a nearby banner, and Raoul's bearers lowered him down so the chit might crown him. Fleur Bosanquet flicked him a vindictive look as though he was the Emperor Caligula. Pointedly, he directed her attention back at the cluster of deputies watching them and saw her shudder. But he had his own misgivings about his audience. What price envy?

461

'*Nom d'un chien!*' That was from his jiggled consort. Unused to military academies and student blanketings, she shrieked as the young men carrying them zigzagged and whooped, clashing their burdens together. Her merriment was cosmetic. Raoul's palm met hers in a slap of triumph but he held her hand now, keeping them parallel.

They were borne down the street in ancient Roman fashion, and might have ended up ducked for entertainment in Paris's version of the Tiber had a military detachment not put an end to it, and bade the students carry them soberly back within an escort of pikes to the Panthéon and the waiting deputies. Fleur Bosanquet looked like a settling top about to keel as they stood her down. Not giddy from the euphoria at all, her grin was wobbly, her eyes wide as she looked up at Raoul. Sometimes he forgot she was only nineteen. He read the subtle relief that mirrored his own. She had been afraid. He had won this round. But the game wasn't over.

The cobbles seemed to shift like tide-washed shingle as he landed feet down. A congratulatory hand, Danton's, clapped his shoulder. Raoul repossessed his pretty royalist's hand. On the other side of Fleur, Hérault staked a sullen claim. They were jostled good-naturedly back up to the coffin, which waited like some monstrous Pandora's box, surrounded, it seemed, by half the Convention.

'So who is it in the bloody coffin?' Danton boomed, yanking the symbolic bloodstained sash off the pike and tossing it at Raoul. 'Is this yours?'

Trying to ignore the dark red blotches marring

the broad stripes of colour, Raoul ran the fabric through his fingers and recognised the familiar snagged thread at one end. Who had stopped a bullet meant for him? Christ! One of the royalists must have . . .

'Well, man?' Marat, the hack, the great sorter through the city's detritus, was waiting.

The glorious taste of power had ebbed and exhaustion was seeping in to replace it. In a controlled voice that seemed very distant, an automaton called Raoul de Villaret responded. 'I am sure this *is* mine,' he said, trying to exert common sense over the emotions rattling to be freed. He would have sold the Hall of Mirrors at Versailles for some solitude to piece the facts together. 'Where was I – I mean, he – killed?'

It was Danton who had read the report. 'Four of them dined at the England Hotel in Lisieux, including this fellow pretending to be you, so it's likely the attack took place next day. Tinkers discovered your coach abandoned in woodland east of Caen the day after that. The man in your uniform was already dead and there were no papers on the body to identify him. The local authorities assumed it had to be you.'

Raoul clawed his good hand through his hair. 'We were attacked west of Mantes-la-Jolie, nowhere near Caen. My papers must have got them through all the pass controls.'

'How very fascinating,' cut in Robespierre, his lawyer's mind sorting the possibilities. 'The first attack might be construed as calculated, but two attacks on the same coach . . . Are we or are we not dealing with mere coincidence?'

'Coincidence!' The scoff came from a Commune official lurking at Marat's shoulder. The printer, Quettehou. 'I can give you another coincidence, messieurs. My uncle was *also* fatally attacked as he travelled to Caen and *she* was behind it!' He jabbed a finger towards Fleur.

Raoul sensed rather than saw the girl recoil. If she had incited her brother to take his life, let them have her; if she hadn't, he prayed the actress in her would carry her through. The hubbub ceased but she didn't speak. And nothing was making sense. *Diable!* The ghosts of his fingers throbbed.

'Citizen Quettehou,' the actress answered with a sigh as though the fellow was a young boy who needed sistering. 'Your open hatred of me is no secret. It is three months since my husband died yet you've brought no charges against me nor challenged his will, so I can only conclude you have no evidence for these unkind, jealous accusations. Why don't you open the coffin and see if Citizen de Villaret recognises the corpse as the man who shot him?' Oh my God, had she any idea what she was asking?

'In *there*,' she brazenly patted the coffin lid, her sea eyes mesmerising the men, 'is the enemy to the Republic who tried to murder the deputy, *not here*!' Her hand splayed her breastbone just above her cleavage. Oh very clever! Every pair of male eyes enjoyed the licence she afforded them. 'Give *me* a knife or chisel . . .' she purred. 'Or are you afraid of what you might find?' The shrug, the challenge to their manhood was like holding out a fresh bone to a hungry street cur. Didn't Fleur know the chance of identifying a two-week-old corpse was like throwing a cow over the moon?

'Well, we've definitely fucked up,' complained Danton, indicting everybody in his stare. 'Being summer, I suppose no one wanted to identify the body.' He grabbed the pikestaff from its pot of earth in front of the coffin, ready to wrench off the blade. 'Let's have a look, shall we?'

The subtle touch on Raoul's arm was from Fleur, her *audacité* gone. The fifteen-year-old child was back waiting for him to rescue her. She flashed him a swift glance sideways. Damn resourceful little chameleon! She didn't deserve a scrap of help.

'Got your perfumed handkerchief ready, Boissy?' Danton chortled, relishing the horror in all their faces. His enjoyment was hard to fathom. There was a story that he had been away from home when Mme Danton died in childbirth and returned so wild with grief that he had had her coffin exhumed so that he might take her once more in his arms. Oh, *bon Dieu*! Now Raoul could believe it.

'Wait, Danton!' Raoul snapped and swung round on the tiresome printer. '*Do* you have the evidence to prove your accusations, Quettehou?'

'Not yet, de Villaret. But I know it. *Here!*' In a mocking echo of Fleur's gesture, the printer thumped his chest between the scarlet lapels. 'Perhaps she intended your death also, Deputy.

After all you've been investigating her.' The fox eyes sought to immobilise him as though he was some barnyard cockerel uselessly guarding a flighty hen, but Raoul had the measure of his audience.

'Since I was present at the fall of the Bastille, Quettehou, no, I rather doubt it.'

For an instant there was puzzlement and then they understood. Ribald laughter pilloried Quettehou's accusation as preposterous. Even Marat grinned impishly; but the printer, excluded by his ignorance, turned an unpleasant, cabbagy red.

'I should remember what happened to the Bastille's governor, if I were you, Deputy,' he ground out, and with a condescending, valedictory nod that went some way in restoring his self-esteem, he strode away, his footsteps echoing ominously.

Marat slapped at a fly. '*Merde!* Hope that's not out of the coffin! So, de Villaret, did he have a name, the *cul* who took your papers.'

'No, we shook hands, exchanged cards, he promised to meet for a beer in Lisieux and then he shot me.' The sarcasm was reckless but the wound in his thigh was aching. He leaned back against the coffin. 'Sorry, Marat, there were four of them, it was dark, they were masked. They shot the other passengers and then me. And it's no good opening this thing.' The flat of his palm scuffed across the flag. 'Even God wouldn't recognise him now.' With that, he thrust himself back on his feet. 'Now I'll bid you all adieu – attending one's own funeral plays hell with the nerves.'

He was almost out the door when Danton

caught up with him. 'There was actually something in the fellow's pocket which the tinkers missed. The Caen coroner sent it on to us.' He dove a hand into his coat pocket. 'Take it, you'll be wanting to investigate further.'

It was Fleur's ring.

18

Non, rien ne peut se comparer	No, nothing compares to
A la sombe Conciergerie,	The sombre Conciergerie,
Le soleil craint de pénétrer	The sun tries to creep between
La grille de barreaux garnie,	Between the solid bars of the grille,
Mais demain, l'on me jugera,	But tomorrow they will judge me,
On fixera ma destinée,	They will decide my destiny,
Et le tribunal m'ouvrira	The tribunal will show me the door
La porte . . . ou croisée.	Or — send me to the scaffold.

SONG OF THE FRENCH REVOLUTION

It was some minutes before Raoul could speak to anyone. He sank down on the steps outside, refusing the offer of Armand's company, and buried his head in his hands.

'Here, Deputy.' A whiskered sergeant crouched down and urged a flask at him. 'Your young woman's round the corner,' the older man chuckled. 'Looks like she's suffering from *nausées matinales* like my daughter. Due to you, eh, you young dog?'

So Fleur Bosanquet's stomach had turned revolutionary. About the only bit of her that had. Revived by the liquor, Raoul clambered to his feet. Discovering her drooped on the step like a wounded singing bird reduced to a sad huddle of feathers, it was hard to think evil of her, to blame her for the pain and death of the last two weeks. The chef was hovering over her like a massive guardian angel and the grisette with the lank blonde curls sat alongside wringing freckled hands. Raoul did not ask them to leave; they read their orders in his face.

Ill-prepared, Raoul stood for a moment, as if trying to find some kind of equilibrium, before he stepped down and, with his good hand, turned Fleur's tear-splashed face to his. 'Tell me, did you commission this?' He thrust out his damaged hand.

'No.' The damp lashes did not close against him. 'Waste of a good hand,' she added. 'I don't hold with revenge either.' His expression was reflected back with no less steel, but the girl made use of weaponry that was hard to resist. 'Is it the tumbril for me, Raoul?'

Oh, he could so easily crush her royalist frailty beneath his republican heel. But of all her despicable family, she should be salted and preserved.

'Suppose –' He set a hand beneath her elbow and drew her to her feet. 'Suppose we were to settle these matters somewhere less public?'

Her humour rose defensively. 'At fourteen paces? Your rapier against my honour?'

'*Eh bien.*' Raoul knuckled the defiant teardrops from her cheeks. 'I was thinking closer than that, but the choice of weapons will suffice.'

Exhausted and defeated, she was a signed treaty waiting to be ratified, or was she? Although Raoul permitted himself to look triumphantly down into her clouded eyes, aware of the childlike tendrils of hair curling against her cheeks and lips that trembled and parted for him, he recognised his own susceptibility. Murder might masquerade behind her loveliness. He had always known that.

With the borrowed coat hooked over his shoulder, he steered her towards the Rue Saint-Jacques. He did not speak. If Fleur Bosanquet had cold-bloodedly arranged his death, he would arrange hers.

'I'm not going in there!' Fleur dug her heels in as she realised he was propelling her towards the Palais de Justice and, worse, the ominous Conciergerie prison. She squinted sideways at the new stone mansions flanking the square, estimating her chance of escape, but not one of the fine front doors was open. Could she evade him among the sacks and bales in Notre Dame? Oh, fine chance! Ahead to her right lay the sprawling, ancient Hôtel Dieu, but de Villaret would know the tricks of the colonnades and passageways better than she, and so would the soldiers he could whistle up in an instant. Damn him!

'Please,' she whimpered, hating herself for this sudden deficit of courage, but the hand on her arm only tightened firmer.

'Let us get this done with, shall we?'

Even in workman's clothes de Villaret exuded a sense of a prowling power that did not require a uniform, but it took a moment for the guards at the barrier to recognise his face, wilder and leaner after his ordeal. 'Lord save us, Deputy! Gambled away your breeches?'

'Nah, *la belle* 'ere stole 'em off him, *hein?*'

Fleur knew the way to where he would interrogate her; she dreaded the terror emanating from those walls, the raw emotion spattered like blood upon the stairs.

'*Bonjour,* Quentin,' her captor said cheerfully, as they encountered a man in a puce redingcote advancing on them down the passageway to the squeaky wince of shoe leather. The autocratic face was one any actor would have envied: dramatic eyebrows, a beaked nose and ebony hair sleeking back from a widow's peak. 'More work for me, eh, Raoul?' the other man quipped as he passed.

The breath of de Villaret laughter's caressed Fleur's cheek. 'Ah, this one's special.'

'*Eh bien, moment!*' Braking halfway along the

upper corridor, the other man spun about. 'You're alive, Raoul.'

'Very much so. I'll tell you all about it later.' He hastened Fleur on, adding, 'Fouquier-Tinville, *accusateur public*. Sorry, I didn't introduce you.' *Sorry!* Oh yes, and there was no such thing as a guillotine. De Villaret would probably hand her over to *cher Quentin* personally when he had finished wringing her like a dishcloth. No doubt they regularly pre-arranged prison sentences over the *vin ordinaire*.

'Any more acquaintances?' she muttered, trying to pull free. 'Sanson the executioner? Marie Antoinette?'

His office was not secured. He arranged Fleur in front of his desk and, striding round to the drawer, removed a key and locked the door. 'We don't want to be disturbed.' The missing weeks had emeried the pity from his face. 'Sit down! There!' He indicated the superior wooden-armed seat behind his desk.

'*Th-there?*'

'Yes.' For himself, he dragged a simple chair with a wicker seat out from the corner, and stood poised to straddle it in reverse, then changed his mind and seated himself in conventional manner. 'Now, go on, interrogate me!'

'P-pardon?'

'*Ma mie*, there will be no peace between us until you stop behaving as though I am a blend of Torquemada and Caligula. Go on, interrogate me!'

'Y-you made me believe . . .' The inkwell was not only within reach but full.

He read her intention and said swiftly, 'Yes, I made you believe that you were under arrest, but you were wrong, weren't you? Just like you are wrong in everything else. Now, leave the inkwell alone and proceed! I'm not feeling patient.'

Damnable trickster! Greasepaint experience allowed Fleur to ease her features into the sympathetic smile she kept for little furry animals and infants. 'You are sure? Your poor hand . . . Don't you feel −?'

His furious look quelled her. 'Part of me feels like pushing up your petticoats and pleasuring you across my desk but I'm sure you'd prefer somewhere softer and with a lover who's not on trial. Stop looking at me like that.'

'You still want me?' The words were softly uttered.

'I have been raddled with lust for you ever since we met in Caen and even more so since that night at your house. I'm burning with lust for you, you infuriating harpy. Now clear your mind and let us get this over with.'

Clear her mind when those golden eyes of his were staring at her with such an intense mixture of exasperation, fondness and desire? He was right; this poison between them needed to be exhumed and destroyed. But he was clever; she was already weakened by the magnetism that charged the air between them, seduced by the thought of his hands sliding upwards beneath her skirts and the wickedness of him taking her between the quill-pens and the books of law.

'Concentrate, citizeness! I'm a regicide and you're a royalist. Why did you want to kill me, citizeness, or is it an ongoing ambition? What crimes have I perpetrated?'

The actress in her rose to the cue. She imagined herself in the public prosecutor's creaking shoes: 'Evidence has been laid against you, Citizen de Villaret. It is alleged that on the day of –'

'*Diable*, Fleur, you don't have to do a formal impersonation of Fouquier-Tinville. Cut to the bone.'

'A witness saw you last September covered in blood at the scene of my father's murder in the Rue . . . Well, never mind, outside L'Abbaye Prison. Prove your innocence, citizen!' The flourish made little impression. 'What are you doing?' she protested. 'You're not supposed to stand up and move around.'

'I'm getting out a map,' he replied with irritating maleness, and selecting one from several propped-up rolls, untied the faded tape and anchored it on the desk facing her. It was dated 1787.

'So, citizen,' she demanded. 'What's this to the point?'

He merely shrugged and scraped his chair up closer.

'Your father's death took place on the second of September last year,' he began as though he was the inquisitor; catching himself out he raised an exasperated eyebrow at her. '*You* are supposed to ask *me* my movements on that day.' But before Fleur could comply, he launched into his defence. 'My poor mother had been desperately trying to find me all morning and it was noon when I returned to my office and found her waiting.'

'Where had you been?'

'Well, it was the day we had to elect the Paris deputies to the Convention and I was one of the candidates, so I had been down to the electoral assembly at the Jacobin Club to vote, and afterwards I attended a meeting at David's house and –'

'But what has all this got to do with your mother?' She received a glare.

'Because, *citoyenne accusateur*, my mother wished to inform me that my father had been arrested that morning on suspicion of sheltering an anti-republican priest.'

'Had he?'

'Hidden a priest? Yes, it probably was true although my mother had no knowledge of it. My father never confided such matters to her. Anyway, she was quite rightly very distressed. She had no idea where he had been taken and she wanted me to find out and pull all the strings I could to get him released. Well, I told her there was nothing I could do until my father came up for trial, except to ensure he was comfortable. The trouble was I could well believe that he had been up to his neck in counter-revolutionary activities. He was an extremely religious man and the Republic's harsh dealings with the Church would have easily turned him into an active enemy.

'I never found out who authorised his arrest but I suspect it was because he was a retired military officer and there were fears he might be one of those likely to take command if there was an insurrection. Anyway, at least I was able to promise Maman I would find out where he was being held. She wanted me to make my peace with him. I told her it was impossible – we hadn't set eyes on each other for years – but in the end I agreed for her sake. In return I insisted she must not return to her lodgings but stay with friends where the authorities could not find her.

'I escorted her to their house. The mood in the streets was ugly and dangerous. The rumour that Verdun had fallen had reached the city the day before and there were placards everywhere with inflammatory slogans.'

'Marat, I suppose!' Fleur interrupted in disgust.

'Marat was behind most of it. People were frightened. We thought that the Austrians and Prussians were advancing on Paris and would put us all to the sword. Lots of men enlisted. Troops were sent to man all the *barrières*. Everyone was whetting their pikes and daggers, wondering how soon the attack would be, and there were so many rumours that we didn't know what to believe.

'Marat had his own agenda. He'd been stirring up the *bas peuple* against the imprisoned clergy for days. He had Paris believing that we had a potential enemy hidden in our midst and that if the prisoners were set free they would turn on us. There was much talk of hidden arsenals of cannon and bayonets. Suspicion was rife. The prisons were crammed and more suspects like my father were being brought in by the hour.

'The hotheads in the sections were like a powder keg with a lit fuse, just burning for the opportunity to make trouble. Once things really started happening, it was anarchy. *Grands Dieux*, the mob you experienced when you first arrived in Paris, Fleur, was nothing in comparison. The city was a hysterical creature out of control. That's why I wanted Maman safely off the streets.'

'But up until then you are saying there had been no –'

'Incidents?' he interrupted dryly, his expression tainted with self-mockery. 'Madame will permit me to rise?'

Fleur nodded with a frown, steeling herself. Raoul leaned an elbow on top of the cupboard where he kept his files and stroked a finger down the grain of the door.

'The first trouble – another nice word – began the day before my father was arrested. The Jacobin Club was buzzing with the news when we met next morning but we all thought it was a single incident. What happened was that a mob of section malcontents saw a party of priests being escorted to L'Abbaye Prison and followed them there and butchered them. Do you know where that is?' he asked, coming across to scowl at the map.

She was trying not to imagine the horror.

'It's here, see, in the Quatres Nations section.' He pointed to the church of Saint-Germain-des-Prés. *Ciel*, it was just a few streets north of the Palais de Luxembourg gardens where she had walked with

M. Beugneux. The tiny block of colour looked so innocent.

'But when that was reported, Raoul, didn't anyone try to prevent the situation getting further out of hand?'

'The Inspector of Prisons, my senior at the time, went to see Danton, who was Minister of Justice, but Danton didn't want to know. No, Fleur, don't give me that what-do-you-expect expression. Danton's always steered excessively close to the wind,' he patted his pocket, 'and it would be simplistic to say he believed that Paris was ill and blood needed to be let to calm it down – he wouldn't have been alone in that – but who knows, maybe he was just bloody scared.'

'And you can respect a man who stood by while innocent people were slaughtered?' Fleur stared sternly up at him.

'All Paris stood by.' He paced to the door before he turned to challenge her. 'You know as well as I that there have been countless circumstances in history when princes and generals, even supposedly civilised ones, have stood by and let innocent people be slaughtered.'

'I reckon he should be brought to trial for it. And Marat. That's really what the Girondins have been trying to get him for, isn't it?'

'And they've failed. How would you prove it, *madame accusateur*? Look, people accepted there was a royalist conspiracy.' *You were not here*, his fierce expression told her.

'So what did you do?'

'My fears for my father were mounting. I made a list of the five most likely prisons he could have been taken to and I went to each of them, but it was hard to get information, to even get beyond the turnkey at two of them, but I finally bribed my way in. I left L'Abbaye to last, not thinking that the militants would return but, oh Christ, they had.

'The light was fading as I crossed the Pont Neuf. I stopped a soldier coming from that direction and asked him for news. He told me he'd heard the mob had been to L'Abbaye a second time. It was happening here.' Raoul tapped the map at the junction of streets south of the church's chancel wall. 'The old place for hangings and whippings. By the time I reached Saint-Germain, it was worse than a medieval painting of hell. Have you ever heard of the Dutch artist Hieronymus Bosch? No? Well, it was utter carnage, beyond imagination, but . . . but it was the orderliness of it, the silent efficiency that horrified me. They were hauling out the condemned prisoners through the turnkey's door, one by one, like beasts to be butchered for market. Any garments and shoes were removed from the prisoners and tossed onto a pile, and then the prisoner was made to run between two rows of sabres. As he fell, the onlookers cheered, "*Vive la nation!*" It was not trial and execution but a process devoid of any humanity, or if this was a new guise of human, Fleur, then it made humanity despicable.'

He returned to lean upon the cupboard rubbing his injured hand as the images rose in his mind. 'I recognised the soldier in charge, a former hairdresser, would you believe, but I did not want to have any dealing with him. Instead I walked straight into the room the committee of inspection were using as a tribunal. No one bothered me so I hung around for an opportunity to question the man presiding. Some of the prisoners waiting to be examined had been brought up into an adjoining room, and I peered through the bars of the grille in the door hoping my father might still be alive, but most of them were priests. I am not sure what I would have done if he had been among them. You see, at that point I didn't know whether I had been elected a deputy and I didn't have any letter of authority. They did actually acquit someone while I was there and the guards escorted him out and we could hear everyone outside whooping and shouting, "*Vive la nation! Vive le patriot!*"'

'Did you have to wait long?'

'It seemed like forever, and all the while I was staring at the pile of pocketbooks, valuables and handkerchiefs piled up on the long table and wondering if Papa's were already there. It was smoky and there were lots of empty bottles and dirty glasses.' He drew breath to add something and then changed his mind. '"Just don't defend yourself from any of the blows, curé," I heard a guardsman say to one elderly man. "It's quicker if you keep your arms down." Oh *bon Dieu*.' He suddenly realised he was offloading the ugly story onto her as though she were a priest.

'Go on,' she encouraged, understanding his need.

'The president of the section told me my father had already been judged and dealt with. Who wanted to know? he asked. I felt like St Peter denying Christ, Fleur, but I was scared for my own life by then. I retorted sternly that I was standing as a deputy and that I was a loyal patriot, unlike some members of my family. God knows, I wished the ground would swallow me up but I was fortunate, for at that instant the local commissaire arrived with a small force of soldiers demanding to know what was going on. My God, he was a brave man or else out to clear his own name from any later repercussions; either way, he had a lot of courage to intervene. He ordered them to halt the executions and demanded to see their letters of commission. I seized the opportunity to return to the street and search for my father's body. He deserved an honourable burial not to be thrown in some mass –' He broke off, and drew his ungloved hand across his mouth, swallowing hard before he continued.

'Many of the corpses had already been carted away but there were still dozens of people lying there. I was stunned with shock. I hardly knew where to start but I had to act quickly in case it all started again, and then I heard a man calling me. I knew the voice and I stopped and turned. In that brief respite when they had all been ordered inside to speak with the commissaire, the poor wretch had managed to drag himself to a doorway – no distance really, just a few paces, but sufficient to go unnoticed. He called out to me again, begging my mercy as a gentleman, pleading with me to hasten his death. It was hard to see his face but I didn't need to.'

'It was your father.'

'No, it was yours.' He held her gaze without flinching. 'I have to tell you this to exonerate myself.'

She swallowed, dreading to hear. 'Then you must go on.'

'I borrowed a lantern from one of the carters. Your father was wounded beyond saving, bleeding profusely and in terrible pain. I hardly recognised him without his wig and finery. I–I wanted to run away, Fleur, not just because it was him, but I was so disgusted with mankind that I didn't want to know or think, or in any way be part of this horror, but your father pleaded with me again.'

'What did you do?'

'I knelt beside him. There was no chance of getting him to safety. There were plenty of onlookers and I'd have been cut down. As it was, one woman yelled out: '"What are you pilfering, fellow? Did we miss something?"

'I pressed my thumbs onto his windpipe and took his life. I suppose that is why your brother wanted my death. *An eye for an eye, a tooth for a tooth.* I looked upwards to the sky cursing God and, believe it, there were even people watching me from the upstairs windows. Perhaps your witness was one of those. God knows, there were plenty of people standing around. And then . . .' he faltered, 'and someone behind me said in execrable

French, "Do you want a drink, mon sir?" And I swear there were two Englishmen there, drunk as lords. One of the carters said they had been swigging wine with the executioners and inciting them to kill faster. The English Prime Minister has deep pockets, don't you know. Anything to make us butchers.'

'Are you suggesting the English agents might have provoked the massacre?'

'No,' he answered wearily after a deep silence. 'No, it was still our patriots who signed the warrants and held the sabres. By Christ, Fleur, the locals were selling wine and lemonade as though it was a fete.'

'And your Papa?' It was a whisper, not enough. She could count a score of heartbeats before he answered. Ah, *bon Dieu*, at least he answered.

'In some mass grave beyond the Porte Saint-Jacques. I'm afraid I did not seek further. It was night and I was world-weary and,' he sighed, 'you may not believe me, Fleur, but somehow helping your father was almost as if I had held my own papa and made my peace. Or so I fool myself.' His chill expression at that moment might have taught lessons to the north wind. 'So it was not quite what you thought, was it?'

Her own guilt rose up like a mirror. Fleur could not answer, not yet. The true horror of her father's death drove into her like a savage arrowhead.

'No, it is not quite what I thought. I played the ostrich while you played the hero.'

'*Hero!*' His self-contempt lashed them both. The

room was silent. Beyond the walls a blackbird fluted; out in the yard heavy boots stamped to attention on the cobbles.

'You are forgetting your lines, madame royalist,' Raoul observed cuttingly, casting her a hostile look. 'What else shall you accuse me of? Ah yes, murdering your half-sister, the Vicomtesse de Nogent, familiar of queens and sycophants.' He came across to lour down at Fleur, leaning his palms upon the printed outskirts of Paris. 'As far as I'm aware, she was held at La Force with the Princesse de Lamballe, and all the world knows their fate. I was in the vicinity, yes, but it was the men's prison I visited looking for my father.'

Fleur stared down miserably at the streets meshing the Chat Rouge. Somewhere there Marguerite had died and nothing was left, no gravestone to lay the flowers on. His breath stirred the curls along her forehead as he ground out: 'Still, never mind, blame me for that as well. I'm omnipresent like God, squeezing life out of the rich and idle. Let me see, who else? Your stepsister, Henriette, who broke her neck when her horse threw her. I was in London at the time but don't let that consideration bother you. Ah, damn, but then you might suspect me of starving Cécile to death in her Soho garret. Do you suppose I gave her the gleet as well or was it Henri de Craon? Marat's written an excellent treatise on gleet and the abuse of mercury if you want to know more but I'm sure Henri de Craon's the expert.'

Fleur flinched, and he mistook her surprise for condemnation.

'Well, you have to blame someone accessible, don't you, Fleur.' His gloved hand clenched. 'I do. In the quiet of the night I forever cross the cobbles outside La Force looking for my father among the dead.' Pulling off his glove, he stared at his hands, inwardly wincing at the partly healed stumps of the two missing fingers. He slowly tilted them palms uppermost as if the life lines were blotched with stains of blood. 'The others, Hérault, Gensonné, they didn't see what happened, didn't see –' His voice grew more ragged with every breath, the brown eyes glinted, fierce as an eagle's. 'What happened to your father and mine is a stain on the honour of France. The unborn will think of this generation with shame. They won't understand how hard we are struggling to get it right. But, Christ Almighty, how can we manage it? In four little years, after a millennium of servitude? It's not just loaves and fishes the multitude want, but finery and carriages. And if we cannot deliver them, September will happen again.'

His hand rose to mask his eyes as if the gesture would shut off the memory. 'My mother blames me for my father's death. She thinks I should have warned him to leave Paris. There are thousands like her and you who abhor the Republic, but we did not want it to come to this, we didn't.'

Compassion was both finite and infinite; it was possible also he might loathe any tint of pity in her voice. She fought the urge to go to him. It was expected and, on her part, offered freely but it was not the answer, not yet.

He sat frozen before her, a breathing sculpture, one beautiful hand steady as though carved from the same wood his fingers touched. She rose and stood with pilgrim patience until Raoul finally spoke.

'Will you join me in hell?' His words ruffled through the peace like golden, wind-blown leaves.

Her heart told her what to say. 'It takes two hands to make peace, two voices, two hearts. It's your turn, citizen. I am guilty until you prove me innocent.' Holding her wrists crossed against her thighs as though some invisible rope bound them, she waited for his questions.

Raoul raised his head slowly as though his mind was being drawn back to the present by her request. 'You want to do this?'

She met his look evenly. 'Isn't it necessary?'

'To assuage my self-loathing.'

'Your guilt and mine. For all your laws, we carry it. From the font and in our natures.'

'Then speak softly, *mon coeur*. The walls listen in this place.' He stood up and his proud stance took her back to Caen. The authority he could exude at will streamed out like swirling energy to engulf Fleur. Power and desire both thrilled and frightened her.

'Begin, sir,' she whispered, moving round to take the other chair.

'When did your brother return to Paris, citizeness?'

It was necessary to swiftly break the lock of gaze. He knew about Philippe! Already she was retreating, fleeing in her mind.

'Answer, Fleur!'

'V-very recently.' Swallowing, she continued. 'My aunt and I quarrelled over my reopening the Chat Rouge. She left to seek my uncle in Coblenz. Philippe was there and she told him about my new circumstances. She felt I was keeping company with the wrong people.' You, her eyes told him. 'Philippe, since he is now the head of my family, felt some responsibility for me and decided to come back to France.' She didn't blame her interrogator for looking sceptical. 'I daresay he had other reasons too. It was actually him who was following me that night you found me at the Palais-Royal. *Voilà*, you see, it wasn't my imagination. Anyway I saw him several times after that. He – he was trying to arrange a marriage for me.'

'God's sake, with whom?' Raoul's indignant reaction pleased her.

Her face dipped in newfound shame. 'Henri de Craon.'

'Christ!' Raoul's curse prickled her flesh.

'Philippe thinks upon him as a friend,' she babbled defensively. 'You really believe that he and Cécile . . .' She gave him a sharp look. 'Oh, *bon Dieu*! Is gleet the same as soldier's pox? Is that what killed her?'

He shook his head. 'No, but it would have set its mark on her child. *Diable!* You've gone as pale as . . . Don't tell me the bastard's back in Paris? Is he? Has he laid hands on you? No? Thank Christ for that! That cur leaves more than his calling card.'

Fleur forced her fists to unclench as Raoul subsided in his chair behind his desk.

'So your brother made himself known to you.'

'Yes, he wanted me to . . . to find out information.'

'From me?' The harsh words were like a dagger slicing through the soft remembrances of hands and lips.

'Yes, Raoul, from you, but I refused.'

'No, you didn't.'

Oh, grands Dieux! The accusation writhed between them like a lit fuse.

'It is doing something for the right reasons that measures us as human beings.' Like a marksman, she held her gaze steady and continued, her voice even: 'It would be a way out to think otherwise, is that what you want?'

The flicking bitterness stilled; the lonely fingers flexed. 'No,' he answered with a long, sad breath that disturbed the papers lying beside the map. His dark lashes hid his soul from her.

Fleur ran her fingers unseeing along the southern boundary of the city. 'The night you held me in your arms, Raoul, was for us, not a dead king I don't respect. Raoul! *Raoul?*' She looked down in astonishment, observing that his shoulders had begun to shake, and then she realised it was not distress that capriciously moved him.

'*Diable!*' exclaimed her mercurial antagonist lifting his face, laughter leaf-veining the corners of his eyes. 'I should hate to think you sacrificed your virginity for the Bourbons.'

Outraged virtue on a pedestal! Fleur's indignation tumbled earthwards with a thud and she thrust a knuckle to staunch her own laughter and then succumbed.

'I didn't interrupt *your* rhetoric,' she protested as her giggles subsided, marvelling that the delicate alliance with this man was stronger than she'd imagined.

'We haven't finished.' The laughter was edged aside like an empty cup and he was watching her again, opening the file once more. 'Where is your brother now?'

A reasonable question. 'He has left Paris. Why, are you expecting him to attack you in defence of my –' She bit her lip, and her glance flew to his damaged hand upon the map. 'Oh no, you don't believe . . . Philippe? *Ciel! Philippe* attacked your coach?'

His face answered her question before he spoke. 'Certainly it was night and he was masked but he's so very like your father, I'm sure I would have recognised him, except he made it easy for me, introducing himself so that every contemptuous word meant something. That was after he and his three associates had shot the coachman and my fellow passengers in cold blood. Ruthlessness calculated to a nicety. They'd make excellent revolutionaries, don't you think? Quite frankly, I don't take kindly to having my hand shot off for daring to touch his sister.'

Fleur could bear it no longer. She fled to his arms and felt them close round her cautiously, then, as though a decision had been taken, tighten protectively in absolution. Snuggling against his shirt, her cheek against his collarbone, Fleur gave a silent prayer of gratitude. Letting go the poison of guilt and regret that had been amassing inside her, she was close to weeping for sheer happiness that he was still alive.

'What's this?'

'Contrition,' she answered huskily, grateful that he had not thrust her away. 'What happened next?'

'They don't allow this at the tribunal,' Raoul murmured. A different intensity was edging out the fledgling kindness. The back of his fingers stroked down her cheek. '*Eh bien*, there were four of the bastards, all armed. They took my . . . rapier – you had my pistols.' The lines of his face were deepening, growing sterner by the instant.

'Go on.' Her arms wreathed his neck.

'Your brother ordered me to give them my papers and take off my uniform before . . . Oh *bon Dieu*! I want you.' His lips closed down on hers and he was kissing her with a glorious desperation.

And Fleur, nestled on his lap, pressed herself against him, surrendering with all her heart. It wasn't just about releasing the emotion that had been building in each of them like a huge wave; no, it was more than that, a deep irresistible undertow that neither wanted to resist.

'Damn.' The male voice in her ear at least sounded cheerful rather than confused.

'Why?'

'It means I am going to have to lay you right

here and now.' He slid his hands beneath her derrière, lifted her onto his desk and skimmed his hands up her skirt. 'Not very comfortable but, believe me, necessary. Is your absolution still available, *mon coeur*?'

'Is this what you do with all your women prisoners?' Fleur murmured, instinctively arching back her shoulders so that her breasts looked fuller. She felt voluptuous, female, and she wanted him between her thighs, filling her.

He kissed her throat. 'Only the pretty ones.'

'On the government map of Paris?' she teased, drawing his face to hers when he raised his mouth from a kiss that told her he would torment her beyond imagination.

'I don't care. Tell me I've found the Île de la Cité? Is that good?'

'Yes,' she sighed with pleasure, 'but it . . . oh, yes, that is purrrfect . . . seems . . . disrespectful on top of a cath – cathedral, ohh.'

'Temple of reason,' he corrected disrespectfully. 'Bells ringing?'

'They're m . . . mmm . . . oh, yes . . . melting down.'

'You know,' he whispered, 'I could have made love to you *over* Paris.'

'In the balloon?' She wriggled back to blink at him in amazement. 'Standing up?'

'Am I not standing now?'

Her lovely eyes were dilated, dusky with pleasure, and she was moist and creamy beneath his adventuring fingertips.

'I missed you. Oh *bon Dieu*, what if I had shot you?'

'Make up for it now,' he encouraged, lifting her hands to the fastenings at his waist. 'It's not every day we feed on glory, *mon coeur. Allons y, citoyenne!*'

The growing vortex of sensation that wildly cast aside all reason was pure recklessness and Raoul knew it, but he could no more stop himself than cease to breathe. Rousseau would have understood, for the surrender was passionately noble, divinely savage and a celebration of being alive in so precarious a world.

Yet as he afterwards tugged Fleur's petticoats down to civilise her ankles, he knew it had been wrong. The ring was still in his possession.

19

Quand j'ai ma mie
Grands Dieux! Que je suis
à mon aise
Quand j'ai ma mie auprès
de moi
A tout moment je la regarde
Et je lui dis: Embrasse-moi?

When I have my darling
Ye gods, when I take
my pleasure,
When I am with my
love,
I can't take my eyes off her
And I say to her,
'Won't you hold me?'

FRENCH SONG

Fleur, content to be squired into a respectable little café close to the quai, lingered beside the stove, shaking her skirts. Outside, the rain, intolerant of plumes and cheap dyes, had emptied the streets of people.

'*Thé à l'Anglaise* and a glass of Tokai,' Raoul ordered, not asking her. With husbandly concern he removed her sagging hat and hung it on a peg, before he led her to a table.

'Are you —?' The helpless gesture was superbly male.

'Damp?' offered Fleur mischievously — after all, they had already shared an intimacy that was quite shocking — and lowered her voice. 'Very, but this is more comfortable than La Force. Are we going there for dinner? I can try and eat with manacles on but I daresay you don't chain prisoners any more. There can't be enough shackles to meet the demand.'

The eyes watching her gleamed appreciatively like tide-shining kelp. It wasn't just the stove that was having an effect. Sighing inwardly, Fleur recognised the hazardous ground she must cross above the row of cherries sinisterly garnishing the *gâteau de pommes à la Bastille* that was served between them.

Raoul's languid mood was gone. The handsome inquisitor was back in place opposite her. The questions would be calm, arranged between forkfuls, and the other customers would think this a simple rendezvous.

'You haven't told me how you got away. I mean, if everyone else was killed and there were four of them. You mentioned a patriot.' The pawn of words edged forwards appeasingly on the board.

Her lover savoured the Tokai and set the glass down easily. She realised now that he was left-handed, that Philippe's cruelty was endurable.

'The coachman, noble fellow. He was wounded in the shoulder but he had a gun stowed beside him and he fired just as your brother was trying to blow my hand to pieces. The diversion gave me a chance to run, so I did.' She could imagine the flares of fire in the darkness; the gasping terror. 'Thank God, it was night. As it was, they brought me down and thought they'd killed me. There was a lot of blood from here.' His fingers pushed up beneath the hair revealing the strike. 'Looked worse than it was, I suppose. It would have been hard to tell unless they'd felt my pulse. I don't remember any more but when I came round, the coach was gone and I heard Jacques the driver moaning. It took me a long time to find help for us. I was badly concussed and they'd winged me in the thigh as well. We'd gone off the road, you see, and I set out in the wrong direction, not thinking clearly.'

'So what happened to Jacques?' She was remembering M. Bosanquet's wounds.

'He died a few days later, God rest his soul. The people who took us in, well, I suppose I wasn't making much sense at the time. It was over a week before I got my strength back and . . . oh, *diable*, the officials in this country enjoy their power. The local fellows made a damn meal of it. I had no papers and they threw me into a cell. Humbling, I can tell you. Don't you dare laugh, *ma fille*. Thank heaven someone turned up who had been to the Jacobin Club in Paris and they hauled me up for identification. So . . .' He gestured palms uppermost.

'Let me be clear on this,' she pursued, and watched him lift an eyebrow at her presumption, 'are you saying my brother and his friends took the coach, everything, and they got as far as Caen and then someone attacked them?'

'It looks like it. I'll find out from Danton. Now it's your turn again.' He leaned forward, arms resting on the cloth. 'Do you know who your brother was meeting with in Paris? Are you sure de Craon wasn't one of my attackers?'

Fleur shook her head. 'Philippe wasn't expecting him yet. He was planning for him to marry me and take over my café and use it as a screen. Over my dead body, I told him! We quarrelled and he said he was leaving for Clerville. He wanted to raise local support and link up with the royalists in La Vendée. There was no talking sense into him. He made me give him all the money I had on me and he took Maman's ring. Oh, Raoul.' Her fingers curled questioningly into his. 'I am truly sorry about what happened to you. It's all my fault. I found your notebook and the painting and it confirmed Philippe's suspicions. You should have handed me over to the soldiers when you had the chance. This,' she slid her other hand over his glove, 'need not have happened and the others would still be alive.'

'But it's not the end of the story.' He dabbed his mouth with the napkin and cast it aside. 'Eat up, citizeness, and I hope you can manage the billet or we'll both be scrubbing pans the rest of the evening.'

Swallowing her last mouthful, Fleur tried to estimate his thoughts. He was reining back on something, something that had to be said where other people could not hear, and then it dawned on her why. The assault in Caen had been meant for Raoul; the man wearing his uniform had died.

She did not prompt him. The penance of the journey back to Paris, his recent injuries and attending his own funeral was showing in the shadows around his eyes. *Ciel*, he must be exhausted.

Pleased that he drew her arm firmly through his as they strolled again towards the Île de la Cité, she smiled up at him affectionately. She wanted to pretend that for the first time in her life, she had a beau. Not just a beau, a lover! Just for a little while she wanted to feel happy, to delude herself that Fortune had at last decided to be kind, that tonight she might curl up beside him.

They lingered on the Pont au Change, the old bridge of jewellers and moneychangers. 'Do you think the Republic will rename this the Pont d'Assignat?' she teased cheerfully, trying to lighten his mood.

'Probably.' He was frowning, waving aside a pedlar trying to sell them busts of Marat. 'You know, I think you should carry a bodkin when you venture out, Fleur. Unobtrusive but effective.'

'Or a stiletto in the quilting of my stays?' She did not want to think about tomorrow. 'I've got a blade in my boot heel.' Her Jacobin was looking as though she had just told him of another Lisbon earthquake. 'No, really.'

'What? *Those boots?* Show me.'

Did he expect her to behave like a horse being shooed? 'Not here.'

They circumvented the building works along the Quai de la Mégisserie and strolled along the riverside terrace overlooking the gardens of the Tuilleries. There were no roars from the Place de la Révolution. Paris was at its most beautiful, the air soft and as gentle as a lover's whisper. Evening light was gilding the mitred rooftops of the palaces, transforming the glass windows to mirrors of fire and making the statues blush. A blackbird, still awake, rippled out its chanson.

'I love this city,' Raoul murmured as they found a bench free of bird droppings in the shadows away from beggars and a drunken soldier singing the Marseillaise. 'I have been to London, Vienna and Florence but this is the city of my heart. Is it not wonderful to be alive?'

'Yes,' Fleur answered truthfully, adoring the flame that lit his eyes. Was this some dark, capricious magic that had granted her deepest desire? To have her mysterious rescuer from Clerville unmasked beside her, heroic as a lover should be. To feast on a man's looks, to find every inch of his profile desirable, to be breathless for his touch, hungry to inflame the appetite for passion. To be in love.

Aloud she asked, 'When did you truly realise we had met before?'

'Our supper at the Palais-Royal, Fleur-de-Lis. All the pieces at last fitted together.'

Astonishment stilled her. 'The toad in your satchel?'

'I am afraid so, Cupid.' He stroked a finger down her jawline. 'Believe me, the girl at Clerville has been clinging to my mind like a burr. Guilt assailed me every time I remembered her.'

'Ha,' scoffed Fleur, 'which probably wasn't very often since she was round and spotty like a fallen apple.'

'But she was brave enough to fire a pistol at me.' Raoul's frown argued against the smile in his voice. He was not looking at her now. 'Your family seems to make a habit of it.' His cuffs were ghostly in the twilight as he lifted his hands, turning them palms upwards as though they were alien objects to be studied. 'They ache, Fleur, my fingers, as though they are still there. Fleur, there's something –'

But not letting him finish, she tenderly clasped his damaged hand and carried it to her lips. 'As I would ache, if you were no longer in my life. I know that now. Raoul, you mean more to me than my very life.'

It was a mistake.

Withholding a lover's answer, Raoul drew away as though troubled. Fleur watched in dismay as his jaw tightened. Clearly she had said too much.

The quiet between them pained Raoul further, knowing that he must throw last week's truth in her face. Would it be wrong to wait until morning? To spend the night in love and then . . . 'Fleur,' he began again. *Diable!* He did not want to hurt her.

'Oh, I forgot,' she exclaimed swiftly, and as if to

cajole him back to amiability set back her petti-coats to pretty ankle height. Then, darting a glance about them to make sure no one was spying on them, the minx took off her boot and twisted its heel. 'A present from an admirer.'

In his astonishment Raoul forgot her hateful brother. 'Where did . . . ?' Lovely wicked lashes flut-tered down, keeping the secret. 'You're not going to tell me, are you?'

'Of. course not.' She tapped her nose like Thomas did when he kept a recipe to himself.

'I can guess.' Raoul played with the boot heel, amusing himself as to how quickly he could extri-cate the blade. 'You'll need to practise if you want to use this in a hurry, *mon coeur*, but it could be palmed, I suppose. You have some very strange allies.'

'It's my *enemies* that worry me,' murmured Fleur, unconsciously turning her face towards the west where, beyond the distant trees, the place of execution was silent.

'The breeze grows chill, *mon coeur*,' Raoul said finally, drawing the darling to her feet and brush-ing his lips across her soft, willing mouth before they turned into the night.

Perhaps, Fleur decided, they did not need words. Each instant was elixir. The lamps of the Pont Neuf threw a diamond necklace across the dark bosom of the river, and the moon was a golden coin spun up into the sky. *Pile ou face?* 'Heads or tails?' she whis-pered silently to Fortune and glanced up at Raoul's resolute profile.

'Supposing . . . supposing I were the only one left of my family, my husband would become Duc de Montbulliou.'

'Only in the palaces of Schönbrunn or Windsor.' Miffed at his indifferent tone, she stowed that insult away for a later quarrel. 'Damn me,' he drawled in imitation of a courtier. 'Do you mean that I have been dining with an heiress. Strap me, and if the monarchy is ever restored – God forbid the return of any of those fat Bourbons – you become a prize. Don't tell me Quettehou proposed in my absence? He did? *Félicitations!*'

'You,' Fleur ground out, 'are the most annoying creature on this earth.' She was tempted to push him off the terrace. 'Yes, he did, after you had left Paris. He knows who I really am. After he tried to force me into giving him the café, he had the audacity to suggest marriage. He gave me two weeks to decide.'

Raoul almost exploded with laughter and held up his hands in surrender. 'Lord, you'd better do it then. His suit leaves me for *dead*.'

Fleur halted as the clapper hit the bell at last. 'Oh my goodness, you were waiting for me to work it out, weren't you?'

Raoul's expression was indulgent, as though she had discovered which of his fists was holding a bonbon. 'It makes sense. Two murders. Both in Calvados. Both on a lonely road. It bears the same signature, doesn't it? And then there were the attempts on your life and the fire.'

'He's not going to give up.' She hung her head.

'I think you should stay away from me. I've already put your life at risk at least three times. You're too valuable to lose. France —'

'France!' The man looked quite irritated. 'Fleur, listen to me. Quettehou can't denounce you, because if he does your entire property will be confiscated by the Republic and he won't get a thing. You are quite safe on that score.'

'But he's getting bolder. You heard him make the accusation this afternoon in front of Marat and the others. Bribe a few people to give testimony that I planned Matthieu Bosanquet's death and I'm sunk. He's quite ruthless. We are not dealing with a man of common decency, you know.'

She looked so adorably perturbed that Raoul could have fought off a cavern full of dragons for her, except that *he* was the one she would be hating before nightfall. 'And another thing,' she persisted, 'the scoundrel actually forged my will, I'm sure of it, for it was after his last visit that I found it among my papers.'

'Not to mention trying to extort money from Monsieur Bosanquet,' Raoul added, remembering the bundle of letters.

'How did y —? Oh, yes! The night you went through my papers.'

He reluctantly hastened the conversation on before she mentioned pythons. The execution blade was whetted. He only had to tell her how to manage the lever. 'I can't prove Quettehou's involvement, Fleur, nor can I work out how he could have so quickly arranged both murders from here in Paris but I will. There's something else.' He dug into his pocket and brought out her ring. He watched the growing horror on her face. The little window of this particular guillotine was readied.

'How did you come by this?' The summer was gone from her voice.

'Danton handed it to me this afternoon. I regret to tell you it was found on the man who was murdered in my uniform.' Fleur's eyes were darker than the river water now, but not with love. 'I can only conclude . . . Dark hair, uniform . . . It's easy for assassins, well, for anyone to make a mistake, I suppose, if you have only a description to go by.' *Diable!* Raoul was not going to feel guilty that her brother had died in his place after what the *cul* had done to him, but he could not bear the hurt and distrust filling her eyes. 'I truly am most sorry, Fleur.'

As her gloved hands gripped the balustrade, he waited for the frost. Below, crouched on the muddy hiatus between the river and the high wall that retained the city, a clerk whistled as he washed his shirt.

Fleur felt the manacles of loneliness and despair snap tight round her heart. Instead of telling her the truth, this smiling Jacobin had deliberately debased her – the Duchesse de Montbulliou enjoyed on his desk like a common trollop, Fleur Bosanquet sweetened for the bad news with *thé* and gâteau, while Philippe lay between them, sprawled across the coach seat with his lifeblood dripping down the leather. Ah yes, her brother had

fallen into hotheaded company and, yes, his character was not what she would have wished, but he
was still her brother.

The winter was back with all its cruelty.

'So now I'm the last on your list,' she said.

20

My dear Marie-Anne,
Be thankful you live nearer the ocean. I have never
known such heat as we have experienced the last week
and it brings more sorrow. The windmills on Montmartre
and Mount Ste-Geneviève are standing idle. The
housewives crowd the doorsteps of the bakeries with
baskets as empty as their poor little children's stomachs.
We ladle out broth in the alley outside the café but it
is not enough.

EXTRACT FROM THE LETTERS OF FRANÇOISE-ANTOINETTE DE
MONTBULLIOU, 1793

As May surrendered to June, Paris was plagued
by more than flies. Raoul, eating a hasty
Sunday breakfast at Hérault's apartment

before they left for the Convention, was too perturbed by his own unhappiness and his country's worsening circumstances to make idle conversation. Common sense was keeping him away from the Chat Rouge. Letting Fleur lick her wounds was all very well but he wasn't sure how long he could endure without her. The aching wasn't just lower down, it was in his heart and mind as well.

Immersing himself in his work helped. The constitution that he and Hérault had been labouring over was almost finished, but the immediate situation was grave and today's debate was likely to make supper in a silent order of monks attractive. Matters were reaching a head like a ripe abscess. He only hoped that Fleur would have the sense to stay at home.

The threats of the Girondin government to move its headquarters out of Paris, the sabre-rattling of the enemy armies still intent on rescuing Marie Antoinette, the royalist uprisings in Brittany and Anjou, and yesterday, the devastating news that Lyons had rebelled against its Jacobin administrators, all these made the citizens irritable, worse than curs with summer itch. Paris's hungry belly was beginning to growl and Marat's vitriol was everywhere. *Enragé* papers screamed of conspiracies. Placards mushroomed each night and survived despite the government's efforts to rip them down before morning.

Armand and the other Girondin orators had been thundering back with their usual self-righteous rhetoric, making no decisions, demanding that the Convention organise armed protection for them, and the ministers were still clinging to the political cliff top with their fingernails. But the situation was almost at crisis point. Last Monday, having learned not a damn thing from their failure to indict Marat, the Girondins had ordered the arrest of some of the Commune officials. Max Robespierre had finally lost his patience and made a passionate, furious speech, accusing twenty-two Girondin deputies in front of the full assembly. The Convention had merely shuffled its feet, muttered about the Commune usurping its role, and no action had been taken – yet. Raoul hoped to hell Armand would not be there this morning. He had warned him to get out of Paris while he still had his liberty.

'Shall we go?' Across the table, Hérault pushed his unfinished breakfast aside.

The tocsin bells were tolling, calling the citizens forth, as the two of them made their way through the Tuilleries gardens. They overtook swaggering packs of armed youths from the western sections, bleary eyed from Saturday drinking; farm labourers, brown and speckled as eggs, wearing their Sunday waistcoats; and *bas peuple* in grimy rags, with pinched mouths and bird's-nest hair. Giggling grisettes in flowered muslins, clustering around a coffee-seller, glanced speculatively over shoulders pink as roses from too much summer flaunting. Straw hats held by ribbons were tossed back between their shoulderblades, and save for cheap bracelets, their soft arms were bare.

'Flags, citizens? Cockades?' Striped skirts swished

out of their brisk path, the *vendeuse*'s red-lipped mouth a fountain spout of disappointment, her jauntier wares sullenly withdrawn.

Some women carried children, a whole new generation of Brutuses and Fructidores come to wave their democratic rattles; and cheerful family groups from Cloud and Germain-en-Laye were trooping in with hampers as though fireworks were in the offing. In a sense they were.

'I spoke with Armand last night. He says that leaving would have made him look like a traitor. I suspect the other Girondins feel the same way. I hope he's changed his mind.'

'Well, it's like sitting on a bloody volcano. If the silly bastards do turn up, we can't very well expel them bodily, not to this rabble.'

'It's going to be ugly.' Fear scraped an icy finger-nail down Raoul's spine. '*Diable!* I'm beginning to recognise faces from last September.' He hoped to heaven Fleur had stayed at home.

'We can't provide bread, but we can certainly do circuses,' his friend answered scathingly. 'Which do you want, Raoul? The broadsword or the trident?' He was nodding cheerfully left and right as though he was making a royal progress, but his smile was as tight as King Louis's when the women had brought the royal family from Versailles, and Raoul noticed him run his fingers inside the neck of his cravat. The hazy close warmth of the morning portended a searing heat by noon.

'I am glad I am not in your shoes today, Citizen Président,' Raoul replied with feeling.

True, Hérault's sangfroid was admirable but there were dark hammocks of fatigue above his cheekbones. The poor *salaud* was only halfway through his two-week term as President of the Convention and this morning was going to be the session from hell.

'If we vote for the Girondins' imprisonment, which is what this crowd want,' muttered Hérault as if following Raoul's thoughts along the same furrow, 'the rest of France will assume we are turning belly up, dead in the water.'

'Surrendering to the dictates of louts and harpies!' agreed Raoul. One of the grisettes blew a kiss at him.

'*Exactement!* You and I didn't kill a lion to be ruled by sewer rats.'

Raoul could feel the sweat already beginning between his shoulderblades. 'The only answer left is to make one of the committees all-powerful, I suppose. You're still thinking along those lines?'

Hérault nodded. 'What alternative is there to anarchy?' The aristocratic nose wrinkled. The ploy was not without risk.

'But it may mean sacrificing the democracy we bought with a king's blood.'

'So we put in safeguards. If the committee personnel are renewed regularly, *hein*?'

'But then you risk a loss of continuity,' Raoul argued. 'Members stepping on and off the board as though it's a carousel! *Mon Dieu*, we'd be giddy with changes of policy. Each man wanting to make his mark, do things his way.'

'But if the goals are to wage the war efficiently,

Raoul, and put a limit on the price of bread. Come on, as an interim measure it has merit, surely?'

'Of course it does, Hérault. It's just that I remember my Aristotle. Democracy can easily degenerate into a tyranny.'

'I don't think we have anyone of dictatorship calibre,' his friend shrugged dismissively. 'Marat might be hopeful but he's about as acceptable as an old boot left out all winter, and that's what we're trying to prevent – mob rule with Marat kicking from the back. Listen, no one living today knows enough about democracy to argue with you, but the Americans seem to be managing.'

'That revolution came from the top and it was against the British,' Raoul argued. 'Rome nearly crowned Julius Caesar and ended up with the Emperor Augustus and a dynasty of tyrants, and Florence suffered Savonarola.' His painter's imagination posed the murderous senators around a dying Julius with young Augustus watching from behind a pillar. '*La gloire* or *la conviction*,' he said aloud. 'Those are the motives that always bring forth a dictator.'

'Well, there isn't a general left with brains for the task so we certainly aren't in danger of a Julius Caesar. Don't count Danton. He's as layered as a gâteau. Too lazy to become a dictator anyway and I'd bet the crown jewels he'd put his head through the little window rather than see France back under a tyrant. Robespierre is single-minded enough. The Revolution's his religion but . . .' he curled his lip, 'not quite your Emperor Augustus, is he? Though the spectacles would look magnificent beneath a laurel wreath. What about you?' he teased. 'The delightful Fleur installed at Versailles. You could resurrect Louis Quinze's old flying chair – save you climbing the stairs to pleasure her.'

'Now there's a thought.' But Raoul's laugh was hollow.

An infant tottered across his path and he turned it gently back to its mama, suddenly regretful there would be no son or daughter to remember what Raoul de Villaret had fought for. An emptiness was growing inside him. *Merde!* Could he be losing his hard edge? Fleur was blurring a horizon that had always seemed so clear. She deserved a husband and children, but he had to resist. Take each day at a time. The Revolution was all that counted; the Revolution must come first, and yet . . .

He lifted his gaze from the path, staring at the people he had risked his life for.

'I see the Amazons are out to a man,' he muttered dryly. And not just in skirts either – he glimpsed brawny women in breeches and jackets, with derrières like broadside warships. *Nom d'un chien!* It would need a volley of cannonballs to keel them over.

'Bonjour, Citizen Président! De Villaret!' Marat, each arm waisting a pretty girl as though they were about to perform a folkdance, waylaid them. The great man looked his usual scruffy self, although the ermine cravat was gone because of the heat or maybe some grisette had stolen it as a keepsake. 'Going to sacrifice your friend Gensonné, *mon brave*? Play safe, eh?'

'Give over, Marat,' retorted Hérault briskly. 'It will be the decision of the Convention that prevails, not yours or mine.'

'The will of the people is all that matters.' Marat added emphasis – one of the girls squealed at being pinched.

'Decided by you, Jean-Paul?' It was risky to poke the great man in the ribs, even verbally, but Raoul could see the fellow was high as a happy drunk on the people's favour.

'*Moi*, de Villaret, *moi*?' Marat made a moué of protest. 'I am the tool of the people, the mouthpiece, but to you I am a prophet crying vainly.' His grin slackened to a scabby smirk. A flaky finger reached out to flick up Raoul's July '89 medal. 'Maybe today will be worth painting. You should be wearing two Bastille medals, *mon beau*. Isn't La Bastille coquetting her dark skirts with you gentlemen today? Ah, I forgot, you are here on business.'

'She doesn't like large crowds.'

'Doesn't she? But I just saw her with Emilie Lemoine.' He kissed his fingers loudly in farewell and swerved off, his arms each a scarlet torque about the milkmaid necks.

'Dirty cur,' snorted Hérault beneath his breath. 'I'd spit if I were not a gentleman. What's the matter?'

'Where is she?' Raoul halted, glowering, and scanned the crowd. '*Diable!*' Hadn't she the sense to stay at home? This wasn't Bastille Day and Quettehou's creatures could easily create a disturbance. 'That fool of a Lemoine creature must have persuaded her.'

'Or the other way round. Come on! If you think you'll find her in this press, you need a strait-jacket. Let's get moving.'

Side by side, like disciplined guards, they walked purposefully towards the convention hall, looking neither to left nor right, giving no one a chance to delay them further.

The familiar foyer seemed no longer friendly but spiky as a cluttered harbour, except the masts were pikes and bayonets and a squall of *sans-culottes* was already in full splash around Boissy d'Anglas who, noticing their arrival, pushed through to them looking ruffled. His usual expensive cravat was inexplicably missing.

'I cannot even go to the privy without being jostled. It's like running the gauntlet,' he complained querulously, tugging his cuffs straight. 'You are president, do something! As an elected deputy of the people, I expect –'

'All right,' cut in Hérault. 'De Villaret, if you please, pray inform the officer over there that if any of the deputies want to go to the privy, he's to send a guard with them.'

'Two!' insisted Boissy.

'Very well, two!'

'And you'd better double it for the Girondins,' Boissy added. 'All twenty-two of them!'

'Double, of course, Boissy.' Only the narrowing of Hérault's eyes betrayed his concern as he said lightly, 'Do you think they will need cannon as well? Or balloons, perhaps?'

Boissy faced him down. The mockery was out

513

of place. 'Take it seriously, Hérault. They'll need a damned army by the time today is over.'

Receiving his instructions, the officer of the national guard muttered a retort that might have made a roué blush but he did not argue. Matters were too serious for that.

Serious! An understatement! Raoul was livid that Fleur could be so reckless. If anything happened to her . . . Where the hell was she? With a window of time before the session began, he hastily overtook the long tail of people that hung down the staircase. If she were indeed here, he would dispatch her home with an escort. No argument!

His resolve strengthened as he passed two ox-like *tricoteuses* marching a frightened woman back to the stairs. By what authority he dreaded to think. Something evil was happening here, swelling like a broken vein beneath the skin. If his little aristocrat fell foul of such creatures . . .

Upstairs the press of people trying to get into the gallery was beyond belief. He elbowed his way through to the entrance where two other harridans had taken it on themselves to inspect passes.

'No pass, no entry!'

Beyond the officious pair, it looked as though the public gallery was crammed to capacity. He stepped past the women without a by-your-leave. Recognising his deputy's sash, they bit their tongues and glared at him viciously as he stood in the doorway and scanned the faces. Fleur was not there. He did not know whether he was glad or not. She might be safer up here than outdoors in that human ocean.

'On whose authority are you here?' he demanded of the doorkeepers in his best imperial tone and received an upturned finger for answer. Trying to move those two from their berth would be like trying to blow a pair of battleships upstream with a pair of bellows. Giving up with a snarl, he marched down the corridor and let himself through a small door to a back staircase which led to the top floor. The attic was dusty and crammed with the detritus of former reigns, old flags and bunting, broken chairs and ancient mattresses. Raoul shoved hard at one of the *oeil de boeuf* windows so he might see out across the courtyard, then he noticed one window was broken with a jagged eyehole.

The sight was terrifying – an ocean of heads all pushing towards the Convention. Upon it floated plank-like, a screeching woman in labour, passed hand over hand back towards the nearest street. Fighting his rising panic, Raoul angled open a window on the other side. It wasn't thousands surging across the Tuilleries gardens to the Cour de la Carousel; it was tens of thousands. All jammed as hell! Fleur could be trampled in such a press.

The lines of national guard, needling like fine threads of metal through the heaving fabric, were useless to hold back this mob if it surged up against the building. There were about fifty soldiers already ranked behind a man on horseback. Hanriot! He recognised the thin shoulders of the former customs clerk. Raoul could hear the military whistles blowing above the hubbub. The fellow must have detached his soldiers earlier and now, thinking better of it, was calling them back. An indecisive expert in charge of the Convention's safety! Oh Christ! Raoul's blood ran cold.

He could only watch in disbelief as the crowd parted in panic. Teams of horses hurtled through pulling cannon, with the gunners running behind, their muskets at the ready. Oh, *bon Dieu*, Hanriot! Whose side are you on? What's going to happen to Armand and his friends? It shouldn't have come to this! When the Bastille fell, we were all on the same side.

With a calm hand that belied his fear, he closed the window and made his way back down and into the Convention's smoky chamber. Hérault was already seated in the president's chair above the rostrum. Catching his questioning glance, Raoul hurried across and mounted the narrow stairs.

'There's at least seventy thousand surrounding us already and Hanriot's brought in cannon.'

'Oh, Christ, Raoul. And look at the silly bloody fools!' Following Hérault's nod, Raoul stared at the twenty-two Girondins sitting in a row like men already on trial; in their midst was Armand Gensonné, reading a book and looking utterly detached. Raoul cursed. If Armand had had any sense, he'd be lying low in Normandy. The cream of intellect. Except that France couldn't live on cream.

Be heroic, lad! Go and sit with the Girondins, the rebel serpent in him hissed. Oh yes, put his own head up for a volley of shot? No, if the damned lunatics wanted to behave like sitting ducks . . .

'Which way, Raoul?'

'Which way?' he echoed dully, dragging his gaze back to today's president.

'Yes, Raoul, which way.' Hérault's golden hair was damp at the temples. Sweat shone on the deepening furrows. 'Which way are the cannons pointing?'

'I don't know, *yet*.' He left his scowling president, and, choosing the uncommitted, sat down gloomily between Boissy and Delacroix as the first speaker took the rostrum. Raoul shifted uneasily and swivelled in his seat; Quettehou was seated with Marat's cronies on the higher benches, watching him with a snakelike intensity. Quettehou! Christ, surely he wouldn't try something today? He searched the gallery again, his panic rising.

It wasn't just the heat; Raoul could almost smell the fear surrounding them. The ploy for a dull speaker to dampen down the tension was not working. Armed *sans-culottes* had infiltrated the floor of the debating chamber. A few were wandering disruptively, eyeing the Girondins with malevolence and fingering their muskets; others had pushed along onto the benches where their prey sat and were puffing pipe smoke in their faces. Hérault shouldn't be allowing it but the president's complexion was pale as unrolled pastry. He was estimating numbers, by the look of him. A waste of time, Hérault. Whatever decisions were taken indoors, it was the cannons outside that would decide matters. Hanriot was the key. The Convention needed something to keep Hanriot on side. Inspiration came suddenly.

'Boissy, Delacroix, listen, what do you reckon to this . . . ?' Raoul's voice fell to a whisper.

Delacroix clapped his shoulder. 'It might just work, *mon brave*. Go ahead. We will support you.'

'I'll be needing your sword for a prop, Boissy.' Now or never! He strode up to the clerk and added his name to the list of speakers. To his surprise, he was summoned to the rostrum next. The other speakers, turning cowards as the *sans-culotte* tobacco fouled the air, were evidently convinced that silence might be safer.

It was necessary to gain attention. Raoul paused, watching them all, and then dramatically drew the dress sword and hurled it point first to the right of Hérault's ear. With no chance of purchase, it skittered ignominiously to the floor in front of one of the tall candelabra. Consternation erupted but Hérault, swallowing, nobly waved the soldiers back.

'It falls, Citizen Président!' thundered Raoul. 'And so shall we!' He had them now. The entire hall was listening. 'And so shall we! And why? Because we have not bound Might to Justice. Citizen Président, fellow deputies, I propose that an army of professional soldiers be formed to protect the Republic.' The pounding of feet shook the hall in applause. 'And, what is more, I propose those men, those brave soldiers of France, be paid a fair wage. Forty sous a day, patriots!' He moved through his arguments briefly, not needing to say what was obvious, and left the speaker's stand to huzzahs.

Deputy Delacroix sprang to his feet: 'I personally will support the proposal and recommend that my fellow committee members do the same.' The vote was taken.

'Carried!' Hérault leaned forward. 'Perhaps, Citizen de Villaret, you would like to convey the good news to the national guard.' Stooping, he retrieved the dress sword from the floor and proffered it to Raoul. 'Next time,' he muttered, 'use someone else for your theatricals. You nearly scared me witless. Go! I hope your idea works.'

Passed to one of the national guards in the lobby, the message of regular pay and permanent status was instantly conveyed to their commander. Any intelligent soldier could read the blatant purpose in the dew-fresh legislation but such lawful bribery might make Commander Hanriot more sympathetic to his civilian masters. Worth a try.

The gallery, too, had done their arithmetic by the time Raoul returned and, restless, were muttering with mistrust.

'Enough shillyshallying, you blockheads! Expel the Girondins!' shrieked a woman with biceps worthy of a laundress.

'*Renvoyez! Renvoyez! Renvoyez!*' chanted the gallery. Their pounding feet shuddered the gallery joists.

The Girondin deputies looked fit to wet themselves. Two *sans-culottes* on the floor of the hall were beating drums, their faces grotesque masks of malevolence leering at the cowering men.

'Order! Silence!' Even God would have needed a thunderbolt to quell the hubbub, and Hérault, far from divine, was reduced to mortal contingencies. He directed an urgent expression at Danton and Robespierre but both men sat immobilised, their faces adamantine.

'Order!' bellowed Hérault once more. 'ORDER!'

'*Ajournez! Ajournez!*' chanted the gallery.

Deputy Paul Barère rose, held up his palm to the gallery for silence and with his other hand pointed towards the twenty-two accused Girondins. The spectators hushed.

'Let those deputies be suspended!'

'Suspend 'em from the lampposts!' guffawed one of the Mountain and the Girondins exploded in protests like outraged chickens.

'*A la lanterne! A la lanterne!*' The deadly drumming crescendoed.

Pushing past the *sans-culottes* who cluttered the aisle, Barère craned up to the president's table. After a whispered conversation, Hérault rose.

'We shall adjourn for an hour,' he announced, ringing the bell, and then he cupped his hands and shouted to all the deputies above the roar of the gallery: 'Patriots, go outside and congratulate our soldier-citizens. They are doing a fine task of keeping order out there. Those of you who need a breath of air, please follow me.'

Barère clapped Raoul's shoulder as everyone except the Girondins filed out.

'Let's see, eh?'

It might work: the calculated fraternising to make it clear to the mob leaders that the army and the Convention held the peace together. Some hundred and fifty or so of the deputies followed Hérault out of the *salle* to cram the foyer, but when the huge doors were thrown open, Raoul wondered if he looked as white as Hérault did. Beyond the small breathing space of steps were the national guard and, beyond them, the mob. The deputies would need to want martyrdom badly to step down into that colosseum. The soldiers didn't look friendly either, but dangerously insubordinate, the higgledy teeth a row of grins beneath the military whiskers. Their shiny Roman helmets, like props from David's paintings, seemed incongruously virtuous. And where in hell was Fleur?

'Play Cupid, will you, de Villaret, since you're obviously feeling brave this morning.' Paul Barère drew Raoul into a triangle of whispers. They wanted him to wing his way to Hanriot! As if that would work!

'Sergeant!' Hérault summoned a soldier over. 'Escort Citizen de Villaret to your commander.'

'Yes, citizen.' The man saluted and led Raoul through the cordon to where Hanriot sat astride his horse, a narrow-shouldered king for the hour. Not a face for a painting. A lampoon maybe. That nose with the pitch of a mitre roof on too small an understorey. The dark eyebrows wriggling towards each other like veering caterpillars.

'Citizen Captain.'

'Citizen Deputy.' The plumes nodded.

'The Citizen President of the Convention sends his greetings and requests that you put an end to this intimidation. He reminds you that the Convention represents the people and it will not be dictated to.'

'I received your message. Forty sous a day! It will take more than that, de Villaret, but a nice try.' The commander leaned down: 'Tell your fucking president that he and the assembly can go fuck themselves, and if he doesn't surrender the twenty-two deputies to the people within an hour, we will blow 'em all up.'

Freezing his features in an inscrutable expression, Raoul resumed his place facing the soldiers at Hérault's left hand. He smiled tightly at Hanriot. Hanriot smirked. And the Hieronymus Bosch faces lapping the horse's flanks were gloating too. All save one. He saw Fleur beyond the cannons, her lips a tight seam of fear. For him. She had come because of him. Oh, my brave girl. He forced himself to appear serene, willing the air to play his messenger and carry his reassurance to her.

'What did he say?' Hérault's voice shook him back to the moment.

'You wish me to say it aloud?'

'Yes,' Barère snorted on the President's left.

'*Comme vous voulez*,' and Raoul repeated the insulting reply with a deliberately flat voice. With everyone watching, it helped his colleagues preserve stoical expressions.

Hérault turned to the deputies crowding the

steps behind him and spoke softly: 'Paul, Raoul, come with me to speak with Hanriot. The rest of you fraternise with the nearest soldiers, and skirt what little grounds are left to us. If any of you discover some exit that has been overlooked or any guards that will guarantee to let us through, come back and tell me.' Then with a smile that had helped to topple a monarchy, he ignored the cannon that were being roped round muzzle-first to face him and bravely stepped forward, walking out past the rank of soldiers, his fingers clasped behind his back like a commander. Raoul and Barère followed like loyal lieutenants.

'Bonjour, Hérault de Séchelles,' Hanriot smiled; the hands more used to handling ledgers were surprisingly at ease with the horse's reins.

'My dear Hanriot, we understand what a difficult job you have here, but you are under obligation from the Convention to keep the exits to the Tuilleries free.'

'And you are free to leave, my dear *Citoyen Président*, we have no quarrel with you. We want the twenty-two guilty men.'

'You are forgetting these men are deputies, representatives of the people. They are not condemned by any court or lawful assembly and I will not surrender them to be torn apart.'

The moustache above the tobacco-stained teeth quirked, highly entertained.

'For God's sake, Hanriot, it is more than democracy at stake here,' protested Raoul. 'It is liberty or death.'

'Indeed, it is, Citizen de Villaret, and I've no quarrel with you either.'

Nor was Barère some lily-livered coward:'Hanriot, we come in peace. If you disobey the President of the Convention, you will be sending France down a very dangerous path indeed.'

'Surrender the twenty-two!'

'No.' Hérault was ice calm.

'On your head be it, Citizen Président.' Hanriot swivelled in the saddle. 'Prime the guns, lads.'

The peacemakers, feeling not in the least blessed, returned proud-backed to the shade of the building and faced the sniggers of the pikemen who had been watching from the steps.

'There's no way out,' the scouting deputies grumbled. 'We've checked everywhere.'

Hérault grimaced and led them back into the *salle* to discover that half the Plain's benches were entirely taken by *sans-culottes* with muskets across their laps. The Jacobin deputies who had not bothered to leave the chamber were nearly slathering like dogs above a rabbit warren; a killing was due. The silence was almost tangible and then it was broken by the familiar clunking of the ratchets that operated the wheelchair of the crippled deputy, Robespierre's close friend, Couthon, as he waggled the two handles above the chair's arms round and round and propelled his way towards the speaker's rostrum.

'Assist me, friends.' Robespierre's brother, Augustus, and his apostle, Saint-Just, hoisted him from the chair and heaved him up the rostrum steps.

Although the strain almost burst his lined face, Couthon anchored his speech notes and hung courageously onto the rostrum.

'Since you have been outside, citizens, and know how "free" we are,' the ironic tone was offensive, 'I suggest we get on with what the people demand and accuse the twenty-two. I have an indictment here against these malefactors.' And he began to read out his list as though it was no more than a student enrolment. Twenty-nine names, he read out, and ten of them were committee members.

Hérault had no choice but to put it to the vote. Raoul knew his colleague well enough to see with what self-loathing it was done, but surely . . . The Girondins sprang to their feet roaring a protest. The Mountain victoriously hurled the invective back. Arms rose like an army of pikes. The men designated to make the tally were wide-eyed, finding it impossible to distinguish the votes of the deputies among the waving arms of the unlawful invaders. No votes were counted.

'Carried!' shouted Hérault with unnecessary haste, more like a harassed schoolmaster than the temporary helmsman of the nation. It was wrong; it was incredibly wrong.

The Mountain were on their feet cheering. One Girondin fainted. Armand blinked as though he had not heard a word. The gallery was whooping. Raoul would have stormed out then and found a wall to fist. The schoolyard was given over to the bullies! Hérault had bought breathing space but at perilous cost. There was still a chance that the indicted deputies could flee Paris but the mob had loured over the Convention like a monstrous thug.

Marat left the *salle* to convey his triumph to the people.

As the tumult slowly subsided, the great orator of the Girondins, Vergniaud, rose with a knife in one hand and a glass in the other. 'Since you are so thirsty for our blood, President, may I offer you a glass of it now. And –'

The screaming beyond the foyer momentarily halted his peroration. It sounded like Fleur.

With a demon on his shoulder, Raoul fought his way through the men pouring out into the courtyard. Marat, perched on a cannon's carriage like an organ monkey, was trying to be heard above the melee.

It was the *tricoteuses*. Like hounds upon a fox, some six or seven had fallen upon a woman with their fists and boots, slamming her head against the pavement. For a moment, Raoul dreaded it was Fleur, but the blood-splashed skirts around the kicking feet were stripped in blue and white. No one interfered, but a hysterical, familiar young woman in black was screaming to free herself from the national guardsmen who held her by the arms. Fleur, oh my darling, *Fleur*!

'Pull those harpies off!' Raoul snarled to the sergeant with such anger that the man instantly obeyed. Some dozen guards ran in and hauled the women, thistly with nails and teeth, back from their convulsing victim. Clothing torn, a young woman lay shuddering on the gravel; her bloodied face was battered beyond recognition, her eyes wide open to the sky in shock.

'What have you done, *mesdames*?' Marat sprang down and in the suddenly hallowed hush came to kneel beside the woman. 'Hush, Emilie, it's over! It's over, pet.'

'The stupid cow was sticking up for a bloody Girondin,' spat one of the attackers, arms like legs of mutton thrust akimbo. 'That dumb Gensonné arsehole.'

'Organise a stretcher,' Raoul barked at the soldiers. Emilie's shuddering had stopped. Going down on one knee beside Marat, he lifted the girl's thin wrist. The pulse, thank God, was there.

'Look after your own,' muttered Marat warningly, and Raoul needed no second bidding. Fleur, struggling against her captors, was yelling angry abuse at them.

'Lucky we didn't start on madame there,' bawled one of the harridans.

It needed drama to satisfy this foul audience. With a surly grin, Raoul strode across and, drawing back his hand, slapped Citizeness Bosanquet to instant silence. 'Now keep quiet! You are under arrest. Bring her inside!'

So he had hoisted up his true colours at last and chosen! If anything would have confirmed her as an enemy of the Revolution, his action had. Unfair! Unjust! Fleur furiously kicked over the chair in her cell, wishing it was Raoul de Villaret. Then she flung herself down on the stained ticking mattress, her forefinger knuckle between her lips to staunch her weeping.

Why was she shut in on her own? Not out there where the aristocrat prisoners sat playing cards and gossiping? Did it mean her name would be on one of the terrible lists in the morning? This was where the long road from Caen had led. This was the only reality – the steps up to the bloodstained scaffold and the little window with the basket ready. Not her make-believe world of the café and the Rue des Bonnes Soeurs. What an imbecile she'd been to think that she could survive.

The Revolution! Had she not been a lady, she would have spat. For a while she'd been deluded, wanted to believe Emilie's dream, to love Raoul de Villaret and even concede some good in Marat, but not now. She could only despise herself for the pathetic way her defences had started to crumble every time de Villaret had turned the full cannonade of his charm in her direction. Curse Raoul de Villaret! He was a snake, watching, waiting in the grass, while she hopped around so innocently.

It was a sullen, silent girl who glared at him from the palliasse in her cell in the Conciergerie with eyes that had seen too much – intensely pained, sea-blue eyes. His hand had left no marks upon her face but there was emotional damage. He could see short-term repairs to her pride had been carried out – that was expected – but he did not like the resilience that newly lacquered her. Patience and sensitivity would be needed to plane it away.

He set the tray down upon the small table and kicked the door shut.

'Go away!'

'*Bonsoir, mon coeur.* Thomas sent this for you.' To tantalise her, he lifted off the covering and fanned the aroma in her direction.

'Take it away!' The slender shoulders heaved, her face was to the wall.

'You are fortunate those disgusting harridans didn't beat you witless as well.' Setting the only chair upright with its back to his sulky prisoner, he straddled the seat and leaned round to help himself to a slice of duckling. 'Have you the sense to stay at home for your own good? No! Whose brilliant notion was it? Yours or the Lemoine woman's?' His tone would have blasted oaks.

'Unless you can tell me how Emilie is, you monster, go away!' Ah, so he was a monster.

'She's in Saint-Pélagie.' He licked the orange sauce from his fingers.

'Prison. *Prison!*' Fleur twisted round, dashing the tears from her eyes. 'But those bitches attacked *her*. Why didn't you lock *them* up? Oh no, don't tell me, they are to receive medals. Liberty, Equality and Atrocity! Congratulations, Citizen de Villaret, what a wonderful new world you have created.'

It was tempting to find some innovative way of stemming the lady's eloquent invective before every troublemaker in the prison heard her, but fortunately she subsided. He raised his glance reluctantly from her lovely breasts, still rising and falling in angry passion, and answered calmly: 'Believe me, your friend is safer there, out of harm's way, for what good it will do her. The poor creature hasn't recovered her wits yet. Aren't you hungry?' Another morsel of duck slid down followed by a gulp of wine.

A female fist hit the mattress. 'Then send me over there, you brute, so I can help. I'll nurse her.'

'I suspect what you know about nursing wouldn't fill one paragraph. Leave it to her mother. She's looking after her. What the hell did you think you were doing at the Tuilleries anyway, you harpy? I thought you had more sense than to be hanging round with the likes of her.' It was unfair, perhaps, to goad her.

'At least Emilie had the courage to defend someone she cared about, which is more than can be said for the rest of you cowards. Convention! You are just a row of windmills, waving your sails whenever Marat blows.' That fist of abuse found its mark.

'I am releasing you in the morning, Fleur,' he declared, rising to his feet as though he was a magistrate delivering a verdict, 'and I am sorry if I had to hurt you but it seemed the only solution considering we were surrounded by eighty thousand people, not to mention the cannon. However, if you prefer to play the martyr tomorrow, I can arrange a place for you in a tumbril. The first one leaves for the Place de la Révolution at half-past six sharp. I expect you'd like to get it over with early.'

'That is not amusing, you devil,' she growled

and, grabbing up the bucket from the corner, stood poised to hurl the contents at him.

He kept his voice low, his gaze on the pail. 'No, nor is there anything amusing about having to rescue you constantly from your own reckless stupidity. That, for instance!' He jabbed a finger towards the pail. 'Stop behaving like a nine-year-old and listen to reason.'

'Reason has become your harlot,' she snarled. 'Get out!' The bucket shifted ominously. He knew her capability. He doubted she'd miss.

'I had you brought to this place to learn sense,' he informed her sternly, dropping the tureen lid back in place with a satisfying clatter. 'Not very friendly, is it?' But his words seemed to consolidate her defiance, for her eyes had become as hard and brilliant as diamonds.

'Adieu till morning. I hope the fleas find you. And from tomorrow onwards you will do as I say if you value your life, citizeness, or you can bloody well marry Felix Quettehou.'

He adroitly caught the bucket before it fell.

He did not come to release her in the morning. One of the gaolers did that, slapping her on the derrière and telling her she was a lucky girl. She arrived home, rumpled and furious, to a message from Citizen de Villaret informing her that he was escorting her to the Comédie Française that evening. She sent a message back saying she was indisposed. The reply that came back was brief: 'I doubt it.'

Her fleabites could not be erased with water or with soap. Not that she had any soap – Paris had run out. With shiny, damp curls and a change of clothes, she marched off to the Chat Rouge only to be confronted with a couple of section officials out for pickings. Ha, so these carrion thought her wounded and vulnerable, did they? She disarmed them of their cudgels by the café door, and although she sweetened them with chocolate and a flirtatious mix of smiles, billiards and careful name-dropping, it was at least an hour before they bumbled off, leaving her free to head for Saint-Pélagie.

The gaoler led Fleur to an unlocked cell. The silence as he opened the door chilled her. The interior, clean and sparse, was bathed in sunlight, very different from the gloomy hole in which she had spent the night, but no brazen cheeriness warmed the air. Poor Emilie lay stiff upon the mattress for all the world like an alabaster monument except for the hideous contusions disfiguring her face. For an instant Fleur assumed the worst and then she saw the rise and fall beneath the coverlet. Untouched, a bowl of potage with vermicelli was solidifying beside the palliasse.

'Ain't stirred all night. Unnatural, ain't it?' Emilie's mother, Mme Lemoine, rose respectfully from her stool, the faded blonde hair and tired face an older echo of her child.

'You've made this homely,' murmured Fleur after she had given the older woman a sympathetic embrace. She heaved her basket onto the table and emptied out two soft-rind cheeses, a platter of fruit and some perry liqueur. 'Emilie will feel much loved when she awakes.' It certainly did not seem like a prison. Fresh dressings lay beside a small vase of honeysuckle, which cascaded onto a bright red cotton tablecloth.

'Me do this, madame? God love you, no, not me. My poor head was running too wild to think of such things. It was the gentleman who sent all this.'

'Gensonné?' Fleur spoke without thinking.

'Oh, not him. Some chance!' The woman spat dismissively. 'No, the Jacobin deputy what's interested in education. Dark hair. Voice to make your insides melt. Seen you talking to him. Arranged all this, he did. Even sent a physician to 'ave a look at 'er. Good, ain't it, but –' She glanced round at her poor girl's battered face, her mouth a trembling arc.

Sad and chastened, Fleur returned to Rue des Bonnes Soeurs. Were there no rainbows in this wretched city? Oh Paris, Paris, what have you done to yourself? Emilie, with her *sans-culotte* dreams and plucky hope, had personified the goodness in the people, but now . . . A curse on Marat and his gutter rabble! And Raoul de Villaret! What use was honeysuckle when Emilie could not smell the flowers or even know they existed? Guilt had prompted the kindness. Kindness, yes, but too late, too late! The Convention should have protected them against those awful women.

Inside her door, she unfolded the strange letter that lay waiting upon the brass tray.

Hoarder! Filthy Harlot! Leave Paris before we hang you!

Each crude pasted word screamed at her as though a rabid beggar stood before her shaking his fist.

'Oh dear Lord,' she whispered, reeling back against the wall.

'*Patronne*, is that you?' Thomas emerged from below stairs and, finding her in tears, took the paper from her fingers and read it.

'Come, *ma petite*. Envy, that's all it is.' He tossed the paper onto the kitchen fire and poured her a brandy. 'So, how's Emilie? Cursing like a sergeant, knowing her.'

'No,' Fleur whispered, pleating her lips, trying not to cry. 'She won't wake up. Madame Lemoine says the physician holds no hope for her. He believes that if she does come to her senses she'll have no more brain than a cabbage. Oh, Thomas, it's not fair.'

His huge arms enclosed her. Her nose encountered a jacket full of pantry smells. 'Things will settle down, *patronne*.'

Eventually Fleur pulled away and sat down, mopping her tears. Scrunching her handkerchief into a soggy ball, she hid it in her fist and said resolutely, 'I've decided I am going to sell the Chat Rouge.' She watched the chef's shiny jowls quiver in appalled disbelief. 'I'm going to send for Monsieur Mansart this afternoon.'

'You have a buyer?' A huffy tone veneered the deep hurt she sensed beneath.

'I believe so.' She reached across the table and patted his huge hand. 'You! You may have it for . . . for a day's wages.'

'*Sacré bleu!*' The blood washed from his healthy complexion. 'But why?'

'Quettehou's going to try to bring me down somehow. In fact, the more I think about it the more I'm sure that letter is his doing. He's just waiting for the right moment. But if you own the café, he won't find it easy to take possession. So if he tries to bribe someone to give false evidence that I murdered Monsieur Bosanquet and if I've already sold the café to you for a mere clip-clop, it gets rid of any motive I might have had for murder.'

'Unless the bastard accuses me of being an accomplice, *patronne*. Have you thought of that?'

'But how could you be? You were selling sausages in Bayeux.'

Thomas stuffed tobacco into his pipe while he digested the matter. 'It's not a bad idea, Fleur, but pulling a pistol on the filthy scoundrel in a dark alley might be better.' His moustache wriggled. 'Or I could brain him with a saucepan next time he comes sniffing around the café.'

Fleur grinned. 'Well, it might make him see sense at last. I've explained to him that *you* are the café, that it's your genius with the food, not four walls and a roof that makes the Chat Rouge profitable, but the man's too greedy to think straight.'

'*Tiens*, it's not just the food, *patronne*. I've seen our clients watching you when you go from table to table asking if everything's to their liking. You banter with them and do it so prettily.'

'Oh, I shall still do that, I promise you, but my mind's made up. We'll have the paperwork ship-shape this afternoon before opening time. Promise me you'll agree.'

'It makes sense,' he said, striking a flint to the tobacco, 'for now, that is. *Alors*, we'll work out an arrangement. As far as I'm concerned, you're still the owner.'

'Thank you, Thomas.' Fleur watched the smoke rise cheerily from the barrel of the pipe.

'Why don't you ask Monsieur de Villaret to deal with Quettehou?'

Fleur shook her head. The thought had crossed her mind but Quettehou was far too much in Marat's company for her liking. She was sure Raoul was quite capable of guarding his back, but Marat was the virtual ruler of Paris now. Besides she wasn't on speaking terms with a certain revolutionary.

'About time you brought the Jacobin up to scratch, *patronne*, if you'll forgive me saying so. You can't go wrong with old-fashioned respectability. Keep him out of the boudoir till he goes down on his knees and swears to make an honest woman of you.'

'Oh yes, and they are going to put Marie Antoinette back in Versailles,' she flared. 'Believe me, Thomas, he merely amuses himself. The Jacobin with his little captive mouse. Why are you looking at me like that?'

'He arranged everything for Emilie's care, did you know that? Asked me to send over some supper for her.'

'To be sure the deputy's a hero. I've written to the Pope to canonise him. Oh, it's no use, Thomas, don't you see? He'll be risking everything by giving me his protection. If Marat finds out I'm a Montbulliou . . . Thomas?'

He had taken her forearms. 'Listen, *patronne*, there's today and there's tomorrow. I know what I'd choose.'

She both dreaded and longed for Raoul's knock on the front door and when it came, she listened behind her boudoir door. He did not disappoint her.

'Not see me! We'll see about that.' She heard his feet on the stairs. The door handle turned.

'Please leave!' she shouted, hands rolled into fists. 'I–I don't want to see you again, you over-bearing republican b-bully.'

There was an outraged oath from beyond the door and some deliberation on the landing. It seemed that M. Beugneux had become involved.

'Are you standing next to the door?' Raoul asked a few moments later.

'No, I am not that desperate. Go away!'

She did not expect the blast of fire as the lock exploded. Her boudoir door shuddered at a further blow and Raoul stepped in across the debris with a smile, his high-crowned hat tilted at a rakish angle and a huge box beneath his arm. He halted, not taking his eyes off her. Had she been more certain of her emotions, Fleur would have basked in his unconcealed appreciation.

'It was easier to borrow a pistol rather than a ladder,' he drawled.

The calculating scoundrel! 'Th-that was extremely theatrical and absurd of you, citizen,' she exclaimed, swiftly recovered from her astonishment. 'Look at my door! You will be receiving a bill for the repairs. I'll send it to the Palais de Justice marked "Urgent". But you can leave NOW!'

Having made such an entrance, her fearless Jacobin nonchalantly tossed the pistol onto the bed, and then spoilt the effect by shifting an uneasy glance from the bed cushions to the armchair before his gaze returned to her and he let out his breath in relief.

The self-deprecating twist of lips alone almost felled her. She would have been a fool not to appreciate the raven hair, the proud, recently shaven jaw above the crisp snowy stock, the finely tailored coat and breeches. Oh *bon Dieu*! He had clearly taken trouble to please her. The man's eyes were a devilish, sensual mirror of the desire Fleur felt just looking at him. The wonderful, slowly tightening arousal. Masculine revenge was clearly planned, a slow, tantalising siege.

'No pythons?'

Fleur drew a deep breath and tried to stay sane. He had made a brilliant entrance but she was not going to turn to liquid honey. Well, at least she was not going to let him see that she had turned to – Oh, *zut*, of all the men in France, why did she have to pick a Jacobin to fall in love with.

Raoul watched with satisfaction. Fleur's lovely eyes had gone quite dusky. Ah, so the little minx was putting him through his paces, was she? And then she blinked at him so wide-eyed and astonished that he was hard put not to kiss sense into her there and then.

'I'm alone, yes, citizen,' she exclaimed, 'and I think for both our sakes it should stay that way. The front door does open. You won't have to shoot it on the way out!'

Merde! He had been stupid in trying to appeal to the actress in her. And damnably impractical! When they made love later, it would have to be in his bed, not here with a door that no longer did its duty. Her words dawned on him. She was seriously giving him dismissal. He could walk out of her life with a shining conscience, except that he couldn't. Out of all the women he had ever met, Fleur stirred him in every way possible.

For an instant Raoul de Villaret looked utterly contrite. His eyes examined her compassionately. 'I'm sorry, are you truly indisposed?' he began. 'If you would rather stay at home . . .' The kindness almost severed Fleur's resolve.

'Raoul, please, please go. We never should have begun this.'

'I see.' Raoul clenched his jaw.

'I hope you understand. In a different world . . .'

'In a different world!' he echoed disbelieving. 'The duke's daughter and the renegade. This *is* the only world, but if you haven't the courage . . .'

'. . . and you haven't the commitment . . .'

Raoul stared at her, perplexed. Every yearning inch of her was telling him she wanted his arms about her. What was he supposed to say? He glanced down regretfully at the immense cardboard package still beneath his arm, and reached out a hand behind him for the doorhandle before he remembered it wasn't there any more. 'My apologies. I will send someone to repair the door.' It was hard to believe he'd done that. He toed one of the splinters with his boot cap and had the grace to look rueful. 'I hope you find someone who will adore you as you deserve, Fleur-de-Lis. Adieu.'

His wonderful voice was forgiving, gentle and it almost broke Fleur's heart. 'W-wait . . .' she exclaimed as she watched him swing round to leave. 'D-did your friend Gensonné get away?'

'Yes, finally,' he answered, and perhaps it was regret that lent his voice a bitter edge. 'Philosophy is the national malady, citizeness. We're going to inoculate against it one day like smallpox. Armand will need it more than anyone.'

Fleur bit her lip and nodded, supposing that the strands of friendship between the two men had almost been strained to breaking point.

'And Citizeness Lemoine has not recovered, has she?'

'No.'

He barely heard her answer. Her aqua eyes were awash with despair. Damn it, why was she still staring so helplessly at him as though this decision was being forced upon her.

'Perhaps,' he cleared his voice, 'perhaps you should keep this.' Striding to her bed, he dropped the large box in among the cushions. He should go. Instead, he straightened. 'Give me this evening and I won't ask for more.' Had he said that? 'We could talk, just talk.' With spread fingertips, he tapped the box. 'This was for you, by the way, to wear tonight. I wanted you to . . . Well, you might want to keep it . . . Black is superbly erotic but . . . I'll open it. You can see if you . . .' Palms raised, he gestured as if the words he needed, but couldn't say, might become airborne of their own volition. Then he stooped to pull the string undone and, setting back the lid, forced her to listen to the tantalising rustle of tissue and taffeta.

Subjected to such exquisite torture, Fleur kept out of touching distance, but she watched – how could she not? – as his artist's hands arranged the shot-silk evening jacket, spreading the bodice across the coverlet. Then, with a stolen glance at her tormented face, he shook out the skirt. Instead of brandishing it like an arrogant toreador, he let the shining fabric run through his fingers with reverence as though a saint had worn it. Long, silken bands of lustrous black redeemed by glistening green. It was costly and unquestionably seductive.

'I won't be bought, Raoul.'

His head jerked round at that. 'How can I buy you?' Each wrenched-out syllable reproached her. 'I who am prepared to die for liberty.'

Gathering the beautiful fabric between his palms, he came towards her and draped the skirt sensuously over her shoulder as though it were a Grecian stole. 'Keep it.' And keep me, his golden-brown eyes warned her. For an unshielded instant, she glimpsed the ambition in his soul at war with an emotion far more powerful.

'It's beautiful.'

'You're beautiful.'

And the universe tilted. She foresaw the loneliness rusting the years ahead, with herself a hollow husk of a human aching for what might have been.

'Your terms,' his light, splendid voice was saying, while his expression, vibrant, alive and yearning, mesmerised her. 'Come with me tonight, *ma mie*. We'll have a hundred chaperones. You may chain my wrists behind my back, blind me, gag me. I'll be as innocent as Adam before the Fall, as celibate as Saint Cecilia, as silent as –'

Her fingers touched his lips. Laughter flowered between them.

'You're being ridiculous,' she told him gently, trailing a finger across his mouth.

'I know.' He tilted his head at the splintered door, and then looked down at her with his heart in his eyes. 'Oh, my dearest Fleur, I just want you to be happy.' He framed her face within his hands, not touching but so close she could feel the warmth from his skin.

If she would not give in, Raoul decided, he would kiss her into surrender but outwardly he maintained a descant eloquence. *I won't kiss you*, he told her with his gaze. *I'll worship your shadow, not even dare to look at you. But it is not what I want. The stoppering of desire for savouring later; that is what you will prefer, believe me.*

A clock in M. Beugneux's room chimed.

'I'll wait for you downstairs.'

With trembling fingers, Fleur gathered up the skirt. The fabric gleamed like peacock feathers beneath her fingers, so seductive, so beguiling, and the girl in her surrendered.

The salon door opened as she reached the lowest stair but it was M. Beugneux who came out. '*Ravissante!*' the old man exclaimed, blowing a kiss from his fingertips.

Raoul, propping a shoulder against the doorframe, could only nod. Yes, she was ravishing and he wanted her as he wanted nothing else on earth. It was tempting to forget the Comédie and steal her back to his apartment. He stared his fill, from the mischievous brown curls framing her face, down over the neat breasts highly thrust, the slender waist and gently flaring hips, to her feet in black moroccan. He must buy her some heeled green shoes to match her skirt.

'Madame,' he murmured, reverting for once to ancien gallantry, and came forward to assist her down the last stair.

'Monsieur de Villaret.' The lady's voice was cool still but her eyes were bright. He could tell she felt beautiful in the gown. He imagined himself already poised in the consummation of the evening game between them, with her thighs sliding like damp silk against his skin. A fantasy yet; they both recognised it must take a few hours to topple her pride before he seduced her with a slow finesse that would have her pleading to be satiated.

He planned to follow the Comédie-Française with supper. All evening she drew men's looks as the beauteous Helen must have done when she shopped for trinkets in the evening market at Troy, and Raoul, like Paris, feasted on more than food.

The conversation was finely balanced not to give offence: a discussion of the play, the tenderness of the viands, the quality of the Bordeaux, the music, the decor, the bombes glacées; but all the while their glances met, at first like the rasp of foils, parrying and thrusting, then offering and withholding; fingers stroked the stems and rims of glass, lips parted and closed.

Imagination primed his body. He had already choreographed the slow unlacing, how one by one each petal layer of her petticoats would loosen and slither down the black silk stockings. He would stand behind her, slide his palm down her satin skin, down – yes – over her mound of Venus.

Oh, God help him. It was an effort to keep his hands from touching her as he helped her into the fiacre afterwards; he had no intention of making love to her in this rattle of a carriage, but . . . Oh, Fleur . . . Her perfume filled his senses now as she arranged her skirts beside him.

'I thought you might like me to come back to your *chambre*.' He liked the breathy way she said it, the modesty gauzing her desire.

'Whatever pleases you, Fleur.' The economy of his answer was a lie. The decision had already been taken. Not to possess her tonight would be like ordering the slow spin of the world to stop turning. 'But please understand the consequences of such an invitation, my darling. You know I desire to lie with you again more than life itself.'

'More than the Revolution?'

His jaw momentarily tightened but he managed to reply soothingly. 'Shall we say that the two are quite compatible.'

'Until –' The lamplight they were passing showed him her anxious profile framed by the window. *Merde*, why could women not enjoy the moment?

The restless shift of taffeta hinted at unhappy decisions still to be made. 'France needs you, Raoul. That's what this is all about. I don't want to stand in your way and if . . .' Raoul wondered where her female logic was galloping. 'If Quettehou denounces me . . . If that ever happens, Raoul, you will have to abandon me, swear you did not know my origins.'

'Oh.' He smiled in the darkness, his heart stirred by her unselfishness. 'Quettehou is just an annoying flea of a fellow. I will protect you against him, I promise.' To his delighted amazement she burrowed into his shoulder. He tightened his arm comfortingly about her. 'Fleur, Fleur?' He tilted her face up. The flicker of street lamps showed the glimmer of teardrops beneath her eyes.

'When you did not come back from Caen,

Raoul,' she whispered, 'I felt so alone. It wasn't the same, the world, without you. I didn't want to go on.'

'But you would have done, *ma mie*,' he replied huskily. 'People do.' Inside he was struggling to stay calm.

'This is so difficult. I'm not sure how to tell you. Raoul, I am . . . in love with you and . . . and because I love you, I must let you go.'

'Fleur, *Fleur*.' Kissing her, he let his passion be her answer, for his answer was beyond more speech.

Could men deceive with kisses? Oh, Fleur hoped not. She so desperately hoped not, for this wonderful man was kissing her as though it was their last moment on earth. When he gave her chance to draw breath, she laughed breathily, and wrapped her arms more snugly about his neck.

It is the truth that there are few moments of utter euphoria for any living creature. For Raoul, the shining instances had been David's consent to accept him, the taking of the Bastille and the glory of being elected a deputy of the Convention. But Fleur's sweet revelation surpassed all else.

Fortune had taken a hostage; now he could no longer work for the Revolution single-mindedly.

'I realise that France must come first,' the aristocrat he adored was saying.

And for the first time in his life Raoul was really afraid for the future.

21

My dear Fleur,
This news may come as a shock to you but the matter is
something I have been deliberating on for some time. My
uncle, who was abbé at Vicques, has taken refuge in
London and assures me that I should be welcome. Much
as it pains me to do so, I have decided to proceed to
England within the week. As I have written to Papa, I do
not believe that one can at present live for very long happy
and tranquil in France. For the Convention not to stand by
those most deserving of men, to eject them unprotected to
be at the mercy of enragés like Marat. Oh, my dear friend,
words fail me. I can no longer tolerate a country where
stupidity and ignorance have usurped reason and virtue . . .
O my native land, your trials are breaking my heart . . .
  Marie-Anne

FROM THE CORRESPONDENCE OF FRANÇOISE-ANTOINETTE DE
MONTBULLIOU, 1793

'Bad news?'

Barricaded behind a small stack of leather-bound tomes, Raoul looked up from the writing desk where the Jacobin constitution of France still resembled more crossings-out than finished copy. The morning breeze from the open windows of Hérault's cottage mischievously blew over a page of Montesquieu's *Esprit des Lois* as though it wanted to read ahead. Fleur watched him reach out for the penknife and idly draw it beneath his thumbnail. 'You've read that letter several times,' he prompted.

She recognised the tiny telltale mannerisms, the wry tug of his mouth that betrayed a twinge of guilt at keeping her to himself these last two weeks. While they had feasted on love, Emilie had slid out of life.

With a sigh, she folded the letter from Caen.

'Is your friend in need of you, Fleur?'

'No, Raoul.' He did not need to know that her dearest Marie-Anne was about to become an emigrée, deliberately thumbing her nose at the Republic and sentencing herself as a traitor. 'It's from a girl I knew at school. She would have made a wondrous deputy. She's descended from the dramatist Pierre Corneille.'

'Would you like me to insert it in the constitution?' he teased. 'All those with a dramatist in their family tree have a prior right to stand for election. Why are you glaring at me, *ma mie*?' She was getting to know when the banter hid a deeper interest. He didn't believe her. His eyes flicked to the letter and then back to her face and his smile was quicksilver. 'And now I suppose this frustrated lady is expecting her third child?' Infuriating man!

'No. Indeed, she has turned down all her beaux.' Then Fleur added to satisfy him, 'But she is quite miffed with you and your friends for depriving France of the continued services of the Girondin government.'

'Let me see.'

'No, I had better not distract you any more.' She brushed the edge of Marie-Anne's letter teasingly across his outstretched palm before sliding it swiftly through the slit in her skirt seam into her petticoat pocket. Marie-Anne had artlessly mentioned which Girondin deputies had fled to Caen. Raoul probably knew already. She bestowed a kiss on his dark hair and danced out of his grasp, shaking her skirts at him skittishly.

Outside, she stood still, the laughter no longer in her eyes. These last two weeks had been the happiest of her life. The dream of a cottage – a well-fitted out cottage! – in the woods with an adoring prince. But it was a childhood game of house. While she gardened and portrayed the housewife, her play husband, busy at his desk, had no intention of putting a ring on her finger.

With sadness in her heart, she drew in the beauty of this moment with all her senses: the heavy scent of wallflowers, the summer buzz of busy insects, the tangle of colours – gold-centred daisies, pink valerian, pansies in mourning, and blue forget-me-nots reflecting the sky like little looking glasses.

The rustle of sleeve betrayed she was not alone. Raoul stood watching her from the doorway, one arm gracefully raised against the jamb. A frond of flowering rose peered at him on face level and he broke it off, twirling its stem, his mind, no doubt, still planing and joining 'equality' to 'right to work' while 'votes for females' lay in wooden shavings about his chair.

'What is wrong?'

How could she collate the feelings scattered in her mind and set them before him? She wanted children who would know their father; a lawful husband, not a dead one; a front door that would not be broken open by soldiers; beds safe from bayonet thrusts and . . . bread she did not have to queue for.

It was impossible to tell this man who cared for France that the world his Revolution had created was for her a terrifying anarchy, a paper dream.

'Fleur?'

The actress bestowed a smile upon him across her bare shoulder, and flouncing to the dappled shade, she scooped up her straw hat and skimmed it to the ground. Then, settling into the cushions of the low-slung hammock, she stretched languorously, her fingers idly playing across the hempen strings.

'The constitution of France,' she declared, 'decrees that all men of goodly proportion under thirty years of age should make love at least once a day.' With a woman's gaze, she luxuriously appraised the gorgeous mesh of dark hair and finely tanned skin laid bare by his unfastened shirt, and moved down provocatively past the sleek line of his waist to his breeches.

'Passed,' he murmured and strode across to stand by the hammock. His face wore the dazed expression of a man intent on fulfilling the clause by every dot and tail.

'The constitution also decrees that such citizens should cook the dinner tonight.'

'Not passed.' The shocked, inverted hammock spat her face down onto the grass and Raoul sprawled across her, pressing her wrists against the cool green blades. His hand slid up her calf and caressed the warm flesh where her stocking ended. 'The declaration of the needs of man,' he whispered, 'requests that all beautiful girls over sixteen surrender to the nearest gentleman this instant.' His kiss between her shoulderblades added a semicolon. It was then a boot nudged his ribs.

'Ha, and I thought you occupied with honing the constitution.' Hérault's amused tone drifted inconveniently downwards.

'Oh, *that constitution*!' exclaimed Fleur, released to wriggle out on her hands and knees.

'Blasphemy!' Hérault's cane took a swipe at her derrière. 'I would not have lent you Le Nid had I realised it would be used for such scurrilous goings-on.' He ran an exploratory finger across the support ropes of his hammock as if looking for unreasonable fraying.

Raoul rolled onto his back and sat up but Fleur was already on her feet, smoothing her grass-stained apron.

'It was most magnanimous of you, Hérault,' she conceded, perturbed that some compelling purpose must have brought him in person to disturb their Eden. Hérault gave her a reproachful stare that implied she could have been sharing her favours more democratically and disappeared back into the modest salon.

'Why is he here?' she whispered.

Raoul clawed back his unkempt hair. 'Maybe the federalist danger. We'll find out.'

She drifted into the cottage after him.

Hérault had already divested himself of his coat and was casting an eye over the desk. 'You've been busier than I expected.'

'Lord, Hérault, there are limits to frivolity.' Raoul's roguish grin had Fleur blushing. 'I've also been teaching my girl here the rudiments of sketching. Whoever taught her before –' He recognised his error. 'Let's just say we've covered a lot of ground,' he added.

'Taught her before?' Hérault sauntered over to stand in front of Fleur like a general suspecting a thief in the ranks. 'The daughter of a lady's maid taking art lessons.'

'I've had other admirers.' Her tone was tart and she sat down pointedly on the chaise longue so the gentlemen might sit also, but Hérault, it seemed, had no intention of divulging his purpose in her presence. She was not to be allowed to play Madame Roland to this particular conversation.

'Make us some coffee, *mignonne*.' The ex-nobleman still gave orders.

Standing behind Hérault's broad shoulders, Raoul lifted a hand to his forehead to mask his amusement. For an instant, the paid-up member of the Société Fraternelle looked fit to give the former *advocat-général* a kick on his aristocratic shin, but Hérault had lent them his cottage.

'Of course, excuse me.' Fleur disappeared to the kitchen before she said something that might give her a fast escort to La Force, and instead took her displeasure out by loudly slamming Hérault's kettle onto the wood oven. Then she tiptoed back to eavesdrop.

'*Sacré bleu!*' Hérault viewed the tangle of greenery through the open window with disgust. 'I'll need to get the gardener in again. It looks like Paris out there. Out of bloody control.'

'Fleur's made a start.' Raoul drew the chair out from behind the desk and sat down. 'I'm surprised to see you. I thought you weren't planning to come here until next week.'

Hérault swung round. 'Let's say I had to get away. Every time I set foot in the street, there is some hairy, stinking lackey of Marat's thrusting a petition at me, calling for arrests or waving some cursed placard, asking me why I haven't introduced this or that. There was a crowd of slatternly Amazons this morning bawling for bread. I'm wearing out, Raoul. And there's no enthusiasm about the new constitution even if we add in your amendments. Mark my words, the bastards'll probably pass it, shove it in a cupboard and turn the key.'

He unwound his stock and peeled it from his throat. 'We've inherited a right mess, my dear fellow, and it's getting worse by the hour. There's no decent leadership and I'm not going to stick my neck out.'

Raoul made no answer. The dogs that yapped loudest were often at the back.

Hérault sniffed and continued, 'I can't see that making an example of Lyons is going to remedy matters and it's getting closer to home. There's a story going round that the town of Evreux rang every bell in the place to welcome Buzot back and that the Calvados army's already in bed with him. We've word that Caen is planning to hold a military rally, and if Normandy forms an alliance with the federalists in Brittany, we'll have to send a force to meet them. Then it will be reprisals. Your name came up as the Angel of Death for Caen. Saint-Just looked so disappointed.'

'Christ!' Raoul thrust the chair back and paced to the door. 'Not your suggestion, I trust,' he growled across his shoulder.

'Hardly!' Hérault's fingers played along the hem of his stock. 'You won't be able to refuse or –'

'Or I'll be seen as a closet federalist. *Diable!* Who did suggest it, then?'

'Marat.'

'*Merde!*' He could already imagine the carts of prisoners trundling along Rue Saint Pierre and turning into the Rue Monte-à-Regret. 'Do you have any *good* news?' he asked grimly.

'Does it exist? Look, what's also nettling me,

Raoul, is that we had the monthly election for this new Committee of Public Safety and there's only Thuriot and me. Georges Danton didn't get re-elected.'

'What! Who the hell's trying to take over then?'

'Two of Robespierre's unholy trinity – Couthon and Saint-Just. We're losing the edge, Raoul. Georges hasn't the fire in the belly he used to have. He's spending too much time with Louise and his children. I wouldn't admit it to anyone else, my dear fellow, but I'm feeling devilish de trop. God, I'm even beginning to understand how Boissy feels. *Boissy!*'

'Oh, come on, Hérault. You're just feeling jaded. It'll pass.'

'Will it? Remember old Sieyès's pamphlet dividing society into three estates – the nobles, the Church and the rest. Well, I'll give you a fourth one. The printers and hacks. It's "Who shall we sink our fangs into today, brothers?" and it's me they're swimming after like bloodied sharks.'

'It works both ways. Would you have us muzzle them?'

'Yes, the dishonest ones! Damn 'em, after all I've done, the bastards can't forget I was born an aristocrat. Believe me, every time I run into Marat he grins at me like a damn gnome, as if he's got my name on a list.'

Raoul took a deep breath. He hadn't planned on returning yet. These last two weeks with Fleur had been Elysium but he recognised the waters of Lethe lapping round his feet. He kicked a toe at the doorstep. Was it just half an hour ago that life had seemed so blissful?

'I've been away too long.'

'*Diable, mon brave*, you deserve your pleasures.' Hérault came to stand behind him. 'There's something else, Raoul.'

'Oh yes,' he turned. 'I can guess.' But he was wrong.

'You've got to let her go,' Hérault jerked his blond head at the inner door. 'The rumours grow more poisonous by the day. She's not worth the risk.'

Raoul drew an angry breath. 'Quettehou, *hein*? What's the bastard saying now?'

'Everything in the hope that something sticks. Murderess, trollop, hoarder —'

'Ah yes, dispensing soup to the hungry is hoarding.' Scowling, he pushed past Hérault and sat down heavily upon the chaise longue.

'Quettehou's saying she's a former aristocrat not an actress. She is, isn't she?'

'I haven't asked.' Raoul leaned back against the tasselled bolster, brazening it out. 'It's not supposed to matter.'

'But it does.' Unflinching blue eyes, hard as flint, strove to stare him down.

'Christ, Hérault. I never thought to see this day. You have got the wind up!'

'Yes, and I'm not proud of it. Sorry, Raoul, I don't want her here on my premises.' He jabbed the air downwards. 'Amusing as she is, I don't want any connection with her any more, and if you'll

556

take my advice, you'll drop her. She'll bring you down.'

Raoul stubbornly folded his arms. 'And what if I'm not prepared to listen?'

'Oh, but you'll have to.' The voice that had persuaded parliaments and assemblies warmed to its purpose. 'You are about the only one left of us that Marat isn't trying to undermine —'

'Ha!' Raoul slammed a hand down on the leather seat. 'Because the beggar doesn't see me as a threat.'

'No, damn it! Because the bastard admires you. You are still the people's hero.'

'And yet he lets his minion Quettehou out like a loose cannon to fire where he pleases.'

'No, Raoul, it's only Fleur that Quettehou's gunning for.' Hérault was wrong; Quettehou would fire at all who protected her. He already had. 'Georges wants you to stand for the committee. We need a counterbalance to Robespierre. Don't look so disbelieving. If his trio side with the *enragés*, they're going to demand the Girondins' execution. You don't want it, I don't want it . . . The Mountain's not listening to me any more. Do you know what one of the committee said to me yesterday? "Pooh, you wouldn't even begin to understand, you've never known what it is to struggle."'

'Hérault!' Raoul chided. Tired men imagined hurts where none were intended.

'No, you listen to me! Read the writing on the wall, damn you! If Max Robespierre is the new man, he's also a stickler for respectability and you're hanging around this actress's skirts like a dog in heat. The chit's already annoyed him when she did that outrageous satire as La Coquette. He hasn't forgotten. You've had your vacation, Raoul, France needs you.' He slammed a hand down on the desk. 'Oh God! Where's that damned coffee?'

Setting a tray and listening at a door were incompatible, Fleur disgustedly decided, forced to abandon her post for sensible reasons. She had heard enough already to alarm her. The Convention wanted to make Raoul its butcher while they lurked lily-livered in Paris. Well, she hoped he'd refuse. If he didn't, then she would not be sharing either beds or breakfasts in his company.

It wouldn't be just the Calvados ringleaders and the fugitive Girondins who would get scooped up in the Mountain's net, but small-fry intellectuals like Marie-Anne and her friends. In fact, Fleur had not the slightest doubt that the insurrection would be used as an excuse to cleanse out anyone with noble connections. Marie-Anne was astute. No wonder she was packing her bag for England.

Halting behind the door with her tray, Fleur could only wonder that the entire female population of France was not heading across the Channel with alacrity.

Raoul opened the door at the rattle of cups. The relaxed lover had vanished; Paris had him once more within its tentacles.

With an expression smoothed into cosmetic serenity, Fleur hid the urgent desire to bounce

Hérault's porcelain off the nearest wall onto his head. Briskly she set down the coffee cups on the small table and straightened, wondering how long the two would brew the news before they poured it out.

'I'm afraid we're returning to the city tonight, Fleur.' *Quelle surprise!* Raoul's hands, light and placatory upon her shoulders, were no comfort.

'May I ask why?' She did not forget to include Hérault in her arched stare but it was Raoul who answered.

'We cannot stay here forever, *mon coeur*.'

No, of course not. The trouble with leaving Paradise was that Eve would never forget what she had lost, when in fact she should have renegotiated the lease with the Almighty and stayed put!

'It's Paris, not the Arctic Pole,' muttered Raoul across the carriage. Hérault had descended to relieve himself against a hawthorn hedge. 'I wasn't elected to make love to you. It's my duty to go back. Besides, it changes nothing,' he added warily and quirked an uncertain eyebrow at her. Why did women need to shake everything out into the open? Some matters resolved themselves without a three-day debate.

'But our future, Raoul?' Fleur hissed. The darling minx was furious that they had not spent another week together. Now she was hurling all the ammunition she could think of: huffs, scowls and silences. He wished Hérault would get back in. When a woman asked a leading question, a man needed time to garnish the answer.

'Ah, *mon coeur*, so we're not talking about the Convention but *convention*.'

'And if we are?'

He had warned her that jingling matrimonial bells would irritate him. Anyone would think his terms had been reasonable. Fidelity with a capital 'F'! Which was more than Hérault could ever manage, leaping from bed to bed like a blasted alpine billygoat. Why didn't the disobliging fellow come back this instant instead of hobnobbing with the driver?

Fleur frowned. Why couldn't Raoul understand? It was true the Revolution had jettisoned hypocrisy in matters of the heart, but bourgeois virtue and respectability were still the measuring stick of polite society. One only had to look at Manon Roland as an example of conjugal stoicism. Despite the efforts of the adoring Deputy Buzot and her other admirers, Madame's *affaires* had been kept at a platonic level.

She kicked sullenly at her black skirt, wishing she was free to wear what she liked, and received a consoling handclasp. He still hadn't answered her question. She dragged her fingers free. 'If we have children, Raoul, then –'

'Children are out of the question, my darling,' he interrupted. 'My livelihood is too uncertain.'

She darted a cautious gaze out the window before dispatching a bitter retort: 'And I am an aristocrat and it's the hunting season.'

'That has nothing to do with it.' His voice sank to a fierce whisper. 'You must understand, Fleur, that much as I adore you, I will give my life to defend the Revolution. If the Emperor of Austria and his allies win through to Paris, I will take my place on the barricades, and if I'm killed, you won't have to suffer the ignominy of being a regicide's widow. You'll thank me for that mercy, believe me.'

'Not if you are dead, I won't, you simpleton.'

The smile he gave her was weary, as though these arguments had been rehearsed a dozen times in his mind. 'Don't make it difficult.'

'I do not understand.'

'Let me quote the English philosopher, Francis Bacon: "*He that has wife and children has given hostages to fortune; for they are impediments to great enterprises.*"'

Determined to be perverse, Fleur stared at him blankly and wished she might give this Bacon, if he was still alive, an earful. 'As long as I am single,' Raoul continued, 'I can fight and die for the Revolution. But if I have a family, I should be torn between my love for them and my loyalty to the Revolution. Don't make me choose, Fleur.'

'But you've already chosen and I'll have to accept it,' she replied. 'Oh, I'm not surprised. Marat warned me.'

'Marat!'

'Oh yes, sweet-smelling Marat. He says that the likes of him and you always put the Revolution first.'

Raoul turned his face from her, leaning his cheek uncomfortably against the leather seat back. 'It's how causes are won, how history is changed,' he said finally. 'Why do you think Max Robespierre won't marry Elinore Duplay? For the same damn reason.'

'Rubbish, the man's a hypocrite. He gave his blessing to one of his friends just the other day. I saw the wedding party returning. And Georges Danton has just got married again.'

'Pah, to his children's nursemaid. He's only doing it because he needs someone to look after them on a permanent basis.'

'No, he's in love with Louise. Emilie said so.' Mention of poor Emilie chilled the air further.

'Yes, all that may be true,' he replied after a moment's consideration, 'but – oh damn it all, my darling,' he grabbed hold of her reluctant hand, 'please understand – if France can kill its king, it can kill its deputies. Georges can marry young Louise but she's just an ordinary chit. If anyone ever arrests him, they might possibly fling her into prison for a few weeks but I doubt they'd give her a death sentence; but you, my *chat rouge*, are a different matter.' He directed a look that was calculated to disarm her. It failed. Not yet thrown, he carried her fingertips to his lips and added, 'You run your café and I will return to politics and we shall be discreet, *hein*. Times will change. When the war is won and our enemies accept that the Republic is here to stay, I will marry you.'

When the Seine finally runs dry!

'I'm not making an excuse. The law doesn't permit girls under twenty-one to marry unless they have the consent of their guardians. There would be questions and you would need to produce the proper papers.'

'I'm sure I could. There must be a few republican forgers left at liberty,' she added scathingly.

'Fleur! I'm supposed to uphold the laws.'

'Stuff your precious rhetoric, Deputy! I know the real message. If you tire of me as your mistress, I can be swiftly set aside, but if I'm your wife, that's a different game.'

Had they been alone, he might have seduced her to silence but for now he was impatient to end the argument. 'Since divorce is easy now, no, it's not a consideration,' he proclaimed icily, and added in a tone that might have frozen lesser company, 'This is France not England.'

The rattle of the door latch stifled further argument.

Hérault climbed back on board and rapped the roof with his cane. 'Cool in here,' he observed.

'Yes,' said Fleur sweetly. 'Absolutely Arctic.'

Since it was Hérault's coach, Fleur was set down alone in the familiar courtyard of the Rue des Bonnes Soeurs. Raoul sprang down and saw her to her door.

'Let's not pursue this quarrel further,' he whispered, brushing his lips across hers. 'It changes nothing as far as I'm concerned, so expect me tomorrow tonight.'

'Of course, Citizen Deputy,' she answered demurely. 'I'll air the divan and plump the cushions.

Would you like the scarlet slippers with the curly toes or the green ones with the spangles?'

'I'd like the houri with the gauzy pantaloons. I'm sure your dressing-room will oblige.'

'To hear is to obey.' His pat on her derrière speeded her towards her door.

He should have known from the dangerous tone that she was not going to dress Citizen Beugneux up as a vizier and serve up camels' humps in rose-water. The next evening she not only let him into her boudoir but encouraged him to divest himself of his entire clothing before she disappeared behind the screen and reappeared in a tiny spangled blue chemise that barely covered her breasts. Matching silken pantaloons were gathered in at her naked ankles. Enough to make a fellow harden instantly.

'Sit down. On that chair! No, the armchair. Put your hands behind you!'

He stretched his arms behind the satin chair back. It was a low bedroom chair without arms. She moved behind him and he found his wrists suddenly looped together.

'What are you planning?' he asked, fantasising already where this game would lead. If she was going to play Salome, this could be sublime torture, and then when she cut him free, he would be so aroused, so . . . Oh, having an imaginative woman for a mistress had its advantages.

'Now one thing more,' she purred.

He never expected her to emerge from behind the screen wearing the blasted python round her neck like a pagan garland. Nor was he expecting her to swiftly drape Machiavelli around *his* neck.

'Fleur? What the –?' Fear froze his tongue as he felt the coils settle against his flesh.

'Machiavelli, *étrangi ek baba kani*. He will bite you if you move, citizen.'

Raoul swallowed and ground out painfully, 'Rubbish, there's no such language, Fleur. You have just made that up.' As if a grown man couldn't cope with a python! After all, he'd overcome his fear of being closed in. But he wasn't going to beg.

'You think so?' She bent forward and teased a finger down his profile. Her half-covered breasts in their sheaths of tight satin almost made him forget the serpent writhing along the nape of his neck. 'Machiavelli, *attention vite, monsieur magnifico mouso, istafan quilla mobile*! I have just told him you are a giant rat. Move if you dare!'

'Fleur, for God's sake. At least, at least put something across me, woman,' he exclaimed. 'This is indecent.'

She adjusted the python's coils closer to his cheek. 'Yes, it is.'

'What in hell are you ... *Diable!* You're not going to leave me here with this monster?' The silk of her pantalons slid sensually against his thigh as she swung slowly round to face him. It was torture to suffer that caressing evaluation. It honed his desire even more.

'I warn you.' Her lovely mouth puckered in amusement. 'Nothing must move. Nothing. Machiavelli might not behave.'

'Damn you!' His voice rose. The game was over as far as he was concerned. She'd had her fun.

'Hussh, if he gets startled or panicky, Machiavelli will tighten his coils around the nearest object. Sleep well, *mon brave*.' She blew the candle out and slid out the door.

Raoul was left alone; the moonlight slashing through the curtain parting showed him the bed. He hoped the damn snake had noticed and would head for the familiar cushions, but Machiavelli showed no signs of moving premises. Raoul gritted his teeth. Adam should have killed the damn serpent before it taught him to fancy Eve. In fact, Adam had been a blasted fool, being seduced by an apple in the first place. And he, Raoul de Villaret, shouldn't have expected any better of a Montbulliou.

Was this because he wouldn't marry her? Jezebel! He'd turn celibate except there wasn't a monastery left in France. He'd strangle her. Put the python round her damn throat and panic it. Make it more panicked than any python had ever been!

At the foot of the stairs, M. Beugneux observed her costume through his quizzing glass. 'Dressing for dinner, are we?' He received an unhappy look and added, 'You do realise that your lover could be slowly strangled.'

'It's all right, I've left some scissors and a knife on the dressing table. It will take him a few minutes to work it out and he'll need to cut himself free rather carefully but I am sure he will manage.'

'Hmm, I still think you and I should eat our

supper in silence on the landing just to be sure. Otherwise they really will be burying him in the Panthéon. The only revolutionary martyr strangled by a python.'

Raoul stirred as Fleur set aside the curtains and let the early morning peer greyly in. The mirrors showed her slumbering prisoner from all angles as though he were some convoluted, exotic sculpture. The python was curled up contentedly on the bed beside him. In fact, Machiavelli's head was actually resting upon his shoulder with a babe-like trust. Very touching.

She gathered the snoozing python up into her arms. Machiavelli opened his eyes dozily. His tongue flicked out exploratively.

'He kept me warm and never once asked when we're likely to have children,' Raoul murmured reproachfully.

'Well, I am glad of that. I did look in regularly to make sure he hadn't strangled you but you were fast asleep.' She unloaded the creature onto its stand with a sigh.

'Do you serve breakfast in this establishment, madame? Coffee, perhaps? I tried ringing your friend's tail for service earlier. Brioche would be good and raspberry confiture if –' He watched her pick up the knife from the floor. 'Lord, truth is a fancy thing. Is that a weapon for slitting throats or buttering?'

It was spoken evenly but retribution was due. She watched him warily as he rose to his feet – like a fine Grecian statue come to life – flexing his stiff arms and stretching. Pygmalion might have understood her trepidation. 'So how much did you hear, Fleur?'

Her lips parted in confusion and then she understood. The clever, exasperating devil! So he had known all along that she had eavesdropped at Le Nid. Well, at least the matter would not fester any longer.

'Enough. I gather I'm to be jettisoned like ballast. It seems whenever Captain Hérault gives the order, it's, "Aye, aye, captain. Three huzzahs for the jolly Revolution!"' She checked to see if he was listening, but the unfeeling man was casting round for his clothes. 'If I have been unfair, Raoul, well, I am sorry. But at least you will remember the final act if nothing else.' Why did he have to look so divinely wonderful even if he was doing nothing more than hunting for his underdrawers? But she would not let the familiar moistening between her thighs weaken her resolve. Her chin lifted defiantly. 'You've thieved my honour. I'm questioning yours.' Fencing with rapiers, one was supposed to watch the opponent's eyes. Raoul's told her nothing. He matter-of-factly tugged on his shirt and shook the sleeves into obedience so he could button his cuffs.

'It seems to me,' and his voice was disgustingly unruffled, 'that what we are dealing with is a drama written for two, and all I'm hearing is a monologue.' He looked up to see her reaction. 'Now I am going to the Convention and whether I come back is up to you. I intend to survive all that life can hurl at me, including pythons and vengeful mistresses. If you want to keep me company, it'll be on my terms not yours, citizeness.' Then he pulled her face to his and kissed her astonished lips. 'Now, you adorable hussy, get me some breakfast.'

But Fleur, loving him, had her mind less on food and more on honesty. 'I thought you wouldn't understand.'

'Then you misjudged me,' he said simply and waited. With a gasp of relief interbred with deep contrition, she stepped through the breach. His arms closed about her. 'Idiot,' he said affectionately.

'I was angry, but I thought it was the best way to let you go.'

'What, me departing with an exit line of hate?' he laughed. 'Lord, my darling girl, you made a whip for your own back by the look of you.' His thumb scuffed the soft crescent of care beneath her lower lashes. 'I think you must have had a worse night than I did. Wherever did you curl up? In Machiavelli's box?' Fleur did not answer; happiness did not have a price.

He kissed her forehead and then the tip of her nose. As though she feared she held a dream, she slid her palms along and up his sleeves, reassured to feel the warm substantial meld of flesh and muscle through the fine weave.

'I'm frightened, Raoul. When I came to Paris, I didn't care. Nothing could have been worse than another winter in the forest at Grimbosq. I really believed I was . . . well, impervious to anything that life could do to me, but now . . .' Her eyes shone with love.

It was, he hoped with all his heart, because Fleur had invested at last in life, and not just in life but in him, and in seeing her predicament, he recognised his own.

'I know, my love,' he whispered comfortingly. 'But the final curtain hasn't come down.'

Not yet.

22

*The Constitution is ready to be presented for
ratification by the Sovereign People. Does it outlaw
speculation? Non! Has it decreed death for hoarders?
Non! . . . Eh bien, we must inform you that you still
have not secured happiness for the people.*

JACQUES ROUX, AN *ENRAGÉ*, SPEECH TO THE CONVENTION, 1793

Machiavelli was difficult to pack that morning, despite the fact that he was sluggish and digesting. As fast as Fleur and Columbine curled his tail end into the blanketed hamper, his head or some other coil overflowed, but eventually the two of them wound him in, loaded the hamper onto a barrow and trundled it towards the Marais.

The python had settled in at the Chat Rouge on a permanent basis. He kept the night guard company and by day he slumbered happily in a box in Thomas's kitchen or rehearsed with Columbine for the evening's performance.

In short he was proving a great attraction, Fleur noted later that morning as she balanced the last two weeks' ledger at her table behind the screen. The café was doing remarkably well. Regular supplies were still a problem but she had kept in touch with the farmer who had helped them with the hot-air balloon and met others through him at Les Halles market, and now the Chat Rouge had its own small grain source, sufficient to let their customers have bread with their soup, much to their competitors' disgust.

'This place is more packed than the Vatican square when a blessing's due.' Raoul tugged down the high collar of Fleur's gown and kissed her nape, and she whirled delighted into his arms.

'You're supposed to be at the Convention.'

'And so I have been, but I want you to accompany me to a military parade later this afternoon.'

He could have sent a message but it was well known in female circles that men at certain times or circumstances displayed behaviour that defied understanding. 'I'm not alone. I've brought some of my colleagues, including David. Talked them into abandoning their usual jaunt. Can you manage? I did not realise you had such a crowd here at –'

'David! Is that wise?'

'Maybe not, but you'll have to come out and greet them.'

Accommodating their distinguished customers required surrendering her own table and some deft manoeuvring but they managed, and Thomas beamed like a glow-worm with two tails when the famous master complimented him on the artistic presentation of the repast.

'Well, that was a success,' Raoul exclaimed later, after Fleur and Thomas had farewelled six replete Jacobins including not only David but Saint-André, the naval expert on the Committee of Public Safety. 'It's very useful having a —' he eyed her warily, 'a friend who runs such a brilliant restaurant.'

If one had to be skating on the thin ice of politics, Fleur supposed it was.

'I've received two more threatening letters, Raoul,' she told him, drawing on her gloves. 'They were pushed under the door – one yesterday and then another this morning. Whoever it was didn't bother while I was away from the city.'

'Show me them tonight. It's time we put an end to this.' He arranged her light shawl round her shoulders and ushered her out the door. 'Pah, not a coach in sight when we need it. Let's pick up a fiacre in the Rue Saint-Antoine.' He drew her arm through his and they strolled along in comfortable silence. The parasol twirled on her shoulder, its fringe brushing the froth of net and satin that served for a hat.

'You know it might not be Quettehou behind

the threats,' he said eventually. 'The other restaurant owners along the Boulevard de Temple must be feeling the pinch.'

'Whoever it is, I wish I might deal with them. I hate such insidious warfare and I have this sense of being watched all the time.'

Raoul didn't tell her that he had an arrangement with Robinet to mind her whenever she ventured into the streets. This afternoon, however, he was playing her guardian angel. He strengthened his grasp on his swordstick and hummed.

'Raoul! Something's happening. *Bon Dieu!*'

She was right. The passers-by seemed to be consolidating. The click-clack of saboted feet behind them was suddenly ominous.

'Don't look concerned. Keep walking.'

'Hoarder!' shouted someone.

'Oh, my.'

'Whore! Filthy harlot!'

The mob of some twenty or so grabbed the words and milled them out in a hideous chant: 'Harlot, hoarder! Harlot, hoarder!'

One workman held a lid, which he beat with a stick. The ugly clanging added venom.

'Keep walking. See that next double gate on the right? If it opens, cross the courtyard! See if you can go through to the next street. If not, hide! Leave me to deal with this. Obey me, darling!' He squeezed her hand.

'Hoarder-hoarder-hoarder!'

Raoul shoved Fleur through the instant they reached the studded wooden gate and spun round to face the mob, his swordstick in his hands, ready for unsheathing.

'Citizens, what's all this?'

'Ohh, the gentleman's stirring for a fight, is he?' The cudgel tapped its owner's palm, mimicking Raoul's weapon. 'We'll give him one, *mes braves*.'

'You want to die in someone else's dispute, do you, citizens?' Raoul asked pleasantly. Were they all hired or had some of them tagged along to relish the spectacle? 'Go back to whoever's stirred you up with lies and tell them the mud won't stick.'

'How come that whore gets bread when our children go hungry?' bawled a young woman with an infant on her hip.

'I've seen *you* breakfast for free outside her restaurant,' retorted Raoul, and scanned their faces. 'Come on, who's behind this?'

'No one's behind this, citizen.' A *sans-culotte* with a face like creased leather was cradling his cudgel. 'An' why are you protecting the silly cow?'

'Your fancy piece, is she?' That was the young woman again.

The wheels of Raoul's mind whirred and halted. The fellow with the cudgel had been the rogue who had seized Fleur from the coach that day he and Hérault had come to her rescue.

'And this young blade is some bloody former noble. I say we hang the pair of 'em. Got a nice set of lamps all ready for you, young sir.'

'And there's a tumbril waiting for you, citizen. Murder a deputy and you'll soon see the straw in the basket.'

'Ho, a deputy, are you?' *Yes, I remember you from last time*, the fellow's eyes told him. 'Well, I'll murder any number of deputies if I lay hands on 'em, starting with the plump old Girondins. Now stand back, lad, and let us have her.'

Had Fleur escaped by now? Raoul was not sure how much more time he could buy her.

'Is this your gratitude, good people?' he exclaimed. 'I was there when the Bastille fell, were you? Were *you*?' He fixed his stare on the agent provocateur. 'I was at the Tennis Court the day they took the oath, were *you*? I signed the warrant for King Louis's death, did *you*? What have *you* done for France?'

'What's *she* done?' A dirty forefinger stabbed the air. 'Lain on her back for *you*?'

There were too many of them. The crowd had swollen with onlookers and some other burlier troublemakers. A pair of national guard lurked at the rear, clearly too cowardly to make their presence felt. He could try demanding they arrest the troublemaker or he could –

He was in the gate in an instant and slammed it shut, reluctantly jamming his swordstick across the old bar supports. What choice was there?

'Raoul.'

Diable, the darling fool. She'd waited.

'Come on!' Seizing her hand, they dashed across the courtyard, into the inner yard and up the stairs, as their pursuers beat at the gate. 'They'll be over it in seconds,' he rasped out. 'Upstairs. We might find ourselves some weapons.' They raced through the succession of shabby, stately, empty bedrooms, locking door after door behind them where there was a key, while down below the mob split up, hounding through the lower floor.

The mansion followed the inevitable quadrangle layout of a former era. If they stayed in here, they'd be trapped by their pursuers coming from both directions. And they found nothing useful for defence. Raoul eyed the curtain rods as they ran through. He could use one as a staff but how long would that last against a cudgel?

'Out of practice,' Fleur gasped, grimacing at the pain in her side as they reached the south-western corner, and turned into the next wing. A discarded dust sheet lay in one corner. Across the broken mirror, a hand had daubed, '*Liberté ou Mort.*'

Cursing, Fleur tried to unlatch the nearest window.

'Let me.' Raoul flung it up. 'Too high to jump and there's no postern.'

'The tree. We can get across to the perimeter wall.'

Hardly, thought Raoul. The oak was at least four feet out of reach. A pity. One branch almost reached above the wall and another sturdy limb was a hand's grasp from the building. She surely didn't mean edge along the stone cornice? She did.

Fleur scrambled out, silently cursing her skirt and, clasping his arm for support, straddled the window recess and set her left sole gingerly on the masonry, testing it.

'It'll hold. Pull the curtain to. Quickly! Come

on.' She pressed her cheek sideways, squashing her breasts against the wall, one hand still clasping the window embrasure. Her free fingertips explored and found a minuscule ledge of masonry, sufficient to keep her balanced.

'*Merde.*' He'd rather look down, keep his heels against the masonry, but then he hadn't a bustle.

'No! Face to the wall! Believe me!'

Oh, indeed! And my mother was an acrobat, he thought, but he obeyed. Clinging to the window frame, he stepped across and joined her precariously on the sill-like ledge. There was scarce eight inches width beneath his soles. *Bon Dieu*, he hoped it would bear them both.

Beneath his spread-eagled fingers, the stone was hostile. Taller, he needed to find different purchase. If he flung himself outwards and jumped, could he lead the human dogs away from Fleur? The charge of sabots echoed beyond the wall. He felt the vibration of the joists and the pain of the panelled doors splintering beneath the blows.

Fleur had miraculously reached the tree. Some fragment of his mind, the piece that wasn't scared or nerving him to inch along, suggested she'd done this before.

'You grab the branch and swing yourself along like an ape,' she whispered and launched herself off the ledge. One leather heel detached and fell. She toed off the other.

The noise brought the human pack. The leader stuck his head out the window and saw them. In seconds a pike was thrust towards Raoul's ribs and whammed towards his hand. He moved then. Oh God, he moved fast. A second window was thrust up. They were trying to get him from both sides now.

Fleur swung her body forwards as swiftly as she could with the twigs snagging her clothing. Her stupid hat caught and she painfully wrenched herself free. Arms aching with her body weight, every inch was a league and the courtyard swam beneath her stockinged feet. If she fell and broke her neck, it would save a lot of trouble.

'Raoul?' The leaves blinded her. She grasped the trunk with relief and felt the branch groan with a second weight. Then she remembered his damaged hand. *Bon Dieu*. This was her folly.

Gasping, she struggled round the trunk and crawled along the other branch, praying that their pursuers had no firearms between them. Her petticoat caught and it took precious time to rip it free. Beyond the thick foliage, the shouts and snarls were terrifying. Where was Raoul?

'Go on, love!' He had reached the trunk of the tree. 'Go on!'

'I'm above the wall.' Now was the hardest part. She lowered herself and saw for the first time the furious faces jamming the lower windows like squashed fruit. The gleam of a gun barrel caught the sun. 'Dear Jesu.' Fumbling out with her feet, she tried to reach the top of the wall that flanked the Rue Pavée. It was at least a foot away and not beneath her.

'Fling yourself.' She did and missed the top,

hanging like a sprawled cat by her fingertips on the inner side. Her arms were screaming silently. A shot smashed into the wall next to her elbow and she screamed.

Raoul kept his nerve. He moved steadily along the second branch, swung and landed forwards, almost tumbling head over heels. But he was lithe enough to recover his balance and with a leg either side of the wall he swiftly leant down and grabbed her by the waist, hauling her up until she was leaning over it.

A second shot drove into her skirt, just missing her thigh.

'Come on!' Raoul's arm across her, they fell together. Heavier, he hit the street cobbles first. Her bustle, the foolish wadge of stiffened canvas, saved her back.

'What's going on?' bellowed a portly housewife, pausing over her broom. A *sans-culotte*, pushing an empty barrow, gaped.

'Eloping, citizen, can't you tell?' muttered Raoul, clenching his fist in readiness against the pocket of his spoilt coat. 'And a right dog's breakfast I made of it.' Behind the wall, the mob bayed, seeking an exit.

'Come on, *mon cher*.' Garbed like a ragged slop-seller, Fleur tugged Raoul's arm and flashed a tremulous smile at the *sans-culotte*. She didn't expect to be hauled in the wrong direction. 'But we're doubling back,' she gasped and then recognised where he was making for. La Force Prison!

'Stop 'em!' bawled someone from down the

sidestreet as they hurtled past the narrow crossroads to hammer on the great arched doors of the men's prison.

The turnkey was slow in coming. 'Let us in!' shouted Raoul, smiting his fist against the gate. 'Hurry, man, in the name of France, *hurry*!' They tumbled into the forecourt and the iron door clanged closed behind them.

'Well,' smirked the fat turnkey. 'Ain't you a turn, Deputy. I've never had any *salaud* so desperate to come in 'ere before.'

The smell of the print works was unmistakable: ink, paper and, mingling in the midst, the odour of beer from the corner tavern. Raoul, plumed and epauletted, with Robinet lurking behind his back like an eager cutthroat, turned into the alleyway from the Rue Saint-Michel. An aproned apprentice, his cheeks not yet settled for kissing girls, was heaving up a basket of agitated pigeons from a delivery cart. Scowling, he jabbed his black signpost of a finger towards a door off the cluttered flagstone passageway. Circumventing two barrows stacked with pamphlets ready to be wheeled out for distribution, Raoul entered the *enragé*'s astoundingly neat realm.

Illuminated by a western aspect, the spacious workroom contained a better press than most Parisian printers could boast of. This was a campaign headquarters par excellence. On trestle tables flanking the wall were the regiments that enforced their general's power: metal rows of alphabet in different fonts, Roman, italicised, serifed and shoeless; the headline characters; and horizontals, ems and dashes, commas, colons, semi and full. And exclusive and happy on their own, a row of shiny exclamation marks – much in demand for silent yelling at a hungry populace. Composing sticks of rumours, riots, victories and victims stood freshly primed. Paper sheets waited to lose their innocence; those ravished with blistering words were queuing for a far more modest guillotine.

The lord of these reams was out the back, busy in the tiny walled yard, but he must have heard footsteps different to his assistant's shuffling gait. The cheerful whistling of 'Au près de ma blonde' ceased in midcadence; there was an irate flutter of wings as though a pigeon was being shoved back into its coop, and Quettehou, bareheaded and with fresh birdshit streaking one boot cap, came in to do new business. If he was astonished to see Raoul still alive, he hid his disappointment.

'Deputy.' A grin a shark might envy welcomed them. 'Want a job done?'

'You get rid of people?' The accusation hit and was batted off court.

'Words,' Quettehou countered, blithely slapping the copy with the back of his hand. 'The new arsenal. Cheaper, too. What sort of campaign do you want and how long? A week in the public pillory brings 'em to their knees better than the cat-o'-nine-tails.'

'Let's not waste each other's time.' With a violence that had been suppressed too long, Raoul grabbed Quettehou by his stock and thrust him back against the press. 'I've got your lackey under lock and key. He's confessed everything.'

'I . . . don't . . . know . . . what you're talking . . . about.'

'Your beloved Aunt Fleur.' Raoul corkscrewed the neckcloth tighter.

'So? Is she . . . OW!'

'Alive? Oh yes. Another of your feckless schemes that failed to fire. Let's rehearse a little catechism, shall we? It goes like this: "I promise not to harm Fleur Bosanquet in any way." *Say it!*' He was being unreasonable considering he was half strangling the man, but when Robinet loomed up brandishing a knife, Quettehou squeaked out a promise and Raoul eased his grip. 'And to be doubly sure, if you try any further tricks, I'll produce your minion in front of Fouquier-Tinville and send you to the guillotine faster than you can say Marie Antoinette.' He dragged Quettehou up from the press, loosed his hold and drove his gloved fist up into the weaselly jaw. The printer went crashing into a poster of a semiclad Liberty in a Phrygian bonnet and subsided in a surprised heap.

Another fellow might have run at his gut. Raoul braced himself but Quettehou stayed put, shifting his gangly limbs lever-like to better order. 'I've been doing some investigating myself, Deputy,' he muttered, dabbing at his swelling, bloody lip. He watched Robinet's fidgety boot cap with respect and added, 'Did you know you're protecting an aristocrat? My honest, theatrical aunt. She's the Duc de Montbulliou's youngest brat.'

'Oh yes, and I'm King George of England.' Raoul folded his arms and leaned back languidly against the trestle table, but beside him Robinet tensed like a dog that had heard its name near suppertime. 'You're a trifle off the bullseye, Quettehou.' It was added with a calm he did not feel. 'The girl's the daughter of a lady's maid who worked at Clerville.'

'Is she?' Robinet interrupted gruffly.

Quettehou rose to his feet, smiling. 'Puts you in the dung up to your neck, doesn't it, Deputy, if she isn't? Unfortunately, I can't turn the bitch in for that or the government will snatch what's rightfully mine, but I can denounce her for murder. You're screwing my uncle's murderess, de Villaret.' He flashed a smirk at Robinet. 'I'd be careful of the company you keep, friend. And there's a brother too. The emigré Duc de Montbulliou, as loathsome as his dear Papa. Or is he a servant's brat as well?'

Robinet's profile skewed round to Raoul. 'I thought you said –'

'That he's dead. Yes, he is.' Raoul's mouth tightened, his gaze pinioning the printer. 'Your men attacked him instead of me, Quettehou, or we'd have finished the state funeral and I'd be comfortably interred beneath the Panthéon. Do you make mistakes with everything?' He picked up a pamphlet, glanced at it contemptuously as though expecting a baker's dozen of errors, and then crushed it in his palm.

'Dead, Deputy? Is he?' Quettehou's sneer swung Raoul's world off its axis. 'I wouldn't be sure of that if I were you. Marat reckons you should ask her, before you totally screw yourself.'

Marat! *Merde!*

Smirking, Quettehou hobbled to the outside door and paused, squinting across his shoulder at his ruined shirt. *Listen to Marat, People of France!* ran jaggedly across his backbone. 'No mistakes in that. Started a new fashion, I shouldn't wonder. Maybe you need it on your shirt as well.' Then he looked pointedly at Raoul's breeches. 'Screwing an aristocrat, eh? Is your little manikin down there doing all the thinking for you?'

The room was silent. The ticking of the shelf clock flicked the seconds.

Raoul recovered his control. 'I know where to find you, Quettehou.'

'Of course, you do, Deputy.' The rising star of the Paris Commune slid his gaze over Robinet like a pickpocket's greasy fingers before returning to Raoul. 'Au revoir, citizens, *we* know where to find *you.*'

23

Par son patriotisme,	*Through his patriotism*
Son amour pour les lois,	*And, to the laws, his loyalty.*
Par un constant curisme,	*Through his great charisma*
Sa haire pour des rois,	*And fine hatred of royalty,*
Marat sut, de la France	*He, more than any in France,*
Préparer le bonheur,	*With all the luck that Life imparts,*
Et par sa bienveillance	*And with his constant vigilance,*
Se gagner notre coeur.	*Marat has simply won our hearts.*

SONG OF THE FRENCH REVOLUTION

'He was threatening you.' Robinet stated the obvious.

'Yes.' Raoul whammed his new swordstick at the churchyard railings and let it clonk against each one.

Marat knew. *Marat!* Perhaps that was the secret of the itchy creature's power. Moral blackmail. Worming through every shadow from the past, opening the cupboards and the hidden drawers. What else could it be? The man's skin made all his associates flinch. His tongue flicked venom.

And now Raoul de Villaret was a name in Marat's pocketbook as well. And what was Raoul going to do about it? What could he do about it? End the *affaire* with Fleur? Plead for a mission to President Washington? A pressing matter of cherry trees? Or to the King of Siam? Sell him hot-air balloons for a flight over the jungle? Now there was a thought for a fool.

'I wouldn't underestimate Quettehou, citizen. The Commune reckons he's the latest thing since the guillotine an' I've seen him 'obnobbing with Robespierre.'

'Oh, to be sure. He's as useful as a dishcloth.'

'Well, you didn't wipe the floor with 'im!'

'No, but I'm getting close.'

Fleur discarded her mending next evening in disgust. The black skirt was snagged beyond redemption.

'Now you know why apes wear nothing, love. Anyway, why bother?' Raoul, sitting with his head leaning against her knees, laid a tapestried book-mark in his volume and set it aside. He picked up the pink striped camisole from her mending basket and held it against his chest. 'I'd much rather see this on the outside. Very charming. It's about time you gave up mourning. All of it!' He clambered to his feet and, bundling up her ruined skirt, tossed it into the empty grate behind the firescreen.

'Raoul!'

'Mourning is no longer à la mode.' He met her defiant scowl. 'It could be misconstrued, and in any case it's sheer hypocrisy, you don't mourn anyone.'

He had gone too far but Fleur was determined not to show her ruffled feathers. Yesterday still bruised the air between them. At La Force he had been ebullient, high on victory, but last night they had not made love. Supper had been a quiet meal. To be sure he had shared her bed but not his thoughts; his arms had held her lovingly but he had lain wakeful. The mob attack had worked its poison.

'We must talk about yesterday.'

'Must we? The man who led the crowd is under lock and key. If you could bring down one of those damn pigeons with your catapult, I'm sure we can prove the link to Caen and find the men who attacked Bosanquet and your brother. We could rent a room opposite Quettehou's yard, spend an hour or two there. What's the matter?'

'To find the answers, you have to ask the ques-tions.' With a deep sigh, she clasped her fingers in front of her as she did when she addressed her staff at the restaurant. 'I've been thinking very hard about this, just like you.' He did not argue. 'I don't think we should continue our liaison.'

He turned away, tapping his palms restlessly against the mantelshelf. The intense passion, the sleeplessness, the horror of yesterday had taxed him. He did not like the man in the looking glass. 'What do you intend to do?'

'Survive, Raoul, but it's only a matter of time.' She slid her arms around him, across the stiff brocade of his waistcoat, her fingers creeping along the links of his watch. 'It's my duty as a good citizen to surrender you to France, who so desperately needs your devotion. Be honest, Hérault is right. You cannot fulfil your destiny if you continue to associate with me.'

'You're being foolish.' His hands sternly strove to sever the chain she had set about him. 'I admit I have a great deal on my mind. I need to finalise the amendments to the constitution and finish some other reports and . . .'

'Exactly. I don't want to be, shall we say, a hindrance.' She loved him too much for that.

Intelligent eyes probed her image in the mirror. 'Then we should give ourselves some air, hmm?' he suggested, hurt and calculation mingled with reluctance in his voice. Fleur hid her face against his sleeve and nodded.

Raoul grimaced inwardly. If he could not give this lovely woman a future, have children with her, then the new France was just as flimsy as an *assignat* – paper instead of gold.

'Raoul?' Brown shining curls teased his shoulder and he turned to kiss the real Fleur. Shadows lay beneath her lower lashes. His fault; the frenzied regime she set herself was just an antidote against the future he refused to share. How damnable of him to keep her to himself, to impose his philosophy of living each day as though there were no morning after, to make her his mistress when he was but a lackey of the Revolution.

'I am wearing you out, my darling. I should let you find some other man who will put a ring on your finger.'

Fleur was trying to keep her voice light. 'Yes, perhaps you should.' With a feigned playfulness, she shook his shoulders as she kissed him back and then pulled away with a sigh. 'Living in Paris is like being in Pompeii, waiting for the Mountain to erupt.'

'The Mountain, oh, a clever play on words, and when does the molten lava start tumbling about our shoulders?' The splendid face was hardening now, hiding his self-deception.

'What I'm trying to say, Raoul, is that you're like a Roman gladiator in the Colosseum, wondering who will come at your back.'

'They don't, darling. It's one on one.'

'But fast as you strike down one, there's . . . You can't stand on your own, Raoul, nor can Hérault or Boissy.'

'Oh yes, I can, Fleur. You're wrong. If poor old Armand had not aligned himself with the other Girondins, he would not be an outlaw with a price on his head. I'm a Jacobin and that displeases you, I know, but I am not an *enragé* and I never shall be.' He took her tenderly by the shoulders. 'I love you so much. Oh, *bon Dieu*, do you really want me to marry you? Is it that important?'

'No,' she lied, absolving him. 'Your life isn't yours to give me.' As her left hand reached out to stroke his cheek, he captured it and kissed her palm. 'Oh, Raoul, you look weary. Go now,' she slid her arm through his and walked him to the door. 'I insist, in fact I do not want to see you for an entire week.'

'Cruel goddess! I protest I cannot survive.'

'Of course you can.' She kissed him and pushed him firmly across the threshold. 'Besides, men can only think of one thing at a time. Just cross me out of your pocketbook until Sunday.'

Then she closed the door quietly behind him and leaned back against it, letting out her breath in a slow sigh. Somewhere she had read that if savages believed a shaman had cast a spell of death upon them, they would surely die. Well, she was too civilised to believe such nonsense but she felt Quettehou's hatred like a shadow stealing over her.

The week dragged its feet. Fleur grieved but it was a living man she mourned. She sensibly avoided the Jacobin Club and the Convention gallery and, above all, the man she loved. Instead, busy as clappers in a mill, she worked frantically at the restaurant. There must be something bourgeois hidden in her bloodline for a future playing Raoul's mistress sat uneasily with her morals. Her mama would not have approved, nor Tante Estelle. But she loved him so. Should she be unselfish and let him go? These days she sadly missed poor Emilie's down-to-earth advice and she longed for Marie-Anne's counsel, even though she suspected her dear friend had never tasted the delights of lovemaking and the little death.

Thinking about Marie-Anne on the Friday two days before Bastille Day as she walked through the Palais-Royal, Fleur stopped stock-still. A short, slender young lady in a polka-dot gown and stout-soled shoes was walking ahead of her, not with the brisk step of someone who knew their way but somewhat uncertainly. Perhaps it was the provincial clothes, but from the back she might have been the very likeness of Marie-Anne, even down to the way the white muslin scarf wreathed her shoulders and the high-brimmed hat with a *tricolore* rosette adorned the chestnut hair. The young lady was pausing outside a bookshop as though she longed to enter. It had to be Marie-Anne. Oh, if only it were. But what would she be doing in Paris when she was on her way to London?

The stranger was enticed inside and Fleur, who needed little urging to enter any bookshop, followed her in. The lady's profile as she gazed up at the packed shelves lining the walls resembled a ravenous beggar's beholding a rich man's feast, and when she hooked down a moss-green leather copy of Corneille, Fleur started forward.

'Marie-Anne?'

The stranger jumped like a startled rabbit and dropped the book.

'May I relieve you of that, madame,' clucked a balding gentleman, bobbing up from behind his sales table. '*Le Cid*. You wish to purchase it?' He examined the spine for injuries with a doctor's care.

'So sorry, I–I did not mean . . .' stammered his customer like a young girl, lifting a hand across her face in mortification. Turning away, flushed, she found Fleur blocking her escape. '*Bonjour*,' she said softly, a slight frown puckering her brow, and hastened past. Fleur followed her out. 'That was embarrassing,' Marie-Anne explained with a nervous laugh, but the familiar vigour was back in her voice.

'So it is you,' Fleur exclaimed with great delight, drawing her into the dappled sunlight of the Galeries de Bois. 'My dear, dear friend.' Embracing her was like hugging a chair back but Marie-Anne had never been one for effusive greetings. 'What is this?' she added lightly, trying to keep the suspicion out of her voice. 'Why did you not write that you were coming to Paris? Oh goodness, have you run away or has something else dreadful happened?'

'Yes, indeed, it was a sudden decision. I've come to present a petition for a friend.'

'Oh, please tell me all about it, Marie-Anne. There is so much I want to share with you. Bookshops and cafés – you must come and have a meal at the Chat Rouge – and all the people you've read about in the journals, I can point them out to you.

Just tell me who you want to set eyes on. And we can go to the Convention, and Dr Curtius's Wax-works, not to mention all the theatres. Talma's playing at the moment and then there's –'Why was Marie-Anne looking at her as though she were talking French like a Spanish cow? Had her breath grown sour or was Marie-Anne hiding some guilty secret? Could a handsome roué have taken advantage of her friend? Was she here in Paris to find her careless lover or, God forbid, a backstreet surgeon?

But Marie-Anne's waist was slender still, the bazin swathed tightly back towards her bustle. Contrite at such a thought, Fleur swallowed and added meekly, 'How long are you spending in Paris?'

'I – look, my dearest, not long at all if . . . if . . . Well, with going to England, you understand,' she whispered, making sure no one was close enough to hear her. 'You did receive my letter?'

'Yes,' Fleur added and waited. Clearly the months apart had put a bridle on her friend's tongue.

Marie-Anne sensed her discomfort. 'That was a wonderful bookshop,' she said, turning her face away. 'I wish . . . Do they know you there?'

'Yes. Why, do you want credit?'

'Oh, I should wish to purchase the entire stock, I assure you.'

'We can go back in. I'd like to buy you some-thing. Truly, I can afford it now. Oh, and there is an excellent glove shop further on but . . .' The immi-nent refusal was evident. 'Perhaps,' Fleur amended generously, 'we could just sit and talk. I know petitions take time but for an instant, please. Over an ice perhaps? Or we could go to my house.'

'I should love to see it but . . . I'm sorry, Fleur, I am short of time today. Yes, let's talk, but somewhere quieter. I'm finding . . . so many people . . . it seems so raucous. Caen is so sleepy in comparison. And the heat.'

Oh, foolish of her not to realise the city was playing cruelly on Marie-Anne's nerves. 'I know just the place. And, here, use my parasol.'

Instead of taking her arm, Marie-Anne preferred to let Fleur precede her through the bustling colonnades. Outside, the noise of carts and hooves in the Rue Saint-Honoré made conversation even more arduous. Fleur wove between the barrows with alacrity, taking care to swish her skirts away from the muddy wheels with their clinging debris.

'You have become quite the Parisian,' applauded Marie-Anne, finally catching up with her. 'One can even catch a trace of it in the way you speak. Where are you taking me?'

'To the Eglise Saint-Roch. Temple of Hay Supplies now, I shouldn't wonder.'

'But that's where –'

'Your ancestor, Corneille, is buried, yes. Not far. By the way, where are you staying? I could have given you lodging and you could still –' She let that matter fall. 'Pardon me, Marie-Anne, I am firing questions at you like an enemy.'

'And rightly so. I should have written to you

about my plans but you know me, Fleur, when I finally make up my mind to do something, I must be doing it immediately. In fact, I only arrived in Paris yesterday at noon and then a most agreeable lady at the diligence office directed me to a boarding house, the other side of the Place des Victoires Nationales. It's fine, truly, clean, and there's even a writing table. I would have felt guilty staying with you, especially when I must devote so much time to . . . the petition.'

'Maybe I can help you, Marie-Anne. I do know some very influential people . . .' Mentioning Raoul or Hérault to a Girondin sympathiser like Marie-Anne might not be diplomatic. Could the petition be on behalf of a denounced acquaintance? If so, her politically-minded friend was skating on paper-thin ice.

'Marie-Anne, you mentioned in one letter that one of your beaux had come to Paris. Is there a man at the bottom of this as well? Something you need to resolve before you leave?'

The older girl's clasped hands flexed with telltale anxiety but her expression was wry as though some irony amused her.

'Monsieur Doulcet, you mean? No, not he. But, yes, there is a man. He fills me with a . . . a madness I have never experienced before. Now,' she set a reassuring hand over Fleur's, 'I beg you, question me on that no more.' The ensuing silence as they mounted the steps of the church was awkward rather than companionable.

'Bother, it's locked.' Fleur shook the iron handle

of the church door indignantly. So, it appeared, were the other doors. 'And I wanted to show you Diderot's grave as well,' she fumed as they gave up and sat down in the shade of an old robinia.

'Never mind, dearest. It truly doesn't matter.' Despite setting a sisterly hand over Fleur's, Marie-Anne somehow seemed impatient, hardly in the mood for confidences but making an effort. 'You are looking so much better than when I saw you last and yet . . . Oh, I wish that man would go away.' A resourceful hurdy-gurdy player had stopped the other side of the railings and was grinding out Mozart for them.

'Poor creature. He used to play for the Queen.' Fleur threw him some coins. 'This is Paris for you. As for me, my fortunes go up and down from week to week. It is like being on a carousel; you hang on until the music stops.' And it would soon. 'So . . . yes, tell me, how is dear Madame de Bretteville?'

'My aunt has just had her sixty-ninth birthday and we managed a little party, Madame Levaillant and her family came, and . . . no, you must tell me what you have withheld from me in your letters. Have you met your poet then, all golden hair and large lovelorn eyes?' The tardy attempt to rekindle the camaraderie in so contrived a manner was as useless as lighting green timber – in any case, poetry had never been Fleur's style, that was an old jest – but it was necessary to locate an answer.

Had she met a poet? One of Danton's circle, the poseur and self-proclaimed playwright, Fabre d'Eglantine, came to mind. He had written more placards than he had dialogue. He sang too, mostly his own praises.

'I am acquainted with one such creature but he is considerably self-centred and quite distracted at the moment revolutionising time.'

The Marie-Anne of Caen would have taken that bait but today's friend showed no interest. 'Oh, Fleur, you are too prosaic. You'll never be anyone's muse if you talk so. Surely you must have –'

'Met plenty of gentlemen? Yes, I have actually.' Oh well, wade in boots and all. 'You remember I described to you the deputy who was in Caen when Monsieur Bosanquet died?'

'All officiousness and stony looks like a male Medusa.'

'Did I say that?' Fleur felt the heat rushing into her cheeks. 'Well, I have aroused his interest.'

'And what's this nonpareil's name?'

'Raoul de Villaret.' She picked up a leaf and idly tore it.

'Raoul.' Marie-Anne made it a mocking growl. 'Wait, wasn't he one of the deputies who voted for the King's death! What do you mean, his interest? Heaven forbid!' Her panic subsided as she recognised the gleam of mischief in Fleur's eyes. 'Oh, you have him at a dangle, then?'

'Yes, I did – to put it delicately – succumb to his ardour. For a while.'

Grey eyes regarded her with astonishment. 'Oh, God, how could you lose your heart to a Jacobin? I must despair of you, Fleur. You, of noble blood.'

'But –' Fleur was about to reassure her that the relationship was at an end.

'Those ghastly Mountain deputies – in my opinion, persons as stupid as they are disagreeable – mercilessly hounded the Girondins from office. Men of ideals and high principles, Fleur, who were doing their best to rule a country at war, and yet no thanks, no pity. Oh, I have heard it all.'

'Please, Marie-Anne, let me assure you that my friend, and he is now merely a friend, does not lean to any particular faction. He moves between them.'

'A fence-sitter then. Just as bad!' The older girl lowered her voice. 'I tell you this in the greatest of confidence. Five of the Girondins are almost my aunt's neighbours. They are staying in the old Hôtel de l'Intendance in the Rue des Carmes. I've actually spoken with them. Monsieur Buzot, Madame Roland's particular friend, was very pleasant, and Monsieur Barbaroux exceedingly gallant. Oh, but you should hear what they have to say about their betrayal by the Convention. They are so bitter.'

'As I understand it, Marie-Anne, they were incompetent and refused to resign. The Mountain indicted them because it was the only way to make them move over and let others more capable take over.'

'No, that's not true. You've been listening to too much of this *enragé* nonsense. Empty, vicious hotheads! Listen to me, Fleur, Paris is trying to bully the rest of France. The Convention is weak as water. That abomination, Marat, is using the mob to dictate to the Convention. Didn't he order the mob to surround the Tuilleries?'

'Yes, it's true. I saw it for myself.'

'If the Girondins had managed to muzzle that revolting man, all would be well, but now nothing will please him but their blood drenching the scaffold.'

'My friend believes France is in great jeopardy and that civil war could easily overthrow the Republic.'

'Oh, and putting France in a Jacobin straitjacket will mend matters, I suppose. I tell you this, the Girondins are the only true republicans. The rest are crude rabblerousers with their own agendas.'

'I've met Marat.'

That struck Marie-Anne dumb but she recovered quickly. 'A crude little beggar, I'm told.'

'Well –'

'Oh, save your breath, Fleur. Tender heart, you'd make a speech to save a sewer rat if it squeaked loud enough.' She stood up, shaking the dried leaves off her skirt. 'Now I'm afraid I must get on with my business.' Her gaze was steady. 'I've always trusted you as you have me. Please do not mention our meeting to any of your new acquaintances. I have no desire to be interrogated about our fugitives in Caen.' The challenge in her tone was hurtful but quite deserved.

Fleur gave her promise willingly. 'I did not mean to anger you,' she added tucking her parasol under her arm. 'Please, come and see me when you have finished your business and if I may help in any way, I will.'

'I have your address.' Marie-Anne's smile was tight, her lip quivered. 'Forgive my vehemence just now. I would not have you remember me so. Paris has turned me into a hedgehog, all spines.'

Remembering her own initial fear of Paris and trying to forget the new terrors that stalked the streets, Fleur took her friend's hands, regretful that she could not be allowed to help. 'Be careful then, and always wear this.' She lifted a hand to touch the compulsory cockade. 'Bastille Day soon. There'll be fireworks.'

'Oh yes, I'm sure there will.' Marie-Anne nodded, her eyes glassy. The arms that wrapped Fleur were like a loving sister's sending a younger sibling away. 'Adieu, my dear friend, and forgive me for being so distrait today.'

It was not a surprise for Fleur to arrive home and find a letter from Mme de Bretteville. An enclosure to deliver to Marie-Anne, she supposed. But she read the contents in growing bewilderment. Marie-Anne's aunt had written to let her know that her niece had discreetly secured a passage on a fishing boat at Ouistreham a week ago and she daily expected to hear of her safe arrival at her uncle's in England.

'And what is the g-gossip from Caen?' asked M. Beugneux, coming down from the salon. 'I have not been playing gendarme. It was uppermost on the tray. Is something wrong?'

'It's very mysterious. I think my friend Marie-Anne may be having an *affaire* and yet she always swore she preferred her books to men. You see, according to this letter from her aunt in Caen, my friend has given away all her possessions and escaped to England but I've just met her by chance this morning. In Paris!'

His lower lip jugged forward. 'Evasive?'

'Very. Edgy too. She definitely implied there was a particular gentleman who aroused her passions.'

Yet her friend had always shown scant regard for romantic notions. Indeed, Fleur had no doubt that if the authorities had permitted the Abbaye aux Dames to continue, Marie-Anne would have remained there assisting with the administration. But people were unpredictable. Joined in matrimony with the right gentleman, it was possible her clever friend could become another Madame Roland. Except, where *was* Madame Roland? In fear of arrest! Fleur subsided on the armchair in her salon, kicked off her shoes and then she smiled. If Marie-Anne had lost her heart at last, good luck to her.

Raoul leaned out of his window, his bare forearms pressing into the sill. There was no session of the Convention today, the eve of Bastille Day, and he had shut himself into his studio. The paint was turgid, the colour was wrong, the brush hairs refused all discipline, the canvas surface was flawed; in short, his skill had deserted him. He could go carousing, drown his cares in an alcoholic cloud but –

'*Holà*, citizen! Look what Papa bought me.'

A plum little arm waggled a wooden horse out of the window across the street.

Raoul waved back. 'Excellent, Jean-Bastille, watch yourself, *mon petit*.'

Born almost four years to the day, the little citizen chortled and was suddenly sucked inside by the vigilant arms of his maman.

'Not at the Convention today, citizen?' she called, stooping to send him a dimpled smile. 'Want to come and share dinner with us?'

'Not today, Gabrielle.'

The window closed. Raoul turned his back to the ledge and let out his breath. What the hell was the matter with him? He was missing Fleur, all of him was. It was not the convenient delight of having a regular woman. *Merde*, no. He just felt, yes, *felt*, that without her, part of his life was missing. He wanted – Gabrielle's laugh reached him – children. Life was not just surviving but the passing on of what he believed in, hopes and dreams, to another generation. He poured himself a brandy and then realised that a distant bell was tolling, and then another and another.

He strode back to the window just as Gabrielle put her head out too. The old man sitting on the doorstep down below straightened. Other windows opened and a great pigeon loft of faces looked out at one another.

'Deputy?' Robinet's wife was in the street, calling up to him. The edge of panic was starting.

'I don't know,' he shouted back and hastened

down the stairs at full pelt to join his neighbours on the street.

'Is it the Austrians, do you think?' Someone's hand plucked at his sleeve.

'A royalist rising. We'll be murdered,' shrieked the next-door housewife.

'No, at least –' *Diable!* What was going on? It couldn't be an invasion, surely. 'It's all right, everyone, don't be alarmed,' he shouted, trying to keep this Pandora's box firmly shut. Oh Christ, keep the city calm.

He reached the Place de Grève before he heard the story from one of the Commune officers at the Hôtel de Ville. *Story*, yes, it couldn't possibly be true.

Someone had murdered Marat.

24

I considered it interesting to paint him [Marat] in the original position in which I found him, writing for the happiness of the People.

JACQUES-LOUIS DAVID

'Where's the d-deputy? How many more d-damn stairs and c-corridors? In there, is he? What do you mean I cannot see him now?'

Hearing that stammer next morning, Raoul faltered in his interrogation of the dentist, Citizen Delafonde, Marat's neighbour from the Rue de l'École de Médecine. 'Excuse me,' he muttered and strode to the door of his office at the Palais de Justice. A line of gloomy people, summoned up for questioning, carpeted the stairs; but astonishingly it was M. Beugneux, pink round the gills and more aggrieved than a bucketed trout, who was causing the quarrel with the guards.

'This 'ere powder puff insists on seeing you, Deputy.'

'Come to give yourself up?' Raoul quipped.

'Oh, very droll,' fluffed Fleur's boarder, tugging his lapels straight. 'I require one minute of your time, de Villaret. In p-private.' He looked round at his escort. 'Well go, d-dear boy, I don't need a chaperone.'

'But *he* might,' muttered the guard and waited for official instructions.

'Oh, very well,' Raoul conceded, gesturing him in.

Despite his aggrieved state, Beugneux scowled with distaste at the sweat-marked seat vacated by the dentist before collapsing onto it and fanning himself. By the sweat dribbling down his forehead, it seemed the exertion and stress were genuine, but the faded eyes were sharp. 'M-Marat, Deputy, is it true?'

'Stabbed in his bath, yes. We've arrested the assassin. A woman from Caen. She's been sent to L'Abbaye. The trial's tomorrow. Bastille Day.' Very ironic. 'Are you here to offer condolences?' His jibe was ignored.

'F-Fleur. I need to get her out of Paris.'

Raoul stared at him in total bewilderment. '*Why?*'

'I-I think the woman who m-murd . . .'

It was an effort for Raoul to keep his voice down. 'Charlotte Corday's her name, yes, so?'

'F-Fleur's f-friend from Caen, Marie-Anne, was in Paris yesterday when she was supposed to have left for England. Fleur ran into her by chance at the Palais-Royal.'

'So?'

Beugneux leaned forward. 'Marie-Anne Corday.'

'Christ!' The implications were lethal. The Corday creature's likeness was on every placard. Raoul pushed back his chair, trying to crack his thoughts into order. Marie-Anne might be Charlotte's sister or no relation at all, but it was not worth taking chances. He pulled open his drawer and took out a headed sheet. 'I can give you a pass to take Fleur out of the city.' He swiftly filled it in and signed it. 'There. What else do you need? Money?' Searching his pockets, he drew out all the coin he had. 'Take this. Where is she now?'

'At the café still. I came here the moment I realised.' Beugneux rose and quickly gathered the money up.

'I'm coming with you, Beugneux.' He started to push his chair back but the older man grabbed his wrist.

'No, there isn't time, leave things to me. *Distance yourself*, Deputy.' The message sunk in like a dagger.

'And if Fleur won't leave?'

'No, Deputy, it's over.'

'Wait, Beugneux, are we being hasty?' Oh God, he needed time to think. 'If she runs away, it implies guilt.' *Bon Dieu, was Fleur guilty?* 'Who saw them together – anyone?'

'The man who's taken over Louvet's bookshop.' *You think I am a fool?* raised eyebrows asked.

'But –' Raoul clawed a hand through his hair. If only there wasn't a day's queue of people outside the door.

'Exactly.' The hobbling speech was gone. 'Imagine the worst and keep your head, Deputy. I have no admiration for your politics, but the Convention needs you.'

Raoul let him go and leaned back against the door in anguish. The old man was right but he could not let – The knocked door vibrated impatiently behind his shoulders.

'What did the old *pédé* want?' the guard inquired amicably before he marched the dentist back in to have the cavities in his memory investigated.

'He thought he had seen the Corday woman, but . . .' Raoul stared at the sketch David had made of her. A very ordinary face. 'God help us, I think half of Paris is willing to testify.'

'Who wouldn't, citizen? Marat was the true Apostle of Liberty. The family and I are going to view him tomorrow night to salute his greatness.'

'See him?' Raoul echoed distractedly.

'Yes, citizen, he's to lie in state, all embalmed like, at the Club de Cordeliers. We're going early. There'll be queues back to the Pont Saint-Michel, I shouldn't wonder.'

'I expect they will.' Raoul's voice was grim. *Imagine the worst.* What did the old man mean? His brain was reeling. *The worst?* The worst was that Fleur was guilty. 'Give me a few minutes before you show the next witness in.'

Oh God, first Armand, now Fleur!

Alone, Raoul sat back against his desk, his face buried in his hands. Was Fleur an accessory to Marat's murder? The suspicions that had run like jagged faults beneath Raoul's faith in her began to crack wide open. Had he been deceived, played like a fish, when all along a conspiracy to murder had been brewing right beneath his nose? Oh God, he needed to talk with Fleur. He would shake out the truth. A murdered husband, a royalist brother, the attempt on his life, and now this. Could these be weighed against mere instinct? He wanted to believe in Fleur just as he had wanted to believe in a benevolent king. But Louis had betrayed France. And Fleur was a clever little actress. Had he seen only what he wanted to see? A woman in love.

'Deputy.' The dentist fidgeted for attention. 'I'm offering you a free consultation if we can get this over with.'

'My apologies.' It was a machine named Raoul de Villaret who asked the questions and noted down the answers. He was halfway through the next interrogation when an urgent knocking disturbed him yet again. Had Fleur been arrested? He rose to his feet, hiding his consternation.

The officer held out an order.

'You are summoned to appear before the Committee of Public Safety. Now!'

Random searches of the Chat Rouge by the military were nothing new. Often it was an excuse to scrounge a free meal and flirt with the actresses, but today it was the Commune soldiers hammering at the door.

'We're closed in reverence to Marat,' bellowed Thomas, and then crossed himself as the door was smashed open and half-a-dozen soldiers with bayonets charged in. Behind them, his heels crunching on the shattered wood, was Quettehou.

Fleur, busy behind the serving counter, brazenly hid her fear. 'Oh, not again, Felix Quettehou!' she exclaimed crossly, marching out, hands on her aproned hips. 'This is the second time this week.' She included the soldiers in her scathing stare. 'What are you expecting? Rat pies? Slug paté? Harassment, that's what this is. Just because your uncle left the café to me. Well, I'm going to complain. What's that?' Bosanquet's horrid nephew was holding out two papers.

'Two warrants for your arrest, citizeness.'

'What, for annoying you?'

Soldiers grabbed her arms and her mockery fled.

'*Françoise-Antoinette de Montbulliou* styling yourself Fleur Bosanquet, I hereby arrest you for the murder of Matthieu Bosanquet and as an accessory in the murder of Deputy Marat.'

Had someone denounced Fleur? Raoul paused on the threshold of the committee chamber wondering whether he would walk out again a free man.

He was not daunted by personal danger but he would be damnably angry if they accused him of antirevolutionary activities after all his dedication to the cause of liberty!

The July members – only nine at the moment – were ranged apostle-like around two tables, shoved together beneath overlapping baize cloths. Robespierre's disciples, the crippled Couthon and young Saint-Just; the war deputies, Lindet and Saint-André, the lawyer Prieur de la Marne, Gasparin, Thuriot, the orator Barère and, of course, Hérault. They did not look as though they were about to interrogate him on his mistress's political inclinations. No, Raoul realised with relief, their attention was centred on what Robert Lindet, the deputy newly responsible for food supplies for the army, was saying.

'So is everyone in agreement about this?' Lindet wound up.

The entire room assented. The order was swiftly passed round for all their signatures. At last France seemed to have men at the helm prepared to make decisions.

Saint-Just, in the far corner, was the last to sign. He passed the order back to Lindet and, ignoring Raoul, murmured, 'Next item.'

'Citizens.' Without waiting to be invited, Raoul confidently took the guest seat next to Hérault, his smile deferential and stern in consideration of the recent tragedy.

Saint-Just lifted his perfect face to quell the assertive visitor with a smug look as though to say: *We are the new masters. You've missed the boat.*

Time will tell. Raoul threw back an equally confident stare.

'Ah, our Lazarus,' chortled Saint-André. 'Good to see you, young fellow.'

'Quite, can we continue?' asked Saint-Just coldly and raised his eyebrows at Hérault to begin.

'Well, de Villaret, since you have served the Republic on previous missions to Caen –'

'Never made it last time, did he?' chuckled Prieur. 'Have you heard the news, de Villaret? Our forces have vanquished the Federalist rebels.'

'As I was saying,' persisted Hérault, 'the committee would like you to leave straightaway for Caen to investigate the background of the assassin Corday. We require you to take everyone associated with the woman in for questioning. Deputy Carrier will be joining you in a few days' time to give you some assistance.'

Work with Carrier! A hard-nosed prosecutor from the Auvergne. Not a man he wanted to be associated with, but it was a chance to get out of Paris. For an instant he was tempted. Disassociation by distance. Certainly Beugneux would take care of Fleur if she was implicated, and by the time he came back from Normandy the storm of revenge would have passed. He might weather it easily, emerge whiter than snow, his integrity intact. But, no, how could he possibly leave Paris unless he knew that Fleur was safe? What if Beugneux could smuggle her to Caen? That had possibilities.

Aloud he said: 'I'm perfectly willing to carry out your wishes, gentlemen, as long as the Committee for General Security concurs, but would it not be better to wind up all the questioning here first? Corday is to be tried tomorrow. She asserts she was acting alone but maybe she will change her story by the morning. It would be useful to have all the information before I depart.' Two-thirds of the table were in agreement with him.

'Hang on a minute!' Couthon's wheelchair rattled. 'The silly cow was caught red-handed and she's pleading guilty, so why dillydally? We need to come down on her associates immediately. Sure as the Pope's a Catholic, Buzot and those other Girondin bastards skulking in Caen put her up to this. If we'd arrested them back in June, Marat would be still alive.'

'Certainly, Citizen Couthon,' agreed Raoul, wondering where Armand was hiding. Not in Caen, he prayed.

'Calvados must immediately be made an example to the rest of France if we are to crush the risings in La Vendée and elsewhere,' declared Lindet. 'We can no longer sit on our hands.' Several members glanced at Hérault, whose hands were now clearly visible. 'We have to be more united now than ever before, de Villaret. The Republic will not endure if we let factional disputes, self-interest and procrastination come before love of our country.'

Procrastination! Saint-Just was smirking. *Procrastination!* Had he just been accused of being a Girondin, a Dantonist or of meandering as a free spirit? On his right, Hérault suddenly found a snag in the tablecloth worthy of study.

Couthon's expression warned Raoul that there was no refusal possible. He was being thrown a rope by these new mariners and he could either climb aboard or thrash around until he found a plank. Plank, indeed. Walk it, or be tied to it and shoved through the little window. Climb aboard? He could already hear his knuckles breaking on the iron rungs beneath Saint-Just's boots. They were making him wield the lash of death. 'The butcher of Caen'? What a wondrous name to leave to history! But better him than another. He needed to be there to temper Carrier's bullish approach. Justice, yes, but no innocent people would be martyred to appease Marat's restless ghost. Not by Raoul de Villaret.

'Citizens, on behalf of France, I accept the commission.'

What choice did he have?

Monsieur Mansart looked as edgy as a rabbit in a burrow with a ferret. It was a wonder he was not standing on his tiptoes lest the dank flagstones of the La Force cell contaminate his soles. Clearly the good citizen did not wish to be associated with anyone who had breathed the same air as Charlotte Marie-Anne Corday.

'I cannot stay long.' For emphasis, he pulled out his watch and read its dial by the candleflame. Fleur could not blame him for wanting to return to the sunlit streets. The smell of a sewer was sweeter than the air in this medieval cell. 'I will see about finding you a lawyer but,' he shrugged, 'I can offer little hope.'

'Thank you.' Paris had more lawyers than a dog has fleas. Hérault, for example, but she doubted he would come within a league of her. 'And if you could arrange something better than this.' The luxury of Emilie's cell came to mind.

'Comfort costs money, citizeness, and you no longer have the means to pay.'

'But that's ridiculous.'

'Must we go through this again? I haven't all day.'

'Please.' She tried hard to concentrate as he reiterated: 'Citizen Quettehou is claiming that you were not married to Matthieu Bosanquet when the will was signed.'

'But –'

'Let me finish, mademoiselle. As I said before, I have examined your marriage certificate again and I can only say that if the priest who heard your marriage vows was the same Abbé Gombault as the outlaw who was executed a month later for being a nonjuring priest and a counter-revolutionary, then he had no authority to marry you and consequently your marriage to my client was unlawful. Citizen Quettehou is entitled to all his uncle's inheritance. Ergo, you are now without funds.'

'I made over the restaurant to Thomas and the house to Monsieur Beugneux.'

'Neither was yours to dispense with. And as to the second charge, there are a score of witnesses ready to testify that you were seen talking at length with the self-proclaimed murderess.'

'Yes, I was, but I had no inkling . . . Oh, please stay longer, Citizen Mansart.'

'Pardon me, Mademoiselle de Montbulliou, at the moment I cannot be of any further assistance to you. Turnkey!' He rapped on the door with his stick.

Fleur leaned back miserably against the wall. She had not been sent to the Abbaye Prison to be with Marie-Anne but to the women's section of La Force. Close enough to her restaurant to smell Thomas's cooking, save that the stale vomit of the cell's previous occupant still clung to the walls and congealed between the paving. The cold seeping in at her shoulderblades was nothing to the ice slowly crusting her soul. Physical comfort had been denied her. There was no mattress, no stool, only a bucket and no privacy. A guard stared through the door grille every five minutes. They had taken her garters and stockings, her apron, sash and neckerchief, her cross, anything she might use to somehow end her life, but because it had been raining that morning, she had been wearing her new boots and she had the small blade hidden in her heel.

Closing her eyes, she tried to imagine Raoul's arms about her. Had anyone informed him of her arrest? If he loved her, he would come to her. No, God forbid, it was selfish to even think it. No, he must stay away. Let him hate her. France had need of him for a lifetime, whereas Françoise-Antoinette de Montbulliou probably had one day left – Bastille Day.

Bastille Day. Of course! Now she realised. Marie-Anne had planned to murder Marat on Bastille Day. Poor deluded, courageous Marie-Anne, fervently believing that with Marat dead, Paris would regain its sanity and the Girondins their liberty. Now she understood why her beloved friend had been so dismayed to see her, so at pains not to involve her.

'The Abbé Flammermont to see the prisoner.'

Fleur straightened. Oh, not some hypocritical churchman who put politics first.

'I have lost my faith in the Supreme Being,' she snapped, her back rigid. 'Go away!'

Two soldiers wearing the Commune uniform stepped into the cell followed by a priest round as a cheese and fat as butter. The tallest soldier took care to position himself sufficiently in front of the grille to block any observation and then he winked. It was Raymond without his usual wig. Outside she heard Juanita's voice low and seductive.

Her actors. Fleur could have embraced them all, especially when she realised the abbé had cotton wadges stuffed against his gums to expand his cheeks and a bolster round his middle.

'*Pax vobiscum*,' intoned M. Beugneux, and proceeded to chant a succession of Latin prayers while he swiftly shed not only a soldier's trousers, but a hat and tunic from beneath his habit. His tiny congregation murmured 'Amen' at intervals while a belt and a curly brown wig resembling Fleur's hair materialised from under Raymond's tunic. A full Grosholz mask made of wax – a woman's face – emerged from the front of Albert's breeches. While Fleur drew on the trousers, Raymond quickly unlaced the back of her dress. He arranged her clothing and the other props so ingeniously that it looked as though she was lying huddled on the floor. It was absurd and wonderful. But if they were caught . . .

'*Nihil carborundum est* we cannot take you from the prisonus, Amen,' chanted M. Beugneux softly. '*Tempus fugit* we were counted in *alleluia*. It'll be up to you how you escape *benedicte filia*, and there'll be a pass *Agnus Dei* waiting for you at the Porte Maillot *et spiritu sancte* ask for Uncle Jules. The string is to garrotte if you have to. Amen.'

They left the cell together. The guards were too distracted by Juanita and the basket of Thomas's bonbons to count the soldiers who emerged. Fleur marched second behind Raymond. With a nod, they left her in the corridor above and it was now up to her. For an instant panic flooded through her but the essence of good acting was to keep one's head and bluff it out. But how? Actors knew their set. She had a very poor idea of the prison's layout and only little time before her escape was discovered, and she needed to give Juanita time to leave as well. Briskly, she marched down the corridor in the opposite direction, wondering if there was somewhere she could hide until the inevitable hubbub died down. And then from out a window she glimpsed the postern in the battlement wall that ran close to the Chat Rouge. Usually there was only one soldier manning it since nearly all the traffic was through the main gates. That was her exit.

'Where's your pass, lad?' Damnation! She recognised the kindly soldier who often played billiards at the café. God forbid he recognised her. She didn't want to tie the string round this man's throat; he had a wife and children.

'*Merde!*' Keeping her face down, she fumbled in her pockets, dredging out an oath that would ripen blushes in a brothel. Surely M. Beugneux had supplied a pass?

The guard laughed. 'Can't let you through without a current pass from the governor.'

'Must have fallen out in the *pissoir*,' she grunted and trudged back into the building, shoulders sulkily humped, only to walk straight into no less than Fouquier-Tinville, Citizen Death himself.

'Look where you are going, fellow,' snarled the public prosecutor.

Oh, this was her death knell. Fleur saluted, trying to nudge her hat down lower over her brow, and attempted to hurry on.

'Wait this instant!' Terrified, she halted and swung round, her mouth dry with fear. 'I need someone to take a note to my wife. Are you off duty?'

'Yes, Citizen Prosecutor.'

'Give me your back then.' She obediently leaned her hands on her knees while the prosecutor rested his writing tablet on her back. Did he not notice her shaking? She tried to think of something mundane. Coffee grounds, sewers, the orange slugs of the Grimbosq forest, wild strawberries.

'There, take that to my wife and tell her I have to question a new suspect about Marat's murder. Why are you wobbling so? You find this amusing?'

'Am-am-am about to sneeze, citizen.' It gave her the opportunity to cover her face with her sleeve.

'Here's a coin for your trouble. Go then! What are you waiting for?'

'Pardon, citizen, I need permission from the governor to leave the prison, citizen.'

'Isn't my letter enough?'

'I don't think so, citizen.'

'Oh, devil take it! Bend down again. And I've only one sheet left in my pocketbook. Here you are, that will have to do. Damn it, fellow, are you still dawdling?'

'You haven't given me your address, citizen.'

Outside the postern gate, Fleur nearly gave a huzzah of pure joy. Forcing herself to march calmly, she set off in what she hoped was the right direction, and then at the next corner she started westwards. The journey was a nightmare of encounters and salutes each time she passed a soldier or a gendarme. Once she was stopped and waved Fouquier-Tinville's letter. Challenged about her destination, she exclaimed that Citizeness Fouquier-Tinville was at a modiste's in the Rue Saint-Honoré. By the time she eventually reached the Porte Maillot, her throat was parched. It was tempting to approach the water-seller's stall. No, she must keep her one coin until she was beyond the city walls. Correction, *if*, for below the portal barring her progress was a pole on cross-supports and the officer and four soldiers on duty were scrupulously checking everyone's passes against a list of wanted persons. *Tiens*, if 'Uncle Jules' wanted to get her past this little contingent, he would need a keg of gunpowder, and what on earth would she do if she could not find him?

Uncle Jules turned out to be a pawnbroker's, a shop with a placard demanding '*Egalité pour tous*' hung up above the name Julius Rosenstein. Inside the shop a merchant with shoulder-length black hair emerging from beneath a skullcap ushered Fleur through to the back room where she found a mirror, some hair shears and the clothes she had worn to burgle Raoul's studio.

When she emerged in breeches with a red bonnet covering her mutilated curls, the pawnbroker pointed her across to a wizened old carter smoking a pipe on a bench outside the tavern nearest the inspection barrier.

'Can I have a mouthful of your beer, beloved Grandpapa?'

'Clever child.' M. Beugneux puffed happily at his pipe and pushed the bottle towards her. 'I knew you'd manage.'

'And if I hadn't?'

'We would have tried again.' He took a packet from the pouch of his leather apron. 'Here's money and a pass, courtesy of your influential friend, to take you as far as Caen. You understand it was too dangerous to involve him further. I'm afraid *my* friends would not appreciate the acquaintance. Cheer up, we shall soon have you out of here.'

'It doesn't look very hopeful,' Fleur pointed

out, grimacing at the barrier and wishing with all her soul she had been able to say farewell to Raoul. They might never meet again this side of hell and he had taken a huge risk in signing his name to the pass.

Her rescuer shrugged. 'There's always the right moment. Be at ease.'

'You and Thomas will take care of Blanchette and Machiavelli, please, won't you? And tell my *influential* friend I shall not forget him. Ever.'

'Of course. Thomas will be all right, you know, and so will I. Go on, finish the bottle, child.' With a hot July sun steaming the morning's puddles, she needed no encouragement.

'Everyone has been so brave,' she whispered, remembering to wipe her mouth on the back of her hand. 'How can I ever thank you all?'

'*Ma petite puce*, if I were of a different proclivity and less creaky, I'd be on my knees begging you to make an honest man of this old fool. We all love you, child.' He stared down the street as if watching for someone and then peered up at a small iron balcony where a coverlet was drying. 'No signal yet, but I'd be surprised if there were. Tell me, while we've still time, how did you get out of La Force?' It was perhaps his way of calming her but there were tears of laughter in his eyes by the time she had whispered how she had been abetted by no less than Fouquier-Tinville.

They sat in companionable silence for a few moments as the bells struck three and then her companion tensed. An officer on horseback was galloping down the street with half-a-dozen infantry running behind him. He swung himself from the saddle and briskly gave orders to the sentries. It seemed a new troop was taking over the gate.

'Stay calm!' M. Beugneux warned.

'Why didn't we leave earlier?' She could have bitten back her bitter tone. '*Bon Dieu*, I didn't mean that, dear friend.'

'Do not panic, *ma petite*. The cooper hadn't finished his rounds. He never leaves the city before three. Ah, see, here comes the wonderful Columbine.' Tricked up as a lemonade-seller, the little actress was actually doing business as she progressed down the street. She rattled her cups vivaciously at Fleur and darted a sidelong glance at the barricade. Then, at a nod from M. Beugneux, she shrugged and meandered across to the new sentries. After two sales and a smack on the rump from the off-duty officer, she was back.

'It's not looking good, *patronne*,' she murmured. 'Even a louse couldn't hide from them now. They are not letting anyone out unless they've a pass signed by a member of the Committee of Public Safety. Anyone would think Marie Antoinette was on the loose. What shall we do, monsieur?'

'You keep moving, *ma fille*. We sit it out.'

After ten minutes, two carts, several barrows and a public diligence were queued up and the irate carters and a score of frustrated travellers waving passes were arguing with the new officer in charge.

Juanita had also arrived dressed as a lemonade-seller and was squaring her shoulders at Columbine.

The coverlet airing out of the first-floor window opposite was removed, shaken and folded. 'There's the signal. The cooper's ready but we can't risk it.' For the first time his voice held the muffled tone of defeat. 'Not without the correct signatures. We may have to hide you till tomor –' He broke off. A coach and six with horn blaring was coming along the street at full pelt, flanked by an escort of military outriders. 'Oh Lord, what now – a general?'

'Oh, this is no use.' In despair Fleur tried to rise but the old man grabbed her arm. 'No, I'm endangering you all,' she whispered frantically, trying to wriggle free.

'No, now's the time.' With a precise movement, he tugged out his handkerchief. Immediately the apple barrow drawn in the queue subsided like a thwacked jelly, toppling its load all over the cobbles. Every passer-by and his dog ran to grab and the oncoming coach was forced to brake, its horses dancing impatiently as the driver yelled for the people to clear out of the way.

Columbine whistled. 'Well, just look who's bowled up. The lad himself. Trying to jump the queue too.'

Fleur glimpsed Raoul's stern profile in the carriage window. He was pale and grim as though the hand of Death had beckoned. 'They've sent him,' she whispered, shrinking backwards into M. Beugneux. 'No, no, this is too cruel.' It was Columbine who grabbed her by the lapels before she could bolt, and then everything happened at once.

Damnation! Now two lemonade-sellers had chosen to have a spat in front of his coach. Had Raoul not been plagued with worry for Fleur, he might have enjoyed the frenzy of petticoats and garters. His escorts were taking bets, relishing the uncensored delights of uninhibited female limbs, but, in foul mood, Raoul shouted out the window for the doxies to be removed at once, along with everything else blocking his progress, and then sat back fuming. Robinet had brought him word that Fleur was still at liberty and busy at the café, but there had been a scornfulness lurking like a sour taste behind the reassurance.

Nom d'un chien! Could Fleur have been part of the Girondin conspiracy to murder Marat? Is that what Robinet really thought? And that all this time, Raoul de Villaret had been behaving like a lovesick poltroon? Christ, he needed time to sort out the truth. He would see Esnault, make inquiries – thoroughly this time – yes, and –

'What the devil now?' he ground out as the door was wrenched open. 'Christ!'

The last thing he expected was to have a boy thrust in, a boy who stared at him from the floor with eyes too wild with tragedy.

Fleur!

'Please, Raoul, forgive me –' She was almost grovelling in terror. 'Please, don't send me back to La Force!'

Horrified, caught on the raw, he snarled, 'You've used me.'

'No, I've used no one. Oh, for the love of heaven.' She flung her arms about his boots in suppliance and time rolled backwards. She was a young girl again, pleading for him to save her. Raoul swung his gaze round the coach in desperation and sprang to his feet.

'In there!' The leather seat hinged back like a music stool.

Fleur needed no second bidding. She scrambled in just as the coach jerked forward. Shutting her in, Raoul sat back down and grabbed a journal from the pile beside him. This could be the biggest mistake of his life but he could not bear the thought of –

'Papers!' The door was flung open. A lugubrious face surrounded by straggly fair hair inspected him. 'Would you mind steppin' down for identification! You or one of your men 'ere may be part of the conspiracy that killed poor Marat, may the Supreme Being bless 'im. We've had people claimin' to be deputies, deputies killed and their papers taken by spies sent by the English. Only a month ago, Deputy de Villaret –'

'I *am* Deputy de Villaret.' It was spoken through clenched teeth. Raoul imperiously held out his pass and letter of authority.

The fellow blinked in astonishment and then chuckled. 'Ah, but *is* you the deputy? You could have brained the real fellow and secreted his body.'

'Yes, that is exactly what I did,' retorted Raoul,

trying to remain unconcerned as the *sans-culotte* officer's shrewd eyes slid over the inside of the coach. 'You will find him lying in the gutter of the Rue Saint-Antoine.'

'Nothing new for a deputy, eh?'

'Listen, my good patriot, I am on my way to investigate the assassin Corday's fellow conspirators in Caen as it states right there. If you value your head, let me pass.'

'All right, you stay put, sir. Let's have a good look at this, shall we?' A gold earring flashed as the man painstakingly checked Raoul's appearance with the description on the pass, then he compared Saint-Just's scrawled signature against a sheet of the committee's signatures. '*Eh bien*, seems to be in order. Won't keep you much longer.'

Eyes closed in relief, Raoul leaned back against the leather upholstery with a prayer of thanks for God's mercy to lovers and fools. But they still were not moving. *Diable!* He grabbed the doorframe and leaned out. The same officer was making a double check of each of his escort's passes. The fellow deserved a commendation even if he was a damnable nuisance. The minutes ticked by.

'You aren't carrying much luggage, Deputy,' commented the fellow, returning. He sprang onto the step and hoicked himself up so he could see the entire roof of the carriage. 'Makes our life a lot easier, that does.' Then he stooped and peered underneath.

'I've got Charlotte Corday strapped down there,' exclaimed Raoul, rising to block the doorframe.

He resisted the temptation to plant his boot on the official backside, but his tone grew staccato: 'Can we leave now?'

The man straightened, signalled for the barrier to be lifted, then his insubordinate gaze once more flickered to the seats behind Raoul. Something more was needed.

'How about you come and see me when I get back from Caen,' Raoul suggested, reaching out for the handle. 'Our new committee will hear about your devotion to duty in my report.' He bestowed a smile of approval and tugged the door from the tenacious grasp of officialdom. 'Well done.'

'That's what they all say. Au revoir, citizen. May Marat prosper your mission!'

So they were turning Marat into a saint already. Fleur, stifled, well, almost, squashed and uncomfortable, felt as though she was already coffined for burial. She tried to push the seat up, but with Raoul's weight pressing it down, she had no strength. It was better than La Force but how long could she endure this? He had a substantial escort with him, judging by the hooves thudding the road, and they were going at a cracking pace, with the horn constantly berating every wretched carter and straggling wayfarer.

It was not until they were well beyond the city's outskirts that she heard him pull the shutters down. Then the lid creaked open but only a fraction. Raoul knelt on the floor between the seats. He did not look at all loving and he was having trouble keeping his balance.

'You are going to have to stay in there,' he hissed. 'I've half-a-dozen soldiers with me, all devoted to the cult of Marat.'

'And what about you?' Fleur asked anxiously, her heart in her eyes.

'Me.' The harsh lines of his face softened. 'I am devoted to liberty.' So he wasn't going to surrender her.

'Oh, Raoul.' Desperately in need of his love, she reached out her arms and felt his fold about her. She wanted to snuggle in beneath his coat and weep for the relief of being with him.

Rubbing his chin across her soft hair, Raoul wondered how in hell he was going to keep her safe. He wanted to kiss her, pull her up onto his knees and staunch the glinting tears, but that way lay folly and he was not a fool, not yet.

'Believe me, I didn't know what Marie-Anne was going to do.'

How could she not?

Fleur felt the limbs beneath her hands go rigid. He disentangled himself, easing up onto the opposite seat, his expression tribunal.

'You surely don't think I helped her, Raoul?' His shoulders flexed; an answer that was like an earthquake to her composure.

'Stop the coach!' she said, struggling to extricate herself from the nest of rope that had lain beneath her since the city.

A firm hand held her down. 'Are you mad?' His voice was controlled. 'Give yourself up and we shall both be sharing a tumbril with your dearest Charlotte.'

The cold words thrust in like a rapier. The reality that she had tried to hide from stared at her from unforgiving eyes. They were going to guillotine Marie-Anne. Fleur trembled. Oh, she had fooled herself that some miracle would prove that Charlotte Corday and Marie-Anne were separate beings. Marat, the coarse, beloved, stinking mouthpiece of the people, had been stabbed by gentle Marie-Anne.

'You can claim I stayed hidden until just now or, better, yes, we can wait until we reach an inn and I can make a run for it. You can let them shoot me down.' She waited, her breath snared, for his verdict.

His hand released her. 'No, I can't.'

Now she saw that his pistol lay beside him on the seat within swift reach. His gaze intercepted hers and held it.

'Later,' he said disarmingly and she had no understanding of his meaning.

His watch dial, manoeuvred into the horizontal stretch of light, slid back within his pocket. 'We'll be reaching another pass control in half an hour.' Reaching into the satchel that lay upon the seat, he drew out a small travel cushion and passed it to her. It was followed by a book. 'This should secure you some air without being obtrusive.'

'Thank you,' she whispered gratefully and rearranged her harsh bedding quietly, fearing the noise of the rope across the chassis, and wishing now she had endured her thirst. It was he who lowered the seat gently down upon the literary wedge like a tender undertaker.

And the hours passed, a nightmare of bruising and hooves, her protector's shift of boots and checking of watch, a blessing and an annoyance. *Ciel!* They should be making this journey as a married couple and not as fugitives.

Across from her, Raoul had reached the decision that if Fleur could survive so far, then she might safely make the rest of the journey. But there were the necessities to be seen to if the lady was to evade detection. Inspired, he crouched again and eased up his own seat, then with great triumph extricated a chamber-pot. The base was crudely daubed with a likeness of Marie Antoinette but Raoul laid it back in its storage place with a grin, certain that given a few minutes of privacy, Fleur's royalist principles would definitely not endure. As for his own, he thought grimly, God help him.

25

Not one among you shall be spared, men, women, children, and the first victims will be your Deputies.

JEAN-PAUL MARAT, L'AMI DU PEUPLE

With constant changes of horses and very little sleep save for a few hours at the inn in Lisieux, Raoul's escort were bow-legged, sharp-tempered and exhausted by the time they prompted a noisy welcome from the dogs of the Place Saint-Sauveur. To safeguard Fleur, the deputy had manipulated the journey so that they would rumble into Caen at dusk, and as his weary soldiers tumbled from their saddles in the Place Fonette, the bells of the Abbaye aux Hommes across the way were booming ten. Raoul, who had scarce disembarked from the coach during the entire journey, stepped stiffly down and took a deep breath of the western wind. The evening air was fragrant with the soft smell of haymaking from the *prairies* beyond the city. His outriders had already ridden ahead to commandeer beds for the escort at the barracks in the old Trinité girls' school, but as he had arranged with Fleur, he made the excuse that he needed to offload his papers at the Palais de Justice, and meantime hustled his disgruntled entourage into the closest inn and set payment on the counter. By the time he returned to the square, his stowaway, who knew the weft and warp of these streets and alleys better than him, had vanished into the darkness.

By morning he had decided his private agenda: to discover the treacherous fisherman who had agreed to smuggle Marie-Anne Corday across the Channel and arrange for him to carry Fleur. As for his public activities: wearing the formidable expression of a representative of the Committee of Public Safety, he held an informative breakfast with the embarrassed President of the Department of Calvados before marching down from the barracks with a detachment of heavy-footed soldiers in his wake to terrify Caen. His intention was to make a search of all the houses from where the river butted the Church of Saint-Pierre down to the Porte Millet, and particularly around the Rue Saint-Jean.

The morning was hazy and breathless. Smoke from the town's chimneys writhed lazily, the welcome odour competing with the stink of the river mud as Raoul and his company crossed the bridge and disturbed the market.

The town gendarmes met him, all salutes, with an obsequiousness calculated to disguise their bile at this taste of authority from central government. Raoul dutifully rattled his officialdom and let them escort him to the hub of their search, but behind his haughty plumes he was worrying whether his brave, resourceful Fleur was safe.

Two dwellings, No 148, the house of the assassin's aunt, Mme de Bretteville, and the former intendant's house in the nearby Rue des Carmes, where the fugitive Girondins had been staying, had already been sealed up by the local authorities with guards on all the entrances. He hoped Fleur had managed to find refuge at her old teacher's house near the place Sainte-Sauveur at the other end of the city. As for the Girondins, the poor wretches must be shaking in their buckled shoes now that one of their worshippers had martyred Marat. If they were hiding out in someone's cellar, he hoped they kept their heads down.

While his soldiers walloped the doors and forced their way in to inspect each trembling family, the local patriots thought it prudent to demonstrate their loyalty. Over a hundred were parading down the Rue Saint-Jean carrying a bust of Marat like a holy icon as Raoul made his own examination of Marie-Anne's house. He had perused some of the papers that had already been confiscated and it was clear that Marie-Anne and Charlotte Corday were definitely the same woman. Dear God, he hoped Fleur was safely off the streets. She had said she would find him but . . . he had so little time. Once Carrier arrived . . .

He climbed a winding stone staircase and progressed painstakingly through the house. Christ, where was the aunt, Mme de Bretteville, hiding? With family? The girl's brothers were emigrés but Charlotte's father and hunchbacked sister had been brought in for questioning from Argenton, a town to the south, and the farm where they lived had been thoroughly toothcombed. Raoul doubted the old lady could have gone that far. In fact, he doubted that she had left the city. The neighbour at the back, Major Lacouture, who had pleaded for the Abbè Gombault's life, was an obvious suspect.

'Nothing, eh, citizen?' Wearing his cockade and scarlet cap, the carpenter Lunel who occupied the ground floor looked the perfect patriot. Sawdust speckled his front and a planed curl clung to a shirtsleeve. He straightened from filling a bucket at the pump. 'Bad business. Who'd have guessed? She gave my little boy some crayons before she left.'

'These things happen, unfortunately,' replied Raoul with deceptive amiability, eyeing the open door that led to the workshop. 'If you're innocent, then you've nothing to worry about.'

'I've already answered a score of questions,' muttered Lunel. From beyond the low arch that led into the courtyard, the crowd glimpsed movement and began chanting. 'See, it's not just my reputation what bothers me, it's m' livelihood. Listen to 'em.

They were threatening to torch the place yesterday morning. Do us a favour, Deputy, and double the guard, eh?'

Raoul nodded and, without the courtesy of asking, stuck his head through the door into the joinery. Several rooms led off.

Mme Lunel, a thumb-sucking child on her hip, was hard on his heels. 'You're welcome to look, but military's been through a half-dozen times already.'

'Of course. Don't let me keep you from your work. I'll see myself through.'

Lunel shrugged and retreated but there was something beyond words that made Raoul suspicious. The workroom was cluttered. He checked behind the propped joists and planks for a cellar door that might have been missed. The kitchen lay off the workroom but between the two was an alcove curtaining-off Lunel's bed. The latter was a stout old Norman creation, the cupboard type, with hinged wooden doors that might be fastened for privacy. A box of books lay beside the wooden bed-steps.

'Deputy?' One of his officers stuck his head through the doorway. 'You still want us to be looking for pigeon coops as well?'

'Didn't I say so?' Raoul answered sternly, dismissing him. He lifted out a copy of Rousseau's *La Nouvelle Héloïse* but it was the Molière that caught his eyes. His finger stroked across the name of Marie-Anne Charlotte Corday and then he quietly drew the alcove curtain, closing off the workroom, and tried the bed doors. A tasselled nightcap and sweaty nightshirt wreathed one pillow and a discarded chemise half nested beneath the other.

'Madame de Bretteville,' he said softly, leaning forward, speaking at the curtain which inexplicably shortened the width of the bed frame. 'You are old and I doubt you knew a thing about your niece's intentions. Speak with me and I shall let you go free.' Was it imagination or did he hear the old woman's breathing? 'Madame de Bretteville, I know you are there.' The slight rustle of petticoat had betrayed her even before something cold and cylindrical pressed shakily against his forehead.

'Don't think that I haven't her courage. Jacobin!' Save for her crouching with a rosary clutched in one hand and a cocked pistol in the other, the old lady could have passed muster in a salon: the mourning gown with the same stitching as Fleur's, the silver hair tightly restricted at the nape, the black lappets draping iron-rod shoulders; but behind the spectacles, her eyes were round with terror. Oh God, he didn't need his brains blown out by a frightened seventy-year-old.

'Kill me,' he warned in a fierce whisper, easing back slowly, 'and my men will haul you to the tribunal and guillotine you with your neighbours watching or –' he lowered his voice further, 'we can make a bargain.'

The shaking hand lifted the muzzle to her temple. 'This is quicker.'

'Deputy!' It was the persistent officer again. Oh, *bon Dieu*, don't let them blunder in here now!

With a finger on his lips, Raoul pushed the

panel quickly back up. '*Moment!*' he bawled. 'Have you searched the church yet! Saint-Jean's over the street?' Then he lowered his voice. 'Please, madame,' he whispered, his cheek against the wood, 'your life for a name, the name of the fisherman who was to take your niece to England.'

'So you can guillotine him, you bastards.'

'No, it's for the woman I love. Fleur, madame. She's here in hiding. I need to get her out of France. This fisherman, for Marie-Anne's sake, madame, if you know his name, *help me!*' He gestured for compassion, suppressing the urge to drag the wretched soul out and violently shake the name from her. His answer was a despairing sob. Had she no sense of urgency?

'*Please, madame.*' The pistol dropped to half-mast.

'But I don't know his name, monsieur. I can't think. Oh . . . try the white cottage near the gypsies' summer camping ground. Yes, try there.'

'At Ouistreham, madame?' Not her fault but it was hard to staunch his irritation.

'I think . . . yes . . . the river mouth.'

'Thank you, madame. As far as *I'm* concerned, you have your life. But this isn't over yet. I'd keep your pistol cocked.'

Lunel waited in the yard with a face that could sour milk, his gaze flicking almost imperceptibly to a cudgel beneath the centre bench.

With an indifferent expression Raoul resettled his beaver hat. 'Be glad I found nothing,' he tossed back over an epaulette, and watched the life flood back into the carpenter's cheeks. 'I've just one further question. Do *you* know anyone who keeps pigeons?'

He spent the next hour interrogating some of the local Carabots, known Girondin sympathisers, who were being held in the castle keep, and then shared luncheon over boned calves' feet in cider and *comme il faut* tripe with officials of the department in the governor's lodge within the bailey. It was while they were enjoying their coffee that a soldier brought him a message.

'Something interesting?' asked the treasurer.

'Possibly.' Raoul shrugged, dabbed his lips dry with his napkin and tossed it onto the table. 'A lead, perhaps. Excuse me.' On the steps to the bailey, he stroked his thumb and finger to the bridge of his nose, wondering if he'd enjoyed too much Muscadet, for there was the boy who was not a boy waiting in the bailey – Fleur, blatantly sauntering up and down right under the garrison's very nose, and with a feather infuriatingly stuck beneath her cockade and a Tree of Liberty badge on her jacket revers. She picked up a stone and skimmed it idly as though bored by the wait. She was damn well supposed to be outside the walls, not tempting fate like a promiscuous doxy. Resisting drawing his features into a thundery expression, he strode down to meet her. Wisely, she didn't snatch off her cap to him but at least tugged a forelock.

'Are you mad, coming here?'

'Absolutely,' grinned Fleur, thumbs in her belt. 'The view's worth it.' Her eyes shone with such engaging delight that his heart missed a beat. 'Don't look so stuffy. You are becoming dreadfully prosaic, you know.'

'Thank God one of us is,' he glowered, trying to keep the love from his voice; even with a streak of dirt on her right cheek she looked adorable. Turning his back to the barracks, he folded his arms. 'How the hell did you get past the sentries?'

'I told them you liked boys,' she smirked and nearly got smacked for it. 'No,' she giggled, 'mention a message for the "important deputy from Paris" and they almost scatter rose petals. You look like a cannon about to explode, or is that too much sun?'

'Will you be serious,' he growled, resisting the urge to kiss her to sobriety. 'Look, I've found Madame de Bretteville. She's safe at the moment. No, don't cross yourself! I'll walk you back to the gatehouse.'

'God be praised. I'm sure she's innoc–'

'What's more important,' interrupted Raoul, acknowledging the salutes as two soldiers passed them, 'is that she's given me the directions to the fisherman at Ouistreham.'

For a moment incomprehension narrowed Fleur's eyes. 'I see,' she said slowly as his meaning sank in. 'Are you coming with me?'

'To England. *No!*' His heart ached at the disappointment in her eyes. 'I'm no traitor.'

'Of course,' she murmured, staring at the stony ground and scattering of puddles before she raised her chin stoically. 'A patriot to the bone, hmm?'

'Yes,' he said firmly, 'except for handing over the woman I love.'

'Thank God for that exception,' she replied dryly, swinging her gaze towards the spires of the Abbaye aux Hommes as if she feared her soul would be laid bare if she so much as looked at him. 'So what's to be done?'

'I'll arrange the passage if I can drum up an excuse to meet the fisherman today.' His hands twitched behind his back. 'I daresay it will be in order to loose my hunting dogs further afield. Don't stay around the Place Saint-Sauveur. We'll have to do a search there as well. You've got the pass I gave you, so what about somewhere safe outside the town? Where can I find you if I need to?'

She sucked her cheeks in as though hesitant in trusting him. 'I've been thinking about that. I'm going to the Enchanted Isle.'

'And I'm going to heaven. Would you care to elaborate?'

'It's an island in the Orne,' she explained, jerking her head towards the south-west. 'You take the Falaise road past the hippodrome, but before you reach the rise to the next village, you turn right down the track to the river. There's a quarry. I've hidden there before and I've enough food,' she patted her satchel, 'to last me a couple of days. Besides, my friends the gypsies may be there. They often are at this time of year. Do I make my own way to the estuary?'

'In two days' time? Can you? If not, somehow I'll get you there,' he promised, 'but if you don't hear from me within two days, make your way to the cottage – the *white* cottage, madame said, behind the gypsies' summer camping place at the river mouth.'

'I know it,' she exclaimed confidently. 'I'm sure it's Pierre Birrot's place.' Her smile lightened his soul. 'Was your luncheon inebriating? You look as though you need a lie-down.'

'So do you,' he muttered, 'preferably with my hand making firm contact with your delightful derrière. Don't take any more risks. Are you sure you can get out of the town without trouble?'

'Want to kiss me goodbye? They'll absolutely love it.' With a pout contrived to look masculine – perhaps it was the wider stretch of those desirable lips – she held out a palm.

'I'm not kissing that,' he said to annoy. 'It's far too grubby.'

'Payment, stupid.' She watched him fumble in his breeches pocket with an extremely mischievous look that conveyed a great deal more. He dropped a couple of livres into her hand. 'Do that to me again and I'll –'

'What?'

'Go absolutely crazed.'

Aware they had an audience, Raoul half turned to go, making his expression deliberately surly, then swung round once more, sketching her face into his memory. 'My darling, whatever happens, know that I loved you and will love you beyond time itself.'

But not as much as your principles, Fleur

protested silently and then instantly regretted such accursed thoughts as Raoul discreetly drew off his signet ring and pretended to put his hand in his pocket again as though she had asked for more money. 'I want you to sell this when you reach England.'

'No,' she protested, remembering the last time she had seen her brother, but he slapped it into her hand theatrically. It had been a different ring she wanted, plain and golden. Oh, this would be a hemlock exile. Already, parting from Raoul was like denying life itself. Hunching her shoulders, she kicked sullenly at a stone as though the deputy was berating her. 'How I envy fickle France your constancy.'

Meeting his troubled eyes, she forced a grin and said swiftly, 'No, say nothing back. There's two corporals coming down the path. It's my last role. The patriot widow. France needs you, Raoul, you were lent to me for a little while and for that I shall ever be thankful. Adieu, you are the truest and best of men.' Then with a mocking salute and a whoop, she headed towards the gatehouse at a full run.

Raoul nodded indifferently at the passing soldiers like a distracted official with much on his mind, and then he followed the path across the drawbridge. Mounting the great battlements, he stood overlooking the city and let his tears at last blind him.

Life without Fleur would be unbearable, but it was his duty to return to Paris without her. What had Robespierre written – '*The soul of a republic is virtue – that is, love of one's country, and a high-minded devotion which subverts all private interests.'*

France! France! He longed to see its people literate, industrious, well fed, an example of wise, compassionate government for the entire world. Only by sacrifice could this dream become reality.

As the breeze dried the evidence of his sorrow, he lifted his face to the southern sky, watching the thunderclouds strengthening into a mighty anvil – another gift of violence from the south! Enemies without, enemies within! But he didn't want to haul men and women to the scaffold in the Place Saint-Sauveur – people with loved ones who needed them. He didn't want to rule with terror.

Did soldiers, weary from war, ache the way he did now, yearning to slide their arms around their wives' aproned waists and feel the swell of babies ripening beneath the skirts? Would he ever know the pleasure of swinging his son into the air, telling a story to his sleepy daughter?

No, I must be strong, he told himself. The Revolution is everything. And yet I love Fleur. I love her so much. I want to wake with her in my arms every day of the rest of my life. And here I am, forcing her to make this same sacrifice.

He frowned at the mob of unruly jackdaws circling the spire of Saint-Pierre and felt taunted by their indifference. *It is possible to change the world,* he shouted silently to the uncomprehending sky. And then he shielded his eyes. A buzzard soared above the Conqueror's castle, eyes and talons intent upon a kill. A Roman might have seen it for a portent but Raoul belonged to the Age of Reason. *It is possible to change the world!*

And if it wasn't?

His pocket watch was showing eight o'clock when Raoul galloped back into Caen that evening, having brandished the republican flag, so to speak, to the unsurprised townsfolk of Ouistreham. The mistake had been to suppose that the obligingly disloyal fisherman dwelt beyond the town, and to forget that rivers like coins had two sides to them. Raoul had commandeered a boat and had himself rowed to the other side. No gypsies decorated any of his horizons but he did discover a single creamy dwelling, quite distant from its fellow cottages along the road, with a rowing boat drawn up on the nearby mudflat. The owner, Pierre Birrot, had been as closed as an unthumbed pea pod, but with a well-judged mixture of threats and advance payment, Raoul had secured a promise from him to take Fleur to safety. So it was with great satisfaction that he eventually strolled back into his temporary office in the courthouse only to halt abruptly as he sensed –

'De Villaret,' came Deputy Carrier's voice. 'At last.'

Two days later, hidden Cleopatra-like on the roof of a gypsy caravan in a roll of canvas, Fleur was unable to join in the singing as the Roma left the grassy upper reach of the Orne and journeyed towards the prospect of fish and samphire at their traditional summer camp. It had been so providential that she should find Paco and his troop near the quarry, especially as her particular Caesar had not arrived with a chariot and some spare horses to escort her himself. She had tried to ignore the anxiety tugging at her, hoping that he might turn up to farewell her with a few *ave atque vales* and a warning not to trust the English, but now she was past laughter.

Perhaps it would hurt less if Raoul did not say goodbye. In fact, Fleur had half a mind not to leave France, maybe find somewhere else to hide until things got better and he would welcome her out of the woodwork. England frightened her. She did not want to die like her sister, forgotten, unloved, alone. Maybe Marie-Anne's uncle would help her, yes, she would seek him out and tell him – Oh, Mother of God, what would she tell him? Fleur's tears flowed into the rough cloth beneath her and gathered, wetting her shirt. Noble, infamous Marie-Anne. She was probably dead now, beheaded while the mob spat abuse and Marat lay decomposing on a plinth. And the gypsies said that Deputy Carrier had arrived from Paris, thundering that he and de Villaret would fill the cemeteries with any who had shared Marie-Anne's sentiments. How could Raoul disobey and survive?

Oh, ambitious dreamers, what have you done to us?

At least he had escaped from his bedchamber without the world knowing. With either leg astride the tiled roof before dawn the next day, Raoul tried not to imagine the swift slide and hurtle to an ignominious end but he was damned if he was going to let Carrier's presence tether him in Caen. Today he would farewell Fleur even if it killed him. Last night he had made complaint of feeling ill and this morning had left a note on his door.

Shielding his eyes with his arm, for the newly risen morning was dazzlingly bright like a perfect Easter Sunday, he considered the possibilities. The hurly-burly of roofs, even the white stork's nest on top the summer chimneypot, failed to please. He edged forward uncomfortably, determined that there had to be some way down from this alien angled world, and then he saw the ladder propped against the dormer window.

For the moment, God was on his side.

26

Carrier, tu vivras dans l'histoire,	Carrier, you'll live in the pages of history
Mais comme y doit vivre un brigand,	But forever inscribed as a villain, you'll be.
Ton nom gravé dans la mémoire	Your name is engraved into memory
Y restera souillé de sang.	As dirty with blood.
Monstre, tout composé de vices,	A monster, of all of the vices made,
Homme scélérat et pervers,	A man so evil, corrupt and perverse,
Ton corps appartient aux supplices,	Your living body haunts those you tortured,
Ton âme appartient aux enfers.	But your soul haunts hell.

'TOUT EST LUGUBRE DANS L'HISTOIRE', A SONG OF THE
FRENCH REVOLUTION

Fleur made her way alone across the marsh of rye-grass and samphire, following the furrowed path that would have been too narrow for two. Behind her the bridle-track, bristled by thistles and nettles on either side, skirted the meadows that sprawled down from the straggle of cottages. Across the river mouth, a row of sparsely limbed trees frayed the horizon and only a church turret offered a hint of the small port of Ouistreham. There was little evidence of the flow of the tide. The earlier wind had dropped and the estuary was placid beneath the hazy sky. Her last small journey in France, and it was taking too long; the path was deceptive, making long meanders around claypans, sunbaked and fractured like aged glaze. No human footsteps had crossed these, only a dog's prints showed a venture and a turning back. Fleur wanted to leave no trace of her passing and stoically pressed on, keeping to where the fishermen always trudged, knowing that the whispering rye-grass, golden-tipped with seeds, hid pits and ruts that would slow her more.

Pausing, she shielded her eyes against the bright sunlight, watching for the rowboat that would carry her to the larger vessel, but she was early. Deliberately early to avoid the pain of parting from Raoul, though to leave without seeing him again was wrenching her soul in two. She had left a letter at the gypsy camp – a few poor lines that could never achieve the love she felt. Better to go alone, unkissed, than put his life in jeopardy. God forgive her, she could wish her own brief life over now, dreading the months of true mourning that lay ahead.

Almost as she glimpsed the oarsman, she heard Raoul's voice and whirled round, in delight and dread, to see him urging his horse along the edge of the salt marsh, his sleeve a frantic flash of white as he sought her attention. Discerning the way she had taken from the height of horseback, he dismounted where the path began, shouting to her to wait, and without even tethering his horse, began running towards her. Fleur could have leapt with joy for he was not in uniform but in shirt and riding breeches, then in dismay she saw he carried no satchel or bag, only his jacket. So he was not coming with her. Of course, but at least he was here to –

Some instinct sent an icy shimmer of uncertainty through her. She hesitated, knowing she should hasten to the shoreline first, but longing to feel his loving arms about her and to say the words she could not trust to paper. Raoul had almost reached her when she saw the blue uniforms rise up from the hedgerow hemming the track and the swift flowers of smoke.

Oh, *bon Dieu*! The shots struck the ground well short of her. It was still far to the water, the boat too distant on the estuary. She ran for her life, glad she was not hampered by skirts, praying that the man behind her would fling himself down out of danger, but Raoul was heedless of the gunfire, closing the distance between them easily, the thud of his boots behind her now.

And suddenly her trust fled. She didn't know the answers any more. In panic, she left the path, blundering her way, her breath ragged, struggling to reach the river, but the boatman was holding off, his oars hovering above the water. And then a heavy hand threw her face down on the samphire as a shot ripped past her ear. The air was whooshed from her lungs.

'Christ, Fleur. I'm sorry.' Raoul's words stirred her hair as he hauled himself forward, shielding her. Her body juddered against his as she gasped for air. Sorry? So this was due to him. More shot skimmed terrifyingly past her shoulders. Hoarse voices shouted at her to surrender. *Bon Dieu*, she could only resolve that Raoul must not be killed defending her. The soldiers must not assume him a traitor. The actress in her broke to the surface.

'You mustn't do this!' She squirmed round, struggling, raining blows against him.

'Come on!' He swore, trying to grab her fists.

'It's too late,' she panted, hearing the heavy feet closing in. 'The final curtain.' Drawing in a deep breath, she shrieked loudly, 'You bastard!'

'Run, damn you!' He shoved her up and gave chase, close on her heels. But the boat was still in midchannel as she sprang down onto the mud and stumbled, gasping, into the river.

'Go on!' Raoul growled, halting on the jut of grass.

'I–I can't swim.'

He winced as though she'd slapped him and swung round to face the bluecoats. 'Halt your fire!'

he roared and, drawing a pistol, pointed it at Fleur. 'The final curtain, my darling? Best make it the greatest performance of your life.'

Confused, she faced him with the muddy water swirling round her ankles. Had she been wrong? *Was* he acting? Had he brought the military to arrest her? There was no time to ask, to understand. The sweating soldiers arrived to find her speechless, disturbing the mud like a lonely, purposeless stake. Their astonished expressions flicked from the pistol to the face of its owner and a half-dozen arms rose in salute. Leather heels smacked together.

'Deputy,' they chorused.

His handsome mouth a thin line of cruelty, Raoul gestured her to climb up the bank. Denied help, the process was ungainly. Squelching onto the tussocks, she spat at his sandy boot caps as she passed, and, in punishment, a vicious prod from a soldier's musket butt thwacked her between the shoulderblades.

Two men – civilians – were approaching. The closest – his top hat plumed and cockaded – wore a dark blue uniform shouldered with braid. Marat's unpleasant friend, the deputy from the Auvergne, Carrier.

Incredibly, the second, to her horror, was Quettehou, his face as scarlet as his trousers from exertion.

'Trying to escape, Tante Fleur?'

'From marriage with you, Felix?' she whipped back like a reflex. 'I'd walk on water!'

'Thought you might need some support, de

Villaret.' Although Carrier tossed the remark at his fellow deputy, he was studying Fleur's body with a hangman's interest.

If silences hurt, this one was damnable. *Had* this been planned? Had the man she loved betrayed her? He was either proving a wondrous actor or a superlative bastard and the trouble was Fleur just didn't know which.

'Good morning, Carrier, and Quettehou, all the way from Paris,' Raoul drawled, housing his pistol in his belt and slinging his jacket across his shoulders. 'Did the pigeons fly you in, citizen?' The obscure question had their attention; even Quettehou managed to look surprised.

'I don't know about pigeons, de Villaret,' he replied, mopping his bony brow. 'I'm certainly not the dove of peace, if that's what you're hoping. I'm here with the authority of the Commune and the Committee of Public Safety.' Fleur's flesh crawled at the smug stare he gave her from behind Carrier's shoulder, but it was the latter's face that made her blood run cold. Intensity and anticipation – a boy who had caught a butterfly and was about to rip off its wings.

'Françoise-Antoinette, daughter of the former Duc de Montbulliou,' Carrier began as though it were a litany, 'also known as the Widow Bosanq–'

'And the actress La Coquette,' threw in Quettehou nastily, lowering her from the salon to the gutter.

One of the soldiers whistled beneath his breath and the almost imperceptible crease of Raoul's forehead augmented Fleur's fear. A bayonet stroked lewdly down the back of her breeches and she flinched and twisted round to give the lout a scathing glare, while beyond his shoulder, she searched the horizon for the boat. Oars resting, Birrot was innocently fiddling with a net out in the channel, and watching events on shore with detached curiosity. Only a fool would intervene.

Did these uniformed beasts surrounding her torment their victims first? Fleur's jaw tensed. She darted another glance at her erstwhile lover. Would he be able to stand by and let these dogs devour her like a leftover from a rich man's table? Or did the note in his pocketbook suggesting a conspiracy brewing in Caen suddenly make dreadful sense?

Had the suppers and seduction all been calculated? Raoul was looking at her now with that same dangerous meld of sensuality and suspicion which had first fired her blood. Even here in the midst of terror, she still desired him. Poison, pleasure, wonderful, beautiful, sensuous; were the kindnesses now the forgotten means to a despicable end?

Aloud, she said: 'Well, go on, Deputy Carrier, this is, after all, your moment of fame.'

'By the power vested in me by the Convention and the people of France, I am arresting you as a conspirator in the murders of Matthieu Bosanquet and Jean-Paul Marat.'

The rattle of shifted muskets answered amen, as the soldiers, realising why they were really here, tightened their hold with disagreeable menace.

'That's not true,' Fleur answered calmly, and then slapped the palm of her heel to her forehead. 'But how stupid of me, Citizen Quettehou, I quite forgot you inherit a successful enterprise and an apartment if I'm guillotined.'

'You shall have a fair trial, citizeness. The Republic of France will see that justice is done.' Raoul, wearing duplicity blatantly now like a comfortable coat, turned to bestow a charming smile upon his colleagues. 'Are we going to stay out in this waste all day while the Girondins crawl out from under our noses? Let's get her back to Caen.'

If it was acting, he was very good.

'Search her!' Carrier ordered the soldiers.

Two soldiers pinioned her arms brutally behind her back while a third slapped his hands down her, feeling for more than a concealed knife. It was not the crude fumbling that concerned her but her lover's studied indifference. He swung his gaze round the desolate marsh, observing the thickening haze seawards beyond the distracted fisherman and, landwards, the scamper of colour as a gypsy child moved.

'Not your day, eh, Tante,' Quettehou quipped, revelling in Fleur's predicament. 'Unfortunately, there's not going to be any trial in Caen.' He grinned at Raoul with the glee of a hyena certain of a feed. 'I have orders from the Committee of Public Safety to hold a tribunal wherever I see fit. We'll do it now. Two members of the Convention and a representative of the Commune, it meets the requirements.'

'How do you plead, citizeness?'

'Since one of you is my nephew and suitor, and the other my erstwhile lover,' purred Fleur sarcastically, 'how could I possibly protest? Undiluted republican justice, Citizen Carrier? Oh, it makes my heart thud. What an achievement!' *Diable, Raoul de Villaret, whether you are treacherous or true, how in hell do we get out of this?*

Standing at Carrier's shoulder, Raoul's face had drained of blood, but he recovered quickly, striding forward. 'Fall back!' he ordered the soldiers and raised a questioning eyebrow at his colleague.

'Do as he says!' Carrier shrugged. The military let go of Fleur and spread out into a watchful, wolfish cordon.

'My former mistress has a point, Carrier. This won't look good, and, in any case, I was going to suggest we try the two charges separately since Quettehou can hardly sit as a judge when he is also a suspect.'

The older deputy's perplexed expression at least gave Fleur some hope of delaying matters. 'On what grounds, Deputy?'

'Quite straightforward ones. I have a man already in detention in Paris for twice provoking the mob to attack the mademoiselle here on the orders of Citizen Quettehou. On the second occasion I was a victim as well, I might add. This scoundrel also commissioned an assassin to kill her at the balloon ascent, not to mention organised the murderous attack on my coach outside Caen.'

'This is ridiculous, de Villaret!' countered

Quettehou. 'Attack your coach? Are you so demented with lust for this trollop that you can't see the wood for the trees? How could I possibly organise such a thing from Paris?'

'You use carrier pigeons.'

'Quettehou?' Carrier was on his guard now.

'Yes, I keep pigeons, citizen, as you've seen for yourself. *For the journal.* It gives me the edge on news. I admit I do use informers as well. Perhaps the man in custody is one of those. But it's Beugneux, her boarder, who killed my uncle, and she,' he jabbed the air at Fleur, 'was in league with him.'

Fleur was too shocked to answer.

'*Beugneux!*' Even Raoul was astounded.

'He keeps pigeons too. Didn't you know? Not at the Rue des Bonnes Soeurs, of course, but as part of his criminal activities. He smuggles royalists out using the Chat Rouge, doesn't he, de Villaret, and you've been turning a blind eye to safeguard her.'

'And *you* never informed the authorities?' Raoul countered smoothly.

'No, too lucrative milking old de Beugneux, *hein?*' Quettehou chuckled. It was rather an ugly sound. 'My pretty aunt looks rather faint. Are you going to play the gallant, de Villaret? But how about we relieve you of these first?' Pushing aside Raoul's jacket, he tugged the pistol free. 'Your rapier too, if you please, Deputy, just to be sure we know where your loyalties lie.'

With an insouciant shrug, Raoul unbuckled his sword-belt.

'I'll take that.' Carrier held out a hand for the pistol and scowled at Fleur as though she was a piece of dung he had trodden on. 'A private word with you, de Villaret,' he suggested grimly and, taking Raoul's arm, led him out of earshot but still within the range of fire. A pity there was no stout piece of wood lying around, thought Fleur, wondering if she could brain this nephew before the soldiers martyred her.

'You really do lie beautifully, Felix Quettehou,' she exclaimed and turned nonchalantly seawards. The boatman was minding his own business but it was the wall of fog moving steadily in that suddenly lifted her courage.

'But it's true, Tante Fleur.' Quettehou took her arm and pulled her to face him. 'You *should* have married me. I'd have looked after you. Tsk, tsk, an old criminal like Beugneux and *him*.' He jerked his head towards Raoul. 'Not a good judge of men, are you, *ma belle*? And your handsome dog there has not got much choice. Return to glory in Paris or die with his whore. Which would you choose?'

'Of course he must choose France,' replied Fleur with cosmetic briskness. 'I'm sorry if I seduced him from the straight and narrow. But if you are right about Monsieur Beugneux . . .'

'Of course I'm right. You're going to die anyway so why should I lie to you? I was behind the mob attacks but *my uncle's death*, no. If you ask me, Uncle got wise to his dear old friend, and when he realised his *cher ami* was using the café for the escapes, he threatened to denounce him. That's why Uncle Matthieu was murdered. And then you arrived, and your deputy started getting too close to the truth and it was his turn to be killed, except it went wrong, and the hired assassins got your brother instead. Such a shame, *hein.*'

'Then why didn't Monsieur Beugneux kill me?' Fleur countered. The temptation to slap that insufferable face had to be suppressed; she was watching the two deputies.

'Because you let him use the Chat Rouge. Very profitable business, smuggling people.' Fleur's gaze snapped back to him in horror, remembering M. Beugneux's museum bedchamber. Quettehou was smiling with spidery delight at her confusion. 'Ha, you don't know what to believe about any of us, do you? Even *him.* You're on your own, *aristocrat.* You always were.'

Yes, she was. *The only person you can rely on is yourself.*

'A clever try, you bastard,' she answered. 'Matthieu Bosanquet condemned you to hell with his dying breath and so shall I.'

Raoul wondered what that *cul* Quettehou was telling Fleur. Not that it mattered. The sea mist was coming up and his unpleasant colleague, with no inkling of the Channel's whimsical habits, hadn't even noticed. No, Carrier was too busy lathering him with phrases like 'past loyalty to the Republic' and 'both committees think very highly of you'. Like hell! Saint-Just would be dancing on the ceiling if he were to be topped in Caen, but Carrier suddenly had a painful grip on his arm and the warning the man was trying to deliver was getting through at last.

'Listen, you young fool! Don't you want to go back to Paris a free man? The chit isn't worth it. You and I have better work to do, rounding up all the Girondin curs and hauling them back for trial. So let me do my job and get this over with.'

'I'm sorry,' someone said and Raoul realised it was himself. 'And listen, I don't give a damn what the blethering committees think, Carrier. I believe in justice. I'll die for it, if need be. There isn't a shred of evidence that says she's guilty of anything and you know it.'

'So I've wasted my breath.' The gold epaulettes rose indifferently. 'Let's dispense with the play-acting then. You're a damned idiot and you can die with her.'

Carrier whistled up the soldiers and Raoul found himself viciously shoved across the grass to join the others.

'I'm sorry, *ma mie*,' he called over his shoulder as they hauled him round to face his judge, 'they didn't like the performance.'

'Well, my darling, there's audiences and audiences,' Fleur answered, her eyes shining with love.

Carrier was rigid with national duty but he looked like an undertaker.

'By the power vested in me by the Convention and the people of France, I hereby find both of you guilty and sentence you to death.'

'What are you going to do? Shoot them both?' Quettehou almost danced in his excitement.

Kill Raoul? 'No, you can't!' shrieked Fleur, launching herself at Carrier in fury, knocking him backwards onto the grass. The soldiers seized her flailing arms and dragged her off him but not before her nails had clawed a fence on either cheek. Carrier shrugged off assistance and struggled back onto his feet with a thundery countenance devoid of pity. Rubbing a hand down his ravaged face, the man was almost rabid.

'We'll see if our fellow patriot starts to think with his mind instead of the little friend in his breeches. Shoot the girl!'

'NO!' Raoul struggled against the cruel arms that held him as a soldier grabbed Fleur by her hair and forced her to her knees. 'Find us a priest,' he roared. 'You can't deny us that.'

'To hear your lies?'

'*No, to marry us.*'

Marry?

Fleur ceased struggling and blinked up at him, her heart in her eyes. 'You truly mean it?'

'Marry? You want to *marry* her?' Carrier stared at Raoul as if his young colleague were demented.

Quettehou was Satan at his shoulder. 'It's just a ruse.'

'Yes, *marry*,' retorted Raoul, enjoying the shock in their faces. 'If I can't save her life, at least I can give her the only gift she ever asked of me – if you'll damn well find us a priest.'

'Oh, I can't give you a priest but I'll give you

marriage.' Carrier had at last realised the fog that was coming towards them. '*Mariage à la Revolution*. Strip your clothes off, Madame Bride, and be quick about it.' He relished the sudden terror in Fleur's eyes.

'But that's not –' Raoul jerked back as Carrier slammed the back of a hand across his face.

'We'll have the clothes off this noble patriot as well. Why not help him, lads?'

'Yes,' Quettehou joined in. 'Pretty him up a bit.'

'Curse you, Carrier!' Raoul roared as the soldiers flung him down, grabbed his boots off and started dragging at his breeches and shirt. They might have kicked him to a pulp except that Fleur hastily began pulling off her shirt. The distraction was instant.

'You'll keep, Deputy,' bawled someone and the pack turned scenting better sport. Even the fisherman was rowing in closer.

'Oh my love,' muttered Raoul, scrambling to his feet, horrified at her selflessness. *Oh, Fleur, no!*

Mesmer could not have given a better performance. Fleur's audience was salivating as she unpinned the towel and slowly unwound it from her breasts. But it was worth her modesty to stop the violence. She tried to forget the soldiers, instead her eyes sought Raoul's, beseeching his understanding.

Gratitude shone in his face. He understood what she was doing to distract them. Oh, how could she have ever doubted him, even for a moment? Of all the men in the entire world. And the contrary smile, light upon his mouth, was for her.

Naked as a Roman wrestler, he stood proudly, undiminished by their attempt to shame him. Dark hair wreathed his brow and the wonderful golden eyes, which had magnetised the Convention and stolen her soul, were gazing only at her. Warmed by the love radiating towards her like sunlight, Fleur knew the courage to continue.

Seductively, she unfastened the right boot, then the left. Shoes would have been more feminine but it was amazing what the flutter of eyelashes with a languorous look could do. Slowly, she untied her garter and peeled down her left stocking. If the fog closed in, then maybe they had a chance. Now the other –

'Hurry up!' snarled Quettehou, guessing her ploy.

'Your last chance, de Villaret.' Carrier, hands clasped behind his back, sneered, clearly despising the soldiers' weakness, and turned to torment his other prisoner. 'A worthy career, a prosperous future ruined, and all for this little bitch. I've a good mind to give her to the –' His voice faltered. Even he was staring now, moistening miserly lips.

'I've a last request,' demanded Fleur, making sure her voice carried. She tried to stand with dignity – Botticelli goddesses did not shiver – playing on the awe that was so briefly her advantage. 'Raoul, you told me they have a custom in Berri that on the wedding day . . .'

Raoul nodded, words beyond him – artist and lover tormented by seeing her beauty displayed to these philistines. If only the fog would veil her.

If he could grab one of the muskets . . . Distract them. Give her a chance to run. They'd shoot blind in the fog. Oh Supreme Being, are you listening? 'On the wedding day,' she was saying, 'the bridegroom comes to the bride's house and fits shoes on her feet. Let him do that, Carrier, and let me die with them on.' Of course! *Her boots!*

'How very pathetic,' shrugged Carrier. 'Well, get on with it.'

Within the hedge of muskets, Raoul picked up her discarded boots, trying to remember which heel the blade was in. The right, of course.

'Is human dignity so unvalued in our new world?' he asked as though it was the Convention he was addressing. 'I pity you, Carrier, if power means more to you than compassion.'

He came to stand before Fleur, and then he knelt with the grace of Paris before Helen of Troy and slid each boot adroitly onto her bare feet. He bent over her foot and, as he kissed it, twisted the boot's heel. 'As you love France, citizens,' he exclaimed, turning his head to address the soldiers while he palmed the blade, 'stand back and give us a few moments to say adieu.' It was Fleur who crouched to secure the lacing.

'Be quick about it!' snarled Carrier. 'Watch 'em. We don't want to lose them in the fog.'

The soldiers stepped back, forming a broad semicircle, their weapons ready.

Raoul's arms enfolded Fleur and he cradled her head to his breast.

'You have it?' she whispered.

'Yes.' His smile against her hair was bittersweet. 'One small blade against a dozen muskets. I am sorry, my darling. I thought to see you safe to the boat not bring these murderers.'

'But you would not have come with me to England?'

'Fleur.' A lifetime was in the sigh. 'I love you more than anything on earth.'

But not more than France.

No time to regret; no time for speeches.

'Oh, my love, hold me tight!' she whispered, but ungentle hands gripped her forearms, turning her away from the soldiers' stares.

'Listen to me, Fleur. There could be a way out. Tell them you are carrying my child. They're not allowed to execute you if you're pregnant.'

And leave him to die alone at Carrier's hands?

'Carrier's offered me my life. A few weeks and I can have you free. Who knows . . .'

'Oh, Raoul, can you believe a man like him?' She stared into his eyes, willing him to see sense. 'My love, I'm an aristocrat, a friend of Marat's killer. Besides, how long could I deceive them? The moment they realise it's a ruse, they'll haul me to the scaffold. I want you to disown me. I beg you, return to Paris.'

'No! I'll not fight on for men like these, nor for the France that they want.'

'Raoul –' He kissed her and then stepped back, holding her hand. '*Here* is my cause.' He carried her fingers to his lips, then together they slowly turned, hand in hand, to face their executioners.

'For the love of God,' he cried, 'let us get this over with! What in hell –'

Gunfire ripped across the water towards the boat. Carrier was shouting.

Pierre Birrot, ordered in under threat of firing, moved the oars with the rhythm of a weary galley slave and was careful to display bland ignorance until he was hauled out to stand with a pistol against his chest while one of the soldiers dragged his boat up.

'Tie our newly married traitors together!' Carrier ordered the soldiers. 'Yes, she can keep her bloody boots on. Stick them both in the boat and row out into midchannel, brain them and throw them in.

'And we'll take this fellow,' he drove his fist into the fisherman's gut and laughed as Birrot staggered back, doubled in pain, 'back for the guillotine in Caen.'

The mist was all around them now. One of the military, improvising, tugged free the leather tie that bound his own queue and with difficulty tied Fleur's wrists to Raoul's so they were face to face.

'Drowning is so less messy than the guillotine,' Quettehou whispered with a leer, his fingers lasciviously stroking down Fleur's neck. 'But I should have much preferred to see your head in a basket.' She shuddered, her skin goosefleshed beneath that hideous touch.

Don't be afraid, Raoul's expression told her. The loving kindness in his eyes warmed her shivering soul and she never took her gaze from his as rough hands shoved them down the ragged bank towards the boat.

'Wait, you cannot execute a pregnant woman!' Fleur exclaimed, whirling round to face the soldiers over Raoul's shoulder; hidden from view, she strained her bound wrists meaningfully. The men closest to them hesitated, looking to Carrier, and in that moment, with the mist closing in about them, Raoul drew the tiny blade through the leather.

'Pah!' scoffed Quettehou. 'Don't listen to the lying cow!'

'Listen?' echoed Carrier with a sinister laugh. 'I heard nothing so – *Merde!*' He roared in warning as sinister shapes sprang from the spiky grass behind them like demons from hell.

'*Down!*' Raoul shoved Fleur to her knees on the mud.

'No!' she protested, trying to grab him back from scrambling up to the monstrous shadowplay. *Bon Dieu!* The soldiers had one shot each and they would shoot to kill.

Crouching alone beneath the jut of bank, she mouthed a frantic prayer. A man screamed, as shots, too close, smashed into living flesh. She smelled the powder, heard the ugly smack of wood, the crack of bone, the shouting and then the battle came to her.

A soldier's body hurtled backwards over her head, thudding down onto the mud. Skewing round, Fleur glimpsed the musket in the dead man's hand. She scurried sideways but as she seized the weapon she heard the splash of boots landing behind her.

'Raoul?'

Merciful Christ! She had barely time to adjust her grip as Quettehou brought the butt of a musket down on her like a woodchopper's axe. Her weapon took the brunt but he came at her again and again, each vicious blow driving her further into the river.

'*A moi! A moi!*' she screamed but the fighting had moved away from the shore and she faced her greatest enemy alone. The butt slammed into her shoulder; she fell back into the water, unable to shield herself against the final blow and, then, incredulous, saw Quettehou's lips slowly open in astonishment as a cudgel crashed down upon his skull. Gasping in horror, she scrambled aside as her enemy, his face a hideous grimace, toppled to his knees and fell head forwards, lifeless, into the water.

Behind him, Raoul, his face iron and implacable, faced her. She could only stare up at him as though he was an apparition. For an instant he seem to be hewn of stone, and then she saw the rigid lines leave his face and the humanity seep back into his eyes.

Between them, Quettehou in his scarlet finery lay in the quiet lapping of the water, a rosette of blood spreading from his brow. Wavelets were washing indifferently through the thin strands of hair as though he was no more than any piece of loosened seagrass.

Silence surrounded them. Somewhere a gull mewed. The encompassing fog was no longer bruised with noise; men's voices, speaking in normal tones, reached her. Not French but Romany, she realised dully. The gypsies!

'Fleur? *Fleur!*'

Raoul's beloved voice restored time to its normal pace, and she let out her breath as he splashed into the water and drew her lovingly up into his embrace. The euphoric realisation that they were still alive burst over her and she began to cry with shock, wild, racking sobs that she could not stop. With his arm around her waist, Raoul helped her back up onto firmer ground. Her face was against his naked breast, her shoulders shaking.

Someone had found her clothes and, sitting her down among the grasses, Raoul crouched, dressing her as though she was a little girl again. She sensed rather than heard the words of endearment as he held her tight, and the tears finally dried to salt upon her cheeks.

'Madame?' Paco, the gypsy leader, striding up behind them, indifferently flung Raoul's clothes to him; his concern was all for her. Fleur climbed to her feet and gratefully embraced him, aware now of his fellow Romanies moving like ghosts through the mist, turning over the soldiers who lay unmoving in the grass.

Pierre Birrot loomed up beyond them. 'We've found the other deputy. He is still alive.'

'Show me!' Shivering now the fight was over, Raoul, half-dressed, dragged on his shirt and flung his jacket about his shoulders as they crossed the marsh to where a man lay spread-eagled, his face in the rye-grass.

'Shall we kill the bastard?' the Romany leader's son asked, toeing Carrier, his knife ready.

'No.' Stooping to retrieve his rapier, Raoul wearily shook his head. 'No, citizens, strip him and carry him to the road, then, in God's name, move camp! Shift your families out of Calvados as fast as you can.'

'Shift him yourself,' Paco retorted, edging his son aside. 'Equality, *hein*?' He spat at the ground contemptuously.

'As you please,' retorted Raoul, flinching at their loathing of his authority. Fleur crept beneath his arm in a show of unity, sliding her arms about his chill waist before she spoke to them in their language, thanking them again and begging them to follow his advice and flee from Normandy.

There was a soft rumble of reply. The Roma chief lifted his jaw at Raoul.

'It doesn't matter to us who rules your country, Frenchman.' *We shall still be outcasts*, his dark eyes told them. 'We did this to help our friend, the mademoiselle.' Then, with a salute to Fleur, he left and the others followed, bearing their wounded comrades.

"We should go, citizen. The tide –' Birrot warned, edgily peering about them. 'The soldiers who ran away may return.'

'*Moment!*' Raoul swiftly knelt, methodically tying Carrier's wrists and ankles using his stock and one of his stockings. The other he bound about the deputy's mouth. 'Thank God for the sea mist,' he muttered and, rising, set a hand beneath Fleur's elbow. '*Eh bien*, let's go.'

And pray God the boat was still there, thought Fleur. Running blindly behind Birrot towards the sound of the river, her heart was in her mouth but no blue uniforms surged out of the greyness to threaten them.

With a thanks-be under his breath, Birrot sprang aboard and took the oars. Raoul swung Fleur into the boat and then, as she settled in the prow, she realised he had not climbed aboard, that he was standing, his mind like Janus, his heart . . . ? Did he believe himself a traitor to his beloved France?

'Come on, citizen. Make haste if we are to join my larger boat! Cast off!'

Oh merciful Christ, surely he was not going back to Paris?

'Please,' she said, trying to keep her voice even as she realised the tempestuous struggle raging in Raoul's soul. She did not dare to breathe now, knowing that this moment might indeed be farewell and she might never see him alive again. And then she heard it, the tiny beat of wings. A pair of sandpipers dipped briefly into sight and were gone. But the words were there now, the certain hope and love that might draw him into her arms.

'No matter how many times the sandpiper leaves France, in the warmth of spring he returns, Raoul, he always returns. Gather up the rope, my love.'

He stirred, breaking out of the regret that sought to chain him; the anchor was lugged up, the rope tossed in, and he landed beside her with sandy feet and his boots in his hand. A damp-sleeved arm curled about her waist and his good hand stroked through her wet curls, down her cheek and tapped her nose playfully as the boat swung about.

'We shall return, Fleur,' he promised.

Behind her, beneath Carrier's grasping hands, the earth of France lay bloodstained, yes, but infinitely redeemable.

'Yes, Raoul, we shall.'

Epilogue

Ton coeur m'est tout, mon
bien, ma loi;
Te plaire est toute mon
envie,
Enfin, en toi, par toi,
pour toi,
Je respire et tiens à la vie.
Ma bien-aimée, ô mon
trésor!
Qu' ajouterais-je à ce
langage?
Dieu! Que je t'aime! Eh
bien, encor
Je voudrais t'aimer
daventage.

Your heart is my
wellbeing, my law.
It's everything for which
I strive,
Truly, for in you, by you,
for you
Is why I breathe and stay alive.
Beloved, what more can
I say?
O my Treasure, whom I
adore,
How I love you! O
God, I pray
That I may love you
even more.

'I LOVE THEE', FABRE D'EGLANTINE

The incense fumes in Notre Dame were decidedly excessive, as though these gilded bishops were trying to make up for the intervening years. Mind, it wasn't every day they crowned an Emperor of France with his Holiness the Pope to do the blessing, Fleur conceded. A shame it was a Corsican. Maybe that other islander, the Sardinian, Marat, would have seen the humour. All those years of struggle to achieve a democracy and here she was in her white satin and golden lace about to see General Bonaparte restore the baubles of royalty. What would M. Bosanquet say if he could see her now? And, M. Beugneux who had lived long enough to welcome her back to France. *Quelle ironie!*

'Where's Papa?' The ten-year-old heir to the Duc de Montbulliou tugged at the gold trimming on Fleur's cuff.

She ruffled the dark hair so like Raoul's. 'He'll be here in a moment, *mignon.*'

And he was, so resplendent in his black and gold that her heart drummed with pride. Their smallest child, Marie-Anne, was in his arms, one thumb in her mouth, the other chubby hand picking at the gold cords of his epaulette.

'I've just been talking to David. It'll take him years to paint this. Keep him out of mischief at any rate,' he added dryly, gently offloading their daughter onto the carpet and straightening to adjust the broad scarlet sash that crossed his breast from right shoulder to waist. 'He's charging to put people in it. Are you interested?'

'But we *are* in it. We're here.'

'Not for posterity, my love, unless we pay.' He laughed and kissed her cheek, and then he crouched down so he was eye to eye with his little boy. 'Would you like to be in a painting with Mama in her finery, Armand?'

'If you paint it, Papa, and let me help.'

'A bargain then, and your *maman* will love dressing up again *à la grande dame.*'

'I'd love to paint *you*, Raoul. You look magnificent,' Fleur whispered, her hand sliding up his shoulder as he drew level with her.

'You know I never did complete my Persephone painting.' The colour of cognac, his eyes teased her, stroking an imaginary finger down her cheekbone, and lower to caress the swell of her breast above the stiffened lace. 'But I will. I want to capture the right emotion.'

'Monseigneur le Duc, you put me to the blush,' she warned, teasing a finger along his lips.

'Later, *hein*, madame,' and his smile promised a late evening, after a magnificent supper at Thomas's newest restaurant. 'Come, Armand, your turn,' and he lifted the child so he could see the notables. 'They may look grand, my son,' he said quietly, 'but they're only people. Just people in fancy clothes. Always remember that.' Then he added grimly to Fleur, his face hardening, 'So it begins once again.'

Fleur's smile was tight. It had taken months of

gentle persuasion before he had agreed to accept the title that marriage had bestowed on him.

'But, Papa, you are wearing fancy clothes, you and Maman, and I am too.' Armand ignored Marie-Anne like a typical brother.

'And once I was not a duke. It's how you behave that's important. It'll be how *he* behaves that's important.' The boy followed his gaze to where Napoleon Bonaparte stood in scarlet and ermine, a wreath of golden leaves upon his forehead.

'And if he misbehaves, Papa? Must we go back to Angleterre?' Armand remembered very little of the three years in England; the foreign land that Mama and Papa had fled to.

'If he misbehaves . . .' echoed Raoul, the old revolutionary gleam back in his eyes.

'Raoul!' hissed Fleur warningly.

'If he misbehaves, I'll send your mother round to tell him so.' He kissed her cheek. 'My courageous, darling Fleur-de-Lis.'

Author's note

Robespierre was appointed to the Committee of Public Safety on 27 July and although the committee gave strong leadership, France became a totalitarian regime. Thousands were killed during the terror that followed, and Deputies Carrier and Couthon became the notorious butchers of the central government. The so-called 'republican marriages' and the drowning of condemned victims at Nantes on Carrier's orders are described in Vol. II of the *Reign of Terror: a collection of authentic narratives of the horrors committed by the revolutionary government of France* (Leonard Smithers and Co, London, 1899).

The Girondin leaders either took their own lives or were guillotined in autumn 1793. Some of them, including Armand Gensonné, were carted to the guillotine together and they sang the Marsellaise, as they waited, one by one, to mount the scaffold. In the following April (1794), Danton and Hérault suffered the same fate. Robespierre and his supporters were finally overthrown a few months later. Carrier was executed in December 1794 and Fouquier-Tinville in 1795 and, yes, he did unwittingly help a woman prisoner escape. David, that pillar of revolution and empire, died in 1825, aged seventy-seven. Marie-Anne's aunt, Madame de Bretteville also survived.

As for the fictional characters: the Commune seized the Chat Rouge but one of Thomas's customers set him up on new premises – good chefs are always needed; M. Beugneux left Paris with Machiavelli, returning in 1794 after the fall of Robespierre; and Blanchette remained with Thomas.

Hérault's constitution was accepted but never used, and it was Boissy d'Anglas who in 1795 completed the third constitution. As a consequence of the extremes and horror that he and France had experienced, it was extremely conservative. It might be argued that the atrocities of the Revolution so terrified England that it put reforms there back forty years and the rights of women back by over a century.

Most of Caen's Rue Saint-Jean was flattened by the Allies during World War II, but the castle, abbeys and old city still retain the flavour of Fleur's world, although it is hard to imagine that a river once lapped the rear of the Église Saint-Pierre.

The Trinité School where Marie-Anne and

Fleur were educated by the nuns still stands but you must not believe the stories that Charlotte Corday sat out under the great cedar and dreamed of a happier France, for the tree was not planted until the 1840s.

In Paris, the Palais-Royal, the Conciergerie and the Palais de Justice still stand. The house that inspired Raoul's lodging is the Maison d'Ourscamp in the Marais, the headquarters of the Association pour la Sauvegarde et la Mise en Valeur du Paris Historique. I should like to thank the ladies of that organisation for their assistance and hospitality.

I have placed Hérault's Le Nid further out of the city but one source tells me it was at Chaillot, which is the name given to the right bank opposite the Eiffel Tower.

You can find the full version of the songs in Pierre Barbier and France Vernillat's *Histoire de France par les Chansons* (Gallimard, Paris, 1956–1961) and in Jean Allix's *Chansons de France* (Paris, 1976). My translations are very rough. 'Ça ira', the popular song of the Revolution is hard to translate. Perhaps the most accurate translation would be the confident Australian expression: 'She'll be right.'

I've been gathering information and texts on the French Revolution over many years, both in studying and having taught the topic at university. It has always been an area of interest for me. Readers keen to learn more will find Simon Scharma's *Citizens: A Chronicle of the French Revolution* (Penguin Books, London, 1989) a wonderful source. Mark Giroaud's *Life in the French Country House* (Cassell

& Co, London, 2000) is fascinating to browse through and – if you can find it – Arthur Young's *Travels in France during the years 1787, 1788 and 1789* (Bell and Sons, London, 1913) is a superb snapshot view of the eve of the Revolution.

My research in Caen could not have been carried out without the wonderful assistance of Deborah Lennie Bisson and Christophe Bisson, who took me to the forest of Grimbosq, the Enchanted Isle and the Orne estuary. I am also grateful for the valuable insights Professor Pierre Gouhier of Caen University offered through cyberspace and over an excellent meal at his home. The staff of the Museum of Arts and Crafts in the Bois du Boulogne, Paris, were very helpful. As for the history of French ballooning, there is probably no better museum than that of Balleroy, Normandy.

Thanks are also due to: Dr Peter Davies and Dr Stephanie Aplin, my gurus on injuries; speech therapist Lee-Anne Biggs; Dr Russell Naughton who kindly agreed to be a sounding board on hot-air balloons; Dawn Bennett for her help with French music; and Craig Adams of the Australian Reptile Park, Sydney, for the lowdown on pythons. Information on costumes, furnishings and portraits came from sleuthing all manner of sources: my thanks to the Research Library of the Powerhouse Museum, Sydney; the Library of the Art Gallery of New South Wales; and to Marguerite Cawte, Antonia Lomny and Kris Alice Hohls. My good friend and fellow writer, Chris Stinson, kindly checked my French and did a first read. *Merci bien!*

Elizabeth Lhuede, Angela Iliffe and Delamere Usher gave me useful feedback, and my supportive critique group offered pertinent and cheeky comments – as usual!

The team at Pan Macmillan, especially Cate Paterson, Sarina Rowell and Julia Stiles, have been marvellous to work with and I thank them for their dedication.

Finally, a thank-you to John, my patient husband, who was my fellow adventurer in working out where Fleur lived and where the Chat Rouge might have stood. Was it more than a coincidence that a business with the name de Villaret (the surname already chosen for Raoul) stood opposite the ideal site!

Isolde Martyn
THE SILVER BRIDE

England 1483. Only the strong rule of Edward
IV prevents the War of the Roses rekindling. In
Wales, Sir Miles Rushden, adviser to Harry, Duke
of Buckingham, is impatient to trust his friend
towards the crown. And in the north, Richard of
Gloucester is growing uneasy at the simmering
intrigue in the south.

The threat to Miles's ambitions is unexpected –
a land dispute that sees him forced at swordpoint
to marry Heloise Ballaster, whose second sight
terrifies people. Miles is determined to be rid of
her but she has powerful allies in Gloucester's
household. Cruelly cast aside by her father, she
seeks out her reluctant, furious husband.

With the king's sudden
death, Miles and Heloise find
themselves at the heart of
treason as the mighty
dukes of Gloucester and
Buckingham manoeuvre
ruthlessly to seize the crown.
In a conspiracy that could
have a lethal ending, can
loyalty, that most elusive,
fragile cornerstone of love,
prevail?

Juliet Marillier
THE DARK MIRROR

When the child Bridei is sent by his parents to live
with the druid Broichan, he knows only that he has
left his home and family to learn to be warrior and
scholar, strategist and sage. He is not aware that in
the divided and wartorn kingdom of Fortriu a secret
council of elders, including Broichan, has long
been making plans for the future of their homeland:
with Bridei himself central to their strategy.

As the only child in Broichan's remote
household, Bridei learns to deal with fear and
loneliness. So when he awakes one freezing
midwinter's night to find a baby on the doorstep,
he thanks the gods for their precious gift of a
companion and takes her in – and with her arrival
Broichan's master plan gains a dangerously
unpredictable new element.

As the foundling Tuala grows from fey child to
beguiling young woman, and Bridei moves ever
closer to his grand destiny, Broichan anticipates
a perilous complication to his long-laid plans. As
well, powerful forces both close to home and in
other lands are ranged against the secret council,
enemies who will employ whatever means they can
to stop the druid from bringing his plan to fruition,
even if they must endanger Bridei's life.